Follow the chieftain Solomon
and the magnificent warrioress Kordelina,
whose wisdom and passion drive an entire Celtic
tribe into new ways of living!

"Her name will be Kordelina," Aonghus' father continued. "She will be part of our family if we agree to recompense the gods for their generosity."

Aonghus' ice-blue eyes darted questioningly to Solomon. He sat stone-faced, staring at the fire as though he were completely oblivious to what was taking place.

"How do we do that, Father?" he asked, visibly distressed at Solomon's condition.

"We must promise something in return," Saturnalia said calmly. "This child lives because we have finally tread down the dark forces conjured by the Black Druidess. In return for the empowerment the heavens have afforded us, we must make a pact among ourselves never to let it be known the circumstances by which the girl came to us. You know that the babe would never be allowed to live, should it ever be known."

The Celtic Heart

KATHRYN MARIE COCQUYT

is a writer of children's and adult fiction. An English literature and history major at the California State University, Long Beach, she has worked as a magazine editor and free lance writer. She lives in Simi Valley, California, where she pursues her other love, working with thoroughbred horses.

This passion has come alive in her writing as well. She has published two children's books, *Little Freddie at the Kentucky Derby*, and *Little Freddie's Legacy*.

Her inspiration for this book came in a dream in 1987, and after more than three years of completing *The Celtic Heart* , she was able to visit the island of Anglesey and substantiate the story with archaeological and historical documentation.

To Write to the Author

If you wish to contact the author or would like more information about this book, please write to the author in care of Llewellyn Worldwide, and we will forward your request. Both the author and publisher appreciate hearing from you and learning of your enjoyment of her book. Llewellyn Worldwide cannot guarantee that every letter written to the author can be answered, but all will be forwarded. Please write to:

Kathryn Marie Cocquyt
c/o Llewellyn Worldwide
P.O. Box 64383-156, St. Paul, MN 55164-0383, USA
Please enclose a self-addressed, stamped envelope for reply, or $1.00 to cover costs. If outside U.S.A., enclose international postal reply coupon.

Free Catalog From Llewellyn Worldwide

For more than 90 years, Llewellyn has brought its readers knowledge in the fields of metaphysics and human potential. Learn about the newest books in spiritual guidance, natural healing, astrology, occult philosophy and more. Enjoy book reviews, new age articles, a calendar of events, plus current advertised products and services. To get your free copy of *Llewellyn's New Worlds of Mind and Spirit*, send your name and address to:

Llewellyn's New Worlds of Mind and Spirit
P.O. Box 64383-156, St. Paul, MN 55164-0383, U.S.A.

The Celtic Heart

Kathryn Marie Cocquyt

1994
Llewellyn Publications
St. Paul, Minnesota, 55164–0383, U.S.A.

Cover painting and illustrations by Michael Kucharski

Cataloging-in-Publication Data
Cocquyt, Kathryn.
    The Celtic heart / by Kathryn Marie Cocquyt.
        p. cm.
    ISBN 1-56718-156-2
        1. Great Britian—History—To 449—Fiction. 2. Brigantes (Celtic people)—Fiction. 3. Anglesey (Wales)—History—Fiction.
4. Druids and druidism—Fiction.   I. Title
PS3553.0292C45 1994   94-13189
813'.54—dc20   CIP

Llewellyn Publications
A Division of Llewellyn Worldwide, Ltd.
P.O. Box 64383, St. Paul, MN 55164-0383

To my Mother, Liv Gilmore,
for her endless labor of love;
To Don,
for doing the "Hat Trick;"
and to my mare, Miss Mardi Gras,
for her tremendous heart
and steadfast friendship.

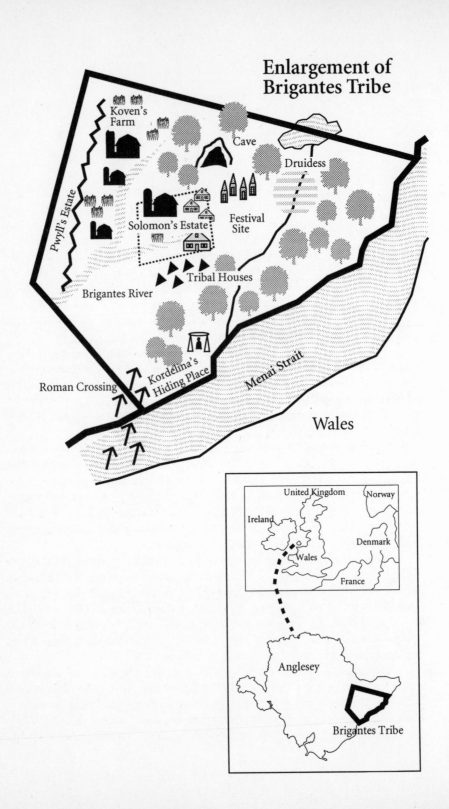

Enlargement of Brigantes Tribe

Koven's Farm

Cave

Druidess

Pwyll's Estate

Solomon's Estate

Festival Site

Tribal Houses

Brigantes River

Kordelina's Hiding Place

Roman Crossing

Menai Strait

Wales

United Kingdom

Norway

Ireland

Denmark

Wales

France

Anglesey

Brigantes Tribe

Preface

ong before the intrusions of Roman civilization and Christianity, the Celts ruled an empire in Great Britain. They lived in tribal groups worshipping the deities of nature and the power of the Divine Goddess. The interlacing boughs of the holy oak groves offered an inviolable cathedral where religious rites were performed and their gods were revered. All facets of the earth and nature were honored—from the animals that became their anointed protectors; to the trees of the forest on which the Ogham alphabet was based; to the sacred lakes and rivers named in homage to their mysterious but powerful otherworldly companions.

The Romanization of the Celtic nations throughout England and Wales began in A.D. 43, when an army of approximately 40,000 Roman soldiers, under the rule of a new emperor, Claudius, conquered Southern Britain. Claudius, who was not a popular choice among the Roman Senate, greatly needed the distinction of a military victory, which he thus seized at Camulodunum (Colchester).

The assault was disastrous for the Celts, and after the initial resistance by the southern and midland tribes, they were eventually overcome. Many of their warriors and chieftains fled westward to the Welsh mountains and Anglesey, situated across the Menai Strait in North Wales. A small but powerful island, Anglesey was known as the granary of the British Isles because of its mild climate and fertile farmland. It was also rich in copper deposits and, aside from being a sanctuary for refugees, it was the last Druidic stronghold.

Years of bitter fighting ensued as Rome focused on neutralizing the hostile tribes in that region. Anglesey remained an imperative target because the Roman army was in need of the food and horses it could provide, and since they possessed tremendous influence over the Celtic resistance, it was vital that the Druids be subjugated. However, protected by a treacherous coastline and dense oak groves, it remained the object of much frustration until a Roman General, Gaius Seutonius Paullinus, devised a method of crossing the Menai Strait.

Utilizing flat-bottomed boats to carry the infantry while the calvarymen swam beside their horses, the Romans landed on the islands' shores in A.D. 61. Although they were met with masses of armed warriors and Druids screeching curses against them, the spectacle only induced a momentary terror in their enemy. The Romans vastly outnumbered the Celts and, following a bloody onslaught, the sacred groves upon the mystical island of Anglesey were ultimately devastated by the battle.

Chronicalling the years A.D. 47 through A.D. 61, *The Celtic Heart* takes place on the island of Anglesey and resurrects the flamboyantly authentic Celtic way of life. It challenges their persistent image as the "great barbarians of the world" while depicting the Druids as the shrewd political leaders, not simply the "Merlin-like" sorcerers many today believe they were.

The glossary of terms and pronunciation guide at the end of this book may enhance your understanding of the Celtic way of life as you follow three generations of the Brigantes tribe in *The Celtic Heart*.

Part One

CHAPTER ONE

D. 47. Steam was rising from the damp ground as a dark cloud left from last night's storm momentarily blocked the sun; droplets on the wet shrubbery clung to the warrior's trousers and boots as he parted the leafy greenery with his horse. It was unusually warm this morning for so early in the spring. The long winter frost had broken prematurely, and it was considered by the tribe to be a good omen.

The Celtic warrior sat straight and broad chested in his saddle. His boots of the finest tanned cowhide laced across the top and went halfway up his calf. His breeches were made of supple, stitched doeskin, and wrapped around his waist was a flamboyant purple and green sash. There was a wide pigskin battle belt secured just above his stomach, where he could easily carry his dagger and arm-length lightning spear in case he encountered hand-to-hand combat. He was wearing a white sleeveless linen shirt that revealed his thick, burly arms. Its V-shaped opening at the neck was fastened by a pair of fibulae, small broaches joined by a chain.

Above the fibulae, he wore a bronze neck torque of thick twisted metal with the heads of two carved birds of prey at either end. This was perhaps his most valuable adornment, since it was given to him upon his anointing as a warrior. It had supernatural significance to the one who wore it, and was the unspoken testimony of his courage.

His hair cascaded down his shoulders, and was bleached a golden red on top. With its true brunet color showing through in places, he resembled an exotic animal. He had a large drooping mustache and a full beard that was the same dark, rich color as his eyes. Born of a Celtic father and a Roman-Christian mother, he had lived twenty-one cycles on this island, eleven of them in this same tribe. He was known to all as the brave warrior Solomon.

He could hear the snorting of Laden's horse opposite him. Moving diagonally, the two warriors narrowed the distance between them with each step their horses took. The pack of hunting dogs accompanying them had their noses to the ground and tails straight up as they followed the boar's scent.

Shifting his position in the saddle so that he could aim his spear, Solomon met Laden's gaze for an instant, signaling his readiness. The hounds began to bark and howl as the wild pig dashed in front of them and ran grunting into the bracken.

Digging their heels into their horses' flanks, both men instantaneously darted after the creature. Solomon's horse was practically clipping the dogs' heels, he was so close behind them. Laden was off to the side in case the boar turned abruptly and needed to be intercepted.

Solomon could see the dark bristly fur of the animal's hindquarters as it scurried through the shrubbery, fleeing the pack of salivating dogs. Tightening his calf muscles, he commanded his horse faster, and rocking suddenly forward, it locked into a violent pace.

They finally reached the meadow, the place Solomon had wanted to be. It would be easier to spear his prey out in the open as he stampeded toward it. Pointing his spear, he heaved it forward, sure that he had easily targeted his kill. To his surprise, the crazed pig swerved, almost as if it were knowingly dodging the weapon, and the spear impaled itself in the ground.

Snorting fearfully, the boar halted, and with a quick turn, charged the pack of hounds. Solomon's eyes widened as he looked at the ugly, snouted hog with two large tusks framing its mouth. Then, realizing that he was in its path, Solomon jerked his horse's head to the side and retreated.

The dogs were scattered and barking, and in a moment of confusion, he saw the pig heading for a small cave on the opposite side of the meadow.

"Head him off!" he yelled to Laden, but the other warrior was too slow to react. The boar disappeared into the dark opening in the rock.

Solomon hit the top of his thigh with his fist in frustration as he retrieved his spear. They had spent all morning hunting, and this was all they had come upon. To lose it now would mean returning to a hungry tribe in shame.

He trotted to the cave entrance where Laden stood beside his horse, resigned and ready to return to the village. The hounds swirled around his feet, anxious to continue their pursuit, as he commanded his stallion to a halt and dismounted.

The cave was a rectangular fissure in a limestone outcropping. There were two massive stone slabs framing the entrance on either side, the faces of which were badly worn from the weather. This place was revered by their clan because it was believed to be an entrance to the spirit world. It was here that a would-be warrior must endure a night alone before being initiated into their elite society. It was a test of courage as well as stamina, since there were horrid tales of fearsome beasts living within that were known to ravage many a brave man's mind.

"You are not going in there, are you?" Laden asked cautiously.

Solomon purposefully grabbed two spears from his saddle. One was shorter than the other, its bronze blade decorated with the imprint of a lightning bolt on either side. It was the warrior's most powerful spear, and he counted on it like he would a faithful friend. It had been blessed by the Druids, and not only could it kill a mortal, but it could pierce straight through a malevolent spirit.

"That is where the boar went," he responded impatiently, "and I refuse to return without it."

Laden looked back at him doubtfully. He was the complete contrast of Solomon. His hair fell in golden locks, and his eyes were a deep green. He was also taller and better proportioned to carry his weight than Solomon, whose brawny build could have used a bit more height.

"This is the entrance to the Otherworld," he argued. "That boar is among the spirits now. Perhaps your half-Christian blood gives you special rights, but as for me, I would rather share the smallest of portions at my table tonight than risk angering the gods by slaying the beast in their presence."

Solomon took a deep breath and puffed out his cheeks as he exhaled.

"This has nothing to do with Christianity and everything to do with my stomach," he replied. "I would like to eat tonight."

Laden shook his head, walked over to a log, and sat down, "As Chieftain I should warn you that —"

Solomon glared at him. "Warn me that I am going in there alone? No need," he said sarcastically. "I would not expect you to tread upon the toes of the mysterious Otherworld."

Laden's face hardened. "Now see here, warrior. I reign in this tribe, and I demand more respect."

Reaching up, Solomon took a broadaxe from the back of his saddle, and scowled back at him a moment before sticking it in his belt.

"You do not reign yet. While your father still breathes, I honor him," he countered, walking to the cave entrance. "If you do not wish to come, at least wait here in case the beast decides to reenter this world as quickly as he left."

He gave an exasperated sigh and snapped his fingers, commanding the dogs to go in ahead of him.

The lead hound was black and gray, with a dark but mischievous expression. The hair on his back bristled as he barked twice, demanding the attention of the other canines. He was stout, with a few hairless gashes on his sides from old wounds that had healed. Of the pack, the warrior liked this one best because he was not only brave but smart.

He reached down to pat the animal on the shoulder. This was perhaps his apprentice's greatest contribution, because the dog was able to pick up and follow a scent for miles, and would go all day until the prey was slain. Admiring this tenacity, Solomon had often wished he was its owner and not the boy, Aonghus.

The warrior gave a low-pitched whistle. Obeying him, the dogs entered the dark opening. Solomon followed, his spear poised in one hand.

The cave was damp and cold, and the sniffing of the dogs echoed off the limestone. There was only a narrow beam of light shining in, making the painted stone walls look eerie. He could scarcely remember the night he had spent in this place, the unwelcome coldness of the ground, or the frightening visions of the animal depictions coming to life that many of the other warriors had recounted. All he knew was that Laden was right; this was a sacred place that he should not be invading in this way. Yet, somehow, he believed that spirits only came at night, and only when they were called, for he had never seen one without the elaborate rituals surrounding it.

As he went deeper into the blackness, he could hear the cowardly whining of a couple of the hounds who refused to go any further. Then, as if completely incensed by their defiance, the black and gray leader nipped at their heels and growled menacingly, demanding they continue on with the rest.

Recognizing the massive painting of the hawk over his head, Solomon wished that he had a torch. If his memory served him right, there was an abrupt drop into a rounded pit of stone, and he would then surely be in complete darkness. He heard the suddenly vicious snarling of the lead dog, then the rustle and snorting of the boar ahead. If it was hiding in the pit, it would be difficult and dangerous to go in there without fire. The animal could be anywhere, and he did not want to risk stepping right on top of it.

The barking and growling of the pack became more intense as two dogs went forward into the ominous basin. Solomon could hear them scrambling back and forth and the raking of the boar's feet against the rock. Anxiously saying a silent prayer to the gods, he moved in closer.

All at once, the wild pig rushed straight at him. He could see the beady eyes of the furious beast in the shadowy light and the sudden flash of his tusks.

Lifting his spear, he heaved it into the pig's back. It dashed away from him, then turned in a rage and bounded back. The warrior was stunned at its sudden recovery as he fumbled for his hatchet. Realizing there was not enough time, Solomon recklessly dove behind a boulder, just as the black and gray hound charged into the swine's chest.

Solomon heard the dog howl with pain as the boar turned and attacked it. There was a mass of snorting and gnashing of teeth as the dog tried to defend itself.

Recovering immediately, Solomon pivoted around the warring animals. His weapon drawn, he tried to save the dog, but the two were a mass of indistinguishable fur.

There was the sound of skin ripping as he saw the hound flung against the wall, bellowing piteously. He could hear the distinct cracking of bones at impact. The boar was standing with its mouth open, squealing madly. Taking his lightning spear, Solomon drove it straight into the animal's eye.

He felt the warm blood squirting onto his legs and quickly lifted the hatchet and brought it crashing down between the boar's eyes. The wild beast fell to the ground dead.

Breathless with fear, the warrior went to the whimpering dog. He ran his hand down its back feeling the crooked, broken spine. Foam was coming from its mouth, and straining his eyes, he saw that its stomach was ripped open. The gash was just big enough to expose part of the hound's entrails.

"You are a brave animal," he said through trembling lips. "Thank you for saving my life."

Standing up, he went over to the boar, and taking its hind legs, dragged it out of the cave. Laden eyed him nervously as Solomon tied the leather thongs around its feet, and then lifted the carcass on Laden's horse.

"What are you doing?" he asked, folding his arms across his chest defensively. "That is your kill, not mine."

The morning sun was getting warmer, and Solomon wiped the perspiration from his face with his dirty forearm.

"This animal was slain because Aonghus' hound sacrificed himself to save me," Solomon said, catching his breath.

"If the animal died in that cave, then he belongs to the spirits," Laden reasoned. "You should leave him there."

Solomon went over to his horse, and took his fur-lined cloak from the back of the saddle.

"He is not dead yet, and he is not my hound," he answered. "He belongs to Aonghus. The boy will be heartbroken if I abandon him here."

Laden shook his head. "That is a bad omen. The spirits gave you the life of the boar, but in return wanted the hound. You should let them have their way; they will only become angered if you refuse the giveaway."

"The animal is still breathing; it would be cruel to reward him with a slow, painful death for his courage," Solomon retorted, walking to the entrance of the cave. "If Aonghus wants him to lie here, then let him bring him back of his own free will."

He did not wait for Laden's reply. Going back into the darkness, he wrapped the dog in his cloak. It gave an agonizing, high-pitched yelp as Solomon picked him up and carried him back into the sunlight.

Laden was already on his horse, looking quite proud of the boar tied across its withers.

"You are a fool to make such a fuss over a simple hound," he said, watching Solomon laboriously tie the cloak around his midriff so that he could brace the dog against him when he mounted.

"He saved my life," was all Solomon said, as he climbed into the saddle and started back to find the dog's young owner.

CHAPTER TWO

The two warriors rode across the lush, sloping hills, their horses breaking the soaking ground where the rain had puddled in hollows of the earth. There were clumps of green in places where the freeze had thawed early, allowing the grass there to grow much longer than the rest. Limestone escarpments scattered about the area gave the impression that the knobby terrain was sprouting faces in the bright spring sun.

Trotting out onto the flatlands, they waded through a narrow stream that ran the length of the hillside. Silver rivulets of the chilly water dipped over the rocks and bumped against the verdant banks as the sturdy equine legs sliced the waves and continued up the other side.

There was a small herd of wild horses grazing to the side of them. Their shaggy winter coats were still wet and muddy from last night's storm. They passively munched on the damp grass as one young, dark brown colt lifted his head and whinnied to them as they passed. He seemed angered by their presence as he pinned his ears back and took a couple of paces toward them. He stopped short, and stood still a moment. Then he began pawing the ground with his front hoof while he flared his nostrils and gave a low, guttural nicker. Had they been riding mares, Solomon would have thought that the young stud was giving them a mating call. But since both men were on stallions much bigger than the colt, he could only assume the rogue was defining his territory.

Bracing the weight of the panting hound against one arm, the warrior started up the incline. The animal's broken body shifted abruptly forward, forcing him to hunch over in the saddle to keep from dropping it. The rest of the pack barked and wove between the two trotting horses, the smell of the fresh blood of the boar, as well as the hound, causing them to foam at the mouth and nip impatiently at one another.

Laden rode at a quicker pace in front of Solomon. The dead game flopped up and down limply in unison with his horse's stride. He and Solomon had not spoken since they started back, and considering that they were not the best of friends, Solomon was relieved that he had not attempted to make conversation.

Laden was the only son of Donnach, the king of their clan. He was assured the position as the tribe's Chieftain upon his father's passing, or when Donnach voluntarily stepped down from his reign. Unfortunately, father and son were not cut from the same cloth. While Donnach was genuinely concerned with the wel-

8

fare of his clan, Laden was rather imperious and self-consumed, and he easily exhausted Solomon's patience. More than once, the warrior would have relished the opportunity to do combat with him, but since Solomon loved and respected the king's wishes, he restrained himself to protect Laden's position in the tribe.

There was one more hill in front of them crowned with alder trees, and beyond that lay the shallows, the lowest part of a rather large lake, framed by hills on all sides. As the biggest known lake on the island, it was believed to be a sacred place of the tribe's patron goddess, Brigantia. There were many accounts of Celts having seen a beautiful woman emerging from its depths during the waxing of the moon. Solomon had never met anyone personally who had claimed to see the apparition, but it was a well-revered tenet among his clan nonetheless.

The lake's water moved in gentle ripples with the offshore wind, causing the sprouting reeds to sway slightly. Solomon could see Aonghus on the furthest shore near a cluster of birch trees, busily coiling in his fishing net.

The boy was seven years old, with dark reddish brown hair and sallow skin. He had a prominent nose, with a few blotchy freckles across its ridge, and the most intense blue eyes Solomon thought he had ever seen on a child. His was a stocky, almost plump build, with hips and thighs nearly as broad as his shoulders. He appeared awkward physically, as though his upper and lower body were developing at different rates, yet he was coordinated, and from the few solemn words he had spoken, seemed smart enough to learn a warrior's ways. Still, Solomon doubted his own skills at teaching the boy. He had no children of his own, and this was his first attempt at raising a foster.

He saw Aonghus pick up a large stone and pound a flopping fish until he killed it. As he came nearer, he noticed a wooden pole leaning against a tree with at least six ducks skewered on it. Even if the child had no stomach for warfare, he could at least keep them well nourished, Solomon thought, as he stopped beside him.

Setting the stone down beside the jiggling net, Aonghus stood obediently and offered the warrior a tight-lipped nod. Then his gaze passed over the dead boar and across the hounds.

"Where is Locwn?" he asked, turning to scan the hillsides around him.

"Who?" Solomon asked, knitting his brows together and craning forward.

Aonghus dropped his hands limply to his sides, looked at Laden and then over at Solomon. His expression faded as he focused on the bundle Solomon held.

"Locwn—my dog?" he asked meekly.

Solomon frowned. He felt a little guilty that the animal had saved his life, and he had not even bothered to learn its name. Pursing his lips, he stared at the boy. This was not going to be easy.

Throwing one leg over his horse's withers, he slid out of the saddle. The hound was so far gone by now that he did not even whimper when Solomon set him down in front of Aonghus.

Unfolding the cloak, even Solomon was sickened by the pungent odor of the bloody, suffering animal. It lay slack-jawed and salivating, with its eyes rolled halfway back in its head. If it had belonged to him, Solomon would have killed it without delay to end its misery.

"This hound you call Locwn is a brave one. Because of him, my life was spared," Solomon explained, watching the boy with a steady, gentle gaze.

Aonghus stood as if in shock, staring at the animal glassy-eyed.

"Were it not for his courage, this boar would not be roast tonight," he continued, gesturing to the slain game.

The boy knelt down and wrapped his arms around the hound's thick neck and hugged it close. Saliva dropped out of its mouth and onto his lap, and the ruddy fluid from its exposed intestines seeped onto his trousers. Solomon could see the end of Aonghus' nose redden as he tried to hold back his tears.

"Oh, get on with it," Laden scolded. "It is only a dog, not a warrior. Is there really the need for such emotion? The longer we delay our return, the longer the time until we can roast this beast. So put the pitiful thing out of its misery and let us depart."

Arching one brow, Solomon cocked his head to the side and scowled at him. "Be off with you," he snapped. "I would not want you to be delayed in indulging yourself."

Laden gave him a vacant look and shrugged.

"Those are my feelings as well," he answered flatly, then gathered his reins. He turned his horse and spurred him to a canter away from them.

Taking his dagger from its sheath, Solomon held the weapon out to his apprentice.

"Some of Laden's words are true," he said matter-of-factly. "This animal should be spared any more suffering."

Sniffling, Aonghus wiped his nose with the top of his wrist, then took the dagger from Solomon. He looked up at him anxiously, as if he did not know what to do with it.

"Drive it straight into the heart," the warrior continued. "It will kill him instantly. Do it as a friend, and afford him his dignity."

The boy ran his tongue across his dry lips and tensed his shoulders. Then he wrapped his fingers so tightly around the dagger that his knuckles turned white. He held his breath, quickly driving the dagger into the hound's barreled chest.

Its body jolted, then went limp, and its head dropped back open-mouthed. Aonghus instantly released the animal as though he abhorred it, and scrambled to his feet.

The warrior bent down to pull out the dagger. Then he handed it to Aonghus, who stood shaking and puffing in front of him.

"You have released his spirit," he said. "This is yours now."

The boy wiped the bloody blade on his thigh and stuffed it into his belt. Then he bolted forward, and taking the four corners of the cloak, tied them together. Knotting it two or three times, the youngster then dragged it along with him as he waded into the lake.

He went out until the water was halfway up his chest and then sent the bundle adrift. It only floated a few inches away from him before it sank beneath the shiny surface.

Twisting the corner of his mustache between his thumb and forefinger, Solomon curiously watched a soaking Aonghus emerge from the water and silently pick up the fish and dead ducks. Tying the net to the end of the pole, he stopped and looked up at him earnestly.

"It was an offering to the Goddess," he said, the tears brimming in his eyes. He put the pole over his shoulder and trudged off in the direction of the village.

CHAPTER THREE

hrough furrowed brows, Solomon stared at Aonghus, shaking his head. He realized how traumatic it would be to have a friend die at one's own hand. But to embrace such an unpleasant duty resolutely, and to grasp its spiritual significance as well, was surprising coming from one that young.

To be so serious at such a tender age was almost alarming. In his youth and even now, Solomon never would have thought to offer the animal's spirit to the gods. He imagined that he would have been more likely to give in to his grief. Perhaps Aonghus would be better suited as a holy man than a warrior, he thought to himself.

Folding one arm across his stomach, he stared pensively at the ground, and pondered what he had been like at that age. Had life and death been that grave a matter, he wondered, scratching his beard. He doubted it, even though, at seven, he was living in a Druidic sanctuary and his only friend was a pretty red-haired girl.

He could still see her devilish green eyes and hear her impetuous laughter. The last time they had seen each other they were but children. Recalling their early days together, he was positive that life had been anything but serious to either one of them.

Solomon's mother, Orphea, was a Roman-Christian who had married his father, Roilan, in an attempt to ease the tension between the Celts and Rome. It was an arranged political marriage. His late father was the eldest son of Oisil, an over king, whose ritual and political functions extended to more than one of the surrounding tribes. As a gesture of peace between the two nations, Roilan wed Orphea on one brief visit to the opposite shore. He obligingly consummated their union, then returned to his tribe the next day by way of a Christian colony, where the young bride was left with instructions to wait until his return.

Roilan, who had a notorious reputation as a womanizer, had no intention of returning for his bride. It would be embarrassing enough to bring a Roman into the clan, but one who was not pagan would only double the humiliation. Therefore he returned alone, satisfied to report to the king that there would be better relations with the Romans in the future.

He soon proceeded to take his second wife, Melena. She was a fair-haired Celtic virgin, perfectly bred to be the wife of a chieftain. Roilan was happy; not only to have a lovely woman to share his home, but one who was the daughter of the single largest land and cattle owner in the territory.

Five years passed before Roilan was ready to assume his duties as Chieftain. There had been no mention of Rome or the Christian, and Roilan and Melena now had a son they named Laden. The Chieftain did not know that Orphea also had borne him a son. He was named Solomon, after the biblical king known for his discriminating judgment and wisdom.

Orphea told her child that he was very much like the biblical figure—his parentage would offer him mixed fortune. He was fortunate to have a brave and respected warrior as a father. Yet he was unfortunate in that there were elements in Roilan's example that would inevitably have pernicious effects on his life. A deeply religious woman, Orphea also believed that her son was a symbol that the two rival nations would someday come to tolerate each other's ways.

It had been twenty-six years since the time of the man known as Jesus Christ, and Orphea diligently tutored her son in the Christian ways. The two were happy enough living in a small Roman colony on the island's eastern coast. For the most part, the Celts did not bother the Romans, nor the Romans the Celts. The two cultures lived in relative peace; save a few skirmishes over whose boats owned the coastline, they successfully established a wealthy trade system.

Their peaceful coexistence came to an abrupt end when one day, in an effort to dominate the trade exchange, Rome demanded that the Celts lay down their arms as a show of good faith in their relations. For a Celt to carry a weapon was considered a divine right. It was looked upon as a friend given to him by the spirits, and to seize it was to take his manhood.

When the tribe refused, a war broke out. King Oisil sent his sons, Roilan and Donnach, with their entire army, to battle the Roman colony. The Celtic warriors won in a single afternoon.

As was his duty, Roilan found Orphea, and promptly, if not gladly, divorced her. He said that since Rome had betrayed its word to the Celts, he was no longer bound to his. He proceeded to sell her as a slave to the first Mediterranean trader who would pay her price in wine. He kept the boy, and, knowing that Melena would never accept a half-Christian child, left him and quite a few bottles of wine with the Druids. He arranged that the child would be raised and educated as a priest in exchange for six of his best cattle each year and a virginal sacrifice every third cycle.

After the initial shock and loneliness of losing his mother, Solomon adjusted to his new home with the white-robed Order. Their beliefs, built on the premise that the soul was immortal and capable of enjoying a close relationship with nature and the gods, were easy for him to embrace. He came to love the open oak grove temples and the elaborate rituals of worship that took place there. He was told that spirits of gods had come down to share their essence with mortals, so that their holy race could thrive and be assimilated into the Celtic societies.

His favorite playmate was a cherubic, red-haired girl his own age who was said to be just such a being. Her education as a Druidess had begun one year after her birth, and since the rigorous, often secretive instruction took twenty years to complete, she was not even half through. Whether spirit or human, Solomon found her fun and normal enough to enjoy playing and sharing interests common to most children their age.

Surprisingly, Roilan visited his son often, taking the time to school him in weaponry and hunting. He explained in great detail the Celtic beliefs and described, time and again, the kingdom in which he lived. After a while, father and son developed a deep affection for each other. Roilan's visits increased in frequency and duration, until one day upon an emotional departure, he informed the boy and the Druids that with his next visit, Solomon would return with him.

Months passed without word from Roilan. Then one day a young king named Donnach came for the boy. He explained to the Arch Druid that his older brother, Roilan, and their father, King Oisil, had been assassinated in retaliation by Rome, and that he was now ruler of the tribe.

With his dying breath, Roilan had made Donnach vow that Solomon would be retrieved and grow up in their clan. Now he had come to fulfill his brother's wishes.

Hearing this, the boy was filled with hate for his mother's people and begged Donnach to teach him the ways of the Celts. The young king embraced his brother's child, and, still mourning Roilan's murder, promised Solomon his loyalty.

He offered the Druids twelve cattle, ten sheep, and two young male slaves in return for Solomon, and a promise of secrecy as to his parentage. According to the precepts of their tribe, Donnach had taken the widow Melena as his bride, and adopted her son Laden as his own. Since no one else knew of Solomon's existence, he would be taken on as the king's foster and raised by him personally. Solomon could not, however, make any claim to the throne.

All agreed to this, and sealed their oaths in a private ceremony. Solomon's memory of it was still vivid. He could see the face of the Arch Druid staring intently down on the piece of raw lamb. His long, dark hair was greying around the temples, and hints of white had already woven themselves into his full beard. He possessed a fierce, disturbing look in his eyes as he cut the bloody meat into small pieces.

At first Solomon did not want to eat it. Not because he did not believe in the vow he was about to make, but because he found the uncooked lamb repulsive.

"Go ahead, boy," Donnach urged, placing a hand on his shoulder.

Solomon looked up at him unsure, and was immediately comforted by the warmth in the young king's eyes. He knew then, by the very care Donnach reflected, that his life from that moment forward would be filled with compassion and friendship from this man. Then Solomon took in a deep breath and choked down the raw offering. He could remember how slippery it felt as he tried to keep it from coming back up. The incident had left such an impression on him that to this day, he demanded his meat well-done before he ate it.

He could still feel the clammy hand of the Arch Druid as he grabbed Solomon's wrist and pricked his forefinger with a knife. He squeezed it until a few drops of blood had fallen into a chalice of wine set between him and the King.

Solomon recalled sucking on his bleeding fingertip as he watched the same ritual performed for Donnach. Then the Druid held the wine high in the air.

"As the blood in your veins has been mixed in the nectar of these grapes," he said in a haunting voice, "so it will be consumed by you. And as it infiltrates your body, the promise we have made will reside forever in the silence of your hearts."

Solomon stayed at the ceremony only as long as he had to, then he fled for the company of his lambent-haired confidant.

"I am going away from here," he told her when he had sneaked by her handmaid and into her private chamber. His uncertainty about this change was evident in his shaky voice.

She returned his frenzied declaration with a languid smile.

"They told me, Solomon," she shyly replied. "I will miss you all too much, but I know you will not stay away forever."

At first light, Solomon said farewell to her with the faintest kiss on her alabaster cheek. She started to cry as he climbed atop the stallion Donnach had brought for him and departed.

Because of Donnach's position, Solomon was easily accepted into the clan. He soon became the leader of the tribe's fianna, an organized band of young warriors who spent most of their time hunting and fighting in other tribal areas. It was a way for them to prepare for the military, as well as an opportunity for an outstanding individual to earn prestige and favor with the aristocracy. Fortunately for Solomon, his prominent displays of courage in the fianna made up for any loss of birthrights he had suffered.

Now, at the age of twenty-one, Solomon had a wife, Deireadh, and had assumed her moderate land holdings. Deireadh's knowledge of ritual practices and soothsayings had endeared her to the king. Solomon's position was further secured because his celsine was thriving. He had proved himself a worthy Celt in all aspects of his life, except for raising a competent foster. Now the only thing left in question was whether he could teach his craft to the waif shuffling up the hillside in front of him.

Solomon looked up at the bright sun a moment, rubbed his tired eyes, and slowly followed behind him on his horse.

The water was dripping from Aonghus' sagging woolen trousers and his wet boots made a squishing noise with each step. From his slouching posture, the warrior expected the boy to be crying, but as he came alongside him, he saw that he was sullen but dry-eyed with his gaze fixed on the ground.

"I can give you a ride if you like," Solomon offered, pulling back on the reins to slow his horse as the boy labored up the hillside.

Aonghus shook his head. There were beads of sweat across the bridge of his nose and upper lip.

"I would rather walk," he said, trying not to appear out of breath. "It will give me time to think of a way to explain this to my father."

The warrior's horse stumbled on a rock, throwing Solomon momentarily off balance, then he resumed his prancing in the next moment.

"Just tell him that the dog saved my life," the warrior replied. "Is that not good enough?"

"No," Aonghus answered.

"No?" Solomon retorted, raising his brows questioningly. "Why not?"

Aonghus stopped and took a deep huffing breath, then he continued walking without answering.

"I asked you, why not?" Solomon questioned again when he realized the boy would not voluntarily reply.

Aonghus remained silent until they had reached the crest of the hill. He set down his game and leaned against one of the alder trees, trying to catch his wind.

"Because although you are important as a warrior, a good hunting dog to a farmer is more important," he explained sincerely. He chose his words carefully so as not to offend the warrior. "Perhaps it will be good for this clan that you should live another day, but for my family the loss of a hound could mean the difference between porridge and meat."

Solomon threw his head back and laughed out loud. He was not laughing at Aonghus' sincerity; he was laughing at the irony of being compared to a dog, and being found less significant. It was perhaps one of the most honest analogies he had ever heard.

At his reaction, Aonghus stood up straight and flashed his eyes indignantly.

"Forgive me," Solomon said, still chuckling. "It is just that I have never been likened to being less than a dog before. It is, to be frank, quite funny."

He could see Aonghus was getting mad by the way he tightened his lips and blinked nervously.

"Ruff," the warrior humorously barked at him.

The boy's face turned red, then he broke into a smile and looked away, trying to conceal his amusement.

"How about if you tell him that it was my mistake," he continued with a half-smile. "Tell him that I was the one who was trying to get killed, but the boar like the hound better."

Aonghus dug his front toe into the ground, making a divot in the moist grass. "It is not funny. Locwn was our best hound."

The warrior's face became sympathetic. "I know, but what are we to do about it? The hound is dead, the tribe is hungry, and we will vindicate your animal tonight by devouring the wretched monster that killed him. You should, in truth, celebrate since by tomorrow the boar will amount to little more than excrement, while your hound rests a hero in the bosom of Brigantia."

The boy's expression lightened. At last his somber face looked its age again, Solomon thought, moving his horse closer to pat the top of his head.

"You are right," Aonghus said, picking up his pole. "But I must still take this game to my family so it will be ready for dinner."

"You are taking all of that home? What about us? You are my foster, and I am entitled to your catch," he said, perturbed.

Aonghus obstinately jutted out his jaw. Lowering his pole, he took off one duck, then reached in his net and grabbed three fish and obediently held them out to him.

"According to the laws you are entitled to part, not all," he argued. "Besides my mother and father, I have two brothers that need to eat as well. You have only a wife, and considering the size of the boar, to demand my entire stock would be gluttonous. If you wish to eat any more fish or foul tonight, you will have to feast at my father's table. I am sure you will be welcome."

The warrior rolled his eyes. "Come on," he said, holding out his hand to the boy. "Put those back, and I will take you home myself."

Aonghus waited a moment, as if he were considering the proposition. Then he impaled the duck on the wooden stick and shoved the fish back into the net. Placing his grimy hand in Solomon's, he let the warrior pull him on the back of the horse.

"Where did you learn these laws so well?" Solomon asked, starting down the slope.

"My father taught me," the boy answered.

CHAPTER FOUR

wisting the ends of her sash together, Deireadh knotted it and discreetly tucked in its corners. Then she pulled back her long dark hair and began rebraiding it methodically.

Lounging on the bed of animal furs, Laden watched her weave her tresses and coil them on top of her head. She had an unusually high forehead that made her hairline look almost as if it were receding. Her hair was so black that her pale skin seemed to glow in contrast. She had sharp cheekbones and rather cold, deep-set, hazel eyes. If eyes are the indicator of the spirit within, Deireadh's were impenetrable.

"I would have you again," Laden said, reaching up and unrolling the braid with one hand. Unlike many of the other Celtic men, he did not have the large rough hands of the common warrior. His were lithe and feminine, almost as if he had never had to labor with them.

Deireadh dropped her head back and smiled as he sat up and began kissing her neck.

"Tell me, does the good warrior Solomon ever smell the scent of another man on his woman, the way he picks up the stench of his prey?" he asked, presumptuously shoving his hand between her thighs.

Deireadh's eyes narrowed and she pushed him away.

"You sicken me," she said in a frigid tone.

Laden laughed as he took a handful of her hair and bent her head backward so he could meet her eyes. "That is not what you said a few moments ago," he told her with a smirk, then he pressed his open mouth to her painted lips. The ruan she had used to redden them left traces on the sides of his mouth when he drew away.

"I like you much better that way," he said, releasing her and lying back down again. The dark-haired woman sat up straight, and tilting her head down, looked at him alluringly out of the corner of her eye.

"Dear sweet Deireadh," he continued, as he scratched his bare chest with both hands. "I do not think that you are quite as calculating or aspiring a woman as you would like others to think."

"That is your error," she responded, running her fingertips lightly over the inside of his calf.

"Perhaps," he replied, scratching a fresh scab from this shoulder that she had inflicted with her nails. "Yet for one so seemingly ambitious, you have condemned yourself to infamy by betrothing Solomon. Do tell me why you married him anyway. You could not have possibly thought he would ascend to Chieftain—or were you truly in love?"

Deireadh jerked her hand away. "It was not such a poor choice. After all, he was your father's foster and—"

Laden burst into laughter. "My father's foster? Well, of course that is a great reason to choose him. Did you think the good King Donnach would offer a portion of his territory to a bastard orphan?" He threw his head back and laughed louder. "You are naive, my precious raven. But I do find it a charming trait."

Deireadh's cheeks flushed with humiliation as she stood up hastily and walked to the window. Opening it a crack, she looked outside. A narrow stream of late afternoon light caught her pupils, making her olive-shaped eyes appear preternatural.

"I could divorce him," she said slyly, then turned her head to stare at Laden intently. "For a king, that is."

"I do not think so," he replied as he picked his breeches up from the floor. "He is half Christian. Their culture does not allow for such matters of convenience. Do you not remember him mumbling a little phrase, 'Till death do you part,' before sealing his marriage vow? I do. I was standing right there."

Annoyed, Deireadh went hurriedly to the bed, and lifting her full skirt, straddled him like a horse.

"The Order would not acknowledge it," she argued, taking his face in her hands. "Not if I had good reason to ask for the divorce. What about you, Laden? You could give me the reason I need. You have yet to take a bride; as your Druidess, it would not be strange for us to wed."

The warrior gave her a pretentious smile.

"No raven, I am set to marry a virgin from the Trinovantes tribe. They are already allied with Rome and rich because of it. They have the most beautiful, full-hipped brunette maidens I have ever laid eyes upon," he boasted. "Besides, my vanity could never abide the public rebuke of assuming tainted chattel."

Deireadh's face turned crimson as she lifted her fist in the air to hit him. Readily catching it with one hand, Laden slapped her across the face with the back of his other. Then he took her by both shoulders and shoved her away from him. She fell clumsily backward, and he leaned over her.

"Do not ever lift a hand to me, Druidess," he threatened, pointing a finger, "or I will have you burned in the wicker man for your dark practices."

Her chest heaving, she rolled away from him and got to her feet. "Any dark conjuring I have done has been for you," she said, rubbing the side of her face.

The fair-haired warrior sat back and propped himself up on one elbow. "They would never take a witch's word over a Chieftain's," he replied.

"You are not a Chieftain yet," she hissed. "Beware, Laden, for I will entreat those same spirits of darkness to prevent it."

Her ears rang with his sarcastic snickering as she impulsively threw her cloak over her shoulders. Promptly walking to the door, she slammed it behind her as she left.

Her cheeks were burning as she walked swiftly down the long, birch-paneled corridor. It was lit with torches and adorned with bright tapestries depicting hunting or battle scenes. Along one wall was a beautifully painted mural of two young Celtic warriors locked in combat with battle-attired Romans. One had already severed the head of his attacker while the other was driving his sword into another's heart. They were each perched atop massive horses, drawn recognizably larger than the animals the Romans were riding. They were wearing crested bronze helmets and wielding large jeweled swords. In the background was a two-horse chariot filled with severed Roman heads and goblets of silver and gold. Villagers were painted on surrounding hillsides with lifted hands and jubilant expressions as they cheered on the noble warriors.

Opening one of the copper screens, Deireadh entered the center room. Her eyes widened with surprise when she saw Solomon seated in front of the hearth with Donnach. He had just lifted a flagon of wine to his lips. His eyes darted to the side and met hers, then he lowered the vessel without taking a drink and grinned.

"Oh, Solomon!" she said, flustered.

"Oh, Deireadh!" he good-naturedly imitated her.

Nervously clasping her hands in front of her, she forced a smile.

"You seem surprised to see me?" he queried, raising the wine and taking a long drink this time.

"No, not at all," she answered, distracted. "I just did not expect you to be waiting. How long have you been here?"

"Long enough to drink a good portion of my finest vintage," Donnach interjected, grabbing the drink from Solomon and frowning.

The older man was dressed in simple red and yellow plaid woolen trousers. He wore a green tunic embroidered with a gold flowery pattern at its hem. Were it not for his thick, flamboyantly jeweled neck torque, his status would have gone completely unnoticed.

The two men resembled each other in that they both had the same close-set eyes and heavy brows, except Donnach's eyes were a shade of greenish-blue, and the younger one's, a deep brown. Their cheekbones were both high and rounded off, giving the impression that they were always slightly smiling, even when they were not. The only pronounced difference between them was that Solomon had a rather straight, blunt Roman nose, whereas Donnach's was long and easily the most prominent feature on his face.

The young warrior leaned back against the pillows, amused by the old king's attempt to feign irritation. More than anyone, Donnach loved these afternoon visits. The two men would sit hour after hour drinking good Mediterranean wine, and Solomon would listen attentively as Donnach recounted stories of his and Roilan's escapades. He had heard the same stories many times, and he knew them so well that, at times, it was Solomon who would correct Donnach as to the proper series of events.

Donnach tilted his head back and raised the vessel to take a drink. As he did this, Solomon purposely nudged the King, causing him to miss his mouth and spill the red liquid down his front.

"Look at that, old man," the warrior said with a gleam in his eyes. "You spilled it. Which of us has had their fair share of drink?"

He did not wait for Donnach's reaction as he sprung to his feet, so swiftly he almost fell, then he staggered over to his wife. She could smell the stale odor of grapes on his breath as he bent down to kiss her, and she awkwardly offered him her cheek. He hesitated a moment, then kissed her anyway, not wanting to appear affected by her reaction. Stepping back, he looked at her questioningly a moment, then he gently ran the back of his hand over the side of her face where Laden had slapped her.

"What is wrong?" he asked sincerely. "You are flushed."

Deireadh shook her head.

"Nothing," she answered, and quickly. "Just a bit of fever."

"And is my son's spirit being well cared for?" Donnach asked in an overly commanding tone. "The soul of a Chieftain should be well wrought in such sacred matters."

"Of course, good King," Deireadh replied, thankful for the distraction. "Your son will be the most deserving of rulers."

She bowed to him respectfully, then started for the door without even acknowledging her husband. Solomon looked down at the floor then ruefully up at her. Perhaps a decent night of feasting would lighten their moods.

CHAPTER FIVE

n spite of the warm day, the evening had taken on the normal chilly bite of early spring. The light of the full moon shone through the gnarled oak branches, casting distorted incandescent images about the grove.

The flames from the bonfire cast a golden crown of light around the center green. It was an open space of grass large enough for the whole tribe, and encircled by oak trees on all sides. It was in this clearing that rituals were celebrated, booty was assessed after a battle, and trials were held when the Druids made their quarterly visits of judgment. It was also the site where weddings took place and warriors were anointed. Located precisely in the middle of the village, it functioned as the meeting place for the entire clan.

On this night, it was the warriors who were celebrating the first full moon since they had observed the three-day Festival of Brigantia. It was considered a good omen to offer up the slain beast in her honor, because they believed it was the Goddess herself who had allowed the animal to be taken.

The members of this elite society were seated in a rough circle, with King Donnach taking the distinguished center place. Next to him was Deireadh. Since she was the clan's keeper of the ritual practices, she represented the Goddess on this eve. She was also the only woman allowed to participate in this event.

It was not that the Celts discriminated against females. On the contrary, the feminine energy was revered, and the women were guaranteed equal rights by law. They could own property, choose their own husbands, and participate in the tribe's political arena. They were even afforded a place on the battle lines. For a woman, to be a warrior or chieftain was not forbidden. It was merely that in this small tribe, there had yet to be a female who showed the desire or expertise to accomplish the necessary feats for initiation.

Opposite Donnach, in the place occupied by the bravest warrior, was Laden. His younger brother, Pwyll, was next to him, where normally the richest tribesman would have sat. The rest of the warriors took their places in order of importance, and much to Solomon's irritation, he was fifth from the center.

Servants and the warriors' young squires moved among them bearing trays of food and carafes of wine. Off to one side were the minstrels, playing lyres and harps. They were accompanied by singing bards, the tribe's historians who composed eulogistic praises for the King and the territorial overlords. They were not only considered part of the entertainment, but were important in perpetuating vital accounts of clan record. No doubt, whatever took place on this eve would be recounted in feasts to come.

Donnach sat complacently in front of the roasted boar. He lifted his hand, gesturing prudence on the part of Laden, who had made more than enough derogatory comments on the quality of Solomon's hunting expertise. Acknowledging the King's request, the blond-haired warrior flashed him a look of pride and snickered, then he put his knife into the piece of meat he had just been served.

It was obvious that the amount Laden had been given was quite a bit larger than the measly portion Solomon had received. Even if he was the King's son, this was not out of diplomacy; it was blatant disrespect to give Solomon so little of the animal he had worked hard to kill. After all, he was the one almost trampled, not his blond opponent. Sacred or not, it had been Laden himself who had cowered at the thought of flushing the boar out of the cave.

With more force than would have normally been required, Solomon speared the meat with his knife and shoved it into his mouth. The piece was much too big to eat all at once, and the juices flowed down his beard as he chewed.

Conspicuously leaning forward, he glared at Laden, thinking all the while that he would like to cut his throat rather than drink the cup of wine he now hoisted to his lips.

"I dare say," Laden declared, pointing at Solomon with the tip of his knife, "This warrior, the one, good King, that you claimed was the best in the tribe, completely lost sight of the animal in the bracken. After he chased him into the clearing and missed spearing him, he failed to head him off and the wretched thing disappeared into a hole in the earth, and this bearded buffoon went into the divine place and tried to steal it from the gods. Of course, I cautioned him that such practices of disrespect could cause the seas to rise and the sky to fall, but he paid no heed. He was lost in the darkness until I personally begged the spirits to spare his life, and hearing my humble supplications, they delivered the already slain animal right onto my horse's back!"

The other warriors threw their heads back in laughter. Berrig, who was next to Solomon, slapped him on the shoulder and roared louder.

Solomon swallowed the chunks of pork and glowered at Laden. "You are not going to make your mistake into my folly," he announced defensively.

Angrily he snatched up his cup, and noticing it was empty, he slammed it down, demanding it to be refilled. Aonghus swiftly came forward. The sallow-faced child looked strangely out of place among the bearded, robust warriors. Responding to Solomon's impending rage, his expression was visibly strained. His eyes, like pale sapphires, nervously darted at anything that briefly caught his attention. He had never been to one of these gatherings, but had heard the many stories of disputes rising from boasting matches such as this, and knew that they usually ended in bloody single combat.

Careful not to spill the wine, he filled Solomon's cup, then stood fidgeting while he waited to see if anything else would be required of him.

"Who is this that challenges my word?" Laden retorted. "The jester who cowered from a bristly swine?"

"Do not be a fool," Solomon growled, a piece of meat dropping from his mouth onto his beard. "It was you who panicked in his sights, not I."

Sweeping his arm across his plate, Laden sent food and drink flying. He sprang to his feet, eyes blazing, as he bounded over to Solomon and stopped abruptly in front of him. Holding his clenched fists waist high, he stood huffing with anger, feeding his fury with each breath.

The only thing separating the two angry warriors was Aonghus, who crouched down so suddenly that he accidently tossed the vessel of wine aside. He could feel the grass stick to his clammy palms as he flattened them against the ground. Moving only his eyes, he looked first at Solomon then skittishly up at Laden. The warrior seemed massive towering over him. From the boy's perspective, his calves appeared almost as big as his thighs. His chest was like an immense boulder, expanding violently, and the veins in his entire body looked like they were dilating.

Tucking his chin to his chest, Aonghus felt his heart swell with fear as he realized that he was trapped where he was. If he did as his instincts dictated and tried to scamper off, he would appear faint-hearted and ruin what might be his only opportunity to ascend beyond his farmer's roots.

"Are you calling me a liar?" Laden's voice sounded like thunder coming through the trees.

The surrounding warriors instantly became silent. Aonghus could hear shuffling as they retreated a safe distance away. Lifting his head slightly, he caught sight of Solomon's hand poised on his dagger. In a flash, Laden's leather boot whizzed in front of his face as it kicked the piece of meat Solomon had just cut out of his hand. Aonghus cringed as the pork flipped into the air and landed on the grass beside him.

"I asked you a question!" Laden roared. "Are you calling me a liar?"

Smacking his lips, Solomon rose to his feet at the precise moment the music stopped playing. Widening his stance, he looked his opponent up and down, then puckering his lips, spit what was left of the roasted boar in his face.

Laden lunged at Solomon and clumsily fell over Aonghus. The little boy flinched in pain as he heard the rest of the warriors burst into drunken laughter. Then pressing his hand to his sore ribs, he scurried out of the way.

Chuckling to himself, Solomon extended the fallen warrior his hand. Laden eyed him suspiciously, his fair skin ruddy with anger, then slapped the hand aside. Realizing that his gesture of fairness had been refused, Solomon shrugged his shoulders. His eyes passed over the line of warriors and stopped at Laden. Then he delivered a swift kick to Laden's jaw.

There was the clicking of teeth as his blond locks were swept backward, then abruptly flew forward again.

In the next instant, the green-eyed warrior was back on his feet with blood gushing from his lips and the shiny blade of his drawn dagger glimmering in the firelight.

Both bearing weapons, the two men pivoted around each other, each one waiting for the other to make the first move. Food was being trampled beneath the cowhide soles of their boots as they sparred like beasts around the bonfire. Finally, Solomon feigned an attack to Laden's right side. Attempting to block it, Laden was knocked off balance, as Solomon quickly changed direction and assaulted him from the left.

Laden lurched forward, trying to regain his stance, but Solomon punched him above his groin. He hunched over in pain, his dagger dropping to the ground. Taking advantage of the reaction, Solomon grabbed him by both ears and smashed his face into his bent knee.

Solomon was raging. He had waited too long to feel Laden's flesh bruise beneath his might. Now that he had started this fight, he was going to take it as far as he could.

This kind of combat was not rare among the warriors. Sometimes it involved a test of dignity, at other times it was simply an excuse to vent frustration, but either way, a warlord who accepted a challenge of single combat was expected to win, or lose respect and standing with the other members of the society.

Laden dropped to his knees, shaking his head from side to side, trying to stay conscious. Running the back of one hand across his bleeding mouth, he focused on Solomon and let out a chilling howl. As if it were a cue to continue, Solomon went forward to kick him again, but Laden caught him in mid-flight and pulled his feet out from under him.

Deliberately turning to avoid a fall into the bonfire, Solomon hit the ground so hard he grunted. Before he could do anything in retaliation, Laden had his hands clasped around his neck and was shoving his head toward the flames. Solomon could hear the ends of his hair being singed by the heat as he felt a panicky shortness of breath. Becoming weak and lightheaded, his vision was a watery blur as Laden mercilessly drove his thumbs into his throat.

Fearing that Solomon would be killed, Aonghus frantically bolted to his aid and began beating on Laden's back with his fists. He could hear his own frenzied voice, demanding Laden to let go of him. Then he felt someone grab him by the nape of the neck and single-handedly drag him off to the side. Twisting around, he found himself looking into Berrig's stern face.

"Keep still boy," he scolded. "You will only get yourself hurt."

Aonghus' face was burning hot, and disregarding Berrig's advice, he started for Laden again, only this time with a rock in his hand. There was the feeling of Berrig's massive arm around his waist as the warrior hoisted him, wiggling and kicking, off the ground.

"Be still, you imp," Berrig commanded, throwing Aonghus over one shoulder. "You can only make it worse."

Desperately forcing his head beneath Berrig's elbow, Aonghus watched an upside-down view of the fight.

Solomon made horrid choking noises as Laden repeatedly slammed his head against the ground. Then Solomon clumsily put both hands behind Laden's neck, and pulling him forward, sunk his teeth into his cheek. He could feel the puncturing of the flesh and taste the salty, warm blood.

Laden gasped at the pain. Taking a handful of Solomon's hair, he tried to pull him away. Solomon dug his teeth deeper, shoved his knee into Laden's groin and flipped him over on his back, pinning him helplessly to the ground.

Solomon picked up his opponent's knife and stuck the point of it into the tip of Laden's nose. Wheezing with his own blind fury, Solomon puckered his lips and spewed the blood from his mouth into Laden's eyes. He wanted to slit his nose up the middle, then drive the dagger straight through his open mouth and impale him to the ground. He wanted to do it; he saw himself doing it. The bloody vision spun dizzily in his head. His heart's wild pounding and his gasping breath overpowered his ears, as he felt his rage boil up and threaten to overtake him. Then he looked at Donnach.

The old King's face was thick with fear. From the piercing look in his eyes, Solomon knew that he would never forgive him, regardless of the circumstances. Yet if Solomon did not kill Laden, he would be considered a coward and suffer a great loss of rank and respect in the tribe.

"You made a vow," Donnach said through quivering lips. Then he raised his hand in the air, signaling the other warriors to draw their weapons.

One by one each warrior lifted his spear or drew his sword, waiting obediently for the King's signal to execute Solomon.

Shaking his head, Donnach looked compassionately back at Solomon. This was the worst of situations, one that he had hoped would never occur. If Solomon were to kill Laden, no matter how justifiable, he would be the proper heir to the throne. Since they had taken an oath never to allow that to happen, it would be impossible to explain to the rest of the tribe why the warrior would be an unfit ruler. Therefore, the only way to avoid such a predicament was to not allow it to take place. In the eyes of the gods, it would be easier to resolve Solomon's untimely death than to disavow a Druidic oath.

"Do not push me to this," Donnach said quietly.

Solomon blindly dropped his gaze then lifted his brown eyes to look at a weeping Deireadh. He could never expect her to honor him after this.

Inhaling deeply, he closed his eyes for a moment, giving the impression that it pained him to look at her. Opening them again, he stared down at Laden's frightened face. He looked docile, almost as if, in spite of his actions, he needed to be protected. Now Solomon knew why he had gone to such lengths to avoid ever having this encounter. He knew, no matter how well he fought, it was a fight he could not expect to win.

For a fleeting instant, he wondered why he had not let Laden's comments go unacknowledged, as he had numerous other times. He knew it was not the accusation that he had failed to kill the boar which had really provoked him. It was more the image of the dying hound that stuck in his mind, and the courage it took for Aonghus to kill it. Or perhaps it was that Deireadh would not look into his eyes that afternoon.

Gritting his teeth, he raised Laden's knife in the air and brought it down wildly into the ground next to his face. Laden's eyes were shut tight, as if expecting a dreaded deadly blow. When he realized he had not been killed, his body went limp.

Standing slowly, Solomon stepped in front of Deireadh. Tears were rolling down her checks and she was nervously chewing on her bottom lip. Gathering her skirt, she hurriedly rose from her place and ran past him to Laden's side.

Solomon could not hide his wounded reaction. His shoulders sagged as mind and body gave way to exhaustion. He knew he was shaking, but his body was so numb he could not feel it. Bringing his hand up over his forehead, he ran his fingers through his hair, then picked up his cloak and wordlessly left the clearing.

CHAPTER SIX

ait, wait for me!" Aonghus called, running after the warrior.

Solomon turned, and seeing who it was, frowned and quickened his pace forward.

Aonghus ran as fast as he could; the excitement of the fighting having given him a rush of adrenalin. Barely able to see the back of Solomon's cloak ahead, he leapt over a tree stump, and cut through the bracken to catch him. The coarse branches of shrubbery scratched his arms as he pushed the bushes aside.

The breathless boy reached out, grabbed the back of Solomon's cloak and yanked on it. The sheer weight of the garment caused it to drop to the ground.

Solomon whirled around sharply and snatched it from the ground. "Go home, child," he snapped. "I have nothing more to teach you."

Aonghus stopped, his arms dropping limply to his sides as he looked back at him open-mouthed. His expression told Solomon that he was not going to obey without more of an explanation.

Solomon's eyes tapered into tiny slits of annoyance. He was still furious, and capable of rendering Aonghus a good spanking if he did not comply.

"Is there something wrong with your hearing? I told you your fosterage is finished. Be off to your parents," he scolded. Slapping a flimsy oak branch out of his way, he felt a pebble strike him in the back of the head. He felt another against his back, immediately followed by a rather large one hitting him in the buttocks.

"You cannot do that," Aonghus was shouting, so loudly that the words came out in a shrill vibrato. "You told my father you would take me under your fosterage. You gave your word."

As he turned to respond, another stone hit Solomon on the side of the face. It pierced the skin on the crest of his cheekbone.

"Ouch!" he yelled, as he touched the stinging area with his fingertips. "That hurt, you little wretch."

Aonghus' eyes widened anxiously. Their color seemed to glaciate to an icy blue as he rocked awkwardly forward on his toes then back on his heels. His expression smacked of a secret contentment at having momentarily gotten the best of one bigger and stronger than he.

"Your father has not fully paid me yet," Solomon retorted. "He has only given me two heifers and a milk cow, not the required six and two milk cows."

"But he promised to give you the rest after harvest, and you agreed," Aonghus hollered back indignantly. "You are a liar and a coward like Laden said. And my dog died because of you!"

The child's face twisted and he began to cry. Solomon stared back at him quizzically; he had never seen a creature work itself into such a state so rapidly.

"I want a chance to be something besides a farmer," he answered, suddenly embarrassed at his emotional outburst. Then he stared red-faced at the ground.

Solomon gave a frustrated sigh. He stepped back, and looked at Aonghus for a thoughtful moment. He had never wanted the responsibility of teaching another man's child or, for that matter, even one of his own.

Taking on a foster was a test of his own skill and reputation to successfully school an apprentice to the point of being anointed by the Druids. The better the warrior Solomon raised, the more accolades he would enjoy. If he failed, he would be looked down upon by the others, and his pride would not allow failure.

"Listen to me," he said, deliberately trying to sound calmer than he really was. "Do you understand what happened tonight?"

Aonghus shuffled nervously from one foot to the other. "You lost a fight to the King's son," he responded after consideration.

"I backed down from a challenge of my own integrity," he said flatly. "And I have dishonored myself and my wife because of it. There is little doubt that when word of this defeat reaches my celsine, they will more than likely take employment with Laden. I will scarcely have any rank if that happens, and it makes little sense for you to continue with me when you could find another capable warrior to instruct you."

Aonghus wrinkled his noise, then frowned as if he found Solomon's explanation unacceptable. "I already did," he replied.

"You already did?" Solomon countered, arching his brows.

"I tried to find someone else to take me before I even asked you," he explained honestly. "None of them would accept partial payment except you. I am not here because I like you the best; you were my last resort."

Solomon put both hands on this hips, eyeing the boy up and down. He was such an odd one, entirely too serious and brutally honest for his years. Still, he came from good stock. Although his family was common, they were earnest, well-meaning people. It would be wrong to go back on his promise to them now, regardless of what his lack of restraint had caused.

"Very well," Solomon said finally. "The arrangement will stand as it is."

The boy's countenance lightened immediately. The little lines at the corners of his mouth and between his furrowed brows seemed to vanish. For a brief instant, Solomon even detected a hint of a smile on his young face.

"Good, my father will be pleased with that," Aonghus replied. "You should banquet at our house tonight; you are entitled to a portion."

"According to the laws, right?" Solomon chided.

The boy looked back at him expressionless and nodded.

The warrior eyed him for a perplexing moment, and Aonghus stared right back, as if he were waiting to be provoked. Then Solomon chuckled and put his cloak back over his shoulders.

"How old are you really?" he asked as they started walking.

"I am seven," the boy answered seriously.

"Oh yes, seven," the warrior replied. "I forgot."

————

Koven's first thought when he saw the two enter the room was that his son had done something wrong, and the warrior was bringing him back to renege on the agreement. From the thin red lines framing Aonghus' eyelids, it was plain he had been crying, and Solomon's tousled hair and ruddy pallor gave the impression that, whether emotional or physical, the two had suffered a rather uncomfortable encounter. Trying not to look too startled, Koven rose to greet them.

"Solomon, so good of you to visit," he said, strained. "I trust all is well."

"All is well enough," Solomon replied, extending his hand to the farmer.

As he shook it, he noticed that the joints of Koven's hands were rather large, like the knots on an oak branch, and very hot. He gripped Solomon's hand precariously, as though it were much bigger than it really was.

"Solomon has no place to eat tonight," Aonghus interjected, as he stepped over to the fire to warm himself. "He lost a challenge at the feast and had to leave, so I told him that we would feed him."

Koven's face reddened at his son's candor, and he gave the warrior an apologetic smile. "Of course," he said. "We would be pleased to have you share with us."

Self-consciously wringing his swollen hands and cracking the knuckles of both thumbs, Koven looked around the small room, embarrassed. There was a defined caste system within the tribe. Aristocrats socialized with aristocrats, and farmers with farmers. It was very seldom that a warrior dined with the lower classes. Yet it was not the house that Solomon found distracting, it was the plethoric condition of Koven's hands. In the firelight, they looked an altogether different color from his wrists down. Every finger was flared out from the knuckles, almost like rotten cornstalks. They were so crooked they looked like they might have been crushed and poorly healed. Only from their waxy, cracking surface was it obvious they were diseased.

"Enda," Koven called into the next room. "We have a guest for dinner."

In the next moment his portly wife joined them. She had soft brown hair coiled in a braid on top of her head. Her face was round, and she had a chunky nose and rather wide-set, light brown eyes. Unlike most of the other women in the clan, she did not darken her brows with berry juice or redden her cheeks and paint her fingernails with ruan. From her kindly expression, she seemed genuinely pleased he was there.

She was leading two pudgy boys by the hand. They were not much younger than Aonghus, but the complete antithesis of the boy. They both had hair the color of their mother's, and her rather nondescript features as well. From their bulky appearance, Solomon though they could probably make a well-matched team if hitched to an ox cart.

"It is well that you should join us tonight," she said, hospitably taking his hand and patting it.

Solomon felt himself smile involuntarily. She was so unaffected that he could not help but find her plainness refreshing. He felt a twinge of sadness as he realized that, having spent too much time caught up in the vanity of life, he had forgotten the attractiveness of simplicity.

"Thank you," he replied softly. "It is well that you should have me."

As he released her hand, he saw one of the boys she had been holding run to Aonghus and throw his arms around his waist in a gesture of affection. Caught completely by surprise, Aonghus stumbled forward, regaining his balance in front of the open hearth. His face flashed with anger for only an instant, then appeared completely calm. He turned sharply and seized his younger brother's arm, and coiled it painfully behind his back. With the other hand, he grabbed the boy by the back of the hair and forcefully escorted the now crying child into the next room.

They paraded in front of Solomon and Enda, Aonghus completely deaf to his mother's admonishment to unhand the boy. When he reached the entryway to what Solomon supposed was the children's room, he gave his brother a hard shove and propelled him, face first, into the opposite wall.

He came back into the room, tight-lipped, and shaking his head in disgust. Briefly meeting the boy's gaze, Solomon noticed that Aonghus' eyes had taken on the same intensity as earlier that afternoon by the lake.

"He always does that," Aonghus said, irked. He then plopped himself beside his father. Gently taking Koven's puffy hand, he massaged it with his tiny fingers. He started at the center of the palm, and with precise movements, worked his way over the joints to the fingertips. When he reached the ends of each one, he would lightly pull on it as if he were milking a cow. After the knuckle had cracked, he would bend the finger forward to keep it flexible.

He seemed completely consumed by what he was doing, and took great care to do it as delicately as possible. From the concerned look on his face, he seemed to actually enjoy caring for this father in this way.

"You need some of mother's poultice," he said in a parental tone.

"Later," Koven replied. "We are being rude to our guest. Please, Solomon, sit with us."

He gestured to the warrior to take the seat opposite him on the mound of tapestries. It was noticeably higher than Koven and Aonghus, and even in these humble surroundings, Solomon knew it was the place reserved for a guest. It sunk beneath his weight, as setting down, he realized that most of what made up the chair was fresh straw. It was covered with a cowhide and adorned with two thread-bare tapestries.

The air in the small house was cloudy with smoke. It filtered in from the middle of the room where an iron cauldron was hung over the hearth by a chain attached to a cross beam. The odors of boiling fish and roasting duck moved along the sloping thatched roof to an oblong opening used for ventilation.

About a foot from the ceiling, the clay walls protruded to form a shelf lining the entire circumference of the room. Along the shelf were arranged bronze and clay vessels and bunches of dried herbs used for cooking and caring for the ill. To one side of the fireplace stood a two-tiered wooden table on which sat a stone quern for milling flour. Opposite that, in the prime location of the room, was a wooden loom with stone weights hanging from each base and filled with thread.

There were two smaller cubicles on either side of this main room, partitioned with wooden barriers. From the visible clothes hanging on the walls, and the fur-lined sleeping ledges, Solomon supposed these were the family's personal chambers. Having been accustomed to the King's lavish household as well as his own, Solomon thought this house barely livable in comparison.

Enda brought each man a large stein filled with corma, a wheaten beer mixed with honey. Had they been better acquainted, they probably would have shared a common cup. But since Solomon was a member of tribal nobility, he was sure she had given him his own out of respect.

Koven, Solomon, and Aonghus sat in uncomfortable silence for a time, each unsure of what to discuss. Mostly, Solomon watched the two younger children playing with broad-bladed hurley sticks. Out of politeness, he offered Koven a few words of praise on their athletic abilities, which, in reality, were not great.

Solomon wondered how Aonghus could be so completely different from them and still be part of the same family. Seeing him next to his father, however, it was apparent that one was the image of the other. The one difference was that Aonghus' features appeared sharper than Koven's. His nose was more prominent, his cheekbones higher, and although their eyes and hair were the same tone, the boy's look was more brooding, and his thick reddish-brown mop a more distinct contrast to his light skin.

By the time Enda served the meal, conversation was so strained that they all seemed relieved for the distraction. Her presence, with the other two children, made the atmosphere more relaxed.

Solomon's portion of the dinner consisted of one entire duck, four fish boiled with mushrooms and scallions, hardened bread softened with warm milk into gruel, and cooked corn. He did not know if it was his own hunger and fatigue that made everything taste exceptionally good, or if, as he believed, it truly was one of the most delicious meals he ever had. As the ale began to relax him and his empty stomach was soothed, life began to appear a bit more positive.

"Sorry about your hound," he said, after a while.

Koven looked up from his plate and offered him a sentimental smile. "It is all right," he said in an obliging tone. "Locwn had been in scrapes like that before, only they did not seem to make him any more cautious. He had to be stitched more than once because he refused to back down. A creature with any amount of sense should know not to take on an enemy he could not defeat."

Solomon flushed as he took an uneasy swallow of beer. He was probably not much different from the dog. Locwn attacked the boar to his own demise, and Solomon's injured pride had caused the same result earlier in the evening.

"You should have seen the fight Solomon lost to Laden," Aonghus blurted, as he reached over to cut his brother's fish for him. Then he picked up the cup of milk the three children were sharing, and helped the youngster hold it while he drank. A small amount of it dripped from the child's chin, and Aonghus wiped it off with his hand. Then he wiped his hand on the leg of his trousers while his brother gave him a milk-glazed smile of appreciation.

"He had him right over the bonfire, choking him," Aonghus continued with a smirk. "Then Solomon kicked him between the legs and threw him on his back. He put a knife to the end of his nose, but King Donnach said he had better not hurt him or there would be trouble. So Solomon gave up, and all the rest of the warriors were laughing at him by the time he left."

The boy's parents exchanged uncomfortable glances as Aonghus picked the fish off his plate by the tail. He let it dangle in the air, then let it flop back down as if he found the sight of it unappetizing. He licked his fingers clean, then earnestly looked Solomon in the eye.

"Maybe you should kill him anyway; nobody in the tribe even likes him," he reasoned with a mischievous grin. "No one would have to know you who did it."

"Aonghus, please!" Enda scolded, offering him a rag to wipe his hands. "You should not say such things about the King's son."

Aonghus took the rag and halfheartedly wiped both hands and the place where he had previously cleaned them on his pants.

"But it is the truth. You think so, too," the boy defended himself, passing the cloth to his brother to play with. "I heard his own brother, Pwyll, tell Megba the elder that Laden was a selfish liar who bedded other men's wives."

"When did you hear that?" Koven asked.

"The other day when mother had me take Megba some bread and eggs," he answered, picking up the fish again, but this time taking a bite.

Koven looked regretfully over at Solomon, who sat not chewing, but with his mouth still full.

"It is true," Koven said, concerned. "I know of your allegiance to the King, but there is talk among the villagers that he is being controlled by his son's ambition. He is old and tired, and he has not been the same since Melena's passing. I fear that if Laden becomes ruler, there will not be much support for it. Perhaps you would consider speaking to the King on our behalf."

The warrior finished chewing, then sat back and was quiet for a long while. He touched his forefinger to his lips, and stared off into oblivion with a most sorrowful look.

"Although nothing would please me more than to see Laden powerless, there is little I can do about it now," Solomon said finally, as he straightened his shoulders and took a deep breath. "I have disgraced myself before the King, and any sort of retaliation against his son would only create further dissention. You would do better to take it up with Deireadh, since she is the spiritual counselor to them both."

Koven and Enda simultaneously stared down at their plates, and Solomon could feel the tension suddenly rise in the room.

"Would that be unacceptable?" he asked, tilting his head to one side.
Koven nodded.

"Why?"

The husband and wife looked at each other, as if each one was wordlessly asking the other to answer.

"I know that she is your wife," Enda eventually answered in an overly polite way. "But there is some question as to the ethics of her practices. Many who have sought her counsel have said that she has turned to the dark arts and considers herself not as a servant of the gods, but as a goddess herself. On one occasion, I went to see her for a fertility charm because Koven and I have longed for a daughter. Since Brigantia is the goddess of expectant mothers, I asked her if she could ask the Goddess what kind of offering I should make so that I would have a daughter. She—"

Enda stopped, smoothing her hair back nervously.

"Continue, please," Solomon said, folding his arms across his chest.

"She said that I should weave her a red gown, and she would answer my request, not Brigantia," she continued. "She told me it was time this clan began to accept the Goddess in a living form and that soon, even the King would acknowledge her power. She said if I did not do this, my womb would go unfilled forever."

"Well did you do it?" Solomon asked, twisting one end of his mustache.

Enda emphatically shook her head. "Of course not, it would be a defilement of the Goddess. But I still do not have a daughter," she said sadly. "I am not the only one who has had such a request from Deireadh. There are many others."

She hurriedly cleared the dishes. Seeing his mother work, Aonghus immediately wiped both of his brothers' faces and hands. He picked up the boys' plates and followed her, then returned with a full carafe of corma.

Setting it down carefully between the two men, he then went to the shelf and brought back his father's fidcheall game.

Koven filled Solomon's glass and flashed an impish smile. "Now on to more important things," he said, in a commanding tone. "As my guest, you move first."

The warrior sat up straight and placed his peg in a corner of the board. Then he grabbed his stein and took a gluttonous drink as he watched Koven make the next play. He felt somehow relieved by what he had heard tonight, almost as if in light of the tribe's opinion about Laden, he would not appear such a fool. There was even a feeling of camaraderie forming between him and this clean-shaven farmer that he would not have otherwise cultivated.

Concentrating on his opponent's next move, he stared intently at the board. Careful not to show any reaction to Koven's maneuver, he promptly countered with the exact opposite move. Thoroughly pleased with his strategy, he sat back and looked around the room. It was not such a bleak place to be after all, he thought to himself. He scanned the room for Aonghus and found him dozing contentedly in his mother's lap, with one arm wrapped around the family cat.

CHAPTER SEVEN

ake up," Aonghus whispered to Solomon as he gently nudged his shoulder.

Solomon opened his eyes a slit and blurrily took in the boy's face, then closed them again and rolled over. He could hear the shuffle of tiny feet walking around on the other side, then he felt small hands patting his cheeks in an attempt to rouse him.

"Solomon, wake up," Aonghus said, raising his voice an octave. "The King wants to see you."

"How do you know?" Solomon listlessly responded, his eyes still shut.

"Because he sent a messenger around the village asking for you," Aonghus answered, taking a wet cloth and dabbing Solomon's forehead. "He said that you should go to his home without delay."

The warrior groaned and covered his throbbing head with the woolen blanket. The last thing he remembered was laughingly dumping Koven's fidcheall board into the fireplace after both men had drunkenly decided that the game made no sense at all. He did not know how they had arrived at that conclusion, but from the nauseous feeling rising in him, he was sure that it had come about after consuming a great quantity of ale.

Turning over again, his nostrils were suddenly filled with a most putrid smell. Uncovering his face, he slowly opened his eyes and found that the youngest child was standing by him. He had taken off his soiled diaper and was holding it out to him.

A look of utter disgust filled Solomon's face as the child dropped the diaper on the floor beside him. Then he turned to the fire and started urinating on it. The flames made a sizzling sound as the child looked back at him with a red-gummed smile.

Aonghus put his hand over his mouth and started giggling at his brother uncontrollably. The lilt of infantile laughter reverberated through the room, causing Enda to come in to see what was happening.

"Cunnedag, stop that!" she reprimanded her younger son, slapping him on his backside. Then she grabbed his arm and dragged him, urine dripping down his leg, into the other room.

"He likes to do that," Aonghus said, still giggling. "He thinks it is funny, and he wants to make you laugh."

35

The warrior pushed away from the diaper as if it were a serpent ready to strike. "That is no way to do it," he grumbled. "What a disgusting child."

Squinting from the morning sunlight, he scanned the room. Finally locating his boots, he went over and pulled them on.

"The King wants to see me," he said, smacking his lips together. The rancid taste of last night's beer still lingered in his mouth. "I'll need a bath first."

"It is all ready," Aonghus replied, wiping the tears of laughter from his eyes. "Mother and I fixed it for you. Come on; I will show you where it is."

He led him outside to a crude earthen building behind the barn. It was conveniently located near a stream that ran through the property. There was a narrow entryway covered with a cow's hide, and stepping inside, Solomon noticed that the walls were lined with straw as well as clay for insulation. There was a small fire burning in the center of it, the smoke escaping through a tiny hole in the middle of the roof. This room was also used as a sweat house for the infirmed if needed. Off to one side was an iron tub filled with steaming water with some soap and a cloth next to it.

"It will be all right if you borrow this," Aonghus said, offering him a clean linen shirt. "But do not get into any fights while you are wearing it, it is my father's best one."

After acknowledging his request, Solomon began undressing in silence. His brow was wrinkled, and from the look in his eye, it was apparent he was in a very foul mood.

Sheepishly turning away from him, Aonghus headed for the door. As he pushed aside the leather shroud in the entryway, he stopped and stared inquisitively at Solomon.

"What is it?" Solomon demanded as he climbed into the bath.

"Do you think he will cut off your head?" Aonghus asked timidly.

"No," the warrior barked back.

Aonghus was quiet a moment. "Then can I go with you to hear what he says?" he asked expectantly.

Solomon looked up at him, perturbed. His stomach was turning and he had the worst possible headache. "Better go back inside, boy," he warned, then ducked his face into the hot water.

———

Aonghus was not allowed to go inside King Donnach's house with Solomon. Instead, he had to wait alone in the front courtyard. He sat down on the wall near the entryway and scanned the estate, marvelling at the beautifully landscaped terraces surrounding the house.

To one side of the porch was an herb garden, and opposite that, a flower garden. The lawn in front of the house was completely untrodden by any, other than human, feet. It would have been impossible to make his house look this way since most of the front yard was filled with livestock.

The dwelling itself was enormous. It was made of stone and finely cut wooden beams, not at all like the log and clay houses in which the tenant farmers lived. It was almost as long as it was wide, and Aonghus had heard stories of the huge banqueting hall that ran the entire length of one end. There were a great many windows dotting the facade, each one ornamented with bronze along the top. It was said to be the most lavish residence this side of the island.

Stone hollows surrounded the doorway from top to bottom, each one containing a human skull. A religious symbol to his people, skulls were believed to be the essence of life and infused with supernatural powers. It was a strongly accepted belief that a human head could remain alive after the death of the body, and a severed one displayed on the entryway of a home could keep evil away while ensuring abundance to its possessor. Skulls of dangerous enemies were often embalmed in cedar oil so they could be taken out and proudly displayed as testimony of a warrior's bravery.

Cocking his head to one side, Aonghus scrutinized the grisly display. He stared at each one as if he were waiting for some kind of response to come from it. It was not an uncommon thing to see skulls in a warrior's doorway, but he had never had the chance to closely examine one that protected the house of a King.

Standing up, he walked over to one that was eye level. Squinting his eyes, he inspected the hollowed-out sockets and nasal passages. Then he ran his index finger over the cranium, wrinkling his nose at the cold feeling of the porous bone.

"Do not do that," the voice of a young boy warned.

Aonghus jerked his hand back, abruptly turning to see who it was. He found that it was Pwyll's only son, Diarmudd. He was a year older than Aonghus, with sandy blond hair and olive skin. He was dressed in fine doeskin pants, fur-lined boots, and a red shirt with blousy sleeves. Clasped just below his neck was a jeweled broach decorated with the symbol of his family. From his attire it was easy to see, even at this age, that he was the relative of a monarch.

"That head was taken by my grandfather in a battle with the Romans," he said haughtily. "It is disrespectful for anyone to touch it without permission."

"Sorry," Aonghus mumbled, looking down at his feet.

Diarmudd stopped in front of him, his stance wide and both hands on his hips. The sole heir of the richest land baron in the tribe, his every mannerism reflected an imperious attitude.

"What are you doing here?" he questioned, taking a step forward to appear more dominant. "You were not summoned."

Aonghus looked up, and then down slightly to make eye contact since Diarmudd was shorter than he.

"I am here with the warrior, Solomon. He was summoned by the King," he answered.

"Well," Diarmudd huffed. "After what that warrior did to my uncle last night, I doubt he will be in this tribe much longer. Even if he does stay, I heard the King telling my father it will not be as a nobleman."

Aonghus looked at Diarmudd sternly, his features appearing to calcify.

"That is not fair," he argued, clenching his fists. "Solomon could have killed Laden, but showed mercy. I do not know why he spared him, but he should not be made to leave because of it."

Diarmudd tilted his head back to look down his nose at Aonghus. Then he uncrossed his arms and turned his back. He walked deliberately to the corner of the house and picked up two carved wooden poles that stood about a foot higher than his head. They had rounded points on either end, and although Aonghus had never used one, he recognized them as training spears.

"Would you stake your honor on that?" Diarmudd challenged.

With one vehement nod, Aonghus accepted the challenge.

"Then take one of these and come with me," Diarmudd said, holding out one of the poles.

Holding it firmly in one hand, Aonghus followed Diarmudd around the back of the house to a grassy area where a handful of the king's servants were doing their daily chores. Seated beneath a shade tree were Pwyll's three daughters. They ranged in age from an infant, being fed by a wet nurse, to a toddler, who was busy petting a fluffy white lamb, and finally, the eldest, looking approximately the same age as Aonghus. She had shiny black hair and the same olive skin as her brother. Her dark brown eyes were heavy lidded, and one appeared to be slightly narrower in shape than the other. It gave the impression that her face was a bit lopsided. She had pudgy cheeks and a short forehead that made her hairline look like it was growing into, instead of away from, her brow.

She was sitting in front of a broad silver washbasin decorated with red and blue carbuncles and golden insets. She held a mirror in her hand, inspecting the manner in which her handmaiden was braiding her hair. Catching sight of Aonghus, she looked up and gave him a mockish smile. The boy pursed his lips, half frowning, as he bashfully looked away.

"The rules are these. The spear can be used in any way against each other. But the first to drop it and be held down on the ground helpless, loses," Diarmudd declared, taking off his broach and gesturing impatiently for the servant to take it from him. "No punching or biting, but kicking is allowed."

"I understand," Aonghus replied, caressing the weapon with his palm.

He carefully watched Diarmudd ready himself, imitating each of his movements. Supporting the spear in front of him with both hands, he bounced on his toes and waited for his opponent to make the first assault.

———

Inside the house, Solomon sat with his elbows resting on both knees, hands dangling between his legs. His head was lightly bowed, and his eyes were lifted as he watched King Donnach pacing in front of the fire. The room was empty except for the two men, and the only sound that could be heard was the rhythmic thud of the King's footsteps as he rambled back and forth.

"Do you have any idea what might have happened if you had broken your oath?" Donnach asked as he stopped mid-step.

Solomon frowned and gave a sarcastic huff.

"No, but do you?" Solomon scoffed. "Do you really? I would like to know. All of this talk about mysticism and destruction is, perhaps, nothing more than superstition."

Donnach's eyes widened, and with a single stride, he stood over the warrior. "You are too proud and stupid for your own good," he admonished. "The oath you took takes precedence over any challenge of pride. To break it would be to break your promise before the gods. And that, you pompous fool, is sacred and inviolable. If you ever do, not only will you suffer greater shame, but you will invoke the forces of your own mortality. I do not care how many times Laden insults you; you may never take arms against him or you will have to be destroyed. I will not have my entire tribe suffer the curses of the heavens because of one arrogant warrior. It does not matter how much I care for you; I will not hesitate to have you executed, not for this."

Solomon could feel his knees weaken as he looked back at him watery-eyed. The justifications he had conjured in his own defense could not stop the sinking in his stomach. He had made a fool of himself in front of the one person he loved and respected. This man had cared for him and raised him like his own son. He had never spared Solomon anything, and often, had seemed to favor him above his own children. But perhaps what annoyed Solomon most was that deep down he knew Donnach was right. There was never an excuse for disavowing a Druidic oath. It had been clearly explained to him from the beginning: if he ever laid heir to the throne, no matter what the cause, he would suffer a maligned fate. Yet he wanted to doubt such superstitions. After all, Christians had the same belief, except they called it penance for their sins.

He put his face in his hands and rubbed it with his palms. He could smell the odor of the lavender soap with which he had bathed still on his skin. Then he rested his chin on the butt of both hands and stared at his feet.

"I am sorry," he grumbled.

"No," the King responded. "I am the one who is sorry. I am sorry that I ever let it get to this point."

Solomon raised his eyes. "That is all right. I know that anything you did last night was not an affront to me personally."

Donnach shook his head. "I am not speaking of the way that you were treated," he answered, taking a seat beside Solomon.

"Oh," he retorted in a disappointed tone. "Then just what is it that you are sorry about? I would like to know so I do not make the same error again."

Donnach looked at him sharply. "I should never have let it go this far. It is understandable that two warriors equal in confidence and ability would quarrel sooner or later. I am apologizing only because I should have been more discerning and made some sort of distinction between you long ago."

"Forgive me, good King, but I have never considered myself his equal," Solomon argued. "I have always thought myself—"

"Above him," the King interjected.

"Yes, above him," he said seriously.

Donnach scratched the center of one hand and grunted dubiously. "But you will never be above him. And you may never kill him either, no matter what the provocation."

In a gesture of concession, the warrior dropped his elbows back onto his knees, laced his fingers together, and silently sunk his forehead into his hands.

"I have decided it is time for Laden to take his rightful place as ruler," Donnach continued. "I am old now, and too tired to be bothered with the pettiness of a title. I would like to enjoy what is left of my days, and Laden is in his prime. He has the energy and more than enough ambition to rule the territory."

Solomon remained motionless. "And?" he asked without looking up.

"And in view of what took place last night, your celsine will be reduced from thirty-seven to ten," he said, rising to his feet and walking to the window. "It is enough to make a decent living for yourself."

Solomon released a low, sardonic laugh. "Tell that to Deireadh, will you?"

There was a long, distressing pause as the King opened the window and looked out at the children playing in the yard.

"That will not be necessary," he said compassionately. "She has requested residence in this house. As spiritual counsel to the King, she has her right. She has also asked that she be permitted a divorce."

The warrior craned his neck forward. His heavy brows came together for an instant, then the twisted expression slowly faded from his face. He stood hastily, throwing his shoulders back and sucking in his stomach.

"Could you please tell my wife that I would like to see her?" he asked in a voice so composed it belied him.

The King looked at him sympathetically. "I will," he said softly. "That is all."

Turning on his heel, Solomon exited through the nearest doorway leading to the back court. He blindly strode past Aonghus and Diarmudd, who were rolling around on the ground in a frenzy punching each other. Vaulting on top of his horse, he absentmindedly broke into a canter. He did not leave by the gates, rather he jumped the wall and two fences protecting the estate.

Halfway up the road, he remembered he had forgotten Aonghus. He made a sweeping half-circle, and headed back in the opposite direction. He found the boy running up the road after him. Still at a slow trot, he held out his hand and pulled him onto the back of the horse. In the next moment there was the strangely comforting feeling of Aonghus' small arms locking tightly around his waist. Without thinking, he affectionately patted the boy's smooth forearm.

chapter eight

n the weeks that followed, Solomon busied himself with virtually
anything that would fill his days. Taking advantage of the sudden
wealth of free time, he used it to school Aonghus in the basics of
weaponry and even helped Koven around his farm. In return, he
was always afforded a place at the family table at meal time, and
Enda had happily absorbed his household duties such as laun-
dry and mending in the absence of his wife.

The warrior found his new freedom almost enjoyable, that is as long as he
did not have to face any of the other warriors or his former clientele. He had been
visited a few times by his close friend, Berrig. These occasions always took place in
the late evening so Berrig would not have to deal with the gossip of the other warriors for choosing to affiliate himself with an outcast.

More than once, Berrig had asked Solomon, in the strictest confidence, why
he had not injured Laden. It was not that he was prying but it usually followed a
long report on the poor quality of service Laden was giving Solomon's former
clients. Berrig would chant the same litany about how Solomon had the gift of
courage, and that after all the years he had known him, and fought at his side, he
simply could not believe that Solomon was a coward.

Solomon's reaction was always the same. He would grind his teeth together,
and discreetly pinch the skin on his bicep until the urge to tell Berrig everything
had subsided. He knew that of all the warriors, Berrig would understand and keep
it in confidence. Yet somehow, Solomon felt that the spirits would listen, and his
exile would only become more severe.

On this day, he had just returned from an overnight hunting trip in which
Aonghus had successfully tried his newly carved spear and killed an elk. Obviously
fatigued from carrying the extra weight of the boy and his kill, his horse walked with
head hung low. The bend of his neck was lathered with sweat and the nap of his coat
was uneven with dirt. They made their way down the path leading to Solomon's
home. It was a stone and wood structure that appeared to be a small version of the
King's manor. There were two barns parallel with the back of the house. One was
used for the pigs and milk cows; the other for the horses. Set between them was a
level space used to school the horses since part of the warrior's income was based on
training them for battle. He had even begun to show some of his techniques to
Aonghus, who seemed to take to them easily.

The boy's chores included grooming the animals, which he did quite meticulously. He showed no fear of the massive creatures, even when one unruly colt had pinned him in the stall. Solomon was impressed that his apprentice did not call for help; instead, he calmly talked to the colt until he was pacified. Solomon would not have heard about the incident if he had not questioned him about the hoof-shaped bruise he had noticed in the center of Aonghus' chest. Like his weapon, a warrior's horse was looked upon as a gift from the gods, as well as a trusted companion. A good horse was crucial to a warrior's existence, not only in battle, but in everyday life. At one point, Solomon had even considered giving Aonghus one of the gentler colts, but reconsidered. It was better to let him choose his own, since he had to work and live with it.

They stopped in front of the house and dismounted. Solomon could see two of his servants in the back tending the vegetable garden. He would have called to them to come and take the elk, but they were out of voice range.

The house would surely be empty by this hour. His handmaid lived in a hut at the end of the property with the other slaves. She would come in the mornings and evenings to prepare his meals, fix his bath, and clean. The time from mid-morning to late afternoon was her own. Deireadh had always complained that Solomon was too lax with his servants. Yet he could not help but view them as a constant reminder of his own mother's destiny.

"Go inside and get the two skinning knives hanging next to the hearth," Solomon said, lifting the elk off his horse's back. "If we hurry we can dress this thing by dinner."

Wiping the sweat from his brow with his dirty forearm, Aonghus started for the front door.

Leaving the elk on the grass, the warrior unsaddled his horse. He heard the front door open and out of the corner of his eye, he saw Aonghus stop short.

Solomon looked over his shoulder to see what had caused him to do this, and found the boy standing open-mouthed in front of Deireadh.

The warrior's chiseled expression melted as he looked upon her. She was wearing a lovely orange robe that revealed one of her soft shoulders. Her hair was pulled back from her face by a gold hairband, and bracelets adorned her wrists and biceps. Solomon was captivated by the vision of her. The two had not spoken since the night of the banquet and seeing her now, after sleeping so many nights in an empty bed, made him all the more positive that he was still truly in love with her.

Feeling his stomach flutter, he dropped what he was doing and walked toward her. There was nothing that could not be forgiven. He felt that if he could have her back again, the rest would rectify itself. Even though he had rationalized that these past days had not been too terrible, the truth was that he yearned to have his wife and his standing back again.

Stepping in front of Aonghus, he took Deireadh by the shoulders. He loved the feeling of her smooth flesh in his hands. Without speaking, he urged her inside, and closed the door in Aonghus' face.

The boy huffed discontentedly as if to say this was all entirely predictable, and any fun the two had shared together would now come to an end. Peering through a crack in the shutter, Aonghus watched as Solomon embraced her and held her close for a prolonged moment. Then to his complete disgust, he watched the warrior drop to his knees, and bury his face in her stomach. Suddenly he felt hatred rising in him. He wanted to take his spear, along with the kill he had made, and heave it all back at the warrior. The feeling made him dizzy and short of breath. He was so angry at Solomon that he wanted to hit someone or something until his fists bled and he dropped from exhaustion. How could he do that, Aonghus wondered to himself. How could he show him how to make such a clean kill, how to conquer, and then be rendered helpless by such an ugly woman?

Unable to watch his master humiliate himself any further, he turned away. After all she had done to him, he was so happy she had returned that he got down on his knees before her. It was too disenchanting—it made him feel crazy inside. He would never do that, he silently promised himself. No, he would find a trustworthy woman when the time came, one just like his mother.

Refastening the stallion's saddle, Aonghus took a rope and tied it around the elk's hind legs. Then he threw it over the pommel and, using all his strength, hoisted the animal back onto the horse. Agitated, he strained to get his legs over the horse's hindquarters, and finally getting into position, he caught a nose full of the rancid odor of his kill. It would have to be cleaned and salted as soon as possible or it would spoil from the heat. And this tired horse had to be fed and groomed despite this silliness about Deireadh coming home, he thought to himself. Heaving a disgusted sigh, he grabbed the reins in both hands and started back to the farm.

Deireadh ran her fingers through Solomon's sweaty hair, the thick brown and red locks tangling around her knuckles. It was odd to be so close to him again. His emotional reaction had provoked mixed feelings of care and remorse in her. She had rehearsed the lines over and over, but when she looked into his languid eyes, they all seemed to evaporate into one lonely void. For the briefest of moments, she even considered staying with him and forgetting about her plans with Laden. Yet she knew that whether she loved him or not, simply being the wife of a titleless warrior was not acceptable. And she knew that she would one day come to despise her husband for being just who he was. She wanted more; she had to have more. It was wealth and power she desired, more of it than Solomon would ever possess. For all his shallowness, Laden was the one who could give it to her.

It was not that she considered Solomon less a man than her lover; it was quite the contrary. Solomon's humor and steadfast devotion, as well as his physical prowess, were not to be resisted. The tingling she felt between her thighs at this very moment made it undeniable, but he was not cunning enough to be a leader. By his very nature, his sense of justice outweighed his ambition.

"Solomon," she said coldly. "Donnach said you wished to speak with me."

She tried to step away from him, but he held her tighter. He ached inside, his heart was so heavy, so mournful, that being near her was debilitating. She wanted to leave, he knew it. He could smell it emanating from her as he inhaled. It was the odor of indifference, even dissatisfaction at his touch. But he did not care because he knew that despite everything, he could make her want him again. He had to make her want him again.

Running his hand down her buttocks and over the backs of her legs, he parted her robe and began lightly kissing her belly. It seemed strangely hard, so he lowered his head and lightly pressed his lips to her soft thighs. Deireadh did not try to resist, but she offered him no response either. She merely stood there as if she were waiting for him to compose himself and let her alone.

Anger rose in him as he found himself wondering if he was as good a lover as Laden. But as quickly as it surfaced, it subsided, and he immersed his face in the silky dark tuft between her legs. Tasting the salt of her, he kissed her again and again, and he felt her knees slightly buckle as she widened her stance and put both her hands on the back of his head, pushing him deeper and deeper.

He ran his tongue across her smooth moistness, until she grabbed a handful of his hair and pulled his face up. As he stood, she backed away from him. The look in her eyes reflected fear as well as desire, and it excited him even more.

He firmly held onto her arms, as she backed herself into a wall. Then Solomon bent his head forward to kiss her, but she stopped him by putting her fingers to his lips.

"I do not wish it to be this way with us," she said.

They looked at each other for an incalculable moment, then Solomon reached up and unclasped her broach. The gown dropped to the floor, exposing her shapely breasts. Taking them in his hands, he caressed her. Their gaze was locked, and unable to conceal his arrogance, he watched the passion rise in her eyes. They looked like stars exploding again and again. Then he felt her hands tugging on his breeches. Looking for and finding the hard part of him that wanted to be freed, she guided him into the promise of her soft, warm flesh.

CHAPTER NINE

here was a rather large group of tribesmen gathered in his father's barn when Aonghus arrived. He could hear the loud voices in a heated exchange as he passed the closed, double-paneled doors. His thoughts had originally been filled with visions of the praise that would be heaped upon him when his parents saw the size of the elk he had killed. But when Enda stepped outside and gestured to him to stay out of the barn, he knew there was something more important at hand.

He stopped the stallion in front of his mother. She gave him a strained look of pleasure at the sight of the elk, then the lines on her face deepened. She helped him lower it from the horse, and the two laboriously strung it up on a beam beside the front door. They were scarcely paying attention to each other; they were too busy trying to overhear the filtering voices coming from the barn.

Aonghus unsaddled the horse and led him to a small, fenced-in corral. He made sure there was hay and fresh water, then latched the gate and started over to see what was happening. He caught sight of Enda dramatically waving her arms in the air, warning him not to intrude. But he pretended not to notice and walked faster, hoping she would not catch him and make him go inside.

From the sound of the many voices within the buildings, Aonghus wondered why there were not more than the few scattered horses in the yard. Glancing about the farm when he arrived, nothing looked very much out of the ordinary.

Not wanting to draw attention to himself, he shimmied up a rope hanging from the roof, and crawled into a second level hay chute. The stalks of oat and alfalfa stuck to his sweaty arms and face as he waded through it, making as little noise as possible. The dust from the dried chaff made his nose itch, and he wrinkled it a few times to keep from sneezing. When he reached the edge of the loft, he peered over and got his first glimpse of an impressive group of tribesmen. In the furthest corner of the breezeway were at least a dozen of the clan's most prominent farmers; next to them were three noblemen who operated a wealthy grainery exchange with the Mediterranean traders. Standing along one of the wooden stall partitions were the warriors Berrig, Ronan, Ogda, and Cwyn. They all had taken on the familiar wide, cross-armed stance, and each wore the same stoic expression. It was said that a warrior's look should never give away his true intent, lest an enemy be able to exploit him. And from the appearance of these four, Aonghus thought, they could have been watching a game of hurley as easily as a battle. Perhaps it was that Aonghus was better acquainted with Solomon than with these men, because, from the varied emotions that flashed across Solomon's face in a single day, he thought his master sorely failed any test of shrewdness.

Seated in the center were Megba, the elder, and Aonghus' father. The boy felt a surge of pride seeing Koven, whose countenance suggested a sense of purpose—almost as if he were a messenger of a higher power. His features had a tough appearance to them as he spoke, and the boy knew by the sharp bite to his father's intonation that what he was saying at that moment was of greatest importance.

"It is true that compared to you, Egan, I have little to lose," he was saying to one of the noblemen. "But I have little to gain either. If Laden proceeds to take the throne, I could easily continue my work with scarcely an outward difference, but the change would be in my heart. It would be knowing that I would serve a man who was not concerned with the welfare of my tribe. Not only that, but would you forsake the gentle Goddess who has cared for us for so long? Because if we do not do something to stop it, that is what you will have to do."

Egan uncomfortably recrossed his legs. "Is it as bad as all that?" he retorted in an unsettling tone. "Could it not be that you are just afraid of change? That you fear the progress and wealth you know Laden will pursue? And that all of this is a desperate attempt to cling to the predictable way of life? Of course the passing on of power from Donnach to Laden will involve some conflict because the old ways are threatened, but the only resolution will be to embrace the new, and then peace will reign."

Koven's face progressively hardened until his eyes settled into a sharpness that told his challenger that he was not only wrong, but a liar.

"I cannot make my offerings to a mortal who is neither capable nor willing to do what is best for me or my tribe," he countered.

There was a tense silence, and all Aonghus could hear was the shuffle of Berrig's feet as he took a step forward in case a fight broke out between the two. Aonghus also readied himself to come to his father's aid, if needed.

Megba lifted both hands in the air, as if invisibly holding the two men at bay. He cleared his throat and slowly got to his feet. He was the oldest man in the tribe, and considered more of a sorcerer than a holy man. He had been King Oisil's advisor from the beginning of his reign, and the men were said to have been friends since childhood. Now gray-haired, with a long white goatee, he had sunken blue eyes that looked like they had crystalized with age, and bushy brows that rose and fell as he spoke. He was loved and respected by everyone in the clan, and, in spite of his corpse-like appearance, he had a cackling laugh so funny to hear that it was impossible not to join in. The tribe met his needs communnally because they believed that when his time of passing came, he would speak to the happy Otherworld of the individual generosities of the living.

He ambled slowly around the room, taking time to look at each man directly. He stared into their eyes as if he could see something unknown to anyone but him, then he would go on to the next one. When he had finished this, the elder stood beneath the loft and looked up. Aonghus felt his stomach drop when their eyes met through the darkness, and he had to fight his instinctive desire to flee. Although it seemed as if they stared at each other for an eternity, no one else seemed to notice.

"The spirits of the future are listening," Megba said, turning back to the men. "They are watching our ways with hopefulness."

He lowered his eyes to the ground and held his hands out, palms down, as though he were warming them over an imaginary fire.

"The spirits of the past are listening and watching," he said, his eyes watering. "They want to know if you remember the doings of the Romans? Their betrayal of our people and the slaughter of King Oisil and the young Chieftain, Roilan? I speak for those spirits now. They caution that the misdeeds of Rome have not mellowed with time's passing. They still seek to conquer our land and control you, my kinsmen.

"Their motives reek with the blood of Oisil and Roilan, and their tongues are singed with untruths when they say they wish to establish fair trade. Equality is an illusion they would have us believe is real, and when they have our complete dependence, they will crush us again."

The old man's mind seemed to drift, and he was very distant for a moment. The afternoon sunlight streamed through the knots and cracks in the wood and caught his form, making the elder look powerful and wise.

"This King Laden and his Druidess are of the most impure stock. They are self-serving and will barter away our clan to their own avarice. Hear my words, all of you who care about preserving us. If Laden and Deireadh are ordained by the Druids, we will plummet into the cycle of our demise."

It was so quiet in the barn that even Aonghus held his breath. Egan stood and started to speak, then sat back down and was silent. He was trying to find a way to discredit Megba, but he could not. Then Cwyn, the oldest warrior in the tribe, stepped into the center.

"I felt the stirring of my heart with Megba's warning," he said regretfully. He gave every indication that he was riddled with guilt by his conclusion. "Donnach was the most deserving of kings, but Megba's words are truth. The son of our King should not be anointed, or all that we have fought and cared for will be prostituted into darkness. Deireadh is a black witch, and I am not afraid to say it. I can give the words of my kinsmen who will tell any who doubt me of her vile ways. She has cast aside the goodness for which her skills were meant, and has sold the light of her soul for the riches the wicked spirits can give. If she is given the secrets of the gods, I can only tell you that I fear for what will become of us."

The boney click of Koven's knuckles cracking echoed through the heavy stillness. What these men were planning was an uprising against their leader. If one betrayed the trust afforded them, and told Donnach or Laden, they would all surely suffer a painful execution. And since the plans were devised in Koven's barn, there was no doubt that he would be one of the first to die.

"What then are we to do about it?" Koven asked, disheartened. "We have assembled here today acting in the best interests of our tribe and to seek a solution."

"But the very way it will be done could inflict greater harm," Egan rebutted. "What good does it do if we overthrow Laden at the expense of such bloodshed? If many die or our tribe is split, we will be no better for it."

Megba hobbled over to Egan and cupped his hand over the crown of his head. He was careful not to touch the man, and the sudden attention given him made Egan noticeably uncomfortable. The older sorcerer closed his eyes tightly, then after a moment, opened them and looked at the rest of the group.

"I hear the questioning thoughts of those of you who think this man will betray you," he said flatly. "If I knew that were to happen, he would not leave this barn with breath in his body. But it will not occur. His questions are divinely inspired to caution us to use temperance. If our tribe is to prosper, it must not be at the cost of needless bloodshed. Our people must want the change, and we must give them a reason to pursue it."

"How? How can we do it in such a way that our people will embrace a new king, even at the risk of war?" Cwyn asked.

Megba smoothed his beard with both hands and nodded like he was listening to unheard voices.

"We bring them one who will love them with a pure heart, and care for each of them as if they were a single important particle of one healthy body," he said softly. "I have meditated on this for many nights, and I believe that there is one of special making waiting to assume this task. But it is one whom we have never set eyes upon except in the deepest crevices of our dreams."

All remained silent as they watched the old man take Cwyn's knife from his belt and slice his own wrist. Aonghus shuddered as Megba held it above his head and let the blood flow down his arm. It made a red stream over his sagging, wrinkled skin, then stopped at his elbow and dripped onto the earthen floor. His eyes were rolled back in his head, and he was mumbling something. Then he dropped his arm to his side and blinked. He whirled around and looked straight up into Aonghus' eyes. His stare was so piercing that the boy felt his entire body freeze.

"It will be done!" Megba shouted, clasping a hand around his wrist to stop the bleeding. "What lies ahead of us will take the bravest of kinsmen. It is ordained that we should reshape destiny. We must make an offering to the Druids to bring this spirit to us. We will entrust the mission to the fallen warrior, Solomon, to take it to them on the opposite shore."

Cwyn's mouth dropped, and Berrig and Ronan simultaneously shifted their weight to the opposite legs. Ronan, also one of the older warriors, but far less reasonable than Cwyn, stepped forward.

"Megba," he said in a most respectful way. "Deireadh is Solomon's wife, and Donnach raised him. Although he is brave enough to undertake this, it would be like asking him to slay his own family. That is why he is not with us today; his loyalty is very clear."

"And so are the edicts of the heavens," the elder stated. "The spirits believe that this warrior has the wisdom to do what must be done. I will take counsel with him at sunset after I have made an offering of thanks to the gods. I encourage you few enlightened men to gather your donations of worship and bring them to my cottage before the sun begins its slumber, for I am sure that Solomon will leave at first light. If he does not, our mission will fail."

Megba dropped his head, and with all eyes still upon him, pointed a crooked finger up at Aonghus.

"Boy, I summon you to come into my presence," he demanded.

Aonghus was sure his heart had stopped. In a chilling moment that seemed to last forever, he did not wonder what the old man would do to him, or even what kind of an explanation he would give. The only thing going through his mind as he climbed from the loft was how severe a spanking he was going to get from Koven after everyone had gone.

His hands were so sweaty he lost his grip halfway down, and plopped to the ground. He could feel the momentary numbness in his buttocks, but the pain was minor compared to the nervous cramping of his stomach. Looking at the mass of intimidating faces glowering at him, he got to his feet. His knees began to quiver as the old man grabbed him by the arms and shook him hard, then gently. Aonghus licked his dry lips and tried to keep from vomiting.

"You have entrusted yourself with much," Megba's voice sounded distant in Aonghus' ringing ears. "Do not be unsuccessful."

He turned to Koven. "I know not why fate behaves as it does. But you must have greatly implored the heavens because they have born unto you a messenger."

Koven's eyes emptied of all emotion as he looked at his eldest son. If Aonghus was frightened before, it went to sheer horror as he glimpsed the desperate pallor of his father.

"I will give him my horse," the farmer said with a measure of disbelief.

CHAPTER TEN

The glowing orange ball of the sun was balanced on the crest of the hill outside his window as Solomon relaxed in the steaming bath. Cupping his hands, he splashed water on his face and shoulders, then took some soap and lathered his chest. He had left Deireadh sleeping in the bedroom, completely satisfied that although they had spoken very little, their marriage was still firmly intact.

Taking a flask of cool honey water mixed with oats, he took a swig, then submersed his face and hair. Popping his head back up, he heard the sounds of Deireadh moving about in the next room. There was the familiar clanking of jewelry before the door to the bathing chamber slowly opened, and she apprehensively entered. Her face was ghostly, and her eyes reflected such sadness that Solomon thought she would burst into tears at any moment. Her hair was disheveled, as though she had repeatedly run her fingers through it to keep it out of her face. The warrior's confusion must have been apparent, because she immediately broke into an explanation.

"I did not come here to have this happen," she said remorsefully. "What I had really wanted to do was to tell you that our marriage is over."

"Deireadh," he replied genially. "If it happened that you were someplace else these last couple of hours, take me at my word when I say that it is anything but over between us."

Deireadh nervously scratched her neck with her long claw-like fingers, and did not respond.

"Did you hear what I just said?" he questioned.

"Yes," she answered in a whisper.

She reached into the fold of her sash and removed her wedding ring. Her movements were quick but unsure as she set it on the table next to the bath.

"You and I," she continued, "we want different things from life. And I realized some time ago that we would not be able to help each other possess them. It is better that we find our own ways."

Solomon felt his left eye twitch as he listened to her incredulously. How could she have been so loving to him, knowing what she was about to do?

"Strange," he said pensively. "I cannot give you what you want, and you are all that I want. Now that I have no rank, I suppose simply loving you is not enough. You have an opportunity to possibly become a queen, or royal spiritual-

50

ist at the very least. Rather than tell me honestly that I am a disappointment, you
are saying that our desires are different."

Even though they were a fair distance apart, he could see his own reflection
in her watery eyes. His hair was stuck to his head and his beard was dripping. And
stuffed naked into a steaming tub, he was sure he could not have looked any more
foolish than he did at that moment.

Deireadh tried to conceal an involuntary frown. Her complexion turned a
whiter, more translucent shade, and for a moment it seemed she did not believe
she had actually said what she had said. By her reaction, it crossed Solomon's
mind that she did not truly mean her words; rather, they were a fleeting demonstration of her fluctuating emotions.

More than anyone, he knew that although Deireadh was a lovely woman
who was seemingly in command of herself, she was not as wise as she liked to portray. At times she was her own adversary, and worse, when she was like this, she
was completely incapable of being rational.

"Is that all you have to say?" she sputtered, going from despair to irritation
so quickly that Solomon wanted to laugh out loud.

"I do not mean to be insensitive," he replied. "You want to end our
marriage, so what can I do? I will not demand that you stay where you are,
unhappily. Only I do not think that you are that unhappy. You are merely
enticed by the vain illusions that flutter around your empty little head."

Her brow furrowed and she looked at him as if she did not understand.

"I do not want you to go," he went on. "When I married you, I promised
you my heart till my life was through. In my mind, we will always be wed."

"You cannot hold me to that," she argued, putting her hands on her hips. "I
am not a Christian, and you cannot bind me as if I were an ox. We are finished,
Solomon."

The sound of her words seemed to pierce his flesh, and despite his desire to
remain calm, he became infuriated.

"Then go," he hollered at her, pointing to the door. "Go and never come to
me again, even when you realize how grave an error you have made. You wish to
divorce me, then so be it. You are a free woman as of this instant. Now get out!"

She stood with eyelids fluttering, stupefied by his reaction. Then her face
deepened with regret, and she tried to speak.

"I told you to leave my sight," Solomon roared.

Biting her bottom lip, she started to cry as she hurried out of the house.

CHAPTER ELEVEN

I need more hot water!" Solomon demanded, slamming his back against the tub. A great amount of water sloshed onto the floor.

His handmaid scurried into the chamber, a bucket balanced on her shoulder. She went to the tub and straining forward, poured the steaming water over his head.

"I said to bring more water, not scald me with it!" he cried.

The woman dropped the bucket and covered her mouth with her hand. "Forgive me, good warrior," she apologized through her fingers. "But please do not yell; it is so unsettling."

Solomon tried to hide his chagrin. This sort of outburst was out of his character. But then again, he reasoned, it was not such a common thing to be abandoned by his wife either.

"I will try to be more polite next time," he sighed.

He puckered his lips and made a strange squeaking sound as he stared at the ceiling. His face was flushed; his attendant could not be sure if it was the hot bath or his own impertinence. She stood, hands clasped in front of her, waiting to be excused.

"Lady, you are married are you not?" he asked, perturbed.

"Yes, good warrior," she answered.

"Then, may I ask why you wear no ring?"

She gave him a sheepish smile. "Because such ornaments come at much cost. I would rather have things of which I am in greater need."

Solomon nodded that he was satisfied with her reply. He twisted his mouth, agitated that his wet mustache was stuck in his lip.

"Your husband is a good man," the warrior went on. "He cares for my horses well. I would hope that he treats you in much the same way."

The maid's face took on a bashful expression at the unusually informal declaration coming from her master. She had always liked him, but found him somehow unapproachable until now. Perhaps he was better off without his wife, she thought.

"Why is it that you stay married to a man who cannot even provide his wife with a proper seal of marriage?" he questioned sincerely.

"Because as you have said, he is a good man," she replied.

Solomon shrugged and splashed some more water over his shoulders.

"I must be sorely lacking, because my wife is through with me," he said.

The woman looked at him sympathetically. "I do not believe that it is your error. One man cannot correct what was flawed in its making."

Solomon's expression clouded, and he looked away suddenly. For a moment she thought he was going to cry. Then he picked up Deireadh's ring and handed it to her.

"It would please me that you should have this—with your husband's blessing, of course—but I would boil it before you put it on," he grumbled.

She smiled broadly as she accepted it. Holding it to her chest, she bowed graciously and left the room.

Solomon closed his eyes and let the warmth of the water relax him. It was hot enough now that the sweat trickled down his face. He felt ill, and he knew that it was more from disbelief than sorrow. He had known many people whose marriages had failed, but he had never thought his would be one of them. Maybe he should not have been so harsh with her; after all, she was a woman of limited capabilities. Yet he had given her weeks to let her disappointment settle. Night after night, he had slept alone with nothing but the thought of her pleasing Laden instead of him.

What was Deireadh doing anyway? She could not possibly think that Laden would take her as his queen. At best, she could only hope to be his secondary consort. He could understand her impatience at his recent setbacks, but he would make good again. He was still the best trainer of horses in the territory and warriors were always in need of competent, well-bred animals for fighting. Not only that, but Donnach had not taken away his personal property, and the clientele he had left him with were profitable. It would only be a matter of time before Laden's slothfulness became apparent, and their dissatisfaction would cause them to seek Solomon's assistance once again.

It was true that he was experiencing one of the darker phases of his life, but he knew in his heart it was all for a reason. He was certain that if he could only endure it from one day to the next, he would prevail. Besides, some good had come out of it. He had had more time to share the company of close friends, and the new friendships he had developed with Koven and a few of the other farmers were of great value to him. Even the time he had spent schooling Aonghus had actually been enjoyable; not to mention that he realized he honestly did have a talent for passing on his acquired knowledge.

Slouching to rest his head against the back of the tub, he started to doze. Impressions of the day's hunt flashed through his mind. There was the silent stalking of the elk through the woods and the pleasure he had felt when he saw Aonghus' stealth as he confidently made his kill. At first, he found it more rewarding than doing it himself, then he felt a little guilty when the boy reached in his pouch for a beautifully hand-painted bead and buried it where the animal had fallen.

He realized how deep the child's conscience bore when, on their journey back, he had explained to Solomon that he had slept with the bead beneath his pillow each night, promising it as a giveaway to the gods if they allowed him to take one of their creatures with the spear he had fashioned. It was then that Solomon was his student. Aonghus told him that only by recognizing the sacrifices and gifts of the heavens did the gods grant abundance, and that often it was not through the power of the spear, but through the virtues of the animal who offered itself to be killed, that needs were met. Then he looked at Solomon with his serious blue eyes and told him that one who takes more than his share is viewed by the spirits as both selfish and crazy.

In light of his foster's humility, Solomon could not help but feel superficial and even abusive of the universal laws. In all of the time he had been a warrior, it had never once entered his mind to make a giveaway. He had always thought that if the heavens had not meant for him to take it, either they would not have made him such an astute marksman, or they would not have put it in his path.

Yet he could not help but consider that Aonghus' oratory described what was taking place in his world at the moment: his life had become a giveaway. He thought he must be recompensing the gods of this tribe, and all the others, for everything he had guiltlessly taken along the way. He supposed he should, in truth, be happy about it. If this were so, it meant that as soon as he was finished giving it away, he would get it all back again.

He would even make Deireadh want him again, even if it were solely for the satisfaction of refusing her. For a moment, he wanted to apologize for his egotism. He thought of how much more attractive it would be to be like his sensitive apprentice, but then he rationalized that he could not change what he really considered one of his better traits: his controlled arrogance. In his life, he truly had not been a better hunter or warrior than the others; he had just believed he was. While they were all equal in ability, it was his inner boldness that made his exploits appear more flamboyant, resulting in greater success.

His meditation was brought to an end by the sound of horses in the yard and the tapping at his front door. Assuming his maid would greet whomever it was, Solomon did not bother to open his eyes. The tapping soon swelled into an impatient knock, but still went unanswered.

"You may enter," he finally bellowed, opening his eyes.

He could see the entryway from where he sat. The door opened, and in walked Megba, Cwyn, Ronan, Berrig, Koven, and last, a grimy Aonghus.

"I am here," he called out.

He supposed he should have gotten out of the water to show respect. But if he did that, he reasoned it would signal that he did not mind the visit, which he did, and they would only stay longer. As far as he was concerned, they had been there too long already.

The group walked into the bathing chamber without hesitation. They all wore the same solemn look on their faces, and Solomon could tell by the way they positioned themselves around him that this was not going to be the quick social visit he had hoped it would be.

He rolled his eyes and gave an ironic laugh at how ridiculous he must have looked. He could not help but wonder why a momentous visitation had to occur when he was in such a vulnerable state.

"I am bathing, if you do not mind," he said to Megba. His tone revealed more irritation than he would have liked.

"I can see that," Megba answered unaffected. "And, no, I do not mind."

"It does me well to hear it," he retorted discourteously.

He watched Aonghus strut from room to room like a shrunken version of a chieftain. He searched every chamber in the house and, had Solomon not been indisposed, would have earned himself a spanking for being so presumptuous. Then the boy came back in the room to look at him accusingly.

"Where did she go?" he asked, as if Solomon were a captured enemy.

"I do not know," Solomon shot back, infuriated.

"Is she gone?"

Solomon hardened. "Yes."

The boy gave him a smug, self-satisfied look as if to say that even in his youthful knowledge, he could have predicted as much.

Solomon squinted and showed his teeth at the same time, giving his apprentice a scowl. Aonghus wrinkled his nose back at him.

"What is this about?" Solomon asked, turning to the others.

The men seemed to shuffle at the same time, as though Solomon's line was a cue to appear uncomfortable.

"We have come about a very serious matter," Cwyn began.

"Can it wait until I dry off?"

"If you would like," Cwyn replied.

"Thank you," the warrior said, starting to get out of the tub, then realizing they were not going to leave, he sat back in aggravation.

"Could you give me a moment's privacy and wait in the main chamber?" he barked, not trying to temper his annoyance.

Cwyn nodded and gestured to the men to go into the next room. Only Aonghus remained. He stood cross-armed in front of Solomon, staring at him like a disappointed parent.

"What?" Solomon snapped.

"How could you do that?" he asked, shaking his head disapprovingly.

"I do not have to answer to you for my actions," he said, pointing at him.

Aonghus' eyes flared and, mumbling something under his breath, stomped out to join the others.

chapter twelve

y the way the men were cloistered together, Solomon knew they were there under duress. Everything about their manner suggested they were concealing something, and when he saw a large leather satchel on the floor between Megba and Koven, all of his suspicions were confirmed.

Aonghus was keeping watch at the window, and he deliberately turned his back to him when Solomon entered the room. Solomon bristled at his reaction. He did not know why, but he found the boy's precociousness particularly irritating. In truth, he found this entire occasion particularly irritating. It was not the timing of it; it was more that he had been removed from the inner workings of tribal politics long enough to find it to his liking. Now this visit evoked sour feelings he would have rather forgotten.

He took out a flask of wine and offered it to Megba. The elder shook his head and the rest of them politely refused. Solomon shrugged off their reactions and gladly helped himself to it.

"I trust by the sorrowful look of all of you, that this is not a social visit," he stated obligingly.

"No," Cwyn answered. "We are here under the worst circumstances."

"That is too bad," he said, sipping his wine. He was not about to offer his assistance willingly.

He felt Aonghus tap him on the arm, silently asking for a drink. Pretending he did not feel it, the warrior took another particularly long gulp.

"May I have a drink, please?" Aonghus asked in a small voice.

Solomon widened his eyes, surprised by the request. He held out the vessel, then quickly pulled it back when Aonghus reached for it, and drank again. Displeasure etched itself on the child's features and he sulked back to the window.

"Solomon, we are in need of your help," Cwyn was saying. He had completely missed the exchange between man and boy. "But I have gotten ahead of myself, I should let Megba speak on our behalf."

The elder bowed his head, taking a deep breath. As he lifted his eyes, Solomon was humbled at their appearance. They looked powerful and wild.

"This is important, is it not?" Solomon asked, noticeably troubled by the old man's countenance.

"It is," he responded, throwing his sagging shoulders back and sitting erect. "But before we go on, I must have your promise that all that we say here on this eve will never be mentioned to anyone outside of those present."

"You have my word," the warrior answered respectfully.

He went to Aonghus and absentmindedly put the flask in his hand, then settled beside the elder.

Aonghus smiled to himself, content that his teacher had conceded, and took a victorious drink.

"Speak your mind, Sorcerer," Solomon urged. His care for the old man was evident by his sincerity. "You know I would do anything for you."

Megba took Solomon's large hand in his withered one, and squeezed it tightly. "There are a great many of us who believe that if Laden takes power, our clan will suffer," he spoke firmly, but considerably softer than normal. "He wants to be allied with Rome, and we feel it is not to our good."

"Laden wants to increase his wealth," Solomon offered. "That can only come with expansion, and the only nation worth expanding with is Rome."

"It is more than that," Megba countered. "It is not as simple as preserving what we have, or unifying with another tribe. Laden has plans to extoll himself as a deity, and the abomination will come at the self-professed hand of Deireadh. She has exalted herself over the heavens, and Laden is in favor of it. The people should never be made to accept such a thing. All that is sacred to us will be destroyed. The gods who have cared for us would be forsaken. It is an anathema. This is not only a political matter, but a spiritual dilemma as well."

Solomon stood looking at each of the men, then he took a long look at Berrig. It was as if he were waiting for his close friend to do something that would indicate his place in all of this. Berrig remained stoically quiet, and finally, Solomon had no choice but to look away.

"I understand your position. But why have you come to me?" he responded, his voice thick with uncertainty.

In his mind he knew exactly why they were there. Something needed to be done before Laden claimed his reign, and whoever performed the task must be expendable. Weighing all the aspects of a political overthrow, he was the best choice, and if he were capable of being more objective, he really would have applauded their reasoning. The only problem was it would break Donnach's heart if he went against his son, and the wicked occultist they were speaking of happened to be his wife.

Cwyn picked up the pouch and set it in front of him. "We have collected an offering from the kinsmen who believe in our cause."

Staring at the weathered face of the older warrior, Solomon could not help but feel inferior. These men had always possessed a sort of heroic immortality. From the time he was a child he had, in a sense, idolized them. They had been the steadfast measure by which he had compared himself.

For an instant, it crossed his mind that they had come to bribe him. They would give him the valuables in exchange for finishing the job he had started weeks ago at the feast. He quickly discarded the thought.

"I am honored by it, but I cannot take arms against the son of the King," he rebutted, placing his hands on his hips.

"That is not what we would ask you to do," the sorcerer countered. "We would ask you to take this to the council of the Druids on the far shore. I would have you speak to them of our situation. Make it clear that it is I who have sent you, and that we are in dire need of a spiritualist whose heart is pure. Such a one must be free of blemish or human guile. It must be a person of great caring for our people could be plunged into unending darkness at Deireadh's hand. You must relay to them that this one, of black practices, has forsaken the Goddess and claimed the powers herself."

Solomon stood, his thoughts racing. "If you bring another Druid into our clan, you are blatantly defying the King's choice to govern his own people. It is treason," he argued. "It will no doubt result in an inner war. Are you prepared to take responsibility for that? Are you willing to wipe the blood from your swords at the actions your claim shall incite? You—all of you—owe yourselves your lives and the lives of your loved ones. But more than that, you owe your allegiance to the faithful King who has cared for you. My conscience cannot be washed clean if I act so deceitfully on another's behalf. Maybe your reverence for the heavens has clouded your reality, and it is temporarily unclear whose rights have been usurped."

Megba firmly shook his head.

"Still, if I am the dreaded sovereign who assumes this mission and who brings back the rebel, it will appear that I have organized this overthrow. There are few advantages of such a position except that if you lose this fight, I will be the first to die for this corruption—if the pursuit even gets that far," Solomon argued. His mind jumped to another point. "There are nothing but warring tribes between here and the sanctuary. A lone warrior would not stand a chance."

"We will send Aonghus with you," Koven nervously interjected.

Solomon rolled his eyes. "The boy? I do not mean to be rude, my friend, but I refuse to take your son to a place from which he will surely never return."

"It is not for you to decide," Megba broke in. "I have sought the spirits' council, and it is predestined that he should accompany you."

The warrior's face went blank. Then in what appeared to be a change of light, he was filled with distress. "I think you have all gone mad," he declared, walking to the door and opening it for them to leave. "Good night."

No one stirred. Each man wore the same determined countenance as he stared back at him. Only Aonghus' young face reflected uncertainty.

"Close the door and come here," Ronan demanded, raising his voice like Solomon was a disobedient child.

Heaving an aggravated sigh, he slowly reentered the chamber.

"Do I have to tell you that it would be unwise for you to refuse this request?" Ronan asked, stepping in front of him.

Solomon was silent. He glanced at Berrig, who gave him an apologetic look.

"You are the best one for this," Ronan continued. "You are a capable warrior, and well acquainted with the ways of the Order. And you are..."

"I am the most easily sacrificed if your plan fails," Solomon interrupted. "Do not expect me to believe that you chose me for my courage alone. If something goes wrong, none of you will be blamed and my actions will appear to be nothing more than a jealous husband acting out his revenge."

Ronan did not flinch. His face remained flat and unreadable. "Those are your words. I would advise you to leave at first light, as it will take at least five nights to reach your destination. Travel with great haste, because if Laden is anointed before your return, it will only complicate matters."

He took Solomon by the shoulders and sought to embrace him, but the younger one stepped back. Their eyes met, and something vile seemed to surface in each of them. Their features were at once filled with resentment; Ronan deplored Solomon questioning his authority, and Solomon despised acting against his will.

Ronan exited as the others rose from their seats and bowed their good-byes. Berrig stopped beside him, and when he was sure no one was watching, put his arms around his friend. Then he placed his personal amulet in Solomon's hand.

"We have been close to each other in times of peace and war," he said sincerely. "I would not have it any different now if I could help it. So please take this part of my spirit, so the distance between us will not be as great."

Solomon gulped down his emotion. Berrig would not have passed on something this sacred if he thought he had the slightest chance of coming home.

"Berrig," Solomon whispered. "A portion of my land should be given to the farmer if the boy and I—"

"I know," his friend reassured him. "It will be taken care of if need be."

Solomon turned away, not wanting Berrig to see his pallidness. He saw Koven down on one knee next to his son. He was speaking to him quietly, and Aonghus was listening carefully to each word. He had the most sober way about him, as he nodded that he understood what his father was saying. Then he offered one of those vague, enchanting smiles that only children possess and put his small arms around his father's neck. Koven embraced him, wrapping his arms completely around his tiny body. He stood without letting go of his son, and carried Aonghus all the way to the door before setting him down.

"I would expect a game of fidcheall with you in a fortnight," he said, turning his attention to Solomon.

"Yes, yes," Solomon replied, walking up to the farmer and lightly taking his swollen hand. "All will be well by then."

"I do not have to tell you to take good care of my son."

Solomon glanced at Aonghus. "I will treat him as though he were my own."

The two were silent a moment, then Koven touched the top of Aonghus' shoulder and left.

CHAPTER THIRTEEN

nly Megba remained after the others had left. He had taken off the white leather pouch he usually wore around his waist and set it in front of the hearth. Next to this he placed a gold jeweled vial of oil. In his hand he held a small, shallow container of herbal powder. He was the keeper of the secrets of the earth, an alchemist whose knowledge of the magical arts spanned all dimensions. He realized the forceful vibrations each plant and oil contained. This understanding had been accumulated through the ages by his ancestors, and when the proper time came, he would entrust it to another whom the stars had chosen.

Knowing what he was about to do, Solomon immediately knelt down before the fire. He motioned to Aonghus to do the same, and the boy took a place next to him.

The sorcerer closed his eyes and lifted his face to the ceiling. The orange glow of the fire exaggerated the wrinkles in his shriveled skin and for a moment, he reminded Solomon of one of the limestone escarpments that decorated the surrounding hillsides. He mumbled a prayer, and while Aonghus reverently bowed his head, Solomon uncomfortably cleared his throat.

Megba put his right forefinger into the powder and pressed it to the center of Aonghus' forehead. Then he opened the vial and dabbed some onto his left forefinger. Humming softly, he streaked it across the entire area above the boy's brow. His voice raised an octave as he swirled both hands around the outline of Aonghus' body and over his head. Then he repeated the same blessing for Solomon, who waited impatiently for him to finish. When he was through, the white-haired man rested a hand on each of their heads.

"Your souls are an endless measure of the life force," he said piously. "The life that beats within you does not commence, nor does it cease. May it be like the breeze that ebbs through eternity and thrives until the end of the wind."

Dropping his head, he engaged in a silent prayer for the two journeymen before carefully returning the herbs and oil to his bag.

Solomon sprang to his feet, rushing to the window for a breath of air. It was a direct contrast to Aonghus, who remained on his knees in private meditation.

"It would be easier for you to accept if you believed in it," Megba admonished Solomon. "Someday you will realize that rituals were not created for their own sake, but as a means of manifesting the spiritual realm that extends far beyond your meager world."

"I am sure they are," Solomon indulged him.

The elder trudged stoop-shouldered to the door. "You think that I am betraying Donnach," he said flatly.

"No, I do not," the younger one half-heartedly denied.

"Do not speak untruths, because I can hear your thoughts," Megba rebuked. "I will only tell you this. It is out of my love for the King that I do what I do. I would rather see Donnach slain than watch his heart break when he sees what will become of his people at Laden and Deireadh's hands. Perhaps you hesitate to take on this quest because you think she still loves you. But take it upon my very word when I tell you she does not. She only lusts for illusions, and if you look deep within your vinegar heart, you will find that you do not love her either. She was a convenience and, like the rest of us, you can easily live without her. After all, you survived all these years knowing the fate of the woman who bore you."

The warrior fought his immediate outrage. But he did not mask it well because no sooner had Megba finished his sentence, than he was gone.

Solomon looked down at Aonghus as if he were expecting a response. Aonghus shrugged off his master's reaction and began piling his sleeping pelts in front of the fire.

"Absolutely not," Solomon grunted. "You are not sleeping in here without a bath. You smell like a sow!"

"I did not have time to wash," Aonghus argued. "I had to groom your horse and help my mother dress the elk."

"That is not my problem. Either you bathe or you sleep out with the pigs. The water is in there," Solomon said, pointing to the washing chamber.

Glowering at him, Aonghus marched over and stuck his fingers in the tub. "It is cold," he announced.

"Warm some more," Solomon snapped.

Aonghus frowned and shot the warrior a hateful look. Solomon knew if the boy had been even a pound heavier or an inch taller, he would have punched him. He stomped back in and picked up two of the animal skins. "I will sleep with the pigs," he grumbled, and slammed the door behind him.

———

It was still dark when the two started on their journey. There was a soft sprinkle coming down as they loaded the pigskin saddlebags, rubbed with lard to repel the water, onto their horses. Koven had lent his son the family's only horse. He was a broad-backed, chestnut gelding named Osin, whose thick chest and haunches looked awkward next to Solomon's sleek steed. Still, he was a faithful, well-loved family pet, and it brought the farmer some peace of mind knowing that his son was with a trustworthy friend.

They left the village through the grove so no one would see them. The beautiful stillness of the massive trees suggested such strength and wonder. The huge sacred trunks ran in an endless row from the edge of their village to the cliffs overlooking the sea. The elegant branches that interlaced with each other formed a canopy to the heavens. Such a crude, yet provocative, fortress this was, the tops of which were adorned with mistletoe.

It was midday before man or boy spoke to each other, and then it was only for Solomon to tell Aonghus that they would stop just long enough to rest the horses. When they finally did have lunch, they ate without acknowledging the company of the other. Solomon, agitated with not only having to go on this mission against his will, but having to drag Aonghus along with him, made no effort to hide his displeasure. Taking his duty quite seriously, Aonghus could not help but be insulted by the way his master shunned him. This, plus the added pressure of each thinking the other was entirely unjustified in his feelings, resulted in a terribly uncordial atmosphere.

By sunset, they were well out of the boundaries of their own territory. They followed a stream to conceal themselves in the wooded areas above the banks. Solomon was not sure how these tribes might greet them. They had as much propensity for being friendly as aggressive, and considering the valuables he was carrying, he thought it best to exercise caution.

They finally made camp on a chilly, muddy spot hidden by boulders and oak trees. There was a fire only big enough for warmth. Dinner consisted of the same salted meat and bread they had eaten for lunch; only this time, the two shared some corma that Enda had sent along with pieces of honeycomb as an extra treat.

Solomon watched Aonghus, amused by the way he had become a bit silly after a few drinks of ale. He was moving about in a loose-jointed way which was considerably slower than his usual precise mannerisms, and he could not stop himself from smiling. By the time Solomon bedded down for the night, Aonghus was staring blankly at the fire and singing softly to himself. Realizing it was time to go to sleep, he picked up his sleeping fur and swayed over to the warrior. He covered him with it, then crawled beneath the double-fur pelts and snuggled up to him.

Taken aback by his unassuming affection, the warrior could not prevent himself from wrapping one arm around him. Although he was not about to admit it to his foster, he was glad he was not alone this night after all.

———

It did not take long for the rations to lose their appeal. After a breakfast of saltpork and tea, the two decided it was time to hunt on their own.

From the lack of ocean breeze Aonghus was accustomed to, he guessed that they were on the interior of the island. The sloping hills were lush with grass, and the trees that lined the top of the ridges were bushier than the ones he was used to seeing. They did not grow in thick groves; instead, they were scattered in clumps of five or ten. Although the terrain made it easier for traveling, it offered little refuge from a pursuer, be it man or beast.

The two riders had stopped at the base of a wooded knoll near a small pond. There were clusters of leafless shrubbery dotting the banks. From the large holes burrowed into the earth, it was apparent it was a haven for rabbits.

Aonghus did not bother to tie Osin since he was a bit lazy anyway, and not likely to run off. The gentle manner of the gelding had even calmed Solomon's high-strung stallion who, much to the warrior's dismay, took a place next to Osin dozing in the morning sun. This behavior was most unwelcome in a war-horse. Their keen eyesight and hearing were often the only signal of an approaching enemy. For a horseman as prideful as Solomon, who claimed to have the best-trained battle horses on the island, to see his prized stud sedated by a farming animal was most disconcerting.

Aonghus had saved a smoldering ember from their fire in the hollow of an ox horn. Taking a branch and wrapping one end of it with a strip of cloth, moist grass, and strands of hair from Osin's tail, he fashioned a torch, and lit it with the live coal. After a considerable debate, he and Solomon found a hole they both agreed was the back entrance of a rabbit den, piled it with twigs, and lit them. Each holding his spear, they perched themselves at the front opening and waited for the rabbits to flee the smoke.

Two small bunnies ran out first; they were too little to eat so they let them escape. Following that, one very plump hare streaked past Solomon who was nearest to the hole. It was promptly speared by Aonghus, who had positioned himself a few paces away in case Solomon missed. Fueled by his apprentice's ease at killing the rabbit, Solomon did not miss the next two that crossed his path. Satisfied that the size of them would sustain them for at least two meals, they tied the fuzzy creatures to their saddles and continued on their trek.

Rabbits and fish were the obvious choices for hunting while on the move. They were many in number, and could be readily caught using spears or horsehair fishing nets. They were also easily stored in saddle bags, and in the case of the rabbits, their hides could be used immediately if needed.

That night, in front of the fire, as Solomon tended the roasting of the hare, he came to an odd realization. They had gone literally halfway to their destination without seeing a single Celt from another tribe. Solomon had chosen their path with great care to be sure to travel in neutral territories, but this was more than unusual. In his days with the fianna, it seemed that as soon as they had left their clan's boundaries, they were in a skirmish. During those times he had not considered his mortality. As long as he had a fast horse and a javelin, he felt invincible. It was ironic now that the first thing he had thought of when Ronan had told him of this quest, was the probability of failure, not success. He did not know if he was becoming more responsible or less courageous with time.

"You do not believe in anything, do you?" Aonghus asked, interrupting his thoughts.

"I believe in myself," he answered without looking up.

"My father says that better men must believe in more if their life is to be good. They must desire higher truths," the boy replied.

"And did your father specify what those higher truths might be?" the warrior asked, sitting down cross-legged and stoking the fire with a stick.

Aonghus smiled as though he had successfully baited a hook that Solomon had easily bitten into. "Sometimes he says that it can come in the way of love. Like the way my father and mother love me even when I am bad. Sometimes he says it is in trusting that everything happens for a reason."

"A higher plan, such as divine providence, you mean?" Solomon asked.

Aonghus shrugged. "I do not know if I understand what that is. I guess it is more like when your wife left you. You might think that it is terrible, but someday, you might see that it was better that it happened. The gods understand our ways better than we do."

"I do not think we are in agreement," Solomon huffed. "I have chosen and understood my path up until now, and it has not been unsuccessful."

The boy cast him a mocking smile. "Then why are you not a King?"

"And why aren't you?" Solomon retorted.

"Because I am not old enough yet. You know that," he answered sheepishly.

Solomon frowned. "Aonghus, there are times when I like you, and times when I wish you were far from my presence."

"I know," Aonghus replied, unaffected. "Sometimes I feel the same way."

Solomon's brows came together irritably. "Then why do you stay?"

The boy waited a moment before answering. "Because it is my duty," he kindly replied.

CHAPTER FOURTEEN

On the morning of their last day of travel Solomon spotted three other Celtic warriors. It was quite by chance that it happened. He had been trying so hard to travel in safe territory that he thought he had gone too far to the east. Climbing to the top of a hill at sunrise, he found himself accidentally perched above their camp. All three were still sleeping, but noting their position in reference to his own, he surmised they had been tracking him for at least a day. Unbeknownst to both parties, the only thing separating them was a small ridge that followed a river.

Without suppressing his alarm, he quickly explained the situation to Aonghus as he haphazardly gathered their belongings. He told him that they were going to have to take advantage of the head start they were getting, and try to outrun them. Stashing their supplies so they could move faster, Solomon and Aonghus hastily left their camp. They did not bother to extinguish the fire in hopes that if the band meant to make an assault, they would follow the smoke. If booty was all they were after, they would be pacified with what they had hidden. If it was not, at least Solomon and Aonghus would have a better chance at positioning themselves for the encounter.

They rode at a steady canter, hidden whenever possible by the rows of fir trees along the ridge. Solomon would have preferred to move more rapidly, but the footing was unsure, and although his horse was bred to withstand the terrain, Osin was a burly farm horse who was used to slow paces and flat ground. If Solomon went any faster he would leave Aonghus too far behind, and probably damage the horse in trying to catch up. Instead, the warrior gave his apprentice a sharp dagger and an extra spear with instructions that if they were attacked, he should pretend that the men were elks.

Tightening his stomach muscles and pressing his calves to his horse's flanks, he gave Aonghus a hand signal to gallop. They exited the trees at full stride and crossed an open meadow. Solomon could hear the labored drone of Aonghus' horse, and glancing over his shoulder, he could see the animal was frothing at the bit and bobbing its head with fatigue. Slipping back into the refuge of a stand of trees, he continued a short distance further, stopping finally at a brook.

Wading into it, he let his stallion drink as he dismounted. Standing knee deep in the chilly water, he sloshed over to Osin. Lifting the upper lip of the horse, he checked the color of his gums to be sure the tired animal was not going into shock. He cupped his hands and splashed water on his chest to cool him.

"This horse would run himself to death," Solomon said, moving his wet hand down Osin's lathered neck.

"He would do anything I ask of him, so I do not ask him without good reason," Aonghus replied, turning in the saddle, distracted.

Solomon went around the horse's hindquarters and doused them in the same manner. He could hear the gelding's breathing start to slow as he walked behind him to make sure the hocks were not swollen. Then for some unknown reason, his torso jerked, and before he could even feel the pain, he looked over one shoulder and saw a javelin sticking out of his back.

He grabbed the spear from Aonghus' saddle and slapped his horse. The sluggish animal did not start to run until it saw Solomon's stallion fleeing recklessly back in the direction from which they had come. Then he was so fear-stricken that he bucked. He almost unseated Aonghus, who grabbed a handful of his mane to keep from falling. As he kicked out, he caught Solomon in the hip with his hoof and knocked him down. The warrior fell on his side, fortunately not driving the spear any deeper.

Floundering about in the water, Solomon was only able to get up on one knee before the first assailant was upon him. In an act of utter desperation, he lunged forward and grabbed hold of the spear shaft that was pointed at him before it could be thrown.

The oncoming horse was moving with such speed that Solomon was dragged across the stream. He felt the impact of the jagged rocks bruising his flesh before the sheer weight of his body pulled his attacker from the saddle.

Neither Solomon nor his opponent would release the spear. Instead, each gripped the shaft with both hands and attempted to overpower the other. This was to Solomon's grave disadvantage since the weapon lodged in his back had weakened the muscles on one side. Sensing his vulnerability, the attacking Celt threw his weight at him, causing him to wilt slowly at the force.

Both men were baring their teeth like beasts. Their eyes were locked, completely consumed with the actions of the other. Then there was a great splashing of water in his eyes, and through his distorted vision, Solomon saw a dark blur of what he supposed was the horse of yet another Celt. He gathered what was left of his strength and prepared for another onslaught. Suddenly, the man he had been fighting went limp, and dropped into the water in front of him. He fell face first, and to Solomon's astonishment, he saw that the man had a dagger driven into the base of his skull.

Instinctively turning to see where it had come from, he found Aonghus down on his knees beside him. His blue eyes sparked with fear as he pointed for Solomon to look in the opposite direction. Then he curled himself into a ball and covered his head with his arms for protection.

Out of the corner of his eye, the warrior glimpsed another approaching horseman. Still holding the spear, he painfully rotated his shoulders and heaved it at the oncoming rider, but he was too weak and it fell short of its target. In the next instant, he felt the tip of the adversary's sword slice through the cloth of his shirt and cut into his shoulder.

Aonghus' head popped up at the same time the Celt circled for another assault. Weaponless, all Solomon could do was attempt to grab hold of him and handle him as he did the other.

"Aonghus, run!" he hollered as the boy scrambled to his feet.

With his eyes fixed on his foe, he suddenly felt an excruciating pain in his back. It was as if someone had parted his skin and shoved a burning torch into his muscles. Dizzy and unable to catch himself, he fell forward. He saw the blue of the sky turn to liquid as he sank beneath the rippling surface of the brook. His eyes were still open as he watched the legs of the horse plunging into the water in front of his face. It was as if he were dreaming the mass of tiny air bubbles surrounding the forelegs, and the only thought he had was that the third Celt had stabbed him from behind. He heard the splash of another body in the stream beside him, and assumed it was Aonghus.

There was a desperate moment when he felt himself swallowing the cold water and could feel the breath escaping his lungs. Then someone had him by the hair and was lifting up his face. Coughing and sputtering, he gasped the fresh air as he slowly dragged his battered body to the muddy banks.

With watering eyes, he glanced over and found Aonghus sitting on the bank beside him. He was taking big breaths of air, and his pallor was stone grey except for the red blotches on his cheeks.

Filled with relief, the warrior lifted his mud-caked face and stared at the boy dumbfounded, then dropped it back down.

"I missed twice," Solomon muttered in disgust.

Aonghus' mouth fell open, then he slammed himself backward, and burst into tears.

CHAPTER FIFTEEN

fter a short crying spell, Aonghus gathered the Celts' horses and their own, and using the dead men's supplies, began dressing Solomon's wounds. The spear had landed between his shoulder blades, just to the left of his spine. The warrior lay motionless as Aonghus worked on him, his droopy eyes fixed on the two corpses floating face down in the stream.

"You are going to have to sit up so I can wrap this around you," Aonghus said, stuffy nosed.

Still dazed, Solomon pushed against the ground with both hands in an attempt to rise from his spot. He was only able to lift his torso halfway. Putting his hands beneath his armpits, Aonghus heaved him up the rest of the way.

Using a long strip of hide he had cut from a sleeping roll, he wrapped it around Solomon's back and chest, and knotted it tightly. He then placed another strip over the top of one shoulder and across the wound, and tied that one beneath the opposite armpit. The sword had only inflicted a minor cut that was easily dressed.

The warrior shook his head and rubbed his eyes, trying to rouse himself from his state. He watched Aonghus rummage through the saddle bags and take out a drinking bag. Bringing it to his master, he braced the back of Solomon's head with one hand and held the ale for him to drink with the other.

"Enough?" the boy asked after he had taken a few gulps.

Solomon nodded, causing a portion of the beer to spill down his chest. Clutching the bag with shaking hands, Aonghus sat back on his heels and took a long swig himself. Then he looked hard at Solomon's face, waiting for some sort of response. Dissatisfied with his master's condition, the child had him drink quite a bit more of the ale.

"All right," he reassured Solomon in a quivering voice. "Everything is fine now. We will just sit here awhile."

Both stared at the gruesome sight in front of them. The corpses' blood was pooling around their bodies. It turned the clear water to red ripples, and strands of their long hair floated like seaweed in the current.

"What happened to the spear in my back?" Solomon asked, his dry lips sticking to his gums as he spoke.

Aonghus nervously wiped his brow with his forearm, then pointed at the spear impaled in the torso of the second Celt.

"That was you?" Solomon questioned. "I thought I had been struck again from behind."

Aonghus shook his head. "You told me to run, but I could not get away in time," he said, breathing heavily. "You missed him with your spear, and the only other one I could reach was the one sticking out of your back. I am sorry, but you would have had to pull it out anyway."

Solomon forced himself to blink hard a couple of times to soothe his stinging eyes. Though he had temporarily blocked out the actual images of the attack, he was beginning to remember their sequence.

"How did you make such a clean throw?" he asked.

"I did not throw it," Aonghus answered, taking another drink and coughing the ale back up. He tried to turn his face away, but it spurt out so suddenly that he spit it onto himself. "When you fell, his horse reared and he was thrown on top of me. He accidently killed himself."

The warrior could see that Aonghus was trembling badly, and trying to quell his tears. He reached out to pull him close. He held him tightly with his one good arm, and Solomon could feel his warm tears fall onto his neck.

"I promise you my lifelong devotion for this," he whispered, and kissed the top of his head.

Then he released him, and carefully rising to his feet, walked slowly into the stream. Swaying over to the dead men, he stripped them of their weapons and pulled out the spear and dagger that had killed them. He drew his sword and handed it to Aonghus. Grabbing a handful of hair, he lifted the sopping head of the first one out of the water.

"You have slain them," he said. "It is your right to take their skulls."

Gripping the sword with both his small hands, Aonghus stepped hesitantly closer. Even the red blotches on his cheeks turned pale when he gazed on the wet, stone-like face of his victim. Water drained out of the man's open mouth, and bits of gravel could be seen in his lifeless eyes. Biting his bottom lip to keep from screaming, Aonghus turned away.

"Please," he said tearfully. "I do not want to look at them anymore."

Solomon felt his heart sink as he remembered that for all his bravery, Aonghus was still only a child.

"I understand," he said, letting the head plop back down into the stream. "We will leave them for the spirits and the wolves."

———

The third Celt Solomon had spotted originally was never accounted for. He surmised that either he was a drifter who had shared the fire for a night, or that he saw the little hellion's display, and retreated of his own free will, the latter for which Solomon would not have blamed him.

By dusk, they had reached the Druid settlement, and seeing Solomon's rapidly debilitating condition, they gave them immediate refuge without any questions asked. The boy and the warrior were taken to a one-room, thatched-roof hut. There, two women removed Solomon's bandages and noting the size of his wound, called for the older medicine woman.

She shuffled into the room, shoulders sagging and flabby breasts drooping over her high sash. She had deep lines across her forehead and dark circles framed her time-shrouded eyes. When she turned to smile at Aonghus, she revealed only gums and a receding chin, making the skin on her neck fold over itself.

Aonghus stood in muted horror in the corner of the room. He watched while she ground up some roots in a stone mortar and mixed them with unstrained wine. Then she held it carefully in both hands as she wobbled over to where Solomon lay, and made him drink it.

Pouring oil in her palms, she rubbed her hands together vigorously, then poking the area around the wound, she examined her patient intently, singing a low melody in another language. Once every third or fourth measure, her voice would rise an octave, then drop, as she lightly touched her oiled palms to the base of Solomon's neck and both of his wrists. Then she placed her fingertips on the warrior's eyelids to close them.

With a sudden ease of movement that betrayed her aged appearance, the hag stood erect, and Aonghus was aghast as she took out a huge, broad-bladed knife and began warming it in the fire.

Aonghus crept to Solomon's side, and sensing what was about to take place, began stroking his master's face and hair to comfort him. The warrior was barely conscious by the time the woman came back alongside him with the smoldering weapon. Aonghus cringed as she pressed the glowing red blade to Solomon's cut. His entire body jerked violently as he struggled to escape from it, but the woman held it firmly in place as the room filled with his anguished cries.

"It is all right," Aonghus was saying, striving to sound calm. "It will be over soon."

Whimpering like a puppy, Solomon clutched the boy's arm so hard that Aonghus thought it would break in half. The repugnant odor of cauterized flesh rose around him as the warrior fainted from the pain.

The medicine woman looked kindly at Aonghus and tried to pat him on the shoulder, but she was such a frightening sight, he anxiously stepped away from her. She continued to look back at him understandingly as her wrinkled lips stretched even further across her toothless mouth. Aonghus thought that he had never seen anyone as ugly and fearfully disfigured by age in his entire life. Yet at the same time, he could not help but stare at her with a morbid fascination.

She gathered her tools of care, and without saying anything, set a bowl of water and a clean cloth beside Solomon. She dipped the cloth in the liquid, wrung it out, then gently touched it to Solomon's sweaty face. She offered it to Aonghus, and as he took it from her, he brushed against her scaly hands. Trying hard to disguise how revolted he was by the feel of it, he began dabbing Solomon's face and neck. Satisfied that her patient was in competent hands, she gave the boy a hand gesture he had never seen before and left them alone.

In the next moment, two tall, very lean, white-robed men came in. They were quiet in their entry, and Aonghus was so consumed in caring for Solomon that they were at the foot of Solomon's fur pallet before Aonghus noticed them. Startled, he dropped the cloth and drew his dagger.

"You have experienced much for one of such a tender age," one of them said sympathetically. He had sharp, elongated features with unusually languid eyes. "We are here to care for you and your warrior. There is no need to be frightened any longer."

Keeping his weapon pointed at them, Aonghus shuffled over to pick up the bag containing the tribal offering. Without averting his gaze, he then moved back to his spot to protect Solomon. He did not know why he had trusted the old woman and he doubted these men. Perhaps he was more accustomed to females caring for the ill, and his last encounter with strange men had nearly cost him his life.

The priests watched him unassumingly, bearing content smiles that Aonghus wished he could slap away. In the last few hours, he had been through a most traumatic experience of life and death, and it had left his emotions raw. Now to see such unabashed tranquility in these men's expressions made him furious.

He felt his heart start to race, then slow down, and he was filled with bewilderment at his state. Without thinking, he put down his weapon, rested his arms in a small space next to Solomon's head, and buried his face as he let out a miserable moan. He hated this. He hated the feeling of killing and at the same time, despised himself for being weak. His stomach hurt badly; it was empty and knotted with shame. He wanted to leave this place. He wanted to feel the comforting touch of his mother and experience the mercy of being held in his father's arms. What had he done when he had thoughtlessly stabbed those men? Had he angered the gods, and been cast out from the heavens for ending their lives? It could never feel good to kill. And he should not be free from the guilt and pain of his actions.

"Drink this, young one," the second priest said as he set the cup Solomon had used beside him. "We will leave you now."

The two were gone when Aonghus looked up. He was crying when he drank the cup filled with wine. The taste of it was strong; he found he needed water to wash it down. Grabbing hold of the bowl next to him, he swallowed some of the cool water he had used on Solomon. It tasted salty from the warrior's sweat, and left Aonghus thirsty for more.

He started for the water pitcher near the door, but he was too dizzy and dropped to his knees in the center of the room. He felt the pleasing sensation of a tranquil current running through his body, and the beating of his heart sounded like a distant drum. Inhaling deeply, he filled his lungs with the fresh air wafting into the room.

Sitting back on his heels, his body suddenly felt too heavy to hold up any longer. He stretched out on the cool earthen floor. As he was drifting off to sleep, he felt the gentle sway of the room as he floated deeper into slumber. Suddenly his body twitched, and he felt afraid again. Through closed eyes he saw the ceiling coming down on him. Then in a spinning revolution, he watched in terror as his body started breaking apart. The tiny particles of flesh evaporated into sparks in the distance. He felt the crawling of the vermin into his cold body, and saw himself sprawled on the muddy river bank next to the Celts he had murdered.

He wanted to scream for anyone who could rescue him. He was not like them; he was not dead yet! There was a glimmer of something far away, and he cried out, "Mother, Mother, help me please."

Yet all that surrounded him was a deafening silence. It drowned out the sound of his own voice and left him sinking, sightless and weightless, into the wet soil. He stretched his arms and began digging at the dirt caving in around him, and felt himself vanishing into unwanted peace. He was becoming part of the ground now, and his ears were filled with the sound of the trees and the flowers sprouting up around him. Then his vision shifted as though he was staring into the very depths of the earth itself.

Molten red it was, like the burning blood of his victims. It moved in a swirl, bubbling and popping from the intense heat. Then he saw the old hag who had cared for Solomon emerging from it. She was coming toward him, and he was struggling to get away from her. He was clawing at the mud, and no sooner did he push it away, then it fell back into his mouth and smothered his frenzied cries. Then he felt it: the chilling touch of this horribly deformed shrew running her hands over his body and tearing away his clothes. Was this what death was?

"Help me," Aonghus wept, surrendering to his nightmare. "Somebody help me, please."

CHAPTER SIXTEEN

She was not sad, nor was she angry. She was simply frustrated at how long it was taking. It did not matter that she was assured an eventual result, but the sooner it came, the more rewarding her destiny would be. After all, it was not as if she did not know what she was destined to do. She had known it since her birth, and the twenty years since then only served as a means of perfecting the craft with which she had been gifted.

She moved around the edge of a small watering hole where she often came at sunset to visit with the wild animals. While she took pleasure at the sight of the majestic elk and wild horses, she loved watching the deer the most. She was fascinated by their gentle manner and oversized, compassionate eyes that could penetrate even a hardened heart. At times, if she remained very still, the same beautiful fawn would come near her, as though it were trying to wordlessly teach her that the power of gentleness could touch the hearts and minds of even the foulest being. How she wished the fawn were with her now, for she was being courted by such wretched forces.

Her strides were long, but unmistakably feminine. She was not a tall woman, nor was she a short one; rather, she was of an elegant stature with sleek legs, beautifully rounded hips, and breasts just full enough to be tempting. With fiery red hair that cascaded down her shoulders in luxurious tresses, and eyes so clear and green they appeared preternatural, she was a striking young woman. Clad in a plain white frock that betrayed the lovely body of one twenty years old, Saturnalia gazed up at the tiny stars enveloping the planet for which she had been named, and gave an impatient sigh.

It was all such folly, all of it—the waiting and pretending that she was ignorant of her purpose, as though her feigned subservience was necessary to appease the vanity of her teachers. Of course, they had trained her, schooled her in the tools of alternate realities. She reasoned that it was by her own talent that these attributes had blossomed, and yet, she had to act otherwise to indulge their petty titles. She felt almost as if they begrudged her her youth and the unwavering faith in her skills. To them, she was nothing more than an idealist whose concept of reality had not yet been dashed by the parasites of old ways.

It was more than true that her teachers were old, but more than the crime of their years, they were guilty of fear. Fear of time's passing, and even worse than that, the fear of a man believed to be the incarnate son of a single, omnipotent God. One whom his followers claimed manifested the divine powers. He was born in a land far away from their island, but his proclamations had crossed the oceans and had been embraced by a race who named themselves Christians.

They told the story of a mortal they called their Saviour, a man who was so loved by his people that he was considered a threat to the Roman government. He had generated open enthusiasm for this teachings; in fact, they were said to have incited a political revolution against Rome. His doctrine espoused nothing more than love, forgiveness, and a spiritual communion for every person with a lone God, not the multiple ones Saturnalia had come to know. Even though their beliefs were different from hers, she could respect the necessity for a separatist faction. Only this faction did not believe such a thing was possible, and Saturnalia had heard many stories of her people being tortured for believing in their beloved Celtic gods rather than the Christian one.

Manner of worship aside, who was this man anyway? This supposed incarnation of God who was somehow viewed as a subversive, and was eventually put to death by Caesar. Was he only a flagrant excuse for a deity with whom she had yet to be acquainted? It would seem insignificant now, since it had been forty-seven cycles since the travesty, yet it was because of him that the Druids lived in constant fear, not only of the religious war of pagan versus Christian, but the condemnation from Rome as well. As a result, an order that had once thrived throughout their land was now more tempered and frighteningly tolerant of the Roman-Christian presence.

Sitting at the water's edge, she studied her reflection. She ran her fingertips across her cheekbones and over her chin. She followed her fragile neck down to her bosom, and opening her frock, looked with secret pleasure at the image of her breasts. There were those in the Order who had said she was not human, that she was put on this earth when the spirits had mated with a witch. But cupping the yielding fullness of her bust with both hands, she felt more human than she could bear. She had felt it even more the night, years ago, when she had stolen away with the swarthy Mediterranean trader who had come to bring wine. His lovely olive skin and his thick curly black hair were too sensual to resist. How liberating it had been when he filled her with himself and whispered the promises in her ear. She did not even care that they were lies, because it was the moment, that brilliant moment of becoming one with another person for the first time, that had mattered most.

How she had shocked her elders and the old witch Jara, who had relentlessly drilled into her head that she was a soulless creation. Saturnalia did so relish the spark of jealousy in her eyes as she graphically recounted the lusty feeling of being a virgin no more. For a moment, she thought she had done it just to spite Jara, to somehow make it clear that there were some parts of her that were exempt from her teacher's rule. All the vicarious fulfillment Jara got from Saturnalia's beauty did, ultimately, stop when Saturnalia wished it so.

Leaning back on one elbow, she dangled a bare foot in the pond. It was so calm tonight; the moon was only a slice of light in the distance, and how glimmering and tranquil the stars were, like a land of dreams too beautiful to be tainted by a waking thought. These flames of the sky were older than the gods, yet still so new. How dare they look down upon her as she struggled for flight.

The sound of an animal came from behind. Casually turning her head, she saw her cat. It was old and feeble, but its shiny orange and grey coat reflected the meticulous care she had given it since she was a child.

"You, beloved friend, are such a well-bred feline," she said, stroking its back as it slinked alongside her. "You are of perfect ear, perfect eye, perfect tail, and such very perfect claws. You have no scar of battle, and yet you never cease to kill the mice and devour their offspring. Dare I say that you possess too much dignity to ever caterwaul at the new moon?"

The cat rolled on his back and let her scratch his furry stomach, and Saturnalia gave still another aggravated sigh.

"I could shriek at those who think that, because I am frail of body, I am also frail of heart. You, you dear cat, know how deep my strength resides, and you have never doomed my impetuousness. How you honor me."

She stretched alongside the animal. With her lithe arms and legs extended, she very much resembled it as she gazed out at the jagged outline of the top of the oak branches. How the Romans and Christians had blasphemed these sacred groves in their descriptions. She had heard them recounted from Celts who had sought refuge from the Roman dominance with the supposed holy Christians, who had demanded that they denounce their true religion or die. These men of God and government who were so audacious as to call their holy Druidic rites savage, and their gods grim and rude. Who said these beautiful groves were hideous, that wild beasts would not lie here, nor birds perch in the oak branches? What good did it do for these Roman-Christians to make spectacles of their worship? And to what end would such brutish accusations come?

How she wanted to rise from her place on earth and become a star. Then she would shine, not as a modern fledgling, but as a gleaming example of the earth's wonders. The elders wanted to keep her here; she knew it. They wanted to keep her away from her people because they knew all too well that she was more spirit and more human than anyone in this Order could ever hope to control. Once she was out of the priestly confines, they could not stop her from doing what she wished. Weren't they strange to create such a one as she, and then fear her so?

"What are you doing, Saturnalia?" she heard Jara call from across the pond.

Saturnalia rolled her head to one side, and covered her eyes with her arm. "I am enjoying the sounds of the night," she answered.

"But there is no ritual here this eve, and you should be mindful of the privacy of the gods," Jara gently admonished as she approached her.

She sat beside her, and began stroking Saturnalia's curly red locks. The younger one did not acknowledge her affection, keeping her eyes hidden.

"He is here, is he not?" she asked.

Jara drew back her hand and looked off in the opposite direction. "There is one who just came this night—"

"I knew it! I knew he was here; I could feel it," Saturnalia declared, shooting up from where she rested.

"Saturnalia, how do you know it is the same one?" Jara asked.

Saturnalia swallowed hard, closing her eyes a moment. "Because I have heard him coming for me. I have heard every step his horse has taken, and it has grown louder and louder until it throbbed in my head and I had to come here to get away from it. The dream—do you remember the dream of which I spoke?"

Jara shook her head.

"I will tell you again. I was in a place so serene that my spirit could leave my body at will," she began. "It had no reason to stay in this physical dwelling because there were many in this place who desired it within them as well. There was a man there. He was not my lover. More, he was my protector. The one whom I could count on for anything. He was faithful and devoted to me—so much so, that I had no fear of giving everything to his people because I knew they would not defile me."

"Had you eaten the brown flowers of the earth before you had this dream?" Jara inquired, trying to discredit her.

Saturnalia looked back at her, wounded. "You scoff at me, Jara. I speak to you from my heart, and you scoff at me."

The old one shook her head reprovingly. "I do not mean to hurt you. It is only that you are young and different from the rest. You will never be a part of this holy Order. Your perceptions are too unorthodox, and I fear that this is yet another scheme concocted by your mind."

Saturnalia stared down at her feet and tried to conceal her hurt. "You think I am crazy, do you not?"

"No," Jara answered, smoothing the back of her student's hair with one hand. "It is only that I have taught you since your birth, and I know, probably too well, what your weaknesses are."

"My only weakness is that I believe in the righteousness and the power of the earth and the sky. And you, you fear it," she responded coldly.

Jara was silent a moment. "Do not be cruel, Saturnalia."

The young woman turned her back to the witch. "If I am not a Druidess, then how would you describe me?"

"You are the ethereal High Priestess," Jara replied. "Your power lies in the realm of the hidden world, and because you can understand both dark and light, you have as much potential for creation as destruction. The mysteries you commune with are far beyond the depths of my understanding. It is as though the hidden darkness abducted you when you were too young for me to rescue, and the invisible rulers you consent to consider me a trespasser. You have never been anointed because your innocence resides in the shadow of our lives. Your dreams and intuitions are real, but they are only to your own purposes. I cannot..."

"Control me," Saturnalia finished her sentence.

"Yes," Jara replied. "And my biggest fear is that your gradually waking consciousness cannot control itself."

The two were silent for a long while, then as if Saturnalia resented her presence, she stood and walked further into the grove. "The seeds of change have been

dormant too long," she yelled. "There are natural laws which govern the unfold-
ment of destiny, and their purpose has been revealed to me, Jara, only to me."

———————

Berrig and Ronan scaled the low stone wall that had originally marked the
boundaries of their village. It had been constructed as a means of protecting their
tribe in times of war, but had long since been abandoned. Because of the growing
presence of Rome in the surrounding islands, a forced migration of many a Celt
had expanded the local tribal territories.

There was an ancient custom that a Celt seeking sanctuary from another
threatening nation was never to be assaulted. He was extended courtesy and hos-
pitality by all clans, and his primary needs of food and shelter were fulfilled before
an inquiry was ever made about the reason for his presence. This custom was even
afforded to Romans in earlier times—until they had betrayed the Celtic open-
heartedness.

The two horsemen descended the uneven face of a rocky hillside, past the
area of their settlement that was occupied by the craftsmen. There were metal
workers and artists here who designed weaponry and farming tools, as well as
horse tack, dining flasks, and jewelry. These people lived in the nucleus of their
tribe because their skills often required very little space, but were viewed as indis-
pensable in fulfilling the needs of everyday life. After the King and the tribe's spiritualist, the safety of these specialists was seen to if there was ever an attack.

Slowing their horses to a jog, the warriors followed a jagged trail down to
the beach. The tide was in, and each time a wave would rush the shore, the salt
water would rise halfway up their horses' legs.

Laden was waiting for them in the exact place he had told Ronan he
would be. He was accompanied by Deireadh and two other mercenary warriors
whose services he had obtained from Rome. As they approached them, it was
apparent that one of the soldiers was quite fatigued. He was droopy-eyed and
dirty as though he had returned from quite an arduous journey. The other was
well-rested and dressed in the flamboyant multi-colored attire of an Icenian
journeyman. Both men were rugged looking. Seeing Laden next to them made
his delicate features and coloring appear all the more pristine.

"He is still alive," Laden announced, as Berrig and Ronan stopped in front
of him. "He and his foster somehow managed to kill the others and escape."

Berrig chuckled to himself; he could not help but be glad that Solomon had
trounced these imposters.

"You find that funny?" Laden challenged.

Berrig chewed the dirt out from underneath one fingernail in the hope of
concealing his smug expression. "Did you think such a one as he would simply
vanish because you overpaid some unworthy assassins?" he countered. "You fail
to realize that he is not a man of ordinary stock. He has the blessings of the gods
of both worlds, and he has many a time scaled the battlements of defeat. Perhaps
when all this is over, he can instruct these men for hire in his ungracious ways."

Berrig eyed the two Icenians with mockish contempt. "Do not trust yourself to the mediocrity of these men."

The well-clad warrior drew his knife and pointed it at Berrig. Berrig looked at him blankly, then threw his head back in laughter.

"Should we do war now?" he scoffed. "Let us end this child's play before it even begins. You and I, warrior, let us perform our feat for the ocean gods, and whoever fails shall live with them for eternity."

"Silence yourself," Ronan commanded, moving his horse between the two men. "We have much to consider here. If Solomon did survive, as you have said, he will have surely reached the Druids by now, and we can only assume that he has told them of Megba's wishes. Since he is safely within the boundaries of the Order, any further assault on him would be construed by the Druids as hostile, and we cannot afford to have them oppose us, yet."

"I agree," Laden responded. "After we have negotiated with Rome and can look to them for protection, we will not be bothered by these arcane men of worship. My concern now is the manner in which we will accuse the intruders upon their return. Solomon and the peasant child will be sentenced of course, but what of the Druid? He will surely have come with the Order's blessing, and will possess all authority according to the laws. To execute such a one could be disastrous."

There was a puzzled moment of silence, each man looking at the other, waiting for him to make the first motion of religious usurpation. All except Berrig, who gazed out into the ocean as if he were oblivious to their scheme.

"Accidents often happen when one is new to a place," Deireadh suggested slyly. "One may mistake the edge of a cliff for a hillside, or misjudge the depths of the lake. Even a holy man could be guilty of such an error. And when he is disposed of, it will only appear to the clan that the spirits did not wish his presence here, and will confirm our rite of power."

Laden gave a half smile and nodded his approval. "Very well. Now we must organize ourselves for the battle. It should be easy to declare a fight without controversy, and I am deserving of the right to demand the death of these men who would seek my ruin. Our success is assured if everyone does as they are instructed. So, which of you will be the good citizen that will inform Megba that I have found out about his plans?"

Ronan lifted one hand. "I will. I will tell him that Deireadh was told by the spirits of his vile intent and that Berrig, Cwyn, and Eagan have confessed and promised you their devotion. I do not think he will pursue a forceful resolution, and after you have burned Solomon and his crop of underlings, the rest of the tribe would never dare to question your authority again. Donnach will be saddened by the actions of Megba and the others, but he will have too much confidence in your judgment to question your desire to include Rome."

"And why will it be you who returns to tell Megba this, and not Berrig?" Laden asked suspiciously.

Ronan's eyes darted over to Berrig, then uncertainly back at Laden. "Because I am too old a warrior to ever be believable in betraying my King. A younger warrior, such as Berrig, would not look as conspicuous taking your side."

Laden studied Berrig's unreadable expression, then dropped his head and stared at the ground considering Ronan's reasoning. "I would perceive it so. A young warrior would stand to gain everything in a new rule, and an older, established one could lose all."

Ronan smiled uncomfortably and there was an immediate change to his manner. "Of what are you speaking?"

The blond-haired warrior slowly lifted his head, his green eyes barely visible through his furrowed brows.

"I am speaking of the manner in which you have tried to play one side against the other without directly partaking in the conflict. You have played the sly fox, coyly waiting for Solomon and me to kill each other and leave you, the eldest warrior, to assume full power. This entire scheme you have devised was not meant for any other reason than that, and it was all under the guise of loyalty to the King. I am aware of that now."

The older warrior glanced at Berrig, who stared back at him regretfully, then moved his horse beside Laden and the others. Ronan took a deep breath, and dropping his arms to his sides, looked to the night sky. As he heard the two Icenians draw their swords, it crossed his mind to make one last plea for his life, but then reconsidered, knowing it would come to no avail. It would be far better to return to this world having departed with bravery, not cowardice.

"Farewell trusted warrior," he heard Berrig say quietly, then he heard the Icenians command their horses to a gallop, and felt the spears being driven into both of his sides.

The two horsemen impaled him on their weapons like a duck on a spit. Feeling himself shrinking back unwillingly, Berrig forced himself not to blink as he watched the sickening sight of Ronan being wisked from atop his horse. The water splashed up behind them as they galloped further up the beach and flung Ronan's still breathing body against the base of the cliff. He was held against the rocks for a morbid instant by a crashing wave. It must have broken bones because his torso appeared to fold over backwards before it fell face first into the water.

He could hear the sound of Laden's laughter, and glancing over, he was disgusted by his gleeful look. He shook the hands of the two men, then extended a hand to Berrig. Berrig gripped it firmly for an instant, and without giving away a hint of his disposition, vowed that he would hate Laden from that day forward.

CHAPTER SEVENTEEN

Beautiful, plump, soft breasts. He did not have to open his eyes to know that it was the enticing bosom of a woman his face was buried in. He touched his lips to them one at a time, then taking the puckering rosebud nipple between his teeth, he nibbled on it lightly. As he did this, he felt soft fingertips down the side of his face, then on the back of his neck as she pulled him close.

The warm flesh gave way to the tip of his nose, and taking a breath, the only smell he could identify was the clean smell of a woman. He ran his tongue across her cleavage while he pressed one hand to her naked rib cage and let out a sleepy but pleasurable groan. He heard her giggle and squirm delightfully closer as she shoved her hand between his legs. She zealously took hold of his genitals, and as he flinched at the tickle of it, he felt a terrible radiating pain down his back that made him gasp.

The young woman immediately pulled her hand away, and held him tightly until it passed.

"Quiet now," she whispered. "You have been badly wounded, and I have come to heal you."

Solomon opened his eyes a crack and tried to look around, but all he could see were mounds of curly red hair. It was in his eyes and mouth, making his nose itch. If he could have resisted the taste of her sleep-warmed skin, he would have pushed her away instead of pulling her closer, as he did in the next moment.

She intertwined her legs with his, and rubbed his hairy calf with the bottom of one foot. Her chest raised as she let out a contented sigh and caressed his neck and shoulders with both hands. Solomon wanted to lift his head to look at her face, but he was groggy and fending off sleep. From the feel of the damp room and the lack of a fire, he reasoned it was just before dawn.

"Unless you are a fabulous witch who can change from beast to temptress, I would say that you are a different maid than the one who tortured me last night," he said, taking a mouthful of her hair and wrapping it around his tongue.

It felt silky and tasted sweet, having been rinsed with honeysuckle. He wished he could rouse himself from his drugged state and make love to her. Even though he had not looked into her face, he knew from the the curves of her body that she was indeed a delectable female. He did not even care if his wound started to bleed, he wanted her badly.

She did not answer him as she put her hand beneath his chin to lift his face. He struggled to open his eyes, but before he could, she lightly kissed his forehead.

"It is you, is it not?" she asked, with a buoyant lilt in her voice.

"Yes," he answered, even though he had no idea what she meant, and kissed her full. He would be anyone she wanted as long as she stayed where she was, and remained unclothed.

"I have missed you," she whispered between kisses.

"I have missed you, too," he humored her, and tried to roll on top of her, but the pain stopped him. It shot down his spine into both legs, momentarily arresting his foreplay. Tucking his face in the round of her neck, he let out another miserable groan.

"Lie still," she said, and began playing with his hair.

In a moment it was gone, and suddenly reminded of her, Solomon ran his hand down her back, and took hold of one buttock. She giggled again as he stroked it, and squeezed the inside of one thigh.

"Promise me something," she said, letting him feel inside of her.

"Of course, anything," he replied, pushing his middle finger further up into her. He relished the slippery wetness of her hidden feminine place.

She tilted her head back and took an aroused breath. "Promise me that no matter what they say, you will let me return with you."

Solomon kissed her neck and nodded. Then she began laughing like a little girl who had just taken something forbidden her. She wiggled down to look at him, and when Solomon finally opened his eyes, he was greeted with the most impish, irresistible smile.

"I have to go now," she teased," but I will be back soon."

She carefully pushed herself away to not jostle him. He tried half-heartedly to hold onto her, but he was too weak and could only smile dumbly at the sight of her unclothed body. He watched her start for the door with such haste that she accidently stepped on Aonghus, who for some reason, was sprawled out in the center of the room. The boy flinched and grouchily opened his eyes. When he realized that it was a naked woman, he sat straight up and did not blink until she was no longer visible through the entryway, then he quizzically looked back at Solomon.

"Where are her clothes?" he asked.

"I do not know," grumbled Solomon, and closed his heavy lids. "But I hope she never finds them."

Three nights passed before Solomon was well enough to sit up and feed himself, and when he finally did eat, he gorged himself to sickening proportions. Aonghus, in turn, had eaten little while his master was ill. Aside from his stomach constantly cramping from nerves, he did not trust anything the odd white-robed creatures brought them. He still held them responsible for bewitching him on the first night there. It did not matter that Solomon had explained to him that the remnants of the drugged wine, and the sweaty water he drank after cleansing him were enough to send a boy his size to a state of permanent dreamtime.

Aonghus found this priesthood a curious lot. There seemed to be a horde of delicately built men and only a handful of women, who ranged in looks from plain to absolutely ugly. They busied themselves with oral study, the gathering of herbs, and wordlessly spoke to each other with crude hand signals. It infuriated Aonghus when they would gesture in his presence—he thought it not only rude, but untrustworthy. When they did speak to him, their voices seemed to lack the vitality of living beings.

The colony was also occupied by a tribe who tended the crops, and seemed to be endlessly repairing the crude fortress surrounding the settlement. Their warriors were intimidatingly warlike in their full leather garments. They must have been from Greece because each member of the clan, save the holy men and the witches, had long wavy black hair, olive skin, and beady, ebony eyes. Aonghus had scarcely seen such dark people in his life. The only person in his tribe who remotely resembled them was Deireadh, and he took that as a warning.

How Aonghus hated it when they would come to check on Solomon. It did not matter what he was doing, be it tending his master, or in a deep sleep, they had such a spooky, otherworldly way about them that it made his skin crawl. He had sat many an afternoon scoping the village from the window of his room because he did not dare to venture out alone. He knew the movements of the tribe, when they would go into the fields, and when the priesthood would take their meditation. It seemed to him that the movements of the population were designed so no one could enter or leave the fortress unnoticed. He had, more than once, entertained the thought of escape, but had no idea where the horses had been taken.

The sun was almost down, and Aonghus sat cross-legged on the floor staring at the platter of food that had been brought for dinner. It had been there for some time, and as was always the case when such portions arrived, Aonghus spent a good deal of time scrutinizing it, vainly trying to identify any signs of poison. He would stick his finger in it, pick it up, smell it, and stir it until he was satisfied it had not been tampered with. Only then would he wake Solomon, who would roar at the sight of his food being sloshed, nibbled, and poked.

"You worry too much," Solomon said, smacking his lips together and reaching for a pitcher of water. He lifted his head up enough to get a drink, then set it back down.

"I would like to leave now," Aonghus announced, getting to his feet.

"Go ahead," Solomon said.

The boy looked reticently at the door, then down at the bag containing the valuables. He did not want to appear a coward, but he simply could not tolerant another day there.

"Can you come with me?" he asked humbly.

Solomon sat up and rubbed his eyes with his fists, then yawned. "I do not think so, but if you want to return home, I will understand. If I remember correctly, the stables are at the corner of the settlement. There is an old man there, not as old as Megba, but close. Tell him that you came with me, and you would like an escort back. He should do it if he can."

"A stranger?" Aonghus asked dubiously. "You would entrust me to a stranger from this place?"

The warrior bent his neck to one side and rotated his bad shoulder trying to ease the stiffness. "He is not a stranger, and this place is not that evil," he answered flatly. "You are being too suspicious."

Aonghus looked at him puzzled. "What do you mean?"

"I mean, has anyone physically harmed you while you have been here, aside from you drinking from my cup?" Solomon inquired.

"No."

"Have they done anything that would make you think that they are going to harm you in the near future?"

"Well, no," Aonghus answered, scratching his head. "But —"

"But what?" Solomon countered.

"I think they are—well, strange," he responded innocently.

Solomon slowly stood up, and rubbed the small of his back with one hand, then scratched his crotch. "They are not strange; they are different."

He walked over, examined his dinner, then looked at Aonghus and frowned. "You know," he said, shaking his head disapprovingly, "I wish you would stop this."

Before Aonghus could get the words out to plead his case, the door opened, and an aged, grey-bearded priest entered. He was accompanied by a docile, middle-aged woman with straggly brown hair and pale skin. Her dark eyes had a cynical, faithless expression.

"Solomon," he said in a gentle but commanding tone, "You have been long away from my sight; let us commune about your presence."

CHAPTER EIGHTEEN

olomon offered a nostalgic smile at the sight of the old man. Even though the passing years had wrinkled his face and bent his shoulders, he recognized him to be his childhood advisor, Gaeren. He stared at him, starry-eyed for a moment, trying not to shed a sentimental tear at their reunion. Then, as if Solomon were still a child, Gaeren wrapped his scrawny arms around him to give him a paternal embrace.

It had been years since Solomon had thought about him. This was the being who had taught him to commune with the gods and the sacred oneness of the spirit. He had tutored him in the praiseworthy traits of the celestial warriors, and had spent many an hour instructing him in meditation, and the ebb and flow of the mystical force. This man knew more about Solomon's inner being than he himself wished to delve into.

Gaeren was the priest who had presided over the ceremony when Donnach and he had taken their private oath. And while this meeting was a happy one, it was also an unwanted reminder that he was defying the generosity of the man with whom he had shared it.

As the two released each other, Solomon could not help but stare curiously into the old man's eyes and touch his crinkly face. He then gave a boyish grin.

"You are a disappointment," Gaeren stated. "You have been away from me for eleven cycles, and have not once bothered to address my spirit in meditation."

Solomon laughed. "That is because I do not meditate. Besides you are the spiritual one, why have you not addressed mine?"

Gaeren's entire face contorted into an obstinate smile and he cackled loudly. "I have. That is how I know what a savage you are. You have had some setbacks, and I sense you are full of your self-worth. I feel as though you do not wish to be here and that your heart is sorely displaced."

Solomon frowned at the old man's candor. Reaching down, he picked up a piece of meat and rudely bit into it. Then, as if to deter any further declarations about his personal life, he haphazardly offered it to the maid accompanying Gaeren. What color she did have in her pale skin faded, and she glared at him for his behavior. Realizing his discourtesy, Solomon bowed his apology.

"Forgive me, dearest maid, I am Solomon of the Brigantes. Please share a place at my fire, and a drink of my wine," he said in a suddenly charming manner. "By what name may I call you?"

The woman looked at Gaeren, who nodded approval. "Jara," she replied, sitting beside Aonghus. "I am known as the witch Jara."

"Very well, witch Jara," Solomon continued, handing her a flask of wine. "This is my apprentice, Aonghus."

The boy stared at the ground self-consciously, and nodded his response. He then waited a moment until he thought no one was watching and scooted a fair distance away from her.

"You would not mind if I lie back down while we speak," the warrior said. "I am better, thanks to the work of your healer, but I am still not myself."

"Do as you wish," Gaeren answered. "But please tell me what has brought about this visit."

Solomon nestled back into the animal furs, and motioned for Aonghus to bring him some drink. Thankful for the distraction and a chance to be near his master, the boy zealously complied.

"I am not here for reasons of my own," Solomon began. "I have been sent by the good sorcerer, Megba, with an urgent message of assistance."

"Continue," Gaeren stated.

"Our tribe has experienced great dissension because of a desired change in rule. As you well know, Gaeren, our people are lacking the ability to defeat other nations, but do well with inter-tribal quarrels. The King, Donnach, has given his reign to his son, Laden. It is an ignoble situation because Laden is seeking a trade alliance with Rome, and has entreated a witch, Deireadh, to intercede with the gods. She has, in turn, deemed herself a living goddess. I assume her tactics have come about in the light of the Christians' successes, since their living God was martyred. It is my opinion that she is using the same artfulness to entreat a great troop of warriors. She has not told me, as such; I only say it now because I know this new rule is in desperate need of tribal support. Trade with Rome is risky, and if I were a new leader, I would do everything possible, physically and spiritually, to increase my strength."

"Do you agree with this declaration?" Jara inquired. "Surely you must know that the gods surround us in all of earth's creatures. For one unsanctified to assume such a position is blasphemous."

Solomon's face tightened. "I suppose I do not denounce the methods. I recognize that Laden is a man who refuses to be broken. He knows he cannot defeat the imperial arsenal, so he is trying to find a way of living with it. It could even be to our people's advantage. Perhaps a Celtic-Roman reconciliation would take some self-sacrifice in the beginning, but if the people believe that his aspirations are divinely inspired, it would make for an easier transition. Yet I can, at the same time, be sympathetic to Megba's plight. Rome inflicted great pain on our people once; what would prevent them from doing it again?"

Smoothing his beard, he shook his head. Perhaps it would be easier if he did not understand both sides. Still, he reasoned that anything done in the pursuit of freedom could not be in error.

"I feel that you share a deep personal commitment to his supposed goddess," Gaeren added.

"Yes," Solomon said, without looking at him. "She is my wife."

"Was your wife," Aonghus quietly corrected him.

Solomon shot him a hateful glare, and Aonghus shrunk in his place.

"They have asked you to go against her, have they not?" the Druid questioned.

"They have."

Gaeren waited a moment. He was gazing at the area above Solomon's head, and his eyes appeared to be moving from side to side as though he were watching a bird in flight.

"Your protection has abandoned you," he stated. "The great hawk you were anointed with has ceased to share his keen eye and bold heart with your spirit. It is because you have locked your mind and not let him circle your dreams. His shrill message to you is that you have become friends with unawareness and have not sought the truth."

"Truth is an individual reality," he argued. "I have my truth; Laden and Deireadh have theirs."

The Druid took hold of the warrior's hand. "What you have described is war. The thoughts of a single man controlling the consciousness of his people, to the point that they are willing to die for his cause whether righteous or not, is ultimately decided when one side conquers its opposition so that the individual reality may flourish. The manner in which it comes about is often sobering, but sometimes inevitable. What exactly is it that Megba desires?"

Solomon swallowed, and motioned for Aonghus to bring the leather satchel to Gaeren. He did not want to be any more a part of this scheme than he had to.

"This is an offering collected by many of my kinsmen who oppose Laden," he explained. "I have brought it under the divine counsel of Megba. He believes the spirits of Oisil and my father have cautioned against Roman sympathy. He says they have warned us not to forget the shedding of their blood, and that when the clan understands what the future will bring, they will oppose Laden entirely."

"And what will the future bring?" Gaeren asked.

Solomon huffed. "You do not know either? I thought all you keepers of sacred truths spoke to the same gods."

"Contain your arrogance," he admonished. "You are acting on behalf of many; do not embarrass them."

Solomon felt a tightness rising in his gut. He did not want to say any more, less he be thought in favor of the uprising, but he had sworn to this duty.

"Megba said I should make it clear it is he who has sent for one whose heart is pure," he said, resigned. "One who is free of human guile and can care enough for his people to lead them from the darkness Deireadh has engaged."

Gaeren looked at Jara, who signaled something to him.

"Very well," the Druid said, turning his attention back to Solomon. "We will take it under advisement, but I must caution you that this request may be difficult to fulfill. As you must be aware, the Imperialists have refused to recognize our immunity, and we have lost a great many of our priests with their conquest. It is hard to satisfy even cyclical tribal visits, much less permit a trained priest to reside with one clan permanently. I assure you, however, that my heart will be open to the desires of the heavens. You must prepare yourself to leave by dawn. Whether you take one of us with you or not, your time here is through. I will bring you an answer before daybreak."

Even though he tried to hide his reaction, Solomon saw Aonghus' eyes brighten at word of their departure. He would have shared his sentiment if only he did not have to leave without seeing the nymph who had visited him. He had wanted to remain there a bit longer, hoping that she would hear of his improved health and visit his bed again.

"I will be ready," he replied, as Jara and Gaeren departed.

Once outside, the two said nothing until they were far from the warrior's hut. "Does this confirm your intuitions?" Gaeren finally inquired.

"Yes," Jara answered. "It will do well. We give them one, and they, in return, will give us many."

"And Saturnalia, will she cooperate?"

Jara smiled to herself. "Saturnalia cooperates with Saturnalia; that is the only assurance I can give, but if we are delicate in our handling of her, she will remain pleasantly naive. Of that I am certain."

———

"I do not think the sound of your voice is strange," Saturnalia declared, twisting a lock of her hair around one finger. "All the keepers of the earth have their own sounds, and so do you. Besides if you cannot hear it yourself, how do you know what it sounds like?"

The elderly medicine woman looked up from her pestle to offer the girl a red-gummed smile.

"Elenai, look at my mouth when I speak so you may understand my question," Saturnalia said, holding her withered face with both hands. "How do you know what your voice sounds like if you cannot hear it?"

Elenai shrugged, then smiled in an even kinder way.

"It is beautiful when you sing," the young woman added. "I love to hear you sing. I think that the chimes of the heavens are carried upon your tune."

The crone's cheeks turned pink as she went back to the herbs she was grinding. Saturnalia knelt opposite her so Elenai could see her lips move when she spoke.

"He is greatly changed from what I remember," she said, resting her chin on the edge of the table. "When he was young, he was a bit of a buffoon, big and clumsy, but he has turned into a sight of a man. He has a child waiting for him."

Elenai nodded agreement and with her gestures, described Aonghus. She pointed to the blue scarf she was wearing, then to her own eyes and blinked.

"No, not that one," the girl shook her head and a lock of hair fell into her eyes. "That is not his child. The one I speak of is his spirit baby. It waits in the shadowlands. I have crossed over there, and we have spoken. It has asked me in my dreams to bring it to the sun. I do so like this one, as though its spirit and mine are close already, but it lives in the womb of another."

She watched in silence as Elenai tied the powdered herbs in a piece of linen. She then mixed a dab of honey into a shallow bowl of water containing three branches of mistletoe. She looked at Saturnalia, her eyes misting, and patted her affectionately on the cheek.

"Now if it is bitter, I will be refused," Saturnalia reaffirmed. "And if it is sweet, he and I will never part."

The hag blew Saturnalia a string of kisses. "It will be sweet," Elenai said in muffled syllables, and took a place in the far corner of the room.

She began to hum softly as Saturnalia disrobed and started washing herself with the honey and mistletoe. She used only her hands, wetting them and smoothing them across her shoulders, down her stomach and over her thighs. The liquid felt thick, and seemed to rapidly absorb into her skin. Then she rubbed herself from head to toe with the oil of frankincense and sat in front of the fire. Elenai had started playing a large pigskin drum. Balancing it atop one shoulder, she fanned it with the tips of her fingers to create a driving tempo that penetrated Saturnalia's veins.

Rocking back and forth, she found herself rubbing the outsides of her knees to the beat, and let its anthem lull her into a hypnotic state. Then she touched a twig to the fire, and used it to light a small bronze bowl set on the hearth in front of her. It was filled with beeswax and ashes because she had used it many times before to burn her offerings. When a small flame ignited and she was satisfied that it would not go out, she tossed the twig back into the fire.

Holding the muslin bag to her breast, she silently invoked the powers of the earth to hear her petition. Then she placed it on top of the flames. The fire enveloped it on all sides, making the muslin sizzle and break apart. Kneeling over it, Saturnalia inhaled the perfumed smoke, pretending to grab handfuls of it and rub it on her skin.

"Now sweet soil is earth, and sweet earth is air," she said, running the back of her fingers down her naked torso. "And sweet air is water; thus sweet water becomes fire. Let all go unto me, and me unto them. And let us arise as one; I be thee, and thee become me."

Clutching her hair with both hands, she breathed in the incense. "I am the fill; the earth is full. Let the Goddess' will abide."

She felt a sensation of gentle mourning come over her, and began to loudly sing the ancient burial hymns. Her voice cracked from the heated air and each time she sang a note, she could taste the herbal fumes. Then there came a sudden feeling of frenzy as she looked down at her breasts and imagined them to be swelling with the milk of the mother. It was a most gentle ache that went from her heart to her womb. Lying down with her eyes closed, she let herself be immersed into the oblivion of her female energy.

chapter nineteen

aeren and Jara arrived at Solomon's hut while it was still dark. Aonghus had been awake long before, gathering their belongings to make sure Solomon would be ready to depart on time. They somberly came into the room and took a place on either side of the warrior. Their expressions were grave and voices hushed.

"We have earnestly sought the spirits about your cause," Gaeren began. "And as I have already spoken to you, there are few in this priesthood who can be spared, but I am sympathetic to Megba's predicament, and do believe the communications of Oisil and Roilan to be true. When one is confronted with such delicate choices, one must be careful to remember that any man is a capable leader, and motivation executed with enough force can be made right. That is why our Order is necessary. We are the force of justice. We are the administrators called upon by the gods."

"Is that what you want me to tell Megba?" Solomon said with a harsh laugh.

Gaeren tilted his head back to look at the warrior out of the corner of his eye. He was an audacious one; Gaeren was never sure if he was taking him seriously or making a mockery of him. Frankly, considering his brashness, Gaeren was surprised he had even lived this long.

"No," he replied in an even tone. "We have decided to send one with you who has yet to be anointed. She has completed the holy instruction, but does not have the proper makings of one who would fit in with our Order. She is superbly schooled but slightly unorthodox in her practices."

"She?" Solomon inquired, raising both of his bushy brows. "I do not think that would work. Not that I am questioning your choice, you must understand. It is only that considering Deireadh's venomous position, another female would only add to the snake pit. You must admit that it is a pitiful sight to see what transpires when two women tangle."

Jara folded her arms across her chest. "I have tutored this one myself since the day of her creation, and I should tell you that she is not an ordinary woman," she said, taking a step toward him. "Her existence was brought forth by the blending of the clay of the earth, the water of the rising sea, the golden rays of the sun, and the breath of the wind. She has no parentage. Her spirit did not come from the flesh. I found her myself, a tiny babe having emerged from Brigantia's womb

89

the sunrise after the goddess' ritual. This Priestess was brought forth by the intentions of the worshippers, so I caution you to view your refusal in another light."

"I see," Solomon said. "Can she swim?"

"Yes," Jara answered, surprised by his question. "Of what matter is that?"

The warrior smirked. "I was curious; if she was created from the elements as you say, she must be able to fly as well."

The woman's eyes smoldered, and she clenched her teeth. "Don't make a spectacle of me, you pompous beast. She is dear to me, and you dare to laugh when I would give her over for the good of your people."

The smile faded from Solomon's face. "You do not have to do that for I am entirely against it."

Gaeren walked over to pick up the clan's offering from the place where he had set it the night before. It was customary that once a donation was touched by a holy man, it was believed to be in the possession of the gods. If one unsanctified laid his hands upon it, such an offense usually resulted in death.

"The decision has been made according to your petition, Solomon. You must trust that the heavens know our ways, and reward us as such. Take heed to their warnings, thoughtless one, for they are gentle in the beginning, but painful if ignored," the Druid cautioned. "Come Jara."

Jara grabbed Solomon by the forearm, and dug her fingernails into his skin. "I am giving you a piece of myself," she warned. "Do not abuse it."

Both Solomon and Aonghus stared after them as they left. Then Aonghus turned to Solomon with a worried look.

"What if it is the wrinkled, ugly one?" he asked uneasily.

"They cannot get any uglier than that," Solomon replied, referring to Jara.

———

Solomon's and Aonghus' horses were brought to them bathed and well rested. The boy was so happy to see his burly equine friend that at the sound of his approach, he threw open the door and ran outside to meet him. He was oblivious that the entire clan and priesthood had assembled for their departure. It was only after he had kissed and hugged Osin's neck that he looked up to find amused faces staring back at his affectionate display.

Releasing the animal, he turned and noticed three more horses set to leave with them. One was loaded with traveling satchels and tapestries and the second with supplies and a cage containing an old cat. The cat sat with his paws drawn up beneath him, staring smugly back at Aonghus. The boy eyed him, then turned to find Solomon, to tell him about it.

He found the warrior in a hushed exchange with Gaeren. His expression was grim, and at the sight of the boy, the conversation immediately ceased.

"What is it?" he asked.

Aonghus put his hands on his hips. "There is a cat out here," he stated.

Solomon retorted, "You have seen a cat before. Why is this one special?"

"This cat is coming with us," the boy answered, pointing behind him.

Solomon squinted and walked to the window. When he saw what Aonghus was speaking of, he turned back around and shrugged his shoulders.

"Yes I suppose it is," he affirmed, then addressed Gaeren. "Now where is this Priestess you warned me about?"

"Jara will bring her when you are ready," the Druid replied.

"I am ready now," Solomon stated. "The sun has almost fully risen, and we have far to go."

The two men and the boy went out into the peaking morning sunlight, and at the sight of the clan and the priests, Solomon bowed gallantly.

"Thank you, thank you all for nursing my health and offering us refuge," he said, as he reached behind him and caught Aonghus by the arm and pulled him forward. The child looked questioningly at Solomon.

"State your appreciation," the warrior advised.

Aonghus' eyes passed over the gathering, stopping at Elenai. Recognizing her to be the woman who had doctored Solomon, he looked at the ground.

"Thank you," he mumbled. He bowed his respects then immediately ducked behind his master.

With tears brimming in her aged eyes, Elenai came forward and took one of Solomon's hands. She looked at him pleadingly, and motioned something in sign language.

Solomon's face softened and he shook his head. "I am afraid I cannot understand your message."

"She says that she would like for you to take very good care of me," a woman's voice sounded from beside him.

Turning his head, Solomon's eyes gleamed as he looked at Saturnalia. "I will," he said. "I will," he repeated, turning to Elenai.

The lovely, red-maned Priestess went to Elenai and put an arm around her shoulders. Unable to control it any longer, the crone let out a stifled whimper, and pulling Saturnalia close, hid her face in her curly locks. Saturnalia's eyes misted and she took a deep breath to conceal her rising emotion.

"It was Elenai who brought you back when you were between worlds," she told Solomon. "She is a gifted healer."

"You must thank her for me," the warrior responded, feeling Aonghus clutch the back of his shirt. He shoved his face beneath Solomon's arm so that he could peer out at the hag, protected.

"I have," she replied, taking Elenai's face affectionately in her hands. She looked deep into her eyes, then kissed both of her cheeks. "I have thanked her for you, many times."

Solomon's eyes met Saturnalia's over the top of Elenai's bowed head. She warded off her tears with a sudden sharp look that said she was no longer able to avoid him, and by the light in his eyes, she knew he would never be able to resist her. The lure of having him so close for these few days and keeping away from him until the proper time had actually left her a little uncomfortable with her own feelings. It was as though she should be more nostalgic at their reunion, but she could tell from the unabashed expression that his only recollection of her, so far, was of the night she had visited his chamber. He had not yet recalled their past.

"Well?" Solomon asked.

"Well, indeed," she answered, puzzled by their behavior.

"Shall we be on our way?" he questioned.

Her lips curled into a smile, and she stepped directly in front of him. She could tell by the way he flinched that he wanted to step back. But he stood there, a thunderous presence of the man she had summoned, looking slightly out of place with the young boy's face peering out from beneath his bulky arm.

"Yes," she pointedly replied. "Now, we shall be on our way."

CHAPTER TWENTY

eireadh wiped the vomit from the corner of her mouth with her scarf, then rinsed it in cold water and dabbed the sweat from her face. Feeling her abdomen contract, she took a deep breath, and let out a quivering moan as her breakfast rose in her throat. She felt unlike herself, as though her turning stomach had initiated an irreversible change in her. She sat huddled behind the curtained alcove of her room. Red-eyed and nauseous, she realized she had spoiled herself, not allowing this to happen sooner. Morning sickness seemed far less severe in women younger than she.

She found herself unattractive these past few days, and listless. Even something simple like washing her hair and applying her face paint was much too demanding for her. Straining forward, she gasped in a breath of air before she let out a dry retch and heaved a gorge of food into the chamber pot. The rank taste of it lingered in her mouth, and before she was able to take another breath, more foul matter erupted in her throat.

Without rinsing her mouth, she curled up on the floor, and pressing her heated cheeks against it, started to cry. She was miserable, so completely miserable that it was almost as if she were paying recompense for all the times she had done away with this child. Only this time, for some peculiar reason, she really wanted it. She wanted to have it as a pledge of devotion to Laden. When he had defeated his opposition, this babe would be the testimony of her loyalty to their future.

Even if he did take his Trinovantes bride, her child would be the one he would hold in his arms first, and boy or girl, she would insist upon a position for it in his rule. It was the only way she could insure her own position for the rest of her life. Of course, Laden would argue that it was Solomon who had taken her virginity, and therefore, her offspring were summoned by that initial union. Yet knowing Laden as she did, he could eventually be coerced into caring for it.

Closing her eyes, she dozed a moment, hoping that if she could sleep a while this sickness would pass. She had tried to heal herself, for she believed that theirs was a specific force in procreation that was dictated entirely by the gods. That is why she had surrendered. This time she wanted to bring forth the life that was inside of her, not drive it away. Perhaps if she could somehow give a life back, she would then be allowed to recreate her own. After feeling badly all night, she had done what she could about invoking the divine power of the higher sources that existed around her. Yet she had worked no magic, and had recognized no emanating presence of vitality within her midst. Now she lay completely drained of her own essence, as if the growing fetus were eating her alive.

It was true that she was a beginner at sorcery. Her spiritual evolution was in its most infantile stages, and she lacked the force to honestly appropriate the power of the heavens on her behalf or anyone else's. But she believed that if she proceeded with her work, she could happen upon an important principle and manifest her power. She had lighted the torches, burned the incense, chanted to the skies, and it had all evolved into nothingness. Even the robe that was meant to be such a sacred garment was stained with her vomit.

Still, she wanted to work with the spirits, and wished more than anything that they would work with her. But after a night of requests going unanswered, she doubted they had much sympathy for her now, not after she had emptied her womb so many times. Now that she wanted to birth this baby, she feared she would be unable to carry it. Lately she had experienced the seeping blood and cramps, and had been unable to fulfill Laden's desires. She thought she would surely miscarry the last time she had been with Solomon, and had been forced to pack herself with a poultice of red clover, raspberry, and peppermint to avoid losing the child altogether.

The rays of morning light appeared to be swirling around the edges of the ceiling as she heard a faint knock on her door. She tried to answer, but was too exhausted to move. It sounded again, and then the door opened, and she heard the shriek of her handmaiden as she spread the curtain and saw her.

Coming immediately to her side, the hefty woman lifted her single-handedly off the floor, and helped her to her bed.

"Quiet now," Deireadh murmured. "Do not let the King hear you."

Her servant lifted a cup of berry juice to Deireadh's lips. The smell of it peaked her nausea, causing her to groan and push it away at the same time.

"Please, I want no food or drink," she whispered. "I want only to sleep."

"Then close your eyes, good lady," her servant replied, covering her. "I will not leave you alone."

Drawing her knees to her chest, Deireadh took a series of slow, rhythmic breaths to slow her heartbeat. She let out an appreciative sigh as she felt her handmaiden begin rubbing her with astringent. The cool, icy feeling was soothing to her heated skin.

"Do you wish to keep this child, good lady?" the maid asked, lifting Deireadh's robe over her hips.

"Yes," she said. "I wish to bring the first life into this new kingdom."

The older woman touched the palm of her hand to Deireadh's distended stomach. She waited a moment, then spread her legs and palpated her uterus.

"Then you must make yourself drink the tea I will make you," she advised, shaking her head with great concern. "Or this babe will not survive. Have you told the father?"

Deireadh felt tears unexplicably running down her cheeks as a sudden feeling of sorrow overtook her. "He has much on his mind," she murmured. "There will be a better time for it I am sure."

When the servant finished bathing her, she rubbed her with an ointment of parsley, henbane, poplar, and hemlock meant to induce sleep and visions. Closing her eyes once more, Deireadh could not seem to drive the image of Solomon from her mind.

The huge wooden doors to Solomon's stable gave way as Berrig entered. He bore the tattooed image of a wolf on his front. The animal's face covered him from shoulder to shoulder with its white and black head, yellow eyes, and a muzzle that was wrinkled into a snarl. His arms were adorned with bracelets, and he was wearing nothing more than a doeskin breechcloth and boots. His hair was bleached with lime and pushed back from his face. From his appearance, there was no doubt that he was anticipating a battle.

Megba, Cwyn, and Koven immediately rose to their feet at the sight of him. Even though they had been warned by the way he had privately arranged the rocks outside of Megba's yard that danger was close at hand, to see the intimidating portrait of him now caught them off-guard.

"Laden has summoned the blood," Berrig declared, his face showing signs of concern. "He has brought forth the terrible aspects of this and drawn his sword."

Koven stiffened at the warrior's statement. Somehow he had always known it would come to this, but he had not mentally prepared himself for the sacrifices it would entail. He felt a confounding tightness in his chest as he turned away so the others could not see his fearful reaction.

"Have you come on his behalf or your own?" Cwyn demanded.

"I have come on behalf of freedom," Berrig answered. "He has sent me in the name of the good King Donnach. He is aware of the way that I have posed for both sides, and has entreated me to secrecy in the name of the memories of ancient wars, and the soul of his father. He beseeches you now to understand that only the scarlet will end this dispute, for his crafty son has learned of our plans through Ronan's cowardice.

"Donnach has requested that I continue to act as servant to Laden, and trust in his judgment to the very end. His faith still resides in the bosom of Megba, and his hope in Solomon's quest. Yet he desires you to know that should you inform his son of this, he will deny it and have you killed. For in my telling you this, your treason is now two-sided. It offers only one resolution: to do as he sanctions in his private thoughts. He cautions you to remember that his people's well-being will yet flourish if his instructions are followed by all."

The sorcerer watched him closely, then moved in front of him. "What does Donnach mean to accomplish if we do as he advises?" Megba asked cautiously.

Berrig rested one hand on the handle of his sword. "He understands the greedy desire for wealth Laden seeks, and that Deireadh is a counterfeit of the mystic force, but there is no way he can persuade them to reconsider their choices. Donnach knows that if he resists too much, he will surely go to sleep one night and not rise again. He has sought my confidence, and is reliant on the bravery of Solomon and the Druidic laws. He brings the message that upon your lives and the souls of your children, prepare to bear all. This hard condition must be corrected by poison, not flattery."

The three men listened intently.

"The gods of battle have stolen the warriors' hearts," Berrig continued without waiting for a response. "Indeed, the adornment of the weapon and the tide of blood will become the ceremony of this throne. Align yourselves to fight, and understand the cure that Donnach seeks will end the jealousy and bring together our kinsmen's hearts."

Megba gravely nodded. "It is a sad time when we must choose such action, yet it has been the way of our people since the lands have risen from the sea. Tell Donnach we will do as he commands, and prepare to fight for our righteousness. I am sure Laden knows of our strategy, and upon Solomon's arrival, the uprising will be complete. Has Donnach any further instructions?"

"Yes," Berrig responded. "He says that he will recognize all territory to the east of the warrior Solomon's estate as separate. He will tell Laden that he relinquished it to bind his anointing. He advises you to use this dwelling as your center, and bring all families that support your cause within these boundaries. They will be hanged from the branches of the oaks if they are left out. All livestock and crops that are left will be ransom to Laden, and should he be defeated, they will be returned to their proper owners. He will give you two nights until he informs Laden of this, so make good use of the darkness."

"And what will become of you and Ronan?" Cwyn inquired.

"To all others I am nothing more than Laden's faithful defender. As for Ronan, the error of his greed has sent him to rest in the sea."

Cwyn was noticeably shaken by the news. Like Berrig and Solomon, he and Ronan had been close friends since childhood and they had studied the warrior's ways together. They had been present for the birth of each other's children, and had fought at each others' sides many times.

"Do not be saddened," Berrig consoled him. "His was of a divided allegiance. He wished to see Laden and Solomon kill each other, and leave him to assume all authority. To be released from his betrayal was merciful."

He watched as Cwyn's features went through a series of changes, finally setting into a determined expression. "I understand," he conceded, realizing Ronan's indiscretion. "So be it. Tell Donnach we will fulfill his expectations."

A hint of sentimentality showed in Berrig's eyes. "This will be my last communication with all of you until this is resolved. I would ask that you not tell Solomon that I am acting under Donnach's command. He is a tenderhearted man whose emotions often cloud his judgments. If it comes to a fight, it is better that he believe completely in the cause, or he could harm himself by trying to spare Donnach or me."

Megba reached out to make an imaginary symbol in the center of Berrig's forehead. "Purify yourself in the lakes and streams until that time comes," he said softly. "Call upon the protection of the Goddess that your soul will be strong and free of stain. Let the blessing she imparts upon you free the paths of your understanding."

A thick silence fell upon them. While they realized they were clearing away the debris inhibiting their future, they also knew that what they were destroying could never be replaced. There was an urgency to say something that would reaffirm the righteousness of their decision, but none could speak.

"So be it," Berrig softly broke the void.

"So be it," the voices of the rest of the men affirmed.

CHAPTER TWENTY-ONE

A cold snap had suddenly moved in. By mid-morning the chilly wind and the rapidly darkening sky had forced the three travelers to put on their cloaks. Saturnalia's was made of finely-woven white wool and lined with wolf fur. Solomon, who had used his traveling cloak for Aonghus' wounded dog, proudly wore a bright purple one Enda had made to replace it. Embroidery decorated its hem and it was double-lined with a layer of extra wool to stop the wind. Aonghus had on a simple brown overgarment that lacked any lining. Still, it had a hood, and if it did not start to rain too hard, it would keep him warm enough.

The party moved hastily through the groves and over the hillsides. In case the weather did get worse, Solomon wanted to go as far as possible now, so he kept the horses at a steady trot. The cool morning suited the animals nicely and the rapid pace did not seem to affect them. The only one who complained was the cat, who would whine now and again to show his displeasure.

The rate at which they moved provided little opportunity for conversation. Solomon found it a bit odd that Saturnalia had offered no indication that she remembered their bedroom introduction. He found it even more strange that she seemed to care little about leaving anyone behind except the old crone, and had exited without a farewell to either Jara or Gaeren. Every time he looked back at her, she offered him a transparent smile, and stared at him so pointedly that it made him look away.

Feeling a drop of rain on his face, he broke into a gallop. If his memory served him correctly, they were not far from a cave where they would be able to wait out the impending storm. Entering a stand of trees, he pushed aside a low hanging branch so Saturnalia could pass. It unexpectedly snapped back, nearly hitting her in the face. Realizing what had happened, he looked at her apologetically, and was pleased to see she was wearing the same unruffled expression as before.

Noticing that the leaves on the shrubbery were facing up, and that the sky had turned an ominous black, Solomon headed across an open field that tapered into a ravine. They followed it to a limestone gorge, and as the rain started to fall, the smell of the moist soil rose up around them.

The rocks were slick and shiny by the time they dismounted, and followed the warrior between some boulders until they were nestled in a rather large cave.

It was dark and deep; the back of it could not be seen, but it was high enough to provide the horses shelter as well.

"This will do nicely," Saturnalia stated, taking her cat out of its cage.

"You had better not do that," Aonghus warned, loosening Osin's cinch. "If that cat runs off you will never find him."

"If this cat leaves, it is his choice to do so," she said, running her hand over his fur. The cat immediately started to purr as he arched his back and stuck his tail straight up in the air. "Cats belong to no one."

"Maybe you are right," Aonghus agreed, scratching his nose with the back of his hand. "But I had a cat I loved so much that I wanted to take him everywhere. My father told me I could not because cats were not like dogs; they do not come when you call. But I did not listen, and one time, I wanted to take him fishing with me because cats are supposed to like fish. So I snuck him out of the house in my bag, and when I got to the lake, I let him out. He acted fine for awhile, then he tangled with a badger and got his throat ripped open. He died right there. I gave the Goddess back all the fish I had caught, and asked her if she would bring my cat back to life. I left him there hoping that when the moon rose, she would see him and grant my wish. When I went there the next day, all I could find was his tail, and my father told me that the wolves had probably eaten him."

Saturnalia's face twisted, and she clutched her cat close to her. "That is horrible."

Aonghus shrugged. "I suppose I should have listened and not taken him at all. But do you know what else happened at that same lake?"

"No," Saturnalia said wearily.

"I had a favorite dog too, and I let Solomon take him one day —"

"That's enough, Aonghus," Solomon interrupted. "I do not think she wants to hear about Locwn's misfortune."

Aonghus wilted, and without uttering another syllable, spread out an animal hide in front of Saturnalia for her to sit on.

The Priestess offered Aonghus a genuine smile at his chivalry, and sat down. She put the cat beside her, then untied the leather pouch she wore about her waist. Unknotting the thong around its top, she emptied its contents in front of her. There were bundled herbs and a small clay vial with a cork top. She had various stones of different shapes and colors, the skull of a hawk, and a strand of white, braided horse mane. Aonghus peered over her shoulder curiously, then forgetting himself, he innocently touched the tip of one finger to her hair. He pulled it back quickly and smiled.

"Would you like to sit with me?" Saturnalia asked.

Aonghus sheepishly took a place opposite her. The cat slinked over and began rubbing against his crossed legs, then nuzzled his way into the boy's lap. Aonghus stroked him gently, causing its fur to shed in all directions, and he had to wrinkle his nose to keep from sneezing.

"What are these?" he asked, lifting the cat and setting him aside.

The cat meowed once, then jumped back where he was. Realizing it was useless to push him away again, the boy resigned himself to scratching it between its crooked ears.

"I will need this tonight," Saturnalia answered. "I must yield myself to the rites of purification."

"Oh," Aonghus politely responded. "Can I help you with it?"

"Perhaps," she said. "I will need a snake and a branch from a willow tree."

Aonghus' eyes widened, and he sprang to his feet. "I can do that. It will only take me a little while."

When he exited into the pouring rain, Solomon busied himself with making a fire, stealing a look at Saturnalia every now and then.

"I would not get too comfortable," he said, blowing on the small flame to light the kindling. "As soon as the storm lets up, I would like to continue."

Saturnalia arose from her place and took a determined stance opposite him. She was absolutely stunning, he thought, as he found himself walking toward her. There was something hidden in her mind that was beckoning him, something that was both delicate and calculating. Something that made him want to give himself to her with no expectation or conditions.

"I would like to stay here tonight," she softly stated. "I have much work to do, and the back of this cave would give me the privacy I need."

"Of course," Solomon heard himself say. She had completely cracked his defenses. As he reached out to touch the back of his hand to her cheek, he felt a peculiar familiarity about her blazing green eyes.

"Here you are," Aonghus' voice sounded from the cave entrance.

Saturnalia and Solomon turned to see the drenched, shivering child proudly holding a dead snake in one hand, and a willow branch in the other. Both were nearly as long as he was tall.

"Thank you, Aonghus," the Priestess said, taking a linen bag from her supplies and putting the snake into it. "A snake must be your animal of anointing. A snake crawls with the fire in his eyes that summons the eternal flame. He has the power of immortality, and can transmute life's poison while integrating the aspects of the soul. We must share this meat tonight, you and I."

Aonghus stared at her open-mouthed. Then abruptly clicking his jaw shut, he shook his head "yes."

While Solomon cleaned the reptile, Saturnalia took Aonghus with her to collect herbs and mushrooms. Even though it was still raining, the two walked hand in hand and found it of little inconvenience. Aonghus was preoccupied with telling her about his tribe, and singling out special people that he thought she would like the most. Of course, they were the ones he held in highest esteem, but he did not clarify that to her. He was thrilled about the way she was indulging his every thought and opinion. When the two returned, Solomon could tell by the vacant look in his foster's eyes that the boy was suffering from his first infatuation.

He followed Saturnalia around, happily doing anything she asked of him, and his chatter was endless. By the time he had hauled her things to a secluded corner alcove and made her a torch to use, she had been briefed on every bit of gossip he had heard, seemingly, since birth.

Saturnalia meticulously prepared the meat, mixing in the fresh herbs for flavor. She rested the basket of prepared food on top of a basket of water where she had added hot rocks to make it boil. Stirring it continually with the tip of her knife, she added the mushrooms last. Solomon watched her cautiously because he recognized them to be vision flowers of the earth, not the ones normally used in the preparation of meals.

When she served the portions, he cast her a disapproving gaze since she purposely gave one to Aonghus.

"He is only a child," he bluntly told her.

She looked at him seriously. "He will grow to be a man. He will have to understand it one day; the sooner he learns what it is about, the better."

Solomon pounded his fist on the ground. "I will not stand for it."

Saturnalia looked at Aonghus, then coolly over at Solomon. "You have not the right to keep him blind. Allow him the privileges of his quest."

The warrior stared at her coldly as she began to eat. Aonghus sat in silence, staring at his plate, then at Solomon, then Saturnalia. He repeated this a few times before he, too, began to eat. Only Solomon refused to partake, as though sharing in the meal would mean condoning her decision.

"Go ahead," she said, sweetly. "You need not worry about the child; such a small dose never hurt either you or me at his age."

Solomon leaned forward to stare at her. She looked back at him, watching the expression on his face go from shock, to nostalgia, to sheer sentimentality as he realized who she was. He reached out and, pulling her into his lap, hugged her close. She returned his affection honestly. "Is it you?" he asked, incredulously. "How could I not have known?"

She smoothed back his mustache with both her delicate hands. "My name is different."

Solomon's brows lifted in surprise. "I do not remember what it was before," he replied, embarrassed.

"It is no longer important. I have taken the name Saturnalia because I was anointed by the spirits at the time the moon passed into Saturn," she explained. "I was not anointed by the Druids because I failed to pass their test of discernment."

"Yes, they told me that you are unorthodox," he chuckled. "What do you believe in, random sacrifice?"

The young woman burst into laughter. "No, quite the opposite. I was refused anointing by the Order because I did not do as they commanded. They gave me a task that would test my devotion to the laws, and I exercised my free will instead. Thus, I was refused a position in the Order."

"What was the task?" he asked sincerely.

Saturnalia seemed flustered. "They instructed me to impale my cat on a pole as an offering to the gods. I refused."

Solomon looked at her tenderly. "That is why you brought him with you."

"Yes."

Solomon looked at her proudly. "Then I am glad of it," he said.

"Then you will eat now?" she asked, wiggling out of his embrace.

The warrior glanced at Aonghus, who was cleaning his plate with his finger.

"Let us now enjoy it together," he said, without taking his eyes off her.

———

Aonghus was asleep before Solomon and Saturnalia had finished their meal. Solomon covered the boy, then turned his complete attention to the Priestess. Humming happily to himself, he followed her to the back of the cave, and waited patiently for her to arrange her altar.

In the direction of the north, she set a carved figure of a goddess. She was sitting on a throne with large, erect breasts, and a baby's head emerging from between her legs. Framing the statue on either side, she placed earthen cups filled with animal fat and a wick. She took the willow branch and placed it perpendicular to them, setting in front of it a silver chalice filled with cakes, meant to symbolize the south.

Placing a cup of wine and a bowl of water in the east and west points, she filled the space between them with her knife. Then she drew a circle in the dirt large enough for her and Solomon, and lit the wicks in the two cups. The tiny flames flickered off the statue that now cast a large shadow on the cave wall.

Raising her palms to the sky, then turning them to the ground, Saturnalia said a prayer to herself. Then she took the willow branch. Holding it in one hand and grasping Solomon with the other, she stepped into the sphere.

"In the name of the blessed Goddess, I do part this halo of power," she whispered softly.

She pointed the willow branch in the four directions, and holding it in her right hand, began using it as a wand.

"Let the Lady of the Elements, who embraces what is wild and free, bless us. Let her presence be known," she recited. "The circle forms the endless spirit from which we shall perform."

She handed the wand to Solomon, who was starting to feel the effects of the mushrooms. He was staring at the ceiling of the cave and did not know she wanted him to participate until he felt her nudge him lightly on the shoulder.

He pointed the branch in the same manner, repeating Saturnalia's prayer. He then set it on the ground between them while Saturnalia picked up the bowl of water. Placing his hands on top of hers, they balanced the bowl between them.

"May this water cleanse our souls," they said in unison. "May the Goddess grant peace and healing. Let her purify the inner being of us all. So be it."

The Priestess dipped one hand in the liquid and ran it over Solomon's face. "I do charge you, in the name of our Goddess, to wash away that which has stained your soul," she proclaimed. "That which has stained your spirit."

Solomon knelt down and outstretched his arms to the end of the circle with his palms up.

"In the name of Brigantia, let my friend be cleansed," Saturnalia said, pouring a portion of the water over his head and shoulders.

Solomon remained there a moment, enjoying the feeling of the room as it began to spin. Then he stood to perform the same rites for her. It took him a bit longer because he could not keep his mind from drifting, and Saturnalia had to continually remind him of the proper word order.

When this was completed, the two stood facing each other with only the goblet of wine between them. Solomon could not take his eyes away from hers, and mesmerized by her beauty, he could not join her in the toast either.

"O Lady of the Streams and Lakes, let the pure and sweet water be our blessing," Saturnalia said, licking her lips between words, "for we are your children. We are of nature. Let the guilt be released. Show us the path of understanding. Lead us to the Otherworld of your mystery and wonderment."

"So be it," Solomon mumbled, watching her lips as she drank.

"So be it," she clearly replied, as he emptied the glass.

He tossed the empty goblet aside, and stared at her for an excruciating moment. Something had been happening in tiny increments in his life, and now he felt it had all finally been swept away to reveal something plain and simple. He had always thought himself too strong to partake of spiritual rituals, but with her to lead him, he was scarcely able to resist. He felt oddly frightened about what the next move would be. He wanted to make love to her, but at the same time he wanted to avoid it. He knew that if he reached inside of her, he would be helpless to her every thought and whim.

Lifting her hand to his lips, he kissed each of her fingertips. Then she ran both hands down his face and neck to his chest, and unclasped his fibulae. His thoughts were spiraling, and he was seeing fragmented moments of their childhood together. He closed his eyes, and smiled to himself at the remembrance, and when he opened them, she was standing in front of him naked. Taking her in his arms, he felt his breeches being pushed down until they dropped around his ankles. He felt the cool air on his genitals as he went down in the center of the circle on top of her, and lost himself in her softness.

CHAPTER TWENTY-TWO

King Donnach stood at the window of the main chamber watching the group of Trinovantes warriors make camp in his yard. There were more than thirty of them, completely outfitted with arms and horses. Laden had hired them knowing they were among the toughest of the mercenary soldiers, and that one Trinovantes was worth two Brigantes when it came to fighting. Considering their number and the extent of their battle expertise, Donnach speculated that even if the entire tribe opposed Laden, he would still win.

Twisting the ring on his little finger, he thought of happier times when his life was full. Ironically, the memory was of this very room; Melena was still alive, sitting peacefully in front of the fire, and Solomon had just given him this ring as a gift for blessing his union with Deireadh. Poor Solomon, he had no idea what he was walking into, and strangely enough, Donnach felt more sympathy for him than Laden. Berrig had explained how Solomon had been forced into taking the journey. Donnach knew that of all men, Solomon understood the delicate balance between war and peace. Considering his battle expertise, it showed great discernment for him to be able to distinguish the necessity and time for both.

He was so different from his own son, and Donnach was sorry only that he had not been born to him. At the same time, he realized that the depth of Solomon's character came from having to endure the radical life changes since his childhood. His mixed background offered him a sort of philosophical objectivity that Donnach found incomprehensible at times. How sorrowful he would be if Solomon did not see this conflict through.

Donnach dredged up the vivid image of his father and brother that awful night they were murdered. Waking to Melena's shrieks of terror, and running down the long corridor, his nostrils filled with the repugnant odor of fresh blood coming from Roilan's chamber. How brutally the assassins had done it. Binding both he and Melena, and making her watch as they gouged out Roilan's eyes, they then castrated him and slit open his torso.

The indignity of it all, to be tortured by cowards in the night while his wife wept at his helplessness. As he lay dying, he did not beg for salvation or revenge. He asked nothing more than the promise that his Christian son would be retrieved. It was such a strange last request that Donnach did not even consider leaving it unfulfilled.

The murderers had been much kinder to Oisil; they simply slit his throat while he slept. Considering the difference in the handling of the two, Donnach took it as a message from the Romans not to get too powerful. That is why he had gone to such lengths to keep peace during his reign. He observed the boundaries of the other tribes, and did not seek active trade with either Rome or Greece. What imports his tribe did get were usually bought from the Trinovantes tribe at twice the cost. He took great care to remain an anonymous leader for he loved his family and his tribe too dearly to suffer the same fate as this brother.

"Why such a sorrowful expression?" Laden asked, entering the chamber. "We are Celts, battle is our livelihood. It is my intention to resurrect our sense of dignity, and allow our people to defend their territories. I can see your worry over this, but you must remember that you have governed a tribe of cowards, I intend to rule a clan of strength."

"This impending bloodshed is nothing to boast," Donnach gently rebutted.

Laden came toward him with long strides, his expression irreverent. Donnach faced him for fear that he was about to be struck.

"King Donnach," Laden said, his voice rising to an angered pitch. "I, Laden, am your most blessed son. I have the honor of my parentage and the right to slay the man who would dare to defy me. It is a mystery to me why you would caution me against killing the half-Christian dog. Solomon has challenged my dignity by seeking the Druids' intervention. He is a fool who tries to rob in the darkness what he is undeserving of in the light."

Donnach looked at his son sadly. His face was red with anger while at the same time, his eyes watered for his father's approval.

"Then may the gods grant you the power of persuasion and the spirit of profit, but before a sword is drawn, we must assemble in the court, and the two of you must state your intentions," he said flatly. "There must be good reason for you to split a tribe that I have kept together for so long, and you must allow every one of our kinsmen the right of choice."

"Why," Laden challenged, "It is obvious Solomon has done his work in secret; why should I have to uphold the laws behind which he has hidden?"

"If you fail to do so, your greatness will be scourged by your own hands," Donnach replied. "There are many among us who have not the eyes to see nor the heart to understand the need of war. They must be afforded the fellowship of free choice. If you are a true believer in your quest, it will do no harm."

The blonde warrior stared down at his feet in silence. Then he lifted his head and opened his mouth to speak, but did not. He appeared suddenly childlike and insecure.

"What is it, my son?" the King asked.

"I am not a true-bred coward or a leader," Laden said, emotionally. "I am both fearful and envious, for I know in my heart that your hopes reside with Solomon. You have viewed us differently since we were boys, treating me like I was sweet as honey, and caring for him like he was already a man. You afforded him your skills in honesty while you left me to be soothed in my mother's lap. No one had to tell me it was he whom you would have chosen to be your son, not I."

"And by making the battle cry, and filling his wife's womb with your child, you have chosen this as your redemption?" Donnach countered. "I have done the best that I could with you and Pwyll. The raising of my sons was not hindered by Solomon's presence. I have loved your mother to the depths of my being, and have never refused my family anything. If my reward for this is the accusation that you were left unloved because of an orphan whom I chose to raise, then I would only wish your heart deliverance."

He turned and started to walk away, but Laden grabbed hold of his arm.

"Father, wait," he said, stepping in front of the old man. "Tell me what it is that he possesses that I do not. Tell me of it, please, that it would rise in my being and just once make you proud."

"Let us not jest with each other. You are as you have always been, and I have never asked you to be any different," Donnach replied compassionately. He could see the struggle in his son's face, and could tell by his trembling hand that he desperately wanted his consent. "My heart is big enough to share with all of my people, Laden, and I have never been able to make you understand that. There is not the need in my being to prove myself by war or theft of another man's woman. Nor will I rebuke you for having it yourself. You and Pwyll are my sons; riches and glory will never change that. As for Solomon, I too have raised him in my bosom, and all the warlords and killing you bring on cannot take that away. I feel that it is an unworthy thing you have done to turn his wife against him, and when the babe you have summoned is brought forth, I fear you will finally understand that. It is never a noble deed to destroy what another one has created, for the gods will always seek restitution."

He started to leave, then sensing his son had something more to say, turned back around.

"Do you seek anything more of me?" he asked.

Laden took a nervous breath. "Father, I need to know what position you will take in all of this?"

"The only position I am left to take," he said, shaking his head regretfully. "I will remain King until you have resolved your differences. And whether you suffer victory or defeat, I will call you my son forever."

Laden put his face in his hands, then dropped them lifelessly to his sides. Much like the little boy for whom Melena had always made excuses, he was visibly shaken by his father's indifference.

"King Donnach," he stated, his voice cracking. "Do not force me to make a political decision to silence you."

The King's face was unchanged as he looked back at his son. "If you did that, my companion in the Otherworld would be the knowledge that all of his mother's love could not save my son from becoming a Roman underling."

———

There was an eerie stillness about the village as Solomon took the rein of Saturnalia's horse and led it alongside him. There had been a hint of unrest as they rode through the damp forest. The deep green leaves of the oaks did not rustle with a sea breeze as usual, and there was scarcely a rabbit or hawk to be seen the entire way through. It gave him the uncomfortable feeling that he was either too late, or walking into a trap. His suspicions were confirmed when he climbed the knoll to Megba's cottage and found it empty. What was worse, as he stood looking down upon the settlement, he noticed there were a number of huts dark and empty as well.

Saturnalia seemed oblivious to the situation as she got down from her horse and walked unannounced into Megba's cottage. Solomon and Aonghus waited, restlessly, for her to come back out, but when she did not, Solomon went in after her.

He found her stoking the embers in the hearth and blowing on them at the same time.

"Where is the elder you informed me of?" she questioned innocently.

Solomon looked around impatiently. "Well, he is not present," he answered, obviously perturbed. "Come, you must not stay here."

"Why not?" she retorted, putting a fresh piece of wood on the fire. The tiny flames ignited and sent a stream of smoke to the ceiling and out the ventilation opening. In the next moment a splash of water extinguished it, and she looked up, surprised to see Solomon standing next to her holding an empty pitcher.

"What is the matter with you?" she demanded.

"This is not a game, Priestess," he snapped. "If Megba has left this place, it is because he has either been killed or it was unsafe to remain here. Let us take our leave, as well."

Saturnalia stubbornly crossed her arms. "Are you afraid?"

"Only a fool would not be," he countered. "You must remember that what we have done is treason. Did you think these people would suddenly lay down their lives for a self-important female who saunters into their midst and demands that they fight for her presence?"

With precise quickness, Saturnalia lifted one of her delicate hands and slapped him. Solomon felt a slight sting on his cheek, but considering her frailness, it was nothing more than a nuisance. He jerked his head back, and looked at her for a long moment. Then using the back of his hand to temper the blow, slapped her back.

Saturnalia gasped, and holding her cheek, glared at him.

"That is your first lesson in the real world, my beautiful Priestess," Solomon cautioned. "In our tribe, men and women are equal. If you choose to start a fight, you may do so."

In an instant she was again composed, and even though a red welt was visible on her alabaster skin, she no longer acknowledged the pain. She stood and stared at him so pointedly that suddenly he felt remorseful of his action.

"Do not ever do that again," she stated matter-of-factly, then walked out of the house.

Solomon pressed his hand to his brow and shook his head. Women had to be the most confounding creatures. They were difficult to resist, yet they could drive an otherwise rational man to extremes, provoking him to the oddest reactions with a single word.

He looked around the empty house; something had to have gone wrong for Megba to leave the dwelling. Solomon was at a loss to do anything but return to his own home and hope it was safe.

He walked out to find both Saturnalia and Aonghus waiting patiently atop their horses.

"I do not know what else to do except take you to my home and wait for Megba there," he said politely, as he tried to make eye contact with her.

She ignored him, and sitting rigidly in her saddle, she kept her eyes fixed in front of her.

"Can I go home now?" Aonghus asked softly.

"You had better stay with me until I find out what has happened," he said.

Aonghus moved his horse alongside him and gave him a worried look. "Something bad has happened, has it not?" he asked in a whisper.

"I cannot say," Solomon answered, rubbing the back of his neck.

The boy frowned and fidgeted with a strand of Osin's mane. "Something bad has happened. I know it. I want to be sure that my mother and father are all right. Let me go, and I promise I will only ride by my house. I will not even stop. Then I will come straight to your dwelling."

Solomon patted his cheek. "Very well, but you must not be long. If my horse is not tied in the front, do not stop."

Aonghus nodded back at him seriously, then trotted toward his house.

Solomon climbed into the saddle, and took hold of the lead ropes of the two pack animals. Pulling them forward, he handed one of them to Saturnalia, who took it without glancing up.

"Well?" Solomon inquired.

"Well, indeed," she muttered, starting out in front of him.

chapter twenty-three

efore Solomon reached his house, it became clear what was happening. The crooked rows of thatched-roof houses were completely uninhabited beyond one invisible point. The boundary line became more evident when they crossed the center court, and one completely abandoned dwelling was right next to one that was lit and filled with people. Herds of livestock were loosely tied together in open areas near the village outskirts. As they turned down the road to the King's manor, they found that there was a trench dug down its center. Sticking up from it were logs that had been carved into pointed tips, and in the center was a red pole with a hawk impaled on it. Since it was Solomon's personal totem animal, he knew immediately what it meant.

Halting his horse, he stared at it a moment, then looked away.

"Do you understand what it means?" Saturnalia asked calmly.

"This is the road to the King's estate," he explained. "This has been dug to show the division of our tribe, and that I am no longer welcome in his home."

"And the hawk?"

"It is the animal of my anointing," he said, moving up to it. "Laden has used the red pole as a way of communicating intent to kill me. That is why he has sacrificed my spirit animal with it."

Reaching out, he unskewered the hawk and tied it to a thong hanging from his saddle.

"I have accepted his challenge," he remarked, trying to disguise his hurt. With eyes downcast, he began stroking its beautiful tricolored feathers. "There is no choice but to raise arms."

Unsure of what to say, Saturnalia contemplated the evening sky. She could feel the tip of her nose getting colder with the setting sun, and the chilly air was starting to chafe her skin. To be greeted by this atrocity was more than a little unsettling. It had been a lovely journey back; at long last she had been able to revel in the feeling of freedom and adventure. Now to see the broken-hearted reaction of Solomon, and knowing that war was inevitable, she was left with a desperate, sinking feeling.

"I would not keep that for very long," she cautioned. "Whoever did this has drawn a black line of ashes down its center, and has removed his eyes. In my teaching, I know this to mean that they have divided the soul between the light and dark sides. His vision was taken away so that he would wander blindly forever in a black void. To assume this bird's character is to give yourself over to their intentions. They are seeking more than physical combat. This is spiritual warfare. Do not give in to it because the fear you will experience will kill your mind."

"What should I do?"

"When you are in private meditation, put all of your unwanted thoughts and fears into the wild foul," she explained. "Then invoke the good spirits to hear your supplications. Tie a piece of raw pork around its neck, and give it over to the fire gods. They will accept your offering, and by freeing his spirit from the darkness, it will free your heart as well."

She studied him, trying to get a hint of his disposition. "Solomon?"

"Yes?"

"Why have you not spoken of your wife?" she gently inquired.

Solomon's eyes misted, and he shook his head. "I do not know."

"Forgive my lack of subtleness. Matters of the heart should be spoken of in times of tenderness, but I must caution you not to follow your instincts when it comes to her," she warned, reaching out and taking hold of his hand. "My motives are not self-seeking, you must believe that; but this one, whom you know as wife, the spirits know as being misled into darkness. She will bring you harm if you are not careful."

He nervously untied the bird from his saddle, and put it in his traveling bag. "When we are in the cradle, we make promises of love we cannot help, Saturnalia. I do not know if you can understand the bond between two people when they care as one."

"I have never had a husband," she answered honestly. "Nor have I experienced such things as you speak. But inside me is a voice that says, 'the hands that build can also destroy.' Protect yourself Solomon. Please protect yourself."

He disguised his emotions by forcing a smile, and in that slice of time between helplessness and sorrowful humor, she saw in him a strength of character that could not be taught. It was a drive that embraced life's changes and turned them into prosperity. He alone embodied the dynamics of the earth with a piousness and unpredictability that would win him the gratitude of his people.

"Solomon?" she said, realizing he was not going to speak unless she did.

"Yes."

"Take me to your home now."

———

It was worse than Aonghus could have predicted. Not only was there no one at his house but every barnyard animal, except the bull, was gone. Even though he had promised Solomon he would only ride by, the sight of his house, cold and dark, left him with no choice but to investigate. Now he stood in the center of the main chamber, his hands dangling loosely at his sides, and his mouth agape. The hearth was cold which meant that his family had left some time ago. He was filled with a horrible numbness in his limbs, and he wanted to scream for his mother as loud as he could. But he just stood still, frightened at the emptiness of the place he knew as home.

Was it he that had changed? Was it being out on his own and even killing a man that made this dreamed-of sanctuary now appear a desolate frame? Or was it that it lacked the presence of those he loved, and without them, it was unimportant where he lived? This must have been what Solomon was feeling when Deireadh had returned. She was like the fireplace, the one thing that provided him light and warmth. It did not matter how much fun he and Aonghus had together, it could never replace the genuine force of someone who truly loved you.

The silence was pierced by the growling of his empty stomach. Going over to the honey jar, he dipped in all four fingers, then shoved the sweet bee nectar into his mouth. He was hungry and disappointed that his mother was not there preparing dinner for him. He wanted to come into the room and be swept up in her arms, and hear how proud she was that he had returned. It did not matter that she would do it eventually. Wherever she was, it was not home now, and that meant there was something to worry about.

Licking his fingers clean, he felt a chill run up his back. He shuddered at the feel of it, then ran out the door without closing it behind him. He felt frightened, as if he was being watched by someone. Leaping into the saddle, he heard a rustle in the shrubbery to the side of the house. Twisting around, he found himself looking into the face of a wolf. Startled, he cried out, taking in the creature's bloody muzzle and the way he was licking his chops. He was immediately haunted by the memory of the two warriors he had killed, and how Solomon had said they would leave them for the spirits and the wolves. What if this wolf was one of them? What if he inhabited the animal's body and came back for revenge?

"Mother!" he cried, kicking and hitting his horse at the same time. Osin broke into his usual lazy trot, and started down the road with Aonghus sitting in the saddle, crying and begging him to run faster.

CHAPTER TWENTY-FOUR

rinovantes?!" Solomon ranted. "How many Trinovantes are there?"

"More than thirty," Cwyn calmly informed him. "And there are a group of Icenians as well."

Solomon stared at him in shock. "Who does he think we are? Rome? Where are Ronan and Berrig?"

"Where is Aonghus?" Koven interrupted.

Solomon looked at him irritably. "He is looking for you. Why are you not at your farm?"

"Because Donnach sanctioned the boundaries east of it. If I had stayed I would have been allied with Laden," he explained anxiously. "If Aonghus has gone home, he will find no one, but I thank the heavens that is all that has happened. When I saw you arrive alone, I feared the worst."

Solomon calmed a moment, and grabbed hold of the farmer's arm.

"He is a good child, your boy," he told him. "He will have much to report to you himself, but I assure you that you have reason to be proud."

In the next moment, the door burst open, and with eyes bulging and tears streaming down his crimson cheeks, Aonghus scurried into the room. He ran straight past Solomon and Cwyn, then threw his arms around his father's waist.

"I think he followed me!" he cried hysterically.

Immediately, everyone in the room was concerned.

"Who followed you?" Cwyn asked, trying to pry the boy from Koven.

"Look outside, you will see," he wailed, burying his face into Koven's stomach and clutching him tighter.

Cwyn and Solomon went hurriedly to the door. Going outside they took a good look around, then came back inside.

"There is nothing out there," Cwyn stated. "Who did you think it was?"

The boy cried harder, and Saturnalia went to him and began stroking his hair. "Aonghus?" she asked softly. "Who did you think was following you?"

"The warrior," came his muffled response.

"What warrior? Did you recognize him?" Solomon questioned.

Aonghus looked up at his master. His nose was so swollen and red, it looked like the rest of his face grew out around it. The tears were flowing, and he had dark circles around his blue eyes.

"No, he turned himself into a wolf," the words came out in sobs. "I know it was one of the men we left at the stream. He was coming back to get me."

Solomon rolled his eyes. "I knew this was going to happen. You took the incident too well," he said, throwing up his hands. "The fear of the food being drugged was only the beginning; now you're envisioning ghost wolves."

"Let the child alone," Saturnalia said, wiping the tears from his cheeks with her fingertips. "It is real to him; do not rebuke him for it."

Solomon scoffed, "I suppose you can see this spirit beast, too."

"Silence!" she snapped. "Why do you not express your anger to the one who deserves it—yourself. If you are upset about this dissension, then direct it at the King or your opposition. But do not inflict it on an innocent child."

Solomon stared at her, appalled. If she had been a man addressing him in that tone, he would have shoved a fist into her mouth. He might have done it, still, if there had not been so many people around, but bruising women was not his way. He was already tense enough to strike out at anything.

"There is something to what the boy has witnessed," Megba intervened. He took Aonghus' face in his clammy hands and looked into his watering eyes.

"Tell me exactly what you saw, boy," he said, gently stroking his cheeks with his crooked thumbs.

"I was at my house, but no one was there, so I got scared and left," he sniffed. "I ran outside to get on my horse, and a wolf came out from the side yard. He looked at me viciously, and his mouth was covered with blood."

"Did he try to attack you?" Koven asked.

"No, he just stared at me and licked the blood on his mouth," he answered, trying to control his tears.

Megba gave Saturnalia a knowing look, then faced Cwyn and Solomon.

"It is time to assemble," he declared. "That wolf was Berrig's spirit guide bringing the message that we must gather the tribe without further delay."

"Berrig?" Solomon asked warily. "What do you mean?"

"The wolf is the bearer of new ideas. He finds the paths, and returns to share them with his clan," Megba explained. "The keen wolf is the power ally of the warrior, Berrig. I believe it appeared to the boy as a sign that it is time for action."

The expression faded from Solomon's face. "Then Berrig has joined Laden," he said, disappointed. "And Ronan?"

"Murdered by Laden's men," Cwyn replied sorrowfully.

Putting his hand over his eyes, Solomon closed them for a long moment. "What am I doing?" he asked aloud. "What are we doing? Donnach does not deserve this calamity. Perhaps I am too tame, but I feel we have brought about this indiscretion ourselves."

"We are doing the only thing we can," Cwyn argued. "We are defending ourselves. You do not see this clearly because you are not viewing it with a warrior's vision. You are seeing only that you have been cast out by those you love. This is not an indiscretion, Solomon—we are fighting to preserve our liberty. And

Laden's pitiful ambition has caused us to prepare the battlefield. You said that Laden sent you the hawk as a message, then you must take command of your madness, and fight the ill forces he has intended. Will you send the messenger?"

Solomon's eyes glassed over and he began rhythmically stroking his torque. "I will, and may the gods cast aside this clan's lesser part."

———

The bonfire was lit, and torches blazed at the four corners surrounding it. In front of the flames, a huge drum boomed, and the entire tribe circled around. They had all come to hear the two warriors state their reasons for the much anticipated battle.

In the middle sat King Donnach. He was dressed in his most elaborate scarlet tunic and cloak. His boots were ornamented with beaver fur sewn over the laces and around the cuffs. Even though Solomon was a good distance away, he could see the weary look on the King's face and his concealed sorrow.

Next to him stood Laden and Deireadh, both beautifully outfitted in matching green cloaks. He was wearing a golden tunic with red trousers, and she a simple red frock with a gold sash around her waist. Behind him stood Berrig and a large group of hired soldiers.

Descending the hillside toward them marched a savage-looking, leather-clad Solomon. He was framed by Megba and Saturnalia. Following a short distance behind were the other tribesmen who had originally come together in Koven's barn. As the crowd parted to let them pass, the warrior saw that some were old, some robust and young, yet all reflected an impressively trusting expression. A few of the women reached out to touch him, and he could hear others whisper at this gesture.

Stopping confidently in front of the King, he bowed, and without thinking, leaned forward to kiss his cheek. He saw Donnach's eyes gleam at his motion of affection while he touched the side of Solomon's face to return it. There was a shadowy instant of uncertainty between the two, then Solomon saw Donnach's expression transform into one that wordlessly told the warrior of his secret loyalty and approval.

"She is a fine one," he whispered, referring to Saturnalia.

"And stubborn," Solomon whispered back. He took a place opposite Laden and met Deireadh's eyes, which glowered jealously at him and Saturnalia.

"Now must our conscience be heeded," Donnach declared, rising from his place and walking around the circumference of the circle. "It is a sorrowful day when kinsmen take arms against kinsmen, and their thoughts form into actions. The quarrel we grapple with now is not for mere entertainment; it is for the rule of our people. We are beset with a time when no man's morality is true, and no woman's intuition must be betrayed. I would ask that every one of my people take heed to what these men pronounce, then let your choices be made. For if we could have settled this with words alone, our presence here would be of little need. This has come to the drawing of blood."

The tribe pressed closer in as Donnach spoke, causing the space between the two factions to narrow. Saturnalia watched the spectacle with a collected, almost disinterested attitude. She could feel Deireadh visually picking her apart, and the one time their gaze met, Saturnalia gave her an unnervingly gentle smile that made Deireadh turn red.

"I would call upon Laden to speak first," the King instructed, taking his seat.

Laden took a moment, smoothed his hair, and straightened his shoulders. The beat of the drum went from loud to soft as he stepped forward, the consummate portrait of righteous dignity.

"My heart is set ablaze at the deceit of this man," he stated, deliberately moving in front of the fire so that his broad-chested shadow was cast on Solomon. "This underling has crept about in the shadows like a sinister vermin to condemn my leadership, for I am the son of his father who has rightly ruled you all. I have the blood in my veins that has not sought wickedness or vanity. As the scarlet runs through my body, I come only to claim my right to the throne. And I pray you all to realize that I am not spotless of error or lacking in desire of wealth. But it is wealth that I will share with all of you! We have spent too much time under the sun's rays, and have not reaped the gold that has shined upon us. For it is there, as you all are here, to be had with great abundance upon Rome's good word. They seek not to bend the spirit of our nation, nor to confound you with their mettlesome religion. They have entreated this merciful clan to no longer doubt their gentle intentions, and to allow them to endow us with our just portion of wealth."

He paced as he spoke, looking earnestly into the faces of the people. When he had completed the area of his audience, he stopped in front of Solomon and looked him squarely in the eye.

"This sad state of a man has divided his people with his trite conspiracy!" he yelled. "He has taken justice to be a comical thing, and has blasphemed the gods by undermining their divine choices. He has set petty traps by which to snare your conscience, and to provoke you to draw blood. The noble binds of power have been cut by this thief. I call upon all of you to stand by me in my right to slay him and in my quest to bring abundance to my people, so that every man and his family would thrive in the breast of good fortune and tolerance of the Roman nation."

The clan whispered among themselves, but not one of them offered vocal encouragement. They seemed more concerned with Saturnalia and receiving an explanation for her presence.

On the cue of Donnach for Laden to retire and Solomon to come forward, the warrior awkwardly took his place before them. He stood with his burly arms at his sides, and nervous sweat pouring down his face. His mouth was slightly open as he stared at the mass of people staring back at him.

"You may speak now," Donnach instructed.

He uttered not a syllable. He was surprisingly overcome by his first attempt at leadership. What reason could he give these people to die for his actions, and what excuses could he offer them that would make them wish to live under his authority? He felt sorely inadequate for this task, and looking over at Saturnalia, he choked down his nerves and prepared to speak.

"Kinsmen," he said in a shaky voice. "To what fair reason could I ask this many of you to die? For as my heart has been pricked by the memory of Rome's past offenses, I state only that they should be resisted to all ends. Within my being is only a warrior who wishes to preserve the good state of liberty in our tribe. One who desires not a title, nor the glory of foreign promises, but a simple mind that desires only to resolve this profane condition. I am not the heat of the fire any more than Laden is the coolness of the breeze. We are simply two men of barren spirit who have cast aside their fears for the betterment of our clan. For it is true that I have sought the covert means of ridding myself of my enemy. But in doing so, I have brought forth the power of the great spirit. I have sought the council of the Druids, and they have sent to you a new teacher, such a one as Megba has seen in dreams, and one who has dreamed of all your faces in her slumber."

Solomon paused, and for some reason, glanced at Aonghus, who stood completely enthralled by his speech. He had made his way to the front, and with arms folded across his chest, stared up at Solomon with an expression of awe. The warrior had never seen such genuine admiration in his young face, and at that moment, he knew his struggle for his foster's respect had finally been put to rest.

"I cannot offer you the gold that Rome will bring," he said, his speech taking on the tone of greater authority. "I can only give the sincere promise that your grief will not be enlarged by them, either. My desire is to preserve our freedom by resisting their trickery, and to keep the preciousness of our spirits by giving you not a self-appointed goddess as does Laden, but a high Priestess sent by the Druids."

Holding his hand out to Saturnalia, he bowed graciously. Taking it trustingly, she came before the tribe a vision of elegance and piety. "The enchantress I have labored in secret to bring to you is known to all as the fair Saturnalia," Solomon said.

There were muted reactions as the clan came still closer, all but swallowing up Laden and Deidreadh.

"Woman of dishonor," came Deidreadh's shrill voice from among them. "She is the adulteress who has bedded my husband! She is the reason why I will no longer share his company. He has kept this one in secret. She is not a Priestess at all, she is the one who has seduced him into leaving me. She is nothing more than a sow who has bewitched my husband."

Deireadh burst through the crowd, her hazel eyes sparked with hatred. Groping forward, she clumsily took hold of Solomon's hand, and forced him to release the Priestess.

"Such punishment should be heaped upon you to stir this man's blood to the point of treachery," Deireadh blustered. "You are not the gem of a woman who could portray the Goddess, nor are you worthy to cause such misery to come between my kinsmen."

Deireadh faced the crowd. "She is a vile stranger!" she shrieked. "Banish her!"

A deadly hush came over the tribe, and they shrank back. Then Saturnalia lifted her hands above her shoulders, and beckoned them to come near. They did, stopping a few paces away.

"I will not lie to you, good people, for I fear you have heard too many untruths these sad days," she said softly. "Rather, I will say that in your ability to perceive lies, you will also be able to discern the truth. Part of what she has said is true. I have become one with this warrior in a ceremony to the gods. We are not man and wife, nor are we concealed lovers. We are simply two people who are unashamed to share our pleasures in private ritual. I have not been his sovereign who has sought to take control of him for my selfish ends. I am only a Priestess who was raised by the Druids for your good. I proclaim nothing more. I have not the viciousness to mislead such tenderhearted beings as you. I am brave only in my desire to create a society where we may all be free to worship the gods of nature, and that is not at Rome's hand. I seek a sacred relationship for all of you to experience in their presence, that you may love the fear out of your souls, and like the gentle breeze, thrive in the presence of your own righteousness, not the distasteful one of greedy mortals. Believe me when I say that I would curse the one who would not restore the valor of your heart, and would draw the blood of their kinsmen for the pleasure of gold."

Stepping past Deireadh, she began touching the people with both hands. She started with Aonghus, who returned her affection so honestly that many more followed. Soon she was surrounded by a great number of the clan, and the circle had split into two smaller ones.

Donnach motioned for Solomon and Laden to come before him. "As brothers, do you still seek to do war?" he asked.

The color was bleached from Laden's face. His eyes narrowed, and he gave a firm nod, "yes."

Solomon stared at him, then Deireadh. "I would seek peace if it were possible."

"It is impossible now," Laden snapped, pulling Deireadh to his side. "When the sun rises, I will seek to have your head for my doorway."

"The evil that is our nature prevails, so let destruction begin its work," Solomon retorted.

He grabbed hold of the King's hand and kissed the top of it. "For my fault, do not suffer yourself," he whispered. "When all the promises we have labored to keep are broken, and whether I am breathing in the sunshine, or a part of the earth, I will forever love the honor of your mighty heart."

"Yet such a mighty heart would be vanquished if it were not so for you as well," Donnach replied softly.

CHAPTER TWENTY-FIVE

he night of waiting was excruciating.

Solomon watched the people trickle into his estate bringing their families, their weapons, and an abundance of food for the warriors' feast. It was customary that, on the eve of a battle, a banquet was held to honor heaven and seek its protection. The ceremony was presided over by Saturnalia, who did not disappoint all those who had labored to make it elaborate in spite of the short preparation time.

She settled in perfectly with everyone; Solomon wondered if there were anything she would ask that they would not do. The women of the clan gave her a beautiful robe as a welcome, and when the feasting and dancing was over, she went to each person and inquired of their name and their supplication, then she anointed them with oil. By the time she was finished, she had endeared herself to the clan; they were completely zealous at the prospect of battling for her cause.

For Solomon, it was quite the opposite. He felt like a spectator in the event. The words he had spoken in front of the King seemed as if they had come from a political stalwart who had temporarily possessed his mind. He had offered them the truth, but had done it in a way far out of his character. He could not help but question if he were not more like Laden than he wanted to be. He reasoned that if he were not, he would have called Laden a liar to his face and settled it all right there. There would not have been the need to have others stake their lives for this issue, and he would not have sought their moral support to begin with.

Yet the forces turning in his life had no regard for his personal apprehensions. And he had not the vaguest idea of what to do about it. Seeing the way the clan had embraced Saturnalia convinced him even more that whether he was right or wrong, the masses had to believe in a principle stronger than themselves. Perhaps that was what worship was all about, the desire to acknowledge a force greater than free will.

Solomon's introspection left him with the hollow realization that life's private pleasures must be neglected when one is in power. He saw that every thought and every motion was completely affected by the fact that it, inevitably, involved his tribe. The only one he found of any solace was Aonghus, and that was the most peculiar thing of all. He could not deny the comforting feeling he had when the child crawled into his arms and hugged his neck. And the only thing Aonghus had told him was that he believed everything was going to be all right. Yet, it was enough to carry Solomon into a few short hours of sleep before the dawn.

It was Aonghus who woke him and told him that the soldiers were beginning their preparations and that Megba was set to do the blessing. Solomon
dressed carefully, and, kissing the tip of his sword, stepped out into the courtyard.

His senses were filled with the smell of wet grass, and the vision of the people
swathed in dense morning fog. The horses were taken up, and more than the sound
of their heavy breathing, Solomon could hear the incessant grinding of their teeth
against the bit. The oak stump used for the banquet fire was still smoldering, and a
few of the children had gathered around it to ward off the early morning chill.

Gazing out at the trusting faces of his tribesmen, Solomon was overcome
with the burden of leading them. At the same time, he felt he needed this stronger
purpose for he was no longer motivated by the solitary desires of his pride. He was
now thoroughly influenced by the needs of this mass who believed in his ability to
make decisions on their behalf.

"They are waiting for you to speak," Saturnalia said, touching his shoulder.

Solomon angled his head and looked into her dazzling green eyes. Their
reflection was confident and bold. He found in her a reservoir of power that he
knew was limitless.

"What brave people you are to stand before me now," he proclaimed, turning back to them. "For if we are marked for sacrifice upon this morn, I could not
find fewer men of greater honor under all the eyes of heaven. I wish that not one
of you should perish, and the outward hope of safety to you all dwells now within
my eyes. Because to look upon you, I see the brilliance of men who understand
that manhood comes at great expense, and were I to die, I could not enter the otherworld in any company of better magnificence. And while it would seem that
glory has taken Laden as a concubine, we here know that her riches rest in the
pure intents of our souls. I am not desiring of gold, nor the acknowledgement of
Caesar. I seek nothing more than to outlive this day with all of you, that together,
we may see old age and stand before the noble Goddess of Bravery. So rouse in
yourselves your courage, and as brothers, let us steal the breath from his body
who would doubt your might!"

Howls of valor came from the warriors, and the women seemed to raise
their hands to the sky at once, and cry out for its blessing. Then the waves of fog
parted, and the dark image of a single horseman neared. The sound of the people
dimmed into desolate silence as all heads turned to see who it was. The click of the
horses' hoofs grew louder, and even though he was at a very slow walk, the volume seemed to increase to aggravating proportions until the shadowy face
became visible, and the horseman halted in front of Solomon.

Slouching in the saddle, completely tattooed and outfitted for combat sat
Berrig. Tears were visible in the corners of his eyes. He was holding his shield with
one hand, and his reins with the other. And draped across the withers of his horse
was a corpse.

Solomon did not have to be told who it was. And when Berrig heaved it to
Solomon's feet, he saw that the fine, angelic features of Laden's face were bordered

by a slit beneath his chin that went from one ear to the other. His jaw was slack, and his green eyes did not show the serenity of one who had passed into the Otherworld. Rather, they reflected the haunting look of anger and surprise at his betrayal.

"The King says there will be no war today," Berrig stated flatly.

Without waiting for him to say any more, Solomon rushed forward. He grabbed him from the saddle and threw him to the dirt. Going down with him, he attacked him with both fists, using quick jabs in his ribs and face to keep him defenseless. He could hear Berrig grunting, and was so close to him that he could feel his breath on his face. Then Solomon felt Berrig shove two fingers into his nostrils, and jam his head back.

In the next moment, Solomon was looking up at the grey morning sky and could hear the shuffling of feet on either side of him as the people tried to get out of the way. Using both legs, he coiled them around one of Berrig's knees and bent it outward. As he did this, he could feel the tip of Berrig's knife beneath his chin.

"Drop it or I will break your leg in half," Solomon fumed.

"If you do, it will be your last deed," Berrig warned, catching his breath.

Solomon looked into his friend's tortured eyes for a prolonged moment. "You served Laden!" he accused.

Berrig shook his head. "I served the King. And if he would have asked me to kill you along with him, I would have done that as well. So if you wish to end up like your opposer, do as you wish. Take heed that a leg will heal, but a lifetime must be born over again."

Relaxing his legs, Solomon kept his eyes fixed on Berrig until he had sheathed his dagger. Then as if he were welcoming home a lost companion, he put both arms around his friend and hugged him. The remorse he felt was overwhelming; at the sight of Berrig's compassionate face, his eyes began to mist.

"Forgive me, good friend," Berrig said, helping Solomon to his feet. "I am a warrior; my duty is first to the King."

Solomon stared down at Laden's corpse, and feeling the tears stinging his eyes, rubbed them with his fingertips and turned away.

"I understand," he murmured.

When he looked up again, he saw that the group of warriors had already tied a rope around Laden's midriff, and carrying him by his arms and legs, they strung him over a large oak tree in the side yard. Then Cwyn swung his massive sword, and severing the head of golden curls, sent it soaring onto the grass. It rolled a short distance into the crowd, and one of the women picked it up by the hair, and howled with macabre laughter.

The blood from his neck smeared on the people's hands as they triumphantly tossed it from one person to the next. And finally giving it to Cwyn, the seasoned warrior held it high in the air, and proclaimed Solomon to be the new leader of them all.

Solomon stood watching the spectacle, disgust rising in his throat. He was alone except for Aonghus. The child had his face concealed in the small of his master's back, moaning at the dreadful exhibition.

CHAPTER TWENTY-SIX

s was his duty, Solomon went immediately before the King to claim the right of power. He found Donnach seated in the corner of his chamber, looking older, more helpless, and more condemned than he had ever wanted to witness. Like a fallen hero, he was dressed in the same clothes he wore the night before, but they were no longer impeccable. They were now soiled with the blood of his eldest son. His face had seemingly aged lifetime after anguished lifetime in these few hours. His eyes were vacant, and his hands trembled profusely.

At the sight of him, Solomon wanted to scream as loudly as he could to release the torture of seeing one he so dearly loved emaciating before his eyes. He was glad they were alone; he could not maintain his facade of strength any longer. He wanted to confess his guilt and self-condemnation, and he wanted to lament the passing of his youth into the monger of self-importance he now considered himself to be. But as he came in front of the man, all he could do was get down on his knees and rest his head in Donnach's lap.

The two men said nothing for a long while, and the only movement in the room was of Donnach stroking Solomon's hair.

"You have made me proud all of these years," he finally said, in a quivering voice. "You have spared me the scenes of demanding your birthright, and I know you had no choice but to do what they demanded. You are the reluctant leader now, and I would only beg you to be their pawn no longer. You have the title you were born to. In the name of your father, and his father before him, rule your people with a just hand."

Solomon listened patiently, no longer trying to stop his tears. He felt like a child again, taking refuge in the strong, but gentle, presence of his surrogate father.

"I had no choice either," Donnach sadly continued. "The needs of the many must not go unfulfilled. And were you to take arms against my son, I know you would have easily killed him. It is not that I love one of you more, it is only that the promises we make before the gods must be kept at all costs. Were I to let you harm Laden, both the promises we made long ago would have been broken. Now you may become leader of my people, but you still may never be king. For you ate of the lamb, and offered your word to the Druids. It must remain this way until your rule is passed on. In the future, you may anoint a king to take your place when you are finished. But you will stay a chieftain only, for I have sworn it to the heavens upon the blood of my son."

Solomon mumbled a contrite monologue of his guilt and confusion. Before he was finished, he found himself begging the King to forgive him for being too weak to face up to his actions.

The King listened to his outpouring sympathetically, then beckoned him to rise to his feet. "You have nothing to punish yourself for," Donnach said. "We have all been traitors to ourselves at one time or another. I felt as helpless as you when I held my dying brother in my arms. The stench of his blood clung to me, as Laden's does now, but this time my solution is much different."

With his shoulders hunched, he went to his bed to lie down. Following him, Solomon took a place next to him. He could feel his sense of desperation swell, and he wanted to remain as close to Donnach as he could.

"Then, I chose to rule my people with a scepter of peace," he continued, setting his hand on top of Solomon's. "And by all descriptions, it did suffice. You must find your own cures, but if I were to impart to you any wisdom, it would be that a vengeful heart cannot be forgiven. Let the deeds of the people rest, and seek to quell this flame of revenge, not feed it. If you do that, you will not prove the villain you envision yourself to be."

"I will seek the virtue you speak of," Solomon said in an uneven tone.

With eyes downcast, he felt the midmorning breeze come through the open shutters. It swirled about the chamber then yielded to a placid stillness.

"That gentle wind is so like the breath of a woman, is it not?" the old man said softly. "It can share our joys and dreams, and can caress us in our downfalls. I have placed a kiss each night since the day she left upon the right place beside me where my beautiful Melena slumbered. Now the breeze should end in her presence, and the sweet poison should carry me there. I will at last have peace."

Unable to speak, Solomon felt Donnach's hand go limp, and shuddered as he heard the faint sound of the breath leaving his body. The King had fallen.

———

Staggering aimlessly into the morning light, the warrior focused his bloodshot eyes on Deireadh. She stood with both hands bound behind her back, staring dry-eyed at Laden's head skewered atop a wooden post. Her long dark hair had been cut down to the scalp, and the rich, dark tresses lay scattered around her feet. Catching sight of Solomon, she glared at him with callous hatred as he approached her.

"This woman has been tried before us for her blasphemies," Megba explained. "She has been accused and found guilty of conspiracy, treason, and unrightfully claiming herself a goddess."

Solomon stood stone-faced and aching as he looked at his wife. How pitiful they both had become.

"And what is her sentence?" Solomon asked with no expression.

"Banishment!" Deireadh snarled, spitting on his feet. "And I want it. I want never to be a part of this wicked band of ignorance you now claim to lead. Send me to live with my own conscience because I refuse to burden your petty court any longer. Or take my head if you have the stomach for it, which I do not believe you do."

Reaching deep inside himself, Solomon found the last ounce of his confidence as he spoke. "So be it," he announced, raising both hands in the air. "This shall be the last of the sentences. Deireadh, let it be known that you are now the Black Druidess who once belonged to the tribe of the Brigantes. Take your soul and dwell among the dark forces for you are forever banished from the tribe of your birth. Your sentence will hold with all the tribes in the Celtic nation of which you would seek mercy. May the rule of the people stand, and may it be known that no others shall be punished. If we are to be united once again, let all who rose against me stand pardoned, and let this travesty slumber from this day on."

He stepped forward and untied Deireadh's hands. "Woman who was once my wife, seek refuge far from me."

"So be it, once brave warrior," she responded, with biting sarcasm.

Keeping her head held high, Deireadh deliberately looked into the faces of her jury as she walked silently into the dim recesses of the oaks.

chapter twenty-seven

he crisp spring succumbed to the robust heat of summer, then faded into the dampness of fall. The clan had matured, it seemed, and it was more from Saturnalia's influence than any decision brought down by Solomon's rule. She was the wealth in their daily lives, their embodiment of inspiration, desire, and compassion, involving herself with their daily triumphs, and sympathizing with even minor dilemmas.

Solomon had done what he could to learn his place as a leader. He had endured the intense spiritual initiation by Megba and had even tried to incorporate it into his days. It had been enough to see the tribe through the celebrations of the vernal equinox, the summer solstice, and the holy grove Festival of Beltaine.

Laden and King Donnach were given an elegant, aristocratic burial. Both Megba and Saturnalia had issued the elaborate rites of passage, and a huge festival was held to commemorate their final resting. As was the custom, the tribe had adorned them with gold and rich traditional banquet foods as offerings. The mourners danced and sang around them for a day and a night, then father and son were enshrined together with their deceased family, all of their weapons, and their best steeds.

As the months passed, the tribe seemed content to enjoy the wealth of the warm summer days, as was Solomon himself. He had taken Saturnalia as his lover, and found the pleasure of her private and public company exquisitely satisfying. Then one eve, convinced that he had accomplished all that he had set out to do, Megba informed Solomon and Saturnalia that he had imparted to them the best of his knowledge, and his time there was completed. When he awoke the next morning, he found Saturnalia sitting straight-backed and stone-eyed in Megba's cottage. She calmly related that the old sorcerer had simply walked out into the center of the lake and disappeared. His corpse was never found, which gave Solomon the uneasy feeling that perhaps there really was something to this religion.

The only accounts of Deireadh had come from kinsmen who had seen her wandering in the groves, or had caught glimpses of her stealing raw corn from the fields. She was said to be a frightening sight with matted hair and dirty, tattered clothing. All who had come in contact with her declared her insane, and believed she was possessed with the spirits of darkness she had befriended.

On this eve the tribe had gathered in the grove to celebrate the sacred Festival of Samhain. This was an important and solemn occasion, because it marked

the time when the creation of the world's chaos was said to have been transformed into order. It also memorialized the spirits of the dead who were believed
to return, and were allowed to roam in the land of the living until dawn. It was a
time of spiritual danger and warfare, as well as a celebration of holiness. It distinguished the year's end, and served as the divider between the mortal and spiritual
worlds.

A large bulk of wood was placed in the center of the festival court, and was
dressed in the clothes of those who had died throughout the year. The wood was
practically concealed as family members draped it with cloaks and robes. Plainly
visible next to the lovely ornamented cloaks of Donnach and Megba, was the
green cloak Laden had worn on the last night he had visited this place. It had been
bundled together with what was easily recognizable as Deireadh's sheared locks.

All had observed the day-long fast before this ritual. There were specially
selected families that had each killed a castrated ram to be eaten, while others took
care of the enormous mass of accompanying food dishes, most of which were prepared with pumpkin and corn. A magnitude of flasks filled with wine and ale were
surrounded by specially prepared cakes and breads.

In front of the stone altar that was set aglow by beeswax candles and burning torches, a horned ram was tied. His collar was made of flowers, and his body
wrapped with ivy vines from his neck to his tail. He would be the blood sacrifice,
a messenger to be dispatched into the divine realm of the gods on their behalf.

The many drums pounding off the oak trunks was accompanied by flutes
and lyres playing a bewitching melody. The men and women drank and sang the
laments of their dead, while dancing with reckless abandon in front of the flaming shrine.

Saturnalia stood anxiously before her altar, scanning the area for Solomon.
She had already waited too long for the Chieftain's presence and would have to
proceed with the holy rites without him. The crowd watched with horror and
curiosity as she firmly took hold of the ram's muzzle and swiftly slit its throat. The
blood flowed freely onto the altar as she chanted the holy rites. Shutting her eyes in
silent prayer for the beast, she felt a gentle tug on her sleeve. She looked down and
saw a pallid Aonghus staring up at her. At first, she thought that the sensitive boy
had perceived her sense of grief at what she had done, but she knew that it was
something more when he wordlessly took her hand and led her into the woods.

They walked a long way, and it was not until they were far from the celebration that the dazed Saturnalia thought to ask him about it.

"Where are you taking me?" she asked. The sound of her voice seemed mis-
placed in the silence of the trees.

"Solomon needs you!" Aonghus responded, his expression deepening.

Saturnalia moved as though she were in a space yet unaffected by her physical being. The grove was hauntingly black, and the dampness of the ground
mixed with the smell of rotting autumn leaves created an unearthly desolate
atmosphere.

When they reached Solomon's manor, Aonghus led her around the back, and into the barn. She found her lover seated on a bale of hay, his ashen complexion and wide eyes confirming her feeling of anxiety.

She could hear the sound of a woman's moans coming from one of the stalls, and walking past him, she found a laboring Deireadh lying on clean straw. She was naked beneath a leather shroud, and Saturnalia could smell the familiar odor of blood and fluid of a travailing woman.

Deireadh was delirious from the pain, but when she focused on Saturnalia, she began shrieking for her to keep away. Her teeth were clenched in a snarl, and her screams came out in raspy growls. Her skin glowed from perspiration, and Saturnalia could see the infant thrashing inside her stomach trying to be born.

"How long has she been like this?" Saturnalia asked.

Solomon looked at her blankly, then hid his face in his hands. "I do not know. She came here on her own. She told me the pains began yesterday."

The Priestess went to Deireadh, and despite her weakened protests, grabbed hold of her wrist and mentally counted the beats of her heart. She was too far gone to resist the attention. Eyes still filled with hate, she looked up at Saturnalia and begged for her help.

Resting her hand on top of her protruding stomach, Saturnalia measured the time between contractions, then turned to Solomon, her face distressed.

"I cannot save them both," she whispered.

Solomon shook his head, and shrank back. "Do not tell me that," he yelled. "You can save both; you must save both."

Saturnalia knew from his strained manner, he had obviously been hiding Deireadh for some time. It was apparent by his reactions to her that he was more surprised than anyone at her condition.

"Forgive me," he said, in a quieter tone. "It is only that the child—it is mine. I cannot make a choice."

Saturnalia went to him, and ran one hand over his guilt-ridden features. "Then I will do it," she quietly reassured him. "The remedy for this can only be one thing, and I will take responsibility for it. Please wait outside."

Gently urging Solomon and Aonghus into the evening, she shut the enormous barn doors, and bolted them from the inside.

Solomon panicked as he heard Deireadh scream for him to help her. Her voice was filled with wrath as it grew louder and louder.

"What has befallen me that you would ask for my murder!" she shrieked bitterly. "As the gods have abandoned me, Solomon, the child I bear is yours!"

Saturnalia's commanding tone soon drowned out her wailing as she began to pray in Greek. Her voice rose higher, and she started to sing recognizable hymns of exorcism to the Goddess. When the Chieftain realized that Deireadh was no longer screeching, he found himself pounding on the barn doors with his fists, begging for Saturnalia to open them. When she did not respond, he began throwing himself against the wooden barriers as Aonghus pulled on his tunic, pleading for him to calm down.

Then with a single thrust, the doors flew open. Rushing in, he found Deireadh writhing agonizingly in the straw, blood pouring out of her slit stomach. She stared vacantly up at him for only an instant, then her eyes rolled up in her head, and clawing at her bedding, she gasped one last tormented breath.

In the same instant, Solomon looked over at Saturnalia, who was washing the bloody newborn in a watering trough. She appeared tired and frail. Blood was smeared over her face and hands.

"It is a girl child," she announced softly.

Feeling sudden fury come over him, Solomon angrily lunged at her. "Give it to me!" he demanded, trying to grab the infant.

Saturnalia turned her back to him, attempting to shield the child, and Solomon found himself shaking her by the shoulders to release it.

"Give it to me," he howled. "I will kill it!"

"Stop! Please, please stop," Aonghus begged, beating against Solomon's back with both fists.

The Chieftain shoved him out of the way, and swinging Saturnalia around, seized the crying baby with one of his mighty hands. He tried to pull it away from her, but she held it firmly and commanded him to stop. In the next moment, Solomon was stunned by a bucket of cold water hitting him in the face. Stupefied, he turned and found himself facing a rattled, desperate Aonghus.

"I am sorry," he said, "but you must not hurt it. It is only a baby."

Numb and humiliated, Solomon stepped past the boy, and took his original place on the bale of hay. He appeared drugged as he placed his palms on his thighs and stared off into oblivion.

"Get it away from me," he said, monotone. "I want never to set eyes on it, lest I crush its head beneath the heel of my boot."

Steadying herself, Saturnalia took a few cautious steps toward him.

"Do not come near me," he growled. "Or the same will happen to you."

"Chieftain," she addressed him in a civil tone. "We have all labored hard to have our tribe remain under the blessings of the heavens. What you have done by taking mercy on one you yourself had banished would be severely punished if it came to light. All you have espoused these months would amount to nothing. As your intimate friend, may we keep this between us, lest the wrath it will invoke in our people be suffered by you."

Solomon made no effort to acknowledge her; instead he kept his gaze fixed on the far end of the barn.

"I would have this child's parentage remain a mystery," she continued, nervously clutching the crying infant close to her to quiet it. "I would give it over to a family who has petitioned a daughter, and say that it was fulfilled with the festival ceremony. Will you agree to this?"

Solomon focused on her. "I will, Saturnalia. But as you have killed my wife, I will ask you, in exchange, to remain my intimate friend no longer," he stated disdainfully. "I will be Chieftain of this tribe in name only. I will fulfill my duty according to your precious laws, but you will be responsible for all decisions from this moment on. I will respond "yes" when you wish, and "no" when you do not."

Saturnalia felt the blood drain from her body with each syllable he uttered. Then she looked into those brown eyes that had once been vibrant and welcoming, and saw them no longer inhabited by the man she had come to love.

"So be it," she mumbled, looking to the ground. "Deireadh must be disposed of. We cannot bury her as we did the others. Banishment carries over into the afterlife, and she must endure this transition alone. It is my suggestion that she be found by the clan in the woods where she has dwelt. All inquiries will be laid to rest because I am positive that the tribe will believe that she burst from the spirits within her."

"If that is what you wish, Priestess," he grumbled, rising to his feet.

He went to Deireadh's lifeless body, and without saying a word, rolled her in the leather shroud. Then he lifted her over his shoulder, carried her to his horse, and laid her across its withers.

"You will have to do it yourself," he stated, looking at her coldly.

Saturnalia shook her head. "This child must be taken to one with milk, or she will surely not survive."

"That is not my problem. You did the butchering, so finish it completely," he declared, then walked away.

Saturnalia placed one hand on Aonghus' shoulder, and pulled him to her.

"I will do it," he muttered, hiding his face in her side. "You tell me where to take her, and I will do it."

Saturnalia got down on one knee beside him, and hugged him close. The boy embraced her and the baby, and even though his remorse was apparent, he strangely shed no tears.

"Will you speak with him?" he asked earnestly. "Explain to him why this had to happen."

"Of course," Saturnalia consoled, shifting the position of the baby in her arms to hold him nearer. "I am sure one day he will understand."

———

Harassed and shaken, Aonghus wove his way deeper into the dark vacuum of the grove. The whites of Solomon's horse's eyes were visible as he darted at, seemingly, every noise or shadow he encountered. Aonghus knew it was because of the smell of the blood that the horse was unruly, but still, the dangerously excitable steed took all of his strength to control.

Struggling to keep the animal at a walk, he waded through a creek and up a hillside toward the sea. Saturnalia had instructed him to leave Deireadh in the woods, but the boy had thought it better that she be rolled off a cliff. If and when she ever did wash ashore, the fall against the rocks would make it almost impossible to detect the precise incision across her belly. And it would make it obvious that she had flung herself into the sea, and had committed suicide.

He was almost at the top of the hill, and was able to detect the thick, salty ocean air when a rather plump rabbit scurried in front of them. It was all the distraction his horse needed; as it reared up on two legs, it jolted Deireadh's corpse backward. The dead weight of it was too much for the boy and he hit the ground with it landing on top of him. Scurrying out from under it, he ran after the horse terrified, finally catching it tangled in the shrubbery on the stream banks.

Hurriedly getting on its back, he ran his hand down the front of his shirt, utterly disgusted at the sensation of cold blood across its front. Yanking the horse's head to the side, he looked up at the shadowy lump of the dead woman on the hillside. It gave him a peculiar sense of relief to know that the last vestiges of Laden's uprising had finally been disposed of.

It was still dark when he awoke to the sound of a baby cooing next to him. He opened his blurry eyes, and focused on the tiny bundle of life nestled in the animal pelts where he slept. Enda was seated beside them, beaming at the sight of the slumbering little girl.

"The gods are good to us," she said, stroking the hair away from her eldest son's eyes. "They have finally offered us a daughter."

Aonghus kissed the infant on the forehead, then carefully cradled her in his arms. She was so fresh and soft.

"It is important for you to rise now," Enda continued. "The sun is not shining yet, but Saturnalia and Solomon have summoned you. They are waiting with your father in the main chamber."

Feeling hesitant of what he would encounter, Aonghus kept hold of the baby while he scooted out of bed and followed his mother into the next room. He found everyone seated around the hearth. His father's face looked untroubled next to the tense expressions of Solomon and Saturnalia, seated at opposite ends of the room. The lack of sleep was apparent on the lovely face of the Priestess, who appeared solemnly lifelike compared to the brooding Chieftain.

"Come here, son," Koven said, reassuringly. He must have sensed Aonghus' confusion at being roused in the night to see the assembly.

Aonghus complied, and took a place beside his father. He noticed a piece of raw lamb and the goblet of wine on a platter in front of the fire.

"She is beautiful, is she not?" Koven asked, referring to the baby.

Aonghus nodded and smiled at the same time.

"Her name is Kordelina," his father went on. "She will be part of our family if we agree to recompense the gods for their generosity."

The boy's ice-blue eyes darted questioningly over at Solomon. He sat stone-faced, staring at the fire as though he were oblivious to what was taking place.

"How do we do that, Father?" he asked, upset with his master's condition.

"We must promise them something in return," Saturnalia said. "This child lives because we have tread down the dark forces conjured by the Black Druidess. In return for the empowerment the heavens have given us, we must make a pact among ourselves never to let it be known the circumstances by which the girl came to us. The babe would never be allowed to live."

"Yes I know that," Aonghus said, rocking the child.

"You also know that one day, Solomon will end his rule, and anoint a king to take his place," the Priestess explained seriously. "All here are in agreement that we should enter into a sacred promise of these events. In return for the raising of this child as a part of this family, and as your sister, you will one day become king if your promise goes unbroken. It is a burdensome thing to rule a people, and even more burdensome to take a sacred oath. For if this oath is defiled, great harm and even death would come to the one who would dishonor it."

"I understand," Aonghus said, trying not to appear intimidated.

"This Chieftain you know as Solomon, has sworn to offer you his rule in exchange for this vow," Enda said to her son. "You would be assured a kingship, and my prayer for a daughter would be fulfilled. Will you do it, son?"

Aonghus looked protectively down at the baby, then rubbed her silken forehead with the side of his cheek. There was something about how she rested peacefully in his arms that made him not want to let her go. Then he looked at the resentful expression of Solomon. This baby would surely perish if he had his way.

"Yes, Mother," he gently replied. "I would promise to take Kordelina as my sister, and never tell another soul. As the gods know our actions, I vow it."

With no further urging, Saturnalia cut the raw lamb into small pieces, and gave some to each of them.

"We welcome the way of the ancient ones every time we honor their will," she said. "Let first our duty be to the laws, that we should not betray the promises we make upon them. Let us accept their will even unto our own death, and swear to abide by it."

Aonghus quickly swallowed the meat. He hated the slippery feel of it going down, and wished he could have a drink to wash away the raw taste.

"In exchange for this life, a new rule will be issued upon the passing of power," Saturnalia declared, holding the goblet of wine above her head. "As the blood in our veins is symbolized by this nectar, let it be know that when the Chieftain Solomon is finished, his foster, Aonghus, having kept his vow, will rule all that we know to be our tribe and its territory."

She lifted the wine to her lips, then passed it to everyone. They all took short drinks, except Solomon, who realizing he was the last one, vehemently gulped it down. He then sharply focused on the bundle Aonghus was holding, wiped his lips with the back of his hand, and exited the gathering without a good-bye.

Part Two

CHAPTER ONE

D. 54. A splendid sun dipped below the hillside much later each evening as the mournful days of winter were, at last, coming to an end. There was a sense of newness; a regained innocence that came when the trees, barren from the cold months, sprouted their pink and white blossoms. The air turned thick with the aroma of wild flowers and lush fields of heather. With spring, came the preparation of the Feast of Beltaine, little more than a month away.

As if they knew what was to come, the girls seemed to walk with more sway to their hips, looking flirtatiously to the men they would lie with when the first dawn of May arrived. Then the long months of waiting would end, as the entire tribe danced around the fertility pole.

The first light of day could be seen as Aonghus groomed his horse. He took great pride in making sure Osin's black coat was clean and shiny. Although the animal's muzzle was beginning to grey with age, Aonghus wanted him to look better than the other horses when he rode him.

Koven had finally given the old gelding to Aonghus when Solomon had provided the family farm with a new workhorse. Even though the trustworthy animal was many years older than the horses the other boys used, Aonghus often thought he held his head higher, and walked with greater dignity.

Rubbing Osin's neck harder, the boy brought the last flakes of dust to the surface. In spite of the brisk morning air, his hard work caused beads of sweat to form on his forehead and upper lip.

The barn door opened, and Aonghus saw Diarmudd rubbing his sleepy eyes as he blindly entered. He drowsily looked at him, and lifted his brows.

"Aonghus, you are early. I thought I would be the first one here this morning," he said, yawning.

Aonghus lifted his horse's hooves one by one, and cleaned out their centers. "I am going to see my family before we leave."

Diarmudd's lethargic expression turned smug. "I thought you might be visiting Bracorina," he teased.

Blotches of red surfaced on Aonghus' cheeks, and he shook his head. Without giving a reply, he lifted his saddle onto the horse's back.

Diarmudd laughed, knowing he had embarrassed his friend. "She thinks quite highly of you. A pretty one, my sister. As for me, I do not think the woman I was meant for was born into this clan. She is waiting for me elsewhere."

Aonghus questioned his friend. "I see, and where might that be?"

Diarmudd shrugged and yawned again. His mouth involuntarily opened as wide as it would go, and his eyes watered. "I don't know," he said. "But when I find her, I will know it in the beating of my heart."

"Perhaps she will find you," Aonghus humored him, fastening the saddle cinch and patting his horse's flank.

Diarmudd threw the rope around his horse's neck, and led him from the stall. "It is a nice thought, but I do not dare think myself that lucky. We cannot all be lucky enough to have one as rich as Bracorina be admiring of us," he jested.

Taking hold of Osin's reins and getting into the saddle, Aonghus' complexion once again turned ruddy. His comrade's teasing about Bracorina could not help but embarrass him. This would be his first Beltaine celebration, and he hoped it would be spent with her. "I will see you in a while," he said, touching his heels to Osin's sides to start into an even-paced walk.

The warm glow of firelight filled many of the houses he passed on his way to his family's farm. The day started early for most of the tribe, and it was not unusual for work to begin long before sunrise. He deliberately passed Bracorina's home hoping she would be awake and offer him porridge, but with the exception of the servants' quarters, it was dark on her father Pwyll's estate.

Osin broke into a brisk trot at the familiar sight of the farm in the distance. Light could be seen from all the windows but one, the children's room. It was still too early for the younger ones to be awake.

Allowing some slack to the reins, Aonghus let the gelding pace himself because he knew he would predictably stop at the front door, which he did. Putting one leg over the horse's hindquarters, Aonghus jumped to the ground.

He was greeted by a wave of warmth as he entered the cozy little house. Since Kordelina had been adopted, Solomon had seen to it that two new rooms were added to the hut. Even with the extras the Chieftain provided, it still only offered the bare essentials for bringing up the family.

"Aonghus," his mother said, embracing her son. "Sit, please, I will bring you your tea."

"Thank you, Mother," he said, kissing Enda's cheek.

He took a place near his father at the oak-slab dining table while his mother brought him breakfast. It had been seven years since he had gone to live with Solomon in exchange for the Chieftain's daughter being taken in; yet Aonghus still considered these humble lodgings his home.

"And where are you off to today, son?" Koven asked, extending his hand.

Aonghus returned his gesture fondly. He dearly loved and missed his father. Although he had never been a warrior, he was a kind and devoted family man, and had never reproached his son for not following in his footsteps. Before he could answer, Kordelina entered.

"And what would you be doing up at this hour?" Enda asked.

The little girl stood in the center of the room in her nightfrock, her sleepy eyes focusing on her older brother. Her hair was mussed, and one side of her face was red and wrinkled from where she had been resting on it. In one hand, she held her woolen britches, and in the other, her tiny calfskin boots.

Ignoring her mother's question, she climbed into Aonghus' arms and hugged his neck. Pleased by her spontaneous affection, he gave a little laugh as she kissed his cheek. Then he kissed her back.

"I'm talking to you," Enda said, frowning at the child's lack of response.

Kordelina looked up at her guiltily, then grabbed a piece of bread from Aonghus' plate, and took a large bite.

"Do not let her do that," Enda scolded. "You are only discouraging this wild boar from using what few manners she has."

Aonghus smiled as he offered her his porridge, "She means no harm."

A broad smile crossed Kordelina's lips as she put the bowl to her mouth and swallowed. Then she handed him her trousers and patted the side of his face.

He scooted away from the table, and held out the trousers while she stepped into them a leg at a time. Then he tied the braided leather laces around her waist. Watching her two children, Enda shook her head.

"You should make her ask. She knows the words, but refuses to say them," she lectured, placing her hands on her wide hips. "Everyone thinks she is a mute. I would think it myself if I had not heard her chirping with the birds the other day. She was singing to them and imitating the way you whistle. Then clear as day, she recited something—not, the heavens forbid, to me or your father, but to the horse and then the cow. But when I ask her a question, she looks to the ground and shrugs. I am at the end of my patience, and know not what to do with her."

Aonghus looked at his mother empathetically. Her family was all important to her, and to be at a loss in relating to one of her children must frustrate her.

He opened his mouth to offer her some words of consolation, but was again distracted by Kordelina curling her toes against the floor. Holding out her boots to him, she giggled infectiously as he helped her pull them on.

"Bring me your comb and the thong for your hair," he said, patting her on the back as she ran to her room. He turned his attention back to his mother.

"She will talk when she is ready," he offered, trying to soothe her.

Koven, who had been silently eating his breakfast, looked up as Kordelina appeared at the table holding a comb in her clenched fist. "She is asking to come along," he said to Aonghus.

Aonghus carefully combed the tangles from her hair. He then pulled it back and tied it tightly with a string of leather. As he looked at Kordelina's small shoulders and sturdy body, he could not help but love her complete adoration of him.

"I can take her if she is not needed here. We are only going to the other side of the lake to scout boar. It would be no trouble," he replied, putting on her fur-lined vest and clasping the plain metal broach at the neck.

"Not today," Enda interjected, emphatically. "The women are making festival garments. It is sewing for her. She cannot always follow you about like the family pet. What kind of wife will she make some poor man if she does not even know the first thing about being a girl?"

She looked at Kordelina sharply. "That is what you are—a girl—not a warrior like your brother, or a horse like Osin. You are simply a little girl who cannot keep from pretending she is another one of god's creatures."

Kordelina wilted as if she had been doused with cold water. Clutching the sides of Aonghus' vest, she stared at him with pleading eyes.

"I cannot take you," he told the wounded little girl, placing both hands on her shoulders, "but if you get all of your chores finished, and do what Mother asks, we can go for a ride before sunset."

Tears welled in her eyes as she bowed her head pitifully.

Enda rolled her eyes, and swiftly took Kordelina from his arms. "I will not have that. You are not going to make your brother feel guilty for not taking you with him."

For an instant, Kordelina was perfectly still. Then her tiny brow furrowed, and distending her bottom lip unattractively, her face darkened. It grew redder and redder until it was at its boiling point, and she began to wail at the top of her lungs.

She shoved her mother away with all her might, wiggled out of her arms, and ran back to Aonghus. The boy, like his father, was staring open-mouthed at the child's display of temper.

"Have you ever seen such a banshee? She pushes my patience to the limit," Enda declared in frustration. "Father, take her out of my sight. If I lay a finger on her now, it would only be to end her short life this very second."

The woman stooped down, eye level with Kordelina, and looked sternly into her eyes. "It would be death by strangulation for you, my little mute," she said, pointing her index finger at her and shaking it to emphasize her displeasure.

The farmer laughed under his breath at his wife. Enda was incapable of harming a soul, especially one of her own children. Placing his hand over his mouth to mask his expression, he reached for Kordelina. Determined not to be caught, she dropped to the ground and scurried beneath the table.

Koven looked at Aonghus with a blank expression. He lifted his brows in mock surprise as they both burst into laughter, then the two turned to hide their humor from a frustrated Enda.

"Now there, I will not have the two of you making light of this. The child has no respect for her elders and encouraging her to act like a wild, a wild —," Enda threw up her hands in despair as she tried to think of a word, "heaven knows what—does not help her in the least!"

Still struggling with silly grins, father and son remained silent.

"Are either one of you listening to me?"

"Yes," Aonghus said, sheepishly suppressing his desire to laugh again. He dutifully got down on one knee, and looked beneath the table. He found Kordelina covering her head with her forearms, vainly trying to hide herself.

"Come out now," he coaxed, extending his hand to her.

Kordelina trustingly placed her hand in his, and holding it tightly, crawled out into the open. Without acknowledging her parents, she obediently walked alongside him as he led her back to her room.

Aonghus smoothed the blankets of her cot and fluffed her pillow. He unclasped her vest, pulled off her boots, then set her down, covering her up to her neck with furs. Kordelina immediately sat back up and pushed them away.

"Please," she said clearly, staring at him with an unwavering gaze.

Aonghus smiled submissively, as if to tell her it was out of his control.

"I cannot today," he said, in a resigned tone, and again took her hand. "But I will bring you something, a surprise to make up for it."

Kordelina's eyes lit up, and she nodded excitedly. She was easily pleased by anything he did.

"Try not to be a bother to Mother. Do as she says, and at least pretend you like it. You can make it a game of make-believe; the time will pass much faster," he said, kissing her on the forehead. "You will try, will you not?"

The girl nodded. She instantly slammed her torso down on the bed and shut her eyes tightly, opening them only once to watch Aonghus leave the room. Before closing the wicker partition, he looked back at her, noticing her bright eyes abruptly shut again to please him.

Not wanting to be left behind, Aonghus did not pass Bracorina's on his way to Solomon's estate. He knew she would be awake by this time, but since they were still getting to know one other, informal visits were not yet appropriate.

Solomon had been surprised when he had first expressed an interest in meeting the girl. It was true that there were prettier girls his age, but they did not have the social standing that Bracorina was destined to inherit. Since Pwyll was Donnach's only surviving son, he had received his father's wealth in its entirety upon his passing. With Bracorina as the second in line behind her brother, Diarmudd, she would be a principle beneficiary when she married. Aonghus reasoned that his guaranteed position of rule, merged with her wealth, would result in a dynasty.

It had already been discussed between Pwyll, Solomon, and Koven, who was more than thrilled at the prospect of his son being promised to the daughter of the richest land baron in the territory. But up to this point, the only contact Aonghus had had with the girl was dinners chaperoned by her father and Solomon.

The etiquette of choosing a mate seemed silly to him. Solomon found the process of courtship ridiculous, and could not understand why Aonghus was perplexed by it. Lately, Solomon found everything absurd. His disassociation from the tribe was becoming more pronounced, and aside from the clan's meetings in the court, little was seen of him.

At first, Aonghus had reasoned that it was a result of losing his family. Even Saturnalia had explained that sometimes it took many years for one to release such a great amount of sorrow. Therefore, considering Solomon had lost so many loved ones, Aonghus deduced that he should be afforded a lengthy grieving time. However, the Chieftain's mourning had become a series of bad events that went from complete isolation, to drunkenness, to a droll relationship with an inferior woman, and back again. This disheartening cycle had occurred at least a dozen times since he had taken power. Lately, his excess was women. He was obsessed with them, and was never alone. Nights were filled with grunting and giggling from his chamber, and afterward, he slept through the mornings. Aonghus had to take care of any work that had to be done before midday. That included training the horses, surveying the crops, and tending to the land of other clients for whom Solomon was still an overseer. He hated the way Solomon took him for granted, knowing that Aonghus would never think of neglecting his duty. And to witness the way Solomon went about baiting his women into relationships was beneath him.

The Chieftain would use his lofty position to seduce mostly farm women, but there were also a few aristocrats who were equally affected by his stature. He would tell them of his lonely life as a bachelor and his desire to find a woman to help share the burden of his leadership. He would have them move in, and they'd live quite lustily until the novelty wore off and he became disinterested. Then he would recite to them his usual soliloquy of how he was part Christian, and according to his belief, each man had only one wife in the eyes of God. Having already been married to Deireadh, he was not able, no matter how much he wished it, to take another.

The reactions of the women were predictable. They would weep, and then for some reason unknown to Aonghus, each would have a private talk with him. When they had exhausted their drama, they would ultimately leave. Solomon would become a hermit for awhile, then a drunk, then he would find another woman to distract him, and it would start all over again.

It pained Aonghus to see the way his master acted. It pained him even more when he would see the way he looked at Saturnalia during one of their now occasional meetings. His eyes would soften, and he would stare at her as if she were not real. Saturnalia treated him with tenderness, as though every gesture, every word spoken was especially for him. She was unaffected by his escapades.

Approaching the Chieftain's estate, Aonghus saw a cloister of warriors and their apprentices. The absence of his master was immediately evident. If he did not arrive soon, Aonghus hoped he'd be allowed to go with Berrig and Diarmudd. He had done it many times of late, and Berrig was accustomed to the added responsibility. He did his best to share his time equally when the boys were being schooled or hunting, but his responsibility was first to his own apprentice, not Solomon's. Although Aonghus appreciated his efforts, his anointing was not far off, and he was not amused by Solomon's lack of interest.

Lifting his hand to wave to them, he felt a rope drop around his midriff. It constricted his breath with one jerk, and in an instant, he found himself face down on the ground. Realizing that the boy was no longer on his back, Osin stopped ahead, and looked casually back at him.

Feeling a tug on the rope, Aonghus involuntarily rolled over, the blue sky spinning above him from his lack of breath.

"Diarmudd," he heard someone call from the tree tops, "that knot really does slip tightly just the way you said."

From the sound of the voice, Aonghus did not have to be told who it was. Then he heard Diarmudd come next to him on horseback, and saw his perturbed face staring down at him.

"You are late," he stated.

"Maybe Bracorina could not wait until Beltaine," came the teasing voice of the boy in the trees, as he jumped to the ground.

He stood over Aonghus, amused at the success of his mock ambush. Gritting his teeth, Aonghus scowled back at him as he loosened the rope and stood up. He detested this boy. He was from the Aedui tribe that occupied a continent territory southeast of their island. This tribe had originally opposed Rome, but because of inter-tribal war, had eventually aligned with Caesar to reassume their position of power. This young aristocrat, once the son of a chieftain, had escaped with a warrior named Turg. The two had been adopted by their tribe, and he was known by the name Conn.

Conn was tall and slender with fair hair and dark eyes. He had a careless way about him that unnerved Aonghus. He treated his warrior's duties, whether in combat or spiritual instruction, with nothing less than irreverence. More than once, he had tried to provoke Aonghus to fight, and Aonghus knew it was because he held an elite place as Solomon's foster. He supposed it was a bit out of jealousy that Conn toyed with him; having once been an aristocrat himself, he knew that Aonghus' position made it impossible for him to vie for future rule himself.

Throwing the rope back at Conn, Aonghus walked directly over to Osin and remounted. His breathing had steadied by the time he reached the group of warriors, and he went immediately to Berrig.

"Where is Solomon?" he asked, irked.

Berrig grinned. "I do not think he will be joining us today. He has other things on his mind."

Aonghus frowned and looked at the house. All of the shutters were open except for the bedroom. "I do not think his mind has anything to do with it," Aonghus grumbled in disgust.

CHAPTER TWO

oven stood at the window looking out at Kordelina. She was sitting on the post at the entrance of the property, waiting patiently for Aonghus. She had been the terror of a child she was that day, having taunted Enda to the point of tears by midmorning. To see her now, looking expectantly up the road, hands folded in front of her and two hunting dogs dozing under her feet, one would never imagine that such an angelic vision could be such a nightmare.

"What are you looking at, Father?" Enda asked, wiping the flour from her hands. "Is that corn we gave the pigs too moldy for them to eat?"

Koven chuckled. "Kordelina did not seem to mind it."

"Kordelina? Is she out there?" Enda fumed. "I put her in her room."

"She escaped."

Enda glanced out the window, unamused. "I am going to get her," she stated, starting for the door.

Koven grabbed her arm and stopped her. "I do not wish to wrestle with her again by trying to haul her back in here."

"She needs a good beating," his wife declared.

Koven shook his head. "She has had two today already. Maybe Aonghus will forget about her, and she will wait there for him the rest of the night."

Enda gave a half smile. "It would be quieter. But what are we going to do with her? With her behavior, no one will take her as a foster."

"Do not worry," he soothed, putting his arms around her plump body. "Solomon spoke with Pwyll. He has agreed that his servants should instruct her. It will be good for you to have something to keep her occupied."

Relief came over the woman. "I always wanted a daughter, but now I am hoping that our next child will be a son," she offered.

"Perhaps," he said, and looking down to her belly. "Are you sure?"

She pressed her lips to his, then stared into his eyes. "What woman does not know the moment a spirit comes into her womb?"

Looking back out the window, they saw Aonghus ride up. Without getting down, he helped Kordelina onto the saddle and started for the woods.

"He is the only one to whom she is devoted," Enda said, resting the side of her face against her husband's chest.

Koven's swollen hand purred over her fine brown hair.

"Maybe we should call her Locwn," he jested.

———

Kordelina made a game out of shifting her weight with the movement of Osin's haunches and balancing herself. Since he was used to it, Aonghus did not comment, and would actually have been surprised if she had not swayed drunkenly from side to side and laughed about it.

It was starting to get dark, and tired from the day-long trek, he had only planned on riding a short distance to satisfy his promise. His thighs ached from the saddle and the dried sweat on his body made him feel dirty and irritable.

He deliberately took a circular path that led nowhere, but ended up back where they started. When they stopped once again in front of the farm, Kordelina looked at him quizzically and stayed firmly in her place.

"It is time to go home," he stated.

Kordelina looked down and shook her head.

"It is almost night," he argued. "I am too tired to play."

"Where is my surprise?" she asked flatly.

An immediate surge of irritation rose in him as he remembered that he had not brought anything for her. "Were you good?" he countered.

Kordelina did not move.

"Well, were you?" he asked again.

The little girl shook her head "no."

"Then I cannot give it to you," he went on, relieved.

"If you take me swimming, I promise to be good tomorrow," she bargained, looking up at him with innocent eyes. Aonghus sighed with fatigue.

"Why do you do this?" he questioned. "Why do you make promises, then break them? Do you not know it is the worst thing you could do? You promised to be good for Mother, and you were not. Then you promise me you will be good tomorrow if I take you swimming, but you know that you will not be. Do you not realize that a broken promise is the most serious offense? The only thing a person has in all of this world is his word. If he goes back on it every time it is convenient, it will be worth nothing. Then the gods will know it, and they will consider him worth nothing, too. Why, if I broke my promises as often as you do, I should be murdered for being such a fool."

His sister's eyes widened. "I do not wish you dead," she responded sincerely.

Aonghus huffed and rolled his eyes. "You did not understand anything I said, did you?"

Kordelina nodded once.

"What part?" he asked, hoping his speech had amounted to something.

"You said if you ever broke your promise, you should be murdered for it," she answered clearly.

"No," he barked. "I said that one's word is all that the gods honor, and you should be mindful of that."

"All right," she muttered. "Can we go swimming?"

"Will you be good tomorrow?"

"I do not know if I can," she replied, resting her forehead against his arm to hide her face.

Touched by her sudden candor, he patted the top of her head. "Well, I guess that is a little better. At least you did not say you would, then not do it."

"Maybe tomorrow I will, and—," she began.

"— and maybe you will not," he finished, and started for the lake.

As they traveled across the verdant slopes toward the water, he could not stop his mind from drifting to Bracorina. While the open sexual frolicking was part of the celebration, he felt a little embarrassed by it. Even though he always knew his first taste of a woman would be there, he felt more self-conscious than enthusiastic about the encounter. He was certain Bracorina was a virgin, too, at least Diarmudd had laughingly told him so. He had joked about the pristine manners of his sister, and had said that she found even urinating daily an imposition. He had gone as far as to bet Aonghus his saddle that he could not get her to spread her legs without a guarantee of marriage.

Aonghus dreaded the thought of two so inexperienced coming together for the first time at such a large gathering. He supposed he should have taken the cue from Solomon and indulged himself before this. But every time the opportunity had arisen, he felt strange and isolated, almost as though he found his vulnerability shameful. He prayed he would not be a disappointment at Beltaine. There were always the ale and herbs to help peak his urges—and the dancing, how he loved the dancing and the lusty feelings it evoked in him.

Going out of his way, he followed a hoof-trodden path over a knoll to look down on a herd of horses grazing. Occasionally, one of the foals would gallop around the entire herd, causing the rest of the babies to follow. It was then that the dark bay stallion would intercede, and with one aggravated, guttural snort, the perpetrator was silenced, and would slink back to his mother's side.

Kordelina let out a contented breath, putting her arms around him from behind, squeezing him as tightly as she could.

"What?" Aonghus asked. "You like this, do you not?"

She placed the side of her face against his back, and kissed it.

"Do you see that stallion?" he said, pointing to the huge stud standing in the center of the herd.

The muscular horse was facing them. His ears pricked up and nostrils flared as he tried to discern the reason for the children's presence.

"He is going to be mine someday," he declared.

Kordelina's mouth dropped, and she stared at her brother awe-struck.

"I will catch him after I have been anointed," he explained. "Then the power of the gods will be on my side, and he will become my companion."

"I will help," she volunteered.

"Help with what?"

"Help you catch him," she answered seriously. "I can talk to horses."

"You can? Then let me hear you talk to him," he humored her.

Kordelina stared at the horse resolutely, and taking in a gulp of air, whinnied as long as her breath held out. Then she licked her lips and whinnied some more until the stallion nickered back and even walked a few steps toward them.

Aonghus laughed delightedly, and joined her. But the moment he let out the sound, the stud stopped. Raising his tail straight up into the air, he swirled around the herd at a canter until he had jostled them from their meal. He darted forward and Kordelina chirped to him as he rose up on two legs, then bolted away with all his mares and foals forming a string behind him.

"What happened?" Aonghus asked, disappointed.

His sister shrugged.

"You said you could talk to him; what did he say?"

Kordelina chewed her lip, thought a moment, and shrugged again.

Thoroughly disenchanted, Aonghus directed Osin back the way they had come. "It is too late for swimming," he complained. "I am hungry."

On their way home, they passed Saturnalia's cottage. Even if one didn't know she was a sorceress, the appearance of her dwelling would give it away. It was made of shiny limestone, and the rooms were oval-shaped, not square, like the rest of the tribal lodgings. It was surrounded by a low stone wall with a wooden gate ornamented with bushels of herbs, animal bones, bronze skulls, and beads. Colorful swatches of material were braided together to make a rope from which they were hung. They were meant to be an open invitation to the spirits, and were taken as a sign that they would be welcome in her home. To humans, it was a signal not to harm the one who resided inside, lest the wrath of the Otherworld be brought upon them.

Saturnalia sat with her back to an oak. The huge moss-covered tree was draped with mistletoe, and was a commanding presence in the center of her courtyard. She was embroidering a cloak, and at the sight of Aonghus and Kordelina, motioned to them to come up.

Aonghus complied, and pointing Osin toward the cottage, he felt Kordelina stiffen. "It is all right," he reassured, "she will not hurt you."

He knew Kordelina had always been afraid of Saturnalia, but never understood why. Every time the sorceress visited the family farm, Enda had reported that the child would make a point of staying in her room. It was odd behavior for her, since she was normally gregarious and not easily intimidated. The only thing Aonghus could determine was that she had witnessed the priestess overseeing holy rites, and had been traumatized by the various blood sacrifices she had performed. It confounded him why they should upset his sister. It was, after all, part of their religion, and it was something every child witnessed and accepted from a very early age. But he had seen the way Kordelina would weep during a sacrifice, and how she would try in every way possible not to attend the rituals.

Helping her off Osin's back, Aonghus led her by the hand into the yard. He was amused at the starry expression in her eyes as she fixed them on Saturnalia's elaborate flower and herb garden. She went straight to the rosebushes, and before she had even paid her respects to the priestess, picked one.

Putting it to her nose, she inhaled it, then stroked her face with its velvety petals and giggled to herself.

"Kordelina, you are being rude," Aonghus admonished.

The child's laughter abruptly ceased, and she looked at him with a blank expression as she shoved the flower into her pocket. Then she looked at Saturnalia and gave her version of a bow which was, in reality, a quick forward jerk of her torso.

Amused by the child's attempt to be well-mannered, Saturnalia picked another rose, and getting down on one knee, held it out to her. "Hello, Kordelina," she said, extending the flower. "Would you be my friend?"

Tilting her head to the side, Kordelina assessed the priestess. She looked at Aonghus, then up at the sky a moment, before going forward to take it. She repeated the process of smelling it and touching it to her face before stuffing it into her pocket with the other one.

Satisfied that the first inklings of a rapport were present, Saturnalia stood and walked into her cottage. When she emerged, it was with a pitcher of milk and a cup of honey set on a platter beside a mound of fresh cakes. Aonghus licked his lips at the sight of them, and following Saturnalia like two pups, the children took their places on either side of her beneath the oak tree.

"Tell me what you have done since I have seen you last," the priestess said to Aonghus as she mixed the honey with the milk, and offered it to him.

He took a short drink, then held it for Kordelina, who gulped it seemingly without end. Feeling a little embarrassed by her lack of restraint, Aonghus quickly nudged her to stop.

"I went with Berrig and some of the other boys to scout boar today," he answered politely.

"Ah, that must have been very successful. I understand Solomon knows that terrain quite well," she said, as she held out a cake in each hand.

Aonghus immediately took his, but Kordelina waited a cautious moment. She looked at the cake, then at Saturnalia, then back at the cake before succumbing to the temptation. Then she bit into it, and with parts of it pasted to her teeth, smiled delightedly at Saturnalia.

"Solomon was not there," Aonghus replied. "Berrig said he had something else to do. But he always has something else to do."

Sensing his disillusionment, Saturnalia lightly ran her hand over his reddish-brown hair to console him.

"I feel that you wish to be Solomon's ward no longer," she said thoughtfully. "But you think you would be betraying your master, and feel you are indebted to him for what he has given you so far. You also are afraid that if you leave his fosterage you will no longer have the affluence of being the Chieftain's apprentice."

Aonghus stopped chewing and looked guiltily down. "Yes," he said softly.

"Do you really wish to leave him?" she asked, picking up the milk this time and helping Kordelina drink.

She took a sip, and sat back with eyes gleaming at Saturnalia's indulgence of her. Wanting to show her appreciation somehow, the little girl held out what was left of her cake.

Saturnalia took it and smiled sweetly before eating. It was only a small step in the relationship she wanted to establish with her, but she found it pleasing enough.

"I do not wish to leave him at all," Aonghus answered, oblivious to the exchange. "I suppose I wish for him to be different. I wish him to be like he used to be, and act like he still cared. I still love him no matter how foolish he has been, but I do not think he feels the same about me. I think maybe I have disappointed him somehow."

Saturnalia felt her heart ache at the boy's confession. He was a complicated one, tangled up by his own thoughts of duty and need for approval.

"Then you must tell him that," she counseled. "It does Solomon no good for you to make excuses for him. Being honest is the greatest testimony of love one can show, and if you think he is neglecting his duties, you should speak with him about it. But do it out of love, for we are all guilty of such things at some point. To afford him caring, not wrath, is a much better thing."

"I understand," he responded seriously.

There was a lull in the conversation. While Aonghus considered her advice, Saturnalia sat staring at a happily munching Kordelina, trying to reach her on an intuitive level.

Think the words, Kordelina, she mentally told her. *You know how to think the words. Think them, and I will understand.*

She imagined an outline of light around the girl's body. It started at her head and completely encompassed her. Envisioning small luminous rays criss-crossing through her, the sorceress attempted to define Kordelina's etheric self.

Speak to me with your thoughts, she said over and over. *You have the power to speak to me with your thoughts.*

For no apparent reason, Kordelina abruptly stood. She looked at Saturnalia irritably, then down at Aonghus. Grabbing a cake from the platter, she exited the yard, much to the distress of her brother.

"Forgive her rudeness," he said apologetically as he hurried after her. "She does not seem to know what she is supposed to do."

Saturnalia walked a few steps to the wall. Sitting on the edge, she glanced down and saw Kordelina descending the knoll, deep in thought.

"Do not apologize," she countered. "She knows more than she realizes."

CHAPTER THREE

onghus did not return to Solomon's that evening. Instead he had a modest supper of boiled pork, corn mash, and bread with his family. It was followed by a heartfelt talk with Koven in which he conveyed his dilemma concerning the Chieftain, and asked if he could stay with them until he found a resolution. Of course, both Enda and Koven were thrilled to have their son remain there for as long as he wished, but it was nothing compared to Kordelina's jubilation.

When she heard her brother would be spending some time there, she immediately took him into her chamber and made up her bed for him to sleep in. Not wanting to take it away from her, he politely declined and said he would sleep by the fire. Insulted that he had refused her generosity, she stomped her feet on the floor and threw herself on the bed. Covering her face with her arms, she proceeded to ignore him until he acquiesced. At that point, she shot up, darted outside, and returned with a fuzzy baby chick in her hand as a gift.

When it was her bedtime, Kordelina audaciously kicked her brothers out of the best spot by the fire and went to sleep. Unfortunately for Aonghus, halfway through the night she snuggled next to him with the cat and the chick, and remained there until first light.

Purposely neglecting his apprentice duties, the boy spent the morning helping Koven with the farm chores. He remembered the routine clearly, and with the help of his two brothers, Cunnedag and Erc, what used to take an entire day was over by lunch.

With Aonghus' presence, Kordelina was nothing less than perfect. She followed him about, helping with meager tasks like opening and closing the gate for him and carrying his tools. Wanting to take advantage of her sudden change of behavior, Enda packed them a satchel of food, and told them they could go to the lake until dinner. Taking his practice spears, Aonghus headed for a meadow of tall goldenrod first, fully confident that he could get Kordelina to act as a moving target for him to practice against.

Outfitting her with his cloak tied to the end of a stick, he instructed her to covertly move through the field and raise the target at any time. He, in turn, would stalk her and try to hit it.

Kordelina took great sport in crawling through the shrubbery and popping the object up in different places. She soon found that her brother was a very good marksman. Each time he hit the target, she would laugh and he would have to demand her to pay better attention. When they tired of the exercise, they went swimming, and gorged themselves with wild berries. Then with full bellies, they napped in the sunshine.

When they returned late in the afternoon, Aonghus was not surprised to see one of Solomon's horses tied in front of the house. It irritated Aonghus that he made a point of using a different horse every day, and had no one special animal to serve him. He thought it was a reflection of the attitude he had toward women. But since Aonghus now solely trained the horses, he found it a personal affront.

The two children were barely on the property when the door opened, and the Chieftain indecorously started up the road to meet them. Aonghus could tell by his flushed complexion and glassy eyes that he had been drinking, and the unnatural length of his stride showed the extent of his rage.

Coming beside them, he pulled Aonghus off Osin, and slammed the back of his hand into his face so hard he was instantly sprawled on the ground. Dazed, Aonghus' nose and mouth began spurting blood. Kordelina ran to lie on top of him, keeping him from being hit again. Taking her by the nape of the neck, Solomon lifted her off him and tossed her aside. Then with one of his huge hands, he took hold of Aonghus' arm, and jerked him to his feet.

The two stood a few minutes staring at each other, both equally fearful in their fury. Then acting as if he had no other choice, Aonghus fired a fist squarely at Solomon's nose. The blood came gushing out, covering his mouth and beard, but much to Aonghus' surprise, he made no effort to retaliate. He only looked at Aonghus with wounded astonishment.

"You failed to do your duties today," he finally said, dumbfounded.

"And you have failed to do yours every day since I have known you," Aonghus retorted.

A look of genuine confusion flashed across Solomon's face. "What are you saying? I have given you every possible chance to rise out of the squalor you were born to, and the one day I rightfully discipline you for your neglect, you assault me!" he declared, flabbergasted.

Aonghus' blue eyes iced over, and he moved forward so there was no space between them. Afraid that he would be struck again, Kordelina wedged herself in the middle of them and elbowed Solomon in the stomach.

"Be off with you!" the Chieftain growled, taking her by the hair and pushing her away.

"Do not do that to her," Aonghus hollered. "It is obvious that you detest her, and I am tired of that as well!"

"That," Solomon argued, pointing a finger in the boy's chest, "is none of your business."

Aonghus took Kordelina in his arms. The little girl's face was red, and she was puffing, but she was definitely not crying. Instead, she was scowling at Solomon in the very same manner in which he was scowling at her.

"It is," Aonghus insisted. "You look at her the way you looked at Laden. I am not asking that you love her, but you do not have to make such a point of despising her either."

Solomon stood there appearing as though his foster's words were draining him. He rubbed his eyes as if trying to clear his vision, then looked at him again. In all the years that Aonghus had been with him, he had never opposed him so blatantly.

"What in the name of the god's of all creation, is this about?" he demanded, in a thundering voice.

Aonghus ran his tongue over his lips. "It is about you," he said, making a sour face at the putrid taste of it. "It is about the fact that you are an imposter who claims to be a Chieftain but is really only a weak, self-indulgent fraud who hides behind his title and his shallow women. You do not care about me, so why should I care about doing my duty to you? I know you did not want me with you from the very start, but I was there, and I did not fail you. But you have failed me with each sunset since the King died. You cry about the imposition of leadership, but you do not lead. You only pretend to lead. Saturnalia has the power in this tribe and she is the only one worthy to claim the rites of the heavens or the earth, not you. I am leaving you now, and I do not care if I am never anointed because I can harbor this dishonesty no longer."

Solomon suddenly appeared sober, even remorseful, at Aonghus' words. Wiping his bloody nose on his shoulder, he turned to walk away from him, then abruptly came back.

"Saturnalia?" he questioned. "Did she put you up to this?"

Aonghus shook his head. "No. She only advised me to be honest with you, and to inform you in a loving way of the fool you have been. But I could not be loving about it. You did not give me the chance to be loving about it."

The Chieftain's face took on a vengeful expression. "Then I will pursue this with her."

Climbing determinedly atop his horse, he spurred and whipped the animal with his crop, and headed toward Saturnalia's cottage.

———

Flinging the door open, he entered the sorceress' home. He found her seated by the fire, a portrait of contented loveliness. Beside her sat two goblets of wine, and Solomon knew she was not surprised by his visit.

"Close the door, please," she said, in an unaffected tone.

Rendered suddenly passive, the Chieftain complied, then slowly made his way to the center of the room. Saturnalia looked at him with equanimity, and waited for him to speak. When he did not, she held out the goblet.

"Will you sit with me?" she asked. "It has been a long time since we have sat and enjoyed good wine and familiar company."

Her composure at his obviously angered condition made him want to shake her. "Are you crazy?" he growled. "You want me to sit with you and drink wine when you have undermined me? When you have made me out to be a fool to my own apprentice?"

Saturnalia laughed. "If Aonghus views you as a buffoon, I am sure it is from your own actions, not anything I have said."

"Always the smug one!" he exploded. "Saturnalia, the Queen of Ice."

"Solomon, let us not come to this," she reasoned evenly. "Let us not shred what is left of our common bond."

"Do not even start that, Priestess," he shot back, before she had finished her sentence. "Do not heap upon me the reasons that I should still care. They were not in your head when —"

"When I killed her?" she retorted. "I will say it again. When I killed her. When I took my knife and cut open the evil woman you wish to think of as a martyr. Do not fool yourself. Deep inside you know what she was; that is what makes you bitter. You know you were merely a convenience for her, and that is the unkindest thing of all because a part of you loved her very much. Do you think I do not know that?"

Solomon raised his voice, "Silence! I have heard enough of your lecture."

"My lecture, as you call it, is the one thing that I have spared you too long," she rebuked, noticeably upset by his remark. "I have let you squander yourself and become a whore to self-pity. If Aonghus and I had not covered for your duties, your slothfulness would have come to light long ago."

"Aonghus, what can you possibly know about my relationship with him?" he interrogated.

The sorceress rose to her feet, and stood before him. She could smell the alcohol on his breath, but she could also detect the perfumed oil of a woman.

"I know what he told me," she answered. "He said that you have no interest in him any longer, and he thinks it is his fault. I told him to speak with you about it when he could do it in a loving way. But from the look of you, I guess that you could not let that happen."

The Chieftain averted his eyes. She was too close to him, and his peaked senses could barely tolerate it. He loved her in a way he could not endure—a love he had never felt before. Unlike other women, she did not need him; her interest in him was voluntary and set apart from ordinary relationships of men and women. Because of this, her beauty and self-determination, he quite simply adored her. That was the most difficult thing of all. It was not what she had done to Deireadh, not really. He had only used the incident as an excuse to alienate himself from someone who left him defenseless.

"How do you know it was me?" he retorted.

Saturnalia's lips curled, and she raised one brow. "Honestly, Solomon, do you expect me to believe it was that sensitive little boy who idolizes you?"

"Idolizes me? He is more concerned with the demon child," he discounted. "Besides, I do not put much stock in his judgment. Do you know that of all the maids in this tribe, he wishes to be promised to Bracorina? Why her? She has got to be the ugliest thing without tusks or horns."

Saturnalia could not hide a slight smile at his analogy. "Perhaps he would like a woman of substance, if you can appreciate that."

Solomon cocked his head to one side, taking personal offense at the reference to his promiscuity. "Well, that does not mean she has to be ugly."

He walked toward the goblets, wanting to avoid any further questioning. Grabbing one, Solomon sat where he could look at her. He did not drink, but made a clicking sound with his tongue as he eyed her shrewdly.

"Why do you not get married, Saturnalia?" he questioned. "Maybe a few years pregnant will give you something else to do."

Saturnalia seethed. "Like what, watching you spread the legs of every other man's wife? The only reason you do not take one yourself is because you fear yourself a failure. All of these empty-headed distractions whose company you keep are just too stupid to realize it. You could not handle a real woman, an equal, because you are too afraid."

"At least we still have that in common," he snapped.

Saturnalia glanced at him slyly. "You still know how to be cruel."

Without waiting for a response, she went to him. Taking the cup from his hand, she straddled his lap, and not averting her eyes, took a long drink. Solomon shifted uncomfortably, but said nothing. Taking another gulp, she bent her head forward, and putting her lips to his, she let the wine flow into his mouth. Unable to keep from swallowing, he drank it, then jerked his head away.

"Why must you always reduce our disagreements to this?" he asked.

"Why must you?" she rebutted, slowly pushing her gown off her shoulders.

His reaction was unusually naive, and she found secret delight in being able to disarm him in this way.

"This is not always the solution," he said hesitantly.

Saturnalia tilted the cup, and let a few drops of wine fall onto her cleavage. "Strange to hear those words coming from such a one as you," she replied, as he licked the liquid off her cleavage and began kissing her neck.

"Why?" he replied, gathering her in his arms. "One of us was going to say it, eventually." Solomon laid Saturnalia down on her bed and buried his face in her lambent hair.

———

At that moment, across the Menai Strait on the coast of North Wales, Flavius, a Roman commander, looked across the sea at the vague outline of a tiny uprising of land. Clenching his teeth, he finished writing the last of his communication to his General, Suetonius. They had taken Deva from the Celts, and Anglesey was at last in sight.

ChAPTER FOUR

he next week was like an exorcism for Solomon as he made love to Saturnalia amid confessions, lamentations, and often humorous descriptions of his own ineptitudes. The two were drunk with each other, making love in every conceivable place and position in Saturnalia's cottage. And somewhere between the sweat and the tears, she found time to indulge his palate with elaborate dishes, singing to him and reciting prose she had composed and tucked away in her memory.

Solomon did not give a thought to his neglected estate and clientele. He reasoned that somehow they would take care of themselves during this euphoric period. If anyone did question him about his absence, he would tell them he was summoned by the spirits to take a vision quest, and that it had healed him of his avarice.

But the long, sensual days of love and nakedness came to a sudden halt one afternoon when a knock on the door revealed a travel-worn Jara. She entered Saturnalia's cottage with the gait of a monarch, and was more than a little perturbed to find Solomon lounging, uncovered, in front of the fire with Saturnalia cuddled in his arms.

At the sight of her, Solomon grinned arrogantly, and held out one hand. "Jara, you are my favorite," he flippantly declared. "Please come and join us."

The Druidess bristled and immediately poured herself some ale. "I have come here with others. They are outside waiting," she retorted sharply.

"Well, they can join us too," he added.

"You pompous idiot," she exhorted. "It never ceases to amaze me the depth to which you will sink."

Solomon could not stop himself from laughing out loud, "Or the height to which I can rise?"

Remaining silent, Saturnalia put on her robe. She moved around Jara, gathering her things but not speaking, and Solomon could tell by her quick movements and the lack of sparkle in her eyes that she was irked by the older woman's presence.

"Why have you come so early?" she finally inquired.

"Because of the anointing," the older one answered.

"That is not for a fortnight," Saturnalia said.

Jara sipped the ale slowly. "It does not matter. Travel is dangerous now, and we had to leave far ahead of time to be sure that we could cross the channel safely. I have been on the continent for quite some time, and the Roman campaign has hindered our journey."

"How is Elenai?" Saturnalia asked, handing Solomon his clothing.

"The last thing I heard was that your wet nurse had died in her sleep," she answered coldly.

The Sorceress' eyes misted. "Are you sure?"

"Quite," Jara dismissed, helping herself to some cheese. "We will remain through Beltaine."

"There is no need. I am perfectly able to oversee the celebration," Saturnalia said sharply. She knew Jara was there for a specific reason, and the longer she stayed, the more she would try to take control away from her. The two had been engaged in a power struggle from the very moment she came to this tribe.

The older one gave Saturnalia a patronizing smile. "Of course, my dear. But I must remind you that you are not a Druidess."

"Of course," she answered, forcing the same smile as Jara. "You may make yourselves comfortable here, but as for me, I will take residence with the Chieftain."

Solomon had barely finished lacing his boots when Saturnalia started out the door and down the knoll. He ran after her.

The fresh air and sunlight was intoxicating after being inside for half a week, and coming up behind her, he lifted her in his arms and kissed her. Then he set her down and the two walked hand in hand, counting the steps back to his home.

By the time they strolled through the gate of his manor, they had their arms around each other, and Solomon was vainly trying to recite one of her poems back to her. He had been doing very well until he fixed his eyes on Kordelina, who was in the chicken coop tossing out handfuls of grain. Completely losing his train of thought, he released Saturnalia and started straight for Kordelina.

The little girl was smiling at the chickens milling around her feet. Every so often, she would purposely throw the grain to one side or the other and laugh at how the fowls would cluck and move away from her in great masses.

As Solomon entered the livestock area, Aonghus stepped in front of him, halting his stride. His smooth face and cool blue eyes had a determined expression, warning Solomon not to start any more trouble.

"She has been helping me take care of the chores while you have been gone," he said firmly.

"The Chieftain's eyes darted in the direction of the girl, who had abruptly ceased her humming and was staring at him warily. Tense, he flinched when he felt Saturnalia softly take him by the elbow.

"Send her home now," he ordered, and walked into the house.

"Why do you insist on doing this?" she asked him as he slammed the door shut, and immediately started undressing her.

"Because I love you," he said, kissing the crest on one bare shoulder.

Saturnalia pushed him away, and looked pointedly into his eyes.

"You know that is not what I mean. I am talking about the girl child. You should see the look on your face every time she is near. Why do you hate her so?"

Solomon turned and went to the window. Here it was, he thought, the end of their blissful encounter, and it was all because of that rancorous girl. "I cannot explain it to you," he said softly. "I look at her and the blood runs cold inside of me. I do not know if she reminds me of my error, or Deireadh's, or both. But when I am near her, I feel I am being haunted by my own inequities. Something inside me says that she is not my child, but Laden's."

"Does it matter now?" Saturnalia asked, going to him.

He turned, and taking her by the shoulders, looked seriously into her eyes. "Yes, it does. I know not why, but it does."

She ran both hands through his hair, brushing it away from his face. "Maybe if you got to know her, that would change," she suggested.

Solomon shook his head. "I do not think anyone can get to know her."

The sorceress glanced out at the two children. "Aonghus seems to know her rather well," Saturnalia offered, turning her attention back to Solomon.

"Yes, but look at him," he rebutted. "He has been with me for almost eight cycles, and I barely even know him myself. They are well suited for each other."

Saturnalia walked to his bed, stretched out, and Solomon followed, lying beside her. He put his face in the curve of her neck as she scratched his back.

"That is not his error," she admonished. "It has been your convenience."

Solomon groaned. "I was waiting for this. We simply could not continue without a discussion. I suppose seven years is worth a few minutes of explaining, so ask what you will, and I will answer as honestly as possible."

"I have no need for interrogations," she replied. "Your actions are clear."

"Oh, I see," he said, annoyed at her casualness. "Then I have a few for you, if you do not mind?"

"Not at all, please ask."

Propping himself up on some pillows, a look of consternation came over his face. "It is a mystery to me how you do your reasoning, woman," he began. "But could you please explain to me why, if all of these problems could have been solved in one confrontation, did it take seven years?"

Saturnalia chuckled. "The time span had nothing to do with you or me. That was governed by the stars."

"The stars?" Solomon asked skeptically. "Explain 'the stars' to me, please."

Saturnalia twisted a lock of hair around her finger. "We are each governed by the stars," she theorized. "As the planets pass in or out of the space of eternity which our soul inhabits, it affects our life events. The night before you were set to fight Laden, I saw in your stars that you would be victorious in defeating him, but that you were destined to begin a cycle of desolation because of it. All of your significant planets were in opposition, and were overpowering the positive influences around you. All I could do was wait for the universe to take its course, and everything would eventually resolve itself. These things usually happen seven or nine cycles at a time. I charted your stars each night until I saw in the sky that the sequence had ended. I was not threatened by the many women you said you were going to marry because I knew that it would amount to nothing. I was only tolerant of your slothfulness because it was not in your power to do anything about it."

Solomon folded his arms across his chest. "I see, and I suppose the stars told you Aonghus was going to punch me in the nose, as well?"

Saturnalia let out an amused laugh. "You are so simple," she offered, unfolding his arms and wrapping them around her. "You fancy yourself so strong, yet you are most vulnerable. I saw in the stars many nights prior that you would be challenged by one of great importance to you, and that it would cause you to reconsider your ways. When Aonghus and Kordelina visited me, I knew then that this period of disapproval was finished, and that you would soon be open to the truth, even if that came in the form of Kordelina."

"Are we back to that again?"

She kissed him on the forehead, and smoothed her palms across his cheekbones. "I am afraid, dear one, that we have never left," she tenderly responded.

"I cannot believe Kordelina tells you anything," he said, unable to keep from returning her affection. "From what I understand, the child is a mute."

"And you hold that against her, I suppose?"

Solomon let out a belly laugh. "No, I find it rather ironic. Deireadh was always talking, and I am not the quietest of individuals myself. For us to have a mute, I guess, is what you would call cosmic justice."

He saw Saturnalia's expression change as she roughly took his face between her hands. Her reaction was unexpected, and his laughter ceased.

"Do not make fun of her like the rest of the people of this tribe," she reproved. "That child says much, but it is only for those willing to listen."

"I am afraid I do not understand," he said, endeavoring to pacify her. "Are you saying you can hear her even when she does not speak?"

"She speaks all of the time, but it is only for those unhindered enough to understand. Aonghus is able to grasp it, although he does not know it yet, but he is completely able to interpret her thought processes," she explained. "It could be something you will never comprehend, but believe me when I say that she is not to be underestimated."

Solomon placed his hand on top of hers. "I will not underestimate her, but please see to it that she remains more like me than her mother."

Saturnalia smiled sadly and kissed the top of his hand. "Yes, I suppose unintentional weakness is more forgivable than corrupted ambition. Do not worry, dearest, do not worry."

———

In the two weeks that followed, it was one confrontation after another between Saturnalia and Jara. From the moment the hag arrived, she badgered Saturnalia about everything from the time and manner of her worship, to the clothes she chose to wear. She made it clear, time and again, that this tribe was not Saturnalia's, and that it was still under the auspices of the Druidic laws. At first, Saturnalia argued with her, then she ignored her, knowing that once Jara finally did leave, she could easily restore her clan to its former ways.

Still, she was glad for the time to stay with Solomon, to revitalize the time-weakened aspects of their relationship. She found it a bit peculiar, however, that while she cared for him deeply, their love was not the passionate, consuming experience it had been at the beginning. It was more a sublime joining of good friends who had weathered hard times together and were now enjoying peace. Neither of them spoke of it as anything permanent, and intentions of marriage or children were conspicuously avoided.

However, there was another luxury of her stay with him. Every afternoon at Saturnalia' request, Aonghus would bring Kordelina with him to help feed the horses. The first few times Saturnalia watched her from afar. But once the girl found her way to her, their visits soon became a habit.

On one particular night, Kordelina stayed for dinner. For the sake of keeping his lover happy, Solomon had endured it in superb measure, and had even made a point of addressing the child once or twice. Later that night, when Saturnalia had commented on it, she found it promising that Solomon did not argue. He rolled over and went to sleep without answering, but at least he did not argue.

The rains that accompanied the tide of spring lessened, and in what seemed an overnight occurrence, the hillsides were blanketed with bright wildflowers and butterflies. It was also a time of testing for the young men whose anointing had finally arrived.

There were eight of them, ranging in age from twelve to fourteen. They had successfully completed the physical and spiritual instruction to become what the Druids described as the guardians of the earth. If they passed their final initiation, they would be entrusted as representatives of the gods.

To be a warrior among warriors was the most elite standing for a Celt. He must be willing to fight and die with an easy attitude toward death, and while he lived, he must embody fearlessness and pride. His years of education were meant to promote the merging of the spiritual, physical, and imagination of body and soul, while empowering him with the ability to move easily between the common world and that of the gods which he served.

His training was culminated upon his anointing, after which he must spend the night with the rest of the newly initiated warriors in the cave of the Otherworld. There, he must battle the forces of the gods, good or bad, depending on which chose to appear to him. More importantly, he was to conquer the demons of his own soul which, if not overcome, would ultimately render him powerless.

The initiation ceremony began at dusk, and with the exception of Saturnalia and Jara, who would preside over it, the audience was composed of men only. It was a secret ritual meant to get in touch with the ancient mysteries of the universe. Therefore, only a select group was invited to attend. This extended to the bards and musicians, and, contrary to the other tribal ceremonies, it was done without the accompaniment of song and dance. It was a somber occasion where the rite of passage from adolescence to manhood took place.

Because the spirits were present, a bonfire was lit outside the cave entrance as the warriors took their places around it in order of status. Solomon stood between Saturnalia and Jara, and the others fell into place according to rank. Facing them, forming an inner circle around the flames, were their apprentices. There was a feast of pork, wild fowl, roasted hare, edible greens, and wild berries set off to the side, for the masters to banquet on throughout the night while they waited for their fosters to emerge from their test at sunrise. It was a celebration for them, of their successful imparting of knowledge onto others.

Those in attendance waited in silent meditation for the sun to set. When the last remnants of its luminous rays had faded from the sky, Saturnalia began preparing the special drink as the Order of four white-robed priests started to pray. These holy men who had come with Jara were present to petition the gods for the well-being of the young men who were about to be tested. From all accounts of the cave in which they must spend the night, it was a hideous place said to be inhabited by wicked spirits and the souls of captured beasts who would seek revenge on any mortal who dared to come inside.

The purpose of this test was meant to create a bond between the warrior and his anointing totem. The animal whose power he called upon would either find him worthy of his association or reject him, abandoning him to the spirits of the Otherworld. This initiation must be endured alone, because in the death of the young boy's old way of life, he would assume a new personal identity through the confrontation of his own fears.

Saturnalia had her hair coiled in braids around her head, and like the rest of the Order, was wearing a simple white robe that seemed to evaporate into her alabaster flesh. The paleness of her dress only served to make her green eyes all the more intense, and they were filled with a wild, almost erotic look as she finished mixing the hallucinogenic drink and handed it to Jara.

The two women had consulted privately with each of the warriors to determine the special totem they believed had revealed itself to their fosters. Upon taking the chalice from Saturnalia, the frumpish Druidess mentally associated each power animal with each of the boys. As was also decided ahead of time, they would alternate the anointing. Saturnalia let Jara begin the ritual so that she would be in the proper sequence to perform the rite for Aonghus.

Jara made the signs of the sky and the earth, then closed her eyes a long moment before starting her speech. She could feel the quivering fear emanating from the boys as they waited with callow faces for her to address them.

"It is a sacred thing to be a warrior," she announced, in a voice befitting the occasion. "For it is blood and feasting that does sustain him, not the commonality of war. You must taunt and overcome your failures, and resist the shortcomings that mortality thrusts upon you. You must ascend the angelic and earthly elements of supreme physical obstacles, and achieve mental balance. For you will die tonight, and if the spirits find you worthy, you will thus abound as a soulful embodiment of the ancient forces. After this night, you are not a man born of woman, but a spirit born of the gods. Every decision, every thought, will follow you on the road of your eternal lifetimes. As the sun rises in the morn, the dead man that was once you will reside in the cave, and you will emerge a being reborn from painful death into a universe that is always asking you to become your own eternity."

Jara took the chalice and drank the strong, bitter brew. Stepping back, she handed it to Saturnalia who, with head bowed, silently walked to the circumference of the fire, looking carefully into the face of each boy.

"It is said that to understand the mystic influence you must comprehend all that is," she said eloquently. "That by understanding the constant that is eternity, you invoke all the attributes therein. As this involves walking a path different from the others, you remain in harmony with the forces that are the earth and the sky, the perfect forces that last throughout all the lifetimes you have lived and will live again. As you are given the precious flight of freedom and the lessons of simplicity, you must also be given the grave responsibility of your power animal. These animals of your anointing will become the strength in which your personal understanding will reside. They will teach you humility and intuition, and reflect the lessons of your human and spirit selves while you seek the pathway to power. To be a warrior, you must have respect for all things, be always aware of your fears, never cease to be wide awake to the dimensions of the universe, and honor your own self-confidence. To be a warrior is to understand that power lies in the wisdom of the great mystery, and to honor all things as your teacher."

Taking a drink, Saturnalia stopped in front of Solomon and handed it to him. The Chieftain gave her a look that instantly revealed he was both pleased and aroused by the sight of her. Then taking it, he straightened his shoulders, and tightened his stomach as he prepared to make the final toast.

"This that we drink of tonight will induce our ancient dream state," he explained. "It will fill your mind with the voice of the ghost warrior whose words are full of omens, signs, and other occurrences individual to each man. For in your mind resides the temple and knowledge of power, and whether this state is one of tribulation or victory, it will mark both the end and the beginning of you. Let the dream state you experience allow the realities of the body, mind, and spirit to merge. Then all of these aspects will unite within you to create a mighty warrior."

chapter five

s Solomon took a drink, Saturnalia passed a sprig of mistletoe to each boy. It had been picked six days prior, and was to be worn as a protective amulet. This, their most sacred herb, held all-healing properties brought forth from atop the trees of the oak groves, and was, therefore, free of the impurities of the world.

The perfect calm of the evening was broken the next moment by the initiation chant of the priests. "Angels of fire," they began in an unsettling whisper. "Fire of tongues, breath of knowledge, wisdom of wealth, sword of their song, song of the bitter-edge."

Over and over they repeated it; each time raising their voices a decibel until they were nearly bellowing out the words as Jara took the dagger from the fold of her sash. She held it out in the direction of the rising moon. She pressed it to her lips and kissed it, then handed it to Saturnalia.

The boys took in breaths of fear while Saturnalia performed the same ritual, then approached Aonghus. As his eyes glittered with anxiety, he could feel himself trembling, but could do nothing about it as he watched her take her place in front of him. Their eyes connected, and in an instant, he mentally professed his adoration of her. Saturnalia seemed to hear it; as quickly as it flashed through his mind, he saw a faint glimmer in her expression before she touched the blade to his chest.

"Let your power ally be the crawling snake," she said aloud. "It is the energy of wholeness, consciousness, and the ability to experience without resistance. It is the knowledge that all poison taken within you can be integrated into creation. So let the fire in your eyes bring forth the eternal flame of life, death, and rebirth."

He gasped when she cut the sign of the snake into his flesh. An unexpected eroticism surfaced in him. He was unable to take his eyes off her as the blood seeped out and began to trickle down his stomach. He would have done anything for her at that moment, and taking a drink from the cup, he was filled with a surge of sensual purpose. Then in an uncharacteristic display of boldness, he moved his head forward and kissed Saturnalia on the mouth. She received him as though he had done it by her command, then she stepped to the side while Solomon rubbed animal fat on the wound to stop the bleeding.

The Chieftain saw Aonghus' eyes catch sight of something in the trees. He flinched with slight surprise, then smiled softly and once again, gazed straight ahead. Solomon peered over his shoulder trying to see what it was, but saw only the blackness of the surrounding grove.

The last of them to be anointed was Conn. He was given the totem of the elk, and as the symbol of antlers was cut into his skin, Jara told the story of how the elk's strength is derived from the fellowship of their own gender. Only at mating time do they seek the company of the opposite sex above that of their comrades. She explained how this power allows friendship to extend beyond competition and jealously, and has the stamina of true, everlasting love.

When she was finished, Conn was handed the single torch by which they would find their way into the cave. As they all fell into line, both the warriors and their fosters were warned that, under no circumstances, could anyone enter or exit the cave after the Druids had left. The warriors must wait outside feasting, while their students endured this night unaided. At dawn, the Order would return to summon them into the daylight.

The newly honored warriors disappeared into the dark hollow in the limestone, and the older ones settled into places around the fire. Solomon found he had little appetite, and while the others seemed to be enjoying the wealth of food, he picked at his. It took great concentration for him to indulge in any exchange with his comrades, and he was relieved when the drink finally took effect on them all, and they retreated into the silence of their private thoughts.

The Chieftain could not prevent his mind from drifting to the last time he had been inside that cave. It was still vivid: the sound of the boar, and the bravery of Aonghus' hound. He found himself feeling a little frightened that, if the spirits did really exist, they would somehow cause Aonghus greater torment because Solomon took both the hound and the boar away from them. Then he reminded himself that he was being overly protective—he had to admit he loved Aonghus more than he had ever thought himself capable.

These years had been good for him, too. In sharing himself with his apprentice, he had been given an education in responsibility and honesty in return, two attributes in which Aonghus was the toughest of task masters, and while he and the boy were very different in their views of their individual purpose in the world, they were much alike in their devotion to each other.

To realize now that this stage of his life was coming to an end, and that Aonghus would be on his own more and more, made the Chieftain feel a sadness and loneliness he had not expected. He closed his eyes and tried to dream, but his mind refused to rest. He recalled the first time he had met this morose little boy, and the series of events that led him to the unsettling realization that he cared for him more than he had ever expected. He had not wanted to see the changes in his manner and his physical body as he matured, but as they had unavoidably come about, it at least made Solomon proud to know that he had contributed to this prize of a human being. Then, as if it were being replayed before his eyes, he saw the anointing again. He saw the way Aonghus had kissed Saturnalia so innocently, and the subtle change of expression when he had looked out into the trees.

Opening his eyes, Solomon stared into the grove. What had he seen? Was it the spirits, or was it the image of a soon-to-be-concluded childhood?

"Aonghus," Solomon whispered, "I wish you did not have to go now. Forgive me for my selfishness, dear boy, but I see in you a tender hope and belief that I have never seen in myself."

There was a wistful longing in him to grab hold of what he had not yet squandered in his life. He had never told Aonghus he loved him, never said he was proud of his integrity, or that he respected his expertise. When the dawn came, and the boy emerged from the cave a young man, the chances he had missed could never be regained. What could he do about it then? Confess his guilt for wasting these tender experiences, for realizing too late that he needed and wanted them more than he could bring himself to admit?

He felt hypnotized as he scanned the blackness of the trees, the elusive mystery Saturnalia had once described as darkness: that space between the spirit and the mind that infected men's souls with truth. Painfully, he understood now that she was right.

His vision rested on a spot of white above the shrubbery, and squinting his eyes into focus, he saw that it was a face. From where he was, he could not make out any details. All he could see was smooth glowing skin, the dark caverns of eyes, and the hollowed cheeks. Startled to his feet, he began walking toward it.

As he left the boundary of the fire glow, he found that the night was bitingly cold. It sent a shiver through him as he crossed the meadow without taking his eyes off the ghostly image. Coming closer, he could see that the face had a small nose and a tiny mouth, and he froze in his steps when the likeness of Deireadh flashed in his mind. Had she come back this night to haunt his conscience? Had she felt his remorse for his wasted time, and was now offering him an opportunity to atone for a single aspect of his life?

"Deireadh?" he called, his voice cracking from the cold air. "Is that you?"

The image was sucked into the shadows, and he started running after it. He could feel the dampness of the ground beneath his feet, and the frost clung to his arms as he parted the greenery. He was heavily drugged; his head felt as if it was splintering apart into thoughts of Deireadh as a child, and as a woman. As his breath formed clouds in front of him, he saw her again as she truly was: a greedy, corrupted being without loyalty.

He suddenly found himself in the darkness of the trees, panting and holding his throat because it ached from the cold air. Then he glimpsed a vague outline of something in the shadows. He could hear the patter of running feet and his heightened state turned it into the sound of waves crashing against the rocks. He could not prevent himself from following it.

"Deireadh, wait! Talk to me please," he was mumbling over and over. "I only want to tell you that I am sorry. I will not harm you. I promise I will not harm you."

It seemed to be running in circles around the trunks of the oaks, always just far enough ahead of him to lure him deeper into the woods. It crossed his mind that it was doing this on purpose, taking him to a place where it could trap him and seek revenge. But he did not care. If this was a spirit, he wanted to confront it and speak to it even if it took his life in return.

Finally, the footsteps ceased, and the only sound that pierced the stillness of the grove was that of Solomon, unknowingly weeping. He found himself repeating the words, 'I will not harm you,' as though it were a premeditated chant.

Wiping the tears from his face with the backs of his hands, he staggered to the silhouette ahead. He felt as if his heart was going to stop as he made out the dark hair and the light skin in the moonlight. He could see that its knees were quivering, but that was the only part of it that moved.

When he was close enough to touch it, he realized how tiny it was. Dropping to his knees, he stared, waiting for it to move or speak. But it did not.

"If you are what I think you are," he said, his numbed lips causing his speech to slur, "I wish only to tell you that my heart would, at last, heal itself of this hardened state if you would accept as truth that my love was once true, and does now ask forgiveness. For were it not for this chance to release the guilt within me, I should find myself a much lesser man with the dawn's light."

He shuddered with fear as the figure turned and took a step toward him, then backed away. But as it lifted its head, he felt a sense of joy at the sight, for he realized it was not a spirit at all. It was Kordelina.

Without saying anything further, Solomon gathered her in his arms and hugged and kissed her. She squirmed to get away from him, but he held on until she finally gave up. Her teeth were chattering from the cold, and her body was trembling.

"Did you come to check on Aonghus?" he asked, but she did not answer.

"Were you afraid he would leave and not say good-bye to you?"

The tears welled in her eyes, and she bit her bottom lip.

"I know," he said, taking her face in one hand. "I do not want him to go either."

Kordelina offered no more resistance as Solomon carried her back to the campsite, and wrapped her in his cloak. Strangely, none of the other warriors commented on her presence. They seemed to be in their own dream states, and did not notice. Solomon could feel himself drifting further away too, and lying down with Kordelina beside him, the last thing he noticed was that she was finishing the food he had left on his plate.

It was Saturnalia who awakened him, a look of quiet surprise on her face at the sight of the child snuggled in his arms.

"How did this come about?" she asked in a whisper.

"I thought you arranged it," he grumbled.

At the sound of the voices, Kordelina's eyes opened wide, and she scrambled to her feet. She looked around for Aonghus, and when she did not see him, became immediately distressed.

"Did he leave already?" she asked, grabbing Solomon by the sleeve.

The Chieftain's expression went from shock to disdain.

"Why you little beast; you can speak," he said indignantly. "But you only do it when it is convenient for you. You are more shrewd than I gave you credit for."

Kordelina flashed him an irreverent look, then turned her attention to the cave entrance. Two Druids stood on either side of it with torches lit as the young men walked out one by one and took a place beside their masters.

Kordelina stood behind Solomon, peering up at Aonghus curiously. He was pale and gaunt. His eyes were swollen with tiny red lines around their rims, and he squinted at the sunlight like it hurt.

"I am all right," he reassured her, without being asked.

She stepped forward and grabbed hold of one of his thumbs, then stared down at her feet.

"Do not cry, Kordelina," Aonghus gently commanded. "You promised me that you would not cry."

Kordelina shook her head "yes" and looked back at him dry-eyed. He gave her a weary smile and turned to Solomon.

"I am well pleased with you," the Chieftain said, then looked at the others. "I am well pleased with you all. As you have proven your courage before the gods, let it then be professed to the world in the symbol of this torque. Take heed to understand that the animal whose power you draw upon is depicted upon its ends. When you are in trouble, you may call for his aid, and as it has been infused into your blood with this, your anointing, this totem will forever honor you."

The older warriors put the torques on their apprentices. Even though they were tired and hungry, their young faces radiated with pride.

"Go now, all of you, and ride together to gather the cattle to be paraded at Beltaine," Solomon announced. "And may the sea not rise nor the sky begin to fall before we are reunited."

As the rest of the young men went to their horses, Solomon pulled Aonghus aside. "Osin is not fit for such a long journey," he said to him. "So I would have you take my steed because my weary nerves would be that much better knowing you would be assured a swift escape if needed."

A sparkle came to Aonghus' eyes. "Thank you," he sincerely replied. "I will see you when the moon has grown full, and the celebration of Beltaine begins."

"I expect a wealth of cattle for the gods," the Chieftain said, hugging him.

"As it will be, Chieftain," Aonghus replied, climbing aboard the horse.

Trotting off across the meadow with the others, Aonghus looked back, not at Solomon or Saturnalia, but at Kordelina. He circled his horse to draw near her, and stopping long enough to see she had shed no tears, he smiled at her proudly. Then breaking into a gallop, he caught up to the band of six young warriors.

CHAPTER SIX

caling the verdurous hillsides and descending to the lush slopes deeper into the forest, Aonghus was filled with the liberating sensation of having shed a tremendous burden. He felt as though the dread he had lived with his entire life was no longer there. He was not going to be a farmer after all, and he never had to worry about it ever again. He knew from the way Solomon had always addressed him that one day he would inherit the tribal rule. Yet, somehow he felt as though he must never take it for granted; that if he did not voraciously pursue it, it would somehow evade him, but in the passing of a single night, all the worry had evaporated into the walls of the most frightening and sacred cave.

Strange, he had always imagined it would be more menacing and that he would be helpless with fear and anguish, not thrive on it, as he now realized he had done. Having come through it to this place, he had actually liked it. He relished the absolute lack of control, and for once, not having to be responsible for his own feelings. He took great pleasure not only in the narcotics taking over his body, but in the emotional purging of his guilt and denial.

But when the distress became too much to bear, he found comfort not in the thought of his parents, Solomon, or his secret idolatry of Saturnalia. No, it was Kordelina who filled his mind, that obstinate little girl who worshipped everything he did, yet expected nothing from him but his genuine care. It did not matter if he was happy or sad when he was with her. Being who he was at that very moment was all she had ever required of him. He now understood why she trusted him and indulged him with thoughts and words she did not share with others: she had never doubted that what she was seeing in him was true. At that moment when he had spoken with her in his mind's eye, whether real or not, he perceived she was the one genuine friend he had.

Steadying his hands, he eased his horse to a swift but even trot as he came alongside Conn. Of the group, Conn's experience the night before had been the most poignant. Aonghus had been surprised to witness his desperation because he seemed to have the most stable and easygoing personality of the boys. But Aonghus knew he would never forget the pitiful sight of him spiraling around the center of the cave in a funeral dance to his family. It seemed he had relived every moment of the Romans invading his tribe and tormented, hysterical cries had escaped his lips as he mourned each execution of his loved ones.

At one point, Aonghus thought his heart would break when Conn had crawled over to him weeping and begging for an honorable death. That was all he had said, honorable death. He repeated it over and over until he was unable to endure it any longer. Aonghus then held him close, and let him cry until he passed out. When they emerged into the morning light, with the incident behind them, there existed an unspoken bond of trust.

They rode still further into the forest, until the leaves on the trees began to turn black with the setting sun, and an evening breeze caused them to flutter in the twilight. Soon the mistletoe atop the trees was nothing more than silhouettes against the starry sky, and the nearly exhausted band settled into a quiet camp. They were on a raid to prove their manhood, and the instructions were the same for them as they had been for all the newly anointed warriors before them. They would ride far into the territory of another tribe, and if they were truly blessed, would be able to steal from the herd enough cattle to ensure prosperity and abundance for the summer crops. When the dawn of the celebration of Beltaine arrived, and theirs were the first cattle driven through the purifying smoke of the bonfires, the gods of the harvest would be pleased.

Dropping halfheartedly to a place away from his group, Aonghus looked up at the stars flaming and dancing overhead. They appeared to leap out of the darkness, defying mortality. To see them through his blurry vision, flickering to the accompaniment of the drawn-out wailings of the wolves and the short articulate hoot of the night owl's song, made something cold and dark stir inside him. It was an irresistible, almost obscene pulse that seized his bloodstream. It was the instinct that had driven the unnumbered generations of his wild, nomadic forefathers. While his body dozed lazily, the restless vision of strange desire was awakening in his mind. He could feel it as though it were a tangible thing infecting him with the murmurings of the forest and the mysterious sounds of his primal being. Like a strong wave, it quelled inside of him until this animal reality exploded, and as he drifted off to a restless sleep, a voice inside of him said this was an addiction to which he was now entitled.

"So that is the purpose of your visit," Saturnalia said, in disgust.

Jara's eyes darkened, and folded her arms across her chest.

"You say it as though I should find it shameful," she countered defensively. "You have not the slightest idea of the atrocities that are taking place across the strait. The imperialists have conquered one tribe after another, and territory that was once exclusively ours belongs to them now. What I am asking is the least that you can do considering the measure by which our people are being annihilated."

Saturnalia arched one brow, and keeping her eyes fixed on Jara, walked a slow circle around her, then stopped where she had started.

"No," she said flatly. "I will ask the warriors, but not the fianna. They are only boys, and they have not had enough experience to fight the Imperialists. To send them to the continent is to send them to their death."

Jara gave an exasperated sigh. "You have not heard anything I have said. Your warriors must remain here. Rome believes the Druids are the cause of the resistance to their rule. They see us as the reason that so many of the tribes have refused their offers to merge, and they have had to resort to military force. They are seeking to destroy this island completely because they reason that once the Order ceases to exist, so will the resistance. The men on the continent are in need of young fighters. No armies have been organized except for small bands of warriors who have had some success in individual skirmishes. I am offering these young men a chance to increase their wealth as well as their standing, because once Rome is defeated, they will be heroes."

"You are lying again," Saturnalia stated. "How can you offer them riches when all the wealth is tied up with the imperialists? Even the Icenians have been unable to fend off Caesar. You told me yourself that King Prasutagus was forced to become a Roman client king. If he had his trade taken away, what makes you think he will not oppose you?"

"He will not," Jara declared. "I have it from a very trustworthy source that he and his queen, Boudicca, would support a rebellion, not try to stop it. Saturnalia, yours is not the only tribe being asked for assistance. The other tribes that have been petitioned have all gladly agreed that the young ones should cross the strait and fight, and the older, more experienced warriors should stay to protect the island. If Rome is not stopped, this could be our only stronghold, and I only thank the gods that the coastline is too hazardous to make for an easy invasion, but if it were possible, I assure you that your guest tonight would not be a Druidess, but an Imperialist."

The priestess was quiet a long moment. She rubbed her lips with the tip of her index finger, carefully considering Jara's argument.

"Your plan has turned on you, has it not Jara?" she finally questioned.

Jara's chubby face turned stoic. "I do not know of what you speak."

Saturnalia laughed to herself. "You and Gaeren thought you would send me here to be your eyes and your ears. You assumed I would be so thankful for your entrusting me with this clan that I would do anything you wished. But you were wrong. I am not a shell of a woman governed by your wishes. No, I am the priestess of this tribe, and you will have to kill me before I will betray these people. They love me, Jara. They love me and respect me because I have never wronged them, and that will not change even with the presence of Rome. Your influence here is subject to my will, not the Druidic laws. So I would advise you that if you wish to work with me, I am to be given full Druidic standing. I should be allowed all the judgments, ceremonies and influence of one of your Order. That means your visits here would be minimal, and I would be left alone to govern my tribe as I see fit. If you do not agree to this, I will actively oppose you, and if you try to harm me, I guarantee that my people will see to it that you never see the sunlight again."

"Are you threatening me, Saturnalia?" Jara asked indignantly.

"No, Jara," she answered truthfully. "But I have taken a broken people and restored them to power. We have a wealth of crops that could feed masses, as well as prime livestock. That has not been accidental; it is the result of hard work, physically and spiritually. My people's hearts are rich, and there is scarcely a hint of dissension among the them, except when you are present. I have given these people my sweat and tears, and in return, I only ask for what should have been mine from the beginning. You can either work with me or work against me. The choice is yours. But I can promise you that in the end, I will get what I desire."

She could see Jara mentally assessing her options, and the ways in which she might further manipulate these circumstances.

"If I do give you full power, then you will offer your assistance?" she inquired, trying to hide her loss her composure.

"I will discuss it with the Chieftain, and will tell the young men of the opportunity. But I will leave the decision to them. I cannot demand that inexperienced warriors fight Caesar's army. They are too young," she said.

Jara considered her response a moment. "Then if you are given what you ask, you must understand that in return, you will be expected to fulfill the offering of a virginal sacrifice of my choice when called upon to do so. Since the Roman invasion has united all the tribes in a common cause, you will also be expected to take a girl from another tribe and educate her in your ways."

"Why can I not educate one of my own choice?"

"You may, but you must also, as a show of good faith, take in another from a neighboring tribe. The teaching of our ways is a precious art, and we must impart it to many, especially now that it is in danger of perishing," she said.

"I understand. Of course I will fulfill these wishes, but my power must not be questioned by the Order, or I promise you that my wealth will become inaccessible. Is that clear?"

Jara stepped up to her and took hold of her forearm. "Do you know what you are doing, Saturnalia?" she asked, completely at a loss for insight.

"Absolutely, Jara. I always have, but you have only refused to see it," she answered. "I still have one question for you, and I would like your honesty."

Jara turned her back, then whirled to face her. "What is it?"

"Are you allied with Rome as well?"

The Druidess lifted a hand to slap her, but did not. Letting it drop to her side, she looked at her wearily. "Always the idealist, are you not?" she said, not expecting a reply. "You wish to be a Druidess? Very well, I will inform the Order that you are now a Druidess."

She made a halfhearted symbol on Saturnalia's forehead with her finger. "You are now anointed," she said dryly, then departed.

Saturnalia felt a sudden chill. Jara's contempt for her was only now awakening.

CHAPTER SEVEN

he sliver of the moon grew full, and the tantalizing sun showed the fullness of summer. Little sounds like the crickets' song and the buzzing of flies were more noticeable, adding a special magic to the lusty atmosphere. The foliage across the sloping terrain offered refuge to a wealth of baby hares, quails, and foxes. The scent of new life was in the fresh breeze wafting from the seashore.

When the silvery dawn arrived on the morning of the Festival of Beltaine, it revealed a clan of gaily attired people gathered around an eight-foot-high pole erected in the clearing of the grove. It had been decorated with ribbons, greenery, and flowers, and in a circle around it were thirteen torches with bronze containers of herbal incense next to each of them.

This was the festival in the Celtic year associated with the fertility of the earth. It was a time when new crops were planted and the cattle were put out to graze in green pastures. It was named for its patron god, Belenos, and the rites performed to him involved the driving of cattle through the smoke of the bonfires as a form of purification and health.

It was the ceremony that marked the division between spring and summer. An occasion when the Druids placated the gods with offerings and incantations, and when young men and women made love in the open air and sunshine as a benediction to the powers of earth.

In the center of the clearing were two bonfires of oak and green yew with a wreath of birch and greenery forming an archway between them. When the first of the cattle could be seen, a Druid priest lit each one with a torch, and as the first steer walked through the smoke, sacred cakes were offered to the flames while the tribe sang the ceremonial song.

"We celebrate the God of Fire, Belenos, Belenos," they chanted to the accompaniment of drums and lyres. "Here we celebrate. We celebrate the sacred Beltaine and the flowering of the woods and the meadows."

There was a provocative carelessness about it, and when the women moved in circular steps around the fertility pole, the chorus of bells sewn to the bottoms of their skirts chimed rhythmically with the music of the bards.

"We here do call and bid to the gods to be with us," their beautiful soprano voices sounded. "We call upon the wild things of trees."

"Of trees," the men echoed.

"Of skies and of waters," the women serenaded.

"Of skies and of waters," the men repeated.

"Be with us here," they rejoiced. "For here we gather to let the sleeper wake, and let the earth and sky be clean."

The women skipped back and the men took their places in the circle facing them. The warriors had their anointed animals depicted on their bodies and were wearing dyed breechcloths and boots. The aristocrats and farmers had adorned themselves in their vividly ornamented festival garments.

"May the touch of the ladies bring forth the flames!" their baritone voices exclaimed. "Let it be the touch of the land that brings forth abundance."

Bounding forward, the males and females locked their arms together and the circle broadened to twice its size.

"We are all friends," they heartily laughed and sang together. "As we look upon this pole, Belenos looks now upon us. He can see into our minds as he rises from the earth. Like the flowers, he blossoms around us, cascades through us, and flows from our bodies out into this world!"

In the next moment, Saturnalia came forth, and with a carved willow scepter in one hand and a bronze statue of the fire god in the other, danced a beautiful solo around her people. Dressed in an elegant yellow sleeveless gown, and masses of fresh flowers in her hair, she twirled around them nine times, and with her lilting voice, called to the heavens for a blessing.

When she finished, she fell dizzily and giggling into Solomon's arms, and they watched the last of the cattle the boys had stolen complain and snort their way through the smoke-filled archway. Then as was the tradition, the Chieftain lit a smaller bonfire of peat turf and yew branches, and as a point of honor, each of the newly anointed young warriors jumped over the flames and then proceeded to dance hand-in-hand with their kinsmen.

Off to the side of the revelry, a cluster of Druids gathered beneath the holy oaks and prayed to a larger, wooden statue of Belenos. Baskets of cakes, fruits, meat, and wine were set around it with a number of human skulls brought from the doorways of the tribesmen's houses. These were meant to bring divine omens and prophesies to the seer who would use them. Strands of beads and warriors' torques were hung from the surrounding branches along with long, thin braids the women had cut from their hair.

By the time the banquet began, the prancing around the fertility pole had turned into a drunken choreography of rejoicing. Aonghus had stepped to the side to have a drink and catch his breath, but before he could make it through the crowd of people around the banquet table, Saturnalia grabbed him by the hand and led him back to the center of the circle.

He stood still a moment inhaling the incense, and smiled foolishly at the seductive sight of her in front of him. Her hair was falling in all directions, with only a few of the flowers that had originally been there still in place. Her neck and shoulders were glistening with sweat, and the smell of the jasmine oil she wore was carried to him by the breeze. He glanced over at Solomon who was watching the two of them, obviously pleased that his young apprentice had earned the full rights of manhood, and that his lover was indulging him in the steps of the earth. Then he looked at Bracorina, who was waiting patiently with the other single girls for him to get up his nerve to take her into the woods.

With the change of the drums to a faster tempo, Saturnalia began whirling around him. When she was at his back, then he pivoted and imitated her motions. There was no exchange of words as she impishly chose the steps, and he drunkenly, but eagerly, responded. They moved in half steps around the fire without touching, and when they had completed one revolution, she placed her hands on his shoulders, and he wrapped his arms around her waist. They swaggered back and forth, laughing and kissing each other. She seemed too tiny to him as he realized the top of her head was only slightly higher than his brow.

Pulling her closer to him, he could not stop himself from lowering his hands to the curve of her hips and stealing a few brief touches of her bosom against his chest. All the while, her eyes sparkled with pleasure at him being a child no longer. They were kind and inviting, and as he felt her move voluntarily closer, he stopped abruptly, and without thinking, began kissing the bend of her neck.

Saturnalia did not encourage him, nor did she discourage him. They were both drunk with wine, and filled with the jubilance of the occasion. Her gaze met Solomon's, who was off to her side dancing with two other maidens at the same time. Catching sight of Aonghus, he laughed amusingly to himself at the once shy boy who had grown so bold as to try to seduce a priestess. Then he nonchalantly wove his way over to them, and coming up behind Saturnalia, he started kissing her neck from the opposite side.

Throwing her head back, she burst into reckless laughter, and when Aonghus saw Solomon he, at once, realized what he was doing, and stepped back in embarrassment. In the next moment, Bracorina had him by the hand, and with an animal skin tucked beneath her arm, led him off into the woods.

She said nothing as she lay the pelt down outside the confines of the celebration. Aonghus was deluged with wine and desire, and glad of it. He watched her curiously as she started removing her jewelry and unbraiding her straight, shiny black hair.

"I will expect a vow of marriage," she said, and looked at him with dull brown eyes. "I do not care how many wives you wish to take, as long as I am the first. In exchange for the merging of my land rights with yours, I will also demand that my offspring be acknowledged as full heir from the beginning. Any children you wish to have after that are up to you."

Aonghus looked at her, perplexed. It was not that he had not expected her to say this, but it did not seem appropriate for the circumstances. "Of course," he replied. "But not until I am king. If you are willing to wait, that is. I would like to have some wealth of my own before I take a wife."

Bracorina wrinkled her pudgy nose then nodded. "Very well, I will wait. But you may not take another wife before me, you must understand."

"I do," Aonghus answered, feeling his euphoria start to dissipate. "You will be my first, and I will not acknowledge any children before yours."

"So be it," Bracorina confirmed, as she disrobed and layed down.

Feeling suddenly awkward, Aonghus stripped and took a place next to her. Running his hand lightly down her side, he noticed that she had not the curves he had enjoyed so much on Saturnalia. Rather, her torso was straight and chunky, and even though her breasts were large, they were shapeless, and were it not for their wide, dark brown nipples, they would have hardly been distinguishable from the rest of her rib cage. Pressing his mouth to her pursed lips, he came to the sobering realization that they would never be in love.

Rolling on top of her, he caught sight of a naked Solomon and Saturnalia under the trees opposite the clearing. He had her propped up against the oak trunk, and she had her sleek white legs wrapped around his hips. Her eyes were slightly open, and she seemed to be mesmerized by the blue sky. Solomon had his face hidden in her loose hair as he thrust into her.

Seeing the vision of her caused Aonghus' waning desire to flare. Without a hint of tenderness, he spread Bracorina's legs, and pushed himself past the barrier of her virginity.

She scarcely made a sound of either pain or pleasure at the feel of him. And while he selfishly kissed her, he never took his eyes off Saturnalia for more than an instant. He found himself responding not to Bracorina's lack of feeling, but to Saturnalia's lusty manifestations. When he saw her tilt her head back and cry out with pleasure, nothing Bracorina could do mattered as he released himself. Then not wanting to shatter his fantasy, he rolled over with his back to his future wife, and closed his eyes without speaking.

CHAPTER EIGHT

he embers of the festival bonfires were still smoldering when Kordelina was ushered off to begin her fosterage. She was escorted by Enda, who knowing that she was going to the estate of an aristocrat, put on her best robe and made sure that her daughter was bathed and had her hair braided.

She had meticulously dressed Kordelina in a robe she had labored over for weeks just for this occasion. Unfortunately, not accustomed to the long, flowing material, the little girl could not keep from tripping on it or getting it wrapped around her legs. By the time mother and daughter reached Pwyll's estate, Kordelina had ripped the hem out of it, and despite her efforts to hold it up, most of it was dragging on the ground.

With Kordelina firmly in hand, Enda humbly made her way to the servants' quarters and deposited her with the eldest handmaid. She thanked her profusely for the opportunity to have her only daughter taught by the head servant of an aristocrat. Then she carefully explained to Kordelina that she would be living there for a time, but assured her that she would return regularly to bring her home for visits.

Expressionless, Kordelina watched her mother start down the road toward home, then scanned the faces of the servants she had been left with, and decided immediately this was not for her. Not bothering to give an explanation, she turned on her heel and followed after Enda. Realizing what was happening, the stern-faced maid commanded her to come back that very instant, but her demand went unheeded. The woman then called for Diarmudd to intercept her at the gate.

Happy to oblige, Diarmudd grabbed Kordelina by the hand, but she jerked it away and tried to kick him. She attempted to run from him, but her efforts were thwarted by her attire, and Diarmudd caught her a few steps away.

"Come on, you ugly little thing," he chided, lifting her, kicking and sputtering, over one shoulder. "You will not get away with that here."

"Maybe we should tie her up with the dogs," Bracorina called to her brother from the porch. "I have heard that she can howl louder than the wolves."

Diarmudd laughed at his sister's comment as he set Kordelina back down in front of her teacher. She was an aged, brooding woman who had raised him and his sisters with a heavy hand. Knowing how obstinate Kordelina could be, he thought they were quite evenly matched.

"There now," the woman said, taking off the leather strap she wore around her waist. "If you wish this to be your first lesson, so be it."

She bent the girl over one knee, and proceeded to give her the worst beating of her young life. "Your parents did you no favors letting you act like this," she said, hitting her over and over. "They should have been more responsible."

Kordelina could feel the stinging of the strap. She squirmed to get away, but two other servants came and held her down. The snap of the leather soon numbed her backside, and biting her quivering lips to keep from crying, Kordelina looked up to see Bracorina and her sisters on the porch laughing at her. Vowing not to make a peep, she shut her watering eyes hard, and when the cracking of the belt finally ceased, she could barely stand, it hurt so badly.

"Now, child, I think you will try harder next time," the maid declared.

Kordelina fixed her eyes on her feet as another servant took her by the hand and led her into the bakehouse. Most of the tribe shared a common oven located in the center of the village, but since Pwyll was wealthy, he had a private one.

The four clay kilns made it very warm inside, and each was manned by individual attendants who stoked the flames constantly to keep it at the proper cooking temperature. There were planks hanging over them to deflect heat and smoke to a hole in the roof. In the center of the building was a slab table with pottery plates, eggs, milk, and flour.

"You will first learn to make bread," the woman instructed. "I will show you once, and it will be your responsibility after that. We are not tolerant of slow learning so please pay attention."

She set two eggs and a bowl in front of Kordelina. "Crack these in there."

Kordelina's eyes darkened, and she jutted out her bottom lip. Her legs ached and her backside still stung, but she was not in the mood to be accommodating. Clenching her tiny fist, she smashed both eggs on the table and sprinted out the door. She ran in the opposite direction she had before, taking cover in the pigsty, and crawling under a fence to get to the woods. She could hear the ripping of the material of her robe, but could have cared less. All she wanted was to get out of that place, lest she get another lesson with the strap.

The maid stood in the center of the yard, watching and shaking her head. "Let the worthless thing go," she said, waving her hand impatiently in the air. "She will not amount to anything no matter who tries to teach her."

It was late afternoon when a concerned Enda and Koven visited their eldest son and the Chieftain. They recounted Kordelina's antics as were related to them by Pwyll's handmaid, then apologized to Solomon that his payment for her fosterage had been wasted.

"That is all right," he said, draping his arms over the fence rail of the horses' pasture. "It was worth a try."

"Where is Kordelina now?" Aonghus asked, obviously irritated. He had faith that if she had fled in such a manner, it must have been for a good reason.

"She has yet to return," Enda said, wringing her hands.

Aonghus bit the inside of this cheek, trying to conceal his anger that his little sister had been subjected to such abuse.

"Do not worry about her," Solomon said, rubbing his beard. "She has proven that she can take care of herself."

Aonghus shot him an angry glare. "She is only a child. I will try to find her myself."

He purposely chose Osin to ride because he knew that if Kordelina was hiding, she would easily recognize the gelding. He put only a bridle on him, and left Solomon with his parents to muse over the condition.

It did not take much thinking to figure out where she had gone. It was evening, and she would surely be at the watering hole watching the horses and other wild animals drinking. He felt a tightness in his chest as he rode, half fearing that she might have actually run further than he thought and he would not be able to find her by nightfall. But his worries were put to rest when he located the herd of horses near the pond, and saw her sitting naked on top of a rock off to the side.

She smiled happily at the sight of him, and when he stopped beside her, she turned around to show him the red welts on her buttocks and lower back.

"Look, they will not go away," she said seriously. "I tried to wash them off, but they will not go away."

Aonghus gave a sympathetic smile. "You cannot wash them off. They are from the strap and they have to heal. Do they hurt?"

Kordelina's eyes watered. "Yes," she answered, trying not to cry.

Feeling sorry for her, he got off his horse and held open his arms. She was in them in an instant, and he hugged her close as she burst into tears. He did not say a word as he let them flow. When she finally stopped crying, he sat down at the edge of the pond and held her in his lap.

"Where is your dress?" he asked.

"Gone," she answered.

"Gone where?" he questioned, again stroking her hair

"Anywhere," she replied.

"Mother worked hard on it," he added.

She was silent a moment. "Tell her I am sorry," she replied guiltily, then scurried out of his arms to look at her reflection in the water.

"Come here and see," she said, waving to him to join her.

Aonghus bent over and looked at the mirror of his face next to hers. "See what?" he asked.

Kordelina moved the tip of her finger in the water over the image of his face. The gentle ripples distorted his features as she went across his forehead, down the bridge of his nose and over his lips. Then she took his finger in her hand, and did the very same thing to her reflection.

"We look nothing alike," she announced, looking at him resolutely. "We are brother and sister, and we look nothing alike. Cunnedag and Erc look alike, but not me and you."

Aonghus' eyes widened, and he gave a nervous laugh. "That is because I am older than you, and you are a girl, and I am a man."

She considered his reasoning a moment, then pointed to the stallion he had said he would catch after he was anointed.

"He will be too old to tame by the time you come back," she told him.

Aonghus' look intensified. "How did you know I was going? I have not told anyone."

Kordelina shrugged and started to cry again. "I do not know. I just know you are leaving soon, and will be gone somewhere far away for a very long time. I will be so lonely."

He felt his heart sink, and had to look away. For a long while, he watched the horses drinking across the pond and studied the stallion protectively overseeing his herd.

"Would it help if I explained to you where I am going?" he asked finally.

"No," she replied, tossing a stone into the water. "You will still be away from here."

He reached out to pull her to him. "Kordelina, there are men called Romans who have invaded other villages, and are trying to kill our people. I want to go and help try to stop them."

"They are not my people," she said shaking her head. "I do not care what happens to them, and you should not either. Your home is here, and the Romans are there. You should stay away."

Aonghus put his hand beneath her chin and made her look at him.

"Do you not see? If the Romans are not stopped over there, they will come here," he argued. "If I go and help these tribes fight them, this will not happen."

She pressed her forehead to his, and looked straight into his eyes. "Bracorina makes you unhappy, too," she stated, completely changing the subject.

"Kordelina," he cautioned.

She stepped back and took hold of his hand. "She makes me unhappy," she added, pulling on his little finger, making the knuckle crack.

"Ouch! Do not do that," he snapped. "I am not Father; I do not like it."

Immediately remorseful, she kissed his hand to soothe him, and he was easily placated by her affection.

"Will it be soon?" Kordelina whispered, in his ear.

"What?" he whispered back.

"When you leave? Will it be soon? I do not know how to measure time, Aonghus," she said. "Will I still be this age when you go?"

Why did she have to make this so hard, he thought. "Do you see that colt over there?" he said, pointing at a scruffy weanling that had the same color and presence of the stallion.

Kordelina looked at it and nodded.

"Before I go, I am going to catch him," he explained. "And while I am gone, you take care of him for me. When he is grown, and ready to ride, I will be back.

That is how you can measure time's passing. We will get him tomorrow, and one for you as well. Show me which one you like?"

Kordelina pointed to a light brown filly with a beautifully chiseled head, and a long neck and legs.

"Very well, but you will have to care for them both while I am gone."

"I will, I promise," she said, with sad eyes. "But if we catch them tomorrow, that means you will leave too soon."

"It is always too soon to leave," he said softly, and forced a smile. "But the sun is nearly gone, and we are due home."

Kordelina frowned. "I cannot go home or they will make me go back to the ugly lady."

"Well, you cannot stay here," he said firmly. "Not alone."

"I am not alone, Aonghus," she responded truthfully. "There are many horses and animals here and good spirits, too. I will stay with them and you can come back here in the morning. I do not wish to go home and be sent away again. It hurts my feelings."

"I know," he said, gently lifting her in his arms as he stood. He set her back on top of the rock she was originally sitting on so that she was eye level with him. "Listen carefully. I will go and tell Mother that you are all right. She is so worried. I will get your clothes and something for us to eat, and we will build a fire tonight, and both sleep under the stars.

Kordelina's face glowed with joy. "Yes, I would love that. But when you come back, you must not bring Bracorina."

Aonghus passively shook his head.

"I do not think she would like to come anyway," he answered, wrapping his cloak around her. "I will be back as soon as I can."

CHAPTER NINE

As he had promised, Aonghus returned a short time later with Kordelina's clothes, some dinner still warm from their mother's kitchen, and a message that if she did come home she would not have to resume her fosterage. Of course, he did not elaborate on the fact that they would not have taken her back anyway, and that she would have to find some other means of working off the payment Solomon had made on her behalf. Rather, he had consulted briefly with Saturnalia on his way home, and the two had devised a plan they believed would appease both father and daughter.

The two made camp a short distance from where the herd of horses had settled in for the night. Since they were not far from their settlement, Aonghus brought only his dagger and his spear for protection.

They ate their dinner in blissful silence, content to be together beneath the stars and near the horses. When they finished, Aonghus took out his hand flute and played Kordelina a happy tune. With a broad smile, she spun and hopped around the fire, imitating the dancing of the older women in the tribe.

At first, Aonghus found it funny, but after he had himself a good laugh at her antics, he patiently showed her some simple steps, humming while they danced together. She took to it easily, concentrating on his movements and trying her best to please him. When he was satisfied she knew them well enough, he played the song he had been humming on his flute, and let her dance alone in front of the fire.

A wistful feeling came over him as he watched her outline in the firelight doing each step in perfect tempo to the music. Seeing the dancing shadow intertwine with the knotted oaks, it crossed his mind more than once that he simply could not leave this child to be brushed aside when she had such potential. He knew that with the right instruction, Kordelina could probably do anything. More than anyone, he had witnessed the extent of her coordination and memory. As a matter of fact, one had to be careful what one said or showed to her, because once it was in her mind, it stayed there. This girl seemingly never forgot a thing, and Aonghus found it worrisome to think of all that he had thoughtlessly said to her long before he realized this.

Moving his fingers along the holes of the hollow-boned instrument, he wondered if he was, in reality, running away. Perhaps there was something that made him altogether unhappy. At this moment, however, it was quite the contrary. Out in the fresh night air with this simple child, he had a warm sense of purpose. It was more than what he had felt with Solomon or the other members of his family, because he knew that while they cared for him, he did not make as strong an impact on their lives as he did on Kordelina's. Then he thought of the sorrowful murmurings of Conn back in the cave. How he had wept and lamented the atrocities of Rome, and it occurred to Aonghus that the fear of losing such precious things as these were what motivated him to go from the start. Not only that, but with the exception of Diarmudd, all of the other boys were going, and he did not wish to be a coward.

Stopping halfway through the second chorus, he looked straight at Kordelina, and without knowing why, he felt suddenly overwhelmed with emotion. His eyes watered, and instantly sensing his need, she knelt down and rested her chin on one of his bent knees.

It had been many years since he had been at the mercy of his feelings. With his warrior's training, he had schooled himself to be disciplined in his perceptions, and not mastered by his sentiments. But as he blinked back the tears, he was too overcome to explain what was taking place inside of him. All he could do was sit quietly and wait for it to pass. He was glad no one besides Kordelina was there to see it. He felt strangely unashamed when she comfortingly put her arms around him and kissed his cheek.

"Will you love me this much when you are gone?" she quietly asked him.

Rubbing his eyes, he could only give his response by squeezing her hand.

"Come on," he said, after a long while of composing himself. "We should go to sleep now; horses awaken early."

Kordelina layed down beside him on the sleeping hide, and he wrapped it around them both. They snuggled in front of the fire, with her running her fingertip rhythmically over the blade of the dagger he had set out in case he needed it. She seemed fascinated by the shiny smooth surface, and was so consumed by it that Aonghus finally had to put it away so she would try to sleep.

"Will it be hard to catch them?" she asked, yawning.

"The horses? No, they are only weanlings," he answered. "We will have to be careful not to upset the mares. If they decide to run, we will spend a fair amount of sunlight catching up to them. You cannot start whinnying and chirping at them even if you get excited, all right?"

"All right. Do you think they will mind being caught?"

Aonghus shrugged. "We will let the Goddess decide. If we have her blessing, we will be successful."

Kordelina's lids were starting to grow heavy. "Does Brigantia rule over the horses, too?"

"No, the horse goddess is named Macha," he answered. "She is a beautiful woman who is part horse. They say she has wings and can soar through the clouds whenever she wishes. Anyone who has ever seen her has been blessed with abundance. We will ask her if we may take these horses, but we must promise to give something back if she is generous."

Kordelina smiled sleepily. "If she lets us have them, I will promise her that I will name mine Macha, after her. Is that enough?"

Aonghus kissed the top of her head. "Ask her in your dreamtime, and we will find out tomorrow."

The young warrior was adept at catching the weanlings; it was almost anti-climactic. By early morning, both the colt and the filly had ropes around their necks, and were following along behind Osin. Aonghus had done most of the work with Kordelina watching wide-eyed from behind a tree.

Surprisingly, the animals offered little struggle, other than the bucking and squealing they had done when the rope was pulled tightly around their necks to draw them in. After realizing the inevitable, the gentle animals dropped their heads and let Aonghus lead them away from their herd.

The only questionable moment was when Aonghus had Kordelina hold onto the colt while he rounded up the filly. It reared up and hit her with its flailing hooves. She was struck once in the mouth and once in the eye causing one to bleed, and the other to swell shut. However, when they came through the gate to their parents' farm, she offered a proud but lopsided smile at the two horses they had in tow.

"They are handsome," Koven admitted, watching the graceful animals run together in the pasture. Once freed, they went in sequence along the back fence, snorting and whinnying for their lost herd.

"Yes, the colt is mine and the filly belongs to Kordelina," Aonghus replied. "She is going to care for them."

Koven raised his eyebrows in surprise. "Why not you—are you not the horseman?"

Aonghus gave a nervous, tight-lipped smile. "Because I have decided to go with the rest of the fianna to Wales."

His father nodded slowly, trying to disguise his shock. "I should have expected it; the murmurings of change have been in the breeze. I suppose it is only natural for a young man to go off to be tested; it is what you have worked for. It is selfish of me to desire it to be for a very short time, but know you will be sorely missed."

Father and son looked straight ahead, too emotional to meet each other's eyes. They watched as the weanlings ran in circles around each other. They kicked their back legs out, then stood straight up and stabbed at the air with their front hooves, as if in a choreographed dance.

"I will arrange it with Solomon for Kordelina to help with his horses, and Saturnalia has offered to school her in exchange for assisting with daily tasks. Will that be all right with you?" Aonghus asked, placing both hands on Kordelina's shoulders.

"That is a thoughtful gesture, son. Whatever Solomon will agree to, I will agree to, as well," he said, the worry still evident on his face.

"Father, I will see to it that he agrees," Aonghus confirmed.

———

"Have you gone mad?" Solomon's voice thundered, through the barn. "Not only will I not have her working with my horses, but I refuse to acknowledge your request to leave."

Aonghus stared at him in disbelief. "What is the matter with you? I can understand why you would be hesitant to have Kordelina here, but what I choose to do with my life is no longer of any concern to you."

"It is not?" he hollered, raising his voice even more. "Of course it is. I have raised you, and taught you all I know. I have given you an inheritance and a guarantee of rule, and you thank me by informing me, the day before you leave, that you are going off to fight a horde of soldiers who wear skirts! I think you are crazy, and that your opinion of your skills is inflated with your new independence. As the heavens have created us, Aonghus, if it is Bracorina you are evading, there are simpler ways of doing it."

Aonghus' eyes grew cold. "That has nothing to do with it. It is Bracorina's decision to wait if she likes. If she does wait, I will honor my promise, as before."

"Now I know you are crazy," Solomon scoffed. "Why do you want to do this? Have you forgotten you are guaranteed a kingship? You do not have to pursue some idealistic quest to get it. I will gladly hand it over to you in a few years."

Aonghus looked at him blankly, then started rubbing his temples with his fingertips. "Please, Solomon, try to understand that this is something I feel I must do. The imperialists are not going to simply turn back when they reach our island. They will keep coming. The only way I will have a kingship to inherit is if I do something about stopping them now. I am not like Diarmudd. I could not, in good conscience, stay when all others have gone. I want to fight for what I love, not stay here and fool myself into thinking it could never be taken from me. Try to understand that, even if it is not what you would do."

The Chieftain put his face in his hands, then without warning, let out a warrior's battle cry, and put his fist through one of the stall partitions.

"It is not my wish to see you die!" he yelled. "And that is what they will do, kill you in an instant. There are masses of them over there, enough to take entire territories. Do you really think your presence will make any difference?"

"Yes!" Aonghus yelled back. "Yes, I believe it will. If everyone thought like you, there would be nothing left of us by now. The Druid's transport leaves at sunrise. I will be on it."

Out of sheer desperation, Solomon took Aonghus by the shoulders and shook him hard. "You fool of a child," he rebuked. "I will not have it; I will not have it. You cannot go and die for Rome. I will not have it!"

With both hands Aonghus shoved him away. "I am not going to die. I am a warrior now, a protector anointed by the gods."

"Do you really believe that? If so, you are more gullible than I thought," Solomon replied irritably. "It is ceremony. It does not make you stronger or more able in warfare, but I guess you are bent on finding that out for yourself. If you wish to go, then go, but I am not taking Kordelina as your replacement. I paid needlessly for a fosterage that lasted a heartbeat and I owe her nothing."

"You owe her everything!" Aonghus countered, coming at him so fast he was backed into a wall. "You owe her the chance to become something besides a peasant wife with a herd of children at her feet. I will not let you sentence her to poverty because of your pride. She is of your line, and could no more become a farmer than you could. You cannot see beyond your own selfishness to realize that is her problem. She has been placed in a world of rules and requirements of which she has no concept. She is too much like you, and cannot perceive of having to do something just because someone tells her to. When she is let alone and given the freedom to do what is natural to her, she is nothing less than beautiful."

"Then take her with you," Solomon answered flippantly, and stepped out of Aonghus' way.

Aonghus ran his hand through his hair and thought a moment. "I am always amazed at how selfish you can be," the younger one stated coolly. "Kordelina will come here to work with the horses. The rest of the time she will assist Saturnalia. If it ends up differently I will take her with me, but not to Wales to fight Romans. I will take her to another tribe along with my inheritance."

Solomon cocked his head to the side skeptically. "If you do that, you will never see your inheritance," he rebutted.

Aonghus shook his head. "You are wrong. We took an oath, and as long as I never tell her that she is yours, you have no choice but to fulfill it."

Solomon looked Aonghus up and down. He was resolute at this moment; Solomon had nothing with which to challenge him.

"You are right," he grudgingly conceded. "You have the laws behind you, and I only have my personal reasons for not wanting it. So, yes, while you are away on your delusion of courage, I will allow Kordelina a place caring for these horses. But please let it be known to you and the gods, that both of your decisions are against my better judgment."

With a look of sincerity, Aonghus approached him. He touched the Chieftain on the arm, but Solomon gave no response. Only his eyes gave him away. They mirrored love, frustration, and fear, all at the same time.

"Solomon, you have given me the best of your knowledge," Aonghus said, his voice both quiet and apologetic. "You must have faith in that. I do."

———

With his leather traveling bags thrown over one shoulder, along with a mass of weapons, Aonghus boarded the wooden ship with the others. Clutching his churning stomach and with sweat streaming down his cheeks, he made himself take a place along the rail where he could see his family. The whole tribe, with the exception of Solomon, had gathered atop the bluff overlooking the harbor. A few had ventured down the cliffs and were perched in different places in the rocks.

Feeling as if he had just made the biggest mistake of his life, Aonghus meekly lifted one hand, and waved good-bye. He was hoping beyond hope that Solomon would reconsider and come in time to see him off.

"This will be a great journey," Conn said, coming up behind him and slapping him on the back. "Very adventurous, fighting Romans. They get incensed by our howling before a battle. The tribes will be glad to see us—we will not have to worry about a thing, and I dare say, that includes women."

Aonghus nodded hesitantly. "Going to an unfamiliar place is always a bit frightening," he said, trying to disguise his apprehensiveness.

"From what I have heard about the conditions over there, you will not have much time to worry about it," Conn replied, reaching into Aonghus' food bag and taking out a cake. "The warriors who are still alive will look out for us."

Taking a bite, he offered a big wave to Diarmudd, who was partially concealing himself behind his father and Bracorina.

"You think Diarmudd's sister will wait for you?" he asked casually.

Aonghus had his eyes fixed on Kordelina as she kissed her fingertips then held them in the breeze so that it would carry it to him.

"If she finds me worthy," he replied, distracted.

"It would do you well to hope that she does not," Conn said, lurching forward as the ship set sail. "There are many beautiful women in these tribes, and when Rome is defeated, you might decide to stay."

Aonghus shot him a questioning glance. He had never considered not coming back, and he completely discounted a woman, of all things, would be the reason for his staying.

"No," he stated. "It is my desire to return. This is my home."

Conn laughed to himself. "Do not speak so soon. There are more worlds than exist on this island."

As the ship carried them further out into the currents, Aonghus did not speak. Instead, feeling the gentle rocking of the water beneath him, he studied the cracks and slits of the coastline and the shapely emerald hills. Saddened at leaving the people and the place he so loved, Aonghus vowed he would return.

CHAPTER TEN

O ver the next few months, Kordelina watched with fascination as her mother's stomach expanded. When she was not busy doting on the horses or gathering herbs with Saturnalia, she would wait impatiently for her mother to let her feel the baby moving inside. As Enda related the belief that babies were summoned by spirits and allowed to come back into the world by the Goddess, she found that she was forming an endearing bond with her daughter.

Kordelina had become nearly delightful with the passing months. Even Solomon had to admit that she took her job with the horses seriously, and was possibly more adept at handling them than Aonghus was at that age. With the emptiness in the Chieftain's life since Aonghus had gone, he found that he actually enjoyed sharing his equestrian techniques with Kordelina. Yet nothing could make up for their loneliness of being without Aonghus.

As was her duty, Saturnalia had begun tutoring a young girl named Edainne from a neighboring tribe. She had taken residence at Pwyll's estate because she was a bred aristocrat. Although she was already promised as a chieftain's bride, Diarmudd had become helplessly enamored of her.

She was a natural beauty, ten years old, with long dark blond hair and doe-like brown eyes. Her manner was gentle and patient, and while she was the antithesis of Kordelina, the two got along nicely. Saturnalia was pleased to see Kordelina had found another girl close to her age with whom she could relate, and that her socialization seemed to be blossoming. The sorceress believed Aonghus' absence was the best thing to happen to her. She could no longer rely on him to take care of her, and was forced to be more tolerant of others. Yet in spite of the young girl's progress, she remained the tribe's conspicuous outsider.

On a rainy afternoon a fortnight after the Festival of Brigantia, Kordelina trudged, dripping and shivering, down the muddy road to her house. What she found there was a gathering of men in the barn comforting a nervous Koven, and an equally concerned band of women in the main chamber.

Closing the door behind her, the color faded from her cheeks as she heard the wailing of her mother in the next room. Not bothering to ask what was happening, she shoved her way past the three women who, with hurried explanations, tried to stop her. Entering her parents' chamber, she found a sight both miraculous and terrifying.

An unclothed and sweating Enda was propped up into a squat by two women on either side. Saturnalia and Edainne stood in front of her, hands held out to the baby that was emerging from between her legs. She could see the tiny crown of its head, as with clenched teeth, her travailing mother bore down harder. She appeared like the image of the goddess statue to whom Saturnalia prayed, the full breasts resting on the protruding stomach as she brought forth new life.

When the child was delivered, Enda was gently eased back on her bed as Saturnalia cut the umbilical cord with a molten-hot knife. As Kordelina made her way into the room, the newborn was bathed and laid to rest in its mother's arms.

Wide-eyed and speechless, the girl knelt at the bedside, captivated by the sight of the baby suckling Enda's breast. Unknowingly, she had begun to cry.

"It is all right, child," Enda said, exhausted. "His name will be Niall. Go call your father now."

Overcome with amazement and delight, Kordelina staggered out into the rain. At the sight of her father, she ran straight into his open arms. He took her face between his swollen hands and kissed her on the forehead. Then he sloshed his way into the house.

Happily, Kordelina stood in the rain with arms outstretched, letting the drops of cold water titillate her skin as she stuck her tongue out to taste them. How she wished that Aonghus were there to share this special feeling. With that thought in mind, she went into the barn, nestled her way into the straw of Macha's stall so she couldn't be seen, and cried herself to sleep.

The sensation of warm breath against her face awakened her hours later, and opening her eyes, she saw Macha's fluctuating nostrils. Wrapping one arm around the filly's neck, Kordelina buried her face in the shaggy mane and tried to go back to sleep. She kept envisioning the birth and could not help but recount the many months that she had witnessed the growth and movement of the infant. Deciding she simply could not live without a baby of her own, she rose, brushed off the straw, and headed back out into the rain to find Saturnalia.

Walking through the wet, misty grove, Kordelina loved the sound of the rain against the treetops. The scent of freshly bathed foliage reminded her of the night of Aonghus' anointing. She had never been able to forget how oddly Solomon had acted, and how he kept calling her Deireadh. She had never mentioned it to anyone, but there were times when it was all she could think about.

Climbing over the stone wall at the back of Saturnalia's cottage, she peered into her sleeping chamber and saw only the snoring Chieftain. Going around the front of the house, she was greeted by the Druidess.

Saturnalia smiled kindly as Kordelina stepped inside, and at her urging, the girl started taking off her wet clothes. Hanging them on a peg near the doorway, she went straight to the open hearth and tried to rid herself of the chill she felt.

Then Saturnalia wrapped her in a woolen shroud and began to rock her gently in her lap. Kordelina placed her head in the bend of the Druidess' neck, and started playing with a strand of her red hair.

"I want to have a baby," she stated flatly.

Saturnalia could not help but laugh at her declaration.

"I am sure that when the time is right, you will," she said.

Kordelina was quiet a moment. "Saturnalia, when will that be?"

"When two people who love each other deeply come together and their joining is pure, the Goddess blesses their union with a spirit. You have much growing up to do before this can come to pass," she explained, holding her closer.

Kordelina frowned. "I could do it tomorrow so I could have a baby sooner."

"Well," she replied, clearing her throat. "It involves much more than completing tasks. Your body must be mature to carry a child. Your breasts must be full enough to produce milk, and your womb must be able to prepare itself for a new life. You must love someone with the very depths of your being, and that love must be returned before the union is pure."

The little girl stared off into space as she pondered her words. Saturnalia could see the reality of it settling in, and her eyes started to tear as she looked questioningly up at her.

"Then I cannot have one now?" she asked.

Saturnalia shook her head. "Not yet. Perhaps later when you are joined with the one that was made for you, the Goddess will grant you a child. Brigantia is very generous."

Kordelina cocked her head to the side and a tear trickled across the bridge of her nose. "How do you know when it happens?"

"The spirit will tell you the instant it is called. It is the spark of life that warms you from inside," she answered.

The girl involuntarily closed her eyes and started to fall sleep. Saturnalia could see that she was fighting it as she continued to rock her back and forth, humming softly.

"Saturnalia?" she asked, interrupting her tune.

"Yes?"

"What is a Deireadh?"

The Druidess took a pensive breath. "Where did you hear that name?" she questioned.

"The night Aonghus was in the cave, Solomon chased me into the woods and he would not stop saying it," she said, sleepily. "I had never heard it before."

"Nor should you again," Saturnalia responded, hugging her protectively. "Deireadh was a black Druidess who used to be in this tribe. She went over to darkness and was killed by the evil spirits whom she had befriended. But that was a long time ago, and her wickedness has since been forgotten."

Kordelina became worried. "Why did he call me that; does he think me wicked too?"

"No," she gently reassured her. "Although he never speaks it aloud, he thinks you are quite the opposite."

CHAPTER ELEVEN

A.D. 56. Aonghus was barely conscious by the time he hit the ground. He could feel the sharp pain on the side of his head where the axe handle had struck him, and as the fluffy white clouds spiraled overhead, the blood flowed down the side of his face and out of his ear like water. With what was left of his energy, he pulled his knife, and knowing that the attacking Roman had turned his horse and was coming back for him, he waited.

With ears ringing and vision impaired, he let the horse come alongside him before throwing the weapon. Luckily, it lodged in its thick neck, and as it reared up from the pain, Aonghus was on his feet the moment the animal fell.

The rider had one leg pinned beneath the horse, and as Aonghus swayed forward, he looked into the tiny, vicious slits that were the Roman's eyes and found his strength. How he hated these Imperialists for what they had done to his people—forcing them to migrate from village to village to avoid the Romans' ever-growing presence.

Passing through these tribes, it was hard to tell who was a true Celt and who was a Celtic-Imperialist. These refugees had seen much slaughter and much of what they loved taken away; most of them simply wanted to surrender. The Roman occupation of the island was past the point of being a threat: it was a dominant reality.

Aonghus himself had fought too long. He had seen scores of others helplessly strung up by Caesar's men, and had come to believe that he could do nothing else to prevent this conquest. He thought if he saw one more maid, docile and meek, being raped by a Roman, he would simply go mad. He felt as if he were nearly there already, forced to live like a beast in the woods for protection. Every time he went into another tribe, he wondered if a Roman sympathizer would try to kill him in his sleep, or turn him over to the other side.

Witnessing the brutality and distrust had hardened him. He had done so much killing that he felt he was decaying from the inside out.

As he yanked the knife from the horse's neck, he nearly tripped and fell on the trapped soldier.

"Come on, you heathen dog," the infantryman taunted. "Kill me."

Feeling his anger peak, Aonghus recorded every detail of this man's dirty face, the pale eyes, the blunt nose, and the way he had one of his front teeth missing so that he whistled when he spoke. Throwing his head back, Aonghus let out a long warrior's battle cry and went forward. The Roman stared at him for a calculating moment, and when Aonghus was nearly on top of him, he quickly pulled his spear from his saddle, and jammed it into the warrior's gut.

Aonghus staggered back as he sent his knife sailing into the Roman's chest before falling back down.

His thoughts went blank as the next moment, Conn knelt beside him.

"Wake up," he said. "This is not bad enough to kill you."

With one rough tug, he pulled the spear out of Aonghus' stomach and lifted him to his feet. Slapping his face a couple of times to keep him conscious, Conn stared at him keenly, and slapped him again.

"Who am I?" he asked.

Aonghus' head rolled to the side, then dropped forward.

"Who am I?" Conn demanded again, jerking his head up by the hair.

"Conn," Aonghus wailed, clutching his wound. "You are Conn."

He then fell to his knees moaning. Again, Conn helped him stand and wrapped one of Aonghus' limp arms around his neck.

"Lean against me," he said. "There are two horses tied in the trees."

Dragging him most of the way, Conn led Aonghus through the mass of fallen warriors and cavalrymen. Some of them were struck with weapons. Still others had been trampled by the horses and left unrecognizable.

"We must get out of here," Conn said, shoving Aonghus into the saddle. "There are bound to be more Romans on the way."

"What about the others?" Aonghus asked, trying to sit up straight.

"Forget about them," he answered, mounting the other horse and grabbing hold of Aonghus' reins. "If they are not dead, they have surely forgotten about you."

His horse started to gallop and Aonghus groaned with pain and slouched forward as Conn led them deep into the grove. He could tell by the way the breeze was blowing that they were headed for the shore. He hoped, according to their original plan, that they would hide in one of the many caves until they could board a ship headed for home.

Making a wide turn to the north, the two warriors were greeted by the awesome sight of two corps of Roman infantrymen headed their way. Conn looked at Aonghus in disbelief.

"They are everywhere!" he declared. "Hold on because we are going to have to do some hard riding to get away."

Aonghus rolled his head back and took in a gasping breath, then once again slouched forward. "Not me," he moaned. "No more, not me."

Unable to stop himself, he fell sideways and dropped to the ground. Conn went to help him, and putting his hands beneath his armpits, he dragged him to a shallow spot beneath a cluster of boulders.

"I will be back for you," he told him, taking his hand and placing his knife in his palm. "Just lie here quietly. If they see you, they will think you are dead. But do not make it too convincing; as soon as it is safe, I will return. I should not be too long."

Aonghus grabbed the torque from around his neck, and gave it to his friend. "Just go home. It is time for you to go home," he mumbled.

Conn stared at the torque uncomfortably. "You fool," he said, putting it back on him. "You are going to need this. If you want someone at home to have it, you will have to get better and give it to them yourself."

Ripping a strip off his shirt, he wrapped it around Aonghus' head. He tried to keep from showing his disgust at the sight of the open wound. The blood had clotted around it, but he was still able to make out a few bits of the shattered skull area. From his condition, he knew Aonghus must have a drive strong and deep within him to even maintain consciousness. Considering the severity of the wound, Conn wondered if it was even worth coming back for a corpse.

"You are a warrior, your soul thrives until the end of the wind," he said gently. "You must remember that."

Barely able to gesture a response, Aonghus watched Conn climb atop his horse. The last thing he heard was a shrill battle cry filtering through the trees, then everything faded into comforting darkness.

He thought he was dead many times during the next two days. How he loathed the indignity of lying there waiting for it to come. He even came to detest the rank smell of himself as the damp ground sank in around the outline of his body. Over and over, he was haunted by the same nightmare he had in the Druid camp as a child. The awful hag laughing wickedly and coming at him as he decomposed into the earth. Only this time, instead of seeing the image of the two Celts he had first killed, he was rankled by the face of the Roman pinned beneath his horse. He had not killed him. Aonghus was sure of it by the way he smiled triumphantly through the shadows of his irrational mind.

In that time between worlds, echoes of his life filtered through his thoughts. He could see vividly what he had left behind: the trusting face of his father and the rough but tenderhearted Chieftain who had warned him he would end up this way. Then there was the gorgeous Saturnalia who, to him, represented the embodiment of a goddess. He could smell her, feel her touch—and how he loved the sensual way she danced before the festival pyre. When all this had faded away, there was only one person who remained untouched in his heart: Kordelina. His precious, innocent Kordelina. What would happen to her if he did not come back? Would she be able to live as a farmer's wife and working the fields like a peasant? He had thought about her so often and spoken with her in his dreams these many months since he had been gone; promising her, always promising her, that he would return. The pain in his heart at not being able to keep his word caused him to groan miserably. Again and again he groaned and wept at failing her.

"I am sorry," he murmured tearfully, not knowing if he was saying it out loud or in his dreams. "I am so sorry."

There were flashes of brightness receding to blackness, and tiny bending rays in the distance that made up the vision of a young girl on horseback. Then he felt the soft touch of a hand to his brow, and opening his eyes, he focused on the fuzzy image of a woman kneeling over him. As his sight cleared, he saw that she had long blond hair and eyes the color of the sky before a storm. They were framed by tiny smiling wrinkles that revealed she was past her prime, but still quite lovely. She seemed pure and undefiled by this war. She was like the untouched icon he had fought to deliver, and he was filled with the sudden, desperate urge to preserve her from these invaders at all costs.

He suddenly started growling like an animal, and grabbing her by her hair, bent her head back. She was too sweet, too virtuous to let them have her. He thought of putting the quivering knife blade to her throat. He was going to kill her and then kill himself because he was weary of waiting for his inevitable death.

"Forgive me, but you must not be touched by them," he rasped. "You must not be defiled."

For a moment she did not move or breathe, and Aonghus could see the blood and dirt from his hand soiling the cascade of gold that was her hair. Perhaps it was that he was frighteningly near death, but as he studied her sympathetic grey eyes, she appeared too much a part of the living. He heard her whisper something softly, but he could not understand her over his heavy panting. Then a foot kicked him in the ribs, a shield smashed his face, and he was again helplessly unconscious.

"Do not kill him, Bov," she quietly addressed her rescuer. "He is not in his right mind, but I think I can save him."

"My dear sister, Klannad," the man said, shaking his head and reaching down to feel Aonghus' pulse. "Always trying to deliver every mongrel that crosses her path. This one is young; maybe he is dumb enough to try to survive."

"Bov, you have seen it yourself. Seen the waste of these boys who would fight for us. If I can make the difference with even one of them, it is worth it to me," she argued. "Brother, by your words I would question if you are still a Celt."

Bov gave a cynical laugh. "I am still a Celt, but need I say that this one would have killed you?"

Klannad looked up at him with a delicate but imploring expression. "Please Bov, he will be of no further bother to you, I promise."

"Nor to you, I hope," he replied.

Lifting Aonghus over one shoulder, the broad-backed Celt started for his cottage with his sister following close behind.

———

For a long time, Aonghus lie motionless in the small bed chamber. It was warm and comfortable, and while he was not conscious, he knew he was safe. He could hear the faint mingling of sounds now and then combined with an awareness of his head being touched by delicate hands that soothed and held him in the dark. Even though all remained black, he could tell when night came because he knew there was the naked body of a woman beside him. That unmistakable murmuring of femininity, and the sensation of enticing softness. For a long time he could do nothing about it until one night he found strength enough to bury his face in her bosom and to caress her bird-like shoulders with his unsteady hands.

He was unsure how much time had passed, but he had grown accustomed to this murky condition of life, and was thankful to be alive for still another day. Then without warning, he felt it—the spark of anxiety and desperate need. It rushed over him like a wave of boiling water blistering his flesh until he cried out. He knew not what anguished words had escaped his lips. All he was aware of were the slim arms around him, whispering something gentle and sweet that let him know he had not been abandoned.

CHAPCER CWELVE

here was a side to Saturnalia that was not all warmth and understanding, and required the keenest sense of self-confidence to approach. It was a side that was astute and strong-minded to the point of being merciless. It was the inner core that she had described many times as the seeker of knowledge and the witness to power.

When she led Kordelina and Edainne out on what she called a night of seeking vision and truth, Kordelina could tell by the simmering look in her eyes that it was going to take all of her courage to receive the mysterious instruction Saturnalia was planning to bring forth.

Kordelina had originally enjoyed these occasions because not only was she liberated from watchful eyes of the settlement, but she found Saturnalia's teachings interesting. The Druidess had begun the instructions by explaining the fundamental theories of the universe, herbal remedies, and the principles of positive magic. But the lessons soon evolved into spiritual quests of enlightenment and the initiation into the art of sorcery. While there were times when Kordelina wanted to skip her sessions with the Druidess, she was nonetheless captivated by what took place.

It was not a case of liking them or not; it was more that she was ill at ease with the altered states of consciousness and hallucinations that often accompanied the sessions. But like any addiction, when it was over, she could not stop herself from wanting to experience them again.

She had been with Aonghus many times during these meditations. She had spoken with him and even created a world in her mind where they both existed untouched by reality. It was during these moments that she was entirely certain he was still alive and would one day return as he had promised. She had also witnessed the peculiar vision of the Goddess Macha. It was so real that she often thought she could conjure a visitation without the use of herbs or wine. She felt that the centaur was ever present, as though she were guiding her in her work with the horses. When she had related this to Solomon, he dismissed it as instinct instead of divine empowerment. But whatever she chose to call it, it was always accessible.

On this occasion, she and Edainne had followed Saturnalia deep into the grove. Unlike other expeditions, Saturnalia had not packed any supplies, nor had she requested they dress warmly even though it was winter. The only thing she had said to them in preparation was to bring the one thing they felt they needed most.

For Edainne that was a simple embroidered bag Diarmudd had given her. For Kordelina, it was one of Solomon's skinning knives. She had not bothered to ask the Chieftain if she could use it since she knew it was forbidden her. But she could not prevent herself from sneaking into the house when she knew he was with Saturnalia and stealing it. She had every intention of returning it once this lesson was completed, but there was something about the way Saturnalia had phrased the purpose of this quest that made her think it would be useful.

Saturnalia seemed to find it amusing to see that Kordelina had taken to thievery, especially from the tribe's Chieftain. It reinforced her impression that father and daughter were equally irreverent. She had been touched by Edainne's choice because it was obvious she and Diarmudd adored one another. The unfortunate fact was that since Edainne was promised to a Chieftain, she was not allowed any other male relationships. If she were not chaste upon her wedding day, she would suffer a sentence worse than death. She would be ostracized by her clan and all others still under Celtic rule. This meant that not only would she be shunned as a curse, but she would not be allowed to partake in tribal rituals. If that happened, it was believed her soul would spend eternity in chaos and never be permitted to reincarnate. So she and Diarmudd loved each other from afar, and were left to indulge their affection on public walks in the daylight.

The trees were barren this time of year, and storms frequent. It was only weeks after the celebration of Samhain, and the harshest months of winter were still ahead. The ground had lost the aroma of rotting leaves that autumn brought, but had yet to yield to the sweetness of blossoming spring. Instead, it lay dormant, as though all signs of life would remain dead forever. How Kordelina hated this time of year, and what she hated even more was that Saturnalia had chosen it for this venture.

The Druidess moved at a quick pace ahead of her students, not looking back to see where they were, or even to address them. At times, she appeared to be walking at such a great speed that her feet were not touching the ground. More than once, the two girls had to run to keep up with her, and since Edainne was unaccustomed to physical exertion, it was very taxing on her. For Kordelina, it was a relief. Her work had made her extremely fit and, out in the woods and fresh air, running seemed natural.

Half a day's trek into unfamiliar territory, Saturnalia simply stopped. She appeared thoroughly unfatigued by the pace she had set. The sun was still high, and without a word, she pulled out a drinking flask and took a long drink. She then handed it to Kordelina, who knew immediately by the bitter taste that it was drugged. After drinking of it as well, she offered it to Edainne.

Everything about Saturnalia today was unsettling to Kordelina. The way she deliberately ignored them, and the intensity in her eyes as she assessed the surroundings. Then as though she were sorry for her behavior, she took a spot atop a boulder and looking kindly at her two students, motioned for them to join her.

Irritated by what she considered rude behavior, Kordelina purposely paid her no heed. Shimmying up an oak, she perched herself on one of the crooked branches and watched a squirrel eating an acorn. Then, half-curious and half-aggravated by Saturnalia's game playing, she focused on her.

This attitude was very unlike Edainne's, who tried with every passing moment to please her teacher. Her tribe had paid a great amount to have Edainne schooled and she desired to make the most of this education. Kordelina's attitude was altogether different. She liked the lovely red-haired woman, but was not sure of the way she tried to introduce her to the spirit world. She had flatly told Saturnalia this more than once, but she was strangely unaffected by it. It was as though the more Kordelina resisted, the more Saturnalia made a point of teaching her. However, despite her complaints, Kordelina secretly yearned for the empowered feeling of communicating with the Otherworld and the peculiar morbidity it evoked.

"You will not join us?" Saturnalia inquired, looking kindly up at her.

"No," she answered, staring at her pointedly. "I do not wish to be here."

"Where would you like to be?" Edainne asked sweetly.

Kordelina thought a moment. "I do not know where it is. But sometimes I feel a strange aching inside of me as though a part of my being were missing. I suppose where I wish to be is not one place or the other, it is—I do not know."

"You do know, Kordelina," Saturnalia insisted. "That is why we have come here: to find out what we already know. It is important to understand that the soul must have a destination. It is what motivates us and directs our lives. It would be folly for us to simply seek out an existence. We are placed here for a purpose, and I would like for the two of you to understand that purpose while you are still young enough to see it fulfilled."

Edainne began wringing her hands nervously, and gave Saturnalia an uncertain look.

"Go ahead and tell her, Edainne," Kordelina urged. "She will not rebuke you for it."

Edainne bowed her head in silence.

"Tell me what?" the Sorceress asked, looking first at Edainne then up at Kordelina. "Tell me what?"

"She and Diarmudd are in love," Kordelina announced flatly. "They have promised their devotion to each other, but since Edainne is supposed to be a Chieftain's bride, she thinks she has wronged the gods. I told her it would be wrong not to do what she felt was true in her heart, but she does not believe me. No one else knows about this, and Diarmudd has said that he will kill himself if she marries another."

"Is this true?" Saturnalia asked, maternally running her open palm over the girl's silky hair.

"The way I feel about Diarmudd is strange," Edainne explained meekly. "I could live with him in this way, only sharing with each other what is lawful for us, until the age of marrying does arrive. But I could not do it if I were to marry the one to whom I am promised because I have promised my heart to Diarmudd. He is honorable in the way he cares for me, and he would never expect anything I did not wish to give. Yet, I am not capable of giving what I truly desire to give."

"Edainne, you brought the bag he gave you as the thing you felt you needed most," Saturnalia said. "Can you explain to me what it represents in your life?"

"It represents the one person who loves me for what I am," she said, her lips starting to quiver with emotion. "Diarmudd loves me not for what I was born to, or what I can give to him. He loves me simply for what he sees inside my heart. I think that is unique."

"Especially for Diarmudd," Kordelina added sarcastically.

Edainne frowned. "Kordelina does not like him, nor does Diarmudd care for her. He says that she, well, it does not matter."

Saturnalia stepped down from her place on the rock, and standing beneath the branch Kordelina was on, looked up at her seriously.

"And what did you bring?" she asked.

Kordelina smirked. "A knife."

"Why a knife?" Saturnalia countered.

"Because we came out here with no supplies or protection, and I, for one, would like to eat tonight," she answered.

"Do you not believe the gods can feed you?"

Kordelina's brows came together, then her expression went blank. "They never have before."

"You fool of a child, they feed us each day—what do you think the purpose of our rituals is?"

"I do not know," Kordelina shrugged. "All I know is that our food comes from the fields that are worked by men like my father."

"And your father works under the blessings of the heavens," Saturnalia confirmed. "Why, you have said yourself that many times you feel the Goddess Macha directing you when you are training your horses.

"Yes," she confirmed, "but I do not know how much of it is just me thinking it is she."

"But what of the apparitions?" Edainne asked. "You have told me of apparitions where Macha and Aonghus have spoken with you."

"Aonghus?" Saturnalia asked, surprised. "Have you elevated him to the status of a god now?"

Kordelina felt her heart sink. "No," she mumbled.

"What?" Saturnalia asked, purposely wanting to make her say it louder.

"No!" she yelled. "No! No! No! There, now do not make me say it anymore. He is not a god. I just miss him. That is not wrong, and even if it were, you could not stop me from missing him. I want him to come home, and I do not care if it is by the blessings of the gods or not. It is what I feel within me that matters, not what the laws say."

The Druidess folded her hands calmly in front of her and nodded a response to the girl's fervent oratory. "If you wish Aonghus to come home, then call him home," she said, unreprovingly. Then she reached into her pouch and took out the dried mushrooms. She handed two to Kordelina, who draped her legs over the branch and hung upside down to get them.

"Why must we always use these?" she asked.

"Because you are stupid," Saturnalia answered, handing some to Edainne.

The two girls looked at each other, and with Kordelina still in reverse, they burst into laughter.

"It is not something to be proud of," Saturnalia added, unable to prevent herself from laughing as well. "You must silence your rational mind to understand that in your unconscious lies the truth. If you were able to do this without altering your condition, there would not be the need. But both of you are too bound by this earthly world to allow any spiritual perceptions to come about on their own. You seek practical explanations for an impractical world, and it is important to comprehend that while the two may exist separately, they are both of equal importance.

"I have brought you out here without food for your bodies or shelter from the elements so that you may become a part of all that is. It will enable you to understand that everything must flow through you and you through it. You must embrace yourself as a product of the earth as well as the sky, and afford yourself the enlightenment that dwells therein. I will leave you now as I am in need of solitude, but when the dawn breaks, we must gather as we are now. It must be in the same place, and you must take special care to remember the thoughts you have at this moment so we may confirm, to our conscious minds, that the dimensions we have experienced are a world apart from this one."

Kordelina rolled her eyes. Seeing her reaction, Saturnalia whirled around and, grabbing her by the hair, pulled her face close to hers.

"Only the ignorant scoff at what they are incapable of understanding," she said coldly. Then with no further explanation, she glided off into the trees.

Lowering herself to the ground, Kordelina felt the immediate effects of the mushrooms. She was starting to feel woozy. Not wanting to fall asleep, she sauntered through the woods, noticing every intricate detail of the bark on the trees and the leaves on the shrubbery.

The sun was peeping from behind a cloud when she happened upon a brook. She followed it a fair distance until she found a spot where it pooled deep enough in which to swim. Captivated by the silvery formations the water made as it flowed into the brook, Kordelina sat down on the bank and stared at it in silence until the sun lulled her to sleep.

"Kordelina," Saturnalia's voice woke her.

Opening her eyes she looked around and realized it was completely dark. "What?" she replied.

When there was no answer, she arose listlessly and looked around, but saw no one. Dismissing it as her imagination, she splashed some water on her numb face and tried to prevent herself from falling back to sleep.

"Kordelina," came the voice again.

This time she said nothing in response as she drew her knife and waited. When she did not hear it again, she suddenly realized she was starving. Crawling beneath a bush, she sat back on her heels and tried to remain perfectly still. She did not know how much time had elapsed when she found herself imagining she was part of the shrubbery concealing her—the branches were wrapping themselves around her, and the water from the earth infiltrating her veins where her blood should be. Then, catching sight of a very plump hare crossing her path, she reached out and with one try, had it by the ears. She shook it hard a couple of times to shock it, and with one whack of a rock to its head, killed it.

She used Solomon's knife to skin it, and too hungry to build a fire and wait for it to cook, started eating it raw. Her stomach immediately felt the effects of the uncooked meat, and feeling it churn, Kordelina vomited it back up. Nauseated by the taste, she rinsed her mouth in the stream, then ate more.

"Kordelina," a deeper voice sounded from the trees.

Still chewing, the girl looked up, but once again saw nothing.

Strangely unafraid, she rose from her spot and started to follow it.

"Kordelina. Kordelina." She could hear it so clearly that she began running after it, but every time she thought she was right at it, she heard the voice in a different part of the grove. Finally out of breath, she dropped to the ground and began stabbing at it out of frustration.

"Who are you that knows my name?" she demanded furiously. "Who is the coward that would call me from the darkness, and not show its face?"

All was silent for a moment, then she heard it again. "Kordelina."

"Saturnalia, if it is you, stop your games and reveal yourself," she screamed, but the only response came in the form of her name, repeated twice as before.

Kordelina was definitely not frightened by this—she was infuriated by it, but she was absolutely not afraid of it.

All at once, there was something warm and wet on the leg of her trousers, and looking down, she realized that she must have grazed herself with the knife because she was bleeding. She watched with fascination as the red stain grew bigger and bigger. She was overcome by the way it seeped into the leather, almost like dead skin being revitalized with the blood of life. Then there was the unmistakable presence of two people standing at opposite ends of the forest in front of her.

Lifting her head, she saw the transparent, ghostly images of a man and a woman. One was Saturnalia and the other was, unmistakably, Aonghus. Both had their arms held out to her and were using a single voice to say her name. Their features were vague but each possessed determination. She knew beyond a doubt that they were beckoning her to make a choice between a life as a sorceress or that of a warrior.

In her mind, the decision had been made long ago. Knowing that what she was about to do would disappoint her teacher, and possibly change their relationship forever, Kordelina nevertheless could not prevent herself from going to Aonghus. She was out of her mind with happiness at the vision of him and the drugs to be able to stand. Instead, she crawled to him and began kissing his feet.

"Come home, Aonghus," she begged, fighting off hysteria. "Come home. I am so lonely; there is an emptiness in my heart without you here."

As she rested the side of her face on his feet, she glimpsed the image of Saturnalia evaporating into a ray of moonlight, but she did not care because it was Aonghus who was there with her.

———

The sun was breaking on the horizon when she awakened and found herself clutching a good-sized boulder. Her neck was stiff, and her face was stained with blood from last night's meal. Rubbing the sore shoulder on which she had slept, she rose to her feet and found her way back through the woods. She had an eerie feeling when she found Saturnalia and Edainne in the exact places in which they had been the day before, and it was very strange to see that their hair was not mussed, or their clothes soiled. Compared to them, Kordelina looked like she had been through a battle.

She stopped in front of them, and as she looked from one to the other, their poise and radiance confirmed to her that she was not of their making. She could not go between worlds with character and humility. Her world had room for only two, and she would not, even if she could, change that.

Deliberately fighting the urge to run away, she made herself appear calm as she turned away and walked back toward the village.

"Kordelina, wait," Saturnalia called.

Kordelina halted, but did not turn around.

"If you are elsewhere when the sun's face shows, the dimension you were in last night will remain your reality," she cautioned.

Kordelina took a deep breath and considered her words. Perhaps at another time, they would have affected her, but on this morning, they did not.

"I have work to tend to," she replied evenly, and continued her pace.

ChAPTER ThIRTEEN

t was the sound of a harp that first caused him to stir. It was like listening to chiming raindrops as the tinkle of the strings penetrated deep within him. When he at last focused his aching eyes, he practically swooned at the sight of life around him. There was a glowing fire and a woman playing the instrument while a girl about Kordelina's age combed out wool at her feet. The room was sparsely furnished with nothing but the bare essentials, and while it was austere in comparison to the way he remembered his own home, all that was held within it seemed to glimmer with vitality.

He opened his mouth to speak, but could not make the words come out. Feeling suddenly panicked at his condition, he attempted to sit up, but could only thrash about in his bed. He was terribly weak and disoriented, and catching sight of his movement, the young girl tugged on the woman's robe and pointed to him. The maid stopped playing and came to his bedside.

Aonghus immediately recognized her as the woman he had tried to kill, and was thoroughly perplexed by her kindness. Frightened by his helplessness, he reached out to her, making muted sounds he thought were words.

"There now," she said, letting him hold on to her. "You have been badly hurt; you must not upset yourself."

Aonghus shook his head and the room abruptly whirled round and round and went black. Then, slowly, the colors faded back in, and when he had regained his vision, he attempted to speak again.

"What is this place?" he asked, the thickness in his tongue causing saliva to dribble from the side of his mouth. "Who are you?"

Using the end of her sash, she wiped his lips and the sweat from his brow.

"I am Klannad, second wife of Daneen. This is my home until I can join him on Anglesey," she said, her voice echoing loudly inside his head, making him cringe.

He covered his face with his hands, curled up on the bed, and began crying uncontrollably at the pain. He felt his stomach cramp as he became nauseous. Klannad called for help, but her voice became more and more faint as the room funneled back into darkness.

What followed from that point on were lucid episodes jumbled together with memories of the past. At times, he could scarcely discern which was which, and it seemed the more he struggled to revive himself, the more intense the delir-

197

ium became. He awakened once to a raging storm with booming thunder—he was sure his head would burst—and he awakened again to snow flurries. Finally, it was a warm beam of light that renewed his spirit, a single melancholy ray of winter sun illuminating a droplet of water suspended atop the window. The shutters were open, and the chilly air had the fresh-bathed scent of rain.

Running his hand over the side of his head, the first thing he noticed was that his hair was cut short. After holding up a few strands of his once long mane as a confirmation, he felt the tender area around his wound still bound with muslin. Touching his hand to the side of his face, he noticed it was numb.

Slowly he sat up, and even more slowly, forced himself to stand. He shuffled weakly over to where a mirror sat on a table, and holding it up, was shocked to see that his face was slightly lopsided. His right eye drooped at the end, and one brow was more slanted than the other. His lips were thicker on the right as well, and he was unable to close his mouth all the way, even when he tried. His hair was so short that it barely covered the top of his ears, and his torque was gone. To look at him, one would think him a peasant farmer, not a warrior.

He was too dizzy to drop his head enough to check his stomach. So he lowered the mirror, and pulling back the bandage, saw that it was healing well. Then examining his face again, he glimpsed the reflection of a woman behind him.

She approached him slowly, and resting the side of her face against his back, ran her hands down the sides of his naked hips. Panicked by her familiarity, Aonghus' body tensed. He tried to step away but was too uncoordinated.

"It is all right, Aonghus," she whispered. "It does me well that you have decided to enter this world again."

He started to shiver from the cold breeze on his unclothed body. Accidently dropping the mirror, he heard it shatter as it hit the ground.

"You are still weak," she said, wrapping his arm around her shoulder and helping him back to bed. "You must not try to do too much."

She covered him up to his neck with the animal skins and started dabbing the cold sweat from his forehead with a cloth. Shaking profusely, Aonghus watched her with narrow, suspicious eyes.

"How do you know my name?" he asked slowly.

"You have said much these days," she answered. "I know of your Chieftain, Solomon, and the beautiful Saturnalia. You told me her hair is as red as the fire of the setting sun. I know you dearly love one named Kordelina. You keep saying how precious she is to you; is she your wife?"

"No, I have no wife," he responded hesitantly. "Kordelina is my sister."

Klannad smiled a radiant, kind smile that was almost too genuine to trust.

"She has been your companion many a troubled night when you have tried to prevent death from taking you," she continued, setting down the cloth and folding her hands in front of her. "She must be strong-willed because you have often called to her to ease your pain. Do you remember who I am?"

"No," he mumbled through chattering teeth.

She smiled and playfully twirled a lock of golden hair around her finger.

"You have asked me my name at least twice each day since you have been here," she told him. "My name is Klannad. I am second wife of Daneen. I live here with his daughter, Grainne, until we can join him on Anglesey. My brother, Bov, lives here as well. He trains horses for the resistance."

Aonghus licked his dry lips, and Klannad immediately offered him water. "I am from Anglesey," he slurred, once his thirst was quenched.

"It is the only place that is safe on this side of the sea," she replied. "Perhaps you will be well enough to return with us. And if we have not left by the time you are stronger, you should work with the horses to repay my brother's good will."

She rose from her place and left the room, then returned moments later with honey sweetened gruel. Propping him up on goose feather pillows, she fed it to him slowly. Aonghus found this demeaning; he could not look into her eyes as he ate. An irrational anger rising in him at her kindness, he jerked his hand up and knocked the bowl to the floor.

Klannad did not seem surprised by this as she picked it up and continued feeding him what was left in the bowl.

"These feelings are all part of it," she said unaffected. "For one as young as you to be this way forever saddens me."

Aonghus' eyes started to flutter involuntarily and his face felt hot.

"I will not be this way forever," he babbled. "I will not live helplessly."

"Nor should you," she comforted, wiping the gruel from his mouth. "Your strength will return, but your mind will always be a fragile thing. My first husband suffered a wound such as yours, and he became crazed by the visions until he took his own life. I tell you this not to frighten you, but so that you may understand and not suffer the same fate. And perhaps because of your age, you will yet heal better than he."

He heard her words trail off into silence as the ringing in his ears grew louder. He saw the chamber door open and the young girl enter. She stood at the foot of the bed staring at him and smiling innocently. Looking back at her, Aonghus grew calm again. She had a sweet, untroubled face of one untouched by violence. After seeing so many abused children in these villages, her naive radiance was irresistible. She had dark hair and eyes, and did not resemble Klannad in the least. She was much younger than Kordelina, as he realized that he had been gone for nearly three years now.

His hearing suddenly returned and he caught Klannad in mid-sentence.

"—my daughter by marriage," she was saying. "Grainne is born of Aisling, but I love her as if she were my own. Since I am unable to bear children, the blessings of Daneen's other wives are my enjoyment."

"I am sorry," he said softly. "Children are gifts from the gods."

"Yes," she answered. "But they have given me another gift of creation. I am an artist. Daneen fell in love with my work and took me as his wife so that I might continue it. If it were not for him, I would be a slave somewhere. When the Romans invaded our settlement, he took me as his wife and told me he would provide passage to Anglesey with the others. But we were separated before the ship departed, so Grainne and I are still waiting for passage to his island. He says it is a beautiful, untroubled place."

"It is," Aonghus murmured, his mind filled with pictures of his homeland. "There is a wealth of crops and livestock, and the herds of horses roam free throughout the hills. The groves are sacred, and the earth itself breathes with life."

He noticed that his speech was suddenly clear, and his mind alert. He touched the center of his chest, where he remembered his anointing symbol was, and felt a bit of regained confidence knowing it was still there.

"Where is my torque?" he asked.

Klannad shook her head. "You had no torque when I found you, and you would do well not to mention it. I cut your hair so you would not appear a warrior; otherwise, the Roman authorities would see to it that you were executed. Let them think you are a farmer until we can leave here. Caesar's men do regular searches, and they believe you were kicked by one of my brother's horses and that we are tending you out of good will. If you wish to see your home soon, please do not take to violence because there is nothing you can do about their presence here but live with it."

Grainne came to the side of the bed, and compassionately touched him.

"Yes, I do wish to see my home again," he said under his breath. "I wish I were there now."

———

Klannad was wonderfully eccentric and lighthearted, which made Aonghus' abrupt personality changes easier on them both. She seemed to be able to handle the way he would fly into a violent rage for no apparent reason, or when he would sink into a deep depression and cry endlessly without knowing why. When his moods reached the point where he might try to harm himself, she would fix him a tea of wormwood and cowbane. Then a gentle euphoria would set in and he could see a way out of his tunnel of madness.

When he was lucid, she would explain to him what he had done and the reason for it happening. She had many times recounted the deep depression that had caused her husband's suicide, and had asked him over and over to trust her to care for him. He willingly did this, even though he was fully aware he was becoming addicted to the herbal concoction she prepared.

Klannad also used hot compresses and massage to ease the paralysis in his face. After a time, he regained the full usage of the muscles and could speak clearly again. But in spite of this progress, his expression was never the same.

The moon grew full six times before he was well enough to work again. In that time, he had grown attached to Klannad and Grainne as the three lived comfortably in that one small room. There were moments when he actually felt happy again, and by the time Klannad had shared herself with him, he had even considered staying there permanently. Their age difference did not seem to interfere; she was exactly what he needed to get well.

Blackouts and nightmares were normal occurrences for Aonghus, causing whole days and nights to go unaccounted for. With Klannad's patience, he was able to endure them until his need for her medicine had tapered to a single dosage each day to placate his dependency.

On the morning he went to the barn to help Bov with the horses, the first thing that came to mind was Kordelina. He could not help but wonder how she had done with the two weanlings they had caught. Knowing she was older now, he could not clearly picture her face anymore, and he was at a total loss to remember what either Solomon or Saturnalia looked like. It was unsettling to draw a blank on the three people he knew had greatly influenced his life.

"I do not spend too much time with them," Bov said, walking up behind Aonghus and pointing to the horses. "Most of them do not live long enough to need to know anything besides accepting a saddle, going forward, and halting on command. Klannad tells me you used to train horses also."

"Yes," Aonghus said, turning to him. He did not trust Bov. He was much too accommodating, even though Aonghus had heard he and Klannad arguing about his presence there many times.

"Good," he replied, slapping him on the back. "I will leave you on your own then. You take four and I will take four. With your help, we should make a profit on them in half the usual time."

"How can you make a profit if they are for the resistance? They have nothing to pay you with," Aonghus inquired.

Bov nervously averted his gaze and stared straight ahead, but kept the same smile. "Freedom," he answered curtly. "Fighting for my freedom is the profit. Now this one here, he is mean and crazy."

He walked into one stall where a chestnut colt was tethered. The young horse tried to strike him with one of his back legs, and Bov delivered two hard kicks to the animal's underbelly as discipline.

"See that. I cannot stand this one," he told Aonghus, as he hit the colt's nose so hard that it pinned its ears and tried to bite him.

"Let me take him," Aonghus offered. "Some horses are just misunderstood."

Bov looked at him coldly. "Is that right? Well then, if you understand him, perhaps I will not have to use this one for food as I had originally thought. Feeding an extra mouth has lessened our supply."

Aonghus nodded. "I understand, and I thank you for your generosity. Because of your kindness, I am well enough to hunt now. You will have no further burden."

The Celt's face hardened; he looked as if Aonghus had insulted him. "I have been able to tend my family without a warrior's help up to now."

"Of course, forgive me, I did not mean that..." Aonghus stopped. "You called me a warrior. When I was brought here, was I wearing my torque?"

"No, not that I recall," he answered evasively and proceeded to show Aonghus the rest of the herd.

Chapter Fourteen

iall was a delicate, pale-faced child whose wiry frame showed the effects of his mother's troubled pregnancy. He was a sheltered and favored son, indulged by both Kordelina and Enda because he was certainly to be the last child of the family.

Despite being pampered, Niall remained sincere and unaffected. Due to his size and quiet manner, he was constantly the brunt of the practical jokes of his brothers, Connedag and Erc. More than once, Kordelina had come to his defense when they treated him too roughly or sent him out to find a nonexistent item they claimed they had forgotten in the woods. The even-tempered Niall took it all in stride, and was glad for the time he could spend with his older sister.

By age four, Kordelina regularly took him to work with her at Solomon's estate. In the same way Aonghus had shown her to care for the animals, she passed her knowledge on to him. It was apparent that he was deathly afraid of horses, though. In their presence, his mouth went straight and his body became stiff. The only horse he would consider riding was Osin, but the sway-backed gelding was now much too old to carry even one rider, no matter how small.

Holding his hand, Kordelina led him past Pwyll's manor on their way to Solomon's. She had originally thought she would stop to say good morning to Edainne, but when she saw Bracorina seated on the porch, she changed her mind.

Bracorina had recently been returned to her family by the husband of her second trial marriage. Her first trial marriage was shortly after Aonghus' departure. She had made an agreement with Berrig's younger brother, but it had failed miserably after a brief period, with Bracorina blatantly rebuking him in front of the tribe. She had accused him of slothfulness, and demanded that their union be abolished immediately.

Afterwards, Bracorina had gone into a period of deep depression until her father had paid for another marital testing period with an aristocrat from a nearby tribe. He returned her a short time later with bruises and a broken nose, saying only that he had found her an unsuitable wife. Now she was awaiting the birth of her first child, making sure that everyone knew what a horrible fate she had suffered at the mercy of another clan. She had also made a point of telling Edainne that she didn't want Kordelina anywhere near her. She considered the girl an underling, and due to her present condition, refused to subject her unborn child to the company of a peasant.

"Be off with you!" Bracorina yelled, catching sight of the two children. Rising from her place, she started after them. "Get away from here!"

As Kordelina quickened her pace away from Bracorina, she happened to glance over her shoulder at the precise moment Bracorina threw a stone and hit Niall in the head. The little boy did not make a sound, but Kordelina could see that it had hurt him.

Turning on her heel, she let go of Niall's hand, and began walking straight at Bracorina. The pudgy girl stood there, arms dangling at her sides, looking a bit threatened by Kordelina's approach.

Kordelina did not say a word until she was right in front of her. Since Bracorina was a good deal shorter than she, she got as close as she could and looked intimidatingly down on her. "You did not have to hurt my brother," she said protectively. "We were leaving."

"Then go! You and that scrawny child were not summoned, nor are you welcome," she hissed.

Kordelina was not affected or surprised by her behavior. Of all the people in the clan who made a point of treating her badly, Bracorina and Diarmudd were the worst.

"Do not speak ill of him," she told her. "He has done you no harm."

Bracorina glared over at Niall who shrank back and gazed at the ground. His meek reaction to her rudeness struck a cord in his sister, and without thinking, she grabbed Bracorina's still swollen nose and jerked it hard. She could feel the cartilage slip out of place, and the puffy sinus area start to bleed.

The young woman let out a wail of pain. Gripping Kordelina's wrist, she tried to loosen her hold, but Kordelina did not let go until someone took her by the hair and yanked her backward. In the next moment, she felt a slap across her face. Seeing a fist come at her, she ducked and started running.

She darted past Niall, who immediately followed her as fast as his skinny legs could carry him. It was not until the two were a fair distance up the road that they stopped to catch their breath.

"Did you see who hit me?" Kordelina asked, bending forward a little to get her wind.

Niall nodded.

"Was it Diarmudd?" she asked.

Niall nodded again.

"Thought so," she told him. Then she saw Niall's eyes widen, and he turned a whiter shade of pale.

"He is on his horse!" he hollered, frantically pointing up the road. "He is coming after us!"

Kordelina took off in one direction and Niall in the other. She knew he would be safer by himself, since it was she that Diarmudd was after. Knowing that the young warrior was on horseback, she purposely ran off the path through soft and rocky footing that was guaranteed to slow him down.

She could hear the hoofbeats a far distance behind her, and could also make out Diarmudd's grumbling at the terrain. There was a part of her that took secret pleasure in antagonizing both the brother and sister. She had always harbored a grudge against Diarmudd for staying behind when Aonghus had gone, and for being completely unashamed of his cowardice.

In Bracorina's case, not only did Kordelina find her ugly and lazy, but she resented the way she had easily abandoned her promise to her older brother. Now that she was expecting a child and was not married, she had conveniently drawn on the Celtic belief that all children came from the initial union with the man who claimed a girl's virginity. Therefore, all offspring were raised in Aonghus' name, and believed by the tribe to be of his line. Kordelina found this thoroughly absurd because Aonghus had been gone for years, and regardless of what anyone said, she was sure that he had nothing to do with the conception. Besides, Saturnalia said the union must be a pure love that was felt by both, and she knew Aonghus had never been in love with Bracorina.

The horseman was coming closer. Not wanting to be seen, she dove into the bracken, and crawled on her belly to a safe place where she was concealed by rocks. In a few moments, Diarmudd galloped by and when she was sure her presence was undetected, she began giggling to herself. She thought him such a buffoon that the simpler it was to outwit him, the more pleasure she derived. Suddenly hearing a rustle of bushes on the other side of the rock, she grew quiet and peered out to see what it was.

What she saw was a pair of beautifully beaded leather boots that led to even more flamboyantly embroidered doeskin breeches. They had connecting half-circles stitched up the legs. The area below the knee, where the boots ended, was garnished with threaded vines of mistletoe. The girl's eyes followed the slender legs to the torso, where a thick belt was wrapped around a slim waist, and a form-fitting leather vest covered most of the curvacious, but muscular frame. Red hair, soft and full of body, flowed past the waist. There were rings on every finger and bracelets halfway up the sinewy arms. And it was not until Kordelina looked into the face that she realized it was not a man, but a woman.

Her mouth dropped open, but then she smiled, thinking she was having another one of the unexpected visions from using Saturnalia's herbs. But the muscles of the woman's body rippled with life, and her appearance was much too keen to be an apparition.

"I am the warrior, Blathnaid," she said in a harsh voice. "I come as messenger for the Icenian Queen, Boudicca. It is with your Chieftain I desire to speak."

Kordelina glanced behind the woman and saw a well-bred steed with a lustrous nacre coat. Its headstall was ornamented with silver and the leather was inlaid with the same design as on the seams of her breeches. The embellished animal made the girl gawk even more.

The warrior grew impatient when she saw Kordelina's reaction.

"Can you speak, child?" she demanded.

Kordelina frowned at her, and without a reply, she went straight to the horse. She ran her hand down its brawny neck, and examined the flexible metal snaffle bit it wore. The rings on both sides of the mouth were much bigger than the bits she used, and there was a leather band fastened around its nose. She inspected the rest of the riding equipment to see what else differed from what she used.

"Why are the rings so big?" she asked.

"For more control," the warrior answered, responsive to Kordelina's interest in her horsemanship. "It is easier on them if they can feel the command with their cheeks and not just with their mouths. They understand it much quicker, and neither horse nor rider has to work as hard."

"And the leather tie around the nose?" the girl asked, sticking one finger beneath it to measure how tight it was.

"It keeps him from refusing my command," she answered. "If he sticks his nose out too far and tries to get around it, he hollows his back and does not use his legs enough for running."

Kordelina nodded, then was distracted by the sound of what she knew was Diarmudd. Ignoring Blathnaid, she picked up a good-sized oak branch from the ground and climbed on top of the rock she had been hiding behind.

The young warrior saw her and approached. She waited until he was at close range, then whacked him across the ribs with the piece of wood. Diarmudd grunted and grabbed hold of his torso, but noticing the woman, did not retaliate.

"That is for striking me," Kordelina barked as she picked up a stone and threw it at him. "And that is for what your sow of a sister did to Niall."

"Ouch," Diarmudd flinched. "Stop, Kordelina, or I will see to it that —"

"That what?" she purposely taunted him. "You can do nothing to me."

Diarmudd's face grew red but he said nothing back to her. Instead, he directed his attention to Blathnaid. "What purpose do you seek here?" he asked in an overly commanding tone.

"That is no concern of yours," Kordelina answered for the warrior. "I will take care of it."

She walked over and grabbed Blathnaid's horse, and brought it to her. Standing like the perfect attendant she had been taught to be, she held the animal by the reins until its master was in the saddle and had raised her stirrup.

"Come with me," Kordelina said, her voice filled with self-importance. "I will take you to our Chieftain."

With Diarmudd watching after them, the two started toward the road that led to Solomon's manor. Both went along without speaking, Blathnaid sitting majestically in her saddle and Kordelina walking beside her on foot. The girl was enthralled with everything about the impressive woman, taking special note of every detail, from the way she outfitted her horse to the intricate stitching on her clothes. When Niall emerged from his hiding place and saw the company his sister was in, he timidly fell in a good distance behind them.

When they were in sight of the estate, Kordelina saw the Chieftain walk onto the porch with Saturnalia behind him. He was still chewing his breakfast and scratching his now slightly rounded belly when they stopped in front of him. His eyes had a humorous glint to them that easily revealed his condescending attitude toward female warriors.

"I am Blathnaid," she said, dismounting and bowing to him and Saturnalia. "I come as messenger from Queen Boudicca. She asked that you would honor her by listening to what I have to say on her behalf. It is of concern to all the Celtic people, and I am only one of the many who has been entrusted to disperse her message to outreaching lands."

"Very well," Solomon replied. "Please take comfort in my home, as I and the Druidess, Saturnalia, rule over this tribe."

Blathnaid looked at Saturnalia and smiled.

"What is it?" the Druidess asked. "Have we met before?"

"No, good lady," she chuckled. "It is only that I find it funny that you should name yourself after that which the Roman's call the All Fools' Festival. It is a time when the slaves assume their masters' attire and roles to make a mockery of them."

Saturnalia could not help but smile at the woman's genuine honesty, even if it was unintentionally insulting.

"In my world I was named for the moment when the moon entered the realm of the planet Saturn," she said.

Blathnaid nodded. "Of course that is a more noble title for such a one as you, and your world is far from such things as Roman mockeries."

Kordelina watched the three disappear into Solomon's house. Intrigued by this visitor, she quickly led Blathnaid's horse into the barn, and took off its bridle so it could eat and drink. She did not unsaddle it because she did not know how long the warrior would be staying, and it was only proper to wait to find out. Niall watched her with his hands politely folded in his lap.

"Wait right here for me," she told him, hanging the bridle on a peg on the side of the stall. "I want to go in to find out why she is here. Maybe she knows something about Aonghus. If anyone comes looking for me, tell them I forgot something at home and will be right back. Then you come and knock twice on that window over there, and I will come out."

"All right," Niall said. "But how will you get in? The shutters are locked."

Kordelina smiled and pulled out the skinning knife she had never returned to Solomon. She walked to the window and opened it to climb inside. The shutters closed again without a sound, and Niall sat patiently waiting for her to return.

"There have been many battles," Kordelina could hear Blathnaid saying in the next room as she cracked the bedroom door and peered out. "They have taken place mostly in woods and bogs. Some have not been planned; they were chance encounters. It is only by our stubbornness and bravery that we have not been subdued. The Romans can be very ruthless and cruel in dealing with our rebelliousness, though. The steps they have taken to establish settlements have only been moderately successful. There are some Celts who have surrendered, declared their loyalty to Caesar, and made a shrine to him. Even worse, a number of Druids are already bargaining with him because they see his rule as inevitable."

"And what has happened to our kinsmen who refused to be colonized after the authorities declared it law?" Saturnalia asked.

"Most have become slaves or been imprisoned," the warrior answered mournfully. "Their wealth has been appropriated to influential tribesmen who have sold their loyalties to the Imperialists. The young virgins are sold as concubines by the Druids, who are already convinced that the only wealth to be had now comes from Rome. It is a more attractive alternative to submit to Rome because Caesar has already assured them independence. He has established a great many client kingdoms from which the appointed king can collect tribute if he maintains order and raises recruits for Roman armies when asked."

"You mean there are Celts fighting against Celts?" Solomon queried in a harsh tone. "To fight tribe against tribe is an altogether different thing than fighting for Rome. We should all be kinsmen."

"Yes, Chieftain," she urgently agreed. "That is why I have been sent by the Queen. Among many of the new generations of Celts who know of Roman oppression, there are a great number who wish to avenge the defeats of their fathers. We have set aside our individual differences and taken up a new common attitude that desires the defeat of Caesar. We have been collaborating in secret for some time now, and all legions have agreed that we can do nothing further—the government-imposed rule has taxed us into dependence and poverty. I have come on behalf of the Queen Boudicca and her husband, King Prasutagus, to solicit your assistance in our campaign against the Imperialists."

Solomon looked at her with sudden indignation, and for the first time since Aonghus had left, Kordelina fully realized how much the Chieftain resented them for luring him away.

"We have already given you men," he stated. "That is not enough?"

Blathnaid glanced at Saturnalia, questioning the reason for his severe reaction. "It is, and it is not," she said firmly. "Most of the young men that were received into our clans are dead. While they fought courageously, it did little to prevent the Romans from seizing our settlements. Now not only are we at a loss for dedicated kinsmen, but we are in need of arms and backing."

Solomon slumped in his seat and stared at the ground as Blathnaid continued to speak.

"I came to this island because it is the next obvious target for the Romans," she went on. "The Silures and Ordovices tribes are yet to be subdued, but if they are, this will become a primary goal of the conquest. It is a gain for the Imperialists because these corn fields can produce enough grain for the islanders and most of the main islands. Everyone knows it has become a refuge for leaders and warriors defeated in southern Wales. Not only that, but it would be a major victory for Caesar, because it is now the only surviving Druid center. The Romans believe our spiritual leaders to be the cause of the resistance. If they are defeated, we know from valid sources that the rest of the tribes in Wales will surrender. Also, the presence of copper in your outlying areas would be still another motive for attack. If you can give us enough support to continue to fight on the main islands, the Romans will be unable to assault you."

Solomon did not seem to hear what she was saying. He sat with his head dropped forward and eyes unblinking.

"I am sorry for your struggle," Saturnalia finally broke the silence. "I suppose I had hoped to hear you had fared better than this. Of course you may tell your Queen, in the strictest confidence, that she may count on our assistance. I would caution you in further dealings with any of our holy Order. This is a time when ambition and guile run rampant, and for the future safety of your people, your discernment will be needed. I do have an inquiry about a young man who left our island for Wales."

"Yes?" Blathnaid said, looking curiously at the unmoving Solomon.

"I realize there are many over there, and that perhaps you cannot be sure of only one. His name was Aonghus. He is of this Brigantes tribe and should be almost eighteen by now," Saturnalia hopefully told her. "He is blue-eyed with hair the color of—"

"Forgive me, good Saturnalia," Blathnaid interrupted. "But I can already tell you that I have yet to know one of that name. I am sorry."

Saturnalia clasped her hands in front of her. "Nor has anyone who has passed through our midst from your parts, but thank you. It would do us well to have you stay to feast with us this eve. I feel our people should be informed of your acquaintance with the Imperialists. While I will say nothing of your conspiracy, your truths will bring you more wealth than I could ever draw upon in secret. Come to my home, and you may rest until nightfall."

CHAPTER FIFTEEN

losing the door as quietly as she had opened it, Kordelina slid down the wall until she was sitting on the floor. She had no idea there had been any inquiries about Aonghus' whereabouts. Now she understood why Solomon had taken many journeys to outlying harbors to pay Greek traders who regularly sailed across the Menai Strait to Wales. She had oftentimes been at a loss to understand his irritability upon return, as well as the way he lashed out at anyone who dared to get in his way. Even Saturnalia was not immune to his moods, and the result of this had been a noticeable demise in their relationship.

Rubbing her eyes with her fists, Kordelina tried to keep from crying. Aonghus was not dead; he could not be dead. She did not know how to communicate it to Solomon, but she was positive that some part of her being, still breathing with life, was entirely shared with her brother. At times, she felt so close to him that she was sure if he died, she would also. It was impossible to explain it to anyone, much less understand it herself. Sometimes she thought herself deranged for believing that she and Aonghus shared the same sphere in the universe, even though many miles and years had now fallen between them.

Resting her chin on her palm, she heaved a worrisome sigh and looked around the room. The shutters were closed, and there was only a small amount of daylight peeping in from under the door and around the window. Still it was enough to make out the finely kept decor in this room and the fact that it was not used regularly. This room had been lifeless far too long.

Scanning the area, she focused on some clothes and weaponry stored in a corner alcove. Recognizing the threaded design on a linen shirt, Kordelina rose to her feet and went to inspect it. A closer look confirmed her first instincts. The garments hanging there belonged to Aonghus. She picked up his sling and the dagger, and remembered how they had fascinated her the last night they had made camp together. Then rummaging through the rest of his things, she found bracelets and more clothes stored neatly in a cedar chest.

She lifted them to her nose and tried to remember the smell of him. Then pressing his cloak to the side of her face, she tried to remember the sound of his voice and the way it used to feel when he held her hand in his. She felt a sudden delight at the vividness of the memory, and suddenly recalled what Saturnalia had told her: 'If you want Aonghus home, then call him home.' It seemed entirely too simple, yet as she sat there completely surrounded by all that was left of him, it seemed entirely possible as well.

Taking off her muslin tunic, she put on the linen shirt. It was slightly big on her so she fastened one of his broad leather belts around her waist, and with the exception of having to cut a new hole in it to make it tighter, it fit her well enough. Then she carefully looked through his jewelry and found a pair of plain bronze fibulae to fasten the shirt's V-shaped neck, and helped herself to two of his bracelets. She thought the visit by the warrior must have been intended as an inspiration because the change in outfit filled her with a new sense of pride. She was comfortable like this, and she learned it was not forbidden for women to be warriors. She was now sure of her purpose in life.

Her thoughts were interrupted by a shuffling of feet in the outer hall, and before she could think to hide, the bedroom door opened and Solomon entered. He wore a melancholic expression, trying to hold back tears. He was so consumed with his feeling that at first, he did not notice her tucked away in the corner. Taking a place on the bed, he affectionately ran his hand over the tapestries that covered the pillows. He mumbled something to himself and shook his head. Then catching sight of Kordelina, he jumped to his feet with a start.

Confidently, Kordelina stepped into the open and looked him straight in the eye. "I want to be like Blathnaid," she declared.

Solomon looked her up and down, and realizing she was wearing Aonghus' clothes, clenched his teeth and scowled at her. "You are a brazen child," he said. "Take that garb off before I give you the beating you deserve. You should not be creeping about in places forbidden to you."

The girl waited a moment, then deliberately put Aonghus' dagger into her belt. "No," she answered flatly. "I want to be like Blathnaid."

The Chieftain widened his stance and folded his arms stubbornly across his chest. "You are going to be like Aonghus in a moment if you do not do as I say."

Kordelina stubbornly jutted out her jaw and assumed the exact same stance. "He is not dead. I do not care what you wish to believe, but he is not dead. I would know it."

Solomon huffed. "How would you know it?"

"I just would," she retorted.

"Then would you also know where he might be?" he asked sarcastically.

Kordelina shook her head. "No, I do not. But Saturnalia told me that if we wish his return, then we should call him home."

The Chieftain dropped his arms stiffly to his sides, and walked over to the window. With one thunderous blow of his fist, he caused the shutters to fly open. "Go ahead and call," he said, motioning outside. "Perhaps a bird will hear and save us some trouble by simply flying across the sea and informing him he is needed here."

When Kordelina did not move, he glared at her indignantly.

"Saturnalia and her mystical truths," he said scornfully. "Why do you not go to the wondrous sorceress and have her conjure your brother out of the air?"

"Stop it!" Kordelina rebuked in a harsh voice. "Do not make a mockery of it. I do not understand her ways any more than you, but I do know that they are not to be laughed at."

"Oh yes, forgive me. I forgot how seriously you take your spiritual schooling with our priestess," he turned to walk out of the room, then remembered that Kordelina had not yet relinquished her attire.

"Are you going to take those off?" he demanded, whirling back around.

"No," she answered. "I already told you, I wish to be like Blathnaid."

Solomon's eyes were blazing, and Kordelina could see him appraising her determination. Then, his expression suddenly shattered and he laughed. "This is insanity. You cannot be like Blathnaid; you are only a girl."

"So is Blathnaid," she countered earnestly. "She made it through the initiation, and so can I. I would beg you, but I think your heart too hard to take pity on me."

"You are right about that," he agreed, again crossing his burly arms. "I know of no warrior that would take on a girl as an apprentice. Even if I did, your family has nothing with which to purchase your schooling. You would do well to remain with Saturnalia and learn what you can from her."

Kordelina looked at the ground, inconspicuously trying to get a hold of Aonghus' sling.

"Do not take that, either," Solomon warned, aware of her actions.

"Aonghus would let me have it," she argued childishly.

"Then when you have called him home, he can give it to you," he once again turned to leave, but stopped when Kordelina began stomping her feet and throwing Aonghus' clothes and jewelry in a tantrum.

It was all Solomon could tolerate. He grabbed her so fast that the girl was already over his knee before she knew what had happened. Using his open palm, he proceeded to give her a painful spanking.

At first, she kicked and tried to bite him, but with one of his massive hands, he held her by the back of the neck and continued. His palm stung with each blow, but much to his surprise she remained perfectly silent.

When his hand was numb, he finally stopped and set her back on her feet. She looked at him coldly and red-faced, but she did not touch what Solomon knew must be her aching backside.

"I want to be like Blathnaid," she said, her voice even more resolute.

Solomon blinked hard a couple of times. For a brief moment he considered disciplining her further, but from the feel of his hand, he was not sure which of them it would hurt most.

"Why?" he countered, throwing his hands up in the air. "Why, why, why?"

"Because I cannot be like Saturnalia, and I cannot be like Edainne, and I cannot be like my mother," she said, at last showing signs of tears. "I have no ability for it. Saturnalia has tried to teach me, and while I try to understand her ways, they are not a part of my being. I thought I could try to be good and sweet like Edainne, but no one takes me seriously. I like my mother, so I tried to be like her, but it was boring. Washing, sewing, and cooking at sunrise and dusk."

Solomon's face softened as he rubbed his sore hand. "Why do you not just be yourself?" he suggested.

"Because it is undesirable," she replied, blinking back tears. She quietly put Aonghus' weapons away and removed the bracelets, the belt, and the fibulae. Then she carefully picked up the clothes and began folding them neatly.

Solomon watched her tenderly. "Why is it undesirable?"

Kordelina shrugged. "I do not know. What seems natural to me, everyone else finds strange. My mother says no one will want a girl who smells like a horse or knows how to track a deer through the woods. But that seems to be all I am good at. When I am with the animals or sleeping under the stars, it is the only time I feel happy. I wish to be like Blathnaid; she has taken the things which others find unworthy in me and made them something to be proud of."

Solomon felt his stomach knot. "And you think if someone showed you a warrior's ways, you would be successful at it."

Kordelina nodded as she picked up one of Aonghus' sashes and touched it to her lips. For a moment, she seemed a world away from Solomon, then as quickly as she had drifted off, she resolutely looked back into his eyes.

"You could show me," she said.

"No, I cannot," Solomon answered as he started for the door. He feared that if he stayed one moment longer, his guilt would make him agree to anything the young girl wanted.

"Is it because of Deireadh?" she questioned.

Solomon stopped short, and with what seemed only one long stride was again standing in front of her. "What do you know of Deireadh?"

Kordelina knew she had struck a vulnerable cord in the Chieftain, and she was not sure how, but she wanted to use it to her advantage.

"I know she is a great mystery," she answered. "She is the evil one by whose name you begged my forgiveness the night Aonghus was anointed. I believe she is the reason why you avoid me. You said yourself that I was the image of her."

Solomon reached out, and taking Kordelina firmly by the shoulders, lifted her from her place and backed her into a wall. He was uncertain what made him do it; all he knew was that if he did not assert some sort of dominance over her, she would force him into revealing the truth.

"Silly child," he said. "You know not half of what you think you know."

Kordelina cast her gaze to the ground. "I am only sure of two things," she said without a hint of intimidation in her voice. "I know that Aonghus lives, and that I wish to be like Blathnaid."

Solomon instantly released her and turned his back.

"You are so stubborn," he rationalized. "You are not stupid like everyone thinks; you are pigheaded! Once you make up your mind about something, you will not change it. Still, you are not my problem. I have made restitution."

He stormed out of the room. Hearing the front door slam, Kordelina ran to the window to see where he was going. She watched him throw a bridle on the nearest horse and vault atop its back. Unfortunately for Solomon, it was Lir, the colt Aonghus had last caught. He was still young and unruly, and at the sudden feel of the heavy warrior, he wheeled around and started bucking, until Solomon hit the ground in a cloud of dust.

As soon as he was off, Lir stood still, looking curiously down at the surprised Chieftain. Then Solomon rose and lumbered into the grove on foot.

———

Three days later, Bracorina miscarried and directly attributed it to the abuse she had suffered from Kordelina. It was an unfortunate incident because Bracorina did become gravely ill from the hemorrhaging. When Kordelina owned up to her actions, she was ushered before a tribal assembly and made to publicly ask for Bracorina's forgiveness.

As punishment, she was forbidden access to Pwyll's estate, and was not allowed to speak to Bracorina unless the girl addressed her first. Her father also had to pay Bracorina a sizeable amount of the future harvest as recompense.

The clan's open hostility and the disappointment of her parents caused Kordelina to withdraw, which not only made her appear more guilty than she was, but further alienated her from her tribesmen. She felt that even her family disliked her now, and save the understanding lecture she received from Saturnalia and the private guarantee that Edainne was still her good friend, Kordelina decided to take her future into her own hands and find Blathnaid.

She was not running away from the humiliation; she was simply getting away while she could, she told herself. She believed the visit from the warrior was an answer she had long sought regarding her destiny, and if she let it slip by without doing anything to catch it, it would evade her forever. Since Aonghus had entrusted the colt and filly to her exclusively, she could perhaps pay the warrior with Macha, and still have Lir to ride.

She tearfully explained her predicament to her horse, professing her remorse at having to use her as payment. Macha was the truest friend she had. Kordelina begged her to try to understand that she had no choice because Lir rightfully belonged to Aonghus, and was not hers to give away. The little filly pricked her ears up, then tenderly placed her furry muzzle in the bend of the girl's neck, and Kordelina interpreted this to be her consent. Determined to escape from her futile existence in the clan, Kordelina stole off one morning before sunrise in the hope of finding a new life as a warrior.

She had not traveled far when she thought she saw the lone female warrior riding up a hillside in the distance. It was too far away for her to be sure, but keeping Lir in tow, she signaled Macha to a gallop and started toward her. The overcast day made it impossible to tell for sure if the horse had the unique nacre coat of Blathnaid's steed. Rather than take any chances that it was a journeyman, Kordelina crossed a hilltop, and cut through a cluster of trees to be alongside the hill.

When she emerged to where she was sure the traveler should be, she was baffled to find no one in sight. Inching out of the trees, she saw a horse without a rider, and felt a chill run down her spine, as if someone were watching her. She looked up and saw a warrior perched in a tree above her. He was young and handsome with sun bleached wavy hair and rich brown eyes.

She drew Solomon's skinning knife and pointed it at him. The warrior took one look at her and threw his head back with laughter.

"What are you doing out here alone, little one?" he asked, jumping to the ground beside her.

His voice had a velvety softness Kordelina almost recognized, but taking a long look at him, she did not know where they had met.

"I am searching for the warrior, Blathnaid," she told him, still pointing the knife in his face.

"I see," the young man said, motioning to the east. "She went that way. I saw her perhaps a day ago. If your filly is fast you may catch her in two day's time."

"She is fast enough," Kordelina retorted, keeping her eyes on him as he walked around to inspect Lir.

"It is dangerous on this side of the island," he said, almost too sincerely. "There could be Romans out here who would like nothing more than to get their hands on a young virgin like you. I would trade you weapons for this colt."

Kordelina shook her head. She tried to keep her expression unreadable even though she felt frightened. "He belongs to my brother and is not mine to give away," she answered, pulling the colt closer to her.

"What about your filly?" he inquired.

"No, she is too small for one your size," she told him. "If you made her work too hard you could injure her."

The warrior nodded his head. "You are probably right. So may I ask why you are in search of Blathnaid?"

"No, you may not," Kordelina answered. "But I do thank you for your offer, and I happen to know there are no Romans in this territory after all."

"Are you sure?" he said, humorously arching his brows.

"Are you?" Kordelina shot back.

He looked at her for a moment, then laughed again. "Yes, I am sure. You are smart for one so young. Will you tell me your name?"

"No," she said. "Will you tell me yours?"

"Yes," he said, bowing gallantly. "I am Conn."

"Goodbye, Conn," she said, gathering her reins and continuing on her way. "I am sure the ladies of my tribe will better appreciate you than I. Continue on your path and you will find them long before the sun falls below the horizon."

"Yes," he called after her. "I am sure I will."

Saturnalia was spellbound by the sight of the handsome warrior entering her yard. It was not that she was unaccustomed to men, it was that the look of this statuesque man awakened something slumbering deep inside her.

Tying his horse, she watched him confidently walk to her door. Before he could knock, she opened it. The two stood a prolonged moment looking at one other, then as if they had read each others' minds, both tried to speak at once. They both immediately stopped to let the other talk, then proceeded to start, laughing when they once again blurted out at the same moment.

"You speak first," Saturnalia finally offered.

The warrior gave her a broad smile, then took her hand and bowed before kissing it. "Dear Saturnalia. It does me well that your beauty has remained untouched."

Taken aback by his charm, Saturnalia pulled her hand from his and smoothed her hair away from her face.

"How is it that you know me and I do not know you," she asked, unable to keep from returning his smile.

"You do know me. It is only that I have been long away from you, and my looks have greatly changed," he answered, straightening up. "I used to be of this tribe, but now have taken residence to the north of here."

"And may I ask your name?"

"I am the warrior, Conn," he answered, touching his hand to the center of his chest. "It was you who anointed me."

He watched her cheeks turn pink, and she girlishly looked away.

"What is it? Am I not a pleasurable sight?" he asked, this time taking both of her hands.

"Yes, you are," she replied, flustered. "But I must confess that the memory of things so long ago makes me feel quite old."

"If it does, time has not etched itself on your face. You are as beautiful as my memory envisioned you."

They stared at each other for another long moment, then Conn released her hands and stepped a polite distance away.

"As I said, I have taken residence with the clan of my wife," he explained, a hint of regret in his voice. "I am only here to inquire of a good friend."

Saturnalia regained her composure. "Who is that?"

Conn looked at the ground, then his brown eyes darted nervously back at her. "Aonghus. I am here to inquire of Aonghus."

A look of despair flashed in Saturnalia's eyes. "He did not return. But please come inside and tell me where you last saw him."

CHAPTER SIXTEEN

he was enveloped in the scent of sunshine as he stepped into her cottage. He was tall and slender, and the contour of his muscled arms seemed to glow in her vision. He stood nervously in front of the hearth until Saturnalia motioned for him to sit as she brought wine and cheese. She sat opposite him, overcome with a sudden sensuousness.

"He did not return?" Conn asked, trying to continue the conversation.

"Who?" Saturnalia replied, slightly distracted.

Conn offered her a tiny smile. "Aonghus."

The Druidess immediately shifted her position and became attentive.

"No," she replied, clearing her throat. "When did you last see him?"

"It has been nearly a cycle since I have been back," he explained. "We— Aonghus and I— had decided to return home. On our way to the ship, we were ambushed by Romans. We happened to come upon a battle where there was still some fighting. I think they thought we were the trackers for reinforcements. A great many of our people died that day."

Saturnalia tilted her head to the side and stared at the flickering orange flames of the hearth. She did not want to hear more, but felt obligated to ask. Perhaps this news, however painful, would at last cure Solomon of his obsession to find Aonghus. She studied the hurtful expression on the young man's face, his beautifully clean hair, and subtle attire. It had been too long since she had seen such radiance in the face of another—almost as if it were a reflection of herself.

"And Aonghus?" she asked in a whisper.

"I believe he died," Conn said, his eyes misting. "A wound on the side of his head was gaping open and he was barely conscious. I had no choice but to leave him. He had been speared in the gut and could not ride. He told me to go on because he knew it was over for himself."

Saturnalia drew in a deep breath and watched a small stream of smoke move along the ceiling. She was trying to quiet herself long enough to discern if what Conn had described had indeed been Aonghus' end. She felt strangely scattered and out of place, as if she had put too much psychic energy into the boy's well-being for it to be over suddenly.

When she turned to speak to Conn, she found him directly beside her. He had a questioning but desirous look as he silently caressed her features with his eyes. Then he kissed her.

His soft lips were like warm water, and she willingly kissed him back. She felt an arousal of her femininity that she had never expressed except alone in the privacy of her chamber. It was a heat that surfaced from deep inside.

A million things ran through her mind at once. At first, she thought he was exploiting her, that somehow he wanted to witness the vulnerability of one seemingly stronger than he. But when she felt him run his tongue down the side of her neck and start kissing the tops of her breasts, his motivation was unimportant.

This was pure passion, she thought to herself as she opened her gown. This was the consuming feeling she had witnessed in young lovers; the carnal urge that set them apart from devotion and was fueled only by lust.

She felt herself break into a sweat as she removed his shirt and felt his skin brush against hers. It was so erotic, so wonderfully animalistic to be suddenly naked in the arms of a handsome stranger and not care about anything else but that moment.

There was a burning between her legs, and as she stretched out on the floor in front of the fire, she spread them for him.

Conn looked at her for an awkward moment as if to say he was sorry for such a hurried seduction, and that he had come only to find his friend.

"I do not care," Saturnalia said, licking her dry lips, "and I do not care that you are married either."

Conn's eyes turned to pieces of onyx as he gazed upon her. She could see him trying to steady himself, and for a moment, she thought he was going to leave. Then he unfastened his trousers. Instead of lying upon her, he took hold of her legs, and kneeling, wrapped them around his waist.

The fullness of him as he entered her made her gasp at first, then it settled into low, pleasurable moans as they rocked back and forth. In a fraction of a thought, she questioned what she was doing seducing a young, married man, and of how Solomon would be hurt if he knew. Then she arched her hips and staring back into his deep brown eyes, her cares sublimated into ecstasy.

They dressed without speaking, and when Solomon did arrive unannounced, there was not a hint of what had taken place. He entered the cottage without his usual knock, and it was apparent by the furrow in his brow that he was irritated about something.

When he saw Conn, Saturnalia could see him trying to place his face. Then his eyes wrinkled into a smile, and he forgot himself.

"I know you," he said to the young warrior.

"Yes, I was raised here, my name is —"

"Conn," Solomon finished his sentence. "I am so glad to know that one of our kinsmen made it home. How long have you been here?"

"Only a short while," he said, his eyes nervously darting over to Saturnalia, then back to the Chieftain. "I live in another tribe north of here. I have a wife and we are expecting a child shortly."

He saw Saturnalia bite the inside of her lip as he finished his sentence, but she gave no other sign that it made a difference to her.

"And you have come to see Turg?" Solomon asked. "He would be happy to cast his aged eyes on you again. Why did you not go to him first?"

Conn said solemnly, "I stopped first to ask of my friend, Aonghus."

Solomon's smile was instantly replaced with a tight-lipped frown. "I was hoping you would have brought word from him as well," he said, disappointed.

Conn shook his head and remained silent.

"Aonghus was alive when he last saw him," Saturnalia offered. She blurted out the words clumsily; she could not believe it was she who had said them. Yet, she took her automatic reaction to be a hopeful sign. "He was wounded but was still alive. Is that not what you told me?"

"Yes," Conn answered, trying to appear confident. "He was hurt badly and had to stay behind. But I can tell you no one was more determined to come home than he. I am sure when he is able, he will return."

A light came to Solomon's eyes. "Can you remember where it was that you last saw him?"

"Well, yes, it was near a small settlement to the south of the trade harbors. Have you not inquired from the ships who have docked here if anyone has seen him?" he asked.

"I have, but none recall him. Perhaps for a reasonable sum you could be persuaded to return," Solomon suggested.

Conn shook his head. "It would be folly to try. There is no Celt who could set foot on that island without having to deal with the Romans. The Greeks are the only ones who have passage, and that is only because Rome keeps the trade lines open and is in need of supplies. Not only that, but as I said, I am soon to be a father. Even Blathnaid is in a tough situation. If she makes it back to Boudicca, it will only be because the gods have granted it."

"So you know of her?" Saturnalia inquired. "Has she been successful in her dealings with your tribe?"

"Quite," he answered, helping himself to the untouched cheese. "Our chieftain has called for a gathering of the clan. He would like to establish a means of total protection of our territory, excluding the Druids."

"That is something you should not be telling me, for I am a Druidess."

"Indeed," he said, unable to keep from smiling when he met her eyes. "But you do yet love your people more than Rome."

"I do, and it will remain so. Chieftain," she said, focusing her attention on Solomon. "It seemed that you had come about a matter of great importance."

Solomon scratched his beard and thought a moment. "Oh, yes. I did," he answered, remembering what it was. "Have you seen Kordelina? She did not come to do her work today."

"No, I have not seen the child in three days. She has been sulking for having to apologize to Bracorina."

"Yes, I know. But the two horses are gone and I thought perhaps —"

"Was it a colt and a filly?" Conn interrupted.

"Yes," Solomon and Saturnalia answered in unison.

Conn laughed to himself. "I should have known. I did find it very odd that one so young would be without an escort. She is headed northeast of here. She said she was looking for Blathnaid."

"Yes, it is odd," Solomon retorted, in disgust. "But so is she. Well at least we know where she is."

"Are you not going to find her?" Saturnalia was irritated by his lack of concern.

"No, I am not," he told her emphatically. "If I bring her home, she will only leave again. Let her return of her free will, and when she does, we will act as if she was never missed. Otherwise, it will only encourage her to be more manipulative."

The Druidess huffed her displeasure. "And what if she does not return?"

"She will," Solomon answered.

"She will not," Saturnalia argued.

"Of course she will," he countered. "If she really meant to leave, do you not think she would have at least said farewell to you?"

"Not Kordelina. If she meant to go, then she is gone," she stated. "You must find her. She is only a child."

"She is only a child," Solomon grumbled under his breath. "If she has not returned by tomorrow at dusk, I will do as you wish."

———

That night, Solomon set out alone to find Kordelina. He found her an impressive distance away from their settlement. She had made camp on a partially concealed knoll and made a fire to ward off nocturnal prowlers. She did not hear Solomon approaching and when the Chieftain peered at her through the bushes, he found her roasting a hare on a wooden spit and musing at the flames. The two horses were munching grass closely behind her. Macha's nose was almost pressed against Kordelina's back as she grazed.

He stayed behind the trees watching her. The firelight had cast an inviting light on the girl's face, making her striking features even more distinct. She had the high forehead and long tresses of her mother, and more than once Solomon had witnessed her running her fingers through her hair in the same manner as Deireadh. Her eyes had the same cast as her mother as well, but they were not narrow and cold. Instead, they were almond-shaped and vibrant. Solomon recognized her nose to be his own, as were her square jaw and high cheekbones.

Thinking of her past behavior, Solomon now found her irascibility almost endearing. There was an honesty in it that, although often misinterpreted, took strength of character to display. Kordelina was not as selfish as she was independent, and what made this trait palatable was that she retained the capacity to be both steadfast and devoted.

Poking his head through the branches, he deliberately made himself visible before entering her camp. He knew she must at least have a knife with her, and he did not wish to risk provoking her to use it before she recognized him.

Her eyes were dark so he was not sure if she had already seen him by the time he stepped into the ring of the fire's glow.

"Hello, Kordelina," he said, disconcerted at the way she ignored him.

She limply lifted one hand and gave a small gesture of greeting, then turned the spit to roast the rabbit's other side.

"You made it quite far considering you had two horses," he said, sitting down on the grass.

"Not far enough for you not to find me," she muttered.

Solomon picked up a small branch and stoked the fire for her. "Are you not frightened to be out here alone?"

She shook her head. "I am not alone. I have Macha and Lir."

"They cannot be much company," he said, tossing the branch into the flames. "They cannot talk."

"They talk all the time, if you listen," she said defensively. "And they do not care about the petty things people do. They do not lie, and they do not try to change me. All they ask is that I treat them the same way they treat me, and I do."

"All right, all right," Solomon replied, trying not to anger her. "Did you have any luck finding Blathnaid?"

Kordelina shook her head.

"Do you think you will?"

The girl shook her head again.

"Then why are you out here?" he asked, perplexed.

Kordelina shrugged. "Because it is better than being back there."

Solomon went to his horse and returned with a leather satchel.

"Saturnalia sent this for you," he said, sitting down again.

Kordelina immediately rummaged through it. She pulled out some honeycomb and fruit juice, and consumed it like she had not eaten for days.

Solomon watched in silence, and seeing that the meat was about to burn, took the spit and turned it himself.

"Did you know I used to be married to Deireadh?" he asked her softly.

"No," she responded carelessly, licking the honey off her fingers. "But it does not matter. It is none of my concern what she did or when she did it. I was trying to use Deireadh that night to make you teach me what I wish to learn. But you do not have to, and you do not have to explain to me why she makes you weep either."

Solomon looked at her and then was silent.

Kordelina smiled broadly as she found some shelled nuts at the bottom of the bag. "Is that finished yet?"

Solomon lifted a piece of the meat on the leg to check it. "It is still pink."

Kordelina took it from him. "That is good enough," she said, ripping off one of the hind legs and offering it to him.

"I have already eaten," he politely refused. He had not even finished his sentence when she had already taken a bite out of it.

"So what are you going to do now?" he asked, stretching on one elbow.

"I am going to eat, then sleep," she answered, still chewing.

The Chieftain was silent a moment. "Then?"

"Anything," she said. "I will do anything; it has to be better than going back."

Solomon twisted his face and rolled his eyes. "It is not that bad; you like your work."

Kordelina nodded. "Yes, I do like working with the horses. I will miss them most of all. Then I will miss Niall, but I think he understands."

Solomon listened to the rhythmic sound of the horses munching. It was peaceful beneath the stars, with nothing but a fire and the horses. It was the time when the mind blended with the sounds of the night, and memories came to life.

"Saturnalia will be hurt if you do not return," he offered, sitting up and tearing off a piece of rabbit to eat.

"Tell her I am sorry. Did Conn make it there?" she asked, changing the subject.

"Yes, did you recognize who he was?"

"Yes. I did not tell him who I was because he would tell you and you would find me. But you found me anyway," she reasoned, drinking the berry juice. "Has he seen Aonghus?"

Solomon perked up at the question. "Yes. He said he was hurt badly when he saw him last, but that he was still alive."

"Maybe we could go find him?" she inquired hopefully. "We could wait for a ship and go over there to see if what Conn said was true. I already know it is though, but you are not interested in that."

She fell silent, lost in thought. Then, she looked at Solomon impatiently. "You should go now," she told him.

"I cannot return unless you are with me," he responded, taking a drink of juice and wiping the food off his mustache with the back of his hand. "Saturnalia has gotten it into her head that you must come back. If I return alone, she will not give me a moment's peace."

Kordelina began cleaning the meat from bones and humming softly to herself. When the carcass was bare, she took it a fair distance away and buried it to avoid attracting animals to the camp. When she returned to the campsite she seemed irritated that Solomon was still there.

"I told you to go," she said tersely.

"Did you hear what I said after that?" he countered.

Kordelina frowned. "It is no concern of mine how you deal with Saturnalia. Tell her I am sorry and maybe she will not be as mad."

Solomon vehemently shook his head. "When she gets of a mind to have things a certain way, she does not rest until they are the way she intended. Now she wants to have you home by dawn, and she means it."

Kordelina spread out her sleeping hide to lie down. Then she turned her back to Solomon and went to sleep.

CHAPTER SEVENTEEN

t daybreak, Kordelina awoke to find Solomon had left and taken everything with him. Macha and Lir were gone, as were her food and supplies. He had even repossessed his skinning knife. Looking at the abandoned campsite in utter disgust, she was angry at herself for underestimating him.

She rolled up her sleeping hide and, tucking it beneath one arm, started back to the village. She had no intention of returning for good; she was merely going back to reclaim what was hers, then continue on her venture. She had definitely made up her mind that there had to be more to life than the limited exposure of her tribe. All reasonings told her that if she did not fit in where she was, she should simply go where she did—even if that meant living alone in the woods with her horses.

Trudging down the hillside, she noticed the overcast skies and the unsparing cold of the wind. She stopped at a stream to wash her face and observed a thin layer of ice forming along the bank. The temperature had dropped drastically from the night before and a bad storm was blowing in from the north.

She jogged back in the direction of her settlement. She was careful to go through the open meadows only when she had no choice, and then she would run as fast as she could for the shelter of the trees. She did not want to risk being seen by a passing journeyman, and with the rapidly darkening sky, she wanted to protect herself from the freezing rain that could start at any time.

When she first felt the large, icy drops, she realized there was no way she would make it home before the squall, so she wrapped herself in her sleeping hide to stay warm. She was sobbing at her stupidity, and her chest was tight from anxiety and fatigue. She was consumed with the thought of being alone and helpless, and could barely make out where she was going. The clouds were blocking the sun and the winds whipping from all sides had completely scrambled her sense of direction. As the skyline blackened, she knew this was not going to be a harmless flurry.

The rain soon turned to sleet as Kordelina plowed her way through the branches blocking her path and headed deeper into the forest. She stumbled over a log once and remained sprawled in the mud, crying miserably. She had scratches on her arms and legs, and was so cold that her teeth were chattering and her feet were numb.

Then she noticed a brief tranquility about the surroundings as the driving sleet turned into fluffy white snow. Lightheaded and confused from her rapidly decreasing body temperature, Kordelina fixed her eyes on a limestone outcropping of a hillside. It seemed a great distance away, but from the looks of it, she was sure it would have sheltered hollows along its base.

Holding her aching side and trying to quell her tears, she headed toward the shelter. The onslaught of snow had washed everything in white, and even though she was sure she was heading in the right direction, the gradually fading surroundings made her question how far away the hillside really was.

With soaking boots and bleeding scratches, the girl crossed the secluded meadow in front of it. She panicked when she surveyed the wall of wet stone and found that it held no cave as she had originally hoped. All she could find was a shallow depression in the rock, just big enough for her to scrunch into.

Too tired and disoriented to go on, she sank into it. She drew her legs to her chest, and wrapped the wet animal hide around her. The area was small enough to contain some of her body heat, but not enough to keep her from drifting off to unwilling sleep.

She remembered waking only once to a blinding world of white. By force of instinct, she ate some snow then fell into a deep sleep again. She had no dreams; she only felt suspended in a dark and chilly void. She recalled the pain from the lack of circulation to her legs, but it was only a vague sensation in her frozen body.

The seeping blackness was interrupted by the frightening sound of snarling dogs. While she was too weak to do anything, Kordelina was sure they were wolves that had caught her scent. She opened her eyes slightly, and seeing a smooth milky wall enveloping her, was urgently aware of paws digging through it. She wished she had not regained consciousness because to die at the mercy of a pack of hungry beasts was the worst possible end she could imagine.

As the ice crumbled, the scrape of the nails sounded in the insulated hollow. Kordelina could see the bright light coming from the rapidly widening hole until a snout was visible. She had scarcely a thought or memory when the whiskered muzzle nosed its way to her, and to her surprise, instead of sinking its teeth into her skin, began affectionately licking her face.

Then there was another one nuzzling her, and the sound of barking from still others. A recognizable voice commanded them away, and soon someone was pulling her into the sunlight. She remained frozen in the same position with the only pain coming from someone trying to uncurl her legs. She yelped from the pain, and her rescuer immediately yanked off her boots and examined her feet. He started rubbing the circulation back into them with both his gloved hands.

"Saturnalia will have my head if you have frostbite," came Solomon's worried voice. He painstakingly bundled her in furs, and gave her water with honey and oats to revive her. He apologized endlessly for leaving her alone without her supplies, reassuring her that he had no inkling of the sudden storm approaching.

"I just wanted you to come back," he said, gathering her in his arms and climbing atop his horse. "I could not drag you back against your will, and I only thought that if you had nothing with which to continue on your journey, you would return. A snowstorm did not figure into my plans. I swear, I would not have abandoned you in such a way if I had known."

"Where are my horses?" Kordelina asked, swallowed up in his warm chest.

"They are at my home, and are fine," Solomon comforted. "We must get you there as soon as we can."

She recalled the uncomfortable jostling of the horse's canter on their trek back. The bright sun irritated her vision each time she tried to open her eyes, but when she was placed in the warm tub of water in front of the hearth, her fear and pain vanished. The only disconcerting thing now was the way Solomon constantly patted her face to keep her awake, and repeatedly asked her ridiculous questions about insignificant things.

After a long sleep, she awakened a bit dazed, but very much herself. She saw Solomon seated beside her, and she could hear her mother and father on the other side of the door. She recognized this was not her own chamber, but the one in Solomon's house that belonged to Aonghus. The family dog and cat had been brought for her and were sleeping on the bed. There also was a platter of food on the ledge above her.

"Where are my horses?" she asked, her voice came in a whisper.

Solomon ran his hand over her cheek and gave a relieved smile. "They are in the stable. How do you feel?"

Kordelina pointed to the platter of food. "Hungry."

"Hungry?" Solomon laughed nervously. "Good!"

He brought it to her and helped her sit up. Then he stepped back and worriedly watched her eat.

Every few bites Kordelina eyed him curiously. She had never seen him act this caring, and his uncharacteristic behavior was unsettling. The purring cat woke up and after arching its back to stretch, nosed its way beneath her arm, causing her milk to spill.

"That is all right, that is all right," Solomon reassured her, immediately wiping it up with a cloth. "I will get you more."

"No need," Kordelina insisted. "There is still some left, I will drink that."

The Chieftain gave a fretful nod and walked to the window. He opened the shutters, and looking out, noticed that most of the fresh snow had already melted, leaving only a thin layer of white on the ground.

"Kordelina, you must understand that what happened was unintentional," he said without looking at her. "I made a mistake."

"Yes," she replied, forgetting about the food and stroking the cat's sleek coat. "I know you meant no harm, so there is no need to apologize."

She lifted the furs to look at her legs, then wiggled her toes to be sure they were all right.

"I have said nothing of the circumstances to anyone, except that we got separated during the squall. Saturnalia and your parents believe I found you afterward. I did not tell them differently," he said, meeting her eye. "When I left you, there was no inkling of a storm. When I saw it blowing in, it was already sunrise. I gathered the hounds and left as soon as I could. No one else knows that I made it back, then went out again."

"All right," she said. "So that is what I will say as well, but only if you return my horses to me and allow me to leave as soon as I am able. You must promise not to follow me."

Solomon frowned. "Are we back to that again? Please explain to me why you wish to leave. Are you truly that unhappy here?"

Kordelina started alternately wiggling her big toes and looked up at the ceiling without responding. From her abrupt change in attitude, Solomon could tell she was not in the mood for compromise.

"I am unhappy with what I am here," she finally declared. "And if I stay I will have no chance to be anything else."

"If you are dead you will not have a chance to be anything else either," Solomon claimed. "And a girl your age stands a very good chance of having something terrible happen to her out there."

"Do not try to frighten me," she retorted, her voice cracking when she tried to raise its volume.

"I am not," he replied. "This is an example of —"

"Of what happens when someone steals someone else's supplies," she interrupted. "Those horses are mine; you should not have taken them from me."

"You are right, I should not have. I already apologized for that," he said, running his hands through his hair to push it away from his face. "And I would like to make it up to you."

Kordelina's eyes narrowed skeptically as she waited for him to continue.

"Will you listen to me for a moment, and consider my proposition?" he asked sincerely.

The girl nodded without a change of expression.

"I have been thinking about the reasons you gave for wishing to be like Blathnaid. And it is only fair that people have the chance to take pride in themselves as individuals," he reasoned. "Everyone is different, and the needs of each person vary according to their personalities. You seem to want to be, well, let us say, unique. And you believe you would be happiest by learning the ways of a warrior. I have the ability to teach them to you, but according to our customs, I cannot anoint more than one. As you well know, I have already done it with Aonghus. Also, I cannot teach you without payment or consent from your family. Now if you stay here and continue your work with me and the Druidess, fulfilling all obligations there first, I will show you what I know in my private time."

Kordelina's face brightened with a smile, and she went to speak but Solomon raised both hands.

"Now wait a moment," he cautioned. "This must be done in strictest confidence. No one else must know, not your parents, Niall, or Edainne. And you must not go around parading your skills and using them inappropriately."

"What about Saturnalia? Can we tell her?" she asked, keeping her smile.

"We should. She will find out anyway," he reasoned gullibly.

"But if it is done in secret, and I cannot use the skills I learn, what is the use of learning them?" Kordelina asked, becoming sullen.

"Because you will be old enough soon, and according to the laws, I must pay you for your time. Perhaps if there is a warrior who sees that you have already developed some skills, he will take my guarantee that all you earn here will apply to an apprenticeship," Solomon explained. "You will have already started later than most of the other boys, but perhaps if you pass your testing, it will make no difference. Will this be agreeable to you?"

"Yes," Kordelina said, folding back the covers and rising to her feet. She took a couple of wobbly steps over to where her trousers were drying by the fire, and using the wall for support, she put them on. "Now I wish to see my horses."

CHAPTER EIGHTEEN

onghus put another log on the fire, then tenderly kissed the sleeping Klannad and covered her bare shoulders. Lacing his fur boots and picking up his axe and spear, he stepped over Grainne, who was slumbering on a pallet near the hearth, and exited the room.

Bov was sprawled in front of a waning fire in the main chamber, snoring drunkenly. Looking at him as he passed, Aonghus hoped he had been too intoxicated the night before to remember that, in an angry fit, Aonghus had knocked him unconscious. The two men had gotten in one of their habitual volatile arguments that, with the exception of last night, were usually about everything in general and nothing in particular.

In the full cycle since he had been there, Aonghus' strength had returned, and he had at last finished paying his debt to the Celt. Not only had he helped him train three more groups of horses in half the time, but had made a point of hunting twice the amount he needed for himself and the girls as payment for Bov's prior generosity. Now after so long a time, Aonghus felt he was entitled to a few liberties, and had asked Bov if he could keep the one rogue chestnut colt he had first taken on.

The horse was returned the first time Bov had tried to sell him, because he was too unruly. Not wishing to see the animal used as food, Aonghus had taken a special interest in training it, and both he and the colt had developed a strong bond. When Aonghus had returned from hunting the day before, he found the colt's stall empty. He was infuriated to learn that Bov had traded it for wine.

Aonghus held his temper and tried to reason with Bov that it was only one horse, and it was special to him. He promised he would break two extra the next time if he would only tell him to whom he had traded it so he could get it back. When Bov drunkenly refused, Aonghus abandoned all control and started pounding him with both fists. He was so angry that he wanted to kill him, and if he had not heard Grainne start to cry at his violence, he surely would have.

Now, stepping out into the icy morning, he whistled for the dogs, and when they came running, he headed into the woods to hunt before breakfast. He was glad for the fresh air and solitude. The incident last night had triggered something that had suddenly made him realize the extent of his mental crisis. He had deliberately overmeasured Klannad's herbs, finding comfort in the drug-induced euphoria. When he had dreamed, he dreamed of his home for the very first time.

It had come to him as clearly as if he were actually there but no one could see him. First, he was soaring over the ocean and could see the small island coming into view. Soon he was able to look down on the emerald hills and the rugged coastline. Then without a hint of transition from the sky to the earth, he was carelessly running through its beautiful oak groves.

He did not have to consciously choose his steps because he knew perfectly well where he was going. And when he cast his eyes on the small settlement, he recognized every hut and individual, even though he was unable to specifically remember their names.

One was a red-haired nymph he was sure he had once known very well. She guided him down a narrow wood chip road to a stately manor. There he felt as though every stone and board of the house was beckoning to him. It was a crazy, haunting feeling to have such a reality simmering so deeply within him, and facing it was the only way he knew he could survive.

Then he followed her to a farm, and stepping invisibly through the doorway, he watched a family conversing in the main chamber. It was his family, but the only way he knew it was because their conversation involved Kordelina's recovery.

He studied their words and gestures, looking for some trait he could identify. Then, their faces stretched into elongated images, forcing themselves in front of his eyes, and taunting him to say their names. When he confessed that he could not, they all scoffed at him. Tormented and lost, he grabbed the hand of his female guide and implored her to help him remember. Her only reply came as she touched her soft hand to the center of his brow, and without moving her lips, told him that he already had.

"What happened to Kordelina? Where is she?" he asked in frustration.

"She is exactly where you left her," she told him.

"Where did I leave her?"

"You know where, you have always known where," she said, her words trailing off as she evaporated into mist.

The sound of his own screams awakened him. "Where, tell me where!" he was demanding and pounding the bed with his fists. By the time he was able to control himself, he saw Klannad and Grainne, frightfully huddled together in the corner of the room. How guilty he felt for scaring them. At that moment, it was perfectly clear he had to leave. The memories were coming back often, and he was teetering on the edge of sense and reason.

The soles of his boots slipped on the icy ground as he made his way to the meadow. He had purposely left some salt there to lure the deer, but had said nothing of this to Klannad. Salt was a treasured commodity, and she would never have consented to his use of it.

Before he reached the clearing, his senses were filled with the rank odor of human blood. It was a stale aroma that made him instantly squeamish. He did not need to see it to know that it was yet another surprise attack by the resistance that had ended in slaughter.

When he got to the meadow, it appeared the same as the many other battle sites he had recently come upon. Romans and Celts were sprawled everywhere, all of them dead.

Aonghus had his own personal ritual for these occasions. In the event that any of the soldiers were still living, he would mercifully end any Celt's misery. However, when he came upon a conscious Roman, he made it a point to inflict further suffering on him. It gave him a perverse thrill to make them beg for their lives. He had only done it a few times these last months, but it had now developed into a sadistic fascination.

To his surprise, some of the Romans had already been decapitated. Looking at the bleached pallors of the corpses, he realized that whether they were Roman or Celt, in death, all men appeared the same. He even reasoned that their thoughts were probably alike, each one wishing he could live another day, and dreaming of the loved ones they would greatly miss.

Surveying the entire field and turning over dead bodies, he looted whatever weapons he could find. As usual, in a situation such as this, there were only a few daggers or slings left. When he was through, he stood in the center of them, and inhaling the pungent odor of dead flesh, threw his head back and let out a warrior's howl. One of the dogs lifted its bloody snout from a corpse and howled as Aonghus did it again and again. When all the breath had left his lungs, he stood with his face to the sky and was filled with a subtle gratification.

A few animals scurried through the grass, then the silence of the meadow was pierced by the sound of human cries. Following it to the edge of the trees, Aonghus found a young infantryman hidden behind the base of an oak. He was curled up with his arms covering his head. A few paces away was his horse. The bone of its foreleg had broken through the skin, and it lay on its side, eyes glazed over and moaning piteously. Aonghus did not have to look twice to know it was the colt he and Bov had fought over.

Overcome with fury, he grabbed the whining soldier by the neck, and jerked him to his feet. He became even more angry when he saw that his uniform was completely unsoiled.

"Please do not hurt me!" he choked. "Please, I do not wish to fight you!"

Aonghus glowered at him, his ice-blue eyes appearing as though they were concealing a demon. He tightened his hold and studying the soldier's young face, realized that he could not have been any older than Aonghus was when he first arrived there.

"Please," the boy begged. "I was going to leave this island this very sunrise. I was going home. That is why I did not want to fight. I was going home."

Aonghus smiled at him coldly, then his mouth hardened and he banged the soldier's head against the tree. "You are a coward," he yelled, spitting in his face. "Say it. Confess to me that you are a coward."

Tears were streaming down the Roman's face, and his mouth was contorted. "I am a coward!" he cried in terror.

"What? What did you say? Say it again, louder," Aonghus taunted. "Say it so loud that the sow who bore you can hear it all the way back in Rome."

"I am a coward!" he screeched again.

"Now confess it to her personally. Say, 'Mother, I am a coward. I hid in the trees like a baby while my comrades died.'"

The boy bit his bottom lip and refused.

Digging his fingernails into the arteries of his neck, Aonghus put his face closer. "Say it, all of it, or I will cut your tongue out and feed it to my dogs while you watch," he threatened.

The Roman gasped in fear, then repeated what Aonghus had said.

"That is good," Aonghus offered, in a calculating tone. "Do you know what the sentence for cowardice is in my tribe?"

The boy shut his eyes hard, and still whimpering, shook his head no.

Aonghus laughed coldly. Seeing that it was evoking greater fear, he threw his head back and roared like a man possessed.

"Please," the Roman wailed, his knees knocking and his teeth clicking together. "Please, I only want to go home!"

For some reason Aonghus' laughter abruptly ceased. He tilted his head to the side and stared at the colt, then back at the Roman. "Silence yourself," he commanded, drawing his knife and slicing open one of the boy's cheeks.

He yelped at the pain, and when he did not arrest his tears fast enough, Aonghus cut the other one. "You make me sick," he told him, as he slit still another gash across his forehead. "Silence yourself now!"

"I want to go home," he whimpered, the blood flowing into his eyes and mouth.

"You are going to go home," Aonghus reassured. "I promise you that."

The boy forced a placating smile through his bloody, quivering lips. "Thank you," he babbled. "Thank you for your kindness."

"You are welcome," Aonghus nodded, then without another word, he stuck his knife into the boy's lower abdomen and ripped him open all the way up his torso. His head rolled back and he slid to the ground.

Then Aonghus went to the colt, and sparing it any more suffering, stabbed it in the jugular vein with his spear. With a single gasp of air, it was dead.

He stood, head bowed, staring at the horse for a long time. Everything became clear to him: not one of the animals he had trained for Bov were for the resistance. They had all been sold to Romans, and Klannad had known about it. She had no intention of returning to Anglesey, and she probably had no husband there either. These months he had lived with her were a lie, and he cursed himself for ever considering he was in love with her.

Holding out his bloody hands, he looked down at them sorrowfully. He knew what he had to do.

He was careful to wash away the blood, and to store the weapons in the barn before going into the house. It was easy to hide the evidence of what he had done to the Roman, but most difficult for him to conceal was the realization of the truth.

The atmosphere was thick with tension inside the cottage. Bov was seated at the table eating gruel, one swollen eye barely open, and his bottom lip swollen as well. He kept a glaring eye on Aonghus as he set down his weapons and hung up his cloak. Klannad was cooking, and Grainne was sitting in the far corner of the room, looking nervous and frightened.

More worried about the young girl than either his opposer or his lover, Aonghus quietly walked over to her and gently took her face in his hands. She would not look at him at first, but when he kept his gaze focused compassionately on her, she lifted her teary eyes and stared at him sorrowfully.

"Grainne, I am sorry for what you saw last night," he said softly. "I did not mean to scare you."

The little girl started chewing on the side of her bottom lip uncomfortably, and looked away.

"What is it?" he asked, disturbed by her behavior. More than either Klannad or Bov, Aonghus had formed the most endearing friendship with the child. She had always been accepting of him and wanting to please. Now he was baffled by her lack of forgiveness.

Grainne shook her head, then spontaneously threw her arms around his neck and hugged him tightly. Returning her affection, Aonghus held her for a long moment, then released her.

As he turned to address Klannad, he focused on her walking deliberately toward him with a well-sharpened, single-edged knife in her hands. It was the one he used for shaving and trimming his hair. He looked at her intently, as if to say he had always known she would resort to this. To his surprise, she gave him her usual light-hearted smile in response.

"Sit now, and let me trim your hair before you go out," she said, placing a hand on his shoulder. "The authorities will surely be making rounds today."

"Why today?" Aonghus asked. "They counted our stock two days ago. Do they suspect we have livestock for which we are not paying taxes?"

"Not at all," she replied, trying not to upset him. "Since last night's fighting was so close, they will probably be looking for any Celts we may be —"

Her eyes met Aonghus' and she immediately looked away.

"Hiding," he finished her sentence for her. "How did you know there was fighting last night, anyway?"

Klannad looked disquietingly at her brother, then back at Aonghus. "While you were gone this morning, a passing journeyman stopped here for some food," she explained, obviously shaken by Aonghus' inquiry. "He informed us of it."

"I see," he replied, glancing at Bov who sat staring at him in vengeful silence. "This journeyman had obviously come from the harbor, and seen these men spread along the cliffs. When I went hunting, that is where I found them."

"Of course," Klannad told him, lifting a strand of his hair to cut it while he was still standing. "Now please let me tend you."

Aonghus felt a wave of despair overtake him at her response. The ambush had taken place in the meadow, not on the cliffs. There was no journeyman that had told her of it. Her knowledge came from Roman maneuvers of which she was already aware. The way she was ill at ease discussing it only confirmed she had been informed of it before or she would have realized that what Aonghus had told her was wrong. Knocking her hand away from him, he caused the knife to fall.

"Get away from me, woman," he barked. "I am not your toy!"

He walked straight to his sleeping chamber. Carefully closing the door, he leaned against it and tried to collect his thoughts.

It was true that the authorities were coming, and he knew this time nothing would prevent Bov from turning him in. He was sure that brother and sister had discussed it in front of Grainne, and that was why she was distraught. Aonghus knew that last night had been the final episode to tip the scales, and he wondered to himself if Bov had deliberately provoked him into it. He was sure he had considered doing it many times; after all, he disliked him, and now the resentment between the two was becoming more violent.

Hearing the front door close at the same moment he heard a horseman stop outside, Aonghus cautiously peered out the window and saw Bov leading a Roman infantryman into the barn. This was no time for poor judgment, he thought, as he climbed out the window and sprinted to the back of the barn where he had stored the weapons.

Taking a broadaxe in one hand and stuffing his knife in his belt, Aonghus tried to make out the muffled exchange between the two men inside. He crouched low to the ground to avoid open windows. The earth was banked around the foundation of the building, slightly elevating the structure so that in the event of heavy rains, it would not flood. Only now it served as a muddy crumbling embankment beneath Aonghus' feet.

Pressing his ear to the wood, he could not discern what was being said because of the blood pounding in his ears. It had been nearly a year since he felt his life threatened, and in that time of complacency, he realized he had lost the ability to handle such situations with stealth. At that moment, he felt terrified, not only of making the wrong decision, but also of being incapable of making any decision whatsoever.

A film of sweat broke out over his entire body, and his hands started to tremble. Tilting his head back, he took in a deep breath of chilly winter air and tried to maintain his composure. He knew the stress had triggered the reaction in his head, the one that would soon send him into one of his dangerous personality changes. It was from his injury, he fully understood that, but what he feared most was that rather than it being an incident of violence, it would be one of fear-stricken hysteria.

He felt what he thought was the earth shifting beneath him, but was really a momentary loss of equilibrium. Trying to keep from falling over, he pressed himself against the back of the building so hard it caused a thud. As the voices hushed, Aonghus wrapped his clammy fingers around the handle of the axe, and when Bov stuck his head out of the shutters to investigate, Aonghus sunk it precisely into his skull.

Bov was too surprised to make a sound as the blood gushed from his puffy face, and he slid down the inside wall. Even though he was inside and Aonghus was outside, he could hear the thump of his overweight body, and the startled hoofbeats of the horse as it tried to get out of his way.

The Roman cautiously walked over to see what had happened to Bov. He was unaware that Aonghus had already sneaked inside, until he drove his knife into the base of his skull, twisting it a few times. Killed instantly, the soldier fell on top of Bov.

Aonghus could feel the tremors coursing through his body. Sweating and clenching his bloody fists together, he fell to his knees and crawled weeping to the very back of the barn. It was not the killing that had caused the tears, it was the helplessness he felt at not being able to react instinctively, no matter how hard he tried.

Wrapping his arms around himself, he slowly rocked back and forth. In these moments of delirium, he felt as if he were two people. One of them was insane and incapable of dealing with reality. The other was safely nestled in the inner dimensions of his mind, trying to help the disturbed body it inhabited.

CHAPTER NINETEEN

t the sight of Aonghus entering the front door, Klannad shot up from her seat behind the harp in shocked surprise. Her grey eyes widened as she looked at him. When he did not move, she propped her instrument against the wall, and awkwardly made her way to the serving table to get his breakfast.

With bloody hands concealed by his crossed arms, Aonghus walked up behind her, causing her to take in a startled breath of fear. Grainne, who had been stirring the boiling pot, dropped her ladle into the venison stew at her stepmother's reaction.

"I would like to speak with you in private," Aonghus said in her ear.

Klannad shook her head. "We can speak here, Bov is away from us."

Aonghus pressed himself so close to her that she bent forward over the table. He was a head taller than she, and now that his body had returned to its muscular form, Klannad was swallowed up by his stature.

"I wish to speak to you alone," he demanded. "I know Grainne is the only safety you have because you know I will not harm you in her sight. But by my presence here right now, we both know that what you had anticipated happening this morning did not happen, and I wish to speak with you about it."

Klannad shut her eyes hard at the reference. "I did not wish it. But there was nothing I could do."

Aonghus purposely pressed the tip of his knife into the small of her back. "Let us go into our chamber, Klannad, and you can explain yourself," he said.

Fists clenched and back rigid, Klannad walked past Grainne and into their room. Aonghus followed close behind, careful not to let the child see his weapon. He had already decided that whether he let Klannad live or not, Grainne was coming with him. If she truly did have a mother waiting for her on Anglesey, he would find her.

Once the chamber door was closed, Aonghus took a place on the opposite side of the room. Klannad stood with her hands clasped tightly together, the small wrinkles around her eyes and mouth becoming more pronounced with anxiety.

"Where is Bov?" she asked meekly.

"In the barn," Aonghus replied.

"Is he all right?" she hesitantly questioned.

Aonghus' expression remained blank. "He is fine, except for the axe stuck in his skull."

Klannad covered her face with her hands.

"Do not worry, he is with his friend, the Roman," Aonghus continued.

"Is he dead too?" she asked, not moving.

"I think so, but if you wish, we can both go out there and check to be sure," he said with contempt.

"You fool, you killed the Roman!" Klannad screamed. "As the heavens have made us, Aonghus, you have no idea what you have done. That man insured that we lived unbothered by the fighting, and he kept us, you and I, out of Roman slave camps. He was our protection, do you not see that?"

Aonghus firmly shook his head. "He was your protector, but he would have been my executioner. Now Klannad, I wish to hear no more about the Roman. What I wish to hear are the reasons I should let you live."

Still clutching his knife, he let his bloody hands fall to his sides and looked at her sharply. Klannad stared at them for a prolonged moment, then timidly lifted her gaze. "I did not betray you," she said softly. "It was not my choice to turn you in; it was your own doing. Why could you not live with my brother in peace? We could have been so happy."

"Happy here?" Aonghus rebutted. "How could we have been happy living with Rome? How could you think that I could continue to bow to them when I am here to fight them? Perhaps I am not entirely capable of reasoning properly, but I do know that begging Imperialists is no way to live. Do you not see that after a time, paying them taxes and pretending to respect them would not have been enough? They would have wanted more until we would not even have had the pride in our hearts left. That Roman was not your guardian, he was your oppressor."

Without offering a reply, Klannad went to a basket hidden in the storage alcove and reached into it. At first Aonghus thought she was getting a weapon. He did nothing to stop her because he reasoned that it would only make it easier for him to kill her if she tried to harm him. Instead, she walked directly to him and held out his torque.

As tears stung his eyes, he took it in one hand and let the cold, smooth feel of it sink in. Then he pressed it to his lips before putting it back on.

"I thought I could change you," she told him defeatedly. "I thought that with enough love, and the passage of time, I could starve the thirst for blood out of you. But as I now see, it was folly to try. My first husband was just like you. He could not be happy to live in this world; he had to try to change it. I gave him everything, everything I could, but it was not enough. He kept talking of honor in death and the need for independence. But he was wrong, like you are wrong. He is dead now, and for what? The Romans are still here, I am still here, and this world knows little of whether he ever existed. Where is the honor in that?"

"There is more honor in dying in truth, than living in lies. Not all the love, hurt, or desire will change what I am inside: a warrior. I have been anointed by the gods, and there is not a being in this world or that of the spirits who could alter my purpose," he stated. "If the inability to fulfill that purpose is what caused your husband to take his life, then I sincerely understand."

He sat down on the edge of the bed, his elbows on his knees. Looking at her softly he said, "Klannad, you must answer something truthfully."

"Yes," she responded. "I will be as truthful as I can."

"Were we ever in love?" he asked with innocence. "I need to know, because right now I could kill you without hesitation. And I believe that if one truly does care for another as they would for themselves, such a thing would not be possible. Deep inside of me, I do not know what true love is, nor do I understand of the love you believed would change me."

Taken back by his sudden honesty and sincerity, Klannad put her fingertips to her mouth and started to cry. She did love him, and that morning, when Bov had insisted that he be turned in or that she and Grainne would be charged with harboring a fugitive, it had taken everything she had to allow it.

"I wanted to love you in the way of which you speak," she explained tearfully, "and I think you wanted to love me in the same way. You and I greatly need each other, but our hearts are in different places. Aonghus, I took you in and cared for you because I needed a reason to go on. When I saw your innocence, your helplessness, I thought perhaps I had found such a reason. It had been long since I had looked into eyes with such honor and willingness, eyes that believed in the good and decent.

"You see, I have lived here with my brother, tending his home, knowing all the while that he was an informant for Caesar. It did not matter because if I ran away from him, I would only have run to slavery. My husband promised me passage, but I have no way of knowing if he fulfilled it—I only had Bov's word to rely on. Every time I asked him about it, he told me Grainne and I had been forgotten. When I found you, it did not matter anymore because I had another purpose. I had a man who needed me, and held me at night while I slept. That was enough. So to answer your question, I do not believe we loved each other as much as we needed each other for a time. If it had been possible, I would have taken all of you, but you were not willing to give it to me. Your heart dwells in a place with your beloved, of whom not even you are aware. It is possessed by one so strong, it will never be shared with another."

A look of sadness filled his eyes at her words, and for an instant, he did not know what to say. He wanted to tell her that he, too, wished it had been different, but he did not.

"Dear lady," he said, rising to his feet. "Were it not for you, I would have died; yet today, you would have let me be killed upon your betrayal. As I feel that I no longer owe you my loyalty, I do understand your truths. I believe you had no other choice but to let Bov act out his vengeance. As for me, I am quite sure that I was deserving of his deeds. I cannot stay here any longer, nor will I leave Grainne. It is my wish that we gather the livestock that can yet be traded, and try to find passage to Anglesey. But need I remind you that if I find anything suspect in your manner or your words, I will either kill you or sell you without guilt."

Klannad's chin started to dimple as she frowned, and cried even harder. "What would heal me of this sadness is knowing that what we shared was not a trifling matter, and you would yet trust me again," she gently pleaded. "For as I have said, sweet Aonghus, I would have loved you with all my soul if you would have but allowed me."

"Do you truly have a husband on Anglesey?" he asked, ignoring her pleas.

Klannad nodded. "And his name is Daneen."

"Very well. I will deliver you to him," Aonghus replied as he put his knife away. "And for your sake, I hope he does exist."

––––––

Klannad knew where her brother had hidden a sizeable sum of Roman money, therefore it was not necessary to take the livestock with them to the trade port. Instead, since he knew they would not be returning, Aonghus opened the gates for the cows, sheep, and pigs, and unfastened the chicken coop. There were only three horses that had not been sold. He saddled one and tied ropes on the other two, and returned all of them to their herd.

It was an awesome sight to see the way they freely galloped, ears pricked up, and muscles rippling with each thunderous stride back to the others. At first, the stallion bellowed at the presence of the defectors. As if they knew they had offended him, the three immediately calmed and humbly approached him. The massive stud flared his nostrils, and gave a dramatic display as he snorted, whinnied, and pawed the ground before finally allowing them back into the band.

Aonghus had expected Klannad to be gone when he returned, but to his surprise, she was waiting with Grainne. She had packed a satchel and bundled herself and the girl for the chilly sail across the strait. Aonghus took the liberty of wearing Bov's flamboyant red cloak lined with wolf fur, and together, the three looked like a family. They had only to board a trade vessel before a Roman decided to inquire of their destination.

In their port, the Romans performed investigations in an arbitrary manner. If they were busy doing something more important, they would not bother passers-by. However, if it was a particularly slow day and they had little to keep them occupied, they would interrogate anyone. An incident such as this usually resulted in the Celt being charged with offending a Roman. He would be sent to a slave camp with no hope of seeing freedom again.

Before Aonghus was hurt, he knew of many men who traveled easily between these islands. They had said that one need only find a trader who liked the price they were willing to pay, and the rest was simple. The Romans never bothered the merchant traders because the commerce from the Mediterranean not only provided them wealth, but supplies. Oftentimes, the sailors who regularly sailed the various Roman territories used their neutrality to sell information to both sides. Rarely were they charged with espionage though, because neither the Romans nor Celts wanted to sever their lines of communication with the mainlands.

There was a large Roman marching camp built in front of the military docking area. It was filled with tents set out in ordered blocks, and the entire circumference of the site was surrounded by a ditch with a rampart erected from timbers and earth. Inside the camp boundaries, a legion of battle-armored infantrymen were drilling.

There were warships interspersed with flat-bottomed naval transports docked along the harbor. This campaign had been going for some time, and the presence of these ships told Aonghus that the island had yet to be secured as an official Roman domain.

As they came alongside the marching soldiers, Aonghus picked up Grainne and tried to walk faster. He purposely stayed ahead of Klannad, thinking he was fully prepared to offer her as a distraction to a Roman who might detain them.

Moving hurriedly past the military vessels, Aonghus noticed the single-manned oared ships were empty. That meant they had brought more men over, and fighting was sure to follow with the increase of troops.

Grainne put her head on his shoulder, and Aonghus looked at the ground as they went by a cluster of Roman commanders. They were discussing the need for greater diplomacy in establishing their client kingdoms, and the need to engage further Druidic influence to insure success. The conversation then shifted to the desire for northern expansion.

Aonghus ignored them until he heard a woman's voice. At first he thought it was Klannad, and he wondered why she was drawing attention to herself in such a way. But glancing over his shoulder, he saw it was a robed Druidess talking. He recognized something vaguely familiar in her manner, and in her oddly rounded face.

"Do not be ridiculous, Flavius," she said, looking without recognition at Aonghus, then looking away. "If they had any idea you were approaching, you would be annihilated while scaling the cliffs."

The tall commander looked down at her, insulted. "Need I remind you, Jara, that this is only one small outpost in Caesar's empire," he replied condescendingly. "We have defeated worse barbarians than those living on that island."

The sound of her name touched something in his mind. Unknowingly, he had turned around to look at her again. He and the Druidess were staring at each other intently when Klannad took his hand and urged him to continue.

When they reached the trade port, they were greeted by the sight of bartering Greeks and Romans, mingled with an array of caged livestock and oak barrels filled with wine and ale. They passed one trader unloading rugs and tapestries, and Aonghus discreetly approached him. The merchant immediately sensed he was seeking refuge, because he pointed to a wooden vessel docked two ships away.

He nodded that he understood and continued on his way as a crate of chickens fell on the dock and burst open in front of him. Feathers flew in all directions as the hens ran circles around each other cackling frantically. Aonghus was thankful for the commotion. It enabled him to pass by two Roman authorities unnoticed and to get to the correct boat.

There were sacks of grain and barrels of ale on the deck of the ship, and as Aonghus and the women boarded, a handsome olive-skinned sailor came up from below. He had the salty, wrinkled skin of a seaman, with a head of curly black hair and a kind expression. He wore a ring in his left ear and possessed the brisk attitude of one adventurous but humane.

"Do you have money?" he asked, looking at the trio.

Klannad nodded and handed him a pouch filled with Roman coins. Since neither Klannad or Aonghus ever had to use money, they had no idea of the extreme value of the purse they were handing over.

"You want to go to Anglesey?" he asked, quickly closing the pouch and sticking it in his belt.

"Yes," Aonghus answered gruffly.

"Very well," the sailor replied. "Get below and do not make a sound. I am waiting for the rest of this stock to be picked up, then we will set sail."

Doing as they were told, Aonghus, Klannad, and Grainne climbed down the ladder to the hull. It was damp and musty, with the smell of moldy grain hanging heavy in the air. Four oarsmen were drinking wine and eating bread, and at the sight of Klannad, they whispered lecherously among themselves.

She hovered close to Aonghus, who took little interest in her presence. He seemed far away as he listened to the men moving the grain off the boat. Sounds of grunting and heaving were followed by the shouts of the sailor ordering them to hurry the job along. Then it became silent, and Aonghus could hear the trader arguing good-naturedly with a Roman inspector who wanted to take stock of the cargo below.

"Oh no," the Greek was saying. "I would not do such a thing. I have a good business running between these islands. Why would I risk it to transport refugees? Besides, they have no money."

"Then what is it you are hiding?" the Roman asked.

The trader laughed. "A few oarsmen, and well, a woman I bought for myself. She is a tender creature, too young to appreciate me yet, but I am working on it. So here my good friend, take this wine and let the fickle beauty have her privacy. It would make my voyage much more pleasant, you understand."

The Roman let out a laugh and started down the ladder despite the protest. Aonghus grabbed Grainne and hid in a shadowy corner, leaving Klannad in plain view. Realizing he was using her as a decoy, she removed her cloak and hastily unbraided her hair so that it flowed loosely down her back.

The oarsmen watched in silence as the inspector stepped down the ladder, followed by the sailor. Fixing his eyes on her, the Roman walked up and roughly took one of her breasts in his hand. Klannad looked fearfully at the sailor then meekly bowed her head.

"If you would like to have her for awhile I can pick her up when I get back in port," the Greek said. "But you must promise to take good care of her, she has cost me quite a sum of wine."

The Roman stuck his hand between her legs and squeezed her so hard that Klannad screamed and tried to push him away. When she could not, she slapped him, and he slapped her back a few times. The sailor did nothing to stop him, nor did the oarsmen, and it took all of Aonghus' control to remain still. They had no more money and if he let his presence be known, not only would the sailor be charged, but they would never have another chance for escape.

Grainne started to cry silently as the inspector shoved Klannad down on a rowing bench. With one hand clasped tightly around her neck, he lay down on top of her and made her spread her legs. The musty hull echoed with the sound of material ripping. Unable to witness her rape, Aonghus lunged out of the shadows and sunk his dagger into the small of the Roman's back.

His torso jerked up in surprise, and as it did, Aonghus grabbed his face with both hands and yanked it hard to one side. The crackling of the vertebrae lasted only an instant, then the Roman fell backward, the weight of his body driving the knife further in.

Panting angrily, Aonghus looked at the Greek, expecting to be reproved. The trader stared at the inspector blankly, then turned to Aonghus.

"We can set sail now," was all he said, then went back on deck.

CHAPTER TWENTY

T he ship creaked and swayed to the changing tides as Aonghus sat in a shadowy corner of the hull. He was watching the men row the heavy oars, their naked torsos glistening with perspiration and their taut biceps looking as if they would burst through the skin of their arms. Aside from talking to the Greek earlier, he had not said a word since he had set the horses free. There was something about that incident that had plunged him into baffling isolation. He wanted no part of anyone, and although he knew Klannad probably felt he resented her, that was not the case. But he was too introspective to take the time to explain his mood.

He supposed it was also the muddled array of memories he had of his home. The thought of returning to a place to which he now had no attachment caused him great distress. Yes, he was going home, but what was home? It was a few vague recollections of his childhood, and a tribe that had been important to a person who no longer existed. He was not the boy who had set sail believing he would be the heroic protector. Instead, these few years had produced a vile warmonger to whom killing was almost as natural as breathing.

Resting his head on his forearm, he tried to sleep, but the rocking of the boat made it impossible, so he climbed on deck and, taking a place along the wooden rail, pondered the small island that appeared in the distance. Had he ever believed he would return to that place? And what had happened there that could have possibly sustained him when he should have died? Trying to remember, he conjured the images of the lush fields of wheat and corn, and the sloping hills that looked like veils of green jewels. He could clearly see a huge lake surrounded by oak groves and alder trees, and could even envision the faces of his parents now. How would they feel about him if they knew what he had done? How would they react if he told them he had slowly tortured men for the thrill of it, and had forced himself on women whom he found loathsome? He wanted to confess the things he had done, the atrocities he had carelessly watched take place. Then he wanted to look into their shocked faces to ask them if this was the son they had raised.

"Have you lived there all your life?" the Greek asked, breaking his thoughts.

Aonghus nodded, but said nothing.

"How long have you been gone?" the sailor asked, standing beside him.

Aonghus shrugged. "Four summers, maybe more. I am not really sure."

"That is a long time for a warrior to stay alive fighting Romans," he replied. "For that, I will share my wine with you."

Taking the leather drinking bag the sailor held out, Aonghus let the unstrained wine filter through his lips. The liquid had been well-aged in oak barrels and would have brought quite a hefty price in trade.

"There is a chieftain over there looking for you," he continued, seeing the surprise in Aonghus' face at his words. "He has visited my boat many times, and pays nicely for any information I give. He has offered a reward to anyone who can locate you. That is why I did not throw you overboard when you killed the Roman. From the description he gave, I recognized you immediately. That, and the snake on your torque. He says you are known by the name Aonghus."

The young warrior was filled with a sudden sense of warmth and emotion, knowing that someone had actually come looking for him.

"Who was the chieftain—was it Solomon?" he asked, breaking into a smile as he said the name.

"Yes," the sailor said. "He is a surly one with long hair and a drooping mustache. He is sometimes funny, but when he eats, it is with the manners of a sow."

Aonghus threw his head back and gave a belly laugh.

"That is him, is it not?" the Greek asked, laughing as well.

"I wish I could remember it all," Aonghus replied uncertainly.

"Well, I have remembered something," the sailor said, slapping him on the back. "I remember that the Roman is still stinking up my ship. We are far enough out to dump him, so you come down and help, all right?"

"All right," he answered, following him below.

———

At the sight of the Greek sailor and the young warrior entering the settlement, Conn handed the baby girl to his wife and started out the door to meet them. He noticed they were being followed by a woman and a child, but the two were of no concern to him. What had sparked his interest was the rocking stride of the young man, and the way he threw his hips forward with each step he took.

When he was close enough to make out his face, Conn let out a howl that seemed to hang in the air forever. Then he ran up and threw his arms around a stupefied Aonghus, and howled again.

"I cannot believe it!" he declared, astounded. "I cannot believe you made it back. I thought you were dead!"

Aonghus stepped back apprehensively. Realizing his friend did not remember him, Conn offered a sympathetic smile and extended his hand.

"It is I, Conn," he said. "We were kinsmen once."

"Yes," Aonghus answered, in a way Conn knew he was merely being polite. "We are searching for one known as Daneen. This is his wife and daughter."

"Daneen is of this tribe," he responded, holding both hands out to the two maids. "These lovely creatures must be Klannad and Grainne. Daneen and his wives speak of you often, wondering why you did not return when he sent passage."

"Then you will take us to him," Klannad said, returning his greeting.

"I would have to," Conn replied. "I am married to his sister. Come, all of you, take comfort with us."

Conn led them to the elegant home he and his family shared with Daneen, his three wives, and eight children. Seeing the way the older Celt received Klannad and Grainne, and the joy it brought to the rest of Daneen's large family, gave Aonghus a peculiar sense of peace. Things would never be the same for him and Klannad, but the time they had shared together had brought them both to a place of reuniting with their pasts. He watched as the women shed their joyful tears and the children giggled with each other.

Daneen was a gracious Celt who thanked Aonghus profusely for returning his missing family members. He tried to pay him for his deed, but Aonghus asked that it go to the Greek as a substitute for the reward Solomon had offered.

"If that is what you wish," Daneen told him.

"That is what I wish," the warrior affirmed. "Klannad saved my life. I am thankful for her, too."

"Then you must stay a time with us," Daneen suggested. "I am sure my dear wife would not want to see you depart so soon after such a difficult journey."

"Nor would that be my wish either, but I am long away from my own family. I would like to return as soon as I can," he said courteously.

"I will go with you," Conn interjected. "You can use one of our horses. If we leave straight away, we will reach your settlement by tomorrow afternoon."

Aonghus looked at Conn skeptically. "No, I—"

"Aonghus, please," Conn insisted. "I know there are probably many things that have left you, but I will tell you of them on our journey. I would ask that you take my offer as we once shared the deepest friendship."

"If that is what you wish," he said, not wanting to seem ungrateful. "Thank you for your kindness."

The two warriors traveled at a leisurely pace while Conn went into great detail about how Aonghus had gotten injured, and what he knew about his tribe. Late in the afternoon of the second day, the two men entered the outlying territory of Aonghus' tribe. Suddenly he was able to discern the groves, the limestone outcroppings of the hills, and even the individual landmarks that he referred to as a child.

They passed over the flatlands, crossing a stream that rambled through the middle, then continued up a hill dotted with alder trees. When they reached the crest, Aonghus immediately recognized the reed-filled shallows and the huge body of water beyond it—he remembered his dog, Locwn, and his burial there so very long ago. He had to stop and wipe away his tears when he recollected the cherished vision of Brigantia, the Goddess his tribe worshipped. This truly was his home.

As Aonghus started down the hillside, he heard the barking of a dog. Following the sound with his eyes, he focused on a young girl lying on her belly at the water's edge, gazing into the gently rippling water. There were two horses behind her; one was almost black, and the other tan and rounded with a foal. The maid was dressed in the work clothes of a boy, but her rolled up pant legs revealed long, trim calves and bare feet. She was staring dreamily at her own reflection, deaf to the sounds of warning her dog made.

Aonghus spontaneously turned his horse toward her, a nervous cramp of excitement in his abdomen. He wanted to make his horse gallop through the swaying reeds to stop in front of her, yet he was careful not to move too aggressively. He took in every detail of her as she came into view.

Her tousled hair was dark and wavy with strands of it so unmanageable that they appeared as though they were growing in entirely different directions from each other. A portion of it was dangling in her eyes, concealing them, but by the time Aonghus stopped a short distance away, he could easily make out the dainty nose and square jaw that seemed out of place with her slender neck.

The hound began to snarl when Aonghus dismounted, and only then did she lift her head to see what it was. As she turned, the sunlight cast an odd illumination in her eyes, making them look like dark, partially flawed emeralds. As he stepped closer and stared into them, it was hard to make out if they were olive-colored, or amber.

Jumping to her feet in surprise, she darted behind the rotund, tan mare, and chewing on the nail of her index finger, eyed him coyly over its withers. The hound was now stalking threateningly in front of her, and it was the only thing that prevented Aonghus from running and gathering this shy waif in his arms. She was beautiful to him—beautiful in a wild, indomitable way. From her stature to the uncontrollably keen expression in her eyes, no one could ever have mistaken her for ordinary.

The girl stood protected by her horse and did not call off her dog. She studied the stranger who silently waited. It was not the expression she finally recognized, because that was altogether different from anything she remembered. It was the unmistakable cast of his eyes, that fabulous, magnetic blue that would deepen or fade according to his moods.

When she realized it was Aonghus, home at last after years of waiting, and that he truly was standing there in front of her in the same way she had pretended so many times these passing years, she gave an unexpected hop in the air. Then putting all four of her fingertips between her teeth, she giggled nervously.

Aonghus was thoroughly endeared by her reaction; he forgot about her furious, growling guardian and started forward. His steps were arrested immediately as the hound lunged at him, its teeth clicking shut as Aonghus jumped back, barely avoiding being bitten. The girl gave a harsh command, and the dog calmed himself and begrudgingly took a place beside her.

She did not move a muscle as she watched Aonghus walk toward her and stop on the opposite side of the horse. It was not until he offered a gentle smile that she came out from behind her equine shield to greet him.

The two said nothing at first. They stared at each other in disbelief. Then slowly and tenderly, Aonghus reached out to take her vibrant face in his hands and stroke her cheeks with both thumbs. She stood there, in complete surrender to his touch. With instinctive, genuine emotion, he ran his palms down her neck and over her shoulders, stopping to affectionately squeeze the tops of her firm arms. She was strong, yet vulnerable and entirely willing to be at his command. With her eyes, she tenderly entered the melancholy recesses of his troubled mind with the brightness of her faith and innocence. She made it clear to him that she was all his—fresh, pliable, and loving.

Finally she spoke his name. Her voice sounded like soft waves to him, waves that told of distant truths and forgotten dreams. When she smiled, it was the white toothy smile of her father, and seeing her, touching her, and listening to the tone of her speech brought back the memories he was convinced would go unrecalled forever. They came flooding back in fragmented sequence, but now, they were entirely comprehendible.

"Kordelina," Aonghus whispered, as she wrapped her arms around his neck and he pulled her close. "My precious, precious, Kordelina."

Lifting her off the ground, he spun in a circle. She kicked her feet out behind her and laughed that distinctly irreverent laugh he easily remembered.

"Aonghus, I knew you would come back," she declared, kissing his cheek. "I always knew you would come back."

Conn had joined them by the time Aonghus set her down. From the way Kordelina looked at him, he immediately understood his presence was an imposition. He lifted his hand to greet her, but she ignored him and taking Aonghus by the hand, led him to the dark bay horse.

"This is your colt," she said proudly. "I kept his name as you intended, and I have cared for him everyday as I promised. Lir is well trained, and ready for you. Solomon says he is a rogue, but he is only stubborn. Because of him, Macha is going to have a baby. If it is all right, I would like to keep it myself. I thought it would be the first of my very own herd."

Aonghus studied the shiny, muscular colt, then looked at Kordelina as his eyes filled with wonderment. Now he understood why setting the horses free before he departed had made such a strong impression. It reminded him of her, and the last experience they had shared together.

"Yes, it is fine," he told her, overwhelmed with emotion. "This animal is too much for me to take from you, not after what you have done with him. He is magnificent."

Kordelina's eyes teared as she shook her head. "But you must take him. I cared for him well and spent much time with him, knowing I would be able to give him back to you and show you I can keep my promises. It might sound silly, but I believed if I could keep him alive and shower him with love and kindness, it would somehow be carried by the gods over to you, wherever you were. When everyone else believed you were dead, I knew you could not be, because Lir was thriving. He is a proud and fearless colt. I would not have given him up for anything; it would be like I had given you up."

"I can testify to that," Conn added affably. "I tried to buy him from her, and not only did she refuse me, but she threatened me with a knife."

"A knife?" Aonghus asked, unable to disguise his amusement.

"Yes," she answered, bowing her head a moment then lifting it again. "But it was only because I thought he was a passing journeyman, and I was alone, and far from our tribe."

"She was far, too," Conn added. "Nearly a day's ride out of the territory. She was trying to find one of Boudicca's messengers to see if she could not get herself recruited. She wanted to fight Romans."

"That is not true!" Kordelina defended. "What do you know anyway—why do you not just go to Saturnalia's cottage and sneak through an open window so no one knows you are there?"

From the way Conn's face hardened at her insult, Aonghus could instantly sense tension between the two, and it concerned the sorceress.

"As you wish, little one," Conn retorted. "Are you coming Aonghus?"

Aonghus eyed the two a moment, then shook his head. "No, not right away. I will be there after awhile. Please do not say anything of my presence yet. I would like to visit my parents in my own time."

"I understand," Conn said, sitting up straight and taking the reins. "I will see you at least by sunset. There will be something to feast about tonight!" He trotted back in the direction he came, and left Aonghus and Kordelina alone.

"What happened to you?" she asked, point blank. "You look different."

Aonghus' eyes narrowed a moment, then resumed their gentleness. "Well you look different too," he stated.

"I look different because I am becoming a woman, but you, you look meaner," she explained. "Did you kill a lot of Romans?"

"Yes," he answered.

"Did you like it?" she inquired, wrinkling her nose.

"No," Aonghus said, smiling at her reaction to her own question.

Kordelina cocked her head to the side and looked at him mischievously. "Did you get married when you were there?"

Aonghus let out a silly laugh and blushed, then shook his head.

Kordelina stared down at her feet, suddenly embarrassed by her prying. "Then why were you gone so long?" she asked.

"I was hurt," he explained hesitantly, "and it took me a long time to remember what my home meant to me. There is still much that I cannot discern about our tribe. I am not even sure that I know what Mother and Father look like anymore."

"But you remembered what I looked like, and I look nothing like what I did when you left," she countered, digging into the muddy grass with her toe. "Maybe you are not as hurt as you think."

Aonghus did not reply as he hopped up and sat on a large, flat rock on the lake shore. Kordelina followed, taking a seat behind him. She rested the side of her face on his back as if it were the most natural thing in the world. She could hear the rhythmic thud of his heartbeat, and from the way his breathing was becoming more irregular, she knew he was upset.

"I did not mean to hurt your feelings," she apologized.

Aonghus took her hand and pulled it around his waist. "You did not hurt my feelings. Many things left me while I was ill, and I have problems reasoning clearly at times. I do not know how I knew it was you when I saw you. I only hope it will be the same when I see everyone else."

"It probably will be," she comforted, opening her palm as he fondly rubbed its center with his fingertips. "But do not be upset if you do not recognize Niall. He was not born when you left."

"Niall? Who is Niall?" he asked, jerking his head around to look at her.

"He is our brother," she replied, taking the opportunity to nuzzle his cheek with the tip of her nose. "I like him. He is almost five now."

"Do I have any other brothers or sisters I should know about?"

"No, everything else is the same, and different," she said, studying the partially visible scar on his forehead. She touched her finger to it, then moved her hand through his hair to feel the entire area it covered. "You were hurt badly. I am sorry for it."

Aonghus hugged her again. For a long while the two of them sat gently rocking each other, silently thankful that they had been reunited.

"Kordelina," Aonghus finally said in a quiet voice. "Will you help me with the things I have yet to remember?"

"Yes, Aonghus, I will," she said. "But I cannot go back with you now. I have to stay out here for one more day."

"Why?" he asked with sudden irritation.

"I already told you. I have started to become a woman," she explained. "Because I have chosen a different path than other girls, when my womb empties itself, I am supposed to spend it in solitude. Saturnalia says it is the most powerful time for a girl except when she is with child. She says I should use this time to entreat the spirits as to my special purpose, and to embrace the seriousness of the world that I inhabit."

"What does that mean?"

Kordelina rolled her eyes. "It means I am supposed to stay out here until I finish bleeding and try to figure things out, I suppose."

"Oh," he replied, a bit baffled. "Is that what you were doing as I rode up?"

At first, Kordelina shrugged like she did not want to admit to something, then she shook her head. "No," she answered. "I was pretending I was a fish, imagining what the world would look like from the bottom of the lake."

Aonghus laughed out loud and kissed her cheek. "I missed you so much, Kordelina. I missed you so very much," was all he could say.

chapter twenty-one

am nothing more than a distraction for you," Conn said, offended. "You take my visits as though it would scarcely matter to you whether I ever returned."

"That is not true," Saturnalia contended, as she made circles in his chest hairs with her fingertip. "I am always happy to see you."

"But you care little when I leave," he argued, purposely dropping his hand from where it was resting on her bare hip. He stared at the ceiling, his wounded pride obvious in his expression.

Saturnalia touched her mouth to his unresponsive lips in an attempt to sooth him, but it did no good. "Now you know better," she said sweetly. "I am always sorry when you leave."

Conn's brown eyes deepened as he looked at her for a moment, then looked away. "But you never ask me to come back."

"And yet you always do," she said, putting her hand between his legs and fondling him.

"Someday I will not," he stated, trying not to give in to her affection. "Someday I will get tired of the way you take me for granted, and you will never see my face again. The way it is between us—I feel like I should be the woman, and you should be the man. You have me wondering constantly if you respect me, and if you are not keeping me solely for the pleasure I bring to your bed. Somehow, I do not think this should be so. I am afraid if I tell you I love you, that I will scare you away and you will want nothing else to do with me. Yet I fear that if I do not profess my feelings, you will never take me seriously, and I will become another one of your affairs."

Saturnalia's eyes wrinkled with a smile. "Another one of my affairs. That is interesting. How many affairs do you think I have had?"

She could see the response in his face from her foreplay as he turned to her. His lids were half closed, showing only the dark sensual orbs that were his eyes. From the way he ran his tongue over his lips and hesitated to respond, the Druidess knew his need for an answer was subjugated by his desire for her.

"I do not wish to think about it," he said jealously, then pushed her away and rolled over. "It is enough that I have to beg for any time with you at all."

Saturnalia propped herself up on one elbow and huffed. "You do not have to beg me as much as you have to lie to your wife," she told him, getting out of bed and putting on her robe. "Do not expect me to tell you that you should leave her or your child. What happens in your personal life is your own doing. What I will tell you though, is that I do not wish to stop seeing you. Yet if the only way it can continue is if I make empty promises that only serve to stroke your vanity, then you had better be on your way now because that will never happen. I refuse to whimper over a man who does not have the courage to decide for himself with which woman he wants to be. You must take responsibility for your own desires, as I do."

"You do? You do?" Conn challenged, throwing back the covers and getting to his feet. "Then I suppose that is why I have to tie my horse in the bushes, and you leave open your window for me to crawl through instead of permitting me to enter through the front door."

Saturnalia smiled sympathetically. "Does that hurt your feelings? I am sorry but that is the way it must be for now."

Humiliated but determined, Conn walked up to her and, using only his naked body, pressed her against the wall. She was small and delicate; he thought he might crush her with his weight alone. But from the defiant look in her eyes, he knew it would be impossible.

Feeling entirely at her mercy, he bent his head forward and kissed the round of her neck. He would not caress her with his hands, though, as he gave tiny nibbles up to her ear. Then he circled it with his wet tongue while he moved the hardened part of himself against her thighs to tease her.

"Do you want me?" he whispered.

Saturnalia gave a small nod, but did not speak.

"Then tell me, tell me that you want me," he continued, barely running the tip of his tongue over her closed mouth. "Tell me, please."

Saturnalia involuntarily rocked against him with her hips, but she did not touch him with her hands either. It was as though the two were sparring to see who would first give in to the seduction.

"I want you," she said through tempered, aroused breaths. "Yes, Conn, I want you."

Conn gave a deep, seductive laugh. "That is all for now," he declared, stepping away from her with a smug, victorious look.

She dropped her head, but then looked up at him with eyes sparked with a fiery light. Seeing her reaction, a horrible thought came to his mind before she spoke: what if this time he really had angered her, and she would send him away forever? What if she had grown tired of his immature sexuality, and he had exhausted the last thread of her patience?

"That is all for now," she said, her voice suddenly polite. The tone of it betrayed the fierce, almost vicious expression on her lovely face. He watched her glide her lithe fingers through her soft red hair, and he felt absolutely foolish for what he had done.

"Saturnalia, I—" he stopped in mid-sentence.

"You what?" she prodded him on.

"I think I love you," he confessed in a shaky voice.

The sorceress kept the same expression, but added a coy smile. "How does one think love? Loving is an action, and the master of the heart," she told him sharply. "I think you are foolish to think of an action that is acting upon you. For, while you may be young, and your wit and body still tender for the future, you waste much time thinking about that which has already mastered you."

Conn felt a sudden longing for her. The way she was standing there made him want to ask her to forgive him for his lack of confidence. But from the very manner in which she tempted him with her open gown to the keen way she looked at him, he knew it was unthinkable.

"In that, beautiful Saturnalia, you speak much truth," he murmured, weakening in her gaze. "For I would forsake my honor for the love of you. I would leave my friends and my child without father with only one word from your lips. I would care little of happiness unless it was the chance to be happy with you. The neglect of my world is caused by the world we have created, and while the musing of my heart may be infirmed, it is only because it is sick for your touch."

She ran her fingertips down the inside of one breast before tying her robe. And when the veil of material closed like a fortress around that which he desired, she turned her back on him and walked silently into the main chamber.

Like a child who had just had his hands slapped, Conn washed and dressed, trying to reason his way out of his humiliation. He noticed daylight was fading, and remembered Aonghus would be coming shortly.

Putting on his cloak, he went into the next room. He was instantly spellbound by the scented oil the Druidess had applied. Wanting to appear unaffected, he straightened his shoulders and went to face her.

"Then, is this farewell?" he asked innocently.

"You should say farewell, if farewell is what you mean," she retorted dryly. "But do not say farewell and banter on my window by the light of the sister moon, for such weakness is unbecoming of one seemingly strong. You stand before me now asking me what you should do, as though I should accept responsibility for that which you are too misled to do yourself. You should willingly do that which your heart and mind can abide. Do not force love where it is not, and do not toy with the hearts of those to whom you wish to endear yourself. For in the end, we all must atone for our creations."

Conn stared at his feet, afraid to look into her eyes. She was an entirely stronger force than he: more disciplined, confident, and altogether more wise.

Slowly opening the door, he turned his head only enough to get a glimpse of her. "I will not be on my way tonight," he said, "as there is need for celebration in this tribe."

"Celebration?" Saturnalia questioned. "What celebrating needs be done?"

"The welcoming home of one who has sickened the heart of your lover and Chieftain," he answered.

"Aonghus has returned!" Saturnalia declared.

———

Solomon sat on the trunk that used to be the oak tree in his yard where Laden was hanged. He had cut it down immediately after he assumed rule, and made sure that the wood from it was used for the Samhain bonfire that year. He had done this at Aonghus' suggestion. After the incident with Laden, the boy had made a point of avoiding any contact with the tree whatsoever. He would go to great lengths to walk around its shadow, and say little prayers to himself when he had to pass by it. When Solomon asked the reason for this behavior, Aonghus had explained to him, in his boyish but intensely serious way, that he thought the tree was cursed and should be given back to the gods. At his request, the oak was chopped down the next day.

Twelve cycles later, at a time when Laden and Deireadh were characters of lore, he used the stump as his favorite spot to sit when he visited with friends or worked on his weaponry. It was situated where he could see the stables and training areas for the horses, and where he could also look up the road to see if anyone was coming.

Joined by the warriors Berrig and Turg on this afternoon, Solomon sat busily carving a new practice spear for Kordelina. All three of the men had spent the day relaxing in the winter sunshine, drinking ale, and telling stories. It had been a careless time, and the trio was content to have more than enough to drink and a comfortable place to sit while exchanging well-embellished stories. As was usually the case, when all the tales were told, the conversation inevitably turned to Rome.

"The Druids are not to be trusted in dealing with the Imperialists," Berrig said, stretching out on the grass with both hands behind his head. "They say it was the Druids who killed Blathnaid."

"Blathnaid?" Solomon said, looking up in surprise. "When did they kill her?"

"Only a day after she left here," Turg told him, pausing to belch before he continued speaking. "Apparently the Druids had been tracking her for a long time. They knew of her dealings for Boudicca, and saw her as undermining their attempts to reach an agreement with Caesar. The Druids are doing the bargaining, not the client kingdoms. Someone like Blathnaid who had the support of the outlying tribes would have ruined all the negotiating that has been done."

Solomon twisted his face. "Do they know who did it?"

"No," Berrig sighed. "But from the way it was done, it was definitely a Celt who knew the terrain well. The assassination was clean, and the tracks well-covered. Everyone believes the Druids hired a local warrior. He disguised his path well; it was impossible to tell where he came from or where he fled. Also, her torque was gone and her hair was cut. Rumor has it that they were presented to the Druids as confirmation of the kill."

"It is a mystery," Turg continued. "Surely one of the tribes must be protecting him. To kill her where he did, then make it to the Druid sanctuary with the proof, he would have to have been gone for at least a few days. Surely, such a one would be missed."

"Perhaps," Berrig answered. "Unless there are those among us who have already been enticed by Caesar."

The three were silent a worrisome moment, then Solomon started to whittle again. He stopped when he glimpsed a young journeyman coming up the road toward his house. When he lifted his eyes to get a better look, he instantly recognized the colt he was riding as the one that belonged to Kordelina.

The Chieftain flew into a panic as, unable to identify the stranger, he was sure his daughter had been robbed. The current conversation and ale fueling his imagination, he thought she had probably been murdered as well.

Solomon dropped his work and taking hold of the sword propped beside him, yanked it from the scabbard. Before Turg or Berrig knew what had overtaken him, he was running up the road at the horseman, swearing.

The two warriors watched dumbfounded as the rider jumped to the ground and began dodging the sword the furious Chieftain was wielding.

"Wait," he was pleading, both hands held up for protection. "It is not what you think."

"I only think I am going to kill you for stealing that horse," Solomon roared, jabbing his blade forward and trying to stab him. "Where is the maid you took it from?"

"She is fine, she is fine," the stranger cried, as he bolted to the side to avoid his maneuver. "As the gods have made us, Solomon, Kordelina is fine!"

The Chieftain was deaf to his words. He gave a low, guttural snort that sounded like an attacking boar, and with both hands, swung his weapon across the young man's knees. He had to leap a fair distance off the ground to escape harm.

"Have you gone mad, Solomon?!" he yelled at him in frustration. "It is me—Aonghus!"

Solomon was in such a frenzy that he ignored him and kept attacking. Ducking out of the way barely in time to avoid injury, Aonghus almost lost his footing. Taking advantage of this, Solomon kicked him hard in the groin.

Aonghus doubled over and dropped to his knees from the pain. Fully aware that Solomon was coming at him again, he desperately grabbed a handful of dirt and threw it in the Chieftain's face.

Momentarily blinded, Solomon sputtered and cursed his opposer as Conn rode up behind him. Using the sole of his foot, the young warrior shoved the Chieftain forward. Realizing he would fall on top of his sword if he did not let go of it, he clumsily tossed it aside before he landed on his belly next to Aonghus.

Aonghus was still on his knees crouching forward from the pain as Solomon wiped the dirt from his eyes. He looked at Conn angrily, then glared at Aonghus and reached for his weapon.

"Do not do that," Conn warned, pulling the javelin from his saddle to get Solomon's attention. "You will be killing the one whom you raised. It is Aonghus come back to you."

Solomon turned white at Conn's words, and crawling closer to his lost apprentice, peered at him curiously for a long moment. Then with hands quivering, he pulled him close.

"I am so sorry, dear Aonghus," he cried. "I did not know it was you. I thought you had harmed Kordelina. She is out there alone, and I am worried about her. To see a stranger riding her horse fueled my worst fears."

"It is my horse," Aonghus corrected him. "And if you worry about her being alone, why do you allow it?"

Solomon's wrinkled brow went smooth and he released Aonghus. He had not expected this terse response and it made him bristle.

"I do not allow it," he firmly told him. "It is the way it must be."

Aonghus' upper lip was sweating as he reached down to cover his genitals with one hand. "That is no way to say hello, Chieftain," he admonished.

Solomon rose to his feet, and crossing his arms, gave Aonghus a blank look. He felt happy and unsettled at the sight of him. The coolness of his manner and the hardened look in his eyes was too unexpected.

"Nor was it the welcome I planned for you," he replied, extending a hand to help him to his feet.

Taking a firm hold of him, Aonghus drew in a deep breath, and with the other fist, he punched Solomon directly in the nose. Solomon felt the warm watery blood flow onto his mustache and he thoughtlessly wiped it with his hand.

"What was that for?" he asked angrily.

"That was for not bothering to say good-bye," Aonghus yelled at him. "And I should hit you again for being too proud to apologize for it."

The Chieftain licked a drop of blood from his mustache, then using the hand that Aonghus was still holding, jammed it straight forward into the young man's stomach. Aonghus grunted in surprise.

"Do not ever greet me like that again," he stated, shoving him backward.

The warrior teetered a moment, and in spite of his anger, Solomon grabbed him to prevent him from falling. This was not at all the way he had imagined their reunion, and the sudden provocation to anger on both their parts distressed him.

He looked at him apologetically, and watched Aonghus' expression go through an odd series of emotions before finally settling into one that was characteristic of the boy he knew.

"There are more important things than what we owe from the past," Solomon said emotionally.

"Yes," Aonghus conceded unevenly. "Forgive my intemperance."

An unforgotten tenderness immediately surfaced between the two men as Aonghus put both arms around the mighty Chieftain and hugged him.

CHAPTER TWENTY-TWO

hat night, amid tears, music, and rejoicing, Aonghus feasted with his family and close friends. They all gathered in Solomon's banquet hall to celebrate the return of their lost warrior. A milk-fed calf was roasted and served, along with freshly baked bread, butter, cheese, and endless amounts of wine.

It was not as difficult for Aonghus to recall their faces and what they had meant to him as he first thought. The mannerisms that either endeared or alienated—all remained. He was filled with happiness at the sight of his parents and was enveloped with the immutable warmth and understanding of his father. His mother wept continuously and fussed over the shortness of his hair and need for new garments. She proceeded to go into great detail about her daily tasks. He did not mind, though, because in her relating what she thought were matters of great importance, he was able to readily grasp the intricacies of his past.

His feelings for his two brothers had not changed either. They shared the same parents, and that was probably all they would ever have in common. And from the moment Aonghus was introduced to Niall, he was instantly unnerved by his effeminate features and the way he hovered about Enda. The boy was so frail that Aonghus thought if he raised his voice to him, the child would simply evaporate. He was further annoyed by the way he spoke in whispers, and when asked a question, would look to his mother first for approval before giving a reply.

"The child has no guts," Solomon said to Aonghus under his breath. "But do not say it to Kordelina as she is very protective of him."

Aonghus looked at Niall irritably. "It is a waste. What is weak in the beginning is always weak in the end. Where does Kordelina sleep when she stays away like this, anyway?"

Solomon shrugged. "The only ones who can know that are Kordelina and Saturnalia, but I can tell you where the girl is right now."

"Where?" Aonghus asked.

The Chieftain walked to a side window and looked out casually. "You will have to pretend you are getting some air," he told Aonghus. "If she thinks you have seen her, she will hide. But if you look beyond the stump to the corner of the fence, she is partially hidden behind it."

Aonghus nonchalantly took a place beside Solomon. He took in a deep breath and stretched his arms above his head then looked to where Solomon had

254

indicated. What he saw was Kordelina sitting on the ground, halfway concealed by the thick corner post. She was clutching her knees to her chest for warmth and had her dog beside her.

"Can we not let her come in and join us?" he asked, sorry for her.

Solomon shook his head. "I am afraid not. These times are tests for her. They are meant to increase discipline and self-reliance. She wants to be a warrior."

Aonghus looked at him sternly. "You are not going to let her, are you?"

Solomon nodded. "Aonghus, much has gone on with her since you left. Perhaps it is no surprise to you that she is different, but over these passing years, I have come to love her for it. I believe that if she is encouraged to develop her natural ability, she will be extraordinary."

"What is this change of heart? You sound almost remorseful for giving her up," he replied with a hint of a smile.

"I fear I am," Solomon admitted. "We make foolish promises in our youth. If we could only know in the beginning what we know in the end, we could benefit from our wisdom. Saturnalia and I discussed telling her everything and giving her the choice of remaining with me. But as Saturnalia advised, the edicts of the heavens must stand and we must continue to uphold them despite our selfishness."

At that moment the front door opened, and appearing elegant and poised, Saturnalia entered. She wore a red flowing gown that fell off one of her perfumed shoulders, and a sash that crisscrossed around her full bust. The room hushed as she stood waiting to be acknowledged by Solomon and Aonghus.

"The world has brought to my eyes what the spirits promised in my dreams would be," she said graciously.

Aonghus looked at her coldly and kept silent. He recognized her as the guide in his dream but along with this realization, a stifling resentment emerged. She possessed the same air of self-importance he had once worshipped. But after all that he had been through, there was little room in his life for exaltations. His experiences had taught him that life was both fleeting and precious, and should be relished in spite of ancient customs and vows.

"Saturnalia, can you believe this?" Solomon exclaimed, gathering her in his arms. He held her in such a way that he had one arm beneath her knees and the other around her shoulders as he began dancing and kissing her at the same time. He was so jubilant that Saturnalia could not help but encourage him. It had been far too long since she had seen him this happy.

However, she sensed Aonghus' disposition, and other than offering him an affectionate greeting, she did not pursue conversation the rest of the evening.

The celebrating ended far into the night. While Aonghus was genuinely touched by the occasion, he was travel weary, and it was stressful for him to disguise his lack of memory for such a prolonged period. Long after his family had gone home and Solomon and Saturnalia had retreated to the Chieftain's chamber, Aonghus found his way to his old bedroom. Much like the reacquaintance with his family, it welcomed him in a peculiar way. From its decor to the personal things he had left behind, he was gradually beginning to feel at home again.

Stoking the fire, he added another log to it, then went to the window to see if Kordelina was still there. He had to strain his eyes through the darkness to see. When he could not locate her, he climbed outside for a better look.

It was clear and the stars were bright; he could scarcely remember a time when they had looked so alive. They twinkled in their vivid colors of yellow, blue, and red, and he thought if he extended a hand, he could touch them. Walking a few paces into the night, he watched his breath form small clouds in front of him. It was too cold and dark for a young girl to be out alone, he thought, looking around for Kordelina. Then hearing a dog whimper behind him, he turned and found her standing there, shivering.

"Did the stars look this pretty where you were?" she asked, her teeth chattering from the cold.

"No," he smiled. "They look much better from here. I thought you would be off in your hiding place by now, sleeping."

"I should be," she said. "I wanted to say goodnight to you. It has been long since I have been able to do it, and it is something very special."

Aonghus looked up at the sky a moment, then abruptly looked back at her. "But I am not sleepy yet," he replied. "So you cannot say goodnight. I have a feasting plate in my chamber; perhaps we could share the fire and banquet in private."

Kordelina's eyes brightened. "I would like that. But you must say nothing of it to anyone. I am supposed to be in solitude."

Aonghus put his arm around her shoulders, and led her back to the window. "I will say nothing," he promised, as they both climbed back inside.

Once in the room, Kordelina went straight to the alcove where his weapons were and picked up the sling Solomon had forbidden her.

"Do you think if this were oiled it would work?" she asked, holding it up.

Aonghus put the platter of food in front of the fire, and sank into a mound of silken tapestries. "Probably. You can have it if you wish."

"Thank you," she smiled, then sat down in front of the fire and started eating. "Osin died while you were gone."

"He did? I am sorry," he replied sadly.

"But I think he is inside Macha," Kordelina added hopefully. "Saturnalia said that can happen. That when a soul leaves one body, it can enter another body and still be the same spirit. I think Osin wanted to be like Macha and Lir because he felt left out for not being able to run as fast as they."

The young warrior flashed a rueful smile. "Perhaps," he said, then fell silent.

Neither of them spoke for awhile. Wanting to be hospitable, Aonghus added more wood to the fire until the room was so warm that Kordelina went to take off the leather vest she was wearing. As she unlaced it, Aonghus could not help but catch sight of the small breasts she had developed. Seeing that he had noticed, Kordelina frowned back at him.

"I do not like them," she declared indignantly.

"Why?" Aonghus laughed. "It is natural that you would have them one day."

"I suppose, but they only get in my way," she protested. "I have to lace this vest as tight as it will go so they will not bother me. Being a girl is not fun, not with the things that happen with your body. You are a man so you would not know what I mean, but I can tell you that if it were not for being able to have a baby, I would rather be a boy."

Aonghus gave her an amused look. "You will make a fine woman, I am sure. But I must know, why is it that you have decided to become a warrior?"

Kordelina proudly sat erect. "Because there was a woman warrior named Blathnaid who came here for the Queen Boudicca," she began excitedly. "She was strong and absolutely magnificent looking. She had a horse that was the most beautiful color and —"

"Blathnaid is dead," Aonghus interjected gruffly.

"No she is not. Where did you hear that?" she challenged.

"Solomon told me about her at dinner," he answered, as he buttered a piece of bread and handed it to her. "He also told me how you ran off looking for her, and how he felt so guilty about leaving you in the snow that he promised to teach you to be a huntress."

Kordelina passively took the piece of bread, and wilted back in her spot. Her face was dissolved of all expression, only her eyes possessed that distant wounded look he remembered her having as a child.

"I told him he should forbid it," he continued sternly. "I told him that he could find better ways of assuring your future than teaching you weaponry."

Kordelina set down her bread and rose to her feet. "I have to go now," she said courteously. "I only came to say goodnight."

Aonghus felt his stomach cramp as he grabbed her by the wrist to stop her. Why had there been this sudden change in atmosphere between them? He had always been able to say anything to her without apologizing for it. Yet staring into her faraway eyes and watching the way the fire glow cast a swirling light on her features, he realized she was now different from the girl he had known.

"Please, wait," he pleaded. "I did not mean to offend you, I was only speaking my mind."

He shuddered as she pulled her hand away from him, and in a desperate flash of force, he gripped her tighter. A tense moment passed between them, and he felt her yield to him slightly before he released her.

"Kordelina," he addressed her, trying to locate a compromising tone. "What I mean is that you have no idea of the savagery that is in the depths of all men waiting to come out. They use their titles and their weapons to slaughter each other in the name of their nations and their trivial gods. I do not wish to see you partake in such blasphemies."

Calmly taking a place at his feet, she looked up at him, her eyes now rich with infinite feeling. "I wish to be a warrior, Aonghus. Will you help me?" she asked, in a way she knew he could not refuse her.

He felt disoriented for an instant, like this was a dream he had conjured and reality was the intruder. Probing deeper into her eyes, he completely adored the way they danced with light, and he found in them a moment he did not want to lose. Then as if she were pulling him through the dark tunnels of her pupils, he was overcome with the feeling that his reason was melding with the shadowy caverns of her mind. He wished he could remain connected with her like this forever, and knowing that if he refused her the one thing she wanted most, this tender creature would never trust him again. He gave a faint response in a whispered laugh; he would do as she asked.

Taking both his hands, she softly kissed the tops of them. "The stars deceive us in the way they have allowed us to be born into such betrayal," she whispered. "As though we would not know ourselves when we looked upon each other."

"Precious one," he said running his hand over the top of her hair. "We are but shadows in their sight."

She rested her head on his lap and watched the fire while he paternally untangled her dark locks.

"Will you go back to Bracorina?" she asked, her voice normal again. "She has much wealth now."

"It is not riches I seek," he said. "I want only to reclaim my dreams."

"But according to the laws —"

"The laws," Aonghus interrupted. "The laws are merely an attempt for man to define himself. I am no longer sure if I embrace them or abhor them. I question how valid something can be when with a few words of truth and a single action, I could wipe away the laws you and I have lived by forever."

"Are you speaking of killing another?" she asked, perplexed.

Aonghus put his hand under her chin and lifted her face. "Perhaps it could be done by killing, and perhaps by simply loving," he answered.

Kordelina stared at him, her expression reflecting the knowledge that he had only confirmed what she had already reasoned for herself.

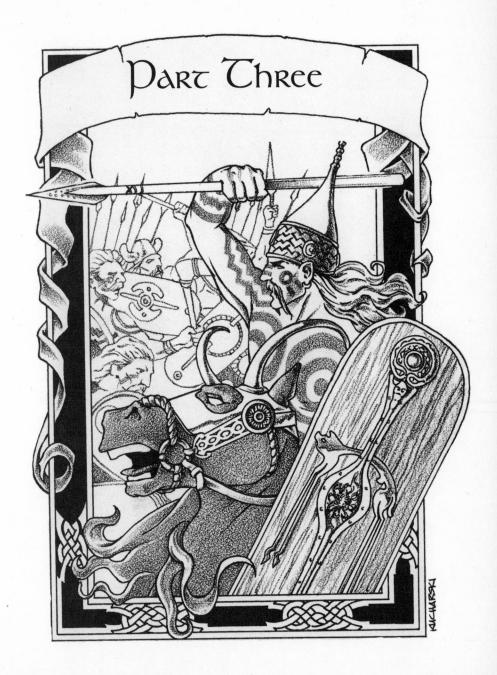

Part Three

CHAPTER ONE

D. 60. Upon his return, Aonghus had told of the horrible conditions in Wales. Disturbed by the tales, Solomon took it upon himself to form a protective alliance with the outlying tribes. The elders of his clan approved of this move because the conquest had recently experienced threatening changes in their military administration.

Gaius Suetonius Paullinus, a Roman commander in his early sixties, had taken up governorship of the main islands. A man with a long history of acquiring military honors, Suetonius was described by Caesar as one of the greatest military generals in his army. He had distinguished himself as a ruler prone to undue severity, and had experienced much success in his dealings with other unsubmitting tribes. In Rome's view, there was little doubt that he would carry out the unfulfilled promises of his predecessor.

The commander had instructed the armies already there that the major strategic point of the conquest would be the midlands. After years of campaigning, the Silures and Ordovices tribes of this region were still unsubdued. His immediate goal was to make it clear, in no uncertain terms, that the tribes should cooperate with the Imperialist expansion. Once this was accomplished, he intended an all-out assault on the Druidic core of the Celtic nation: Anglesey.

News of this came by way of Conn who, since Aonghus' return, had taken part-time residence with the warrior of Turg's family. Since it was Turg with whom he had originally fled the Roman oppression, the warrior's home was always open to him. It worked well; by traveling between both tribes, he was able to relate information that came from Daneen's sources in the trade harbors. It also gave him a reason to see Saturnalia, with whom, by this time, he was helplessly enamored. It was so blatant that Aonghus was not only embarrassed for his friend, but could not understand why Solomon was blind to it. Solomon, however, only concerned himself with the matter at hand, and that was Rome.

He had organized a gathering of the tribes by sending Aonghus and Conn on a month-long tour of the island. They were entrusted with a message from the Chieftain that all those wanting to resist Rome should gather at his settlement on the next full moon. He took special care to extend the invitation to the kings and chieftains directly because he did not wish to give the impression that he was trying to covertly expand his territory.

For Aonghus, it was the opportunity to enjoy the prestige of being a warrior returned from war. In each settlement he visited, he was afforded a hero's welcome. He was given the best accommodations and his choice of any maid or maids who interested him. For a young man in his prime who had seen only fighting from puberty to manhood, the luxuries of bachelorhood were a novelty.

For Conn, it was an appreciated break from his gradually cooling relationship with his wife, and the tedium of fatherhood. But more than that, he saw a chance for adventure, while further endearing himself to the sorceress.

When the moon finally did grow full, visitors were greeted by escorts Solomon had appointed to guide them to their village. The center clearing was prepared with specific areas for each tribe to make camp. Tribal chieftains and aristocrats would be accommodated at either Solomon's or Pwyll's estates.

There was an aura of excitement about hosting the great number of guests; an actual summit of chieftains had never been done. Because there was no specific ruler of the Celtic nations, many dictatorial chieftains and a few ruling kings led the tribes. As with the hierarchy of Solomon's clan, status was earned according to individual wealth. Many attendants at this gathering were also young maids and warriors anxious to marry outside their tribes in order to form stronger political bonds with other rules. Combining the wealth of one tribe with another was, in most cases, beneficial for all.

For three days, a mass of Celts filtered in for the conference Solomon had initiated. The Chieftain was pleased; for the first time since he was a young man, he was actively taking responsibility for his clan. He was even more pleased to find there were clan members who had been sent in proxy for chieftains on some of the smaller surrounding islands.

By day, there were games and contests among the men, and the women exchanged recipes and cooked for the upcoming full moon festival. At night, the air was filled with music, dancing, and the exchange of clan histories. Solomon told the story of Laden and Deireadh, and made a special point of speaking of Aonghus' bravery as a boy. He went on to recount how such character had sustained him through many years of fighting the Imperialists. This elevated Aonghus to heroic proportions in the eyes of the girls who were vying for his attention.

There had been more than one wealthy offer from a visiting chieftain to purchase his promise of matrimony. While Aonghus was flattered, he was enjoying his life too much to take any one of them seriously. In addition, Bracorina was doing everything possible to endear herself to him. She had been careful in her pursuit, not demanding that he fulfill his original promise of marriage which, if she had decided to insist upon it, would have been within her rights. She tried continuously to spark his interest; having been alone these many years, the fear of never having a husband again was now hanging heavily on her mind. Bracorina also understood that Aonghus would one day inherit Solomon's title.

The abundance of female attention had, however, gone to Aonghus' head. He donned flamboyant clothes, changing outfits often then sauntering conspicuously through the center court where the contests were held. He commanded great presence there, not only for his skill but for the proud way he carried himself. It was as though he knew the eyes of the tribes' women were adoringly fixed upon him.

Aonghus' new personality greatly aggravated Kordelina. She felt he sorely lacked as a hero; he had little more on his mind than flirting and stealing from one maid's bed to another. And, as his apprentice, she was left to absorb the entire burden of work he neglected during the gathering. Combined with her daily chores, this left the girl so weary that she often fell asleep before the nightly festivities began.

Saturnalia had problems of her own. The Druidess of her clan, she was required not only to act as hostess and spiritual overseer of nightly rituals, but also as private counselor for visiting tribesmen. From the time the sun rose, a steady stream of Celts filtered through her cottage seeking everything from herbal care to spiritual healing and the conjuring of spells. To add to the chaos, Jara arrived unannounced before the celebration, claiming she had heard of the gathering and saw it as her duty to help the sorceress direct it.

"I have come because I care," she said, looking out the window of Saturnalia's cottage at the great mass of tents and people moving about. "Our tribes are at a grave loss for morale on the main islands and it is well that you and your Chieftain care enough not to let it dwindle here."

Saturnalia could not help but cross her arms defensively. "I am from the Druidic line," she said calmly. "It is my duty as well. My knowledge of the other islands only comes from refugees seeking sanctuary with us. While I know that they have suffered greatly, it is with the preservation of this land that I am most concerned. We must be able to sustain ourselves before we can oppose Rome."

"Do you think it is possible to take on Rome?" Jara asked, turning to her with an unreadable expression.

"Always trying to bait me, are you not, Jara?" Saturnalia responded, keeping her gaze fixed on the aged woman. "What is it that you wish me to tell you— that we plan to attack the Imperialists by crossing the strait before they invade us? Your precious Caesar would pay nicely for such information. Would he not?"

She gave an ironic laugh that came from deep in her throat. "But I can tell you no such thing. We are a few worried tribes who can find only comfort now in unity with each other."

Jara seemed thoroughly unaffected with Saturnalia's answer. "How is the child you were teaching?" she asked, changing the subject.

"Edainne is well," Saturnalia replied with a heavy sigh. She was suspicious of Jara's queries, knowing there was a calculated method to them.

"She is set to be returned to her tribe soon," Jara smiled. "That is one reason I am here. I plan to take residence with her clan and perform the ritual myself."

Saturnalia felt a chill at the thought of Edainne's departure. Of course it was an honor to be chosen as a chieftain's bride and to be sacrificed in the name of the gods. But Edainne was a sweet, kind girl, who could do much in this world, too, Saturnalia thought to herself. And Diarmudd, for all of his pompous ways, would greatly feel her loss.

"Prepare yourself, Saturnalia," Jara continued. "For when the time for another virgin is needed, I will call upon you for the maid. It is your turn."

There was a soft knock on the door and Saturnalia was immediately thankful for the distraction. While she knew it was her duty to prepare a maid for the gods when asked, she had neglected to do so. She somehow felt Jara would never expect it of her. Edainne was an entirely different situation. From the time the girl was a baby, she had been raised with the idea that she would one day be the virginal offering for her tribe. In Saturnalia's clan, she had yet to find one selfless enough to willingly give herself over.

"You may enter," she said.

The door opened and Aonghus stepped inside. He bowed to Saturnalia respectfully, but when he cast his eyes on Jara, he was speechless.

"What is it, warrior?" Jara asked.

Aonghus' eyes tapered angrily for a moment, then they resumed their former expression. "It is nothing, forgive me, Priestess," he said, and bowed again. "It is just that I thought the sorceress was alone."

"She is alone," Jara stated, putting on her cloak and moving toward the door. "Saturnalia, there are other chieftains with whom I must speak before sunset. Let us resume this conversation by moonlight."

She looked at Aonghus intently for a moment, then walked out the door and shut it behind her.

"Yes, Aonghus," Saturnalia said, wearily taking a seat.

She eyed the handsome warrior dressed in his linen shirt, leather trousers, and high boots. In the time since he had returned, he had taken to his position in the aristocracy quite easily. He enjoyed adorning himself in expensive attire, and indulging in fine women and wine.

"She is a traitor," he stated.

Saturnalia's brows came together, and she looked at him reproachfully. "You had better never say that outside of this room," she cautioned. "Accusing a Druidess of treason is a very serious matter."

"Perhaps," he replied. "But I can tell you that while I was trying to find passage back, I saw her speaking with Romans."

"That does not mean she is an informer, Aonghus," she responded, pushing her hair out of her eyes with one hand. "The Druids have tried to establish a dialogue with Rome for the benefit of all our people. Jara has gone to great lengths to earn political immunity. I realize there are those in the Order who have been less than gracious in their dealings, but I cannot accuse anyone until I have proof. Jara has done nothing except come here on behalf of the order. I must allow her that."

Aonghus stared in the distance, purposely cloaking his expression. His change of manner was enough to tell Saturnalia that he did not believe her explanation, and suspected her as well.

"Aonghus, can we have a moment of honest conversation?" she asked, still too tired to rise to her feet. "I would like to speak with you not as a Druidess to a warrior, but as one who was once near to your heart."

The warrior did not move. Time had built a wall between them and it would take more than a few sincere words to break through it.

She looked wistfully back at him, as though she were trying to reclaim the soul of the stranger standing before her, that by some miracle the animosity that had become commonplace would dissipate with her heartfelt desire to relate to him.

"What is it about me, Aonghus, that you can no longer accept?" she asked.

Aonghus blinked nervously, taken aback by her bluntness. "Saturnalia, you are the Druidess of this tribe. I do accept you for that," he answered without a trace of feeling in his voice.

She studied him cynically. "You have indeed mastered your insincerity. The boy I used to know would never have said that," she told him, putting her elbow on the table and resting her forehead in her hand.

Still Aonghus said nothing as he impatiently put both hands on his hips and waited for her to go on.

"When I looked into your eyes the night of your return, what I saw was a brash young man without the slightest inclination toward kindness," she said, with a worried sigh. "But you now seem to truly enjoy the status for which you sacrificed. I am baffled as to why you resent me because while you were away, I did nothing except hope and pray that you would remain well."

"For that, I thank you," he replied. "And I would yet speak to you if I knew that what I had to say would not come back on me. But while you profess to abandon your title at this moment, you and I still cannot speak freely. Because when I walk out that door, what I have said will not remain on the mind of a trusted friend; it will be in the mind of a Druidess."

Saturnalia felt a craziness rise inside her. He was so terribly poised in contrast to her weariness that she wanted to force him to succumb to her. She wanted to crush the barrier that made him untouchable and make him speak the truth.

"I must confess," she snapped. "You have the benefit of being able to isolate yourself from me. I am unable to do the same thing with you. I keep looking for the child who used to believe in me, but I find nothing of him in your soul."

Aonghus kept his gaze locked with hers. She was trying to read his mind, but he would simply not allow it.

"Perhaps the being that so distresses me is not the one whom I mourned. Perhaps the warrior I now address is an addicted murderer," she said coldly.

A look of disgrace fleetingly crossed his features, then he was again composed.

"Aonghus, I know of the herbs Kordelina gathers for you, and I know why you need them. Please do not misunderstand and think I reproach you for it. I only raise these needs as an explanation for your present state."

Aonghus' face seemed to change entirely. She knew she had hurt him, and perhaps that was exactly what she had intended. Maybe she wanted to see if there was a vulnerable part left in him, or if he was an empty shell who had survived too long a time killing Romans.

"Yes, Saturnalia," he finally said in a gruff voice. "As a man speaking to a woman, not a warrior to a Druidess, I will confess my dependence. What Kordelina brings to me I cannot live without, but I would not offer that as the reason for the tension between you and me."

"Then what is it that sparks this tension, as you say?" she asked, pleased he was finally going to speak his mind.

He paused a moment, and she could see an inexplicable anger rising in his eyes before he turned to speak. "When I was ill," he said, making a conscious effort to temper his words, "it was not your customs or vows that I clung to while I hovered between worlds. It was not the laws that you espouse, or the rituals you perform. There was nothing in those things which you find of such great importance that offered me a single thread of comfort. What did keep me believing that I wanted to go on was not you or Solomon, or all that I would inherit here. No, what kept the force of life within me was a little girl who I promised I would not forsake. And when I look at you, I see the culmination of all those things that will yet keep her from me, and I hate you for it."

The sorceress gazed at him, shocked, and shook her head.

"Yes, Saturnalia," Aonghus said, in a forceful tone. "When I look at you I do not see the woman I used to worship. I only see betrayal. Do you think Kordelina does not already know that what she has been told her entire life is untrue? She is getting older now, and I am aware of the questioning glances she gives you and Solomon. She has no attachment to my family. It is the three of us who command her world, and she is too innocent to call us the liars we are."

The sorceress rose to her feet. For an instant, she stood motionless as she carefully considered what to do next. She was amazed that he challenged her in this way; it maddened her. In the next moment, she slammed her fist down on the table and looked at him with stringent, green eyes.

"Do not deny her happiness because of your selfishness," she stated bitterly. "The child has a right to it. Dredging up her past would not only make a spectacle of her, but would break her heart. And most importantly, you made a vow to the gods that can never be broken."

Darkness fell on Aonghus' blue eyes as he moved menacingly closer to her. She turned sharply to face him, and by the very strength of her expression, he stopped.

His words were ice. "Kordelina is mine."

In an instant, she understood that all Aonghus wanted to do was make Kordelina as much a part of his life as possible. She suddenly felt great pity for this young man, who could never fully have what he so desired.

Noting the sudden pureness of his expression, she said, "She will be of marrying age soon. I hope you will not prevent her from happiness."

Aonghus turned away from her. He was an imposing figure with his full reddish-brown mane falling below broad shoulders, and a sleeveless shirt revealing taut muscles. Aonghus had a more threatening appearance than either Solomon or Conn. It was not only because of his intimidating stature, but because he possessed a frigid, unpredictable glint in his eyes that indicated he was equally strong and devious.

"I would never deny her anything she wishes," he said, wheeling around. "She may marry whom she loves, not who is chosen for her. And when she finds one to whom she is endeared, it is I who will purchase the union for her. Not you; not Solomon. Me."

"For her sake, I hope you mean it," the Druidess said, neglecting to hide the anger in her voice, "because there are visiting tribesmen who have already inquired about her future."

The warrior's demeanor instantly weakened.

"I do hope that you will allow her to partake in the festivities tonight," she continued. "Because even though she is your apprentice, she is still a young girl. Do not forbid her the pleasantries of it."

"I will not," he forced a reply, but Saturnalia had the impression she was destroying him with her words alone. "But all talk of purchase must be done through me, as she is still my foster."

"I will relate that to all who ask," she said, taking her seat again. "Now warrior, what is it that you came to see me about?"

Aonghus did not answer immediately. He walked to the entryway, opened the oak door, then turned to her. Saturnalia shuddered at his appearance. He had gone through a drastic change in their time together. He was pale and meek, drained of vitality.

"I came on behalf of our Chieftain," he stated. "He would like you to be present when the races begin."

CHAPTER TWO

y milk cow could beat that animal!" Solomon jested, pointing to one of the other warrior's horses.

The warrior tightened his fists and stood erect, preparing to fight.

Seeing his reaction, Solomon tossed his head back in waggish laughter.

"Are you willing to prove that?" the warrior challenged.

"That is what I came here to do, is it not?" the Chieftain quipped. "So may I caution you, warrior, since you are about to be embarrassed."

A wary look came into the warrior's eyes. He was slightly shorter than the Chieftain and quite a few years younger. He had the reddest hair and most freckled complexion Solomon had ever seen, and that was probably why he singled him out of the group of riders to tease.

Still smiling broadly, Solomon stared back at him for an expectant moment waiting for him to make a hostile move. When the warrior offered none, he ceased his heckling and motioned for Kordelina to bring his horse.

The girl complied and confidently held onto the animal's reins while he mounted. Then she ran to fetch Lir for Aonghus, and helped him mount.

"You promise that if he starts to feel bad, you will not go on with him?" she asked her brother with pleading eyes.

"I promise Kordelina," he reassured her. "But do not worry, Lir is strong and should have no problem beating these others."

The young girl gave a worried frown, but nodded her head. "I trust you," she said. "I do not think you would actually try to do him harm, but —"

"Kordelina," Aonghus broke in, "These are horses; running is what they are meant to do. You pamper them too much. Lir will be fine. Do not give it another thought. Think well of us and I will see you at the finish."

"All right," she acquiesced.

She turned to walk back to where the tribesmen had gathered to one side of the designated race course. They were clapping their hands and cheering as the horses fell in line. Solomon's laborers had cleared a path around the settlement for this event. He knew the last and most prestigious test was the one of horsemanship, and he wanted to give everyone a chance to shine, especially himself.

The competition route started on a gentle slope that continued in a straight line for a short distance, then made a sharp turn to the right. The curve was rather wide because it had to go around a cluster of oak trees and continue up the back of the knoll by Saturnalia's cottage. From there, it followed a trail through the forest before reaching a stream that had to be crossed or, preferably, jumped to save time. The last obstacle before the home stretch was a portion of rough terrain meant to slow the horses before they came to the finish, which was just beyond the starting line.

Each tribe had selected two of their tribesmen with the best horses and expertise; sixteen riders in all participated in this most exciting and honorable of contests. Because this event was a display of appreciation for the horse goddess, Macha, the winner was afforded a hero's portion of that night's feast, was given the place of honor, and allowed to pick any eligible maid with whom he wished to celebrate.

The air was thick with anticipation as the animals lined up at the starting place. Kordelina tried to get to the side where her parents were, and was almost stepped on by Conn's horse as it bolted out of line.

"Step away, little one," he yelled, jerking his horse's head to one side to avoid her. As he did this, the animal kicked out its back legs causing the rest of the horses to scatter. The riders reined their animals to a halt and struggled to get the unruly beasts back in the proper positions.

Kordelina darted out of the way unhurt. But as she took her place at the finish, she noticed that Conn was riding a horse she had never seen. It was a tall, leggy chestnut with a short back, bulging eyes, and a neck quite a bit thinner than the others. When she saw the high-spirited horse was extremely lathered around the chest and between its hindquarters, she realized the warrior must have added an ingredient to its feed.

When they were all assembled, Saturnalia glided up to the starting point with a torch in her hand. The spring sun had added a lovely blush to her cheeks and she appeared entirely consumed by the excitement of the moment.

"May you always remember that these are the children of the goddess, Macha. She has entrusted them to you," she said, raising her voice above the crowd. "They are her creations and we do this in her honor. Let the race begin."

She swung the flaming torch in a downward motion and the field of runners broke into a thunderous gallop. Divots of grass flew in the air behind them as each one tried to get clear of the pack for an early lead. The crowd screeched and cheered excitedly as they passed, and when they rounded the first turn, a mass of children stampeded across the court to the far end of the village to glimpse them when they emerged from the forest and headed for home.

Kordelina stood on her tiptoes watching them disappear into the distance. When she had lost sight of them, she stood fidgeting next to Saturnalia.

"Go on, child," the sorceress told her with a smile. "You know you would rather watch them with the other children than wait here."

"It is not that," she offered, trying not to offend her. "I was worried about Lir, that he might—"

"Go ahead," Saturnalia urged. "You do not have to make excuses. If you hurry, you will still be able to see them come out of the woods."

The young girl gave her a sweet smile of thanks, then sprinted after the others to the other side of the course. She kept her eyes on the ground as she ran, taking special care not to step on anyone's camping area. In every bit of space there was either a sleeping hide or a fire ring surrounded with personal belongings.

In a distracted moment, she felt someone grab hold of her arm and try to stop her. Lifting her head, she looked straight into the face of a young warrior. She could tell by his smooth skin and clear green eyes that he was only a few years older than she. He had light blond hair, and apparently, was only recently anointed because his torque was still shiny and new. He was flaunting the lively look of one enjoying the privileges of the fianna.

"Where are you going in such a hurry?" he asked, making her halt. "The horses are supposed to be running, not you. Why do you not stay here and watch the race with me? I am the warrior, Aiden."

Kordelina gave him a look of irritation. She tried to take her arm back, but he would not let go of it.

"I said I am the warrior, Aiden," he repeated, with a smile. "You are supposed to tell me your name as well. It is rude not to introduce yourself, Kordelina."

She looked down at his hand, then impatiently back at him. "You are the one lacking manners, Warrior Aiden," she snapped. "I have a horse running and I would like to see him."

She yanked her arm away, but as soon as she took her first step forward, Aiden was in front of her. She tried to step around him in one direction then the other, but every time she did, he blocked her way. Finally, she stopped and gave him a blank stare.

"What do you want?" she asked.

The young man gave a laugh. A pink hue came to his cheeks, but he did not reply.

"Are you stupid?" she demanded, putting her hands on her hips. "Either speak or get out of my way."

Aiden mischievously lurched forward and taking her by the shoulders, kissed Kordelina on the mouth.

At first she tried to shove him away, but he was solid and young, and she did little more than make him sway slightly backwards. She felt the soft tip of his tongue along the part in her lips, tenderly opening them.

She tried to step away from him, but he pulled her still closer. When there was no light left between them, he gently slipped his soft, wet tongue the rest of the way into her mouth.

There was a baffling surge of warmth in her body that went from her feet to the top of her head. It was a frustrating but delightful sensation as she felt him run one hand over the front of her leather vest to touch her bosom. She was struck with the great dizzying feeling of being a girl, and while she knew she probably should have resisted him, her instinct was to return his affection.

The pleasure of the moment was interrupted by a great rush of children. She knew they must be headed back to watch the finish, but for some reason she could not make herself care. She was too entranced with the sensation of his hand on the square of her jaw and his fingertips fondling the back of her hair. It was wonderful and frightening, and she would not have turned away from him at all if she had not heard Aonghus commanding her to get his horse.

Like a chilling wind, his voice scattered the exquisite feeling inside her, and she cringed. With control she had seemingly abandoned, she carefully pushed Aiden away from her. She did not look in his eyes as she turned and headed in the direction of her brother's voice.

"I will be looking for you at the banquet," he called after her. "We should share a dance together."

She gave no response as she ran her fingertips over her lips. Then she turned to glance at him before starting back to where Aonghus was waiting with Lir.

There were so many people and horses around the finishing area that, at first, she did not know who had won. She looked for Solomon and saw him still in his saddle glowering down at Conn. In perfect contrast, Conn stood alongside him, his hand held out amiably.

"Why are you congratulating me?" Solomon huffed. "I lost."

"But you ran a game race," Conn said, trying to be chivalrous.

Solomon jumped to the ground and grudgingly shook his hand. "Not game enough," he grumbled.

He handed his reins to a servant, then took the jeweled chalice filled with wine and gave it to Conn.

"Let it be known to all here that the warrior, Conn, has won the test of horsemanship, and is blessed by Macha," he announced in a diplomatic voice. "He is awarded the place of honor at tonight's feast, and should choose his maid for the evening."

Conn was beaming as he took a drink of wine, and wiping his lips with the back of his hand, went over to wrap his arm around Saturnalia. An immediate hush fell over the crowd as they seemed to back away from the couple. Saturnalia's skin lost its color, and she looked uncomfortably at Solomon, then down at her feet.

Sensing her displeasure, the Chieftain approached and taking her wrist, pulled her away from Conn.

"You may choose a maid," he said in a quiet voice. "But not a Druidess."

Conn's proud smile disappeared, and he gave the wine back to Solomon.

"Then if I may not have Saturnalia's company, I will concede my victory to you. I am sure you will have her in your chamber when the banquet is through," he said arrogantly.

Jealousy painted Solomon's features as he took the chalice. It was obvious that he wanted to say more, but he did not want to make a scene. He and Conn glared at each other for a moment, then Conn mounted his steed and rode away.

Kordelina watched as the tribesmen traded suspicious glances, and grumbled their displeasure at the young warrior refusing to honor Macha in the traditional way. She wondered if Conn knew he had shunned the goddess' blessing in his refusal.

"Where were you?" Aonghus barked, putting a hand on her shoulder.

Kordelina was suddenly too flustered to look at him. "I was over there," she answered, motioning behind her with one hand.

Aonghus said nothing as he studied her gesture. Lir was breathing hard and when Kordelina started to walk the horse, Aonghus grabbed the reins from her and lifted her face to him. She kept her gaze downcast.

"Where exactly?" he demanded, pinching the tip of her chin to make her look up. When their eyes met, Kordelina was nothing less than mortified by the severity of his expression.

"I was just over there," she answered, pointing to where Aiden was still watching her.

Aonghus locked onto him immediately, and as he released her, he turned his body so he was purposely blocking Aiden's view. Widening his stance and crossing his arms in front of him, he gave the young warrior a withering glance.

"Go back to the barn," he commanded, handing Lir over to her.

"But Aonghus, it—"

"Go back to the barn!" he shouted, and shoved her away from him.

Tears of humiliation stung her eyes as bowing her head, she started walking blindly in the direction of Solomon's manor.

It was cold and too late in the day to bathe Lir, so Kordelina walked him around the barn until his breath steadied and he had his fill of water. Then she mixed his grain with warm nectar and honey as a special treat, and hung the feed bucket inside his stall. She then nestled into the straw to watch the young stallion eat. She thought Lir and Aonghus were very much alike; they were both prone to anger, and demanded to have things their own way. She often wondered what could have possibly happened while Aonghus was away to make him so hard. There were times when even Solomon went to great lengths not to upset him, because when he did fly into a rage, it could be either minutes or days before he got over it.

She saw the long shadow of someone entering the barn and could tell by the pattern of the footsteps that it was him. Still unsure of what to say, she remained silent even when he stopped in front of her.

He made no effort to speak to her either, and the only sound in the barn other than Lir munching his grain, was the tinkling of bells. Finally looking up she saw that he was holding a lovely multi-colored skirt with bells sewn to its hem in one hand, and a silk blouse with lace on the front and a braided sash in the other.

"What is that?" she asked, unable to keep from smiling.

"They are for you," he said kindly.

He wore the gentlest expression, and to see him now affable, one would hardly imagine he could ever have behaved the way he had earlier.

"Why?" she questioned suspiciously. "Why would you give them to me after shoving me like one of your hounds in front of everyone?"

Aonghus got down on one knee beside her, placed the clothes in her lap, then kissed her forehead in silent apology. Kordelina could immediately smell the cowbane and wormwood on his breath.

"You should come to the celebration and dance tonight. There are those who would like to be introduced to you," he said, smoothing her hair away from her eyes.

Kordelina twisted her face. "I think I would rather stay with the horses. There is no one I wish to meet."

Perceiving her anger, he grabbed the outfit. He walked across to Lir's stall and leaned against the partition. He stared at his horse for a long moment.

"Aonghus?" Kordelina addressed him, the pain still evident in her voice.

"Hmm."

"If my parents were here, you would tell me who they were, would you not?" she asked.

The warrior jerked his head around to look at her in surprise. "Mother and father will be there," he answered, trying to dismiss her question.

"No, I mean my real mother and father," she replied. "I thought perhaps they would be here. I have been looking at everyone hoping I would recognize them when I saw them."

"Your mother and father are my mother and father," he snapped. "They would be hurt if they knew that —"

"I know," she stopped him. "I already know how hurt they would be if they thought I did not appreciate them. I love them, Aonghus, and I love you, but I know that we are not from the same line."

"What in the name of all the gods are you talking about?" he asked, whirling to face her. "Who has been filling your head with such nonsense?"

"No one," she answered. "It is only that I have thought it for a long time. Not that it really matters, but I am only curious as to who they were. I would not say anything to them. Perhaps if I was more like them it would explain some things. I had Edainne ask Diarmudd if he remembered the day of my birth, but he told her that our mother was never with child. He said one morning I was just here."

Aonghus was speechless. It made his heart ache not to be able to tell her the truth. Of all they shared together, this was the only lie between them, and his betrayal of her was far more intense than any vow he had ever made.

"If they were here, you would tell me; I know you would tell me," she said, looking up at him with pleading eyes. "I would not love you any less if I knew you were not my real brother. I only thought that perhaps if I were from a different clan, it would explain why I used to want to leave this settlement."

"Do you still want to leave?" he asked, worried.

"Not as much anymore," she answered, scratching the back of her head. "But every time I go into solitude, you leave. Where do you go?"

"Who told you that I leave?" he countered.

"No one had to," she responded. "Every time I come back, you are not here until the next day."

He looked fearful for a moment, as if he wanted to confess something, but when he spoke it was defensively.

"You go into hiding; am I not allowed to do the same?" he argued.

"I go because I have to; you leave because you want to," she told him. "I would tell you where I go, but it must remain a secret. Not even Saturnalia knows. When I see her, we meet at a place decided on ahead of time. But I can tell you that where I hide, someone else used to hide as well. A woman used to live there, and she knew how to write because symbols are scratched on the walls. Her hair was the same color as mine, too. I found a lock of it in a place that looked like it was made for a baby. Why would anyone hide a baby? I think that is odd. I want a baby more than anything, and if the gods gave me one, I would never hide it, or lie to it."

Overwhelming confusion showed in his eyes as they darkened almost to the point of tears. He focused on her, then turned his back.

"I am sorry," she whispered. "I know you would never lie to me. If you knew my parents were here, you are the one person who would tell me."

"Of course," he mumbled. "I understand your need for honesty. But we, mother and father and everyone else, love you so much that—well, we just love you very much."

"I love all of you, too," she told him sweetly. She started to braid her horse's mane while she waited for his grave mood to pass.

After a troubled pause, he walked to her and held out the skirt, making the bells jingle. "This would be nice for you to dance in," he said, suddenly light-hearted. "I would like to see you wear it tonight."

Kordelina gave him an embarrassed smile, and shook her head.

"For me," he persuaded.

She eyed him skeptically and frowned. "All right, but I will not have you introducing me around. There is no one here I want to meet," she stated.

"If that is what you wish," he agreed, and gently reached out to hug her.

CHAPTER THREE

Solomon could sing. He possessed a resounding baritone voice that enveloped the night as he extolled the blessing without the accompaniment of musicians. His words were rich with passion as they cut the air, becoming beauty itself.

He closed his eyes when he released the last refrain about the heavens never falling and the seas ceasing to rise against his people. As the words erupted in his throat, tears appeared in his eyes. He wished all who surrounded him would be as endless as the wind. A fluttering soul whose purpose was at last at hand, Solomon became one with the emotional faces, and held out his arms to invisibly embrace them all.

A wave of applause and cheering immediately followed the fervent song. Then his audience broke into delightful laughter and wished each other well. A few children flipped a circle of cartwheels around the fire, and the sound of musicians awakening their instruments rang out.

Suddenly a ripple of shouts broke out over the clapping as the honey-glazed boar was set on the banquet table. The Chieftain carved the meat and motioned to the servants to feed the other kings and aristocrats before him. The noise of the masses singing and laughing was overwhelming. Combined with the bantering of drums and the playing of instruments, the mood was one of reckless jubilance.

The men of power were seated in the center of the gathering, and in front of them, their wives. Behind each chieftain, his heir to power was seated. The row of handsome, virile young men was more of a sight to behold than either the massive feasting area or the line of beautiful maidens now dancing for entertainment.

Proud to be framed by Aonghus and Saturnalia, Solomon appeared more than pleased amid the pandemonium. The only one who looked out of place was Jara, who was glowering indignantly at having to preside over the priestly order instead of the aristocrats.

Kordelina had to reckon with the incredulous stares and gaping mouths of the women in her tribe when they saw her dressed in the outfit Aonghus gave her. Pwyll's daughters mocked her when she passed their dining site, and a few of the other girls in the tribe made noises to taunt her. She was determined to ignore their curious glances because, although she had never participated in the women's gatherings and had never worn a skirt before, she felt pretty and feminine for the first time. She had even darkened her brows with berry juice and reddened her lips and cheeks with ruan.

She knew the clan's women thought her strange for wanting to be a warrior, but their opinions mattered little, since she had seen other tribes' girls taking the same path. Oddly though, not one of them spoke to her or she to them. They went about their duties with the habitual seriousness they had been taught by their masters.

Stopping discreetly near her parents' table, she took a long, amused look at the celebration. Hordes of people had assembled to enjoy the company of other Celts. She saw Edainne hovering meekly near her father, and across the flames, Diarmudd sat staring at her woefully.

Looking to where her mother was preparing her family's table, Kordelina saw her two brothers drunkenly slouching together. Niall brought her some bread and ale, and she was thankful that he did not say anything about her outfit. Koven and Enda must have guessed how conspicuous she felt as well, because they did not comment either. They only smiled proudly when she joined them.

Catching sight of Aiden watching her, she felt suddenly more nervous and uncomfortable. Fearing he would want to speak to her, she instinctively averted her gaze without acknowledging him. She was too full of self-doubt to deal with him tonight.

Pretending to be intrigued by the assembly of leaders, she glanced up and saw Aonghus speaking with Daneen. There was a casual familiarity between the two men, and she could tell by the way Aonghus gestured freely with his hands that he was more than comfortable with the older Celt. It was difficult for her to understand how they could have developed such a rapport in this short time, and an unexplainable jealousy rose in her.

The delicious aroma of the meal was beginning to make the crowd restless. Kordelina knew she must be hungry but her stomach was so tense she could not feel it. The thought of walking to the serving area in front of everyone dressed the way she was, made getting a plate of food entirely out of the question. The noise of the crowd temporarily subsided as the leaders simultaneously lifted their chalices high in the air, commanding everyone's attention. The music abruptly ceased and, save for the rhythmic beat of a single drum, everything fell silent.

"We have gathered as one people to support a common cause," Solomon announced, rising from his place to face his peers. "We have set aside our individual quests of power to rally for a solitary goal. For while we are ordinary men who have been entrusted with the welfare of many, we have promised to turn our backs to dissension and quarrels. By the grace which has been given us in this beautiful land, we will dream of serenity and abundance among us. When we all bid each other farewell by the next dawn's light, it will be with the covetous honor we all desire, and let not a soul alive offend it. For if any poor wretch should do so, they will find repentance at the mercy of the torch.

"Let it be known to all here, that in the name of the gods who have blessed us, I will abide by the common laws we have agreed upon, and seek abundance between our tribes. Because we live in a time of great testing, and the days ahead may hold danger for us all, I would seek the testimony of everyone here that together we shall resist Caesar and his Roman invaders."

A screech of support sounded throughout the campsite as all the leaders rose to their feet and shared the single chalice Solomon held out. When it was emptied, a servant refilled it, gave it to the heirs, then passed it to the women.

"Let the celebration begin!" Solomon bellowed when it was handed back to him. "Let us reap the beauty of our people."

The music resumed and the priests materialized around the fire. A ghostly sight of gaunt, elongated faces and angelic voices, they chanted with eyes fixed on the heavens and their hands lifted to the sky to invoke spiritual powers. Seeing them, one could easily believe that the men were conduits to the Otherworld.

When they were finished, a silence fell on the court as each man, woman and child offered private supplications. Then the dancing began, and Kordelina was jarred from her thoughts by Saturnalia. The sorceress grabbed her by both hands and dragged her to the center of the twirling women. At first the young girl resisted her, then as she realized it was useless, Kordelina began to laugh and sing with her freely. She suddenly could not help but wrap one arm around Saturnalia to hug her as they moved together to the beat of the drum.

Soon they were joined by the men and Kordelina ducked out of line to avoid Aiden. No sooner had she slipped over to her place near her family than she was beckoned forward by Solomon. The girl, anguished at having been summoned to the front of the crowd, pretended she did not see him. Solomon rose and walked over to her.

She let out a startled gasp when he took hold of her arm and led her back into the circle of high-stepping men and women. He looked endearing with his red cheeks and nose and his bushy eyebrows. A smile soon formed on her face, and the Chieftain returned it with bellowing laughter.

"To see you like this, Kordelina, I must confess, stirs happy memories of my past," he said kindly, then whirled her around and handed her to another warrior.

Concentrating on her steps, she locked eyes with Saturnalia, who was on the other side of the flames. The wisps of smoke and fire framed her lovely face, and the intensity of her beauty bore through the heat and the crowd, straight into Kordelina's mind.

Think the words, Kordelina, you already know how to think the words, a voice sounded in the young girl's head.

Kordelina was stunned by her message. She stopped to stare at the sorceress in astonishment. What was she doing, she wondered to herself. How could she speak to her without her knowing it? In the next moment, she was forced back into line by Aiden, and realizing who he was, refused to look up.

I do not want to think the words, she said in her head. *I do not wish to learn your ways, Saturnalia.*

As if she had heard the message, the Druidess spun around the fire until she was next to Kordelina. She had a sudden kind-hearted look about her, and a smile that was impossible to distrust.

"Do not worry, child," she said softly. "It is already done." Then Saturnalia turned to Solomon and let him gather her in his arms, as he began dancing for them both. Caught off guard by her exit, Kordelina giggled at their open affection, but she still would not look at Aiden. She wished he had not taken her as his partner because she knew it would only provoke Aonghus to confront him. Then almost as if he, too, had heard her thoughts, Aonghus stepped between them and pushed Aiden away.

The younger warrior protested vehemently, and Kordelina saw Aonghus point a finger in his face then shove him once more to assert his dominance. Turning away from them both, Kordelina finished the last measure of the song, then sat down beside her parents, bewildered.

"What is the matter, my little girl?" Koven asked, putting one arm around her shoulders.

Kordelina shrugged, then shook her head.

"Come now, you can tell me," he told her, patting her cheek. "You can always tell me."

She tucked her head in the round of his neck, and let him playfully run his fingers through her hair.

"It is nothing, Father," she said. "I guess I am just tired."

"As well you should be," he comforted. "You have been working too hard for too long. But your struggles are soon to end; your anointing has been decided upon."

Kordelina lifted her head. He looked weary, too. The lines around his eyes and on the sides of his mouth appeared deeper in the shadow of the firelight.

"When you are a warrior, you must not forget about an old man. You have to promise me that," he continued, arranging her curly locks around her face.

"I would never forget about you," she smiled, and kissed his cheek.

Koven's eyes misted. "You look so grown up tonight. It makes me feel good and bad."

"Why?" she asked, tilting her head to one side.

"It makes me feel good that my daughter is a beautiful woman now," he explained with a silly grin. "But it makes me feel badly to know that she is not my baby anymore. Do you like that warrior over there?"

Kordelina shrugged again and fell silent.

"You had better make up your mind before your brother kills him," Koven said, pointing to where Aonghus and Aiden were squaring off to fight.

It was Aonghus who kept trying to close the space between them. Every time he took a step forward, Aiden took a step back. It was obvious to everyone, particularly Aiden, that he was no match for Aonghus, a seasoned battler.

"I do not care. They are both acting silly," she replied, shaking her head. "They are foolish to fight over such things, as though I were chattel. Forgive me, Father, but I am going for a walk."

"Do you want some company?" Koven asked, as she rose from her place.

"No," she answered gently, heading for the darkness of the grove. "I will return shortly."

She followed a footpath through the oaks and out onto the cliffs overlooking the strait. She sat on the very edge of the rocks to see the splashing waves in the moonlight. Running her fingers through her hair, she could not help but feel disgusted with herself. She wanted nothing to do with the warrior who had kissed her, and she rebuked herself for dressing like the other girls. She was not like them at all; she knew she wanted more from life than they did. She did not know exactly what it was, but it was more than simply a husband and family.

There had to be more to be proud of in life than what the laws defined, and while the desire for a child of her own was growing stronger, she believed it came from the need to show that the core of one's integrity went deeper than what the Druids and chieftains espoused. She did not want to share a world constructed within their laws; rather, she yearned to impart the captivating beauty and freedom that existed outside of them.

She suddenly sensed someone watching her from the trees, but no one was there. She had felt it before when she was in solitude—a spirit following her who was searching for an invitation to speak. She wanted no part of it though, and she wanted no part of Saturnalia's manipulation, either. Her mind was her own, and her power, good or bad, belonged entirely to her; she did not want to be a vessel for anyone. Leave that to Edainne, and the other long suffering women of the clan.

"It is selfishness that makes you think so," Saturnalia said from behind.

Kordelina turned to look at her, then stared back at the strait as the sorceress sat down.

"And it is selfishness that makes you deny your gifts," she continued. "Because you know once you claim them, your life will never be your own."

Kordelina began to tap her foot impatiently. "There was someone here ahead of you, did you know that?" she asked.

"Yes, and I know who it is," Saturnalia answered. "She must be the reason for this."

"For what? I do not know what you are speaking of, and I do not know why you insist on talking to me inside my head when I do not wish it either. It is unfair to go where you are not wanted," she said, her voice thick with aggravation.

"Perhaps, but I do it because I fear that if I am not the one to instruct you on using your powers, enlightenment will come by the spirit who follows you," she said earnestly. "She is a dark one, given over to the lusts of blackness."

Kordelina dropped her head for a long moment, and Saturnalia thought perhaps she was about to experience a change of mood. But when the girl looked up at her again, she was the same as before.

"Could you please explain to me how you did what you did when we were dancing in front of the fire?" she asked.

"Is that all you are interested in? Do you not want me to tell you about the spirit that you feel?" the sorceress said, slightly perplexed by her reply.

Kordelina chewed her lip and shook her head. "No," she answered. "Because I am not sure what I think about your spirit world, and I do not wish to be influenced further by your laws and what you and the Order believe it to be. If this spirit is really a spirit, as you say, and has come to me, then I will listen to it when I want to, not when you tell me." She gave a heavy sigh. "I grow weary of all of these laws, Saturnalia."

"Why?" the sorceress countered, noticeably unsettled by her answer.

"I do not want to say," she mumbled.

"Why?" she demanded again.

"Because if I do, you might think I am unworthy of anointing. And if I do not become anointed soon, I will go crazy," she responded heatedly. "I am tired of doing all of Aonghus' work."

Saturnalia was unable to hide her pain of not being Kordelina's confidant. More than anyone, she believed she had gone out of her way to understand the girl, and was now confused by her distrust.

"I do not distrust you," Kordelina said, then fell silent when she realized she had read the woman's thoughts.

The Druidess arched her brow and nodded. "Then you do already know how to do it," she stated.

Kordelina ignored her and looked out across the water. The fullness of the moon cast a haunting light on her face, transforming it before Saturnalia's eyes. The sorceress was unsure if it was Kordelina's personality coming out, or if she was seeing a manifestation of her own conscience. In the next instant, she flashed to the horrible sight of Deireadh growling and cursing her as she cut open her stomach, and the Druidess had to blink hard to stop it. Folding her arms, she shuddered, then stared out at the water as well.

"Who was that?" Kordelina asked.

Saturnalia shook her head and said nothing.

"I have seen her before, I think," Kordelina went on. "But I am not sure if it is in a dream, or something I remember from my childhood. It comes sometimes in quick flashes. I hesitate to speak of it because I do not know what it is."

"I have never encountered it before this," Saturnalia said, licking her dry lips. "I think it is part of you coming into your own. You must decide for yourself which of the spirit world you choose to confide in. But I will tell you that I am going to give you a powerful animal upon your anointing. You will need to draw on it, as I realize now you will encounter much more than I had first thought."

CHAPTER FOUR

The last time Kordelina was required to go into solitude was after the vernal equinox. Her anointing was to follow immediately thereafter, and then she would no longer be obligated to sequester herself when she menstruated. As soon as she spent the night in the cave, she would have earned the right to her powers, and would then be responsible to the gods for her actions.

She felt some remorse about ending this phase of her life. She had gotten used to being alone during these times, and had actually come to consider them a well-earned break from her daily chores and the monotony of training. Aonghus had schooled her well—almost too well—since his return. Having been in battle for so long, he was well acquainted with Roman tactics. He did not let even the slightest error on her part go unnoticed, and he had been severe and demanding. But the result was a confident, hard-muscled warrior, capable of thinking and acting with more stealth than a man. She was aware that even Aonghus was sometimes unnerved by her skill at hunting and the way she took to weaponry. She derived a certain lusty satisfaction from killing, although she never did it needlessly or out of anger; she loved the animals she killed and never forgot to thank them for giving themselves to her. Like the plants and wildlife that inhabited the woods, Kordelina seemed to have been spawned from the land itself. Her instincts, thoughts, and beliefs came from the nature surrounding her.

As was usual during these times of solitude, she collected herbs for Saturnalia in the morning, remembering to keep a share of wormwood and cowbane for Aonghus. Having been instructed by the sorceress in herbal care, she fully comprehended the effects of the combination her brother used.

The mixture of the two plants was a toxic, lethal mixture, but one would not suspect that by looking at Aonghus. There was no residue to his pallor, nor the convulsions and loss of coordination that often accompanied the use of these herbs. He had built a tolerance to them, and was a master at strengthening or diluting them to suit his particular needs. The only hint of their presence came from his perpetually dilated pupils.

Sometimes when he did use a very strong dose, he would develop stomach cramps and a hacking cough. But neither Solomon nor her parents seemed to question it; they attributed it to the fact that Aonghus had always had stomach problems from nerves.

It made her ache to know what he had gone through while in Wales. When he had explained how this need had come about, there was no way Kordelina could refuse to help him. She did not care that to others Aonghus might seem weak. What he had overcome in order to survive was enough to hold him blameless. Besides, she understood something unexplainable happened inside a person when he saw too much bloodshed. From the conditions of both Aonghus and Conn, and knowing of the refugees who had come to her tribe, she understood that they all possessed a cynical distrust of people in general.

She placed the herbs in the white leather pouch that Saturnalia had made for her. The Druidess had given it to Kordelina the first time she had bled as a token of her womanhood. It contained only a piece of jade that had been given to Saturnalia many years before by a Mediterranean trader. The stone was said to have controlling powers, and Saturnalia had been saving it for one she believed could use it without abuse or fear.

Since then, Kordelina kept the bag tied around her waist and had collected several other personal power pieces as well. Also in it was everything she needed to conjure the spells she had been taught during her early years with the Druidess. Kordelina did not have the elaborate understanding of the craft as did Edainne, but she was still able to use it in basic ways to aid her when needed.

By the time the sun had burned away the morning fog, she had finished her chores. Wood was gathered for the night and the herbs were bundled and hung to dry. She got on her unsaddled horse, and with her dog close behind, headed for the strait. It was late enough that she knew the tide would be down, and she wanted to catch shellfish and eggs from nesting cliff birds for dinner. She hoped there would be enough to give some to both Saturnalia and her own family.

She trotted down the wooded path and across the flatlands, then back through the grove that bordered the cliffs. Spring had come early this cycle, and the ground that normally would have been wet and slippery was firm and green. There were blossoms on the trees already, and aside from the heavy rains that were still frequent, the temperature was pleasant most of the time.

When she reached the bluff, she dismounted and, allowing the reins to dangle, let Macha graze freely. She signaled her dog to follow, and together the two started down the rocks to the stretch of beach below.

The dog let out a long howl and a series of quick, happy barks. His lighthearted spirit reflected Kordelina's carefree attitude as he leaped from rock to rock, sticking his nose in the air and sniffing the breeze. His tail was wagging endlessly and every now and again he would stick his snout in the air and let out a long howl. Kordelina howled with him. She was thrilled; at last she was able to claim the privileges of which she had desperately dreamed. Her servitude and inferiority in her tribe were soon to be behind her.

The hound was nosing his way into a cluster of rocks, tail pointing straight out. Kordelina walked to where he was, and peeking into a shadowy crevice in the cliff, she saw a nest containing four eggs.

Removing it from the rock, she held it with both hands and followed her dog to where he had found another one. This time she took only two eggs and placed them with the others. That would be enough to feed her and her dog for the next two days. Taking more would be difficult to carry on horseback.

"You are the best dog in this tribe," she praised the hound and patted his head. The animal gave a whimper, then affectionately licked her face. "But let us see if you can smell fish."

They started toward the beach, the dog barking and prancing around her, stopping every so often to look protectively in one direction or the other. By the time they had almost reached the sand, he began to snarl and the hair on his back bristled. He darted onto the beach and disappeared behind a crag, growling and showing his teeth.

Kordelina's first instinct was to go after him, but before her feet touched the sand, two strange men on horseback came out from behind the rock with her dog nipping at their horse's heels. They were fitted with chest garments of overlapping metal strips and plates strung together with leather thongs. Woolen tunics stuck out from beneath their armor, and their trunks and legs were covered with leather trousers that went down to their calves and had metal studs strapped around the outside of their thighs. On their feet, they wore leather sandals with thick soles and straps across the tops. Their heads were covered with helmets that followed the shape of their heads, but extended to a protective flap on the backs of their necks.

Both men were carrying rectangular shields that curved around their bodies. They were slung from their left shoulders, and in their right hands one man was carrying a sword, the other a javelin.

Kordelina ducked behind a rock and watched them fearfully. She knew no Celt would dress in such a way, and from the appearance of the thick-necked horses they rode, she knew they had to be Romans.

She looked up the beach and saw a small flat-bottomed transport boat with still another Roman waiting inside. She could hear the two share a cold, threatening laugh as they commanded the dog away from them. When the hound continued to try to bite their horses' heels, the one with the javelin wheeled around in the saddle, and aimed his weapon.

Kordelina instantly rose to defend him, but the moment she got to her feet, a hand on her shoulder shoved her back down. Drawing her knife, she turned to attack, but someone grabbed her arm, and put another hand over her mouth.

"Be silent," a voice commanded.

At first she struggled, but when she saw it was Conn, she obeyed.

She pushed both his hands away and turned around just as the Roman heaved the javelin and struck her dog in the side.

The animal yelped with pain, and fell in the wet sand. Then the other soldier whipped his horse around and trampled him. Both of them laughed harder as the dog howled with pain, then went limp.

Kordelina cried silently as the horsemen continued up the beach to their boat. She hid her face in her hands so she did not see them push off. By the time Conn nudged her on the shoulder, she knew she had been weeping for some time.

"They are gone," was all he said, then walked out on the beach.

He was standing over the dog sorrowfully shaking his head when she got to him. The animal was a mass of bloody fur, with a Roman javelin still sticking out his side.

"I am sure he died instantly," Conn offered, trying to soothe her.

"That is not good enough," she said, the tears streaming down her cheeks as she pulled out the javelin. With Conn's help, she carried the hound to the edge of the rocks.

"He died here, so I will leave him for the ocean gods," she said, trembling. "Perhaps they will give restitution to the Romans who did this. The next time they head for this island, I pray their boat will be swallowed by the rising tides."

She began piling rocks on top of the corpse. When it was completely covered, she sat down beside it and looked up at Conn accusingly.

"What were you doing here, anyway?" she asked.

"I saw them land," he explained. "I was following them to see where they would go."

"Following them?" Kordelina asked, perturbed. "You should have gone back to the village for help. Now they will surely return, and there will probably be more of them."

Conn shifted uncomfortably and stared into space. "It is strange that they only rode halfway around the beach and did not even go as far as the harbor," he offered, guiltily. "If I had thought they were not going to leave, I surely would have gone for help. I did not think —"

"Silence yourself!" she yelled, her fear now apparent by the way she lashed out. "Save your excuses for Solomon. You will have to tell him about this because I am in solitude, and all I see and hear I may not speak about. So be off with you, and if I do not learn of you telling of these events, I swear I will kill you myself."

Conn's soft brown eyes widened and he looked at her, astonished by the display of temper. He had never imagined that such a young girl could be intimidating. Her furious expression made him grateful no one else was there to witness her rebuke.

"Kordelina, you may not speak to me like this. I saved your life," he rebutted, obviously insulted.

"Saved my life?" she screamed, jumping to her feet and facing him. "You did not save me, you almost got me killed. You should have gone for help. If you had not been sneaking around in the rocks like a coward and doing what you were supposed to do, my dog would probably still be here."

She glared at him a moment longer and shook her head disdainfully. "Help me to remember, brave warrior. How long did you really spend fighting Romans?" she asked, in a biting tone.

Conn bit the inside of his cheek, and his complexion reddened. As much as he was trying to understand her outburst, it took all of his control to keep from slapping her.

"I will relay these events to the Chieftain," he said, struggling to keep an even tone. "And I am sorry about your dog, little one."

———

"Aonghus!" Solomon yelled, riding up the road after him. "Aonghus, wait for me, please!"

The blue-eyed young man turned in his saddle. Seeing it was the Chieftain, he halted his horse and waited for him to come beside him.

"I am glad I caught you," Solomon said, trying to get his breath. "Were you headed off alone again?"

Aonghus nodded, but did not speak.

The older warrior wiped the sweat from his brow with the palm of his hand and smiled. "Tell me, if you will, where is it that you depart every time Kordelina is away?"

The younger one's eyes glazed over and he looked straight ahead, and Solomon knew that he was not in a mood for volunteering information.

"What is it that you have to speak with me about, Chieftain?" he asked, ignoring the inquiry.

Solomon cleared his throat. "Well, she must be a lovely one to be kept such a mystery," he replied. "In truth, Aonghus, I have come about another matter. Perhaps we can sit awhile, and share some drink while we talk."

A faint smile crossed Aonghus' lips as he climbed out of the saddle. Solomon did the same, and both men took a place on the grass beneath one of the oak trees. Solomon handed Aonghus the bag of corma first, and as he drank from it, the Chieftain fidgeted nervously with one of his bracelets.

"It is going to be a warm spring, is it not?" he asked, trying to strike up a conversation.

With his head still tilted back, Aonghus nodded his reply. The bright spring sun caught the strands of red in his long hair and seemed to reflect off his eyes as he took a quick breath, and started drinking again.

"I remember the first spring I met you," Solomon continued. "Now that was a warm spring. It is hard to believe it was thirteen cycles ago, but need I say you have fared nicely, and I am a better man for having known you."

Aonghus abruptly stopped drinking, and looked curiously at the Chieftain. "What do you want, Solomon?" he asked. "If you truly want to know where I am going, I will tell you. If there is something else on your mind, please do share it with me as your odd behavior is making me uneasy. Please feel free to speak your mind."

The Chieftain frowned and stared off to the side for a moment. Then he grabbed the drinking bag and took a long swig. "I do not know how," he confessed. "I am at a loss at how to tell you."

Aonghus rubbed one eye with his fist, and let out a compassionate laugh. "It must be awful, because you are acting like a fool."

Solomon nodded and took another drink. "Yes, I suppose I am," he conceded. "I should tell it to you the way I heard it."

Aonghus grabbed the bag from him and lifted it to his lips. "If that will make it easier, please do," he replied, and started gulping down the ale.

"All right," the Chieftain began with a burdensome expression. "It is Bracorina. She is considering marrying a king's son from the midlands. If she does, Pwyll will have to offer a sizeable amount of his land to purchase the vow. Bracorina is not that young anymore, and there is some doubt as to her ability to produce an heir. The girl is so upset about never marrying again that she demanded all her land be given over as a seal. She reasons that if she gives the young man enough of her wealth, he will stay with her even if she cannot give him a child."

"So, what is the problem in that?" Aonghus asked, leaning back on one elbow. "It seems like a wise offering."

"Wise for Bracorina, but unwise for us," Solomon replied. "The merge of such a great amount of territory would leave our tribe with little. We would not only lose our standing, but would eventually be forced into becoming part of the midlanders. If that happens, you will have no kingdom to inherit, and I will have no title. I came to you about this because it is no secret that Bracorina has always had her sights set on you. She still holds your original promise close to her heart."

Aonghus rolled on his back and put his hands behind his head. He stared at the clouds and the deep blue sky as his body gradually drained of all feeling. He knew what Solomon was about to ask of him, and he knew why. Political marriages were important in maintaining tribal boundaries and power, and since he was Solomon's heir, and Bracorina was destined to be the largest landholder in the clan, the union was only logical.

Sensing Aonghus' thoughts, Solomon comfortingly placed a hand on his arm and offered a tight-lipped smile. "Aonghus, may I share with you something of my parentage?" he asked.

"Of course," Aonghus replied, his voice cracking as he tried to disguise his sudden desperation.

The Chieftain drew in a heavy breath, and puffed out his cheeks as he exhaled. "My mother was a Christian, who was wed to a Celtic heir in an arranged political marriage. It was a long time ago, about thirty-four cycles now, that it happened. But it was during a time when Rome and our people wanted to bridge their differences. My father never loved my mother, and for all her devotion to the good of her people, my mother felt nothing for him. Yet they did what they had to, and it was in the best interests of their people."

"Did it work?" Aonghus asked, still looking up at the sky.

Solomon guzzled more of the liquor, then burst into laughter. "No. The only thing that came out of it was me," he said, slapping Aonghus on the arm.

The younger one looked at him, and even though he showed signs of tears, he laughed as well. "I understand, Chieftain," he said, his laughter abruptly ceasing. He felt like all of his visions and hopes were now nothing more than wistful projections of the one whom he had wished to be. He covered his eyes with his forearm so Solomon could not see them watering. It was true that he was only one lone man, a tiny mortal, whose duty was forever to this tribe. He had deceived himself in thinking that he could somehow have his status and happiness too.

"Make the proposal to Pwyll, and I will be there upon his request," he said, his lips quivering. "My one condition is that the vow will be made upon my assuming power. You can decide between yourselves when that will be."

CHAPTER FIVE

wo days passed, and Kordelina left her hiding place for the last time. It was an abandoned burial chamber that had never been used. Excavated from a hill of limestone, the entrance to the dwelling had at some point been blocked by a sheet of fallen rock. It appeared as nothing more than a sheer piece of stone propped against a hillside that faced the sea. But there was space enough for a horse to fit through while still shielding the chamber from the offshore wind.

Inside, there was only a small hearth, because the limestone kept it well insulated. The walls were covered with Celtic symbols and Druidic inscriptions painted by the one who used to live there. It had been inhabited previously by a woman because Kordelina had found strands of long dark hair, and an alcove had been carved in rock to make a baby's crib. There was also a pallet near it that served as a sleeping area.

Kordelina had replaced the moldy animal hides she had originally found with new ones, and had also stored a few weapons, watering vessels, unshelled nuts, and salted meat. There was a large doorway on the back wall that led to an even larger room. Although it was probably intended to be the main worshipping chamber at one time, the young girl had piled it with straw for Macha. Because of its location, disposing of the animal refuse was easy. Kordelina shoveled the manure out one of the larger air holes each morning. Outside she had dug deep compost areas that were easily flushed out when it rained.

She was somehow sorry to leave her secret place. It was almost as if someone had made it especially for her. And absolutely no one, not even Saturnalia, knew where it was. Kordelina herself would not have found it if her dog had not been nosing around. She laughed as she remembered how the animal's barking had come from inside the rock, and she thought he had been swallowed by the earth.

She purposely left the chamber stocked with wood, and did not remove any of the supplies or weapons she had stored. Instead, she carefully folded all her animal hides and stuffed them into the small wooden chest she had stolen from Solomon's barn. Deep inside, she knew that she would return to this place, and only hoped it would be for pleasure and not out of necessity.

Upon her departure, she stopped to do one last thing. With her knife she carved the symbol of the grove—one straight line with two smaller ones crossing through it—on the side of the rock that covered the entrance. Every Celt knew it stood for the interconnection of all creation, and that this lifetime, and all lifetimes in the future, revolved around each other. Whether she was the one to inhabit this place again, or perhaps another young girl, she wanted to leave her mark so that on the day she was to be anointed, she could believe and understand this sacred concept.

"Thank you, Great Spirits," she said quietly. "Thank you for this place and for caring for me."

She climbed atop Macha, and started somberly toward her settlement. It was strange that her dog was not with her, and she could not help but shed a tear at the thought. The animal had been with her a long time, protecting and helping her to make it through the lonely times when Aonghus was far away. In her heart, she understood why he had been taken. A part of her would die tonight, as well: the little girl. She must now assume the rights of womanhood. Through her hound, the naive child had been carried into the Otherworld, and she was glad it had gone with her most trusted guardian.

The excitement and anticipation of the occasion had evaporated with the incident on the beach. It was a brutal initiation into the world everyone had warned her about. The Romans were coming, and they were going to try to conquer her people just as they had conquered others on the main islands. They had already killed something dear to her, and she despised them for it.

Her spirits were further diminished when she arrived at her house and saw four horses tied outside. She recognized Aonghus' and Solomon's stallions, but was not able to place the other two. Tired and upset about her dog, she did not want to be polite to guests. She wanted to get as much rest as possible to make it through the arduous night ahead.

She was careful to lead the two studs to a small side corral away from her mare. Macha was coming into season, and if they were too close, a mating was certain to occur. She walked inside the house and was stunned to see her parents, Solomon, and Aonghus gathered around a banquet table with Pwyll and Bracorina as guests. She made no effort to hide her displeasure at seeing the two in her house, and she took it as an especially bad omen on the day of her anointing.

"Kordelina," Enda greeted her, rising from her place and walking toward her. "Come sit and eat with us, dear girl; we have much to celebrate."

Kordelina looked at her mother questioningly. "Much to celebrate? What are you speaking of?"

"Kordelina, do not be rude," her father reprimanded. "We have guests. Kindly pay your respects and sit down."

The girl gave a bitter laugh. "I cannot sit and eat with you, because according to my restrictions, I am not supposed to be within striking distance of Bracorina. So either she goes, or I go."

An uncomfortable silence fell over the room, and Bracorina glared at Kordelina from behind her heavy-lidded eyes.

"I think we can waive the laws this once," Solomon interjected, trying to smooth things over. "Please Kordelina, do join us."

Kordelina did not take her eyes off Bracorina. "No, thank you," she said, and walked around where Solomon was sitting to get to her bed chamber.

The Chieftain grumbled something irritably, and when she was alongside him, he reached out one of his brawny arms and grabbed her by the wrist, yanking her down beside him. He gave her a look that told her she had better sit there and like it.

"That is better," he said, forcing a smile and shoving a plate in front of her. "Now eat."

The girl let her arms fall loosely at her sides, and glanced across the table at Bracorina. "I said, no thank you," she repeated, in an overly polite tone. "But do tell me, what are we celebrating?"

Enda was beaming, as she looked at her husband and gestured for him to make the announcement.

"Well," Koven cleared his throat, "Aonghus and Bracorina are to be wed."

Her father's words reverberated inside her head, and her mouth dropped open. She looked at Aonghus and he met her eyes for only an instant, then looked away sheepishly.

"It is something to be happy about," Bracorina said condescendingly. "Aonghus is."

The girl flashed a vain smile that made her pudgy nose spread across her face. Kordelina snapped. She could feel the color emptying out of her face, and when the last drop of blush had been extracted from her cheeks, she stared at Aonghus. It was as though time had stopped, and all the private thoughts they had shared had been demolished. Aonghus also suffered deeply, feeling as if he had betrayed them both. She knew how strong his pain was because he would not look at her again.

Then she turned and maliciously looked into Solomon's eyes. Before anyone could stop her, she took hold of his drooping mustache, and pulled his face close to hers.

"You made him do it," she accused, gritting her teeth.

Solomon's mouth dropped and his upper lip contorted as he grabbed her wrist. He gripped it so hard that her hand went numb until she let go.

"Enough!" he said. "It was of his own choice."

Kordelina lost all control. "Liar!" she screamed. "You are a liar! You made him do it, you made him do it. He never would have consented to marry her if you had not arranged it. You and your laws. You have laws about who we can love, who we can kill, who we should respect—and they are all merely excuses to keep yourself in power! If we did what we wanted, what we truly felt in our hearts, there would be no reason for you at all, now would there, mighty Chieftain?"

Everyone was too shocked to speak, especially Solomon, whose eyes were wide with surprise at her outburst. Kordelina thought he was probably going to hit her, and in an instant of rationality, she could not blame him. But sensing that she was going to be disciplined anyway, she decided to take it one step further. Leaning across the table, she got nose to nose with Bracorina and looked her directly in the eye.

"He will never love you," she snarled. "All you bought was a piece of a man to stick between your legs."

For a moment, Kordelina thought Bracorina was going to cry. Then she drew her hand back and slapped Kordelina hard across the mouth, causing her to bleed.

Kordelina lunged forward, and tipping the table, she sent the food and drink flying. She did not care if she violated the restriction of never striking Bracorina. She wanted one chance to give her exactly what she deserved.

She almost had a handful of her hair when Aonghus grabbed her. Wrapping both his arms around her torso so that she could not get free, he dragged her kicking and screaming away from Bracorina and out the front door. Then he heaved her atop her horse and placed the reins in her hands.

"Silence, Kordelina! You are only harming yourself," he commanded.

The girl instantly quieted, then burst into tears. "So are you," she cried. "They have no right to barter your happiness."

Aonghus grabbed his head with both hands. She could see he was trying to stay calm, and she suddenly felt guilty for upsetting him.

"I am sorry, Aonghus," she wept. "As the gods have made us, I did not mean to hurt you. I would never hurt you."

Closing his eyes, he rolled his head back and forth. When he at last opened them again and looked at her, his blue eyes were full of remorse.

"Go, and stay away until the sun sets," he told her. "If you do any more, I fear they will refuse your anointing." He slapped her horse's hindquarters, and sent it galloping out the farm gate.

Sobbing, Kordelina rode directly to Saturnalia's cottage. She was nearly hysterical when she reached the door.

The Druidess opened it before she could knock. "Kordelina, dear child," she said, taking her in her arms. "What has happened to you?"

Kordelina could not stop crying long enough to tell her, so Saturnalia led her inside. There she found Conn looking through her conjuring bag.

Kordelina was shocked; a sorceress was never to allow another to fondle the tools of her craft. She peered questioningly at Saturnalia, her respect for the sorceress quickly dissipating. By the scene in front of her, Kordelina realized the common warrior could reduce this powerful woman to a lowly handmaid. She honestly could not understand what she was doing with him; their pairing not only made Saturnalia look foolish, but desperate.

"I am sorry," she stammered. "I did not know you had company."

"No, no," Saturnalia soothed her, wiping the blood from her mouth. "It is all right. Come in here, and we will talk."

She took the girl into her sleeping chamber. Once inside, Kordelina threw herself on the bed, and burying her face in the pillows, began to cry.

Saturnalia covered her mouth with her hands and paced worriedly around the bed. "Please, child, do tell me, what has happened?" she asked.

Kordelina lifted her head, and took a deep breath. "Aonghus is going to marry Bracorina," she lamented. "They were all there at my house, and when I found out, I went crazy. I should not have done it, but I called Solomon a liar and I pulled his mustache and—"

"You pulled his mustache?" Saturnalia broke in, then she threw her head back and laughed incredulously. "You pulled his mustache?"

Kordelina nodded, then hid her face again and cried even harder.

"Do not weep," Saturnalia comforted, sitting on the bed beside her and stroking the back of her hair. "You must not weep like this over your brother. He is not dead, and he is perfectly able to make his own decisions. Perhaps he loves Bracorina."

Kordelina jerked her head around and glared at her with red, puffy eyes.

"He does not," she stated. "I know he does not. Solomon made him do it because he is afraid Bracorina will give her land to another tribe. She has always wanted Aonghus, and she knows Aonghus would never go against Solomon's wishes. So Solomon told him to do it. I am sure of it. Oh, Saturnalia, if you could have seen the look on Aonghus' face when they announced it."

Saturnalia wiped a tear trickling across the bridge of Kordelina's nose. She knew that deep inside, the girl's heart was breaking.

"Nevertheless, did you think you could keep Aonghus all to yourself, forever?" she asked.

Kordelina rolled over on her back and stared at the ceiling. "I wanted to," she sniffed. "I thought that once I was anointed, and he did not have to be responsible for me anymore, it would be like when we were children."

"But you are not children anymore," she gently argued. "He is a man, and it is only natural that he would take a wife. You, too, will marry one day."

Kordelina burst into tears again, and shook her head. "But I will never marry anyone who hates him like Bracorina hates me. She is going to get him in that big estate of hers, and I will never get to see him again," she wailed.

Saturnalia gathered her in her arms and began to rock her gently. "That will never happen," she tenderly reassured her. "Aonghus loves you too much to ever let that happen. I know him well, and believe me when I say you are forever strong in his heart."

———

When Kordelina stepped before Solomon, it was with swollen eyes, a red nose and a split lip. Staring down at her, the Chieftain thought that for once, she appeared too frail to endure the test that lay ahead. She lifelessly went through the motions of ceremony, and in spite of the anger he still harbored for her, he wished she did not have to do it alone.

Since Kordelina was the only girl ever to be anointed in their clan, the elders had decided that she must survive the test of the cave without assistance. It was a grudging compromise, considering that after a heated debate, Aonghus finally got them to approve his apprentice's status. Originally they had refused her altogether, saying that not only was she female, but she had a number of disciplinary measures against her. The tribe had never forgotten what had happened with Bracorina, and they hesitated to allow her access to the elite privileges of a warrior.

But after hours of prodding and promises, Aonghus secured Kordelina's anointing—on the condition that the test of the Otherworld be done in solitude. The only ones who would be present for the ceremony itself were Saturnalia, Solomon, Aonghus, and one other warrior: Conn. Aonghus had chosen him as his guardian for the night. It was the only way that the elders could be sure that Aonghus did not try to rescue Kordelina. Such a severe violation of ceremonial laws would result in death for both the master and his foster.

As he presided over the vows, Solomon had little to say to Kordelina; he was still furious about the earlier incident. He could barely wish her a kind word, except to say that he hoped she would be well when the dawn came. Even then, he said it through tight lips and with his fists clenched at his sides.

It was Saturnalia who took special care to perform a unique ritual for her student. With her artful wisdom, she designed a ceremony that combined not only the warrior's way and expectations, but the mystical realm. Using a torch of scented herbs, she anointed the girl with Otherworldly blessings. She was careful to ask the heavens to endow her with the strength of wisdom, bravery, and sorcery.

"For you are a woman made from the womb of Mother Earth," she said, swirling the torch above Kordelina's head. "You have the lessons of the female energy within your soul. The elements of earth and water comprise all women, and you are the personification of both. Graceful Kordelina, let your traits of beauty balance with the creation of the huntress within. Long ago it was decided by the mother of our land that it should be woman who would bring forth life. She blessed them with love, vitality, and the gentle powers of the universe.

"Because you were born of woman energy, you are already acquainted with your intuitive self. You are able to respond to the voices deep within your being, and because you are readily able to receive these messages, they are a gift passed down to you from Mother Earth. To lie about these gifts and to humiliate their creative force, is a great disgrace. And since you have taken on the burden of one female warrior in a tribe of men, to lie about anything from this moment on, and to deny your kinsmen your courage, would amount to permanent exile from the tribe. Should such a crime ever be done by you, we will turn this ceremony of happiness into one of mourning, and the treasures you have earned will be consumed by the very flame that has empowered you. Take care to use your talents and inner strength to support your kinsmen. While you may reveal your inner self to your sisters only, you may never show your total face to the outer world. This will cause the trust of your intuition to flourish, and will protect the forces that flow to the rhythm of the water and earth."

Handing the torch to Solomon, Saturnalia crushed the herbs in the chalice and filled it with wine. She set it beside Aonghus and took the knife he held out.

"This weapon that has been made for you by your master will be what draws the sweet red river from your flesh," she said reverently. "And when it has marked you with its spirit, it will be yours to carry and trust forever."

Kordelina nodded and humbly bowing her head, unlaced her shirt and exposed her cleavage.

"For you, little one, the animal of power is the horse," the sorceress declared in a commanding tone. "Let the mighty horse reign within you, that you would have the power to run across the grasslands and bring the vision of our dreams. For the courage of the horse anoints you with physical and unearthly power. And like the Goddess Macha, who you must forever obey, it will enable you to fly through air and leap into the heavens. Were it not for the horse we would all be earthbound. Noble horse will give you the strength to carry the burdens of others for great distances, and it will be done with ease. But in understanding the power of this animal, you must also understand the importance of balancing wisdom with the wind. You may never forget the acts of humanity that are your purpose."

With that she cut the symbol of the horse between Kórdelina's breasts. Eyes on fire, Aonghus then came forward with the animal fat to rub onto it.

For a long moment, he and Kordelina looked at each other, tears welling in their eyes. Then he touched the place that was bleeding with his finger, and moved it to his mouth before applying the stinging ointment.

Kordelina was trembling by the time the drink was handed to her. It had been made so strong she thought she was going to vomit. She covered her mouth with her hand to stop it, and looked helplessly at Aonghus.

It will be all right, she thought she heard him say. Then in the next moment, Saturnalia handed her the torch and kissed her on the forehead before directing her into the cave.

"Many people fail their dreams," she whispered in her ear. "To be the warrior you must be brave. Let your passions emerge as you watch through this night, and open your heart and mind to the vision that calls you. For I do pray by the very gods who are with us here, that when you come back into this world, you will have discovered it and devised a way to possess it."

ChAPTER SIX

he walked slowly through the stone opening, her knife in one hand, a torch in the other. She could feel the effects of the drink, and in a moment of cowardice she thought of turning back, but she made herself move forward.

She had completed the sacred ceremony of the highest power, and as Saturnalia had told her, she was a woman, and life everlasting flowed from her. To go back now would be to give it all up. Taking a deep breath to calm herself, she considered what this ritual meant. She was somehow skeptical; having recently seen her loved ones in a true light had left her disillusioned. Aonghus would marry Bracorina even if he did not love her. Solomon would never have a responsible relationship, and Saturnalia was destined to prostitute herself to a common warrior. Perhaps by themselves, these realizations would not have had such an impact, but combined with the righteous attitude each possessed, she saw that perfection was only imperfection justified in their minds.

Steadily continuing down the stone slope toward the center of the cave, she shivered at its dankness. Having previously thought through her strategy for this night many times, she had only one goal, and that was to make it to a safe place where she could stay warm until dawn. She found herself instinctively scanning her surroundings for wood or anything at all to build a fire. But there were only scattered bones of men and animals. Many warriors had died here, of that she was certain; she could almost hear the sound of their groaning in the walls around her, waiting for their presence to be acknowledged.

She was startled at a portrait of a hawk looming over her. The magnificent bird of prey had its wings spread and short, hooked beak half open, as if it were about to attack. Lifting her torch to examine it closer, she noticed that caught in its strong, sharp claws, was the tiny painting of a man. He was writhing and screaming as he reached out to his escaped soul, plummeting into nothingness. The piercing eyes of the bird were a deep yellow, and its red pupils, the image of a flame. She peered into them for a long moment, and as she did, she realized the dark spots at the very centers were silhouettes of tormented beings burning alive.

"I do not fear you, Hawk," she said, her voice echoing off the stone and surrounding her. "You are the messenger of dreams, and with your eye, you view the omens and the spirit. I know you are not destroying that man out of anger; you have saved him from his a soulless vision. You, Hawk, bring honor to the sky, and I am privileged to have you with me tonight."

295

Cutting a small strand of her hair, she dropped it as an offering, and walked further. Her legs were numb, but she was still able to make out the uneven ground beneath her. The rugged contours of the cave walls appeared shadowed with gold. She knew it had to be the reflection of her torch, yet she could not help but consider that this heightened vision was the way it truly was, but she previously did not have the perception to realize it. There were also many inscriptions painted on either side of her, some of which she recognized from her own hiding place.

Her hearing was gradually becoming magnified; the sound of her feet against the earth was painfully loud. Stopping a moment to take off her boots, she wiggled her toes in the dirt, and was at once fascinated by the movement. She could feel and hear every intricate part of her body working, and she thought of what a miraculous creation it really was.

She could feel the beating of her heart sending blood through her veins. She could sense the pumping of her lungs as she inhaled and exhaled. Even more phenomenal, every pore of her skin was able to perceive the atmosphere. She pressed both her hands to her womb and tried to imagine what it would be like to have a baby inside. A tiny spark of life warming her, as she nourished it with her own flesh and blood. Tilting her head back, she began to cry. To bring forth a life was the most honest, natural thing a woman and man could do—it transcended the laws of the Druids, and ascended into the realm of eternity. Forever there would be a person who would have transformed a feeling of love into a complete being, and it would have taken place within her.

Distracted by a noise in the darkness, Kordelina quickly got to her feet. She held her breath and listened a moment. An unearthly calm had fallen about the cave. She fearfully remained still.

In her peripheral vision, she saw the haunting image of a dark-haired woman standing in front of the cave entrance. She had cavernous eyes and a deeply disturbing way about her. Kordelina instantly realized she was the one who had originally lived in the burial chamber she had found.

"You, dark woman, did no harm while I was within your chamber, and I do not believe you will hurt me while I am here," she said through slurred speech. "What my mind knows of you, my heart does not yet perceive, but I am certain that I am stronger than you. And if I wished, I could walk through your spirit, and you would have no choice but to vanish. For what I see now is only the residue of your soul."

The young girl did not know where she was getting it, but a courage was rising in her. She now understood that the real demons of men were the repressed desires and vengeful lies that dwelled in their hearts, not in the apparitions of the gods. Good and evil were not warring entities, only different aspects of the same feeling. What men could not explain with their need to destroy and regenerate, they blamed on the gods.

Taking up her torch, she saw light emanating from the vicinity of the noise. At first it was faint, but as her vision cleared again, the light became blinding. Whether this was real or not was insignificant.

It glowed as if someone had taken the sun from the sky and forced it into one place on earth. Her eyes widened and a smile came across her face as the spectacle emerged.

The dirt from the cave floor seemed to be dancing in a whirlwind as the luminous power grew brighter, then suddenly dim. There was something there, something beautiful and gracious that Kordelina knew came from the deepest part of her mind. It made her want to spin in the air with delight. Then she saw the face of another woman peering at her from the center of the cave. Her eyes, large and benevolent, invoked the girl's trust.

As she stepped out to where Kordelina could see her, she saw that she was half-woman and half-horse. Her hair was the color of the gold that had highlighted the stone. The tiny wisps flowed in all directions, as if carried by the stars themselves. Her face was exquisite, with a strong jaw jutting out just far enough to make her eyes look like splendid orbs sending greetings from another world. She sprouted two transparent wings in the space between her shoulders, and they fluttered so quickly that the girl fancied them to be the wings of a rather large hummingbird.

The centaur was naked to the waist, with firm, almost masculine breasts and stomach muscles that rippled with vitality as she moved. Her arms were lithe and delicate compared to the rest of her build.

Beyond her waist, her body was white, sleek, and well-proportioned. Her back was shorter than most of the horses Kordelina had seen, and it appeared to be a cross between a full-sized horse and a pony. The ribs of her human body melded nicely with the flanks of the horse's body as her torso extended down to a bulging gaskins, straight cannon bones, and shiny black hooves.

Her tail whipped wildly from one side to the other, standing high in the air each time the wings on her back fluttered.

Kordelina was awed at the sight of her. "I have seen you before; you came into my dreams when I was a child," she said.

The woman bowed her head in graceful acknowledgement.

"You are a goddess, you are Macha," Kordelina continued with a brilliant smile. "You were not a dream; I really did see you, but it was with my silent mind. You helped me catch my mare. I named her Macha because Aonghus told me all horses are your children."

The goddess nodded in agreement. Then with a tiny sparkle of her wings, she lifted herself across the cave and landed closer.

Kordelina was enveloped by the warmth of the light she radiated. It was as if she were in a bubble of air separating her from the rest of the world. "Why have you come here? Did you answer the call of Saturnalia's herbs?" she questioned.

Macha's eyes grew larger as she opened her mouth to answer. "You were taken from my world and placed in this world," her voice lilted through the air, the pitch varying slightly with each word. "It is a troubled place you come to now.

I have come to tell you that all the answers you need are within you. Do not seek the counsel of others; be true only to your heart."

The smile left Kordelina's face. "But what if my choices are wrong?"

The goddess' jaw jutted out further, then retracted. "For you, there is no right or wrong choice," she answered, blinking her eyes and bowing her head.

"I do not understand of what you speak," the girl replied.

The centaur stood suddenly erect, cocking her head to one side to listen. Kordelina had seen her own mare do this many times when she sensed someone coming. "You will understand. Be aware that your enemy can be your greatest ally," she replied gently.

There was a strong flash of white and blue light that caused Kordelina to cover her eyes. Squinting them open enough to see, she could make out darkness where the centaur had once stood.

Invigorated by the visitation, she eagerly explored deeper in the cave. What did she have left to fear? In an instant of enlightenment, she comprehended that this place held man's view of himself, and as much as he resisted the dark and destructive parts, thus was he tormented. Because Kordelina had faced that part of herself long ago, she was at peace with it. She knew she could be cold and violent, and capable of killing anyone who dared to prevent her from getting what she wanted.

As she approached the back of the cave, she saw a painting of three warriors hunting a boar. The boar was facing them with bloody tusks, ready to attack. The men had their spears poised as a group of hunting dogs snarled at the beast. Then she remembered Aonghus had once told her his dog had been killed in here. Dear, sweet Aonghus. Did you think of him on the night you were in here, she thought. Did you know then how much you would love me?

Her ears were suddenly filled with the magnificent sound of a flute. She recognized it to be the one Aonghus used to play to her as a child. Focusing on a stone altar, she saw a man crouched on top of it with the instrument in his hand.

Approaching him, she sensed herself slipping from reality into a dimension of her own heart and mind. It was a link to the highest realm of the spirit, where one could simply relinquish earthly desires and disappear without a care.

She watched the man step behind the altar and motion to her. At first he appeared to transform into part fish; his skin now was gills. The gills then turned into feathers as he became part bird. Spreading his multicolored wings, they metamorphosized to fur and he appeared to be part animal instead.

He beckoned her with eyes like star beams; their color flickered and changed with each step she took. She sensed instantly this was a violent, depraved being who was capable of destroying her. Yet there was something about him that made her want him to give herself over; something that made her want to embrace the agony of her soul.

Completely enamored of him, she dropped her torch and began unwillingly walking to him. She was bewitched by the music in her ears and his gleaming eyes. Without thought, she began taking off her clothes until she was naked and stretched on the altar in front of him. Closing her lids, she felt as if he were caressing her with his hands. The darkness was making love to her, wrapping itself around her legs and arms until she was paralyzed by it. It was a deeply sexual feeling, and soon the gentle pulsating of her womb was too pleasurable to abandon.

This is what sacrificial virgins must feel, she thought, because it was a deeper form of ecstasy than could ever be brought about by union with a man. It was like making love to herself, and this image standing over her was her own male energy demanding to come forth. For a moment, the sensual contractions of her uterus were so strong she thought that she had conceived. Then she realized she had taken the two parts of herself and allowed them to come together to create a new entity, yet one that was still entirely herself.

She woke up shivering, and in a whirling moment of music and hallucinations, she thought she had evaporated into the cave walls. She rose from her place on the altar and saw a mass of gentle faces peering at her from the dark. Walking to the center of the circular cave floor, she started to dance.

She spun naked around the altar, fondling her breasts and running her fingers over the round of her hips and between her thighs in a fertility dance. She was merging with herself, becoming first the woman, then the man, until she was finally a combination of both. So free, so complete was she as she turned and turned for her onlookers—until everything went black.

Outside, Aonghus took a puff off a pipe filled with hemp. He suddenly felt a sharp pain in his head that forced him to cover his eyes. His stomach wrenched, and the pain forced him to leave the campsite. He had only gone a few steps into the woods when it emptied itself of the food he had eaten. Wrapping both arms around his abdomen, he swayed back and forth to keep from falling over. Conn followed his friend and helped him back to a place near the fire where he could lie down.

Aonghus drew his knees to his chest to relieve the pain, but it persisted. He was drugged; he did not know if this was another one of his episodes, or if it was the effect of the herbs. He felt his head was in a vise; the pressure behind his eyes was so strong that even the light from the fire was agonizing. Closing them tightly, he saw a vision of himself as a child with his dog, Locwn. He began to relive every detail of the day he was killed in the cave.

He was overcome with anguish at seeing the crushed animal in front of him, and the horrible realization of what he had to do as Solomon placed the knife in his hand. He cried out loud when he stabbed the dog in the heart, then screamed with terror as the canine turned into Kordelina, and the body that had been the dog's was now her tender, pubescent frame. She looked at him sorrowfully before she took her last breath. Not knowing if it was a dream or reality, Aonghus began to shriek with horror.

He was writhing in the dirt when Conn grabbed him by the shoulders and shook him hard. The warrior took the small leather drinking bag from Aonghus' supply pouch and helped him to swallow. Aonghus was trembling violently, and his long hair was soaked with sweat.

"What is it?" Conn asked. "What did you see?"

Aonghus reached his shaking hands out to warm them over the fire, and Conn could tell by the way the muscles of his back were tensed, that his friend was struggling with madness.

"It is Kordelina," he answered, his voice quivering with fear. "She is going to die in there."

Conn's face faded of all expression. "How do you know?"

Aonghus stared at the fire with glazed eyes. He moved his hands dangerously close to the flames. When he was about to reach straight into it, Conn lunged forward and shoved him away.

"You are insane," he said, slapping both of Aonghus' cheeks to rouse him from his nightmare. "Is there anything that will cure you of this?"

Aonghus began to laugh maniacally. His tone was hollow and unattached to this world; Conn slapped him again to quiet him. It did little to silence the warrior who drew his knife from its sheath and handed it to his guardian.

"Kill me," he said, his voice suddenly a whisper. "I should never have lived. Kill me, please, then let me rest with her inside the cave. It would be mercy for us. Please, dear friend, I beg you."

Conn's face flushed, and he, too, started to tremble. Aonghus truly was deranged, and his suffering had grown worse. Now the herbs and the seriousness of this night were magnifying his debilitated state.

Taking him by the shoulders, Conn pulled him to his feet and led him to the dark stone entry. "You will not make me responsible for any more," he shouted, "as the burden of my deed to Blathnaid is forever wearing on my conscience. If you wish to die with Kordelina, then go inside and kill yourself in her presence. As your friend, I do wish to see you by the light of the sun, and should you return, I will say nothing of this. But trouble me no further with your madness or your love for her, as I am struggling with too much guilt of my own."

With all his strength, he shoved Aonghus into the cave. Aonghus stumbled and fell to the ground just inside. Getting on all fours, he looked at Conn for a lucid moment, and smiled, coldly.

"You did kill Blathnaid, did you not?" he asked, comforted by his friend's admittal of transgression.

"Yes," Conn murmured. "I owed favors. I had no other choice."

Aonghus stared at him through hard, calculating eyes. "Then if I should bring Kordelina from the Otherworld, I trust that upon my silence, it will not be told by you either"

Conn nodded. "If by the morning light we are alive, I will say nothing—if my confession remains a secret as well."

"So be it," Aonghus said, then crawled into the blackness.

CHAPCER SEVEN

On his hands and knees, Aonghus crawled into the murky darkness. His dragging cloak forced him to stop every few feet to untangle it from around his legs. He wanted to take it off altogether, but knew he would need it later to fend off the cave's dampness.

His stomach was tight with fear, and his respiration short and labored. He knew he had just broken a sacred law of his tribe, but it mattered little now. He had to get to Kordelina, had to find out if she was still alive. What a fool he was, how could he have let them send her in here alone?

"Kordelina!" he yelled desperately. "Where are you? Answer me!"

He heard nothing but his own voice reverberating off the limestone, and he cringed at its loudness. He was overcome with an intense fear as the walls of the cave faded and he found himself fighting to stay conscious.

The ground beneath him was moist, and the dirt on his hands smudged his sweaty face as he rubbed it. Stopping a moment to steady himself, he glanced around and saw a multitude of dazzling creatures coming out of the rock—some appeared part human, and others were exotic animals. All possessed gleaming, preternatural eyes that watched him as he crawled forward. He sensed they were waiting to receive him and transport him into eternity.

Dropping his head forward, he moved deeper into the ominous stone hollow. The earth felt as if it were swaying from side to side, and by the time he reached the abrupt drop that led to the ceremonial pit, he thought he had been swallowed by a black abyss. Suddenly he was lying on his back and rolling from side to side. Each time he rolled, he believed he had stopped himself only inches from the chasm of the underworld. Once he thought he saw decaying hands reach up to grab him. He screamed in terror and they were gone, only to be followed by the barking of his dog coming from one side.

"Locwn? Locwn is that you?" he called, squinting into the shadows.

The barking suddenly ceased, and Aonghus listened to the sound of the vicious snorting of a boar. The pig scrambled against the stone, and he knew instinctively it was coming right at him. He could smell the wild sow and soon looked into its beady, furious eyes. Then a mass of indistinguishable fur was on top of him, and he was groaning and crying out for help. In a final moment of terror, he begged for his life. The beast disappeared.

Lying very still on the earthen floor, he laughed deliriously, then abruptly stopped as if it were not allowed. A silent moment passed, but unable to hold it in, he let out a long howl of thankfulness. The spirit of the boar had gone by him.

Catching his breath, he gave a warrior's battle cry and it was answered by the wailing of supplications on all sides. They pierced his mind with their cries. They were coming from the furthest reaches of the sky and the deepest cracks of the earth: they were the entombed beings whose souls had not yet returned.

Listening to their prayers of forgiveness and release was sheer torture. He clamped his hands over his ears and screamed as loudly as he could to drown them out. When he let go, he was distracted by the clattering of bones above and below him: it was the spirits—the old ones, young ones, the spirits of men and women who wanted to stop him, but could not.

He tried to stand once, but his knees buckled, and he found himself lying prostrate in front of a woman. He could smell the terrible stench of her as he saw that she was clothed in the rotting remnants of a robe. Her skin was caked with earth and her feet were bare. She had dark locks of hair, matted and tangled with dirt. She looked down on him with darting, black eyes as she opened her filthy garment. To Aonghus' horror, he saw her stomach was a bloody, gaping wound.

Disgusted, he got to his hands and knees and tried to go around her. He had only gone a short way when he found she was standing in front of him again.

"Stay in your grave, Deireadh!" he commanded through clenched teeth. "Suffer me no further!"

In an instant, she evaporated and he could see an incandescent light ahead of him. It had to be Kordelina's torch.

He weakly dragged himself forward with this hands, holding his knife between his teeth. His awareness of what was occurring dimmed, and he once again struggled to stay alert.

When he reached his flickering vision, he saw more than one. They seemed to be spiraling around each other, and he attempted to grab the one he thought was real. More than once, he sluggishly grasped for thin air. One time he burned himself before he was finally able to take hold of the torch actually there.

She was near, he could sense it. Extending the flame, he focused on the shadow of her, lying unclothed in front of the altar.

Before he could consider what was happening, he was standing over her. He removed his cloak and wrapped her in it, then he held her to him and began rocking her back and forth. He thought of the tiny bundle of life that had fit so perfectly into his arms the night she was born. It was still like that, almost as if they had grown out of one other.

Her eyes were rolled white, and her breathing was silent. She was slipping away from him and he could not bear it. He no longer felt his own pain; he was consumed by her fading condition.

Leaning forward, he kissed her on her open lips, and he felt a yearning rise in him. His arms slipped around her body as distant memories came flooding back. He could hear the songs of his childhood and sense the happiness that had filled those years. He was intoxicated by the scent of her breath, and reaching beneath the cloak, he ran his hand over her naked flesh.

He did not merely touch her; he became her—her breath, her blood. He could hear her voice in his subconscious. He knew, at that very moment, they were forming a visceral bond. He listened to her speak to him in his mind, and could perceive her silent cry for life.

She was no longer sister or apprentice; she had gone beyond these roles. He felt a terror about it, feeling that somehow they had committed an unforgivable offense against the gods, and to be able to hear her speak without talking was a strange form of punishment. How could he ever pretend that she did not affect him now—that he was not utterly mastered by her devotion?

He found himself sobbing outwardly. "Oh, Kordelina," he wept, wiping the jewels of sweat from her face. "I wish we had never started this lie."

He hugged her unconscious body tightly; he thought he might smother her, but he did not care. If she was going to pass to the Otherworld, he wanted to prevent it so that he might absorb her weakness and sustain her by his love alone.

Aonghus shivered as he considered the release of death. Perhaps they could make the transition together. If this cave was to be their tomb, then let them embrace it. While they would never have the ecstasy of the blending of their flesh, their union would ascend to divinity itself. They would become each other, and no mortal would ever separate them again.

Her life had always been his, and now he could not help but want to preserve her innocence. She was his enemy and his friend; their care for each other went beyond physical passion to limitless devotion.

He cradled her close to him, one arm supporting her limp head. He groaned as loudly as he could to drown the sound of her voice in his brain.

We are not two beings anymore, she repeated. *That is our secret.*

"Kordelina, Kordelina," he answered. He swooned as he listened to the rhythm of her breathing. She was resisting death; he could feel her struggle.

Then her eyes flashed open and her lips began to quiver. She frantically reached out to press her hand over his heart, her body tensed and trembling. "Do not leave me, Aonghus," she pleaded, as she put her arms around his neck. "Promise that you will never leave me."

Her weight against his chest caused a burning sensation, and he could feel the thunderous beats of her heart sink into his skin until he was sure their pulse was sharing a single measure.

"I promise, Kordelina," he whispered, then closed his eyes.

———

Kordelina was alone when she regained consciousness. She was completely clothed, and her boots were back on her feet. Groggy and fatigued, she scanned her surroundings and saw she was so close to the cave entrance that she could see the morning light shining outside. Her torch was propped on a stone hollow above her and the braids of her hair had been loosened.

Running her hand down her torso and over her thighs, she was disturbed by the feeling that someone had been with her last night. A mortal had caressed her flesh, and she was angered at the thought. It was to have been her night. No one should have interrupted her seclusion.

She tried to think of who it had been, but drew a blank. She could remember the man with the flute and the erotic sensuality she had experienced with him. After that, she recalled nothing.

Wrapping her arms around herself, her anger dissipated as she was filled with a sudden feminine contentment. It was almost as if her visitor had made love to her without consent. She reached into her trousers and touched herself between her legs to be sure. When she was satisfied that nothing had happened, she stood and faced the entryway.

An awful sadness rose in her at having to leave this place, and a feeling of doom lay heavily on her heart. She did not want to go out to face her life; she knew it would never be the way she had envisioned it last night. The people and the conditions had not changed, even though she had. And now she would be forced to accept life with a greater understanding of its futility.

She thought back to last night, when she had believed she was going to die and had reveled in the contentment of it. The transition would have been easy, but Saturnalia was too adept at concocting her brew, and she would never have given Kordelina more than she could take. She administered only enough so the girl would sleep through what should have been a frightening test of character. Kordelina smiled at her show of tender mercy.

She felt suddenly guilty for not wanting to see the sorceress again. It was not only Saturnalia; it was all of the people she knew. Her aversion was not because they had wronged her in any way. She merely wanted to be away from them at this point in her life. As she walked toward the light, she was more convinced than ever that her time as part of the tribe was soon to end.

At first, the glare of the morning sun made it hard to make out who was waiting. Placing her hand to her brow, she saw that besides Solomon, Saturnalia, Conn, and Aonghus, Diarmudd and Edainne were there as well. There were horses for each of them.

Solomon was still angry; he stood in stoic silence holding Lir and Macha as Aonghus stepped in front of her, a torque in his hand. He looked sickly, his skin jaundiced to the point that his lips had no color at all. His eyes were swollen and red. When Kordelina looked into them, she could tell by the way she started to tear that she had become something he had never wished for her to be.

He was too overwhelmed with emotion to say anything as he held out the torque for her to see, and Kordelina smiled broadly when she noticed the two horses' heads ornamenting the ends of the twisted metal neckpiece. Forcing a wistful smile, he put it on her and stepped back a moment. She could have sworn she heard him say her name, but she never saw his lips move.

"Thank you, Aonghus," she said softly as she touched the torque with her fingertips. "Thank you for believing in me."

He turned away from her, and for a moment, was lost in his own world. Then he wheeled back around, and taking her by the shoulders, kissed her forehead and arranged the hair around her face.

He did not speak as he stepped to the side and let Saturnalia approach. Oddly, the Druidess looked more lovely than Kordelina had ever seen, and she could not help but wonder if her newly-acquired vision would remain as perceptive. She was now able to grasp the entirety of all she saw: the weakness in Aonghus, and the true beauty of Saturnalia. Then the Druidess took her by both hands, and gazed deeply into her eyes, waiting for Kordelina to tell of the evening's events. When the girl shrugged and laughed, Saturnalia laughed as well, then hugged her close.

"Did truth come to you in the night?" she playfully whispered in her ear.

Kordelina laughed again. "Yes, but it left in the morning."

"It always does," Saturnalia remarked as she released her. She stepped back and lifting her hands, smiled proudly. "As you have fulfilled your test, you will now be entrusted to escort Edainne back to her clan. May it stay in your mind that all differences between us and that tribe have been set aside, and we are considered at peace. Let it reflect in your actions and words when you are there."

Kordelina nodded and looked at Edainne. She was terribly frightened. The dread she felt at what was ahead of her blazed in her eyes. Then Kordelina turned to Diarmudd, whose vision fixed sorrowfully upon her friend, and she knew this was going to be a much harder task than spending a night in a cave.

CHAPTER EIGHT

A vague melancholy swept over Saturnalia as she watched the group of three men and two young women ride away. The scent of spring rose in the air as she crossed her arms in front of her and let out a muffled but worried groan. There was little she could say to anyone about what she knew was going to happen— what she had seen in her dreams the night before. There was no tangible reason to dread the future, but she did. She knew very well that every detail of her vision would come to pass, no matter how hard she tried to change it in her mind.

She heard Solomon come up behind her, and putting one arm around her waist, he pulled her to him. She could feel his calloused hands through the material of her robe—those rough palms that she no longer wanted to have on her body, that she no longer yearned for in the dark. He kissed her lightly on the cheek, and gave a boyish laugh. He was happy this morning, happy because it was all finally over. Kordelina was a woman now and she had earned rights of her own. That meant he no longer had to be responsible for her. He no longer had to wonder if his secret would ever be told.

Saturnalia laughed, too, but it was not the carefree laugh of a lover or a person lifted of a heavy burden. Instead, it was an ironic laugh; after thirteen years, the two had successfully staged the drama of their lives. They had kept hidden their personal treason, transcended the overthrow of a kingdom, bribed the only person who knew the truth, and pretended their lives were unaffected by the only remnant of their wrongdoing: Kordelina.

Saturnalia knew deep inside that Solomon was not as happy that Kordelina had been anointed as he was relieved. From this moment on, he would never have to answer for her actions again. She secretly wondered if Kordelina's desire to live in another place was not an idea he planted. After all, the one time the child had left, Solomon had to be threatened before he would retrieve her. Saturnalia had realized then that no matter where Kordelina ended up, as long as she was away from him she could not be a constant reminder of his past.

For Saturnalia, Kordelina was not a nuisance; she was a reason. Through teaching the girl, Saturnalia had come to know herself not as a sorceress, but as a woman. As Kordelina had attained a realization of her purpose in life, so too had the woman within Saturnalia come of age. For a brief moment, she wanted to apologize to Solomon because she realized she no longer needed him.

Unsuspecting of her thoughts, the Chieftain held her closer and stared at the band of riders as they disappeared over the crest of a hill. Then he turned her to face him, and offered her a genuine smile.

"I am an old man now," he told her quietly, almost embarassed by his openness. "Perhaps I have realized it too late, and perhaps you would do well to silence me, but Saturnalia, as I look at what my work and life has amounted to, it comes to little except for that which I have done with you. As the years prey upon us both, and our past is probably greater than our future, I would ask that you grant me the presence of your love and tenderness for what still lies ahead."

A great feeling of despair filled her as he spoke. Looking into his soft brown eyes, she knew he was seeking in her what he had never been able to find in himself. He came to her not as a lover or a Chieftain, but as a man who had finally atoned for his past indiscretions and wanted to resume his dreams.

She felt the pangs of regret in her, and she was overcome with genuine sorrow. What he was searching for in her no longer existed for him. It had been given away bit by bit over the years until there was nothing left but memories.

She looked up at the gleam of sun in the blue sky and watched a few clouds drift into the distance. Then she filled her lungs with air, gave a little shake of her head, and gazed down at her feet. Sensing his dismay at her reaction, she refused to let herself look up even when he brushed the side of her cheek with his hand.

"What is it that you offer me, a touch of compassion or pity?" he asked in a sad tone. "I know of no way to tell a woman such as you what is in my heart, and I am at a loss for the phrases that would even make you listen. What I hold in these eyes that look upon you, are not the inclinations of a leader, or the urges of the young man who once sought you only for his bed. What is in my eyes are the years of learning to live with what I am, and what I am not when you are away from me. While I possess no words to make this sound better or worse, I will say directly that I love you, and I have prayed that you would one day find me worthy as your husband."

Still Saturnalia could not look at him. More than the surprise at his sudden honesty, she was confronted with the lack of honesty in herself. She did love Solomon, but not as a woman loves a man whom she would call a husband, or even as an equal partner who shares the pleasures that come in the darkness. In truth, she had never wanted to marry him, and these many years, she was relieved he had never asked. What they had in common was this tribe, and Kordelina. That was all. Aside from enjoying the unbridled sexuality they both possessed, there was little in her heart or Solomon's that would ever have inclined them to be husband and wife.

"Once, Solomon, you and I shared our ambition, and once we shared a love that was beyond marriage. It was a love that encompassed the souls over which we ruled, but little else," she answered softly. "While you would ask me now to share your later years, I would dare to say to you that your earlier years were far too dangerous and temperamental to dismiss. Of those years, I am glad that I was a part, but as you say, the face of age is shining upon us both, and the recklessness we owe to our youth is little to speak of now. So, my dear Chieftain, let us not complicate each other's lives with commitment for we are too much alike, and there is no place for vows to come between us now."

She stared at him with sincerity and kindness. What she saw was a man who knew that she was more like him than any person could ever be. He gave a small nod but did not take his eyes off her. What was lurking in him at that moment was the deep fear that his twilight would amount to less than his youth.

"You have a place for a wife in your home now, but she does not bear the name Saturnalia," the Druidess said with misty eyes. "For Saturnalia is the dearest and most loyal friend of this Chieftain, but she may never know him as his wife. It is true we have achieved much and have made restitution for the follies of our fledgling times, but we must build now with others. I will confess, Solomon, it will pain me to see you promise to another what I once cherished for myself. Yet, I am too much your friend not to be happy for you when it is done. The season has come for you to marry again, and bring forth the children you once thought you would share with me."

Shock showed on his face, then it faded to resignation. "You woman, do know me better than I would like. How grand it would have been to consider it for ourselves."

Saturnalia stroked his cheeks then kissed him ever so softly on the lips.

"You and I, Solomon, are now and always will be, something grand to consider. For what we have shared will never be breached by another living soul, and what we have built in this place will remain a testimony to it," she told him, relieved that he understood how she felt.

Solomon flashed the infectious smile of one unapologetic of his arrogance. "Yes, Saturnalia, one day they will say that once on this island lived two people who had the courage to dream better dreams. You, Druidess, are the portion of my soul that will remain with this kingdom forever." His eyes began to tear, but keeping the same smile, he took her by the hand and led her back to their settlement.

———

Fixing her sight on a herd of wild horses, Kordelina pressed her calves into her horse's sides, and streaked down the hillside past the rest of her party. Until then, she had been lagging a good distance behind, mostly because she could offer no words of comfort to the lovesick Diarmudd and Edainne, and Conn and Aonghus had been talking quietly but seriously between themselves. She did not know what the topic of their conversation was, but from the way they would both glance back at her to be sure she was not listening, she was certain it either involved her, or was none of her business. Either way, she did not want to be bothered about it. She was too happy to be out in the sunshine away from the rules of her tribe and the watchful eyes of her kinsmen.

It was impossible for her to put into words how liberated she felt. She found pleasure in everything from the warmth of the sun to the lovely, bright colors of the grass and blossoming trees around her. It was all a vision of beauty and a revelation of life. She knew she was probably still under the effects of Saturnalia's herbs, but it mattered little. On this day, just being alive was something captivating.

She heard Aonghus call to her to stop, but she ignored it, and headed straight into the center of the herd. Forgetting herself, she let out a long warrior's cry, the one she had practiced in seclusion, the one she had never dreamed she would be allowed to use.

The spooked horses darted in all directions except for the stud of the herd who stood up on two legs, screaming indignantly at her intrusion. Purposely staying to the side of him, she focused her attention on a yearling who had bolted off alone ahead of the others. He was clumsily galloping across the meadow with long, spindly legs, terrified at being alone.

Howling again, Kordelina tried to catch up with him, but he ran even faster. She could hear Macha's heavy breathing as she quickened her stride. Glancing to the side, she saw Aonghus was next to her. Since Lir was so much bigger and had longer legs than her mare, the stallion had easily caught up to them and was able to match their pace.

It was an odd, but irrepressible feeling as she looked into his unforgettable blue eyes. Abandoning the pursuit, they found themselves consumed with each other's presence.

A blush rose in Aonghus' cheeks as he threw his head back and laughed; the pleasure of its sound caused her heart to swell. He moved his horse closer to her and held out his hand. As Kordelina took it, his skin against hers told her that he was the one who had been with her in the cave the night before. He was the one who had touched her and kissed her in the darkness. The one who had made her feel like a woman in the morning light.

She laced her fingers in his and as they slowed their horses to an even canter, she was overcome with her feelings for him. It was not the admiration that a student has for a master, or the care that she had been told to feel by those who insisted they were brother and sister. No, this was a love possessed by a man and woman whose desire to share themselves was stronger than their need to be discreet. By the time Macha and Lir had settled into a walk, Aonghus and Kordelina had wordlessly confessed with their eyes what they had refused to admit from the time of their childhood.

It was the intrusion of Conn that jarred them to reality. As he good-naturedly rode up and saw the look on their faces, Aonghus and Kordelina knew he was aware of their love, too. He smiled kindly at them, and turned his horse back in the direction from where he came, purposely distracting Edainne and Diarmudd until the pair rejoined them.

"You sound as though you have practiced that yell for quite some time," Conn remarked to Kordelina as she resumed her place behind Edainne. "Perhaps you will have a chance to use it one day. From what I hear, you have much stealth as a tracker, and a good stomach for a kill."

Aonghus jerked his head around to address his friend. "Kordelina is not going to do battle," he stated firmly. "There is no need; we are at peace now."

"At peace with each other, but at war with Rome," Conn argued, intentionally aggravating him further. "When Caesar does arrive, I am sure she will be of great value to us both."

Aonghus scowled at him then stopped his horse. Since he was the leader of the group, everyone else stopped as well. "She is still under my charge," he barked. "You would do well not to include her in your lust for battle."

"She will not be a part of my lust, if she is not a part of yours," Conn said, loud enough for only Aonghus to hear.

There was a prolonged tension as neither the two girls nor Diarmudd knew what had been said between the warriors. Then Aonghus fixed his gaze coolly ahead of him and resumed a steady pace.

The hush around the fire that night was insufferable. Aonghus said nothing to Kordelina with the exception of barked orders for her to gather wood and bring water for the others. By itself, it was not odd behavior; Kordelina had the least rank among them, and it was her duty to take care of incidental chores. And as she was the only girl besides Edainne, it was her responsibility to see to it that everyone was fed before her. Luckily, Saturnalia had packed her supplies and included food that was easy to prepare: meat, aged cheese, fresh bread, and curds. She had gone so far as to include a vessel of fine Mediterranean wine, but the girl never had a chance to taste it because the warriors consumed it before she sat down to eat herself.

She tried not to look at Aonghus during the night— it was not the time or place for them to discuss their feelings. He went to great lengths to avoid her as well, and when he did address her, his tone was unusually harsh. She drew on her composure and prayed to the horse spirit for inner strength. Saturnalia once told her she had the power to carry the burdens of another for great distances, and tonight she tried her best to believe it.

There was no conversation while they ate, and when everything had been cleared away, Aonghus started to play his hand flute while Conn lit the pipe filled with hemp. Only Edainne and Diarmudd moved away from the firelight. Strangely, they sat on opposite sides of the camp, immersing themselves in the shadows of the trees.

At first, Kordelina thought they wanted privacy, so she rolled out her sleeping hide near the horses and tried to rest. She listened to the sound of night animals, and the herd eating grass. Every now and then one would sigh contentedly, or an owl would hoot, but soon it was all drowned by the muffled sobs of Edainne. She sounded desperate for a comforting word. Kordelina could not prevent herself from going to her.

She found the young woman huddled behind a tree trunk, her face buried in her arms. Uncertain of what to say, Kordelina sat beside her and gently patted her back to soothe her.

"There now, Edainne, I know you do not wish to leave Diarmudd," she said softly. "I do not know why, but I do know he is very dear to your heart. Please, dear friend, tell me what I can do to ease your pain."

Edainne looked up at her with tears streaming down her cheeks. She had dark circles beneath her eyes, and when she opened her mouth to speak, she appeared so anguished that Kordelina thought she was going to scream.

"There is nothing you can do, there is nothing anyone can do," she wept. "I chose my destiny long ago, yet it seems unfair to me now. If I had known of Diarmudd then, my decision would have been different."

Kordelina untied the scarf from her neck, and gave it to the girl to wipe her tears. "Can you not go to your father and tell him this? I am sure he would want you to be happy, and what father would wish his daughter to marry a man she did not love? Diarmudd has never been my friend, but to you, I am sure that he is kind and devoted. It is not as though he were a peasant. He has wealth and a title," she offered optimistically.

Edainne shook her head. "The man I am to be with is not an ordinary man, and he would not be happy with an ordinary offering instead of me. Kordelina, I have been preparing for this since the day of my birth. All that I have learned, all that I have worked for, were meant to increase my worthiness for my wedding day. It is a great honor to do what I will do."

"There is no honor in marrying someone you do not love, Edainne," Kordelina admonished. "The intentions of the heart are greater than the actions of men. Perhaps you can find your betrothed, and speak to him of this. Maybe if he is a decent man he will be merciful and release you."

Edainne took in a tearful breath. "I do not know who he is until the sacrifice is complete. Then it will be too late."

Kordelina's eyes widened and she craned her neck forward to stare at Edainne, astonished. "Sacrifice? They are going to sacrifice you? No, Edainne, it would be folly. You have spent your entire life learning the ways of a sorceress, so what good would they be in the Otherworld?"

"I do not know. I only know I took the path of honor to the gods knowing that I was preparing to be with them for eternity," she admitted in defeat.

Kordelina sat back, speechless. Then she gazed at Aonghus and Conn, and peered through the darkness at Diarmudd's shadow. How could they all have been nice to her friend, and cared for her when they knew all along they were readying her for an execution? It made Kordelina sick to think about it.

"Go now," she whispered to her friend.

"What?" Edainne replied.

"Leave now before we reach your tribe. If you wait until everyone is asleep, you and Diarmudd can get away," she told her in a whisper. "I will leave your horses untied so that all you have to do is take them. If Conn or Aonghus ask what has happened, I will say I know nothing of it. You head to the south shore, and I promise to track you to the west as a decoy."

Edainne bowed her head. "They would kill us if they found us."

"You're going to die anyway, so better to be with your lover than give up," Kordelina reasoned.

There was a long pause, then Edainne started to cry again. "Thank you for your concern, Kordelina, but it would never work. There is peace in our tribes and we would eventually be found. I cannot make Diarmudd give up his life for me."

Unable to offer any more encouragement, Kordelina stood up and took in a frustrated breath of air. "I am sorry for you, Edainne, I really am. But I think you are crazy to let others decide your fate. If you have any strength within, use it, because no one can rescue you but yourself. Good night," she said, and went back to her place near the horses.

CHAPTER NINE

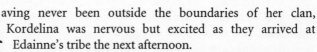

aving never been outside the boundaries of her clan, Kordelina was nervous but excited as they arrived at Edainne's tribe the next afternoon.

She sat atop Macha, scanning the circular settlement that filled a clearing of dense oak grove. Unlike her own tribal area, there was little open land for livestock or crops. Instead, most was used for extravagant estates, and the livestock occupied one common area near the back.

Although she had seen many of Edainne's tribesmen at the clan gathering, the few people who came out to greet them were for the most part fair-complected with blond hair and light eyes. They filtered out of their huts a few at a time until a small crowd surrounded the group. They greeted Edainne, and Kordelina found it a bit unusual that they treated both Aonghus and Conn as fond acquaintances as well.

She watched with an aloofness that betrayed her uncommon urge to go forward to embrace these people. It did not matter that they were strangers; she felt drawn to them as though they were lost friends. She saw them as Saturnalia had taught her: each man was a part of a single body by which all were nourished. The years of her friendship with Edainne made the inclination much more intense.

Outfitted in a warrior's dress, she wore her customary leather vest to hide her bustline, but found the people of this clan staring at her as though she were a spectacle. Perhaps the members of her own tribe were used to her appearance, or she had grown accustomed to being an outsider in their midst. Now to be greeted with the same reaction by ones who did not even know her was bewildering.

She had wanted to make a good impression, and even thought of asking to stay for awhile. It was no secret to her that the alienation she felt with her own people would grow stronger with age. The tribes on this island were unlike those on the main islands that found it a hindrance to have a woman warrior among them. When Kordelina had been asked to escort Edainne home, her expectations had risen in the hope of finding a new home.

She saw an older woman weave her way through the people. She was pretty, with soft features and compassionate brown eyes. She had the same freckles sprinkled across her nose and cheeks as Edainne, thus Kordelina did not need an introduction to know it was the girl's mother. Walking quickly to her daughter, and in a sudden burst of tears, she embraced her. Diarmudd stood expectantly behind

Edainne, waiting for the two to release each other. When they finally did, the young warrior bowed gallantly to the woman and extended his hand.

"Mother," Edainne said. "This nobleman is known as Diarmudd."

The woman offered him a subdued smile.

"It does me well to meet you," she obliged, putting her arm around Edainne's shoulder and turning her back to him. "Now, sweet daughter, we must take you to the King. He is awaiting your arrival."

Edainne looked apologetically over her shoulder, and Diarmudd's face took on a deeply wounded expression. His reaction reflected such helplessness that Kordelina could not help but pity him.

As she turned her head to look away, her eyes focused unbelievingly on Aonghus in a full embrace with one of the tribal women. She had golden blond hair and was dressed in a lovely violet robe. She wore many beaded necklaces and rings on all fingers, including her thumbs. Her slender arms clanked from the multitude of bracelets, and when he let her go, Kordelina noticed that her eyes were a sparkling color of grey.

Kordelina felt her blood turn to ice as she watched Aonghus take her face in his hands. He gave her a long lingering kiss on the lips before pulling her close to him again.

Taking a staggered breath, she covered her mouth with her hand to hide her shock as the pieces fell into place. This was where he had gone every month when she was in solitude. This fair-haired beauty was the reason he arrived the day after Kordelina returned each month, and why he was always in such a good mood. Kordelina had only flattered herself in thinking he was happy because it was her company that he had missed.

She felt foolish seeing him with her now, and as he took her by the hand and led her over, Kordelina saw that even though she was much older than he, the woman was stunning. She had a flawless, radiant complexion, and hair like finely spun gold. As Kordelina scrutinized her through watery eyes, she could scarcely find any imperfections.

The look of pleasure on Aonghus' face frustrated and revolted her. She had never evoked that reaction in him, regardless of how well she threw a javelin or trained his horses. Whatever feelings had surfaced in him the day before while they were riding seemed a mockery now.

The two stopped alongside her. Realizing her lack of manners, Kordelina immediately dismounted and extended a hand of greeting. The woman took it between two of hers and squeezed it affectionately.

"You are Kordelina," she said kindly.

The girl bit her bottom lip and nodded her head yes. Tears filled her eyes, and she could not speak.

"You are just as Aonghus described you," she said. "He boasts of his beautiful Kordelina to everyone. He tells of your special way with his horses, and of the magnificent huntress you are."

"Thank you," Kordelina mumbled, looking down.

"Thank you for coming to meet my kinsmen this day," the woman continued, taking a step closer to embrace her. "My name is Klannad."

Kordelina pulled her hand back and offered a bow of acknowledgement. She felt ugly standing next to this feminine creature. She was one who had caused a likeness in Aonghus that she had never before seen. She was the treasure kept so secret that neither she nor Bracorina had suspected. It was agonizing to be in the presence of someone she so envied.

"Kordelina, are you not well?" Aonghus asked, trying to make eye contact.

"Forgive me," Kordelina answered timidly. "The long journey has left me tired. A bit of fever perhaps. I am sure a cleansing in the lake will help."

"I will go with you," Klannad offered politely.

"Please, good maid, I would do better alone," she replied, climbing onto Macha's back and spurring her to a gallop.

Aonghus looked at Conn, puzzled. "I do not understand her sometimes," he offered, trying to dismiss her reaction.

Conn untied his traveling bags. "Yes, you do," he said accusingly. "You always do."

Aonghus' eyes widened then narrowed. "Explain yourself."

Conn put his bags over one shoulder and gave his friend a pointed look. "It would be better to talk in private. No offense, dear maid," he said, giving Klannad a courteous smile.

"Of course," she answered, returning it. "I would like you to join us tonight. Your wife has asked that I relay to you that she is now with another, so there is little reason for you to stay away from our hearth any longer. He is a good man, and in case you were wondering, cares well for your child."

"I am glad to hear of it," came his charming response. "I am sure she has fared well for herself."

Klannad and Aonghus could sense his relief now that he was free of his family commitments.

"Then may I tell Daneen you will be present with us tonight? He has greatly missed his conversations with you," she continued.

"I would be honored," Conn replied.

Without losing her expression, Klannad left them for the company of the other women.

The two men waited until she had gone, then Aonghus looked at Conn and questioningly held up his palms.

"Kordelina is not a child anymore, Aonghus," Conn scolded. "And for as long as she has lived, the only man she has ever wanted to please is you. She more than adores you, my friend, and I see it in you as well. It is plain in the way you react to the attention she heaps upon you. The way she likes to make you laugh, and to make herself praiseworthy in your eyes is deeper than simply a relationship between master and apprentice. I offer not only my own insight as evidence, but the exchange between the two of you yesterday, and your behavior on the night of her testing. Whether you mean to or not, you encourage her feelings, and because you seem not to even know your own heart, you go to both extremes and either treat her as though she is the most precious thing in creation, or you test her ability to the point of cruelty. She is tender inside, and you only make it more difficult for her now by thoughtlessly shattering her naivete. You bring her to another tribe, and the first one you introduce her to is your beautiful distraction. Perhaps you realize that Klannad is an occasional fancy, but Kordelina does not. The only one she has ever considered you with is Bracorina, and I do not have to tell you that your fiancee does not create such an affectionate reaction in you. Kordelina probably thinks that Klannad is your everlasting love."

Aonghus rubbed the back of his neck and said nothing.

"The cruelest thing about it," Conn continued, "is that I think you meant to do it. You have a need to manipulate the women around you until you achieve dominance over them. You make them want you, then you tell them they cannot have you. It is a morbid way in which you amuse yourself."

"No," Aonghus countered. "I did not mean it to be cruel. It never entered my mind that she would be hurt by this."

Conn laughed to himself and shook his head. "I do not think you would even know it if she were," he stated. "You do not know how much she adores you. If you did, you would not play this game of making her prove her love to you. The heavens be silenced, man; that child you raised is more loyal to you than to herself. You are the one who helped her escape the futility of becoming a farmer's wife, and she has not forgotten it. You are the one who saw her through her anointing. You have made yourself her god, and you like it that way. Do you think anyone could ever cause her to act without your approval?"

"She is not a slave to my word," Aonghus argued, running his hands through his hair and pushing it back. "She has earned rights now."

Conn put his hands on his hips. He could sense by his friend's hurried responses that he was reaching him. "But she would never act against your will. She loves you too much to be able to endure your disappointment in her, and you could not stand having no control of her," he rebutted. "There is more between the two of you than either Klannad or Bracorina, and you prostitute it."

Aonghus did not respond.

"If it is as I have spoken, you had better get yourself together and go after her," Conn continued, taking hold of his horse's reins. "She is probably half the way home by now, or lying with her own throat slit to stop her tears."

Aonghus' eyes filled with concern. "I am blind to this," he stammered.

Conn shook his head and started leading his horse to the stables. "Do not expect me to believe that—I am not afraid to call you the liar that you are. When you do find her, be honest with her. She has at least earned that."

———

Trying to silence her whimpering, Kordelina led her horse deep into the woods. As she passed through some jutting rocks and climbed a grassy slope, she found herself at the head of a waterfall. The glare of the sun hurt her eyes and she put up her hand to block it. Jumping off Macha, she went forward and saw that the cascade of water tumbled into a deep pool. It was bordered by tree-lined banks that made it impossible to see from anywhere but the point from where she was at.

She stood looking down on it, feeling thoroughly confused by her emotions. It was not as though Aonghus had hurt her directly, but there was something about the way he concealed this lover that Kordelina found threatening. Not only was Klannad beautiful in every way and openly hospitable to her, but she had an effect on him that Kordelina had never witnessed before.

What was worse was that Klannad seemed to know a vulnerable side of Aonghus that Kordelina had never seen. This was not petty rivalry she felt, as it was with Bracorina. This woman exceeded them both in beauty and wisdom, and Kordelina could not possibly compete against her for Aonghus' attention. How silly she must have appeared to that delicate creature, sitting atop her horse, dressed like a man.

She felt suddenly embarrassed by what she had become, as though striving to be Aonghus' equal was going to endear her to him more. She had thought if she could be a better warrior, he would forget about his secret lovers, and desire only her. At the same time she also wanted to change for herself. She wanted to scent her skin, and wear the lovely skirts with bells on the hems, not the leather vest that concealed any evidence of her femininity.

Ripping open its laces, she hastily lifted it over her head. Then she took off her shirt, boots, and trousers. How disgusting she found herself, as if she was part male and part female, and neither was acceptable.

Hugging herself, she was sickened with the way her breasts bulged over her arms. She wanted to punish herself for it, and digging her fingernails into her sides, she pinched the skin on her rib cage until it stung. Then whirling around, she began shrieking and waving her arms to drive Macha away. She did not want the mare to witness her indignity.

The whites of the horse's eyes showed and she cowered, but refused to leave. Seeing the expression in the animal's eyes, Kordelina was suddenly ashamed of herself for scaring her. She ran to the horse, and even though she could tell Macha did not understand, the mare remained steadfast. Putting her arms around her neck, Kordelina gently stroked her mane. She could feel her racing pulse as she hesitated to trust the girl's affection.

"Oh, Macha," Kordelina lamented. "Why can I not be more like you? Why can I not accept the love he gives to me and not want for more? I hate myself for it. I hate the way it makes me feel frightened and discontented with all that once brought me joy."

She pressed the side of her face against the horse's massive jaw. "Except you, Macha," she said, softly. "You will always bring me joy."

She went eye to eye with the horse, and tenderly stroked her face. Then the mare suddenly pricked up her ears and looked back as if she were expecting to leave.

"Not yet," Kordelina said, answering her behavior. "I will go into the waters and ask the gods to cleanse me of this envy. Wait for me here."

Walking to the edge of the bluff, she flung herself forward. She felt a sinking sensation in her stomach, and the shock of the cold water as she plunged into the pool below. There was a moment of abandonment as she felt the water caress her skin. Letting herself go limp, she floated slowly to the top. Lifting her head out of the water, she started to cry again.

She filled her lungs with air, then submerged and started swimming toward the base of the falls. She could feel the currents pushing against her, but she swam further into them until the water was pounding above her. She reached for a rock to brace herself, but it was too slippery, and she drifted backward. Her lungs pressed against her ribs as they hungered for more air, and diving forward, she went beneath the plummeting water and surfaced in a small alcove hidden by a curtain of transparent liquid.

Climbing on top one of the rocks at the back of the recess, she buried her face in her hands and struggled against tears. She did not understand why the pain was so bad. She just knew that she had to find a release from it.

It was more than meeting Klannad that had caused it. It was the realization that the one person she truly believed cared for her, cared more for someone else. It was knowing that Diarmudd loved Edainne, Conn secretly loved Saturnalia, and that everyone had someone to care for them, except her.

Until now, it had been Aonghus who had filled that void, and she knew that even though he was engaged to Bracorina as a political decision, deep down he enjoyed her company over his own fiancee's. But with the unveiling of Klannad, Kordelina now believed he preferred her over them both.

At the thought of this, she openly wailed with sorrow, and wrapping her arms around herself, she rocked back and forth until her lament turned to a whimper, and she had no tears left. It was cold in there, and her teeth chattered as her flesh started to shrivel.

Rubbing her eyes, she focused on a small grotto at the back of the cove. There were rocks piled into a mound, and on top of them was a bronze statue of a goddess. She was green with algae, and the fissure in which she was nestled was overgrown with moss. To all sides of her were jeweled flasks, necklaces, and weapons. Lying beyond that was an ornate bronze burial seat that held the skeletons of two people.

Moving from rock to rock, Kordelina wanted to see them closer. What she found were the bones of two corpses who had their arms and legs entangled, as though they were one person. She had to look carefully to determine if they were men or women, but one had a much smaller frame, and by the way they were lying, chest to chest, she surmised it was one of each. They wore no clothing, and all that remained of their adornments was a strand of beads around the neck of the woman, and a torque around the neck of the man.

Kordelina stared at them with macabre fascination, then reverence— she realized that she had invaded someone else's sacred resting place.

"Forgive me, sweet lovers," she whispered, looking adoringly at the two. "What peace you must have found in this place together."

She was disrupted by the sound of Aonghus' voice calling her name from above. It bounced off the rocks, and was swallowed by the water, but Kordelina could tell he was atop the falls and had found Macha. Her tender moment interrupted by the force of reality, she refused to answer. She could hear him calling more frantically, begging her to come out from her hiding place. But she remained silent, as though she wanted to punish him.

Then his calling ceased and Kordelina saw a flesh colored blur dive into the water in front of the falls, and she saw Aonghus' head bob up. Fearing that she would be seen, she moved behind the lovers' bed and stretched out on her belly. He looked around as he treaded water, then he dove beneath the surface. He was down for a long while before coming back up for air.

"Please Kordelina," he said to himself. "I hope you did not do this."

He submerged again and arose on the opposite side of the falls. Pulling himself onto the rocks, he sat down and tried to catch his breath.

"Kordelina, where are you?" he asked, noticing the burial shrine.

She could see him shudder at the sight of it, and purposely look away. Aonghus was afraid of death, that she knew. The one place he would definitely not look for her was in the gravesite, so she rested perfectly still.

"Kordelina, this is insanity," he said, tilting his head back and closing his eyes. His dark hair was plastered back on his head, causing his rugged features to appear even stronger and more handsome. She adored his face, and the powerful frame that sat naked and dripping in front of her. How she wanted to go to him and beg him to go away with her to a place where no one knew their names, or could forbid them their love.

"This is so crazy. It means nothing," he mumbled to himself and slumped backward. "All of this means nothing. I wish you could understand that."

He started talking with great bursts of emotion, and confessing his guilt to himself. Placing his fingers on his temples, he began rubbing them furiously, and she could see the water dripping through the deep furrows of his brow. Suddenly his eyes flashed open; he sat erect and scanned the area. He looked maniacal, and the change in him was so drastic that she dared not let him know she was there.

Holding her breath, she saw him quickly shake his head, then clamp his hands over his ears. Poor Aonghus, she thought. He did not deserve to be in such poor condition, but she was at a loss to pinpoint which caused him greater damage these days: his original injury or his present addiction.

"Did you hear me?! It means nothing!" he yelled at the top of his lungs.

Clenching his fists, he put them to his eyes and hollered again, but Kordelina could not make out what it was. All she knew was that she was not about to do anything now but hide.

"I could kill you for this!" he bellowed, then his head dropped forward, and he moaned sadly. "I could kill myself for this, too."

At that moment, Kordelina's fear transformed into determination. She had to find a way to stop loving him, find a way not to care because Aonghus was surely going to die. He wanted it too badly—wanted the release, and the chance to start over. What he was doing by marrying Bracorina and giving Kordelina a rank as a warrior was securing for her and Solomon the things he could before it came to pass. She understood that now, and the pain she felt because of it brought forth a desperate desire to prevent it. But why should she or anyone else try to stop him, it was what he wanted. He was gravely ill, and no matter how he tried to disguise it, no one was more aware of it than he.

She saw him slouch forward and fall back into the water, then he was gone.

Chapter Ten

I t was long after sunset before Kordelina returned to the settlement. She had spent most of the time soul-searching and trying to determine whether she should leave for home immediately or wait until first light. She finally decided to rejoin her party and face the reality that was set before her. She knew she could not spend her life avoiding the fact that Aonghus was who he was. He would become king of their clan, and love her or not, would marry Bracorina and have children with her. There was nothing she or his future wife could do about the women he chose to keep secret.

She hoped personally to find the strength to deal with these life changes, and to try her best not to involve herself in the matters of Aonghus' heart. As she approached the outer boundaries of the tribe, she struggled to repress the fear and insecurity of seeing him again. How she prayed for deliverance from the pain erupting in her heart.

The evening celebration had already begun, and as Kordelina tied her horse with the others, she was relieved that Lir was not there. She secretly hoped that Aonghus would not return until long after she had found an escape from her shattered dreams.

The music and scent of the food floated on the air, and the light of the bonfire was omnipresent. Its glowing rays stretched out like fingers caressing the many faces it shone upon, and she could make out the line of dancers around its circumference. Approaching the clearing, she saw Edainne dressed in an elaborate ritual garment. Her hair was braided on top of her head, and a small jeweled crown held it in place. Her skin was powdered a ghostly white, and her lips and eyes were heavily made up, making her appear older than she really was.

Kordelina felt her stomach hollow as she realized that this would be the last time she would see her friend. After the festivities ended, Edainne would go into a time of meditation and purification before the actual sacrifice took place. For a moment, Kordelina felt as though she had somehow wasted these years of friendship being distracted with her warrior's pursuits.

Contemplating these thoughts, she did not hear Conn approach. When he touched her shoulder, she was gasped and jumped back at the same time.

"Calm yourself," he said, with an amused grin. "It is only me."

Kordelina put her hand to her chest, and tried to steady herself.

"I have someone here who wishes an introduction," he continued. Before she had a chance to speak, Aiden stepped out from behind him. "Kordelina, this is the warrior, Aiden."

The girl's eyes darted to him, then instinctively dropped. She gave a quick bow of acknowledgement followed by a moment of silence before the brash youth took both her hands and kissed them. She was taken off guard by his action and could not prevent a nervous giggle from escaping her lips. She looked up at him for only an instant, then jerked her hands away and folded them behind her back.

"Kordelina," he said softly. "It has long been my desire to be properly introduced to you. I would ask that you feast at my table tonight."

Kordelina did not reply. She knew she was being rude, but she could not get the words out to accept his invitation.

"Did you find Aonghus?" Conn asked in an attempt to ease the awkward situation. "He went looking for you."

The sound of his name made her stomach churn, and she shook her head.

"Good," Aiden remarked. "Maybe he will not make it back until morning."

Conn gave him a knowing glance, then turned his attention back to the girl. "If you wish to go to the banquet," he said courteously, "you will have to outfit yourself in a maiden's attire. It is the custom of this tribe. Come, I will take you to Klannad; I am sure she will be of help."

As Conn took Kordelina by the arm, she could not keep from stealing one more glance at Aiden. He returned her uncertain gaze with a warm smile as she stepped past him and followed Conn to one of the estates.

When they entered the richly decorated household, they were greeted by Klannad and her handmaid. Kordelina noticed that the woman was lavishly adorned in beaded necklaces, and was wearing so many bracelets that she could be heard before she was seen entering the room. She was dressed in a lovely silken gown with a bright sash wrapped tightly around her small waist.

"Kordelina," she said, putting an arm around her shoulder. "Dear girl, I was worried. I thought perhaps something had happened to you. Aonghus went to find you, but has not yet returned."

"I am all right," she mumbled, as she resisted the woman's affection.

Sensing her displeasure, Klannad smiled at her kindly, and took her hand instead. "Then come with me," she said sweetly. "We will prepare you for the celebration."

Leaving Conn in the main chamber, Kordelina followed her through a long, beautiful corridor. The mural painted on it depicted the history of their tribe as it led them past room after richly decorated room. Even Pwyll's estate could not match this elegant manor.

Kordelina tried to hide her reaction when Klannad led her into another huge chamber that belonged only to her. It was nearly as big as the entire house in which Kordelina lived, and was considerably more unique in its furnishings than the rest of the home.

"I am Daneen's third wife," Klannad explained, as she went to a dressing alcove full of beautiful clothing. "So my accommodations are more modest than his other wives."

Kordelina gave no response as she perused the room and focused on an embroidered leather warrior's tunic that was only half finished. She knew it belonged to Aonghus, and she could not prevent her resentment from showing.

"If you have a husband, Klannad, why do you still take my brother inside of you?" she asked bluntly.

Startled, Klannad's face flushed and she pursed her lips as she stared at Kordelina with chagrin. Then she took a green and orange robe and held it up in front of her. "I think this would look lovely on you, Kordelina," she offered, ignoring the question.

Kordelina felt suddenly guilty for not appreciating of the woman's kindness. "Yes, thank you," she replied as politely as she could, her jealousy still evident in her speech.

She watched as Klannad set it out on the bed. "You may take a bath if you wish."

Kordelina shook her head. "No, I have been swimming all afternoon; I am clean enough."

An awkward silence fell, and for a long moment, neither of them spoke.

"Kordelina, I know you are wondering how I know Aonghus," Klannad finally said. "When he was in Wales, he was badly hurt, and I cared for him until he was well."

"But he is not well," Kordelina snapped. "He is sick, and it is not from his injury; it is from the potion he drinks. I suppose I do not have to ask to know you are the one who first gave it to him."

Klannad's face hardened. "He would have died without it."

Kordelina shook her head. "It is killing him now. If you care for him, you will show him a way to get over it. I am not schooled enough in the use of herbs to know of it, but I do know there is a way to ease his needs without them. If you wish to continue to see him, you would do well to use it because my brother is not long for this world."

Klannad crossed her arms over her chest, and started toward the door.

"In case you have not heard, Klannad," Kordelina said, arrogantly as she passed. "Aonghus has decided to wed Bracorina."

The older woman was already at the entryway when Kordelina finished the sentence. She stopped a moment, and whirled back around to face her.

"Then you and I should both be sorry," she said. "I do not know what Aonghus has told you about me, but from your reaction, I would think it is very little. Yet I would offer to you, Kordelina, my knowledge of how deeply he does care for you. When he speaks your name, it is with a voice of happiness, and I must say that I am perplexed as to your place in his heart. For what I do see in his eyes when he looks upon you is complete and total love. There have even been times in my bed when his thoughts were not of me, but of you. He has intimately called me your name too often a time for me to ignore."

Kordelina did not have a chance to respond before Klannad slammed the door, and left her to consider what she had said.

————

The feasting was half finished when Kordelina finally emerged from Daneen's home, and entered the celebration. She felt awkward dressed the way she was, she could not bring herself to come any sooner. She had spent most of the time before that trying to determine how the robe was to be worn. Fortunately Klannad's handmaid came in to check on her and draped it correctly.

When she walked into the clearing, she was glad to see Conn. Even though they had had their differences, and rivaled for Saturnalia's attention, he was still a familiar face. Since her anointing, he had been extremely considerate to her; she was sorry for all the times she had been rude to him.

He came straight to her and bowing graciously, took her by the hand and led her into a dance. His chivalry and charm soon had Kordelina laughing and singing as he danced effortlessly by her side. When he put his arm around her, she noticed that he purposely ran his palm over the round of her hip and smiled. Then he unsuspectingly pulled her close to him.

Kordelina thought he was about to kiss her when she suddenly focused on Aonghus standing at the edge of the clearing. He was entering the camp, and from his weary expression, she could tell that he had been very worried about her. Stepping away from Conn, she could not take her eyes off him as she saw him make a sign with his hand that meant 'truth.'

Then with his head cocked to one side, he swayed over to her. The yellow glow of the flame gave his skin an eerie tint. He approached her directly, and she became suddenly apprehensive that he might discipline her in front of everyone. When he looked at her, the pupils of his blue eyes dilated with such intensity that even Conn stepped out of his way.

The music seemed to fade into the background as Kordelina watched Aonghus give her a small frown. Then he took her hand, and in a disturbing change of personality, offered her a shy smile.

"I have to talk to you later, in private," he whispered, through slurred speech. "There is much I need to say."

Kordelina unintentionally tried to move away from him. Her intuition told her she wanted no part of his confession—it would only serve to deepen the feelings she was trying to avoid. Aonghus had too great an effect on her, and she knew she would do anything he asked, regardless of the consequences. That is not love, she told herself; it is imprisonment.

"Do not go," he said, his voice having regained its tone.

He kept hold of her hand, and started to dance with her. He moved around her so smoothly that it was impossible to detect any resistance on her part. Finally, unable to do anything but give in, Kordelina's tense face broke into a smile, and she joined him.

As Aonghus looked at her, he appeared as a ghost whose pale vision had discovered life's sweet delight. She locked her gaze with his, a gleam of self-indulgence in her eyes. Yet, she despised herself for loving him so, and for the way she weakened now when she had vowed to herself only hours before that she would remain strong.

Reaching up with one hand, Aonghus ran his fingers through the back of her hair, and grabbing a handful of her dark locks, discreetly pulled her face closer to his. They danced to a song that would never again raise the souls of a man and a woman as it did for the two of them.

Their lips were almost touching when the music ended. It left them standing in front of the fire, staring at each other with the anticipation that is reserved for lovers only. Then Daneen touched Aonghus on the shoulder, and said something to him, breaking their trance.

"What did you say?" Aonghus questioned, releasing Kordelina.

"Good friend," the older Celt replied. "This is a sacred celebration. You must dress if you are going to be present. It is out of respect to the occasion."

Embarrassed, Aonghus answered, "Forgive me, I will tend to it straight away." He turned to tell Kordelina he would return shortly, but she was not there, and as he started for Daneen's house with Klannad close behind him, he could not prevent himself from looking back over his shoulder to see where she had gone.

CHAPTER ELEVEN

gnoring Klannad's questions and gestures of affection, Aonghus dressed quickly and returned to the banquet. He took a place beside Daneen and Conn, and searched about for Kordelina, but she was nowhere to be seen.

He was too distracted to join in his friends' heated discussion about Rome, so he sat silently drinking his wine, watching the dancers, and listening to the music. The servants never allowed his chalice to empty; he quickly felt the effects of his drink. He knew he had far exceeded his limit when both Daneen and Conn eyed him, wondering how much more he could consume. But even when his head began to droop forward and his lids got heavy, he did not refuse the steady refills of his cup.

Involuntarily closing his eyes, he was haunted by the vision of Kordelina. He could see her questioning eyes, and her sudden mistrust of him earlier. He was not sure exactly what he had done to shatter her confidence in him, but he knew that if it was as Conn had stated, he would find her and vindicate himself.

The realization he had experienced when he was in the cave with her, and earlier that day when he thought she had left him, plagued his mind. Aonghus now completely understood that all he had ever wanted was to be with Kordelina. He was thoroughly frightened at the possibility of living without her.

A sweat broke out across his forehead, and wiping it with his forearm, he noticed that the heat from the fire had grown too hot to bear. Struggling to get to his feet, he spilled his wine on Conn.

The warrior laughed lightheartedly at his condition, then extended a hand to help steady him. "Where are you going?" Conn asked. "Not too far, I hope."

"I need some air," Aonghus mumbled, then turned to Klannad and pointed a finger in her face. "You stay here. I will be back."

Staggering from one side to the other, he accidently stepped on the hand of a warrior who was seated on the ground. The man sprang to his feet ready to fight, but seeing Aonghus' state, instead shoved him out of the way.

Slurring an apology, Aonghus nearly fell backward, but spread both arms for balance and stayed on his feet. He ambled into the woods, thankful for the cool night air and the serenity of the oak trees. Resting against one of them, he knew he had to find Kordelina to tell her what had been poisoning his conscience all these years. Instead of more herbs or another lover, he needed the release of telling her all he had hidden since her birth.

He followed a footpath that led deeper into the grove. Off-balance from the excess of wine, he first heard her voice coming from trees off to the side. Aonghus thought his mind was playing tricks on him, but listening closely, he heard it again and pursued the sound to a dense cluster of oaks.

Squinting to clear his vision, he peered through the knotted branches and focused on her sitting on a tree stump with her back to him. He noticed that her back was arched, and her head tilted to the sky. Her position seemed strange to him; at first, he did not know what she was doing. As he drew near, he saw that her robe was open, and she was running her fingers through a mop of blond hair that was nestled between the spread of her legs. He blinked hard, and was further able to make out the shadowy outline of a young man down on his knees in front of her.

Shocked, he stopped dead in his tracks. For a moment, he considered going back the way he had come, but when he saw her eyes close and heard her erotic gasp of pleasure, he lost all control.

He leaped out of the darkness, and grabbing the warrior by the hair, pulled him backward. Both were so surprised by his attack that neither could react. Aonghus shoved his knee into the young man's face and blood spurt from his nose. He let out a warrior's howl, and recognizing the younger one to be Aiden, flew into an even greater rage.

Pulling him to his feet, he kicked him, and when Aiden doubled over, Aonghus kicked him again in the face. Kordelina had hold of Aonghus' arm, pleading with him to stop. But pushing her aside, Aonghus tried to attack Aiden once more.

Using his legs, Aiden was able to knock Aonghus' feet from under him. Aonghus, as drunk as he was, could not prevent himself from falling. He reached for his knife as he hit the ground, but Aiden delivered a two-fisted blow to the side of his head. Aonghus could hear himself groan as he tried once to get back up, then everything went black.

He awakened in Klannad's bed with her sitting attentively beside him, wiping his face with a wet cloth. "Where is Kordelina?" he demanded, touching the side of his head.

Klannad frowned, pointing to where Kordelina was sleeping by the hearth. "She has been waiting for you to wake up," Klannad told him, as she continued to dab his forehead. "She wants to tell you that she is going to stay here for a time. She is very angry with you, she says that —"

"Silence!" Aonghus irritably commanded, as he pushed her hand away and got to his feet.

He swayed back and forth a moment, then regaining his equilibrium, went directly to Kordelina. She was still in a deep slumber when he grabbed hold of her wrist and jerked her to her feet. Her eyes flew open in surprise, then narrowed angrily as she looked at him.

"Fool!" she snarled. "I have rights, and I can be with whomever I choose."

Aonghus tightened his grip. He knew she was baiting him into raising a hand against her. She could then give the elders of her clan the reason she needed to make this tribe her new home.

"If you wish to be with him, then let him pay me for what is still owing for your fosterage," he angrily demanded. "Do you think I schooled you for free? If Aiden wants you, then let him purchase your vow because your debt to me has not been paid. If he refuses, you can give me your horse as payment, and I will gladly leave you here!"

Kordelina looked at him a moment, then wilted and did not reply.

"Now gather your things," Aonghus told her in a chilly tone. "I am taking you home while you are still a virgin and can bring Father something for it."

———

By the strained look on Conn's face when they met him at the stables, Kordelina could tell he wanted no more trouble. They had come to show that peace between the clans was truly possible, yet so far there had been nothing but problems. Not only did Aiden and Aonghus fight but, unknown to anyone but Conn and Daneen, Diarmudd had been caught sneaking into Edainne's chamber. Fortunately, Daneen exercised his influence and cleared the young warrior of what would have been execution for this crime, and when Diarmudd entered the stable a short time later, it was with a warrior's escort.

He was a tormented sight, his face bruised from the beating by the guards. Kordelina had to look away. To distract herself, she checked her saddle to be sure it was tight enough. She listened carefully as the guard informed Aonghus that if Diarmudd was seen again before the sacrifice, he would not only be killed, but the tribe would interpret his actions as hostile and consider it a declaration of war. Aonghus gave his polite assurance that there would be no further problems, and mounted his steed.

As was proper, the four rode through the center of the village to pay their respects, and Kordelina was happy to see that Aiden was there to say good-bye. His face was cut, and his bottom lip swollen, but when he saw her, he grinned and waved as he signaled to her that he wished she would return soon. Kordelina could feel herself blush, and catching sight of Aonghus scrutinizing her reaction, she purposely signaled back to Aiden that she would return as soon as she could.

The tribe's King had stepped outside to bid them farewell also, and when they passed in front of his estate, no one noticed that Diarmudd had stopped his horse and dismounted. Since he was the very last one of the party, they had no idea what was happening until they saw the King's guards rush forward with their weapons drawn. Then the air was filled with Diarmudd's anguished screams for his ill-fated lover.

"Edainne! Edainne!" he wailed pitifully. "Edainne, I love you! Just tell me that you love me too!"

Raising his arms above his head, he tried to run straight into the guards' poised spears as a suicide, but Conn and Aonghus were there in an instant to stop him. They grabbed him by both arms, but he fought against them so hard that Aonghus had to wrap his arm around his neck before they could pull him back.

The King commanded his warriors to halt, and he watched with tears in his eyes as Diarmudd dropped to his knees and pleaded for his lover to come to him. In the next moment, Edainne ran out of the house, weeping and screaming his name.

"I love you too, Diarmudd!" she lamented, as she tried to pass the warriors blocking her path. There were more than four of them between her and Diarmudd. Realizing that there was no escape, she threw herself face down on the ground and started clawing at the grass when they tried to lift her.

"Please, Diarmudd, do not leave me!" she cried, as they carried her back inside. "I will come back to you, Diarmudd! I love you. Promise you will wait for me because I swear I will come back!"

Diarmudd gave a long howl, and even with his two friends and one of the King's men holding onto him, he rushed toward her. Everyone yelled at once for him to stop; their cries combined with those of the ailing lovers reached a feverish pitch.

Diarmudd reached for his knife, but before he could use it, Conn struck him on the back of the neck, rendering him unconscious.

Kordelina's blood ran cold as she watched the spectacle from atop her horse. The suffering pleas of her friend could still be heard from inside the house, and as Edainne grievously begged for her lover to come to her, Aonghus and Conn heaved Diarmudd's limp body across his saddle.

This had to be wrong, Kordelina thought to herself. Two people who loved each other like this should never be kept apart. As they exited the settlement boundaries with Diarmudd and his horse in tow, Kordelina could feel a suffocating anger rising in her at the injustice she had just witnessed.

CHAPTER TWELVE

It was late in the evening before any reference was made to the incident with Diarmudd and Edainne. Strangely, the young warrior had not regained consciousness until they had made camp in the early afternoon. The others feared that his failure to awaken signaled something seriously wrong. When he finally did become coherent, he was thoroughly distraught. The first noises he made were the painful laments for his lost lover, and before he had even opened his eyes, he was begging the gods to take him.

This was so unnerving that it was decided by both Aonghus and Conn that someone should be with him at all times. Not only did they fear he would harm himself in some way, but since their departure, they had been steadily tracked by a party of Celts from Edainne's tribe. There were three of them, and they stayed just far enough back to not be noticed. But Conn had easily detected them, and told Aonghus that they had likely been sent by the King in the event that Diarmudd tried to return before the sacrifice was completed.

"We should post lookouts, two at a time," Conn stated. "If they intend to make an assault, it would be easy enough to kill one of us, but the other would still be able to make it back to camp."

Aonghus scratched the sweat and trail dirt from beneath his jaw.

"Somehow, I do not believe they intend to cause any problems," he replied. "If they had meant to seek revenge, would it not have been more convenient to do it while we were still within their borders?"

"Unless it is only these few warriors who seek covert amends for the insult to their Goddess and King," Conn added. "What Diarmudd did by violating Edainne's purification is a crime, and implies a blatant disrespect for their King. If these few engaged in a skirmish with us, they could justifiably kill Diarmudd without it being construed as a motion for tribal battle. I know this clan, and you have only been acquainted with the elders who have become reasonable with age. I would caution you to consider that the competition between the young warriors for territory is still fierce, regardless of what Solomon's bonfire was meant to accomplish."

Aonghus knew what Conn was saying was true. As heir to Solomon's power, he had used his visits with Klannad to endear himself to the elders of that tribe that he might develop strong ties with them for the solitary purpose of one day expanding his own borders. He understood full well that the rivalry for

Celtic-dominated terrain was mounting. This fertile region of land was a sore spot with Rome because it had yet to be conquered and remained rich in resources that the Imperialist outpost needed. The one Celt who was finally able to rule it would have a great deal of bargaining power with Caesar, and Aonghus was too shrewd to let the opportunity slip by.

As he let his mind wander, he unintentionally made eye contact with Kordelina sitting quietly near the horses. He had purposely ignored her all day, not because he did not have anything to say to her, but because he feared that, in spite of himself, he would be the first one to apologize. She had consumed his thoughts though, and he could not keep from replaying the incident in the woods. He could still envision it clearly. When he watched her pleasure peak, something inside ignited. She had transformed, seemingly overnight, into a woman. And as unfair as he knew that it was, he refused to let her be enjoyed by another.

Sensing he was watching her, she looked up at him, her olive eyes ablaze with innocence. She stared at him, fully aware and unapologetic for what he was thinking. It was almost as if she had interpreted his thoughts, and refused to be sympathetic to them in any way. As he saw the workings of her mind behind the greenish mirrors that were her eyes, he was filled with a sudden urge to beat this rebelliousness out of her. She infuriated him so, yet he knew he could never lift a hand to harm her.

"Aonghus, do you agree?" Conn asked, noticing his thoughts were drifting.

Aonghus looked at him, distracted. "Your advice is well taken. It will do us no harm to watch through the night. If they do take action, we will be prepared, and if they do not, we are no worse for remaining cautious."

His eyes shifted back to Kordelina. It was impossible for him not to admire the way the evening light cast a lovely shadow on the contours of her face. For a moment, he indulged himself in the memory of the way it felt to touch her naked skin. He tried to determine if he had known this would happen between them all along. When his mother placed her infant body in his arms so long ago, he some-how realized that this baby girl was an extension of himself, and his desire to pro-tect and care for her all these years was only in preparation for his future. Yet, it seemed implausible. Their fate was sealed that night when he had eaten the lamb and vowed his silence. He had promised with the very depths of his being to keep her secret.

"I will stay with Diarmudd," Aonghus suggested. If he was alone with her, he would do something more regrettable than the night before. "You and Kordelina take the last watch, and Diarmudd and I will start."

"I think that is a wise decision, my friend," Conn replied, and sat back on his sleeping hide. "Wake me when our turn has come."

Aonghus picked up his weapons and without thinking, walked across the camp and stopped in front of Kordelina. She had her head down, and when she looked up, he suddenly could not remember what it was he had meant to say.

"Why are you leaving?" she asked quietly.

Aonghus' lips went dry, and an ache erupted inside him, but he did not speak as he got down on one knee beside her. He lifted his hand to touch her face, and saw her cower a little, so he pulled it back and tried to smile.

"To keep watch," he answered. "I came to tell you that if you need me, I will be within shouting distance."

The expression in Kordelina's eyes sharpened.

"Brother, I do not need you anymore," she said, so coldly that he knew it was meant to hurt him. "Do you not already know that?"

The sound of her words stung, and no matter how he tried to pretend he was not affected by them, he could not conceal it from her. He felt a gnawing in his stomach, and his inclination to simply blurt out that his actions were nothing more than that of a jealous lover, brimmed within him. But as he stood and walked away, he did not open his mouth to speak again.

Conn was stretched out by the fire, impassively watching the exchange. Occasionally, a slight breeze would blow about the camp causing the leaves to rustle and the fire to crackle a bit more. He did not know if it was his expectation that something was about to happen that made him unable to sleep, or if it was the sadness of the events surrounding Edainne and Diarmudd, but he knew deep inside that this night would not pass without irreversible consequences.

Glancing at Kordelina, she appeared translucent and expressionless, as though without the presence of Aonghus, she was lifeless. He felt a sudden urge to change her thoughts—to find a way he could initiate an independence in her that would lessen her bondage to her master. She reminded Conn of a wild animal who was shackled in Aonghus' arbitrary boundaries, and the only way she could be released was to break them entirely.

The thought of making love to her entered his mind. He fantasized about them naked in front of the fire and the wonderful sensation of her silky, virginal legs wrapped around his waist. But as much as he would have loved to do it, he could not seduce such beautiful chastity into a brief sexual encounter. He knew Kordelina too well, and was certain that the man with whom she would share herself had to be the man she loved. Not only that, but in his own heart, it was only Saturnalia he desired now.

"You think what they are doing to Edainne is wrong, do you not?" he asked her casually.

"Yes," she answered, and rose from her place to sit next to him.

Conn was caught off guard by her sudden openness with him, and as he watched her movements, he could sense that she had developed a deeper trust of him. As she stared directly into his eyes, he felt as though she were trying to read his mind, and that there was no way that he could keep her from doing it. At the same time, he was attracted by the sudden strength that emanated from her, as if she wanted to reveal her thoughts to him as well.

Lowering his sights, he gazed at her bosom and tried to imagine what it would be like to reach past the leather of her vest and caress her. She was so pure, so robust that he knew she would be a delectable creature indeed. He could sympathize with Aonghus always having her near him but being unable to do what his natural instincts dictated.

"I wish I could help her," she continued, unaware of his musings. "But I know that our people have long sought peace and —"

"Long sought peace?" Conn broke in, then began to laugh. "We have never sought peace. War is the way of our people, and if it were not for the presence of Rome, we would be killing each other right now. Caesar is a distraction, an excuse to try to ease our differences. The truth is we are long overdue for a war. These territories have remained static for so long a time now that the leaders of these tribes are lusting for an opportunity to exercise their power."

A spark came to Kordelina's eyes as he spoke. "That is not what our Chieftain says."

"Our Chieftain is only fooling himself," Conn told her, amused by her naivete. "Solomon would prefer to think we can live without exercising force, but that is a lie. I think he is afraid of war between our people because he has too much to lose. He would rather bargain peacefully than use his sword to take what he wants. That is why he has been so long in letting Aonghus assume rule. Aonghus is a sly battler who would not directly confront the tribes on either side of us, but would do it in such a way that he would have the influence and the force to win. What Solomon is doing by trying to make treaties with these clans is to insure that Aonghus will be kept from initiating bloodshed. They are two entirely different leaders, and their minds work in opposite ways.

"You see, I understand exactly what Aonghus means to do, and that is why I have left my tribe for this one. Although he has not said it aloud, when he takes power he intends to challenge the tribes one by one. When Caesar finally does land on this island, which he will, Aonghus intends to possess more power than even the Druids. That is the only way he will be able to insure the rights of his people with the Imperialists. He knows that if he maintains the largest territory, Rome will either find a way to deal with him, or kill him, and I think Aonghus is crafty and brave enough to take that risk. Solomon knows it too, but he is afraid to see Aonghus murdered. He is trying to find a way to force him to keep the peace. Without expansion, Aonghus will be one of many small leaders, not the supreme one."

Kordelina looked off to the side and smiled faintly. "Has Aonghus figured this out?" she asked.

Conn gave a clever laugh. "If I have, do you not think he has? He loves Solomon, and does not wish to hurt him. He is going along with his decisions, and quietly waiting for the right time to strike. I think Aonghus is more worried about Saturnalia trying to stop him, and so the reason for their chilly rapport. But I will be able to take care of that, I think."

The girl's eyes darted back to him. "Conn, I am protective of Saturnalia. If your desire is only to abuse her power, I cannot —"

The warrior placed a hand comfortingly on her leg to quiet her.

"Do not worry, little one," he offered sincerely. "My love for the Druidess is deeper than even your own. I want only to see her future assured in this time of threatening change."

"Perhaps your motives are pure, but I will warn you that I will atone for any corruption of her open-heartedness," Kordelina said. "Saturnalia deceives many into thinking she is strong and without needs of her own, and maybe as a leader of a tribe, that is true. Nonetheless, as a woman, she is all too vulnerable. I hope you will not defile that, because if you do, I will kill you."

Conn looked at her seriously and nodded. "There is no doubt in my mind that you would. But I promise you there will not be the need. Get some rest now. We have to keep watch, and the penalty for falling asleep on duty is death, as well."

"As you wish," Kordelina answered, and went back to her place.

She closed her eyes, and while she thought of Edainne at times, her conscience was mostly barraged with Aonghus. She was dreaming of him, a stream of emotions crossing his face, and she realized that unknowingly, she had intercepted his present thoughts. She sensed the despair in his soul, and knew that what he feared more than battle or success, was his own loneliness. Deep within was the soul of a man who could find no rest. She could clearly see the vision of him entering the cave the night she was inside, and ached at the inconsolable expression on his face.

She was overcome by the despondency in his eyes as he came toward her. As he reached out for her, his hands were so warm, so gentle, that it was as if the membrane of her skin were diffusing his dread, and gradually transfusing him with life.

It was his touch on her arm that awakened her. And from the foreboding look in his eyes, she thought something terrible had happened.

"What is it?" she asked anxiously.

"It is your turn to keep watch," he whispered, and gently squeezed her arm.

How she wanted him to hold her at that moment, and to tell him that she did not care about wrong or right, and that all she had ever wanted was to be his and his alone. But the fear of exposing her weakness made her draw away, and rise aloofly to her feet instead.

"Kordelina, are you rested enough to stay awake?" he asked in a disquieting voice. "Because falling asleep on lookout is —"

"Punishable by death," she broke in. "Yes, Aonghus, I know that and I am rested enough."

He looked her up and down for a moment, reconsidering whether to send her at all, then he held out his sword and scabbard for her to use.

"I am worried, Kordelina," he confessed uneasily. "I am afraid that they will see you are only a girl, and harm you in some way. You may have made it through your training, but you are still only a child, and I am afraid for you."

Kordelina looked at him disdainfully. "You are like all the others. You no longer want what I am; you want to keep me simple. You would prevent me from realizing my power because then you could forever be the stronger of us. How unfair you are not to take me seriously. You think I am playing some sort of game until I grow up. Well, I am grown up, Aonghus, I am grown up."

Aonghus held up his hand trying to calm her. An unwanted separation was taking place between them, and he had to stop it. "No, no that is not true. I only want what is best," came his only response.

"Do not speak of that to me; you are only humoring me again," she said, raising her voice so Conn and Diarmudd looked over. "You want me to do what is best for you, not me. You forbid me any happiness outside of your wishes; you even forbid me the chance to know love."

"What you had with Aiden was not love!" he snapped. "He was only looking for someone to keep him warm in the darkness. It could have been anyone. Do not flatter yourself into thinking you are special to him, or that he could truly love you. He lusts after you, nothing more."

Kordelina's eyes narrowed fiercely. Aonghus realized she was about to unleash a fury he had never experienced from her before.

"Dear brother," she addressed him insolently. "More than anyone, you have shown by your actions and your personal choices of the heart, that you would not know true love if you had it. All you understand is your own vanity! I am sure you tell all your women that you love them, and when you say it, I am convinced that you do. For there is no one better able than you to disguise lust for love. So do not speak to me of caring, or worry for my well-being, because I no longer believe a word you say."

Hostile and confused, she turned on her heel and walked away from him. She could hear him say her name only twice as he tried, inconspicuously, to get her to come back. Ignoring him, she went to her lookout point, and sat down in the dark.

Her thoughts were reeling as she fondled his sword, and tried to reason with herself as to whether or not she should apologize. Then she rationalized that no one had ever told Aonghus the truth unless it was something he wanted to hear. She was tired of it, tired of the way everyone was afraid to offend him, always worried he would be insulted by something that was just a fact of life. Sick or not, Aonghus was the only one hurt by it.

Clasping her hand around the sword's handle, she noticed everything was distracting her. The moonlight made it easy to spot the dying fire in the other Celts' camp, and combined with the nocturnal voices of the woods, it seemed an unintentional invasion of privacy. Far away, she could hear Aonghus' thoughts and, for a moment, she frightened herself. She did not understand how she had the ability to intrude upon his mind, but she knew that if she wanted to, and practiced it, she could probably speak to him in the same way Saturnalia often spoke to her. But she did not want him to feel intruded upon, the way she felt when the sorceress had demonstrated her powers to her.

Inclining her head to one side, she pulled her hair back and heard the rustle of bushes from the other direction. Glancing over, she saw Conn emerge and take a place beside her.

He smiled with soothing brown eyes, then offered her his drinking bag. Kordelina took it, and without interrupting the silence, started drinking. She was surprised to find that it did not contain corma, only unstrained wine, and she loved the taste of the woody liquor draining into her open throat.

Conn studied her as she drank, and even in the dim moonlight, she could tell there was something bothering him.

"They hate us," he said, in a hushed voice. "Hate the way we seek false peace, hate us for our riches. They have not come as an escort, but to make us their victims."

Kordelina gave him a perplexed look, and took an anxious breath.

"Edainne does not want to die, and we do not truly want peace with them, either," he told her, and looked seriously into her eyes. "Aonghus will not go against Solomon lest he endanger his chances at swiftly assuming rule," he went on, his gaze never faltering.

As Kordelina looked back at him, she felt as if she were realizing fragments of a bad dream, but still remained silent.

"If you and I challenge this so-called treaty between the tribes in an act of planned self-defense, there would be nothing to keep Diarmudd from rescuing Edainne. Not only would Aonghus never have cause to visit Klannad again, but there would be no reason for him to marry Bracorina either. No rival clan would accept a combining of boundaries after a bloodshed, no matter how great the land ransom they offered for marriage," he explained.

"But what of Solomon's work and all he has done to bring the tribes together?" Kordelina argued uncertainly.

"It will eventually be shattered anyway," he answered, holding on to her. "Once war broke out, the competition for leadership would be too great to adhere to petty agreements made during a drunken celebration. You and I, Kordelina, have more to gain by initiating destruction than maintaining peace. It is for the good of everyone."

Leaning forward, he brushed his cheek against hers in a faint gesture of seduction. Then moving his mouth to her ear, he circled the inside of it with his wet tongue. He could feel her pulse start to race, and he was charmed by her unbridled response. This one was so in need of feeling loved by someone.

"We will tell them that we heard them making plans to assault us before sunrise, and that is why we killed them in their sleep," he whispered.

He ran his hand along the bend of her neck and down her front. Then stopping at her waist, he put his arm around it and pulled her trembling body to him. He could tell by how unsteady she was that she could not resist his affection. He started kissing her neck lightly and pressing himself closer until she yielded to him completely, and he knew that he had triggered the savage part of her.

"Come Kordelina," he said in a whisper. "Let us save Edainne."

CHAPTER THIRTEEN

hey found their victims in deep slumber when they entered the encampment. The fire had gone out, and as Conn and Kordelina slinked forward, they were only faintly aware of the outlines of the three men's bodies.

Conn could tell Kordelina was watching him, waiting for him to show her what to do. He was aroused by his ability to lure the girl into usurping her master's authority, and to be the first one to show her how to kill a man. He loved the intimacy of it, the taking of this sweet womanchild into a situation where her loss of innocence would never be regained or witnessed by anyone but him. He found it even more fascinating because adolescent girls dreamt more often of birthing life, not destroying it, as she was so willing to do.

He moved soundlessly to the warrior closest to him, and with an elegant sweep of his knife blade, he quickly slit the man's throat. His victim's eyes flashed open, and he made a faint gurgling noise. Other than the body's survival responses, his death was instantaneous.

He could tell by the dazzle in Kordelina's eyes that she was intrigued by what she had just seen. She was feeding on her power now as without a word from him, she moved to the second warrior. Squeezing his nostrils, she pulled his head back, exposing the tender flesh beneath his chin. He awoke instantly, but it was only to experience the cutting of her knife. Conn shuddered at her tactics. They were more insidious than his own, and when she voluntarily repeated the process with the last Celt, he despaired at how easily she had murdered them—as though it were natural for her.

Taking the cloak off one of the corpses, Kordelina put it on, then proceeded to loot their weapons and jewelry. Conn sat back and stared at her. He found the images she conjured in his head almost too erotic as he took in her stealth movements and considered her inexorable nerve.

The two did not speak until they were nearing their own camp. For some reason, Kordelina purposely stopped as though she did not wish to return. Conn looked back at her realizing that at this point, the night had lost all ordinary boundaries of conduct.

He could feel the desire emanating from her as he walked up and gave her a long, wet kiss on the lips. She submitted to him so easily that they were suddenly in a full embrace. With the blood of his victim still on his fingertips, he reached

338

into her breeches and stroked between her legs.

He did not have to persuade her to open her blouse to him, and as he felt her wetness churn into a deeper eroticism, he found himself kissing the nipples of her firm breasts.

Her hips were rocking against him when her pleasure climaxed. How he loved the sound of her naive but lusty moan of surrender. Then she lifted his head so he could look at her, and he found himself captivated by her eyes. What he saw in them was the soul of a child seeking refuge from dreams of love that could not come true.

The sky seemed to blacken, but then he realized it was only that his face was buried in her hair. It was so soft; she was so soft, so young and untainted.

"Help me, Conn," she said in a carnal whisper. "I want not to love him anymore. You can free me of him, and I will never speak of it to Saturnalia. Please help me to know what it is to be wanted by another."

At that moment, he understood that this seduction was nothing more than a powerful cry for deliverance, and he was its imposter. Kissing her once more, he drew back, and stared at her a moment.

"It feels good, does it not?" he asked. "Feels good to have the power of life and death. That is all this is, and we are only intoxicated by it."

Kordelina seemed to compose herself at his words, and she moved away from him. "Yes, Conn. It feels good to kill."

They stood still a moment, half-contemptuous of their self-restraint. Then he took her bloody hand, and lifting it to his lips, kissed it. He could see his smeared red handprints along the fair skin of her neck, and across the top of her chest. And as he let go of her, she started lacing her vest.

"It was only the moment that we felt, Kordelina," he said softly. "Only a moment of lustful indiscretion."

She gave a tiny smile, then went to the spot near her horse, where she had been sleeping. Without looking at either him or Aonghus, she laid down and closed her eyes.

———

"Oh, please, as the gods have made us, Kordelina, what has happened to you?!" Aonghus' worried voice sounded.

She was jarred from her sleep as he took her by the shoulders and held her in his arms.

"I knew I should not have let you go," he continued apologetically. "Precious, Kordelina, what did they do to you?"

Kordelina pushed him away from her. She was tired, and to be roused in such a manner was too startling. "I am all right, Aonghus," she said irritably. "Please let me go. I cannot breathe."

Aonghus only partially surrendered his grip, and when she got to her feet she looked down and saw that he still had hold of her wrist. He was examining her closely with a dreadful expression.

"You have no reason to worry, my friend," Conn's groggy voice sounded. "She would have made you proud."

"What are you talking about?" he asked, rising to his feet and facing the warrior. "What happened last night? Why are you here, and why is she such a bloody sight?"

The brown-eyed warrior yawned, and pushed back his sleeping fur. "Those Celts will be of no further bother to us," he stated flatly. "They are dead."

Aonghus' mouth dropped open, and he looked at Kordelina in complete horror. "No, Kordelina, you did not do this," he said, his voice nearly to the point of tears. "Oh, little girl, do not say to me that you have murdered them."

Kordelina was repulsed by his sudden emotion; she stood stiffly when he put his arm around her, and hugged her to him.

"I did not want this for you," he mournfully declared. "I did not want this for you!"

She could feel her knees start to quiver at his words, and she had a sinking feeling in her stomach that she had injured him without knowing it. Clenching her teeth, she squirmed out of his arms, and turning her back to him, began gathering her supplies.

"I did what you taught me," she said coldly. "I did what would keep us safe."

She could hear Aonghus' labored breathing as she saddled her horse. She knew he was still watching her, but she could not find the courage to look at him.

"Stop this," she heard herself say. "I did nothing that any other warrior who was threatened would not have done."

Wheeling around, she fixed her gaze coldly on Aonghus. His fervent look deflated, and for a curious instant she was unable to determine how upset he really was. "You will not make me ashamed for doing what I was trained to do," she said. "Because you did not have the stomach to help Edainne, does not mean I do not. She does not wish death, and if it costs some lives to save my friend, then so be it."

Diarmudd listened to her declaration as though it were a command to battle. Mumbling a few words of support, he sprang to his feet and hurriedly began outfitting his horse.

"Where are they?" Aonghus stammered, looking accusingly at Conn.

"Saddle your horse, and I will show you," Conn answered, and proceeded to gather his belongings.

Aonghus was in misery as he looked upon the camp of slaughtered Celts. Slowly getting off his horse, he approached the strewn bodies slowly.

In the early morning fog, the men appeared a ghastly sight. Each was lying face up with a long, burgundy gash framing his chin. Their cloaks and tunics were wet with blood, and their faces were hideous images of hollow mouths and vacuous eyes.

Kordelina could see Aonghus' shoulders rise and fall as he took deep breaths to remain calm, and when he turned around, his face was so pale it appeared as though his veins had been sucked dry. His blue eyes had lightened, and reflected both panic and disbelief. Nervously, he rubbed his temples and the strain he felt was evident in his every move.

"Aonghus, I told you already. I heard them say they would attack us before dawn. We did nothing to warrant such a reaction from you. If you had been in our position, you would have done the same thing," Conn offered, scratching the back of his head.

Aonghus managed to nod. He looked at Kordelina for a moment, then stared uncertainly at her victims. "What has happened here is more than the killing of a few men," Aonghus said, his voice quiet and deliberate. "This incident has broken the treaties of the clans, and disavowed our morality."

Kordelina gave a disbelieving laugh, and shook her head.

"Morality?" she retorted. "Morality is for foolhardy heroes; to live is to kill or be killed, and if you trouble yourself to the rights and wrongs of death, Aonghus, you will drive yourself mad. How is it that you have taught me all I know, and I have learned this better than you?"

Kordelina did not wait for his response as she jumped to the ground. She strode past him as though he were invisible, and her lack of acknowledgement could not be interpreted by the others as anything less than total disrespect.

Casting off her stolen cloak, she pulled Aonghus' sword from its scabbard. Then lifting the dead man's head by the hair, severed it from his neck. She swaggered lopsidedly back to Conn, and tied it to his saddle.

The warrior watched her young but hardened face intently. He took such delight in having shown Kordelina her instincts that he was unable to conceal it from his friend.

Aonghus stared at him with jealousy and disgust as Conn took Kordelina's arm and pulled her into the saddle facing him. Like a contented lover who had stolen her virginity, he kissed her deeply on the lips. He was unsure if he had done it as a reward for her display, or as a challenge to Aonghus, whom he knew was concealing deeper feeling for his foster than he would have liked.

Aonghus was nothing less than stunned by their actions; he could not bear to see something he had created surpass his own control. Seeing the sensual gleam in Kordelina's eyes at Conn's affection, he instinctively turned away.

"There will be war because of this," he announced, his voice a trifle weaker than he would have liked.

Diarmudd let out a long howl. It was not a cry for war; rather it was the sound of rejoicing that he and his lover would be together once again.

"Then there are no agreements still to be honored," he hopefully proclaimed. "And Edainne should not have to stay with a tribe that is destined to be defeated."

Conn's smile broadened. "We must rescue the maid before that happens."

Fully intent on being a part of her doomed friend's liberation, Kordelina started for her horse. When she passed Aonghus, he suddenly whirled back around and stepped in front of her.

Jutting out his jaw, he looked at her so hatefully that she knew if she had been a man, he would have challenged her. "You will stay with me," he commanded. "We must take word of this to Solomon."

She glanced over at Conn, as if to say that by his word, she would disobey her master's authority.

Conn discreetly nodded his consent. Then he deliberately locked eyes with Aonghus, and shrugged off the warrior's threatening glare.

"As you wish," Kordelina replied coolly, and stepped around him.

She could feel the tension radiating from him, and was surprised when he made no other physical gesture to show his displeasure with her.

"We will see you in a day's time," Conn said, turning his horse.

Diarmudd followed, and for the first time in days, Kordelina saw his face had regained its color. "And dare I warn you," he said, his countenance rejuvenated. "You should be prepared, because we will surely be followed."

CHAPTER FOURTEEN

onghus and Kordelina continued their journey in silence. They traveled quickly, choosing a path beneath the heavy, low-hanging branches of the oak trees, and eating and drinking their meals on horseback. They kept the animals at an easy trot, watering them as needed. By sunset, the tension between them was replaced with serenity as they took in the red and orange sunset. Neither felt the need to speak; being together like this was all too familiar. They had done it many times before—working together, acting as a single energy.

The evening air was thick with the scent of spring flowers and the pleasant voices of the birds floating upon it. Occasionally, the bracken would rustle frantically, and a rabbit would scurry across their path, or a squirrel would dart out in front of them.

Weaving through the trees, they heard the sound of babbling water, and continuing toward it, they reached a brook overflowing from the rains. A doe and her fawn who had been drinking, looked up at them startled, their gentle eyes growing even larger as they leaped into the shelter of the trees.

Bowing their thick necks, both horses took long drinks of the cool water. Their familiar slurping only ceased when they would lift their heads and prick up their ears at the sounds of the forest animals.

Kordelina let go of the reins, and put one leg over Macha's withers, turning her torso to the side. Heaving a quiet sigh, she patted her horse's neck, then began to braid her mane.

"I miss this," she said to Aonghus. "Making camp with you reminds me of when I was a child. I used to live for the times when you would let me come with you; it made me feel so special."

He laughed shyly, and moved his horse a few steps until he was next to her.

"When I have a baby, I hope he is like you," she continued, her eyes gleaming. "Then you could teach him to be a warrior like you have taught me. He could be under your fosterage."

Kindness radiated from Aonghus' face. "I would like that. Are you planning to have this baby soon?"

Kordelina became sullen. "No. But someday, I will. I ask the spirits everyday for a child, but they do not answer. Bracorina told Edainne that they never will. She said because I am a warrior, my spirit is too masculine."

Aonghus' brows knit together. "It is not for her to say; the gods will fill your womb when the time is right."

"Do you think they will answer sometime?" she asked. Her change in temperament from earlier in the day made Aonghus realize how young she still was. Placing his hand on her thigh, he patted it affectionately.

"Why would they not?" he offered, looking into her eyes. They were dancing with a sparkle he had never noticed before. "And when they do, I will give your offspring the best of my skills."

"Even if you are Bracorina's husband?" she asked sharply.

Aonghus pulled his hand back. It sounded as if she were daring him. "That does not matter," he answered curtly. "I wish you would not speak of her as you do."

"I am sorry," Kordelina said. "She cannot tolerate me, and I know that will not change with your marriage. I fear that once you have committed yourself, you might feel the same."

"Your judgment of me is harsh," he replied, wounded.

Kordelina was silent. She felt his impatience and feared if she said anything else, he would only become angry again.

He gave her a look so potent that she had the inclination to cry. "It will always be special between you and me," he said. "I give you my promise."

He pressed his heels gently into Lir's side, and started up the bank to find a spot for the night. Kordelina lagged far behind him. At times, all she could make out was his horse's black tail as it moved deeper into the woods. She knew everything she had done from the moment he had introduced her to Klannad had been for the sole purpose of hurting him. His gentleness now, and his concern when he had found her with blood on her clothes that morning, made her feel almost wicked.

The sun dipped into the shadow of a knoll, and the further they got into the dense foliage, the more the filtered streams of light cast a peaceful tint on the surroundings. Taking it all in, Kordelina felt a strange contentment wash over her. She knew that by the time she and Aonghus returned to the tribe, the metamorphosis of their relationship would be complete. However frightened she was of its outcome, in her heart, she understood that this was the way it was meant to be for them.

She finally joined him in a small clearing nestled in a cluster of enormous oaks. Aonghus had already unsaddled Lir, and tied him loosely enough to graze on the patches of grass between the tree trunks. The bay stallion craned his neck, and flaring his nostrils, snorted loudly when Kordelina rode up.

"Macha is in season. I should tie her further away from him, lest they mate," she said, dismounting.

Aonghus did not look at her. "Let them do what their instincts tell them. They are not bound by our laws," he answered ruefully.

From the tone of his voice, Kordelina knew that melancholy had already set in. He would be taciturn and demanding soon, and it was useless to try to speak to him until it passed. Trying to keep out of his way, she unsaddled her mare and grabbed her watering bag. "I will bring us water," she said.

"Take your spear," Aonghus commanded.

Deliberately ignoring him, Kordelina disappeared into the woods.

Aonghus could feel his frustration mounting once again, and he did not know why. Kordelina had meant no harm with what she had said about Bracorina, he knew that. Still, her words had gone deep beneath his skin.

Beyond what had occurred that morning or the night before, Aonghus found that, whether she was challenging his authority or trying to please him, all he had found dear about Kordelina was suddenly abhorrent. For the first time since he had lived with Bov and Klannad, he felt thoroughly out of control with his own life. But why? What had brought this about so suddenly? Was it the thought of marrying Bracorina? He could not be sure. His emotions were surprisingly numb about that because as much as he consented to being her husband there was an equal part of him that would never be true to her. But by listening to the other warriors and aristocrats talk of their wives, his feelings were not that unusual.

His mind drifted to the events of the last few days as he collected enough wood to last them through the night. Placing a portion of it in a pile, he stacked what he needed into a pyramid. Then, taking the flint stones from his saddlebag, he rubbed them together in a violent, circular motion. As he bruised the rock, he vented his emotions until a small flame had ignited.

Cupping his hands around the flickering blue fire, he blew on it lightly until it lit the kindling. Soon an intense, yellow heat had erupted and spawned an inviting fire. Sitting back against a boulder with one knee bent, he closed his eyes. The muscles in his thighs twitched with fatigue as he let the radiating warmth lull him to sleep.

He awoke in a stupor, and jerking his head up, he felt the hardness of the rock against the back of his skull. He grabbed it with his hand as the pain crested then subsided. Squinting his eyes open, he saw that it was nearly dark, and Kordelina had not yet returned.

Getting to his feet, Aonghus felt the dull ache in his head and the stiffness in his weary joints from sitting on the damp ground so long. How long had he been asleep, and where was she?

He felt a tightening in his stomach when he saw her spear lying on the ground next to her saddle. Something must be wrong, or she would have been back already. Grabbing his own spear, he hurriedly went to find her.

Any remnants of daylight were unable to pierce the density of the oak branches. It was almost completely dark as Aonghus prowled through the trees, alert to each sound and movement around him. Remembering her last words, he moved noiselessly toward the scent of water.

Beyond a thicket of alder trees, he noticed a small pond. Approaching it, nothing appeared out of the ordinary. But sensing the need for caution, he crouched behind a boulder at the water's edge to survey it. The sound of faint splashes chimed against the trees as an owl hooted above him. Peering over the rock, he saw Kordelina swimming happily, oblivious to everything around her. At the sight of her, so carefree, Aonghus felt a violent surge of anger. She had worried him needlessly.

Picking up a handful of pebbles, he tossed them one by one into the bushes opposite him. They sounded like the rustling of someone moving toward her, and it immediately caught her attention. She submerged beneath the water, and surfaced a moment later at the bank in front of him where her clothes were.

As she stepped out of the pond, Aonghus was caught off guard by the sensuousness of her body. Her rangy build suggested a tough resilience with her long legs and strong hips. Her belly was slightly rounded and soft, and her breasts invitingly plump. He felt a flash of desire at the sight of her, and for an instant, the thought of forcing himself past the tuft of hair between her legs enticed him. Then he was completely maddened by her sexuality.

Kordelina was wiping the droplets of water away from her eyes when she felt someone grab her roughly by the back of her hair. Her chin involuntarily went up, and she felt the cold metal of a knife blade suddenly pressed against her throat. She gasped out loud, then stood paralyzed with fear.

"I am going to kill you," a voice growled in her ear, "but I am going to enjoy you first."

In the next instant, she was thrown to the ground, a rock hitting her hard in the chest. She felt her assailant hurl himself savagely on top of her, bruising her back with the weight of his body.

Kordelina tried to see if it was a Roman or a Celt, but her attacker shoved her face into the dirt, and wedged her arm painfully behind her. She was face down, almost choking from the dirt in her nose and mouth and unable to move.

"You are careless—I told you to take your spear and you disobeyed me!" he yelled.

Realizing the voice was Aonghus', a wave of relief came over her, until he tightened his hold, and inflicted more pain. "I could kill you right now, and no one would ever know. Your foolishness could cost you your life one day," he threatened, pushing against her harder.

For a moment, Kordelina thought he really meant to harm her, as, panting with fury, he put his face against the back of her wet hair. He wanted to make her suffer, not for her defiance, but for the feelings she evoked in him. He cared about her beyond his own control. Everything about her excited him, and he hated her for it.

She began to cry, and he was suddenly sickened by his own brutality. Loosening his hold, he got to his feet, and was filled with guilt as he looked down and saw welts rising on her back. Tears streaked the dirt on her face as she looked at him. She seemed vulnerable to him now as he extended his hand to help her up. Taking it, she stood slowly then turned away from him.

"Do not cry," Aonghus said gruffly. "I was not really going to hurt you."

Snatching her clothes off the ground, he tossed them at her. "Wash the dirt from yourself; I will wait for you," he told her impatiently.

He sat with his back to her while she splashed the cool water onto herself. He could hear the muffled sobs as she tried to stop crying. How he wanted to run from her, pretend she never existed.

She was still crying when they started back to camp. Aonghus led the way and Kordelina followed, deliberately keeping away from him. She sensed that he was in some way repulsed by her presence. Aonghus had taught her lessons like this before, but her impetuousness had never enraged him as this had. He could be absolutely terrifying when he wanted to be, and he knew it.

Her thoughts were interrupted by the sound of her horse neighing wildly. The high-pitched squeals gave her a chill, as the adrenalin coarsed through her body. Macha's cries were almost painful as Kordelina sprinted past Aonghus to see what was wrong.

"Kordelina, wait!" he commanded.

She paid no heed. All that mattered was her horse was in trouble.

Macha gave another shrill whinny and Kordelina, with a burst of energy, ran faster. She could hear Lir snorting loudly as she reached the clearing, and found the stallion straddling her mare. His teeth were sunk into her withers as he thrust himself forward on his hind legs.

The two animals were locked together in a moment of carnal delight. Macha's nostrils were flared and her upper lip lifted. Then her squeals became soft, irregular moans as Lir pushed deeper into her.

The stallion arched his hips higher as the mare bowed her head letting out a long, low groan, then he dismounted. Macha let out a heavy sigh, and Kordelina could not help but giggle at the horse's open contentment.

In the next instant, she felt her body jerk as Aonghus grabbed her by the shoulders and shook her hard. "You can be so foolheaded!" he yelled, his face red with irritation. "If something would have been wrong, you would have run right into your enemy's hands. Will you never learn?"

Kordelina pursed her lips as she felt her temper about to flare. Aonghus was too contentious, and he had pushed her too far.

"Stop!" she screamed in his face, and pulled away. "I do not know why I anger you to such lengths, but I will not let you hurt me any further."

"You ungrateful wretch," he retorted condescendingly. "What I am saying could one day keep you alive."

She returned his icy stare. "You did not mean to help me. A few minutes ago you only meant to hurt me, and you enjoyed it," she countered. "I hate you when you are like this."

She tried to turn away, but he grabbed her arm. Clutching it with what seemed all his strength, he pulled her to him.

"Do not ever speak those words," he sneered, looking into her eyes.

Kordelina forced herself to look back. This was a battle of wills she was not about to lose. "Release me," she hissed.

Aonghus tightened his grip so hard that she thought he would snap her arm in half. Then he shoved her away from him as he let go of her.

She almost lost her footing, but caught herself in time. Throwing her shoulders back, she walked with deliberate confidence to Macha. Stroking her softly, she pressed her face against the mare's neck. Macha nuzzled her affectionately, and Kordelina was thankful for her gentle understanding.

She stood secretly peering at him over her horse's withers. He was sitting with his legs drawn up to his chest, staring at the fire. Its glow made his high cheekbones and prominent nose look like the carving of a god. She found him so handsome, and she wished they had not fought. His bursts of frustration had become too frequent and increasingly violent. But she could not help but consider that it perhaps was her fault—maybe she was not a deserving warrior.

Aonghus must have heard her thoughts because he abruptly turned to her. Without thinking, she flashed an impish grin, and the hardness in his expression melted as he smiled back and sheepishly turned away.

Her perception of him was changing with each passing minute. She watched closely as he reached into his leather pouch and took out some dried meat. He held up a piece, offering it to her, and when she shook her head, he shrugged and began eating alone.

This was unlike any encounter they had ever had before. Their emotions had ranged from utter hatred to gentle acceptance within minutes. At this moment, she wanted to beg his forgiveness. She wanted him to promise again that she would always be special. Only this time, she would tell him that she could not bear to see him marry Bracorina. She had defied him because it was her way of pushing him to show his feelings for her. As she gazed upon his chiseled profile, she wanted to conquer him and surrender to him all at once.

Aonghus suddenly picked up her sleeping hide and rolled it out next to his. Then he took a long drink of ale, and wiped the foam from his lips with the back of his hand.

"I would have you sit by me, and share my fire," he said softly.

Feigning obedience, Kordelina cautiously sat down by him. He handed her the ale, and she drank as much of it as she could without taking a breath. The strong, lukewarm corma was soothing; she had to make herself hand it back to him.

"Have more. You need it," he said, with a little laugh.

She moved it to her lips, and gorged herself for another long moment. "That is enough," she remarked. She held it out to him, then reconsidered, and took another drink before he finally took it back.

Aonghus lit the pipe filled with hemp as Kordelina stared up at the sky. She wanted to sleep, but the mood between them was too disquieting.

"Macha loves Lir," she blurted out.

"She does? Did she tell you she did?" Aonghus playfully responded.

Kordelina shrugged, then flinched at the pain. She had forgotten about her bruises. Aonghus looked at her, his eyes filled with concern.

"You are hurt; let me see your back," he said.

She shook her head. "No, I would like to forget it happened."

Aonghus averted his eyes to the grove, and for a long time sat remotely, deliberately, silent. "I am your harshest teacher only because I know you have the ability to be a great warrior," he finally said, taking a pensive breath. "If any harm ever came to you because of something I have failed to show you, I would offer myself as a sacrifice to the gods in battle."

Kordelina closed her eyes. "I understand," she said. The drink had relaxed her too much, and she was fighting off sleep.

"I love you," she whispered, not knowing if she had said it loud enough for him to hear. "I love you and I cannot help myself. I feel like I am torn in half, and the other part of me is you."

He covered her with his hide, then crawled between the furs to lie beside her. The warmth of his body felt good as he cradled her in his arms.

"Yes, I feel it too," he admitted quietly as she surrendered to sleep.

CHAPTER FIFTEEN

hen she awoke, the sun was already up and vapors from the moist ground were rising around her. Scanning the camp for Aonghus, she saw that the horses were gone and he had left some tea and bread warming by the fire. Kordelina thought he must be feeling repentent for getting so angry the night before, or he never would have allowed her to sleep while he worked.

Sitting up carefully, she noticed that her body felt tighter, and her back ached even more than she had expected. Rotating her neck and shoulders, she tried to stretch the muscles before reaching out for her tea.

As she lifted the steaming brew to her lips, she could not keep from thinking about Aonghus, and the way he had held her close while they slept. Shutting her eyes for a moment, she could recall the feeling of his warm breath on her neck, and his arms wrapped tightly around her. She did not exactly remember what words he had whispered to her in the darkness, but she knew from the feeling she had inside, that he had revealed something she had longed to hear. She noticed that his scent covered her tunic. Breathing it in, she did not want to leave the confines of the furs lest his sweet aroma did not linger.

She heard the sound of horse hooves coming from the trees, and her heart raced at the thought of seeing him in the morning light. Still, she did not look up as he tied the animals; she did not think she could conceal her joy at his nearness. Instead, she sipped her tea and stared straight ahead in silence.

"Get up, Kordelina, you have slept too long," Aonghus barked. He walked to the fire, and carelessly tossed some water on it, soaking her food.

Looking up at him accusingly, she saw that his face was stern. How he incensed her at that moment. Standing quickly, she tossed her tea at his feet, then picked up his hide and flung it at him. He easily caught it with one hand, and began laughing arrogantly.

"You did not sleep well?" he taunted.

"I slept well enough," she replied flatly. "But you are right. I have slept more than my share, but we must hurry back, because my brother's fiancee is waiting."

Aonghus bristled at her answer; she could be so insolent. "Watch yourself, Kordelina. It is a long way back on foot," he snapped.

She laughed aloud. "Do not threaten me, Aonghus. It does not matter what you say now, because I know the words you spoke last night to be truth," she told him as she put the saddle on Macha's back and loaded her supplies.

"You were dreaming," he countered.

She climbed into her saddle, and looked down at him. "As you wish," she replied coolly, then digging her heels into Macha's girth, she deliberately galloped ahead of him.

This time she stayed in front of him, although more than once he tried to come alongside her, but she quickened her pace. Finally, he gave up and let her go. It was obvious that she wanted no part of him.

Kordelina arrived back at her settlement by mid-morning. Because she had never been involved in a tribal war, she was unsure of how to prepare for it. More than that, she feared Solomon's reaction when Aonghus explained to him how it had come about. So she proceeded to perform her daily tasks in the same manner as she had when she returned from a journey.

Unbridling her horse, she stroked the mare's face with the palm of her hand where the leather straps had been. "Thank you, Macha. You were kind to carry me so faithfully," she praised.

The equine rubbed her head affectionately against her. "I love you too. You are a loyal friend." She hugged the mare's neck, and inhaled the exotic smell of her fur.

"I think she loves horses more than people," Bracorina's voice sounded from behind her.

Kordelina turned and saw Aonghus still on his horse with Bracorina seated behind him. Her arms were around his middle, and she held a bouquet of heather in one hand.

Aonghus brought Lir to a halt next to Macha. Dismounting, he then turned and put his hands on either side of Bracorina's waist, and lifted her to the ground. She smiled at him flirtatiously as he embraced her, and gave her a long kiss.

Kordelina could not help but laugh to herself at his open display of affection. If she had thought it was genuine, she probably would have done the opposite. It was so out of his character than she could not help but think it was to make her jealous.

She walked into the barn to get a feed bucket. When she returned, she found Aonghus slipping Macha's headstall back over her sweaty ears.

"What are you doing?" Kordelina questioned.

"Bracorina is going to ride her. Solomon is out hunting, and I am going to have to find him and tell him what has happened. Bracorina is going with me," he answered.

Kordelina's eyes glazed over. He was going to allow Bracorina to ride her horse; that was betrayal. "I will not allow it. She needs to rest. This morning's ride was hard on her," she told him adamantly.

"If she was ridden too hard, it is your fault. You should have been more considerate of your animal when you were galloping ahead," his words brash as he spoke. "We need a horse, and she is already saddled, so she is my choice."

Macha cocked her ears back as if waiting for Kordelina to defend her. She was lathered, and her eyes were dull with hunger and fatigue.

"She belongs to me, and I forbid it," Kordelina declared.

Aonghus threw his head back and laughed disdainfully. "You can forbid me nothing. You may have been anointed, but you have not recompensed me for your training yet. Under the laws of this tribe, I still have a right to all that you own until that is done."

Kordelina was seething. He had committed the ultimate outrage in her eyes by making Macha suffer for his bruised pride. Not only that, but he had broken his promise and let Bracorina come between them. She owed him no further loyalty.

"I will not forgive you if you do this, Aonghus," she said, in a low, chilly tone. "You promised me that you would never let this happen."

"What?" he countered. "You are worthy of no special treatment. Go now; Saturnalia has summoned you."

Kordelina watched as he helped Bracorina into the saddle, and got on Lir. He turned to look at her only once with a triumphant glare as he rode toward the woods with Bracorina at his side.

Kordelina's thoughts were muddled as she started up the hill to Saturnalia's cottage. At this moment, she detested the very thought of Aonghus, as in her mind she again saw him helping Bracorina onto her mare. The jealousy it evoked was unbearable, and it simmered deep within her heart.

She knew his motives had been deliberate from the very start. He had treated her cruelly this morning, and yet, when she remembered the feeling of his body against hers in the night, she was filled with hate as well as pleasure.

The closer she got to Saturnalia's cottage, the narrower the footpath became. Few people in the village frequented the Druidess' home. She was much too powerful and reclusive. Unless summoned by her, the only one with an open invitation was Solomon.

By the time Kordelina reached the gate, the grass was trampled by single imprints. The air was heavy with the smell of rosebuds and jasmine. Suspended in time, it was an entrance to another world.

Her cares evaporated as she entered the courtyard. Here she could set her spirit free and soar above the mundane concerns of daily life. She often wondered why Saturnalia had chosen her to befriend because there were many others in the clan more worthy of her teachings than she.

Knocking softly on the door, she entered when she heard the Druidess permit it. She found her cross-legged on the floor, resting her hands on her knees with her palms open to the ceiling. She was dressed in a soft green gown with flowing sleeves and gold embroidery around the neckline which sparkled in the light, giving her an eeriness that exuded the mystery within.

"Do not worry. Aonghus would never hurt Macha. He knows harming your mare would mean his own mortality," she said calmly.

Kordelina stared at her blankly. She gave no reply; Saturnalia probably already knew what she was going to say.

"Sit," she motioned to the spot opposite her.

Kordelina sat down as Saturnalia closed her eyes and rocked from side to side to a soundless rhythm in her head.

The young girl watched her curiously for a moment, then reclined on the rug and let her own thoughts wander. She was vulnerable now, but she did not worry, because she trusted Saturnalia in spite of herself. Not only could the sorceress penetrate any guise that Kordelina might amateurishly construct, but there was no need to be defensive in her presence. She was her secret friend and confidant. Communication occurred between them without conversation.

The Druidess hummed to herself, then opened her eyes and smiled knowingly at Kordelina. "You frightened him," she said.

"Who?" Kordelina asked, propping herself up on one elbow.

"Aonghus," she answered, her smile broadening.

Kordelina bit her lip, and tried to conceal her amusement. She could not help but relish the idea of having had even a slight dominance over him.

"Do you think it funny?" Saturnalia asked, her voice and manner evasive.

Kordelina's eyes widened. "Yes, a bit, but it also makes me sad that we treat each other in such a way."

Saturnalia maintained her seriousness for a moment, then burst into laughter. At first Kordelina was injured by her insensitivity, but Saturnalia's amusement was too infectious, and she could not help but join in. Soon tears were running down both their cheeks.

"Why are we doing this?" Kordelina asked, catching her breath. "My heart is heavy with his deeds, although I act as if I find them humorous."

The Druidess nodded, wiping the tears away with her fingertips. "Yes, I have seen your thoughts. Joy is the medicine you need. A heavy heart will lighten with happiness. Understand that Aonghus' fury comes from his fear, and that is why he is an intimidating warrior. He has the ability to change his personal demons into courage. Do you understand?"

"I understand your words, but I cannot understand his reaction to me. I fear he despises me," Kordelina said with a frown.

Saturnalia lightly touched her leg. "He sees the change in you. He only pretends he does not notice your independence or your womanhood, but lurking deep within him are the eyes of his heart. They see all things clearly. Those eyes love what is before them, and want it, but know it will never be his. You have been the object of his wrath because he is afraid of losing what the eyes of his heart see. When he tries to conquer these fears, it comes in the form of hurting you. It is a difficult place to be, especially since you are his sister as well as his foster."

Kordelina looked away in distress.

"I sense you want to ask me something. Please, child, speak it aloud, and I will answer all the questions that are expedient in your search for the truth," she said.

Kordelina's expression became even more serious.

"If I speak freely to you, I must have your word that what I say will never come back against me," she stated.

"I give you my word," Saturnalia assured her.

Kordelina clasped her hands nervously. She took a deep breath, gathering her nerve before she spoke.

"Druidess," she began in a hushed tone. "There will be no sacrifice of Edainne, and there will be war between the clans. I have killed on this journey, killed men with whom we had promised peace."

Saturnalia raised an eyebrow. "Go on," she said, trying to remain calm.

"Edainne did not wish to die," Kordelina explained. "And it is a defilement to the gods if the virgin does not go of her free will, is it not?"

"Yes," Saturnalia answered, as a knot rose in her throat.

"Then she should not have been made to do it. Yet, her tribe held her captive even when she tried to escape to be with Diarmudd," the girl said, shifting her position uncomfortably. "They sent three warriors to track us so that Diarmudd would not try to rescue Edainne. Conn feared they would try to avenge the insult to their King, so he and I killed them in their sleep."

Saturnalia pressed her hand to her chest to steady herself. "Where is Edainne now?" she asked uncertainly.

"Conn and Diarmudd have gone to retrieve her," Kordelina answered. "Aonghus says revenge will be sought because of this, and I know he is right."

Dropping her head back, the Druidess stared at the ceiling for a long moment, then looked back at Kordelina. "What else?" she inquired.

"I think myself deranged," Kordelina stated.

Saturnalia started laughing again at her declaration, then abruptly stopped. "You think yourself mad for trying to help your friend?" she asked.

Kordelina nodded, then her eyes began to water. "For that, and because I am in love with my brother, too," she said. "But Saturnalia, I know that he is not my brother. He knows it too, but refuses to speak the truth to me—refuses to tell me he feels the same. Now because of the things he has done to hide his emotions, a portion of my love has turned into hate."

The sorceress slowly nodded her head. "What has he told you, exactly?"

"Very little," she responded. "But his lover speaks of him saying my name while he makes love to her. I know for myself, by the very way he looks at me, that he loves me. But the moment he lets his feelings show, he covers them with cruelty. Then I find hostility surfacing in me as well, and I can do nothing about it."

"What do you want to do?" Saturnalia asked quietly.

Kordelina giggled nervously, then looked down.

"What do you want to do?" the Druidess repeated.

"I want to be his lover," she admitted. "I want him to, well, never mind."

"To take you as his wife," she added. "I am sorry, child, but that may never happen. Aonghus has long been destined to rule this tribe as King, and there is no possible way that our kinsmen will ever accept him marrying his sister. It would not be right in the eyes of the gods."

"But I am not his sister," she argued, her face strained. "I am no more Aonghus' sister than I am Diarmudd's or Conn's. There are those in this tribe who knew my parents, but they never speak of it. They must have been very bad people, or there would not be the need for so many lies."

Saturnalia cringed, then got to her feet and walked to the window.

Kordelina stared at her, expectantly. She knew Saturnalia was patiently indulging her. "There is something else that troubles me, Saturnalia. Conn has spoken of his care for you," she said quietly. "What will become of Solomon if you are with another? Perhaps I am young, but I see that you and the Chieftain love each other deeply but you have never married."

Saturnalia turned, and Kordelina could see in her face that she was glad to confide the affairs of her own heart to another.

"For many years, the responsibilities of our people were the bond between the Chieftain and me," she explained. "As wisdom has come upon me, I can see that I am unable to give Solomon all that is required to be his wife. My heart is devoted to him now as a friend, not a lover."

"Then you will never have his child?" Kordelina asked, disappointed.

Saturnalia's eyes darted away from the girl, and she became defensive. "Kordelina," she said, "If I were meant to bear the Chieftain a child, it would have happened by now. But I can assure you that our two souls have manifested themselves in a magnificent way.

"If Solomon were to be slain in battle, my womb would forever be waiting to receive his spirit. I would bear his soul in a new body with great joy. Then our caring would be shared not as lovers, but as mother and child, and that is the most intimate blend of love there is."

Saturnalia saw the fascination in Kordelina's eyes as she spoke. "Do you understand what I am speaking of?" she asked.

The girl nodded.

"Then we should prepare our minds for the coming conflict," she said, as she started to grind the herbs for the drink.

Kordelina drank it as she had many times before, immediately feeling its effects as it irritated her throat and numbed the crown of her head. Her eyes watered, and Saturnalia turned into a languid mystical image. The energy radiated around her like slow waves of lightning, and Kordelina was mesmerized by the subtle transition in her appearance. Her cheekbones were suddenly higher and more refined. The sockets of her eyes became dark caverns and their greenness turned into luminous pools of water.

She watched apprehensively as Saturnalia took out her ceremonial dagger, and removing it from its sheath, fondled it. She ran her fingers down the blade, then grasped it skillfully with both hands, and held it above her head as an offering. There was a sudden malice about her that was intriguing, and as she stared pointedly at Kordelina, the girl began to feel frightened. Hastily, she moved a safe distance away.

In the next moment, the knife seemed to embed itself on the floor between them. Kordelina jumped to her feet at the impact. It sounded like thunder in her ears. She found she had already started toward the door, but Saturnalia grabbed her by the wrist to stop her.

"Be not afraid," she said calmly. "The spirits speak. Listen to them."

"No," Kordelina answered, alarmed. "I feel afraid, and I do not wish to be a part of these visions. I have seen too many visions these last days."

"You only fear your own feelings," Saturnalia countered. "You are afraid to love Aonghus because it beckons you to vindicate his disloyalty."

Kordelina looked away. "It was wrong for him to break his promise to me," she said with an ache in her voice. "He took the one thing I cherish, and he gave it to Bracorina. It does not matter if it was only for a moment. He swore that she would never come between us."

Saturnalia held onto her as she began to sway. "Close your eyes, and you will see the sacrifices that your momentary hate will bring," she whispered.

"I do not want to see, and please, Saturnalia, I want to have no more visions," she pleaded. "I wish only to feel like myself again."

"Dear child, you will never be that girl who entered the cave," Saturnalia explained, her voice dropping an octave. It took on a hollow pitch as if it were coming from a tunnel deep within the earth. "The price is great for the truth. Can you pay it, warrior? Many have failed before you."

Kordelina felt her place the dagger in her hand. It was hot to the touch as though it had already melted into her palm. She shuddered at the sensation.

Before she knew what had happened, Saturnalia had taken her to her sleeping chamber, and placed her down on the bed of silk and furs.

"Open your soul, and lie quietly," she instructed. "When you emerge, you will face the battle. I hope you are victorious."

The younger one blinked hard at the sight of her. She appeared to levitate, a breeze shimmering through her hair. Then Kordelina felt like she was falling, and about to be swallowed by the lush bedding. She was panicked by her state. This was not at all the way it had been in the cave. For a moment, she feared that she had forsaken her view of life and was being tortured by her own refusal to admit it to herself. She tried to call to Saturnalia to help her, but she could not speak. Her eyes closed, and she prayed that she would never feel abandoned again.

Certain that Kordelina was safe in bed, Saturnalia opened the shutters in the main room. She consumed the colors of the orange and yellow rays of the sun, and let them permeate her flesh until she was part of the colorful streams of light.

She envisioned herself as a vapor slipping through a crevice from reality into the dimensions of her own power. It was a tremendous liberation; she became engulfed by the sound of her own laughter and happiness.

Visions of a past lover—the sensual, wild-eyed Mediterranean seaman with a well-muscled physique—filled her senses. She could see the festivals of her youth, those sweaty, pagan celebrations and offerings to the gods. Then the dagger was before her, and she recalled herself ripping the side of the whimpering, blonde-haired virgin for the first time, and the salty taste of the blood she licked from her fingertips. She was inebriated with the power of life and death, believing she was its messenger and liaison.

––––––––

When she opened her eyes again, she focused on the wisteria vines clawing at the rising moon. The fire was practically out, and the room was seeped in darkness. She was prostrate on the floor, a clump of her fine red hair in her hand. Rising slowly, she went to Kordelina's bedside.

The girl was sweating profusely and murmuring words that made no sense to Saturnalia. Her hair was soaked, a great mass of it stuck to her forehead, and the dagger still rested on her chest.

"Child," Saturnalia said gently. "What do you see?"

Kordelina furrowed her brow, then laughed recklessly. "I am dancing for you—for everyone, around the fire. I feel free; I can do anything I wish," she told her, opening her bloodshot eyes. "But my spirit does not want to return to this tribe."

Saturnalia took a cloth and wet it with hyssop and water before wiping Kordelina's face. "Try to come back now," the Druidess persuaded, in a worried tone. "You can make your soul return at will."

Kordelina closed her lids and rolled her head from one side to the other. "Jara says 'no'. She says you have let me go too far."

Panic flooded Saturnalia's eyes. "Jara cannot have you," she said sternly as she reached for the knife. "Look into her face right now, and firmly tell her 'no'. Tell her she has no place in your heart."

She yanked the knife from Kordelina, the blade hot from her body heat. Accidently cutting herself, Saturnalia watched the blood ooze through her fingers, and she was struck with a feeling of doom.

"Not this time, Jara, not this time," Saturnalia mumbled.

The atmosphere was suddenly heavy, then the murkiness evaporated as quickly as it had come. Taking Kordelina's face in her bloody hands, the Druidess looked hard into her cloudy eyes.

"Sleep, and I promise she will not trouble you again," she assured her. Then she saw that her fingers had streaked Kordelina's face with blood. The sight of it had a chilling effect on her as she slowly backed away. She wanted to expel the picture from her mind, and she turned to leave the room. Her heart almost stopped when she ran into Solomon at the doorway.

Even in the darkness, he could tell she was fleeing from something. Everything about her suggested fear, from the way she was trembling to her dilated eyes.

Taking her by the shoulders, he studied her expression as she held up her bloody hands for him to see. "What is the matter?" he asked. "You are bleeding. What happened to you?"

Saturnalia composed herself in an instant. "Nothing," she replied, trying to sound calm. "I only cut myself. How long has the sun been down?"

The Chieftain stared at her, then walked deliberately to the hearth to stoke the dying fire. When a flame rose, he added more wood until the room was engulfed in warmth.

As the golden firelight shown upon him, Saturnalia could see the stark lines of worry on his face. "It has only just set," he replied. "I would have come to you sooner, but I have been meeting with the elders. It is time to assemble and prepare for what will greet us at sunrise."

Sitting down wearily, Saturnalia held onto her bleeding fingertips as Solomon wet a piece of doeskin and wrapped them. He knelt at her side, and she held out her hand for him to dress.

"I think they are glad about it, about the prospect of war," he said, visibly distressed. "They never wanted peace. I suppose I never wanted it either. I remember when Donnach explained to me his reasons for never challenging another clan unless they challenged him first. He said he did not want to give Rome reason to do his people harm. Yet, it is our nature to destroy before we can replenish."

She looked deep into his eyes, then kissed the top of his head. "There is nothing wrong with your dream of one nation for our people," she said softly. "Do not mistrust your own integrity because of the actions of others."

He nodded, but said nothing in response.

"Have Diarmudd and Conn returned?" she asked.

"Yes, and they have Edainne," he replied. "Conn says to expect to meet with battle at first light. I do not wish to endanger our settlement, so we will challenge them at our borders."

As his face suddenly became fierce, Saturnalia delicately glided her fingers through his hair.

"Then it is time for the ceremony," she responded, rising to her feet.

CHAPTER SIXTEEN

he bonfire was already raging when Saturnalia descended the knoll on the back of Solomon's horse. She could see the mass of warriors milling around the clearing dressed only in calf-high boots, and scant leather breechcloths. They had their hair spiked with lime, and with the exception of their mustaches and head, had thoroughly shaven their body hair. Their skin was dyed blue with woad, and each was intricately painting his body with his anointed animal symbol. The accompanying banging of drums was meant to infuse the warrior's spirit with courage and strength as he readied himself to face his foe.

At one end of the oak-hemmed clearing, the elders and the older women of the tribe would pray to the gods throughout the night for their warriors' victory and protection. Opposite them was a banquet table where an endless stream of maidens were bringing the men roasted turkey, boar, cheese, bread, and curds.

Off in the darkness were the young fosters and newly anointed members of the fianna. Their sole task was to prepare their master's horses. Each warrior would need three; the first was to be used for the primary attack, and if it was slain, the foster's duty was to bring him a fresh one, completely outfitted with weaponry. Should the second horse also go down, then the warrior's best and fastest horse was brought forward for a swift retreat.

The apprentices generally viewed the battle from a safe vantage point where they could easily see the warriors and aid them when needed. Fixing her eyes on the tender youths, Saturnalia noticed that their naive faces were etched with nervous anticipation.

"Kordelina should be here," she whispered in Solomon's ear. "Tell Koven to send Niall to my house to rouse her."

Solomon nodded. "I will tend to it at once."

As the Chieftain stopped in the center of the clearing, the entire gathering bowed and the drumbeat ceased. Only when Saturnalia held out both hands and motioned for them to rise, did they continue what they had been doing. As was customary in priming for battle, she would bless each warrior individually, leaving them to the quiet of their thoughts and rest before they were called to action.

Silently walking to the stone slab altar, she saw that everything she needed for the holy rites had already been provided. Unfastening the broach that held her gown in place, she let it drop to the ground, then slipped her white robe over her head. There were two young female attendants, Sile and Ina, recently placed in her charge, who assisted her and were also being instructed in the holy ways. Examining the arrangement of the altar, Saturnalia was pleased with what they had done.

She remained in silent prayer as one of them ground the herbs into a fine powder, and the other mixed it into the animal fat used for the blessing. When this was finished, Saturnalia unwrapped the hand she had cut, and squeezing the wound, she let some of her own blood drip into the ointment. Taking a vial of oil, she blessed the two girls as they knelt at her feet.

No words passed between them as they rose and took a place on either side of her. One would be in charge of the oil, and the other the ointment.

They both followed Saturnalia over to Solomon, and when the Chieftain got on his knees in front of her, she first touched the oil to his brow, then streaked his forehead with the animal fat.

"We fear nothing lest the seas rise, and the sky begins to fall," she said softly. "You are the supreme warrior, and your soul is as endless as the wind."

She was overcome with the sudden urge to wrap her arms around him and protect him from seeing his own dream of peace shatter before his eyes. But she could tell by the stoic, unwavering gaze he assumed that the usually affable Chieftain was already of a mind for the violence of battle.

Leaving him to the solitude of personal meditation, she proceeded to each of the other warriors to perform the same blessing.

When she stepped in front of Aonghus, he treated her casually; at first, she thought he was not going to kneel. But when she locked eyes with him, he wordlessly acquiesced, and got down on only one knee. When she spoke the words of the blessing, he did not bow his head. Instead, he looked straight at her, his blue eyes reflecting off his dyed skin, and Saturnalia found herself almost intimidated by the sharp, rejuvenated look he had about him. She realized then that Aonghus was ruthless, and these rites meant nothing to him. In the end, he would slay his enemy for his own purposes, not the ones of the gods.

When she was finished with the warriors, she proceeded to bless their horses. An entire herd was now gathered, and she was relieved to see Kordelina was there with Macha, Lir, and two other horses she had trained for Aonghus.

"You must promise that you will not get involved in the fighting," Saturnalia advised, when her ceremony was complete. "Your only purpose on this day is to bring a fresh horse for Aonghus, nothing more."

Kordelina nodded. "I hope they do not injure Macha while I am doing it."

"If they do, you must not try to save her," Saturnalia cautioned. "You will only harm yourself. There is one other thing."

"Yes," Kordelina replied.

"What you saw in your dreams has no place on a battlefield," she said, taking hold of her hand.

"I understand. I hope to see you again in the daylight," the girl said. "And Saturnalia, if something should happen, please take care of my parents."

"Nothing will happen, but if it makes you feel any better, I will certainly watch over them," she said with a strained smile. "You are as strong as the mountains, Kordelina, and you are as free as the wind. Do not forget that. Please, child, do not forget that."

The hours before the final call to depart were centered on the warriors' needs. After they had put the final touches on their tattoos, donned their jewel-studded armlets, bracelets, and rings, and received the Druidess' blessing, they again consumed huge quantities of food, then slept around the fire. When the announcement was made that it was time to leave, each one was thoroughly awake, and craving a slaughter.

One by one, their apprentices brought out the war-horses, and when all were mounted, the warriors stayed in a single, intimidating line as they started forward. The fosters followed a short distance behind, each leading two other horses beside them.

The sun had barely risen when they reached the outlying border, and as predicted, the dew-sprinkled rays of light shown on a mass of naked, tattooed, and weapon-clad warriors approaching them.

The two tribes stopped atop facing knolls, and looked down on the lush green clearing that was to be the site of the bloodletting. As the streaks of gold-tinted light bathed the men's colorfully painted bodies, the air was pierced with the sound of long, shrill battle howls coming from both sides. The roar of their voices seemed to meet in the middle of the meadow. Then the vivid warriors drew their great swords, and hoisted their jeweled shields as each commanded their horses toward their enemies.

A mist still hung low to the ground, concealing the lower part of the horses' legs, but the translucent morning sun seemed to flash a shade brighter when the first line of fighters locked blades. The horrendous clashing of metal mixed with the grunting and howling of the men. The horses squealed wildly amid the chaos, and in what seemed only an instant, two of the animals fell to the ground, fatally wounded.

A timorous Kordelina sat atop Macha, looking down from the crest of a ridge. She watched the boy to the right of her as he galloped out to one of the warriors, leading a fresh horse. And as quickly as he was gone, he was sprinting back up to his place again, his face flushed with fear and panting to catch his breath.

Sickened by the brutal sounds rising from the meadow, Kordelina scrutinized the field, trying to pick out Aonghus. The mist was so heavy beneath them that if a warrior went down, he would surely fade from view, and what might only be a moment of delay would certainly cost him his life.

Suddenly a chorus of frenzied male screams came from behind, and turning around, six two-horse chariots headed straight for them. She recognized one of them to be Berrig as she hastily moved her horses out of the way to let him pass.

The wooden wheels ground down the incline, and the manned chariots surrounded the fighting. They spread out to attack the other tribe from three different angles while protecting the backs of the warriors already engaged in combat.

She heard someone shouting her name, and looking to the side of the clump of bleeding bodies of men and animals, she saw that Aonghus' horse had been wounded above the knee of its left foreleg. It was hopping on three legs, and Aonghus was wildly maneuvering his sword while kicking the animal hard to prod it on.

Dropping Lir's reins, and taking hold of the second battle-equipped warhorse, she bolted down the hill to bring it to him. She halted when she reached the meadow, unsure of which way to go. Acting entirely on instinct, she made a wide turn around the center of the fighting, and was swiftly at his side.

She cowered in her saddle as she saw Aonghus make a desperate swing of his now crimson blade, and cut off the hand of his attacker. The blood spurted from his wrist, covering his horse's mane, as Aonghus shoved his spear into the man's chest with so much force that he was jolted from the saddle. Aonghus gave a defiant howl and jumped atop the horse Kordelina was holding.

He did this with such impetus that the injured animal he had just abandoned lurched to the side, causing Macha to rear up unexpectedly as she tried to get out of its way. Grabbing a handful of mane, Kordelina felt her legs slide backward. Then she felt a hand grabbing hold of her ankle and looking down, she realized it was Aonghus' victim trying to pull her from her horse. With a single innate response, she drew her spear and drove it into the man's cheek.

The smell of blood and damp earth was welling up around her as she whipped her horse to a desperate gallop. She could feel the wet ground give beneath Macha's hooves as though she were going to lose her footing, and Kordelina kicked her hard in the flanks to keep her going forward. She was not going down in the middle of this slaughter.

Taking one jarring step to the side, Macha found her balance, and with ears pinned, darted straight up the side of the knoll, clearing the fighting.

When Kordelina got back to her position next to Lir, she looked down and saw that the peaceful grassland had been transformed into a melee of staggering, wounded men and bleeding, shrieking horses. Half the warriors were now fighting on foot, and the ones still on horseback were making driving spear-headed attacks on them. The echoes of men dying rang in her ears, and combined with the horrible cries of mutilated animals, she could feel herself start to shake.

She focused on Solomon, and became quickly absorbed with an abrupt maneuver he was making toward the center of the battle. With spears poised in both hands, and frantically kicking his horse to go faster, he bore straight through the fierce combat, and took aim at the other tribe's chieftain. An enemy warrior spotted him, and heaved his own spear to stop him. It lodged itself in the side of Solomon's horse, but the animal did not seem to feel it. It kept moving at

Solomon's command, and when he released the first spear, it missed the chieftain altogether, and caught the back of another warrior fighting behind him.

Solomon let loose of the second spear, but the opposing chieftain saw it coming. Rotating his torso to the side, he was struck in his shoulder. Bellowing at the pain, he raised his sword with the other hand, and the two tribal chieftains proceeded to spar.

Their horses trampled the men who had fallen in their path, and sparks came from their weapons each time they collided. As Kordelina watched, another warrior rode up behind Solomon, and out of sheer desperation, she screamed for him to beware. She saw the warrior point his javelin at Solomon's back.

Before he could release it, Berrig swooped down on him with his chariot, and with one swipe of his sword, decapitated him. He jumped from the chariot, leaving a kinsman to steer, and assaulted the leader from the opposite side of Solomon. Then, the two stabbed and killed him. Berrig pushed him out of his saddle, and climbing into it, directed the white-eyed steed back into the battle.

Taking in a gulp of air, Kordelina searched the field again. She was desperate to find Aonghus, but it seemed almost impossible. Most of the men were wounded in some way, and the once ornate animal paintings began smearing down their sweaty and bleeding torsos. They all appeared the same to her, but as she looked to where she had brought his second horse, she saw a lone, wounded man staggering toward the cover of the woods. At first, he had his back to her, but as he turned his blood-streaked face around, Kordelina realized it was Aonghus. He had been speared in the side, and the end of it had broken off. She could tell by the way he was swaying and gripping the bloody wound that he was badly hurt.

"Aonghus!" she yelled, as she started forward.

An apprentice stopped her. "He is going to die," he said, grabbing hold of her reins. "Do not waste the horse on him. It will be needed by another."

Kordelina covered her face with her hands, and when she looked up again, Aonghus had collapsed on the grass. He was lying motionless as the fighting shifted to the area directly in front of him, and pressing toward the ridge where she stood. It would be impossible to make it down to him, even if she did try.

She stared at him for a helpless moment, and unable to bear the scene of him dying before her eyes, she turned her horses in the opposite direction, and galloped away from the fighting.

CHAPTER SEVENTEEN

I t was nearly dusk when the clearing saw the first stragglers return from the battle. The fire was still burning as the fringes of the trees brought forth the injured, bloody men, and a few riderless horses. The drumbeat sounded, and an unending stream of tribesmen came forth to discover which of the clans had triumphed.

When the first man limped into the fire glow, everyone could tell by his high spirit they had been victorious. He walked to Saturnalia, and as he took her soft hand in his grimy one, he offered her a worn smile.

"The goddess was with us today," he said through slurred speech. "They drove us nearly all the way back to this grove, but Brigantia would not let her people be defiled. Praise Brigantia, praise Brigantia."

"Praise Brigantia!" the kinsmen cheered. "Praise our Goddess Brigantia!"

Two of the tribal women started caring for the man. Leading him to a place already prepared for dressing the wounded, they treated his lacerations while giving him food to restore his strength.

Saturnalia stood rigid, arms crossed. She was trying to see past the cloud of smoke rising from the fire to make out which of the warriors had indeed survived. She began to cry silently as one of the young fosters was led past her by another apprentice; he had been blinded when a knife had streaked across his eyes. He was wailing his lover's name. When the maid saw him, she became hysterical and ran into his arms.

"I cannot see you," he cried. "But I can remember your beauty. I can still remember your beauty."

Someone put more wood on the fire, and a great sheet of flame lit the surroundings so the wounded could be tended. The sound of men's voices and the shadows of their bodies continued emerging amid the confusion of scurrying maids and crying women hoping their loved ones had been spared.

Although she said nothing, Saturnalia tried to hide the misery growing inside her. She could see neither Conn nor Solomon, and from the way the young attendants wobbled back from the wilderness, only a few of them still on horseback, it appeared as though they had taken more of a beating than many of the warriors.

She could see and hear the many things happening around her, but she was so nervous, so seized with dread, that she felt entirely removed from it all. She wanted to ask someone if they had seen Kordelina, but she was too afraid that they would tell her something she did not wish to hear. Then she saw a young warrior walk up to her, stoop shouldered, yet he wore a victorious smile. She stared at him disbelievingly as she realized that this sagging, dirty-faced man, with dried blood covering his arms and legs, was Conn. He had a dazed expression, but from the way he was holding himself without swaying or moaning, she knew he looked worse than he really was.

She could not speak. She could only press her fingertips to his bleeding shoulder and try to hold back her tears.

"They drove us all the way back into the wilderness," he said, his mouth so dry that his lips stuck to his gums as he spoke. "They slaughtered most of the attendants, and it was that injustice that turned the tide. When we saw our youths so thoughtlessly murdered, we could do nothing but avenge such wrongdoing. They were only children, Saturnalia; they should have been spared."

Saturnalia could hardly keep from weeping. Looking away to hide her reaction, she noticed that, one by one, each of the returning wounded was being looked after by their families. Those who had yet to find their lost members were waiting anxiously at the edge of the woods. She saw a great number of heads piled in front of the flames, as well as the weapons they had stolen from their slain enemies. It was a brutal, sickening sight as the stench of ripped flesh and dried blood filled the air.

Then she saw a young apprentice enter the clearing from the opposite side. She could not help but notice that his clothes were hardly soiled, nor was he hurt in any way. However, he was completely distraught, as, weeping, he shuffled in front of his wounded master, and got down on his knees.

"Forgive me," he whimpered. "Forgive my unworthiness."

The older warrior, who had been slouching against a tree trunk, sat erect and looked at the young boy with burning eyes. Then he got to his feet, and drew his sword.

"Coward!" he shouted. "You fled like a lamb in the face of your enemy!"

The other warriors fell silent; they knew too well the penalty for such a crime. Then the master stared disdainfully at his foster, and with a single glide of his weapon, decapitated the boy. His head was sent rolling toward the bonfire, and his body instantly dropped forward onto his master's cloak.

Letting out a horrified gasp, Saturnalia turned her head and saw a horseman ride into the light carrying a wounded man. It was Solomon, and he was holding Aonghus' limp body. He had skulls tied to his saddle on both sides, but had apparently abandoned his weapons so he could safely hold onto the unconscious warrior.

When he stopped, Enda and Bracorina were promptly at his side, followed by Aonghus' two brothers. As they lowered Aonghus' body, Saturnalia could see that his lips were a pale green, and the sockets of his eyes were black circles. His midriff was wrapped in a saddlecloth, but it was so soaked with blood that Saturnalia could not imagine how he could still be alive.

She tried to approach Solomon, but before she could reach him, he threw back his head and bellowed Kordelina's name. Then he walked his horse around the circle of people as he furiously demanded she come out of hiding.

"You wretch!" he hollered. "Show yourself. I command you, Kordelina, show yourself!"

Saturnalia quietly prayed that Kordelina would not make an appearance until he had calmed down. But she felt a shock run through her as the young girl emerged from the darkness. Her knees were quivering, and she was leading Macha and Lir.

When Solomon set eyes on her, he jumped out of his saddle, and was in front of her before anyone even knew what was taking place. He stared at her for a violent moment, then lifted her off the ground by the shoulders and carried her, with feet dangling, before the tribe. Then with one of his massive hands, he slapped her so hard across the face that she fell to the ground.

Forcing her to her feet, he struck her again and again, each time harder than the last. The girl was in such a stupor when he let go of her, that her knees buckled. She fell forward, but knowing he was only going to make her stand again, she tried to crawl away.

Grabbing her by her long dark hair, he yanked her up and delivered another blow to her already stinging face. This time it sent her rolling into the pile of decapitated skulls. She was still a moment, too disoriented to move, then focusing her eyes, she saw the green, waxy faces of the dead warriors, and she let out a terrifying scream.

Solomon seemed to have temporarily gone insane, and when he lunged at her again, she was so frightened that she tried to drag herself back, only to send the heads rolling in all directions. She could see Saturnalia and Berrig trying to hold Solomon back as he kept screaming that he was going to kill her for being such a coward.

"You abandoned him! You abandoned him! I will kill you for this," he yelled, the veins in his forehead protruding. "You should never have been a warrior! You are too fainthearted!"

Kordelina was in such a state of shock that she could do nothing but stare back at him. Her mouth was bleeding, and her tunic was covered with the fluid and blood that had pooled around the severed heads.

The faces of her kinsmen told her that they were about to make an example of her. This was their chance to discourage any girl who ever dreamed of becoming more than a wife and mother. They would make a spectacle out of her cowardice, and condemn her for her show of emotion.

One by one, the villagers and any warrior who could still stand surrounded her to prevent an escape. Saturnalia watched Solomon closely. She did not trust him; he was still full from battle, and capable of anything. If Kordelina had abandoned her post, Saturnalia did not want her arbitrarily executed for it.

The tribe formed a half-circle facing the girl, each of them exchanging opinions in muffled tones. Having just won one battle, there was the savage anticipation of further bloodshed. The Druidess could tell by the look in their eyes that they wanted justice in a most morbid way.

Saturnalia stepped between Solomon and Kordelina. Holding up her hands to quiet the crowd, she waited for silence. She was a commanding presence, deliberate and unflappable, the master artisan of diplomacy.

"There will be no punishment before I hear the circumstances," she stated, tilting her head to the sky and taking a calming breath. "Chieftain, declare the charges."

Solomon took a step forward, rivulets of sweat streaming through the dirt on his face and chest. His eyes blazed with contempt as he stared at Kordelina.

"This warrior," he began, pointing at her, "failed to do her duty. She cowered in the face of danger, and refused her master his horse in battle. Her brother beckoned her to come to him, but she retreated in fear, and left him to die. Now he hovers between worlds because of her lack of courage."

A single line of weary fighters had emerged at the front of the mob, each one eyeing Kordelina menacingly. They were undoubtedly on Solomon's side, and would gladly participate in her execution if that was the sentence.

"Do you know this as truth?" Pwyll asked from the crowd.

Solomon cocked his head to one side, and looked at him curiously. His sudden change in expression suggested he was surprised that it was Pwyll who questioned his judgment.

"I saw it myself, Father," Diarmudd interjected, before Solomon could answer. "I heard Aonghus calling her name, and saw his horse go down in front of me. I tried to save him, but he was already wounded, and even when he retreated to the woods, Kordelina was not in sight. Any one of these warriors will bear witness to what the Chieftain has charged."

The air became thick with the sudden jeering and scoffing of the clan. They were feverishly demanding revenge for their future King's condition.

"And if she is guilty, what do you ask as atonement for this crime?" Saturnalia asked, raising her voice above them.

Solomon clenched his fists, and took in a deep breath. "Aonghus has been the bravest of warriors!" he shouted. "He has battled the Romans; he has staked his life for his clan. He has proven himself an honorable warrior in all ways, and has even taken Kordelina as his foster. I want justice! She should be sentenced for her cowardly deeds like any other."

The tribe echoed the Chieftain in unanimous agreement as the line of warriors pressed closer. The entire clan was the verge of rioting as they called for Kordelina's immediate death. Some were screaming for her to be beheaded, and others wanted her burned in the wicker man. Saturnalia winced at the thought of that ominous wicker figure that was constructed from logs and willow branches. It had been years since she had thought of the huge wooden framework being filled from top to bottom with condemned men and women. The thought that one of those writhing bodies, screaming for release as it was set ablaze, could be Kordelina filled the Druidess with despair.

"Silence!" Saturnalia ordered. Lifting an eyebrow, she turned to look at Solomon accusingly. She could not believe he would demand his own daughter's death.

"If she dies, you will be sorry," she threatened under her breath. "I will make you sorry."

Conn came forward, and took a place beside Kordelina, facing the tribe. "I saw for myself that Kordelina brought Aonghus his horse when he called," he stated seriously. "She did as all the other apprentices until the fighting prevented her from giving aid to her master."

He looked at Solomon as he spoke, fully aware of the relief he was bringing to Saturnalia. "I will give my word that I saw her, with my own eyes, deliver Aonghus a horse when she was called. We cannot kill her. Even if she is accused, she has a right to speak for herself, and she has the right, under our tribal laws, to have a viewing with her master to make clear her actions."

"But what of Aonghus?" Diarmudd shouted. "He cannot speak for himself, and it is because of her. If he dies, so should she! I would kill her myself this instant as Aonghus' suffering calls for revenge!"

"Yes," the crowd echoed. "Kill her! Destroy the coward!"

Saturnalia whirled around and faced them with furious eyes. Seeing her malicious stare, they shrank back and fell silent.

"Which of you would challenge me?" she shrieked, purposely frightening them. "I am the caretaker of the laws in this tribe, and this warrior has the right to speak in her defense to her master. It is he who will decide her fate."

She turned to Kordelina. The young girl was staring straight ahead, as if she were watching this scene from a distance. Her eyes were barely visible as they began to swell from the force of Solomon's blows.

"Do you understand the charges against you?" Saturnalia asked.

"Yes," Kordelina answered. She looked to Koven, his eyes reflecting only mercy as he looked back. He offered her a faint nod of encouragement, urging her to stand up for herself. She knew that to him it did not matter why she had done what she had done. His love as a parent would remain steadfast in spite of the conditions. Taking in his trusting expression, Kordelina suddenly felt ashamed.

"Do you have anything to offer in explanation?" the Druidess asked.

Kordelina looked at the ground.

Saturnalia stepped directly in front of her, and taking her by the shoulders, looked urgently into her eyes. "I do not know exactly what you have done," she whispered. "But you must defend yourself or they will kill you."

"I did not want to harm my brother," Kordelina blurted out, so suddenly that she was not sure if the words were her own. "I tried to help him, but —"

She stopped abruptly, and threw herself on the ground in front of Saturnalia. "I ask for mercy," she wept. "I ask that I may speak to my master before my punishment is decided."

"She is a liar!" Diarmudd accused. "She is not a stranger to killing. She has proven that before my own eyes. Her actions are always deliberate, and she purposely failed her brother. I was witness to the way she spoke disrespectfully to him on our journey. She wanted him to die! She wanted him to die!"

"That is for Aonghus and the elders to decide," Saturnalia countered, wiping the beads of sweat from her upper lip. She was using all of her finesse to save Kordelina's life.

"Stand, child," she said, bending her fingers upward and motioning for the girl to get to her feet. "Begging cannot change the truth. This will not be your moment of judgment. Yet, I must tell you that if Aonghus awakens and agrees with what this Chieftain has accused you of, you must pay retribution to him, even if it is by your death."

Kordelina lifted her head, and was overcome with the thought that she was trapped in a cesspool of her own disgrace. She saw people all around her, glaring at her with hungry, bloodthirsty expressions. It was true that Aonghus was not dead, but his chances of staying alive were slim. Now all that was left for her was execution by those who had always considered her unworthy. As she realized these truths, all the tears, all the rage, all the love she had felt for Aonghus turned to ice in her veins. Truly, she was only a shadow in his light. Yet, deep inside, she knew there had been a time or even only a moment when he had loved her, too.

Slowly, she raised her torso and sat back on her heels. Tilting her head to one side, she focused on Solomon, her eyes pleading with him over this meaningless display. She saw the intensity of his expression fade to nothingness. Then looking over her shoulder, she again gazed into Koven's forgiving face.

"I am sorry," she said, moving her lips but making no sound.

"Stand, you wretch!" Diarmudd demanded.

There was the aching thud of his foot in the small of her back.

"Diarmudd, let her be!" Solomon shouted, pushing him away from her.

Pressing the palms of her hands on the ground, Kordelina braced herself and slowly got to her feet. Straining to catch her breath, she stumbled as she took a step forward. She looked again at the impatient mob, then at Solomon.

"I will make it easy for us both," she said with icy composure.

Solomon did not reply as his face hardened, and his eyes glassed over.

She grabbed Diarmudd's knife from the sheath at his side, and started running. Pushing her way past the women, she was nearly at the edge of the woods when Solomon caught her and dragged her to the ground. With all her strength, she tried to thrust the dagger into her chest, but he caught her arm in midair.

Placing her other hand on the knife handle, she attempted to lift her chest to the point of the blade and impale herself.

The hideous look on Solomon's face above her made each moment she struggled for her death unbearable, and she began to cry.

"Kill me," she whispered. "It is what you want to do; it is what I deserve."

Solomon's arm trembled as he held onto Kordelina's wrist. His teeth were clenched tightly, and his eyes, bulging. Part of him did want to kill her for what she had done to Aonghus. The other part felt great sorrow at her state. She would never be able to walk with pride in this clan again, and she would be better off dead than persecuted.

His heart ached as he realized this was not an ordinary individual he had accused. It was his daughter. As his anger dimmed, he knew he did not wish for her death any more than he wished Aonghus to die. Then he felt a firm grip on his forearm, and looking up, saw Saturnalia.

"Enough of this," she hissed. "The child will remain in my charge until the outcome of Aonghus' health is known."

Kordelina's grip on the weapon relaxed, and with tears streaming down her cheeks, she allowed Solomon to take it from her. "Please, Chieftain, do not let anything happen to my horses," she begged softly. "It is not for my well-being, but for theirs. I know they will surely belong to Aonghus now."

Solomon's eyes became teary as the reality of what was taking place set in. As he stood to walk back to the crowd of people, he offered a fervent silent prayer that Aonghus would live to save her.

CHAPTER EIGHTEEN

our days passed before any word came of Aonghus' condition. When Solomon at last visited Saturnalia with news that he had regained consciousness, the Druidess advised Kordelina without delay.

Saturnalia had spent these last few days frightfully worried about the girl. From the moment Kordelina had arrived at the cottage, she found a place in the darkest corner of the sleeping chamber and collapsed. Since then, she had remained in a seemingly unchanged position, staring at the ceiling.

Saturnalia had provided her bedding and brought her food, but Kordelina was unresponsive. She appeared as though her soul had left her body and the physical shell was all that remained. So gaunt and depressed was she that the Druidess thought she was trying to starve herself to death. It was only when Saturnalia spoke of Aonghus' health that any light showed in her eyes.

"The Chieftain says that he has awakened," she said, sitting next to her. "He has taken food and drink, and is able to sit up on his own. All who have seen him say he is very ill, but will certainly recover."

Tears welled in Kordelina's eyes, and she turned her head away.

"Child, I am going to speak with him," Saturnalia continued, smoothing Kordelina's hair back. Even though the girl made no sound, she could see that she was crying. "I am going to talk to him about what happened, but first, I must hear your view of what took place."

Kordelina drew her legs up to her chest and, covering her face, let out a grievous moan.

"Please, child, I know how badly you feel, but there has been enough time. You must recount your actions to me," she gently persuaded.

Quelling her tears, Kordelina looked at Saturnalia, and nodded. "When I was on the ridge watching the battle," she began, in a quivering voice, "I did bring Aonghus his first horse as Conn testified. But when I returned to my position, I did not keep my eyes on him. I was distracted by Solomon and the attack he was making on the other chieftain. A warrior was going to kill him, and I was screaming for him to protect himself. I thought Solomon was surely going to be speared, and even though I knew he could not hear me, I kept screaming for him to guard his back. Then Berrig helped him, and the other chieftain was killed.

"When I remembered about Aonghus, I looked for him, but could not find him, at first. Finally, I saw he was wounded and seeking refuge in the trees. I called to him, but when I tried to bring him Lir, one of the attendants told me it would be a waste of time. He said Aonghus was going to die, and then he grabbed my reins, and told me to save the horse for someone who was still living."

Saturnalia nodded that she understood. "Do you know this attendant's name? Perhaps he will state this to the elders."

Kordelina shook her head. "He was killed later on. No one else heard what he said."

The Druidess frowned. "Then what did you do?" she asked pensively.

Kordelina rubbed her watery eyes with both fists. "I could not bear to bring Lir to another because he is Aonghus' horse," she explained sincerely. "And I knew that if Lir stayed alive, so would Aonghus. I thought that if I took him to a safe place, and begged the gods to save Aonghus' life, they would. That is what I did when he was in Wales. I knew deep in my soul that as long as I cared for Lir, somehow, Aonghus would remain well, too. It worked then, and it worked now, as Aonghus was spared by the gods."

Saturnalia's eyes misted at the honesty and simplicity of Kordelina's actions. "Then what?" she questioned.

"Then I thought that, perhaps, I should go back and do my duty to my tribe. So I left Lir hidden, and took Macha back to where the fighting had been," she replied. "When I got there, all of the apprentices had been killed, and the sounds of the fighting were faint. I had no idea where my tribe was because the sounds were so far off. I even went down to where Aonghus had fallen, but he was not there, either. So I went back to get Lir, and waited in the woods near the clearing for the warriors to return."

"Can anyone else support this story, any one at all?" Saturnalia asked.

Kordelina shook her head. "Only Macha and Lir, but you cannot understand the way they speak. Are they all right?"

"Yes, they are fine," Saturnalia reassured her.

"They will both be given to Aonghus, will they not?" she asked.

"Yes, and any land rights you would have inherited will go to him as well," Saturnalia told her dryly.

"And will the elders ask that I be stripped of my status?" she questioned.

"Worse," the Druidess answered. "They said if you are not executed, they will demand that you be treated as a curse and ostracized from all tribal functions and rituals."

"Then I will be a slave," Kordelina stated, weakly.

"You will be even lower. Your existence will not be recognized by any of your kinsmen," she explained sympathetically. "You will not be spoken to, or allowed any privileges at all. Your family will only see you if it is their desire, and you will be forsaken by the gods."

Kordelina was motionless; it was as though she had already known what Saturnalia was going to say.

"Before I speak to Aonghus, I must know one other thing," the Druidess stated. "This tribe will demand that you be punished in some way, regardless of what Aonghus thinks. If he is going to remain a credible leader, and keep the people's support, he is going to have to make some public display of your punishment. The clan will not allow this to pass just because you are his sister. Actually, it is because you are his sister that they are so adamant about seeing justice done. They reason that if he is too weak to control his own foster, he will certainly be too weak to rule a tribe. But if after a time, we could arrange a place for you in another tribe, would you agree to that? You have long expressed a desire to live away from here."

Kordelina was too emotionally drained to react. "I will agree if it is what Aonghus wants," she said dully. "Tell him I will do anything he asks, even if he asks for my death."

Saturnalia pressed her hand to her brow. "I would like to prevent that," she reasoned. "I would rather arrange a home for you with someone else. I will use all of my influence with the Druids to do it."

"Why is it so important to you, Saturnalia?" Kordelina asked. "It is not to me. I failed my master, and they are right to demand that I atone for it."

Saturnalia took her hand. "Please, Kordelina, let me take care of it," she reassured, then left the girl to her thoughts.

The Druidess was an altogether different person when she entered Aonghus' chamber, and asked to speak to him in private. With one look, she cleared the room at once.

When she turned her attention to Aonghus, she no longer displayed the sympathetic expression she had shown Kordelina. Instead, she was the determined, unyielding woman who was sure of getting exactly what she wanted.

She found the warrior, pale and weak, in his room, staring out the window. He did not acknowledge her when she entered, and like Kordelina, he had dull, vagrant eyes. Seeing him like this, Saturnalia could not help but wonder which of the two was in worse condition.

"I must say you appear the vision of life compared to what I saw of you after the battle," she commented, taking a place by the open window.

He looked at her listlessly. "I will survive in spite of what they do to me," he stated. "As it was you who gave me my power."

"It was I?" Saturnalia asked, raising her brows. "I am flattered to hear such things; yet I do not know of what you speak."

"I cast off death for rebirth, as I am anointed with the power of snake."

"So it is a new man I look upon?" she questioned.

"It is a stronger being than before," he answered.

"Is this stronger being still in love with Kordelina?" she asked.

Aonghus sorrowfully averted his gaze. "Is she well?" he asked softly.

Saturnalia shook her head. "She is closer to death than you are, and in more than one way."

A glint of despair showed in Aonghus' eyes. "Solomon has already told me what took place upon his return. Her death is not what I want."

"It does me well to hear that," she responded, keeping her eyes fixed on him. "However, after the way she was publicly accused, there certainly must be a punishment rendered. If you let her actions go unheeded, this tribe will think you laughable as a leader, and there are those who are already planning to exploit your vulnerability. This would be all they would need to test your resolve. The success of days ago has proven there is not the need to maintain treaties any longer and so it is an open invitation for you to be challenged by other clans as well."

"I realize that," he said.

"Did Solomon tell you what the elders decided upon in dealing with Kordelina?" she inquired.

Aonghus nodded.

"If you do not find her worthy of execution, they will accept nothing less than banishment and total loss of status as a tribesman. That means she will bow to the slaves," she explained, as she watched the lines on his face deepen. "They have already decided that all she owns will go to you as recompense. That includes any land rights she would inherit and her horses."

She saw him gulp down the knot rising in his throat, and faintly shake his head. "Yes, Aonghus," she continued. "And I would caution you to do as they say, lest you find yourself lacking in your assumption of power. This tribe will not tolerate any show of vulnerability when it comes to her."

The warrior closed his eyes for a long moment, then his head dropped forward and he covered his face with his hands.

"I am sorry for you, Aonghus, but it is one of the pressures that comes with leadership," Saturnalia stated curtly. "Your private affairs are not your own when you are in a position of power. I hope you realize that."

Aonghus gave her a painful stare. "Kordelina did no wrong," he responded. "It was impossible to see anything. I was lucky the first time she brought me a horse, and I will testify to the bravery she showed doing it. I do not know what stopped her the second time, but there was so much commotion that it would have been hard for even a seasoned warrior to come to my aid. They cannot persecute her for that."

"They can, and they will," Saturnalia countered. "They never wanted a female warrior, and this is their chance not only to rid themselves of one, but to do it in a way that no other girl would even consider it again."

"I know you are right," he mumbled, pushing his hair from his face.

"My advice to you, Aonghus, if you wish to retain your title, and be deemed a worthy ruler, is to accept the offer of banishment, and assume all of Kordelina's property. As further payment, she should be your indentured servant for a time until I can arrange for her to be purchased by another clan where she can live freely."

Aonghus was dumbfounded. "You want me to make her my slave, then sell her as chattel? I will not do it!" he declared, raising his voice for the first time.

"I am sorry, but it is the only way I can see to get her out of this situation," she replied. "And it is the only way you will retain your integrity with the tribe."

Tilting his head back, Aonghus covered his eyes with his forearm and groaned. Then he let his arm fall to his side, and he looked at her indignantly.

"I can think of another way, a way that has never even been considered by you or Solomon."

Saturnalia placed her hands on her hips, seeing he was no longer going to be receptive. "What is that?" she asked.

"Tell her the truth," he declared. "Finally, tell her everything. Tell her that she was not born of my parents but of Deireadh and Solomon. Explain to her that she is not my sister, and that she is the rightful heir to Solomon's holdings and title. Then Solomon can hand over his power to her, and I will make her my wife."

"Have you gone mad?" Saturnalia challenged.

"Have you?" he yelled back at her. He tried to sit up straight, but the pain from his wound caused him to slump back down. "Do you think for one moment that I could tolerate her being my servant, and allow her to be sold to some farmer when I could have her as my wife? That is what I want. I want to marry her, and she wants to marry me.

"Saturnalia, I nearly died this time. I glimpsed the other side. While I was in the trance between life and death, suspended in that void, out of the darkness the spirits brought me a beautiful instrument. It was not a lyre, a harp, or a flute. Rather, it was all of them combined and none of them as well. When I went to play it, I fingered it like a lyre, stroked it like a harp, and blew into it like a flute. In those times when I would lean near to the blackness of death, I would play this music. It filled me with vigor and so much love that my waking mind cannot begin to fathom it.

"And as I held it in my arms, touched it with my fingertips, caressed it with my mouth, I watched what I had perceived to be that very same instrument transfigured into Kordelina. I realized then that the notes which made my heart swell were the music of our souls. If only they could be joined together, I would be able to bring forth with my voice the music that I was playing, and no matter where I was, it would be carried on the air to please her ears. Once did I try to steal her, and take her through the ring of fire with me to dwell where our love could flourish unfettered by worn out oaths, but Solomon prevented it. Each time I listened again to the beauty of the music she created within me, she did whisper ever so sweetly for me to whisk her away once more. Saturnalia, Kordelina would die for me if I asked her."

Saturnalia's parchment-like skin drained even whiter. "Yes, Aonghus," she said in a low, pained voice. "She did try to kill herself, but Solomon stopped her.

What you saw in your vision was him preventing her death. You are wrong to do this to that child, and that is what she is—a child—with a right to a life outside of your selfishness. She should have —"

"My selfishness? My selfishness!" Aonghus ranted. "It is you who are the selfish one. It is you who keeps her ignorant! It is you who murdered her mother!"

"So she could live!" Saturnalia screamed back at him. "I killed Deireadh so that Kordelina could live. If I had faltered for even a moment, your precious little sister—"

"Do not call her that!" Aonghus broke in.

"Yes, I will call her what she is. Your sister," Saturnalia countered, "would not be alive today. I do not apologize for bringing her into this place, nor will I ever!"

"You wretch," Aonghus accused. "You keep her dependent on you because you can bear no children of your own. You are just as selfish as I."

With one step, Saturnalia was in front of him, firmly slapping him across the face. She glared at him contemptuously, then walked to the door and called for Solomon.

The weary Chieftain lumbered into the room, obviously uneasy at having to be a part of their quarrel.

"Aonghus has something to propose to you, Chieftain," Saturnalia said, with scarcely a trace of her momentary fury.

"Speak, Aonghus," he said compassionately. "I will listen sincerely to anything you have to offer."

The line of Aonghus' strong jaw became more pronounced as he stubbornly jutted it out and clenched his teeth. Solomon could see he was trying to calm himself.

"Solomon, I would never betray you," he began. He tilted his face and took a steadying breath, then looked furtively at the Chieftain. "Yet, I am torn between my loyalty for you, and my love for your daughter."

He saw Solomon blink hard at his straightforwardness. For a moment, he thought he was going to say something, but as soon as he opened his mouth, he swallowed his words and waited for Aonghus to continue.

"I can find no way to relate what has burst in my soul that has made this so undeniable. I can only say that the futility of seeing something so precious to me bartered away, sickens me," Aonghus continued. "This baby girl you refused to accept has long etched her name upon my heart. So strong is this that I am unable to live this lie of being brother and sister any longer. I offer to you this proposition. I will abdicate my right to a kingship on the condition that Kordelina be told of her parentage, and thus be rightfully given all rights that you would offer to me. I will take only what my father would hand over, and the celsine that I have developed on my own. I will have Kordelina as my wife, and as payment for the marriage, you will give me back all that I have originally given up. Kordelina has lineage to a throne, and when she assumes it, I will be King as well."

Solomon stared at him blankly, then looked at Saturnalia and shrugged. "And what of her crime in battle?" he asked warily. "What excuse will you offer for not sentencing her for cowardice?"

Aonghus gave a hint of a smile. "I dare say the shock of her revealed parentage will wreak such havoc that everyone will forget about the petty mishap in battle," he replied.

Solomon twisted the ends of his mustache, and considered Aonghus' proposition. Then he looked at the warrior, and sorrowfully shook his head.

"It can never come to pass, dear boy; I am sorry," he said regretfully. "The promise we made that night takes precedence over all we lust for today. There is no way we can ever tell Kordelina what we swore to keep secret because there is never a reason to disavow a Druidic oath. I am sorry for you, truly I am. Maybe you have forgotten that long ago I, too, had to give up something very dear to me, and endure the pains of my heart to keep an oath I had made. These are the laws of our people, and it is the way it must be. And, Aonghus, I caution you, that should you ever find reason to go against what you have sworn before the gods, I must and will put an end to you. Forgive me, but as I have said, I have been where you are now, and I know how painful the sacrifice can be."

At that moment, Solomon cringed at how much like Donnach he sounded, and how greatly the troubled young man before him must have resembled him years before.

"Kordelina must be held accountable for her actions, and even if it causes your heart to wither, it is you who must render it. For if you fail to do as the laws command, you will be viewed as an unworthy ruler by your clan, and I cannot guarantee that you will not suffer for it. The future is unsure for our people, and what you have is an opportunity to redeem the masses and increase your wealth, while being a great leader for your kinsmen. Do not forsake them, Aonghus. Your personal losses must not defeat the people you have vowed to serve. I am compassionate of your burden, but this is how it must be. You will never be able to fade quietly into the background after you have conditioned yourself to be a ruler. That is your destiny."

Aonghus' head dropped forward, and he closed his eyes for a long painful moment. Then he lifted his chin and stared at both Solomon and Saturnalia with disdain.

"Then what you are telling me is that you have sentenced Kordelina and me to live as unfulfilling a life as the two of you," he said coldly. "That I should be a strong leader, but a weak human being. That I should forsake the integrity of my heart for the antiquated promises that matter only to the order and the two of you. That I should not take the wife I love, but the one that is best for the people. And that my children should be brought forth in a loveless house of duty and lies.

"For I know, Solomon, that if I go against you, you will put an end to me, as you have said. And if I die, so then will the clan have reason to make suffer all that was mine, and that means Kordelina, who is now, as you have informed me, to be my servant. And when I have assumed power to the good of our tribe, and Kordelina is growing corn and birthing children to some peasant, I should take solace in the fact that I did not disavow my Druidic oath."

His voice quivered, and his eyes began to mist. He paused a moment, then swallowed his emotion before he continued to speak.

"So then," he said, resuming his former tone. "It has been decided for us already. She should have no status, and be banished from all ceremonies and rituals. My father will give her land rights to me, and also her horse as recompense, and what is lacking, she will work off as my indentured servant. Is that correct?"

Saturnalia slowly nodded her head. "And as soon as a reasonable period of time has passed, and all believe that she has paid her debt, I will arrange that she be purchased away from you."

"A reasonable period of time," he said scornfully. "Long enough for the tribe to see that I can stand firm as a leader. It is so strange that by my punishing her they will see how strong a fiend I can be. That is the reason for it, is it not?"

"They must believe in you, Aonghus," Solomon reasoned with him. "They must have faith in your ability to make decisions on their behalf. If you let Kordelina's transgression go unpunished, they will have no faith in you at all. It is only for a short time, as short a time as possible. Truly, my boy, you will both be the better for it. For if you do not make the decision, they will, and I do not have to tell you that it is the wicker man to which they will sentence her. If you cannot do it for the people, do it for her, because they are thirsting for an execution."

Aonghus leaned back and stared out the window, just as he had when Saturnalia had arrived, with one hand covering his wound, and the other now dangling from the bedside. His eyes were half shut and wistful as he gazed out at the brightness of the spring day.

"Then assemble all that you must so that her punishment will be rendered," he said, lifelessly. "And Saturnalia, I would ask you guarantee that I never know to whom she will be sold. For I cannot promise that I would be able to keep from killing him."

The sorceress seemed to soften as she slowly approached the bedside. She tried to meet his eye, but he looked through her as if she were not there.

"You must believe that this is for the best, Aonghus," she consoled. "It truly is for the best."

"Yes, Saturnalia," he said flatly. "It always is."

CHAPTER NINETEEN

It was as though the entire world had fallen silent as Kordelina was escorted through the settlement to Solomon's estate. Guarded by Conn and Diarmudd, she kept her eyes fixed on her feet as she walked. She could feel the scrutinizing glares of her kinsmen as she passed, each of them already knowing that she was not to be acknowledged ever again. Saturnalia had told her what her punishment would be, and the clan had been informed of it long before she was ever brought in front of Aonghus.

She found it all too easy to block out the hissing sound of their malicious whispers as the older ones claimed she was Deireadh come back to haunt them. She did not truly care what her tribe thought, because she had always been an outcast among them. To be in this situation now was like an unspoken prophesy come true. She knew her parents would still care for and forgive her. Solomon would certainly try to be tough, but in the end, he would be kind to her as well. That is the way he had always been. Saturnalia had also assured her that their meetings and her study would continue privately. Nevertheless, it was all of little consolation. To be forsaken by Aonghus was by far the most excruciating punishment she would ever have to endure.

Of all these people, he was the only one who mattered. He was the one she had loved as a child—the one who never betrayed her and always rescued her from pain and loneliness. He was the one she adored now as a woman, the man with whom she dreamed she would share herself and love in the darkness. He was the sole entity who could make her want to freely give to him every last particle of her being—the only man she would ever beg to kill her instead of abandoning her. Death would be more merciful than life without him.

When she entered the massive oak doorway, and walked through the long corridor to his room, she was thankful that Bracorina was not there to witness her demise. The people present were Solomon, Saturnalia, Pwyll, who represented the tribal elders, and her parents. The only awkwardness she felt was that Conn and Diarmudd kept their weapons continually pointed at her.

As she stepped inside Aonghus' chamber, she could smell the pungent odor of dried blood and the stale aroma of sickness. When she gazed on him for the first time, and her eyes met with his, she forgot all of it, and began mentally pleading for his forgiveness. She scurried to his bedside, and getting down on her knees, she took both his hands and kissed them. She could tell by the way his cold fingers were so yielding to her that he was no longer angry, and that he did not want her to stop. But before either of them could speak, Diarmudd had her by the shoulders, dragging her backward.

Aonghus impulsively gripped her hands tighter, and tried to pull her to him. Then, he realized what he was doing, and he suddenly released her. She started begging out loud for him not to stop loving her, and she kept groping forward to get back to him. For a moment she freed herself of Diarmudd's hold, but in the next instant, another set of hands on the back of her neck pushed her down and kept her there.

"Calm yourself, little one," Conn's voice tried to soothe her. "This will be easier if you remain silent."

Kordelina tried to obey, but when she looked into Aonghus' watering eyes, she let out a wail and tried once more to run to him.

She heard the faint ringing of Saturnalia's voice commanding her to compose herself, but it sounded like the Druidess was calling from another world. All Kordelina wanted to do was to touch Aonghus again, touch him and relay to him that she would never forgive herself for what she had let happen. She wanted him to believe that there was no one in this world, or the world of the gods, that she could ever love as much as she loved him.

She felt Conn and Diarmudd seize her again, and this time, instead of making her kneel, they forced her to lie face down on the floor. Each had one foot on her hand and the other on her ankle, and the tips of their spears were pressing into the back of her neck. She found it strange that she was not speaking or crying now. The only sound of which she was aware was the pounding of her heart and her labored breath. Then she recalled the horrible scene between Edainne and Diarmudd, and how it must have been a dreaded premonition. Only now, Aonghus was not trying to rescue her the way Diarmudd had Edainne. He was lying there, seemingly disassociated from what was going on around him.

Be still, she told herself. They cannot break you; they cannot break you.

She dug down into what seemed her last reserve of inner strength, and willed herself into a perfect calm. She felt her hands and feet freed, and heard Solomon order her to kneel.

It was by force of instinct that she did as she was told. Lifting her eyes, she stared straight into Saturnalia's face. She was emitting vibrations that Kordelina understood to be especially for her because in a single beat of her heart, she was entirely in command of herself.

"By your actions, warrior," she heard Pwyll's aged voice booming inside her head. "You have been judged a coward by the elders of this tribe and your master. You failed your obligations during war, and tried to escape the fighting. You deserted your master, and refused him the horse intended for him. As a result of these actions, he was nearly killed."

A cold sweat broke out on Kordelina's brow as her momentary confidence evaporated, and she felt a sudden inclination to run. At that moment, she did not care if Conn and Diarmudd skewered her to the wall. She wanted release from this travesty.

Saturnalia sensed her thoughts because she lifted her hand gracefully in the air, and gestured for Kordelina to look only at her. The girl felt a strange, involuntary pull to her, and she stayed in her place as Pwyll continued.

"Yet your master is a merciful man," he went on, in a stately tone. "He has asked that in atonement for your actions, he be recompensed by having all of your land rights given over to him. He will take your horse as well, and as further payment, you will serve him until he deems that your debt has been paid."

A tiny rustle came from Aonghus' bed as he uncomfortably shifted his position. Kordelina thought she heard him say something, but whatever it was, it whirled inside her muddled brain and was so fragmented, that she could make no sense of it.

"Still, because you are an anointed warrior, under the laws, you must also be held accountable to your kinsmen," Pwyll's unwavering voice continued. "The laws of this tribe are clear. They have been upheld for generations before you, and will stand on this day. Any warrior who has forsaken his master must be made to suffer for his crime by the will of the gods. Your transgression has wronged not only the one you have sworn your loyalty to, but the very spirits with which you were anointed. To satisfy what should be an execution, you will be sentenced to a death of a different sort. You shall be cursed by the heavens, and be held accountable to the gods. Never should you attend a tribal ritual as a free woman again; never will you be allowed to share in the privileges of the living. You will not be acknowledged by your kinsmen, and should there ever be occasion for sacrifice, you will be under obligation to fulfill it. For the judgment of your soul, according to the laws, shall be delivered in the Otherworld."

A deadly silence fell over the room, and all hope drained from Kordelina's body. She heard her mother keening behind her, begging the sympathy of the heavens so her only daughter would not hover in a godless void forever. She felt a strange confusion rising in her as her eyes darted to Aonghus.

"But as our tradition demands your death," Pwyll said, "you must accept your sentence out loud. It must be stated by you, in the presence of your family, your master, and the lawgivers, that you understand fully the reasons for this decision and your obligation to adhere to it."

For a moment, Kordelina thought she was going to laugh at how ridiculous it sounded. How could they possibly entreat such vast, unknown powers to rise against her, as though they had the power and knowledge to do so? Then she realized the gravity of the judgment, and she made herself frown instead of smile. There was no escape from this inane demonstration of human aggression, and she knew it. Solomon approached her to remove the torque from her neck, and her heart began to ache.

"Is this what you want, Kordelina?" Aonghus asked, his voice hoarse with emotion. "You must state it out loud."

"You know what I want, Aonghus," she answered. "I want only for you to love me."

The very sound of her voice caused his tears to erupt. But seeing her innocence triggered something within him. He knew that, in spite of all this, her character would not be defeated. She would resist authority even in the smallest degree—and that would be her salvation.

The firelight caused her eyes to glisten as she looked back at him, and it was more torment than he had ever endured. The unique bone structure of her face became sharper, and her black tresses suddenly appeared more rebellious. Behind her olive eyes, he found a certain gratification in her relentless nature. It was something no living being would ever be able to steal. She was as much the object of his desire as she had ever been, and for a moment he wished he could endlessly take in the vision of her.

As if she had read his thoughts, there was a subtle change in her manner. It told him with that certain nerve, that certain reserve of insubordination and independence, she could now survive anything.

"Do you accept your sentence, Kordelina?" Solomon asked.

With her gaze fixed on Aonghus, Kordelina shook her head. "No, Chieftain," she said. "I will accept nothing. I will surrender my body to the judgment that has been rendered, but what remains in my soul, you may never confine."

She seemed entirely absorbed in Aonghus for a moment as a faint smile crossed her lips. "All that we worked for is now folly," she whispered to him.

Enda began to keen even louder when Conn pulled his knife, and Diarmudd gathered her hair to be cut off as a public statement of her crime. It was only then that Kordelina really began to cry.

"Please, Aonghus," she begged through quivering lips. "Do not let them cut my hair."

When Aonghus held up his hand for them to stop, he was so distraught that he could barely get the words out. "It is enough that she be forced to live without her torque," he said. "Let that be the symbol of her unworthiness."

He looked away from her, and placed his hand to his brow. "Take her away from me now, please," he said, then motioned that everyone else leave the chamber as well.

———

It was twilight when Saturnalia returned to her cottage. The purple and orange lights of dusk caressed the oak branches, but she felt such an emptiness within her she was scarcely able to appreciate its beauty. Spring had always signified that rebirth was an eternal journey. What was killed by the winter frost and the harsh cold was always revitalized with the promising sun. Only now, after all that had taken place this day, such blissful notions were nearly impossible for her to grasp.

She had settled Kordelina with one of Solomon's handmaids. She was an aged woman who had been with the Chieftain long before Saturnalia had come to this tribe. Now a widow, the woman had originally been married to one of the grooms, and had asked Saturnalia personally if Kordelina could be allowed to live with her.

At first, the Druidess found this an odd request since Kordelina was considered an anathema, and would certainly bring ill fortune to anyone who associated with her. But the woman had assured her that her time in the world was short, and she had special reasons of her own for wishing it. This was good for Kordelina since the handmaid's dwelling was cozy, and she seemed a tender-hearted sort.

"I believe this child is a special one," she had told Saturnalia. "And I do not wish to see her have to submit to tribesmen who might force themselves upon her. I will keep her safe with me even if it is from her own master."

Saturnalia felt an odd resentment surface as she spoke. This woman secretly knew more about Kordelina than she was letting on.

"As you wish," she had hesitantly agreed. "But you must uphold the ruling as well. She must not be indulged with either speech or former liberties."

"I will uphold it, I can assure you," the woman said. "I have been devoted to this family for all my years, and I know that by Kordelina's very blood, she is worthy of my loyalty as well. Deireadh was once as tender a creature as she and it was only through the mistreatment of her desires that she went to darkness. I do not wish the same thing to be suffered by her daughter."

A jolt coursed through Saturnalia. It had never occurred to her that there would be someone who had known Deireadh so well, that her daughter would be easily recognized.

"I would ask then, that your loyalty extend to that which the Chieftain and I have not revealed these many years," she said, trying not to be defensive. "This tribe never embraced Deireadh, and they would surely bring suffering to her offspring."

"I have always understood that," the woman replied, a certain bitterness evident in her voice. "For Deireadh was as misunderstood then as Kordelina is now. You can trust me. I am such an old woman anyway, that if I did speak out, they would think I was suffering from delusions. My desires are only to protect the girl, not to harm her."

"You are trustworthy, good maid," Saturnalia said sincerely. "I do thank you for that."

As she entered her gate now, she could not help but replay the conversation in her head. She was unsure if she was disconcerted by the idea that someone else knew what she had believed to be successfully concealed, or if it was a slight jealously at someone else now being closer to Kordelina than she.

Then there was the argument with Aonghus, and the way he had accused her of keeping Kordelina ignorant because she had no children of her own. Perhaps that was the truth, and he had voiced a personal fear that she had tried to discount all this time. Perhaps when Jara had told her long ago that she was inhuman, she was telling the truth, and her inability to bring forth a child was a testimony to that.

Weary and confused, she entered her cottage and immediately started taking off her clothes. She wanted only to escape from such realities—they were sucking the life from her.

By the time she entered her chamber, she was completely naked. Desiring sleep, she did not build a fire. Instead, she kept the shutters closed and crawled beneath the covers. Closing her eyes, she suddenly felt a hand on her rib cage, as the sound of Conn's voice cut through her troubled thoughts.

"I should remain with you now," he said in a hushed tone.

Saturnalia clung to him so desperately that for a moment, she felt as though he was her only salvation.

"Yes," she replied, wrapping her legs around his and burying her face in his hair. "We should be together now."

CHAPTER TWENTY

inter A.D. 61. Edainne was already expecting a child when she and Diarmudd were wed at the festival of Beltaine the following May. It was a grand celebration, and even though Kordelina was forbidden to attend, she secretly watched from the woods.

Her friend wore a lovely embroidered robe of many bright colors, and her long hair was adorned with wildflowers. Diarmudd looked undeniably handsome, and radiated joy as he recited his vows. They appeared so thoroughly in love with each other that one could scarcely resist the happy sight of two such enamored people joined together for eternity.

With the exception of her loss of status, Kordelina's life was much the same as it had been before her crime. She was no longer allowed to attend tribal festivals or worship, but that was a relief, not a burden. She rather liked the fact that she no longer had to pretend they meant something to her when they really never had. The one thing she did miss, though, was the loss of personal freedom. No longer could she come and go as she pleased, since leaving the estate without permission was entirely forbidden.

There were times that she did venture beyond the confines of the manor, and it was usually at Aonghus' request. Although he never asked her to do anything directly, word would come by way of another servant that he desired shellfish from the seashore, or wild berries or radishes for his meals. She would always include tiny gifts of her affection, a seashell or a hawk feather, with his requests.

As the months went by, she watched from a distance as Aonghus regained his strength. He would lounge in the sun or take short walks around the estate. His wounds were taking a long time to heal and he was still too weak to ride.

He seemed remote and separate from the world around him. When Beltaine arrived, he was barely able to stand on his own, and only visited the celebration long enough to dispel any rumors in the clan that he was going to die. The summer that followed was used to regain his strength physically and emotionally. He expended little energy during that time, and it seemed as though he was content to appreciate the life going on around him. He would sit for hours on the stump of the old oak tree, and simply listen to the wind or the sound of the birds singing. There were many times when Kordelina wanted to rest her head on his lap, and visit with him quietly. But her intuition warned against it. She knew, somehow, that her presence would bring him more pain than comfort. If she truly did love him, the best way she could demonstrate it was by letting him have the time he needed, without aggravating his already debilitated condition.

He had made her torque into an armlet, which he wore on his left bicep. While some interpreted it to be his public statement of dominance, she knew differently. It was merely his way of showing that he had not lost faith in her, and thus, he wore it on the arm closest to his heart.

With the arrival of autumn and the festival of Samhain, Kordelina's sessions with Saturnalia had accelerated to a level of spiritual expertise. Since she was no longer hindered by her warrior's duties, and spent most of her time caring for the horses Aonghus could not yet ride, she was given to long periods of meditation and works of sorcery.

It was in these trance-like states that she enjoyed the most freedom because in her mind, she could travel unhindered to any place she wished. Sometimes, she would seek out the places where she and Aonghus used to play as children. During those times, she would try to contact him telepathically, and somehow include him in her experience. Often it was the only release she had from the monotony of daily life, and she had come to adore Saturnalia's visits because of it.

The old woman she had originally lived with was named Airann. She was a feeble old crone who died shortly after the harvest. Ignoring the edict which forbade the indulgence of speech, Airann had gone to great lengths to share much of the tribal histories that Kordelina had never heard before. She went into considerable detail in relating the story of a King name Oisil, who had once ruled their tribe. She gave wonderful descriptions of his two sons, Roilan and Donnach, and related how they had once tried to develop a political affiliation with Rome. Airann also explained the story of the black Druidess, Deireadh, and Kordelina had surmised on her own that she was the one whose cave she used to visit while in solitude. The young girl had confided to Airann about the apparitions she had seen of her, and Airann had reassured her that Kordelina's soul was strong and rooted in good, and that she should never fear such things.

On the night Airann died, she called Kordelina into her chamber. She was drifting in and out of consciousness by then, but before she transcended into the Otherworld, she held Kordelina's hand in her crooked fingers and looked at her with an unsettling expression.

"You are the vision of Deireadh before she crossed over," she whispered to her. "I knew Deireadh, and I knew your mother, as well."

Then the breath went out of her body. Kordelina never repeated what the woman had said, but she found it strangely comforting that someone knew her real mother, and that the two of them had at least shared an acquaintance with the same person once in their lifetimes.

As Kordelina had predicted, the Chieftain was inhospitable and unpleasant in the beginning of her servitude, but as the months went by and the seasons changed, so did his ire mellow. He left Kordelina to care for the horses and to pursue her studies with Saturnalia.

Of her family members, only Niall visited her every day. He was so sincere and happy to spend time with her that Kordelina could not help but be thankful for him. He would wait quietly in her room, sometimes bringing food their mother had prepared, and he would tell her everything going on in the tribe.

Lately, it had mostly concerned the Romans. There had been many incidents of Caesar's scouting parties landing on their shores, and their tribe and many others were now posting guards to keep watch throughout the night. He said that most of the Imperialists had either been killed or turned back, but it had happened with such frequency that their father had told him an invasion was certainly in the future. There had also been much unrest with the surrounding tribes, and since the battle in the clearing, many small skirmishes had taken place.

Hearing this, Kordelina could not help but worry that Aonghus was still too weak to endure any challenge for his authority. Solomon was troubled by this, too, because he had insisted that Aonghus' health be fully restored before he assumed power. The Chieftain found it very difficult to see the thin, frail-looking warrior still helpless and dependent. The short walks Aonghus took were noticeably draining, and he was so withered looking for a time that even Kordelina could barely stand the sight of his suffering.

Yet as the moon waxed and waned many times, he was gradually revitalized. And as he regained his stature, so too had the light returned to Solomon's eyes. It brought even greater satisfaction to both of them because they knew that Aonghus had done it without the use of the wormwood and cowbane that had once been such a vice.

Often, when Kordelina saw Aonghus gazing pensively out at the woods, or staring up at the sky, she wondered if he was thinking of Klannad and missing her. She now realized what a lovely and forgiving creature she really was. And whether it was true love, such as she had witnessed in Edainne and Diarmudd, or just a fanciful affair, she had been able to make Aonghus happy.

This became more evident when she saw the way he behaved when Bracorina was present. He was impatient and demanding of her, oftentimes sending her home as soon as she arrived. He would tell her that he wanted no visitors on that day, and no matter how Bracorina tried to dissuade him, he would order her to leave his presence. The woman had only spent the night with him a handful of occasions, and when she did, Kordelina never heard laughter in the house.

Many times during Aonghus' recovery, he and Solomon would share long visits in the sunshine. They would eat bread and drink wine, and have conversations about specific desires for their people, and even about the meaning of life. Often they would reminisce about the past, and both would laugh freely, and affectionately pat each other on the back at their recollections. At those moments, the two looked actually happy and free of the present problems with Rome and the surrounding clans.

There had been many meetings concerning these problems between the warriors and the elders, and that was the case on this particular afternoon. Mostly warriors filtered into Solomon's estate, accompanied by a few of the elders. Saturnalia was not present; Jara had arrived the day before, and had caused her much distress with matters of the holy order.

It was only a few weeks until the festival of Brigantia, and a nearly robust Aonghus presided over the gathering. All present had come together to consider the intentions of the hostile clans surrounding them. The men had assembled in the main chamber, some sitting and others standing near the hearth or by the open window. The one thing they all shared was a common dread on their faces.

"They want war," Conn stated as he paced in front of Aonghus, who was sitting in the center of the room next to Solomon. "They are slowly moving into our territory, and if we do not make some show of strength, they are going to perceive us as afraid to fight. If that happens, they will make an outright assault on our settlement."

"I do know that this clan that has posted warriors on our borders, is aligned with the clan to the north of us," Berrig added. He had taken his regular spot behind Solomon, and the two leather-faced warriors who had once looked menacing, now appeared stately and wise in comparison to the others. "If we attack them, we will also bring on their wrath. Our warriors are not strong enough to handle an assault from both sides. We can only be victorious if we take them on one at a time."

Conn glared at Berrig a moment, then folded his arms across his chest and addressed Aonghus.

"Do you agree with him?" he asked, with hostility. "Are you, also, afraid that we are not strong enough to withstand war?"

Aonghus stared back at him a moment as though he were trying to understand his belligerence. It was no secret that their friendship had diminished since he had become involved with Saturnalia. The tension between Aonghus and the Druidess had risen to intolerable heights since his injury, and Conn interpreted it as a personal affront. Not only that, but Aonghus knew that Conn was ambitious, and that ambition was being nourished by the Druidess' political aspirations. Actually, he had long since anticipated Conn challenging his power, especially during a time when it was obvious that Aonghus was not well enough to survive it.

"I think Berrig's assessment of our fighting power is correct," he stated flatly. "We have the might to defeat one tribe, but not two at the same time."

Conn laughed sarcastically. "It is not what I would have expected from you, Aonghus. I thought your desire was to increase our territory, not give it away."

Aonghus remained decidedly calm and unaffected by his antagonism. "I am suspicious," he said, ignoring the comment. "I think that perhaps these two tribes do not perceive Rome to be the threat it is. I wonder if perhaps Caesar would have us war among ourselves so that all tribes would be weakened, and we would be a minor imposition, should they decide to invade. Conn, I question if that might not be your intention as well."

Conn's brown eyes quickly looked away from him, then he regained his confidence, and took a step closer. Since Aonghus was sitting, Conn towered intimidatingly over him.

"I would like you to make clear that of which you speak," he challenged.

Aonghus looked at him with cold blue eyes. "What I am speaking of is that I think your speculations may be slanted," he answered. "And I think your ambition outweighs your better judgment at this time."

An arrogant smile crossed Conn's lips. "And I think your courage flowed out of you with the blood you spilled in battle. It must have seeped into the ground beneath the tree where Solomon rescued you," he countered. "Perhaps you should go back to that same tree in whose shade you sought refuge, and chew on its bark, and perhaps then you will be nourished by your lost bravery."

Aonghus did not even have to wait for him to finish his sentence to realize that it was only a matter of time before he would have to do away with Conn. It was irrelevant that at one time they had fought the Romans side by side. What was of overpowering importance was that, politically, Aonghus could not afford to have someone who knew so much about him moving covertly behind his back. Conn had killed Blathnaid, and Aonghus had never forgotten that. Whether he owed favors to the Imperialists or not, no one could be sure that they had been paid with that one deed. More than that, Conn had been present when Aonghus had broken a devout tribal law, one that was punishable by death. He was the only person who knew that he had gone into the cave the night of Kordelina's anointing.

Of all the warriors, Aonghus had always known it would be Conn who would try to usurp his rule. From the time they were boys, Conn had always made a point to openly defy his favored position as heir to Solomon's power. It had been only briefly suppressed during the years they fought the Imperialists. At that time, neither had anything to gain and only their lives to lose.

If Conn wanted to invalidate him, this would be the time to do it. Aonghus had not yet fully regained his strength, and was still vulnerable both physically and politically. He was aware there was some question in the minds of his kinsmen as to how much of his courage remained intact after such a vivid brush with death.

The situation with Kordelina had not helped him earn his tribe's confidence either. Even though he had sentenced her for her crime, and made a public display of her punishment, they still remembered that he had gone against their wishes in anointing her. He had demanded, even threatened them to approve it, and it had evolved into a travesty. Now he was viewed as a warrior who had not only resisted the wisdom of the elders, but had done it to his own harm. Raising a competent foster was very important for a future ruler, and Aonghus had failed miserably at it.

"Assuming that we do not have the manpower to take on both tribes at once, Conn, what then would you suggest?" he inquired, making a point of disregarding his insult.

Conn tilted his head back slightly to look down his nose at Aonghus. "There are many Trinovantes and Ordovices who would fight," he answered confidently. "My suggestion is that we take advantage of the great number of refugees surrounding us, and bolster our tribe with hired warriors."

Aonghus almost laughed at his proposition. It was as if history was repeating itself in front of his eyes. Lifting his brows, he looked at Solomon, Berrig, and the older warriors as if to indicate how ridiculous the suggestion was.

"Then I should ask the rest of you, and you Chieftain, how seriously should we consider the solution Conn has stated?" he addressed them.

Pwyll shook his head, and rose to his feet to face Conn. The older man was in direct contrast to the warrior. His face was wrinkled with age, and his hair and beard were almost entirely grey. He still possessed the compassionate eyes of his father, Donnach, and when he looked at Conn, Aonghus could envision his childhood remembrance of the King.

"I am the largest landholder in this tribe," he stated. "I have more to lose than any man here, save the Chieftain, and I have more wealth to purchase fighting power than anyone else, as well. I refuse to hire any men outside of this tribe for I know, from experience, what comes from manipulations of men such as you. You would have us think that you are seeking to protect us, but it is only your way of gathering a stable of battlers to support your desire for insurrection. For I do agree with Aonghus when he says that Rome would have us kill each other so that they may assume our land. And I feel, in my heart, that your ambition in resisting Rome is not as fervent as your desire to rule this territory."

Conn looked at him angrily for a moment, then a smile came to his face.

"I am sorry, Pwyll," he replied. "But you misinterpret my motives. I seek only to protect my kinsmen."

"And rule them as well," Pwyll added. "Warrior, more than you can ever know has gone on in this tribe. And there are greater loyalties that make up its core than you can ever overcome, even with the support of your Druidess."

Pwyll promptly turned, and went back to where he had been sitting, leaving the offended warrior standing in the center of the room. Neither Aonghus or Solomon spoke; both reasoned it was better to let this be the arena to voice the intentions of the others.

"I am in agreement with Pwyll," Berrig said. "Perhaps Conn does not know that such a thing was proposed before, and it was resisted to the good of our tribe. For I have not forgotten the deeds of Laden or Deireadh, and the sacrifices the good King Donnach had to make for his people still reign in my heart. So I will come out against this proposition of including the Trinovantes and Ordovices because it reeks of ill-fortune."

"I am of the same opinion," Turg announced from his place by the window. "Conn, I have long since loved you as my own. I have raised you as my foster, and would wish that the gods bestow only goodness upon you. I knew nothing of this tribe before it took me in, so the actions of Laden and his cohorts are foreign to me.

But this tribe did embrace me, and did give me a home when I had none, and it is not my desire to destroy it needlessly. My opinion is that we avoid petty entanglements with the clans on either side, and that we remain strong to fight the Romans."

Conn put his hands on his hips and looked around the room in disgust. "I think you have all become too complacent, and have let yourselves grow soft," he responded indignantly. "I have no cause for personal gain or insurrection. I want only to protect my boundaries. My worries are not with Rome, for we have turned them back each time they have come. My concerns are with the tribal borders, and if the mass of you wish to sit back and allow this clan's territory to shrink, there is little I can do about it."

He fixed his gaze on Solomon, and shook his head. "This warrior you protect has done more to abstain from our laws than he has to uphold them," he said bitterly. "But then, that is an altogether different matter."

Solomon returned his stare with fiery eyes. "You may go now, Conn," he said. "We will consider such things another time."

Embarassment rose in Conn's cheeks as he quickly bowed and exited the room. He was followed, shortly thereafter, by the others, leaving Aonghus and Solomon to speak in private.

"I feel as though I am reliving a nightmare," Solomon said to Aonghus.

Aonghus went to the window to get some air. "I know," he agreed. "I suppose men like Laden and Conn are not unique, and perhaps men like us are quite common, as well."

"What do you mean?" Solomon questioned, sitting back and putting both hands behind his head.

"I mean only that we think we are doing good, and so does Conn," he replied, catching sight of Kordelina near the barn.

She had apparently just finished the afternoon feeding of the livestock, and was now amusing herself by throwing a stick for one of Solomon's hounds. Her cheeks were a lovely rose color from the chilly air, and her long hair hung loosely down her back. She was dressed in servants' clothing, plain woolen trousers and a fur-lined jerkin. He could hear her giggling as she held the stick out at arm's length, and the dog jumped in the air trying to take it from her. Then she threw it as far as she could, and laughed again as the animal caught it before it touched the ground. Seeing her enjoy something so simple made him realize that all the enthusiasm of his youth had dwindled into petty legalities.

"If Conn is allowed to do as he wishes, you and all our tribesmen will be purchasing him an army that he will use for our people's demise," Solomon told him. "He is a sly one. He would have us think that these mercenaries are to fight for us, but I dare say that they would be our undoing."

Aonghus nodded. "Conn has always had his own matters at hand, and you are right, they are not for our betterment, but his own. I hope Saturnalia realizes that, as well. She is only one more thing for him to exploit."

Solomon sighed. "The eyes of love are many times unclear," he offered.

Aonghus looked at him out of the corner of his eye. "Are they really?" he replied, staring outside again. "I do not believe that. I think that the eyes of love are the only true vision we have. Such is the reason for you waiting for the Druidess and not taking another wife. You keep her alive in your heart, but I do not condemn you for that."

Solomon was too stunned by his statement to respond. What Aonghus was saying was true. He was waiting for Saturnalia to tire of the young warrior and find her way back to him—a wish he had never voiced.

"You know, I used to find her quite lovely," Aonghus went on, thoughtfully. "I remember that when I could not find beauty in loving Bracorina, I would imagine I was making love to Saturnalia, instead. Strange, how I only just remembered that."

He gave an embarrassed chuckle. "Forgive me," he added, running his fingers through his hair. "I do not know what made me say that. I guess it came to me so suddenly that I did not consider you might be offended."

"Not at all," Solomon said, after thinking about it a moment. "I still find her lovely."

Aonghus laughed, then slowly made his way across the room to the door. "I know you do, Chieftain. Strange how a man's idea of his true love never changes," he answered, as he exited through the main entryway.

He walked through the yard to where Kordelina still stood waiting for the hound to bring the stick back to her. Stopping a short distance behind her, he remained silent as he watched her pick up the gnarled piece of wood and throw it again. She was wearing that jubilant, toothy smile that so resembled her father, and the light in her eyes, from the gray winter sky, made them look all the more mysterious.

She sensed he was near, because without turning around to look at him, she started hurriedly toward the barn. For a moment, he considered letting her go, but he followed her instead.

It had been so long since they had spoken. But Aonghus believed that it was time to heal their differences. He wanted to tell her how sorry he was, wanted to explain to her exactly why it had come about. He was well enough now to be able to handle the pain of hearing her say his name, and of gazing into her eyes.

CHAPTER TWENTY-ONE

Kordelina disappeared so quickly that Aonghus had to run after her. When he entered the barn, it took a moment for his eyes to adjust to the shadows. After they had, he saw she was more than halfway to the back exit. He tried to open his mouth to call her name, but it stuck in his throat, and he started running after her again.

She had her hand on the door latch when he reached her, and he instinctively held the wooden bar down to prevent the door from opening. At his action, Kordelina stood still, and kept her head bowed so he could not see her eyes.

Aonghus could feel a wild, nervous energy at being so near to her after such a long time. A current of unbridled desire rushed through him, and for a moment, he could do nothing but stare at her profile. He saw her hand start to tremble, but when he tried to touch it, she jerked it away, and crossed her arms defensively in front of her. He could hear the rustling of footsteps behind him as two of the other grooms walked into the shedrow to see what was happening. Glancing over his shoulder at them, Aonghus could see their vague, unreadable expressions, and he felt suddenly awkward.

"Good warrior," the older groom addressed him. "Has she done something wrong that you would seek to discipline her? Kordelina is a good worker, and I am sure she meant you no harm."

Aonghus licked his dry lips, and tried to look composed as he faced the man. "I do not seek discipline," he replied, nervously clearing his throat. "I was only going to ask the maid to saddle Macha and Lir. I will be waiting outside for them."

He looked back at her for another moment, then rubbing the back of his neck with one hand, he opened the barn door, and stepped past her.

Kordelina was shaking so badly that the other two men had to help her prepare the horses. It was apparent that she was flustered, and they did not want Aonghus to wait any longer than was necessary. When she emerged to face the fading winter afternoon, Aonghus was waiting just outside the door. She could feel him watching her, trying to get her to look at him, but she could not.

She held onto Lir firmly as he mounted, and the animal was so excited to have his master in the saddle, that he immediately started prancing in place. Kordelina broke into a smile at his reaction as she held out Macha's reins for Aonghus to grab hold of.

"I would like you to come with me," he said softly, then before she could refuse him, he turned his horse and started out the gate.

Gathering a handful of mane, Kordelina climbed atop the mare, and filled with misgivings, followed. She stayed far behind the warrior and his steed. More than once, the excited stallion reared on two legs, and squealed his delight at having Aonghus as his mount. As he did this, Kordelina saw Aonghus wince with pain. There was one time when the stallion threw his head back with such vigor that it caused him to jolt in his seat. Aside from these few incidences, the warrior was simply beaming at his horse's antics.

At one point, Aonghus allowed him a loose rein, and let him gallop as far as he wished. Kordelina did the same, letting the cold evening breeze chill her face as she tried to release her rising tension.

The shiny bay horse finally halted at a watering pond, but he approached it with such fervor that all the other wild animals drinking there scattered in an instant. Aonghus was sweating and out of breath as he slumped slightly forward, and gripped his side with one hand. At first, he appeared to be in great pain, but when Kordelina got closer, she could tell that his eyes still possessed a wonderfully carefree expression.

He dismounted carefully, then walked over to a rock, and took a seat. His breathing was still labored as he dropped his chin to his chest and tried to slow it down. Both arms were wrapped around his torso, but his countenance was glowing.

"You have probably kept him too fit," he said with labored breath. "He is very difficult for me to handle. Maybe we should have let him rest the same amount of time as me. At least then we would be in command of each other."

Kordelina was unsure if Aonghus was talking to her directly, or just thinking out loud, so she did not reply.

Straightening up, Aonghus took a deep breath, then released it. He did this repeatedly until his respiration was normal enough for him to continue to speak.

"Do you want to know why I brought you here?" he asked.

Kordelina shrugged, but still would not meet his eyes.

"You may speak, Kordelina; you do not need permission with me," he offered. "Now please, come sit with me awhile."

"No, Aonghus," she softly refused. "I do not wish to sit beside you. I would like to return to my quarters."

The sound of her speaking his name made him ravenous for her. All of the emotions he thought he had quelled came rushing back at him so suddenly that for a moment, he was disoriented.

"Please, Kordelina," he gently persuaded. "Indulge me for a time."

Kordelina considered his words a moment, then climbed out of the saddle and reluctantly sat down a short distance away from him.

"You really would have nothing to do with me now, would you not?" he asked, obviously hurt by her actions.

Kordelina nodded, but did not speak. She could feel Aonghus' joy evaporate as he looked away from her and stared straight ahead.

"You are no doubt angry about all that has happened?" he asked.

"Not angry. I have no cause to be angry," she replied earnestly. "I failed you, and you were within your right to punish me for it."

"I had no choice," he responded in a troubled tone. "The clan wanted you dead, and I could not let that happen. This was the only way that I could prevent them from hurting you, and still appease them."

"You had a choice. You always have a choice," she said, wringing her hands. It was so awful, yet so thrilling to hear him speak to her. The safety in the sound of his voice evoked a dreadful longing inside her. To see him now sitting beside her, made simply being in his presence an experience of curious excitement. "You could have told them the truth. At least then, if they had killed me, I would not have had to watch my care and respect for you slowly wither away. I would have been dead, but that death would have been easier than making my heart die within my body while my body is still alive. That is in the past now—but there is one thing I wish for you to know."

"What is that?" he asked, nervously rubbing the tops of his thighs.

"On that day when you were hurt, I left the battle, but not because I feared for my own life. I could not bear to see the life drain out of you while I helplessly watched," she said, her voice cracking with emotion. "And I would not give your horse over to another, so I took him where he would be safe. That is all I wanted to say. I do not care what the tribe thinks of me, and a part of me no longer cares what you think, either. For I am only what I have always been, and all the punishment and public rebuke in the world will not alter the spirit that dwells within me. If they wish to make me suffer for it even further, so be it, because I can do nothing to prevent it."

Aonghus cocked his head to one side, and eyed her remorsefully. He was torn between crying and restraining the relentless fire surfacing from inside of him. He tried desperately to stay collected.

"This has made you bitter," he said quietly.

"Not bitter, only smarter," she said, folding her hands in front of her.

She tilted her head down slightly, and he was enamored of the gentle bend of her velvety soft neck. It was like a vine of paradise he could nibble on while he drifted into the blissfulness of her scent.

"I feel nothing for these people who needed to see me shamed for my deeds," he heard her say. "It is their lack, not mine, that makes them rebuke what they do not understand. I do not hate them for it, because I have never loved them. And I know that of all the souls who have come to this world, I am not the only one who has experienced this. Still, I would rather have it be so, because to be what they want is to force myself into deception. That is what they have done with you. You have become a hypocrite, and I pity you for it."

A terrible grief washed over Aonghus. It was as if he were locked inside himself, and could not get out.

"Then you are saying you do not care for me any longer?" he asked humbly.

Kordelina covered her mouth with her hand, as though she regretted saying it, and shook her head. "No, Aonghus," she answered meekly. "What was once joy at the sight of you has turned into pain, but it is the pain of life. I used to believe that there was nothing you would not do for me, but I was wrong: you will never speak the truth to me. You will never be able to allow me to be free."

Aonghus could not take his eyes off her as she spoke. She looked so delicate, yet what coursed through her was an incredibly fierce heart. He watched her eyes move over him as though mentally trying to caress him with her vision, then she offered him a tiny, sad smile.

"May I go now?" she whispered.

Aonghus put his face in his hands, and looked down at the earth between his knees. He could see the small fragments of dried leaves rustle with the evening wind and the pale cast of the dormant grass. Then the whole world dimmed before him, and he began to feel lightheaded. He shut his eyes for a moment. He wanted to talk to her more, but her subtle hostility made him reconsider. There was something different about her, something that refused to yield to him. Rather than aggravate a situation he wanted only to nurture, he gave her a small nod that she was free to go.

He could sense her in front of him, and for a moment, he thought she had reconsidered leaving. He wanted to raise his head to look at her, but it felt numb and heavy. Then he heard her soft footsteps as she moved away from him, and his heart swelled with despair.

Aonghus stayed in the same spot long after darkness had set in and a light mist had begun to fall. He did not understand why her words had seemed so brutal, but they had left him drained. She was almost foreign to him now; there seemed to be an intrinsic being that had developed and grown into one so different from what he remembered. No longer did she trust and believe in every word he told her. Instead, she was a sensual creature who also bulged with inner power.

He thought of the disturbing darkness in her eyes when she looked at him. It was a shadowy reflection that left him helpless.

As he mused over their meeting, he tried to find some relief in the thought that he should not be afraid to lose what was never meant to be his. Perhaps Kordelina really was over him now; perhaps these months that he thought she was waiting for him, she was instead purging herself of him. Did she really mean what she said about him never allowing her to go free? He felt his head start to pound at the thought of it. It caused such excruciating pain that for a moment, Aonghus thought he would lose consciousness.

With the flat of his palms, he pressed his temples, hoping it would ease the ache. It had been months since he had experienced such an episode, and he wanted to stop it before it got worse.

"Do not think about it," he told himself. "Quiet yourself for a little while."

The ringing in his ears grew louder, and he became dizzy. Still rubbing his temples, he stared straight ahead into the shadowy grove, and for a moment, he thought he glimpsed tortured faces imprinted on the tree trunks. Visions of skulls lurked in the shadowy recesses of the bark, and he thought he was being flanked by glowing, insidious beings. He shut his eyes hard to drive the illusion out of his mind. When he opened them again, everything had disappeared, but he still had the feeling of many eyes invisibly fixed upon him.

Aonghus guiltily thirsted for the herbal potion and the delirium the mixture could bring; he wanted desperately to feel the euphoria. Shaking his head, he tried to reason with himself that he had worked too hard to achieve this state of sobriety, and should not give it up so easily.

Looking down on the fine droplets of water on his hands, he was fascinated by the way the transparent gems seemed to sizzle with his body heat. He wished Kordelina had not left him like this, wished she was there to remind him why he had to remain sober. For Aonghus knew if he surrendered to his addiction, he would do more damage than was reparable in a single lifetime.

"You must clear your mind," he told himself. "You have to be stronger."

Lir walked slowly up to Aonghus, and with ears pricked forward, looked directly at him.

"I need allies," he said to the horse. "I have lost most of them, and I need to gain them back again."

Lir let out a sigh, and started pawing the ground with one hoof.

"I must regain the trust of those near to me," he said, softly ignoring Lir's impatient gesture. "This tribe is important, and I should remember that more than once I have been willing to lay down my life for it. Conn must not take power because we will be the weaker for it. I can stop him. I know I can find a way to stop him. As for Saturnalia, she is still a woman, and she can be enticed into favors. I should not have forgotten that. I will make her want to help me, and make her desire to see Kordelina realize her true happiness—but it will take all of my cunning to do it."

He stood up slowly, and brushed the dirt from his damp breeches. Reaching out, he patted Lir's forehead.

"I am talking to horses now," he said, slightly embarrassed. "I'm as bad as Kordelina."

He stopped to consider what he had said. "Bad as Kordelina, what an untruth that is. Oh, my precious one, there will be a time for us, but it is not now. I will give you your freedom, and risk that one day you will return to me at your will. I will make Saturnalia help me do it.

"There is a way to accomplish it, but I must be in command of myself. I cannot afford to allow the stirring you cause within my soul could condemn us both if harvested before its time. You must somehow trust in my love for you, and understand that the well-being of our people still weighs heavily upon me. Yet, I do understand that such a divine soul as you cannot be guided by untruths, so I must not burden you with deceptions that I have yet to concoct. You are unaccustomed to such things as this. I can only pray to the heavens, Kordelina, that when I have done all that I must for my people, and brought down that which divides us now, you will still find me pleasing in your sight."

He mounted his horse so slowly that Lir was already in motion by the time he threw his leg over his broad back. Aonghus lurched forward and grunted at the sudden stab of pain in his side, but by the time he was at a full trot, it had passed; so too had the hallucinations, and Aonghus felt the traces of wholeness start to return.

When he entered the manor, he met a very well-dressed Solomon at the gate. The Chieftain was on horseback.

"You can ride again," he commented with a broad smile. "I am pleased because the atmosphere in the village might call for it sooner than we think."

Aonghus nodded his head, and looked at him warily. "Such unrest should be commonplace now," he remarked. "Have you a special meeting? A maid perhaps is the reason for such adornment?"

Solomon rolled his eyes. "If I have come to the age when Jara is considered a fair maid for me, death cannot be far off. I have to meet with the Druidesses, and to be advised of the decisions of the order. It comes with the title, you know."

Aonghus shifted in his saddle. "Could you then relay to Saturnalia, that I would like to see her privately as soon as she is able?" he asked.

Solomon cast him a questioning gaze. "Are you that ready for battle?" he jested.

"No," Aonghus replied sincerely. "I want no more battle. If we are to face troubled times ahead, healing the rift between us will benefit us both. I want to try to ease our differences now."

"Very well," the Chieftain said. "I will tell her, but I dare say with Jara present, it could be well into the night before she will be free to meet with you."

"Tell her that is fine," Aonghus responded, instinctively looking to the barn to see if Kordelina was there. "Tell her I will meet her when and where she likes. Good luck, Chieftain."

ChAPCER CWENCY-CWO

he succulent scent of roasted pork greeted Aonghus as he entered the house. The room was warm and inviting, and he could feel the hunger pangs in his stomach as he removed his cloak. A handmaid came to assist him, carefully hanging the fur-lined cloak and helping him remove the thick leather belt from around his waist. He thanked her quietly as she handed him a loose woolen tunic. Then he walked into the main chamber, and sat down by the hearth. He did not bother to put on the garment because the heat from the fire felt too good against his bare skin.

Setting a drinking flask in front of him, the servant filled it with wine, and Aonghus motioned to leave the full vessel within reach. He was fatigued from trying to handle Lir; his muscles in his back were tight, and his hands ached from gripping the reins so hard. He noticed his fingers were the color of bleached linen, and hating the sight, he rubbed them together vigorously. Then he grabbed his chalice, and with one swallow, emptied it. Reaching over for more, he did not bother to fill his cup, but instead, drank the wine out of the vessel. He loved the taste of the hearty, full-bodied nectar rolling down his throat, and could already feel it start to settle in his empty stomach.

By the time his dinner was served, he had finished the wine and asked for more. He wanted to smother his emotions, wanted to dull the harsh edge of this present reality. He wished Solomon had not gone. It would have been such a relief to have someone to talk to—someone to keep him focused on the responsibilities of his people, not the afflictions of his heart.

Taking a bite of meat, he stared off into oblivion as he chewed. He was thinking of the soft whispering of Kordelina's voice and fantasizing about his seduction of her. He could see himself enveloped by the particles of her body, like she was a beam of light whose glow was all encompassing. Then in one wondrous flash, he could feel her warm hands touching him ever so lightly that his skin began to tingle. It was an overpowering presence, as though she were fondling him from the inside out.

Suddenly the sensual feeling was gone, and his anger and misery over not being able to consummate his love boiled within him. A pain stabbed in his chest, and he pressed one palm over his heart until it passed. For an instant, he wished he were able to visit Klannad to release this passion in the safety of her chamber. She always understood such things.

Then he slammed his fist down, and tried to regain control of himself. There was more at stake than simple desire, and he had to find a means of silencing this primal need for release. He understood that for him to get all he wanted out of this situation, he was going to have to re-establish a trusting relationship with Saturnalia.

Long ago, they had been valued allies, even if it was a pact formed on deception alone. He knew she was now under Conn's influence, that she was supportive of him not as much politically as she was emotionally. It was the nature of love to be so, and he could not fault her for it, nor could he fault her for insisting that he honor his vow about Kordelina. After all, Saturnalia was a Druidess, and her duty was to uphold the laws and customs of her people. She believed in them wholeheartedly, and had it not been for his personal feelings about Kordelina, he would have commended her integrity.

He could vaguely recall the day when Deireadh had come back to this house to visit Solomon. It was an afternoon when he and the Chieftain had returned from a hunt. He was disgusted by the way Solomon submitted himself to his estranged wife, dropping to his knees in front of her, and burying his face in the round of her belly. It seemed wrong to him now to have judged the Chieftain so harshly because at this moment, Aonghus was fighting his urge to do the very same thing.

If he had his way, he would go to Kordelina and speak the truth about her parentage: to tell her she was really a princess, not a servant; that her father was the man to whom he had been devoted all of his life, and to have his only daughter in marriage was his ultimate dream. He would confide to her the sentimental dream he had of being at her side as she birthed him a son, then proudly setting the newborn heir in front of Solomon for him to admire. At night, they would sleep with their child nestled between them, and he would be a magnificent blending of both their souls.

He could easily envision Kordelina with their baby, imagining the way she would cradle him in her arms while he nursed. And he pictured himself taking great pride in educating his son to be a ruler.

Still, he knew Kordelina. If he revealed everything, she would despise his reasoning because she had never honored the laws, only rebelled against them. And if he told her that it was Saturnalia who prevented him from telling her, she would think him a liar. Kordelina was far too loyal to the Druidess to rise against her.

Aonghus emptied the holder of wine once more, and as he set it down, he realized he was crying. Rubbing his eyes with his fingertips, he tried to suppress his tears, but they flowed without ceasing. He felt as if he were going to burst with his despondency, but he smothered the sound of his pain so his servants would not hear. What kind of a leader would he appear to be then? Certainly rumor of him sitting in front of the fire, getting drunk, and weeping would spread through the settlement, and with the action he was about to take, he could not afford that.

There were certainly turbulent months ahead: war with Rome, and much bargaining between their nations. He truly believed that he was the warrior who could see them through this, and the one who could make good the promises of his forefathers. The Celtic people had always held themselves in high esteem, and he wanted to be sure that Caesar did the same.

He did not know how long he had been sitting there before he realized his food was cold, and he had downed two more flasks of wine. He had not even been aware of the servants bringing it to him. All he knew was that it would take a great amount of the drink before he could endure doing what he was about to do.

Sitting near to the fire now, he ran his hand across his chest, and noticed he was sweating. How he dreaded going into Kordelina's room to tell her that she had to leave him. How would she ever understand that he could not confide to her what action he was about to take because he did not yet know himself? The only thing he could be certain of was that if she was too close by, his desire for her would obstruct all reason.

Allowing Kordelina—the one who, in the tribe's eyes, left him to die—her freedom would make him a hero in the eyes of his kinsmen. But in his heart, he did not want to risk that she might find a life away from him. He wished Solomon had returned so he could tell the Chieftain he was going to let her go, and Solomon would be there to make sure that this was exactly what he did. If she were an enemy, it would have been easy; but she was his obsession.

Rising to his feet, he swayed dizzily from side to side. Bracing himself against the wall, he waited for the room to stop spinning before he started for the door. His stomach was bitter with despair, and his body was numb. He was afraid of what he might do when he was alone with her, and for a moment, he hated her for it.

He was still perspiring when he walked out into the rain. It was so dark that he stumbled once, and drunkenly fell to his knees. He felt a sickness rising in him, and he did not know if it was from distress or from all the wine he had consumed.

By the time he pulled himself to his feet, and reached the small room off the side of the barn where Kordelina lived, he was shivering so badly that he stood outside the door for a long moment telling himself that what he had to do was for the best.

"It is only for a little while," he reassured himself. "Only until I can get everything straightened out."

He knocked lightly, and when he heard her voice bidding him to enter, he thought his heart had stopped completely.

Taking in a breath of cold air, he slowly opened the door and entered. He did not shut it behind him because he did not trust himself. The room was filled with the orange glow of the hearth for illumination. He saw her standing near the window, wearing a loose-fitting sleeping frock. He walked a few steps closer until her face was visible.

When he focused on her almond-shaped eyes and her beautifully sculpted face, he wished he had not come. She was too lovely, and it made him ache just to look at her. How he cursed himself at that moment for overestimating his ability to resist her, as he stood groping for his diminishing strength. His hair was disheveled and loose strands hung in his face. His eyes were red and tormented, his cheeks taut. His whole manner reflected weary confusion.

Kordelina stepped away from her spot at the window to face him. She knew by his expression that whatever he was about to say to her was something she did not wish to hear. Wrapping her arms around herself, she bit her lower lip and waited impatiently for him to speak. Aonghus remained still for a time, unaware that the dim firelight made him appear so bewildered.

"Take your freedom," he said in a lifeless voice, "and your horse. You are no longer in my debt, and you should go home now."

Kordelina moved closer to get a better look at him. His voice sounded empty; she was unable to determine if he really meant it, or was only drunk.

"I keep hearing what you said about why you did not bring me my horse," he sighed as the words stuck in his throat. "And I must tell you that I am sorry. Sorry for making a spectacle of you and sorry for encouraging you to care for me in a way that I cannot fulfill. It was wrong.

"I go over it endlessly in my mind, trying to understand why I did it. For you to become a warrior was absurd. You are a beautiful girl, Kordelina, and you should have been a princess, instead. When I took you in my charge, I believe I did it out of my own selfishness. I enjoyed your deep devotion to me and you brought me such happiness all these years that I wanted to find a way to keep you to myself. Deep down, I knew you were not a child anymore, and out of my own covetousness, I toyed with your desires to suit my own wishes. I should have refused you in the beginning, and should have let you live the life a young girl deserves. So you are free. Your debt is paid."

Kordelina stepped even nearer so that she could see his eyes. His words caused her more sorrow than she had experienced on the day she was dealt her punishment.

"I want freedom, but only if it is the freedom to be with you," she replied softly. "I have lived the life that I wanted to live except for one thing, I cannot be yours. However unreasonable or foolish it may sound, you must believe that there is not a man who has been born beneath the heavens that could ever compare to you. My love has, perhaps, shaped me in odd ways, and provoked me to perform deeds peculiar from other women. Still, neither death nor punishment could ever cause me to forsake what is in my heart, and that is that I love you more than spirits can lament."

Her honest words made Aonghus feel like he was dying inside. With the same intuitive precision that she could make a kill, Kordelina was gutting him alive.

"No!" he shouted. "You do not understand! We can no longer be a part of each other's lives the way we once were. What has happened between us has made it impossible to ever recapture such things as we used to know. You are a woman, not a child. You are not deceived in what your beauty can bring you, nor am I. I have to let you go. It is not what I want, but this must be the time."

Undaunted by his display, she started toward him again. The golden tint around her body made her a strange illusion in his drunken sight.

"It is only time to speak the truth to each other," she insisted, stopping a few paces in front of him. Her eyes were clear, and her manner determined. "You do not want me to leave. Even when you are angry with me, you are still glad I am here. How is it that we have come to such a place as this where loving is a transgression, and the only redemption is found in untruths? It is a mystery to me, for I know by the light in your eyes that if I were to leave you, it would be more sorrow that you could endure. If I were to choose another man to whom I would share myself, I would be more guilty of trying to kill you than anything I ever failed to do on the battlefield. Why can you not love me as I am? Love me the way you have imagined it in spite of what others might think."

He stared at her supple lips as she spoke, and in the instant that he blinked his eyes and tried to clear his thoughts to speak, he found she was so close that they were almost touching. Her smooth face was so overflowing with emotion, that it consumed him.

He said nothing as he opened his arms to her, and when she put her arms around him, he could not resist pulling her nearer. The feel of her body created desire inside him; it was like a river overflowing onto parched ground.

He lightly stroked her cheeks with his trembling fingertips, and feeling her soft skin, he could not keep himself from wanting her completely. His arms slipped around her, and he embraced her roughly. Yet as he tucked his face in the round of her neck, he began kissing it ever so tenderly. Too much time and pain had passed between them.

As she rested the side of her face against the top of his head, her body submitted to him completely. "Even when I was a child you were the only one who really cared for me," she said, in a hushed, sweet voice. "When we were together, I was happy. I always wanted to go with you, and it did not matter where, just as you always wanted me to follow. That is still our desire, Aonghus. It is everyone else who keeps us apart; it is not what we want."

"I know," he sighed, holding her tighter. He could feel the throbbing of her heart burrowing to the core of him, and the rising of her breathless passion. She was so silky, so voluptuous that he was as aroused by his need to make love to her as he was by his need to protect her.

"And now you would send me away again. It is not what you want," she continued, lightly kissing his forehead.

Aonghus knew he should draw back, make himself step away from her, but it was useless. He was kissing her throat over and over, nibbling on her neck, sucking on the taste of her skin. He was engulfed by the sensation of her body next to his, and slipping his hands under her gown, he ran his palms over the outside of her thighs. Then he gathered the flesh of her meaty hips with both hands.

Hers was not the slight body of a common maid; it was robust and sensual. The only thing that seemed fragile about her was the intense honesty of her emotions.

Kordelina pressed herself into him harder. "We are meant to be. I know that, Aonghus," she said, sounding as though she were about to cry.

A wave of confusion came over him, and he despised his weakness. She was not weak; she remained steadfast to her truths and she had enough courage and honor for both of them.

"You do not understand; it is more than choice," Aonghus softly protested. Lifting his head, he looked into her stormy eyes, then fixed his gaze on her half-open lips. He was lost in his passion now. What a fool he had been to think he could refuse her.

He put his hand on the back of her neck, and crushed her mouth to his. The flavor of her lips was like a nectar that rendered him spellbound. Kordelina's head dropped back slightly, and she pushed herself against his groin in response. For what seemed an endless measure of time, he fondled her tongue with his. He could feel her palms beneath his breeches as they slid over the round of his buttocks, lightly caressing them.

He kissed her harder as his hands made their way up her rib cage until he was cupping her breasts. Their ivory fullness yielded to his grasp erotically, and he began kissing her nipples through the thin cloth of her gown.

"Aonghus, our love is pure. We can have a child. I want to have a child," he heard her whisper, and he feverishly sucked her nipples harder. She was ripe for childbearing, and the thought of making her body swell with life overwhelmed him. He would lie with her, call her precious, call her lover; he could not help himself.

Taking her in a full embrace, he felt her bare knees clamp onto either side of his hips. Holding her tightly, he carried her to her bed.

The two were thoroughly consumed by each other; they did not hear Solomon ride up, nor were they aware of his entry. He stood in the doorway staring at them in shocked silence, not knowing what to do. Their passion seemed so complete that for an instant, he thought it would be a defilement to stop them. He felt like an intruder, and his first inclination was to disappear quietly into the house, and never mention what he had seen. But when he saw Aonghus start to lift Kordelina's frock over her head, he knew if he allowed this to take place, their union would violate all emotional laws of expedience.

"Stop this!" he told them in a low, menacing tone that caused the startled lovers to pull away from each other. "It must not ever happen."

Aonghus and Kordelina were silent. A long, embarrassing moment passed as Solomon stared accusingly at Aonghus' profile.

"The two of you cannot change your worlds by fulfilling your lust," he said. "I do not care what the reasons are for such things as this. Aonghus, you should be stronger, and Kordelina, you should not offer yourself to your kin in such a way. It is not meant to be so."

Aonghus' face flushed red as he frantically sought his composure. "He is right. We cannot do this. It is destructive to us both," Aonghus said, unable to make eye contact with either Solomon or Kordelina.

Kordelina ran her hand across his face. "Yes, yes we can. He does not matter! He may be Chieftain of this tribe, but that does not give him the right to govern our hearts. If it is love we feel, then one man alone cannot condemn us for it, no matter what his title. All that matters is you and me. If you have not the strength to resist his commands, then lean on me. I can sustain us both," she said in a voice noticeably strained and on the verge of tears.

Aonghus shook his head, and glanced at Solomon for an instant, then looked away. "There is more to it than you know," he argued softly. "You must not hold this Chieftain accountable for our desires. It is not his fault. Kordelina, I want you to go home. I should not have come here; I should have stopped —"

"Stopped what? Stopped me from loving you? You cannot," she said, as she put her hand under his chin, but he turned away.

She saw his features harden and his body become rigid as he tried to step back from her to leave. Yet she adored him far too much to suffer such separation.

"Do not go, Aonghus. Stay with me, please," she pleaded, suddenly dropping to her knees in front of him.

He looked down at her bitterly. She was clutching his legs like a desperate animal. She had no strength now, no pride, and he loathed her subservience.

"Kordelina, get up," his voice was hoarse.

"I will beg if that is what you want. I only possess what is in my heart, I have no riches to offer you. I can exist alone, but I will not love another. I want a baby, Aonghus. Please let me have our baby, and I will never trouble you again," the phrases came out in hysterical sobs as she bowed her head into her folded arms. "I will leave you to wed your aristocrat if you will only give me something of my own, something of my love for you. Oh, how I wish they would have killed me that night."

"As the gods have made us, man, do something," Solomon interjected, emotionally. "You started this, now stop her suffering. If you cannot, I —"

"Enough, Chieftain!" Aonghus shouted, motioning for him to leave. "Allow us privacy, and I will take care of it."

"You had better take care of it," he heard him threaten as he turned on his heel, and left the room.

Aonghus shut his eyes tightly, swallowing the nausea rising within him. Kordelina wept hysterically, crying about children and her love for him. His heart was pounding so fiercely that it felt as if it would burst through his skin. In the next instant, he could still hear everything that was going on around him, but his mind flashed on a gruesome opening in his chest, where his heart had been ripped from his body, and the image of Kordelina, lying on the ground beside him, lamenting. It was so vivid that he thought it was actually happening. Then he placed his hand over his eyes, and shook himself back into reality.

Looking at her pitifully, he bent down and gathered her in his arms. So childlike was she that trustingly, she rested her head on his shoulder as he carried her to her bed.

Gently setting her down, he covered her with a fur and folded it back below her chin. He sat on the edge of the bed, his elbows resting on his knees, eyes downcast. He would give her as long as she needed to calm down before he said anything.

When her breathing had steadied and her tears were only a trickle, Aonghus took her hand and held it tightly.

"Do you know what I was thinking?" he did not wait for her to respond. "I was thinking about the time when you were little, and you had a nightmare. You woke up crying because you thought it was real. I told you everything would be all right, and when the sun rose, it would be the same as it was the day before. You made me promise to stay with you until you fell back to sleep, and I sat with you just like this until you did. Do you remember that?"

Kordelina's face was so pale she looked like a corpse.

"Do you remember that?" he asked, again squeezing her hand.

She nodded a response, and he reached over and stroked her hair, blinking back tears. Would she ever forgive him for this?

"If you have any love left for me, I am asking you to do the same thing now. Go back to Mother and Father, and try to forget this ever happened. Would you do that for me?" he questioned in a shaky voice.

Kordelina looked away. "I do not want to. I want to catch wild horses with you again; I want to make you laugh. Is what I did so unforgivable that you would destroy me like this?"

Aonghus pressed her hand over the scar on his side.

"Feel that? You did not do that to me. Another man did; it had nothing to do with you. Never blame yourself, and never think that I have ever held you accountable for it, but please, my precious Kordelina, you must do this one thing for me. You must return to Mother and Father, and put this out of your mind," he persuaded. "Please?"

"Yes, I will do it. What choice do I have? I cannot make you want me when you do not," she answered, without looking at him.

He lifted her hand and kissed her palm, but she made no effort to acknowledge his affection. "If I were to tell you what I was thinking right now, you could never understand. But you must believe what we are doing is for the best, right now."

"How can I believe you anymore?" she said in a deeply sorrowful tone. "You tell me you love me, then you ask me to pretend that you do not. You hate me with one breath, then you desire me with the next. What is left inside that has not been abused? You claim you are incapable of understanding why you do it. Aonghus, I can no longer discern your truths from your lies, and I do not think you can either."

He felt a desolate burning grow within him as he stood up, and without responding, went slowly to the door.

"Aonghus?" she called.

"Yes?"

"I believe you were honest about one thing," she said coldly. "You are selfish."

Her words were like daggers in his heart.

Solomon went back into the house and sat by the fire, strangely displaced. He waited for Aonghus, wondering what he would say to him when he returned. Deep within, the Chieftain wanted to condone their actions, even encourage them. For he could not bear the thought of what Jara had just told him about his daughter's placement.

His daughter, he thought to himself. When did she transform from simply Kordelina to his daughter? Why could she not have remained so from the start? How could he ever explain to his child that he had been so impassioned with her mother that he could not stand the pain of having any reminder of her near him? That he had wanted to kill Kordelina at birth and stamp her out of existence because any memories of Deireadh were pure agony. That his love for the raven-haired woman who bore her had caused the death of his loved ones, and nearly ruined a kingdom. For he realized now that he had always been aware of Deireadh's zeal for power, and somehow even knew about her conspiracy with Laden. Only he had loved her so deeply, that he could not accuse her. He had let the people do it, and let their lust for destruction command him to make the decision he could never make by himself.

Still, it was too late for confessions now. Too late for atonement. It made no difference that he secretly wanted Aonghus to steal Kordelina away from this place before she was a victim of destiny. But now the Druids were involved, and it was not that simple.

He heard the door open and Aonghus entered. Solomon was glad to see that he did not cower in his presence. Unashamed, his eyes met Solomon's with a cold disassociated glare.

"I have released her from her servitude. She will return home in the morning. Maybe it is not important now, but it was not what you think. I did not intend for that to happen," he said, as he turned to go to his room.

"Aonghus," Solomon said curtly.

Aonghus stopped, and looked at him indignantly.

"You truly are in love with her, are you not?" the Chieftain asked.

"Yes," he answered. "Have you been blind all this time, old man? Have you not seen love blossoming before your eyes? While a skilled warrior you may be, as a man of feeling you have no might. For such griefs, such sorrows of love that I have known, have made me an older man than you."

"It is wisdom, indeed, that comes from your young tongue," Solomon admitted. "And perhaps my response should be to speak even greater truths than

I have ever spoken to any man. For since Donnach has long since died, and Gaeren is no longer a word in the priestly order, my promises to them no longer serve any purpose. So let me share with you, for only a moment, the dispelling of a lie I have lived my whole life through.

"I was born not of a common Christian who was simply violated by a Celt. No, Aonghus, I am the son of the slain King Roilan, and Orphea, a Roman-Christian aristocrat. When Donnach took me in, I made an oath very much like the one you made. It was a promise of secrecy of my parentage, and a vow that I would never assume the title of King of this tribe. So, please, do understand that I am well acquainted with the drudgeries of the heart.

"When you took the oath before your parents and the Druids, it was with this in mind that I so opposed it. For I know the way a man's soul can rot from untruths, and to conceal them a lifetime through, is an infirmity. Yet, you did as you wished, and like me, your true love has become your affliction. I say this not to evoke any sympathy in you, but rather to show that as men, we are very much the same. What is in that raven hair and those emerald eyes can bewitch a man, and drive him to the edge of his own reason. Still, as I have held fast to my honor, I need to know now if you can do the same. If you cannot, speak it to me in private that you might spare yourself public rebuke," Solomon said.

Aonghus' indignation turned into a simmering hate. "I have done it all these years," he said with contempt. "I will find it within me to keep it so."

"She must remain a virgin," Solomon stated, trembling at the words.

Aonghus shot him a questioning glance. "Why?"

The Chieftain stared blankly at the flames dancing in and out of the wood in the hearth. "Because it is part of her sentence," he replied, as he saw Aonghus' expression fade in the fireglow.

"Where will they take her?" the warrior questioned.

Solomon shrugged. "Jara did not tell me specifically. She only said that it was across the strait."

"Is there not anything that can be done?" Aonghus asked, suddenly panicked.

Solomon shook his head. He could not speak anymore, nor did he wish to listen, as perceiving his hopelessness, Aonghus retreated to his chamber in silence.

Once inside, he immediately went to the corner alcove, and took out the potion of wormwood and cowbane for which he had so thirsted earlier. He did not care that it would be difficult for him to stop once he had tasted it again. He had never known such anguish, never felt such a tremendous futility as he did at this moment. He had not considered that the Druids would enter into this, and he was sure that Saturnalia had not considered this either. This news was surely the reason she had been so upset since Jara's arrival. She was probably equally as despondent as he.

Taking the cork out of the small ceramic flask, he drank as much of the bitter liquid as he could hold. It tasted almost as if it were fermented, but he wanted it that way; wanted it to send him off into oblivion before his emotions undermined his strategy. He felt his brow go numb, then the immediate shortness of breath before euphoria.

Making his way to the window, he opened the shutters, and looked to the barn. He hoped Kordelina would somehow let him know that she had forgiven him. He did not know how she could do it, but at times he had actually heard her speaking in his thoughts. He was sure there had been nights when she held him captive in a dream state so that they might experience this visceral communication. But her room was dark, and all he could feel was a cold, drizzly wind blowing at him from outside.

Kordelina, he called her softly in his thoughts. *Please try to understand this is not what I wanted to happen.*

There was no response, and for the first time ever, he felt no connection with her. She had forbidden him access to her soul. For a moment, he hoped she was only angry. Closing his eyes, he focused on her image beckoning her to let him inside, but his thoughts were devoid of feeling. She had taken back the part of her that was once exclusively his.

He felt an emptiness as he drank what was left in the flask of herbs. His mouth was so numb that he could barely keep his lips closed enough to swallow. Throwing the container against the wall, he put his head in his hands, slid to the floor, and wept. He now fully comprehended that she was like the center stone of an archway around which all else was built. Now removed, the rest of the stones rumbled aimlessly to find something else on which to lean.

It all made sense the minute she was in his arms. The pleasurable touch of her strong hips thrust against his hardness and the inviting scent of her breath. It was total rapture as they experienced the blending of their spirits. This was why the many women he had known had only amounted to superficial experiences, not something enthralling and instinctive.

So consuming was his desolation that he knew he could not live with it as his daily companion, even for a short time. He would go to her, and do anything she asked. Beg her to forgive him, beg her to understand, and promise her anything he could if she would just wait for him. But how could she wait? Surely Jara had decided on a time when she would take her. What would he do then, ride aimlessly through the Roman-occupied territory in search of a love that had probably long since been slain on a stone altar somewhere, or sold as a Roman concubine?

Calling out her name, he sobbed even harder. He suddenly felt delicate hands rubbing his shoulders. Yet, the only sounds he was aware of were of his own crying and raving about the need for his lover. He looked up, hoping to see Kordelina, but instead, found himself looking into the face of Saturnalia. He was startled at the sight of her; she stayed perfectly still waiting to see what he would do next.

Aonghus was not sure if she was real. He was hallucinating—one minute he was with Saturnalia, and the next, it was Kordelina in front of him. He felt afraid of his inability to control his grief. His fear must have been a plea of comfort because he realized that she was moving her hands over his chest in a circular motion, trying to relax him.

"How did you get in here?" he asked, touching the center of her forehead with one hand to see if she was real.

Saturnalia ran her fingertips lightly down the back of his outstretched arm. He was isolated and needed care—she wanted only to soothe him.

"It does not matter," she answered, kissing him lightly. "I have come because you asked me. I am here not as an adversary, but as one who wishes to heal your trust. You will be able to love your people only when you release yourself from loving her."

She could feel the tension in his body mount as his eyes narrowed, and his lips tightened. He was so disoriented that it would have been easy to corrupt him. Yet that was not what she wanted. She desired only to establish an insight into his resentment of her and plans for the future. But his consciousness was a mass of whirling images.

Aonghus was entirely confounded by her affection toward him, unable to discern if it was actually Saturnalia or Kordelina. He saw the silhouettes of their two bodies on the wall, but hundreds of candle flames surrounded them.

He realized he was focusing on the uneven limestone entrance of the cave, once again journeying inside to seek his lover. But he did not want to see the hideous visions or hear the voices that plagued him in the night. They were there, whoever they were— the ghastly fiends he had seen in the grove earlier that day, the revolting faces of guilt, duty, lies, and murder.

At this thought, he suddenly became weightless, and was spiraling in another world. He could hear voices whispering in the air, but he could not understand what they said. One was behind him speaking in his ear, then there was another in front of him. In an instant, the faint sounds grew louder, inviting him into a sieve of nothingness. Shutting his eyes and opening them again, he saw that the rock walls were melting. He reached out to touch their pliable surface, but he could not make contact.

Saturnalia tried to take his hand, but he pulled it away. He wanted no part of her; at this moment, he wanted only to hide.

The Druidess sensed his vulnerability. She knew she would have to be very careful because he was hovering on the edge of madness.

"Calm yourself; I will not hurt you," she reassured him.

Aonghus eyed her suspiciously. "Why are you doing this?" his words were laced with melancholy. "I am defenseless, and you know it."

She clasped his hands, and opened his palms, kissing the center of each one lightly. "I know that, and I will not harm you for it. Your emotions will drive you insane if you do not release them. You have no resistance left because it took all your strength to deny Kordelina tonight. Her hold on you is only briefly arrested. When she comes back, it will be stronger. Love has the greatest power of all over the soul. You must free yourself from the passion conquering you; it is for the good of everyone. Release your hurt into me. I can take the shock, and your spirit will be rejuvenated."

She held his hands tightly. "You must experience the pleasures of other women. Each time you do, you will further purge yourself of your feelings for your sister. For I know that you want to do what is right and honorable, Aonghus. It is your nature," she told him empathetically.

"For my sister," he mumbled the words and closed his eyes at the biting pain of their sound. He was struggling to hold back the helplessness setting in, trying to dislocate from this dark reality.

He felt the tears again, and then the soft touch of fingertips wiping them from the corners of his eyes.

"Aonghus, look at me," the voice was Kordelina's.

"No, this is not real," he answered sadly.

"It is as real as you need it to be," she said soothingly. "We can make love. We must make love, or you will never be free of me."

She moved her hand down his neck and over his shoulders. He felt her kiss him tenderly before she opened her blouse to offer him one breast. Wrapping his arms around her, he felt the ends of her hair brush his hands as he buried his face in her bosom.

Reaching up, he took a fistful of her mane. Then he moved his lips to her ear, and circled it with his tongue.

"Tell me that you love me still," he whispered.

She pulled him closer. "I still love you, Aonghus," she answered. "I will always love you."

Her words unlocked his fantasy, and he pushed her back onto the floor. His hair fell in her face as he lay on top of her, kissing the rounds of her arms. Unlacing the top of her gown, he moved it down her waist and fumbled clumsily with her broach. Finally he ripped the material from her body.

Taking his face between her hands, Saturnalia gazed into his eyes to perceive exactly what he was seeing. He stared back at her, his dilated eyes a deep blue. She did not want to look away; she liked the feel of him, his taut muscles and his compelling soul. He had always been special. In her mind, she could be whomever he needed at this moment. But when his body was spent, this warrior would look into her eyes alone, and his vision would be clear.

She could feel the roughness of the skin around his healed wound as she held his waist, and urged him on his back. Bending over his torso, she slowly moved back and forth letting her nipples brush against his chest. He shivered a bit as she loosened his breeches, and sitting back on her heels, she pulled them off one leg at a time.

Taking her hand, Aonghus brought her back to him. Kissing her hard on the mouth, she felt a searing heat overtake her as she let his fingers explore her body.

She moved lower, making wet circles with her lips across his stomach. He mumbled incoherently as he put his hands on her head, and pushed her face between his thighs.

He groaned as her warm mouth engulfed him. Then as if he did not wish to restrain himself, he lifted her head by the hair, and rolled on top of her.

Spreading her legs, she felt him within her, and the frenzied sensation of it caused her to lift her hips to meet his thrust. He moved back and forth, and she became one with his thoughts, allowing him to have all he could consume of her power. As her heart grew heavier with his sorrow, her body moaned with his fervor, finally crying out in pleasure at his hot release.

She stayed beside him a long time afterward, watching him. He was floating listlessly in a trance, murmuring Kordelina's name. His face was serene but at the same time, tormented by his mind's workings. She tried to perceive the source of the turmoil, but found him unreceptive.

Probing deeper into his thoughts, she caught glimpses of what had taken place earlier, and discovered the painful encounter between him and Kordelina. Skillfully extracting bits of his mind, she felt a sharp jab in her chest.

Aonghus' eyes flashed open, a glint of anguish in them as he instinctively pushed her away and rolled over on his side. Saturnalia kept her eyes fixed on the back of his neck, hoping he would receive her again and allow her to penetrate his suffering.

He remained motionless, resisting her entirely. She had invaded the hallowed ground of his secret love, and the white light of her intuition was now aware of his intentions.

"Your purpose is not to give her up at all, is it?" she asked, propping herself up on one elbow.

"I cannot," he confided.

Saturnalia ran her fingers through his long hair, sweeping it away from his sweaty neck. "Innocence must be balanced by wisdom," she said sympathetically. "As naivete is lost, it must be replenished with the understanding that we cannot always change our destinies. You left a part of your innocence behind tonight. You crossed over the barriers you had set up all these years, trying to convince yourself that you did not want her as your lover. Now you must accept that, no matter how much you care, you cannot bridge a chasm fate has ordained."

She saw the muscles in his back tense at her words.

"And what is that? To have a dagger tear open her side, and let her blood cover the altar of a chieftain who needs a virgin?" he asked caustically. "I will be a king, and she should be spared for me."

Saturnalia's blood ran cold. "I wish no harm to come to Kordelina either; we cannot be sure this is what will happen to her. Jara has told me that she is assured a good home. We must take solace in that."

She moved closer, slicing the light between them. Pressing the side of her face against his, she wrapped her arm around his waist.

Aonghus sighed at her nakedness against him. He was still so far off that Saturnalia was not even sure he would remember this. Reaching around, he ran his hand over the outside of her thigh, then intertwined his fingers in hers.

"Let me rest now," was the last thing he said, and she knew it was useless to reason with him further.

————

The afternoon sunlight flooded through Aonghus' open window, jostling him irritably from a deep sleep. His head was throbbing, and he was drained of energy. Closing his eyes again, he had the feeling that he was still painfully intoxicated; even the fur covering him made his body ache.

He swung his legs over the side of the bed, and when he could feel the floor beneath his feet, he lifted his torso. A rush of blood to his head caused such an intense pounding that he put his face in his hands until it subsided a bit. Why did he feel so badly, and why had Solomon let him sleep so long?

Rubbing his eyes a moment, he picked up his pants, and slowly put them on. What had happened last night? He saw images of Saturnalia, her lithe nude body on top of him, and a heartbroken Kordelina weeping in the darkness. Then a stream of pictures trickled through his mind until he remembered everything.

Rising to his feet, he stumbled to the door, and started making his way down the hall to the main chamber. The house was empty. When he reached the entryway and opened the front door, he squinted at the sunlight as he stepped outside. The cool air made his flesh tingle, as he instinctively looked toward the barn.

"She is gone," Solomon's voice startled him. He was sitting on the porch carving a new shaft for his spear.

"When did she go?" Aonghus asked.

"I am not sure. Sometime before sunrise, I think. She was not there when I awoke," he answered, without looking up.

Aonghus shuffled from one foot to another. "Did she go home?"

Solomon shook his head. "No. I checked, but she has not been there."

Aonghus was perturbed. "Then where is she?" he snapped.

The Chieftain gave him a chilling glare. "It is no longer any of your concern," he replied flatly.

His words filled Aonghus with fury, and without thinking, he grabbed Solomon by his vest. Lifting him to his feet, he shoved him against the wall. The two warriors stood chest to chest, both ready to fight.

"Where have they taken her?" Aonghus snarled.

Solomon stared at him with icy composure. "You are mad," he said, emotionless. "If I did not think so, I would kill you this instant."

Aonghus' blood was still rising. "I need to know where she has gone. If you know, please tell me," he said, gripping him tighter. "I do not want to fight, but I will if I must."

Staring into the Chieftain's eyes, Aonghus realized how foolish he was being, and wanted to confess that it was only fear that made him react like this.

"She is with Saturnalia. The Druidess will see to it that everything returns to normal, if you let it," Solomon answered calmly.

Aonghus released his hold, averting his eyes in embarrassment. "Forgive me," he said gruffly. "I am not myself this day."

"Nor were you last night," Solomon remarked, with a bit of jealousy.

A look of shame filled Aonghus' face, then he abruptly turned and stormed back into the house. The door slammed behind him, and Solomon could hear him raging like a fiend.

PART FOUR

CHAPTER ONE

ate Winter A.D. 61, Wales. "We could kill them if you wish," Flavius said to Jara.

The colony of white-robed Druids stood in a line facing her. She could see by their expressionless faces that it made little difference to them if they died now or later. Wrapping her arms around herself, she turned, and looked at what was left of the settlement. A few huts still smoldered with fire, thin yellow and orange flames licking their thatched rooftops. The black smoke spiraled up to the sky, making black streaks against the white morning clouds.

Cattle were crammed so closely into the center court that they groaned impatiently to each other for more space. Pigs and goats roamed loose along the small dirt alleyways, and chickens cackled nervously, fluttering in all directions each time a horseman crossed their paths.

The palatial yard of the tribal chieftain was filled with women and children. Their low sobs and dirty faces made her feel guilty, and her eyes watered for only an instant before turning away from them. She could not stand to look into their defeated faces without wanting to tell them why she could not change their circumstances. It was their unfortunate destiny to watch as their civilization was destroyed. No amount of reasoning could spare them this fate.

After all, Romans were not that terrible; they were simply more powerful. It was the futile resistance of these tribes, miniscule in comparison with Caesar's army, that made the political transition so brutal. Jara could not understand why they persisted, against all hope, to cling to the last vestiges of their world with bitter and pitiful contempt.

She was perspiring from the heat of the huge bonfire in front of her. The branches of oak and green yew, once used to complete sacred rites, now played host to the human embers of warriors who had been cast into the blaze. On this dawn, instead of cattle passing in front of those fires to be sanctified by the pungent smoke, it was prisoners.

Roman soldiers were everywhere with their bare calves, bawdy armor, and beautiful horses. The cavalry numbered in the hundreds as they rounded up stray Celts, mostly women and children, and forced them into the chieftain's yard.

It had not been much of a battle between the two sides, since the Celts were sorely outnumbered by Caesar's men. Attacking them in darkness had made it much simpler, and these warriors showed little ability to grasp the calculated

417

Roman warfare. Jara had witnessed this time and again with these people. The warriors would work themselves up to a rage, and the women would shriek to the sky for divine empowerment. Yet the result was never any different. The Celts would run straight into the Roman battery and were easily slain. This particular tribe was only one of many that had agreed to accept Roman rule, then refused to relinquish their weapons when asked to do so. It is their own fault, Jara thought to herself. If they had been sincere about pledging their loyalty to Rome, they would not have needed weaponry.

"Do you want them executed or not?" Flavius asked again, brushing ash off the sleeve of his jersey.

Jara turned to look at the Order once more. Whether young or old, each possessed a contented look that seemed to say this was only one lifetime. It was unimportant if they died today or years from now; another lifetime was awaiting each of them.

She walked up to one young seer whose particular brooding look had caught her attention. He was the same height as she, unusually short for a man of this day, with fine, almost feminine features. His eyes were dark and intense. They looked like polished onyx, so black that she could almost see her own reflection in them.

He wore a thick torque of twisted metal around his neck. It was embellished with gemstones that had once belonged to a chieftain.

"That is not the necklace of a seer you wear," she said, reaching out to touch it with her forefinger.

The man's look did not change as she spoke.

"It must have belonged to a chieftain. Why was he not buried with it?" Jara questioned.

The young seer studied her with an evasive expression. It was almost as if he considered her interrogations only a minor distraction. How she despised these martyrs.

"Because I was once the chieftain who wore it. It was kept by my tribe until I could return to claim it," he replied flatly.

Jara narrowed her eyes skeptically. "Why would a chieftain return as a holy man?"

The young priest offered her a glib smile. "That I might see your demise with clearer vision," he responded.

His eyes darkened even more, then they appeared as though ablaze, and he lifted his arms to pray. The rest of the white-robed men joined in, solemnly entreating the heavens with the ancient Greek phrases.

They chanted in unison, and it unnerved Jara to see how beautifully composed they were. Each word was in as perfect harmony and intonation as the last, making it apparent that they had diligently studied their craft. What a shame, she thought, that all of the illustrious training of these fundamental zealots would amount to nothing. Had they been women, they surely would have been used as clairvoyants or concubines, thus bringing a handsome price from Rome.

Stepping back, she turned sharply to Flavius. He had not the slightest mark on him, and the only soiled part of his attire were his sandals. He was so clean that Jara could not help but be disgusted that he had let his men fight alone while he watched from safety. A Celt would never have done that.

"I have no use for them. Do with them as you wish," she answered, her voice unaffected.

She caught sight of a young soldier entering the courtyard, accompanied by his commander. The two men scanned the crowd of women, the whites of their eyes looking bright against their dirty, smokey faces. Setting his sights on a pubescent girl with auburn locks, the Roman officer motioned to his soldier to seize her.

Realizing they were coming for her daughter, the girl's mother flung herself on top of her, and began to beg for mercy. The young girl's sobs immediately rose to a hysterical pitch as the soldier cast the mother aside, and grabbed the girl by the wrist. Dragging her screaming and crying across the grass, he dropped her at the commander's feet.

The mass of women rustled anxiously, but to Jara's surprise, made no attempt to protect her. Instead, they shielded the faces of their children as the Roman reached down and jerked the girl to her feet.

"Centurion," he called to Flavius. "I like this one."

"That is the Chieftain's daughter," he replied, waving his hand impatiently.

"She is a common slave now. She has no special rights unless she earns them," he retorted, taking the girl by the arms and pulling her to him.

"No, please! I do not want to do that! I do not want to do that!" she begged piteously, the tears streaming down her red cheeks.

The Centurion put one hand on his hip and nodded. "As you wish," he sighed. "You have done well in command of this army. It is your right to take any woman you like."

The commander gave a lascivious smile, and forced the girl down on all fours. A handful of infantrymen immediately surrounded him, half of them pointing their weapons threateningly at the group of prisoners in the event they started an uprising. The others pointed their spears intimidatingly in the girl's face should she try to escape.

Her sobs were reduced to a whimper as the Roman tore the sleeping dress from her body. She bowed her head, naked and humiliated, as he knelt behind her, and opened his breeches. Her mother was screeching to the gods, her hands held up, and her eyes shut so tightly that her entire face contorted.

The officer looked at the rest of the prisoners with uncaring eyes as he roughly took the girl by the hips, and impaled her on his erection. Her mouth opened wide in anguish, but she made no sound until he began stroking her hard. She moaned painfully as in a few moments, he jammed himself forward, and came into her. Her virginal blood smeared on his thighs as he withdrew, and then he shoved her face down on the ground.

Only a moment later, the girl's mother came at him so fast, it surprised his guards. She seemed to fly through the air, an avenging angel with fists clenched as she screamed for revenge. Before she could reach the commander, one of the infantrymen stabbed her in the side and she stumbled back a step. She covered her wound with both hands, the rush of blood oozing through her fingers. Then she turned and flung herself into the bonfire, weeping.

The fire caught her garments first, climbing up her body to her head. Her hair became a torch as she opened her mouth wider, wailing in agony. Her eyes turned into dark caverns; then she wilted into the flames, and her crying ceased.

Her daughter curled up like a baby, her hands over her ears. Not one of the prisoners stirred. They were too horrified.

"Silly woman," Flavius said. It was as if he were personally offended by her dramatics. "Female prisoners are always raped. Except for you, my dear."

He scrutinized Jara. Trying to hide her shock, the Druidess smoothed the front of her cloak and forced a smile that appeared more like a frown.

"It is our custom that a girl of great status remain a virgin if she is to wed a chieftain," she said, her voice quivering slightly.

Flavius laughed obnoxiously. "The days of chieftains and kings are finished, that is unless they are Roman, then we address them as Senators. Should you still be among the living when this conquest is finished, that is how you will address me."

He walked briskly toward the Chieftain's dwelling. His pace was so quick that Jara had to trot to keep alongside him.

"Druidess, do you still have my virgin stored safely away until I need her?" he asked presumptuously, as he entered the abandoned house.

"Of course," she answered. "That is, provided we discuss the terms of the trade."

The Roman walked around the massive feasting room as if it had always belonged to him. Intricately carved pillars were placed in strategic positions to hold up the high roof, and small cubicles were separated from each other by wicker partitions for privacy. Spread around the earthen floor were animal pelts and woolen tapestries. A long wooden table in the center of the room rested on stone supports. In the middle of it sat a silver flagon with inlaid carnelians that was filled to the brim with red wine.

"Yes, I think I shall be quite comfortable here for the time being," he replied, throwing himself down on the couch of silk pillows and tapestries. Its position in the center of the table obviously denoted a place of honor for the one who occupied it. "Now what terms do you wish?"

Summoning all of her composure, Jara looked him in the eye. "I will escort you to this island as you have requested, giving the impression that your presence there is by consent of the Order. I will tell them that because of my political immunity, Rome, in good faith, has provided me safe passage. A festival is to take place very soon. It is a three-day celebration. I will arrive with you on the second day. Tell your men to prepare the invasion for dawn of the third day, lest it look suspicious."

"The Druidess of the first tribe you will come in contact with is one I raised from a babe, and she is very dear to me," she continued. "The terms are these: I will assist you in taking this settlement provided you do not touch her. She must not be harmed in any manner, and under no circumstances is she to be taken prisoner."

Flavius folded his arms across his chest, and twisted his lips as he pondered her offer. "Very well, but you must keep the Druidess with you from the beginning. I will not be responsible for her; that is up to you. As long as she is with you, she will be safe," he replied carelessly. "Now what of the jewel waiting for me there? Is she worth this?"

Jara took a relieved breath and nodded. "She is a young, dark-haired virgin who I am sure will bring you pleasure."

Flavius slapped his hand on his thigh. "I did not request a brunette," he yelled, causing Jara to flinch at his tone. "I asked for a golden-haired nymph. Rome is full of dark-haired beauties. What makes this one worthy of me?"

Jara's teeth chattered, and she clenched them tightly to hide her fear. It was true that the Romans owed her nothing. The only reason she had been spared was because she had a small influence among these Celtic tribes. As a result of her quarterly visits to these clans, she was acquainted with many of the chieftains, nothing more. She had only nurtured the impression that she had a lofty position in the Order so that she could spare herself. Jara did not wish to be one of the many people persecuted by this conquest. Through her cooperation with the Romans, they had used her as one of many liaisons between themselves and the Celts. It was a delicate position to be in, and one that required her greatest wit and diplomacy.

"This maid is a special one," she said, offering a charming smile. "She is an anointed warrior, and educated in the ways of sorcery as well. She will be of great worth as a mistress because she possesses insight in the ways of her people. Think of what pleasure her tender flesh would bring. I could sanctify her in a special ceremony that would make you exalted above all Celtic chieftains before you. The people would view you as a god, and clamor at your feet."

Flavius sat back, cleaning his fingernails with the tip end of his knife. He was so smug that Jara wished she could kill him herself. However, that would benefit no one, and Saturnalia would likely suffer the same degradation before her tribe as the young girl in the court. If someone were to be the ransom for their freedom, better it be the young transgressor who had tried to kill her master. She would surely be most capable of assassinating this loathsome Roman.

"A god? Yes, I fancy myself deserving of such stature, especially among these savages," he said, with a grin. Then he poured some wine in a chalice, and set it in front of Jara. "Yes, I will agree to your terms. One life is nothing in exchange for an entire territory, and you must arrange a meeting with the client king of this tribe as well. Be sure my Celtic bride is a virgin, and the ceremony should be very elaborate. If it takes sacrificing her to make me look more powerful, then so be it. But I demand that when I have secured this clan, that you claim will be so easily taken, the ceremony to follow must be more elaborate than the festivals to their gods. You will be responsible for organizing the feast, and I want you and your sorceress to perform it. That would only be fitting, would it not?"

"Yes, Centurion. The people would never doubt your worthiness then," she replied, looking away from him.

Jara knew that Saturnalia would be more difficult to deal with in this situation than this Roman. After all, it was Saturnalia who had educated Kordelina, and for her to witness this transgression would be like Jara watching Saturnalia become Rome's prostitute. Nevertheless, some ransom had to be offered to insure their liberty. After watching the brutal onslaught of this village, Jara would do anything to save the one who had been like a daughter to her.

"Very well," Flavius said, noticeably pleased with himself. "Then listen carefully. I do not think I want the maid killed, I would rather take her chastity myself. She should be prepared elegantly, sparing no cost for her ornamentation, and it must be immediately following our victory. This insignificant island has caused us much grief in refusing Caesar for so many years. This ritual will show them that I am their, let us say, savior, and my bride, being a peasant girl, will be a symbol of my generous nature. I would like her clothed in the jewels of the tribal chieftain, and a robe of silk made in the colors of Rome. When we take this tribe, she should remain with you and the Druidess. I do not want there to be any mix-up. Do you understand?"

Jara nodded, still not meeting his eye.

"You will be there before us," he continued, "so I am counting on you to take care of this ahead of time. When I arrive, if she is not with you and this Druidess, I will kill you both. These heathens have truly exhausted my patience, and if I cannot make an impression on them by adhering to their rituals, I will do it by torturing you and your prodigy."

Startled by his threat, Jara involuntarily looked into his eyes. They were the shallow eyes of a fool, who was so self-possessed that he imagined himself a god. How absurd these supposedly civilized men were, thinking they could possibly ascend to divination. Giving him Kordelina was more than compensation. It was her assurance that this Centurion's life would be short, indeed. The child Saturnalia raised would be sure to avenge her tribe's defeat.

"As you wish," she said under her breath, and helped herself to the wine he had poured for her.

———

Filling the clay holders with beeswax and scented herbs, Jara settled back on her sleeping pallet with her legs crossed in front of her. She took a poker, placed it in the fire, and watched as the end of it lit up with a tiny flame, and then extinguished itself, leaving only a smoldering orange tip.

She lifted it and lit the incense. The scented smoke rose around her, and she inhaled it so deeply it made her cough. Her eyes watered as she reached for water, and drank until her throat was soothed.

The room was comfortable enough. Still, as with all of the other places she had stayed while traveling, little of life's essence existed within its walls. Not enough people had walked across these earthen floors, or made love in its confines, nor had the spirits ever been invited into it.

Jara took another long drink of water, and helped herself to bread and cheese. It had been a taxing week, and she welcomed this solitude. The fighting had been constant, and the slaughter of these clans seemed to go on forever. Strange how it no longer had any effect on her, and all of their faces had begun to look the same. Perhaps it was the hopelessness and defeat they all mirrored in the last moments before they died — that sorrowful pallor when they realized that it was finally over, and no amount of warring or pleading could change the outcome.

It hurt her to see her own callous reflection in them because each and every one had once been a particle of her own body. These beloved hedonists had, at one time, been the very reason for her existence. With their wild characters and humble spirits, they had endeared themselves to her like kindly beasts offering complete devotion for the simple satisfaction of sharing with them her love. What simpletons they were, believing that she could somehow possess the secrets of the gods.

Deep in her heart, she no longer believed it. Now she had purposely divorced herself from them, and she found their impoverished reality revolting. Even the land reeked, and the once spectacular groves seemed to cry out at this travesty. And the dream, that same dream she had over and over, the one that caused her to sweat and cry until she shrieked in pain. Only now, no one was there to comfort her because she had ordered them executed. There was only room enough in this new empire for a chosen few, and she thought it better that those few were the ones she had chosen personally.

Closing her eyes, she tried to meditate, imagining her entire body filled with white light as she took each deep breath. Again and again she did it, trying to satisfy that emptiness that felt like it was boring a hole straight through her. Maybe the slaughtered really were the lucky ones, she thought. At least they died believing in their gods, not selling them to the highest bidder as she was.

She focused on the image of Saturnalia, that fiery, idealistic child she had breathed life into as her real mother lay dying. She should have let her die then, because it would have prevented her from suffering the utter desolation of knowing that all she had once stood for and believed in would amount to nothing more than defeat. There was no place in this new world for their rituals, no need for these pagans who now so valiantly accepted their death.

Her mind flashed to a beach in Massalia, and warmth came over her. The day was hot, and the sky and water were so blue that it was hard to tell where one ended and the other began. She was sitting in the white sand, weaving Saturnalia's curly red locks. She was still a child, and Jara fancied the look of her own skin, so smooth and without a wrinkle. How different from the weathered hag she was now.

Jara was softly singing a tune she did not recognize, as Saturnalia made the same symbol over and over again in the sand in front of her. Jara suddenly realized that this was not a memory at all, that somehow Saturnalia was allowing her spirit to be shared. Whether it was voluntary or by accident, it had been many years since she had consented to such intimacy.

Shutting her eyes tighter, Jara had tried to determine the feeling of urgency coming from the child. Her mind was recording each detail, vainly trying to comprehend its significance.

"What are you writing, Saturnalia?" Jara asked aloud.

Saturnalia turned, her lovely cherubim face looking strikingly mature for one so young.

"This symbol is mine. It belongs only to me, not you," she answered, her voice chiming on the gentle ocean breeze.

"What is it?" she questioned, whispering this time.

Saturnalia stood and looked at her accusingly. "I will not share it with you," she said defiantly, then turned and ran down the beach away from Jara.

Not wanting to lose the vision, Jara watched her far into the distance until her tiny body was a speck on the horizon. Only then did she look down to where Saturnalia had been sitting.

Drawn in the sand over and over was the symbol of one straight line with an "X" precisely through its center. It was the symbol of the sacred grove. It represented all knowledge, a holy place where everything in the universe came together for a common purpose.

Saturnalia was telling her not to come. That no matter what place she had once held in her heart, she was no longer welcome in her presence. Her grove was forbidden to Jara.

Opening her eyes, Jara was filled with remorse.

"Sweet Saturnalia, we have no choice," she said softly. "We will never achieve harmony again."

CHAPTER TWO

nglesey. Conn watched from behind the half-open bedroom door as Saturnalia tied a muslin bag filled with decongestant herbs, and handed it to the old woman who stood waiting politely. She had come to see the Druidess because her grandson was sick with fever and a respiratory ailment. Saturnalia had been to see the boy many times to offer her healing powers, but she had known from the beginning that the boy would probably die.

A wave of guilt came over Conn when he saw her hug the woman. Saturnalia really did love this clan with the deepest part of her being. Conn only hoped that when Rome finally took over this island, she would find it in herself to adapt to their presence, and forgive him for bargaining with them ahead of time.

All he would have to tell her, he reasoned, was that he had formed alliances with certain influential members of the Imperialist nation long ago when he had been in Wales, and that he saw this conquest not as a defeat of the Celtic race, but more as an opportunity to acquire the wealth of a new world. After all, Rome ruled the continent, and while the transition may have been bloody, the tribes over there had adjusted to it for their own good. Caesar only wanted to be recognized as ruler of these islands, and as long as the tribes upheld Imperialist laws, everything would be fine.

Conn knew that political upheavals were opportunities for the ambitious, and he was an ambitious sort. He felt no embarrassment about his genuine aspirations of greatness. He had been endowed with it from birth; no matter what defeat his family had suffered, he was a born aristocrat, and whether his action proved lucrative or not, those were the principles that directed him.

Still, he wanted to be a credible choice for assuming this client kingdom, and that was where Saturnalia figured into the plan. If he could get her to make a commitment to him, it would secure a position in the eyes of Rome and his tribesmen. That had been his strategy in the beginning, only he had not counted on Saturnalia's independence, nor had he expected to fall so deeply in love with her. Yet, he understood fully that if he had her on his side, he would also have the support of the Order. And even if some shed tears as to Aonghus' seemingly tragic and untimely end, it would be overlooked when Conn was elected to power in his place.

Naturally, Aonghus would appear a hero and the reasons for his death would surely make him a character of lore in this clan. Reasons had always been important to his friend, and duty had remained his aphrodisiac. Still, Conn felt no remorse at having told the informants where the guards would be posted for the festival of Brigantia, and he had heard Jara conveniently inform Solomon that Aonghus should assume the last watch to avoid any unsavory displays when Kordelina was taken.

He could not say anything to Saturnalia about this because he was counting on her innocence in effectively dealing with the tribe. He knew that with Aonghus out of the way, and Kordelina gone, Saturnalia would need him. He was not expecting problems from Solomon either since the Chieftain was old now, and said to have been the offspring of a Roman mother, anyway.

When the woman left, and Saturnalia closed the door, Conn walked into the main chamber and gave his lover a small frown. She looked at him, perplexed.

"Is something wrong?" she asked, going over to him, and tenderly running her palm across one of his cheeks.

"Everything is wrong," he stated, purposely trying to sound more perturbed than he actually was. "I truly can no longer abide this clandestine existence you have forced on me. Every time there is a knock at the door, I have to scurry out of sight, lest a tribesman find me in their Druidess' abode. I really do not know how much longer I can live like this."

Saturnalia gave him an apologetic look. "I do not do it to hurt you," she replied, full of compassion. "It is only that I would like to keep my personal affairs as private as possible."

Conn cast her an offended gaze. Crossing his arms over his chest defensively, he sat down in front of the fire.

"I think you are ashamed of me," he said. "Ashamed to let the tribe know we share the same bed. You are afraid they will think less of you because of my youth, and that I am not an aristocrat. You fear you will be discredited if they know that you and Solomon have long since gone your separate ways."

Saturnalia knelt down beside him. Taking his hands, she stared up at him with placating eyes. "That is not true," she said, trying to appease him. "I am not ashamed of you, Conn, I love you. I suppose I am unaccustomed to making a spectacle of my affairs of the heart. It is not my nature to be so bold."

Conn shut his eyes slowly, and gave a fervent shake of his head. "How can I believe that?" he questioned, looking back at her sharply. "I only know that I sneak about like your concubine, and I truly do not know if I can do it any longer. You say that it is your nature to desire privacy; well, it is my nature to desire self-esteem, and you have nearly exhausted it. I can only tell you that you should greatly consider making an open statement of our love, or it should be forsaken."

The Druidess' eyes took on a dismal cast. "Conn, this is not a time to seek open displays of our love, as my heart is aching for one I am soon to lose," she offered. "I am preoccupied with what will become of Kordelina. Perhaps that is the reason my thoughts have not been of us. I give you my apology if I appeared to take you for granted because I do not. I love you, kind warrior.

Conn sighed. The words she spoke mattered to him, and what he was saying had more worth than he would have liked to admit. He had courted her in deception, yet it had blossomed into true love. At this moment, he was doing what he had to do, but he took some comfort in the fact that it was partly based on truth.

"Come sit with me," he said, pulling her into his lap.

Saturnalia wrapped her arms around his neck, and kissed him on the cheek. He could not help but smile at her girlish affection as he bent his head and kissed the top of one breast. He heard her giggle mischievously. It sounded so odd to him, then he realized that it had been days since he had seen her smile. Since Jara had left, Saturnalia had been deeply depressed.

"I do love the chime of your laughter," he said, looking into her eyes.

She smiled at him, and he kissed her.

"To look into your eyes now, I would like to forget the words I have just spoken," he told her seriously, "but I cannot. You mean too much to me to love you in secret any longer. I have been asked to keep watch over the far settlement borders throughout the night. So, I will say to you that when dawn's light shows, I pray that you will have come to some decision about us. You will either find it in your soul to marry me, or release me."

A strange, protective silence came over her. "I understand," she softly acquiesced. "But please, give me the dark hours to consider it."

Conn gently released her, and got to his feet. He looked down at her a moment, finding great insecurity in her enigmatic expression.

"You may consider it until dawn," he told her. "If you make a decision before that, you know where I will be."

"Yes, I will find you," she said, as he walked into the late afternoon sunlight.

———

Kordelina was curled up on her bed, stroking the family cat who slumbered beside her. Since her return to her parent's home, she had assumed many of the duties that Koven was now too crippled to do. His knotted hands were so stiff they were barely usable, and although Cunnedag and Erc were there to help him, Kordelina thought them lazy, and believed they took no pride in their work.

She could not seem to get Aonghus out of her mind. She had thought of him unceasingly since the last time they were together, and she knew he truly did not want her away from him. Still, she did not understand his present state or the motives behind his actions. All she knew was that a few days after she had come home, Bracorina visited the house. She wept as she told Koven and Enda how Aonghus no longer wanted to marry her. She said she thought that he had been consumed by the spirits because he was violent and cruel to her. She begged them to make him reconsider, and she would give him anything he wanted if they could still be wed.

Nobody told Kordelina about this, nor did she mention it. But she could not help but worry about Aonghus even more when Solomon had come by days later, and spoke to Enda. He said Aonghus was delirious with hallucinations and stomach cramps that made him weep from the pain. Kordelina knew by the symptoms that Aonghus was taking the herbs again, and these reactions would eventually subside after his body had adjusted to them. She could barely keep from asking her mother what was happening, especially after Enda had spent the last few afternoons tending him.

Once Kordelina thought she would try to reach Aonghus telepathically so that she could look into his mind, and with her intuition, determine how ill he was. She reconsidered; if she opened up to him even slightly, he would consume her, and she could not bear pain like that again.

"Would you like some air, child?" Enda asked her from the doorway.

Kordelina shrugged and smiled at the same time.

"It has been a beautiful day; you should enjoy the sunset," she went on, going over to the window and opening the shutters.

"Thank you, Mother," Kordelina said.

She did not say anything when Enda sat down on the end of the bed. She affectionately grabbed hold of Kordelina's toes and shook them playfully.

"What is it that has turned you into such a shy one?" she asked kindly.

"I am not shy," Kordelina answered, stroking the cat's fur. "I have just gotten in the habit of keeping my mouth closed. You forget, I have had a lot of practice these past months."

"Yes, dear I suppose you have," Enda conceded. "But tell me, child, what is it that troubles you?"

Her daughter ran her long fingers through her hair, and thought a moment. "Mother?" Kordelina questioned. "What is going to happen to me? I have no status. The only skills I possess are weaponry and horsemanship, and I have no land rights to purchase a union, not that it matters if I did. No one in this tribe would take me, not after what has happened.

"I have been wondering if I am going to stay on this farm for the rest of my life. It is not that I mind being with you or father, but when I think about what life will be like when Cunnedag and Erc take wives and start their own families, well, it makes me shudder to consider the quality life will take on."

Enda patted Kordelina on the leg.

"Little girl, I will tell you something that might ease your cares," she said. "Before you came to us, your father and I wanted a daughter so badly that we used to make constant offerings to the goddess that our desire would be fulfilled. Many days and nights passed, and nothing happened, but we did not lose faith in Brigantia's power and love for us. Then long ago on the night of the festival of Samhain, the gods answered. Children born and conceived on festival nights are begotten of the gods. I tell you this, that you might have faith; you were born of higher powers, not of the inconveniences of men. Accept it, Kordelina, and know that in spite of your deed, you will have a divine fate. You will redeem yourself and your tribe. I have been assured of it."

Kordelina looked at her mother with a perplexed expression. What Enda was saying seemed strange to her. Born of the gods? Divine redemption? What was all this nonsense?

"Mother, please tell me exactly what —" she stopped midsentence. Aonghus was outside.

Jumping up and looking out the window, she saw him talking to their father. She could tell by the way that Koven was pointing to the fields that they were discussing the crop rotation. Aonghus listened to him, attentively, then said something in reply, and they both laughed. He looked awful; his hair was unwashed and stringy, his eyes were hidden by dark circles, and his pallor was sallow and waxy.

"What is he doing here?" Kordelina demanded, looking at Enda with fiery eyes. Her mother stared back with her usual compassionate expression.

"He is to feast with us tonight," she stated firmly. "And all of us, especially you, Kordelina, should make him welcome."

"I thought Bracorina said he had gone crazy," Kordelina argued. "I do not want to dine with a crazy man."

Enda walked over to her daughter. Taking her by the shoulders, she looked at her pointedly.

"He has been ill," she stated, "that is all. Dear child, your brother has been more than generous with you. Of all people, you should understand that he is not himself, and you should show him your kindness. He is deserving of it for he has never treated you wrong. What he did to punish you was little of what he could have done. He could have demanded your death, but instead, he let you live unhindered by the requirements others in servitude have had to suffer. As your mother, I am asking you to offer him the same courtesy he showed you."

Kordelina wiggled out of her hold, and flopped down on the bed. "I am not hungry," she countered, burying her face in the pillows.

Enda was quiet a moment, then she gave a frustrated sigh. "Kordelina, you can still test my patience," she declared. "I am telling you right now that you had better get hungry, or I will have your father whip you until your appetite returns."

"Oh, Mother," she sputtered, looking up and rolling her eyes. "I am too old for that."

Enda pursed her lips as she reached over, and gave her a slap on the behind. "Do not ever think you are too old!" Enda declared. "Now, as the gods have made us, child, you had better find that appetite of yours. Do you understand?"

Kordelina said nothing as she hid her face again.

"I asked if you understood, Kordelina?" she repeated.

Kordelina nodded her head, but did not look up as Enda left the room.

The men were seated in front of the hearth by the time Kordelina finally found the courage to come out of her room. She had been listening to the sound of their talking, too flustered to make out what they were saying. All she could hear was the rhythmic sound of Aonghus' tenor voice, and it filled her with absolute desolation.

When she entered the chamber, she could not bear to look at him, lest she do something entirely foolish. He was giving Cunnedag a graphic description of three Roman scouts he and Conn had killed a fortnight prior. She heard him stutter, and briefly lose his train of thought at her entrance, but he completed his sentence smoothly, elaborating on how they had encountered them on the shore, and slain them before they could even speak. He said they had left the transport stored in a crag, and that it appeared seaworthy enough to carry quite a few men and at least a few horses across the ocean.

By the time he had finished his story, Kordelina was helping Enda serve the food. She felt as if she were moving in a dream, carrying out anything her mother handed to her. Setting down the flask of corma near her father, she felt him take her hand to prevent her from leaving again.

"Greet your brother, child," he gently exhorted. "He is a guest tonight."

Kordelina sighed worriedly. She tried to say something to Aonghus, but could not find the words. Then she saw him rise and slowly come over to her. It seemed a tortuous span of time before he reached her. Please do not touch me, I cannot stand the pain I feel when your skin touches mine, she thought to herself.

He reached out and hugged her to him for a brief moment. Kordelina's body went rigid as she felt his warmth, and she shied away.

"Kordelina, it does me well to look on you again," he told her, slightly agitated by her response.

Kordelina bowed respectfully, and hurried into the other room. When she got behind the partition, she took in a deep breath, and tried to slow her heartbeat. How was she ever going to make it through an entire evening with him in the same room?

Her mother stuck a bowl of greens in her hand, and turning her around, sent her back out again.

"The more you do it, child, the easier it will be," she told her.

CHAPTER THREE

O pening her linen tunic and loosening the laces of her leather vest, Kordelina arranged the front of it so that her bosom was almost entirely exposed. She was alone in the woods, just beyond her parents' farm; she had only been able to endure a brief appearance at dinner. The tension between her and Aonghus was consuming, and she thought it better that she leave him to enjoy their parents' company without the added pressure of having to deal with her.

It was so odd the way they interacted, and Kordelina could tell by the admonishing looks of her mother and father that every gesture she made was under scrutiny. Yet, she could not erase the frustration she felt toward him, nor could he conceal his feelings for her. It did not matter how hard he tried; Kordelina could tell by his tender expression that he still loved her deeply.

She had quietly escaped out her window. The atmosphere in the house was draining, and if she had stayed, she certainly would have done or said something she would regret. So she decided to wait for him and ask him one last time to tell her the truth. She wanted the chance to show him that there was never a secret so dark that it would cause her to forsake him.

Kordelina had never hated herself for anything in her entire life except causing him pain. The open rebuke, servitude, and cursings she had suffered were insignificant in comparison. She loved Aonghus with the very depths of her being, and she would do anything within her means to prove it to him. All these years, she had tried to find a way to ease her feelings for him, but it was impossible. If there was a way to get over him, she had not found it. Even if she had, she was sure she would never use it.

She felt her stomach churn as looking up, she saw his silhouette in the distance. Nervously closing her cloak, she stood as closely as she could to the oak tree towering over her. Deep inside, she believed that if they could only consummate their love, he would be able to tell her what was such an ordeal.

Aonghus sat slightly hunched over in his saddle, as though it was a hardship to ride the huge bay stallion. His hair was pushed away from his face, and one arm rested on his stomach like he was in great pain.

He seemed listless, his head bobbing forward with each step of his horse. For a moment, Kordelina thought he was going to ride past her without taking notice until she saw Lir prick up his ears, and snort loudly in her direction.

431

Aonghus came to attention immediately, and sitting up straight, peered into the woods. He drew his spear and strained his eyes to see what had caught the stallion's attention.

"By what name are you known?" Aonghus demanded, moving a few paces into the trees. "I can see your shadow; answer me in friendship, or I will slay you as an enemy."

Kordelina stood facing him in nervous silence. She could see his ankles stiffen and his heels point to the ground, positioning himself to be ready for any sudden movement.

"If you answer me not, I will kill you without delay," he yelled, as he switched his reins to one hand and prepared to charge.

Touching her fingertips to her lips, Kordelina tried to find her voice. She knew that he would be upon her in an instant if she did not respond. Lowering her hand to her side, she stepped forward.

"Aonghus, it is I—Kordelina," she answered in a timid voice.

The warrior relaxed, and urged the horse closer. Stopping in front of her he dismounted, spear still in hand.

"Why have you come here? It is very dangerous to be in these woods at night without a weapon," he admonished, stepping toward her.

Kordelina did not respond, rather she stared blankly into his eyes, then lowered her gaze. She appeared distracted, as though he were a stranger.

"I asked what you are doing here in the darkness," he said again.

"I had to get away from the house; I felt like I was suffocating. I wanted to see you alone to tell you that I —" she stopped abruptly.

Letting the spear drop to the ground, Aonghus touched her lightly on the shoulder, then reached over and opened her cloak. He leaned his head to one side as he studied her cleavage, his eyes dancing wantonly. Kordelina breathed in deeply as if his gaze was the warmth of the sun itself, and she was basking in it.

"Tell me what?" he coaxed, his voice almost a whisper.

"Tell you that I want to go back with you," she said reaching out and grasping his forearm. "I want to be one with you."

Aonghus let her pull him closer. As their bodies touched, a bolt of heat ran through him like a flame igniting, and he was filled with a furious lust. It felt like knives sticking into his gut, and he needed to be soothed by her. Retreating into the memories of their unfulfilled seduction, he reached into her open garment and fondled her breast. It felt so hot in the palm of his hand. Taking her by the arm, he slammed her against the trunk of the oak. He wanted her, wanted to rip her apart for rekindling this passion.

Kordelina closed her eyes at the impact. She had not expected him to be rough. Perhaps Bracorina had been right when she had tearfully told their mother he was losing his mind. She felt his hands grab her beneath her buttocks, lifting her high enough to wrap her legs around his hips.

"Rape me, if that is the only way you can justify it," she taunted, looking into his dilated eyes. "I will love you all the more. I do not care what manner of deception you concoct in your mind, that you may consent to do what our hearts and bodies desire. I want only to have you fill me."

Taking her face between his two hands, he stared at her with an almost sadistic contempt. Her skin was warm, and so enticingly soft, that he wanted to make her suffer.

Squeezing her head harder, Kordelina saw the grove begin to spin, and a bright yellow outline surround everything she looked upon. Then he moved his head forward and kissed her with his wet, open mouth. Again and again he kissed her, letting the touch of her tongue to his bemuse him.

Kordelina ran her fingers through his tangled hair. She could not stop her hips from pushing rhythmically against his loins. The bristly whiskers on his face chafed her skin, and she could taste the stale traces of meat and wine on his lips. Tensing the muscles in her legs as though she were riding a horse, she pulled him so close to her that she could feel his stomach contract as he breathed.

It was a long while before Aonghus forced himself to pull away from her, and then he gave her an even more intensely violent look. Using both hands, he touched her face, examining the shadowy bone structure, the deep set eyes that were at once innocent and challenging. How could this titillating creature hold him so powerless?

Running one hand across the square of her jaw, he lowered it, and clasped his fingers around her neck. He could see her eyes glittering anxiously in the dim moonlight, and he relished his momentary dominance. Watching as her jugular vein swelled, he thought how easy it would be to tear it as though it were a piece of meat, and rid himself of this insufferable obsession. Squeezing tighter, he pressed just hard enough to constrict her breath.

"Kordelina," he murmured. "Help me to understand."

"What, Aonghus?" she forced out the words. Her jaw was tight, and he could tell by the way it clicked as she spoke that she was afraid of him.

"Can love and hate exist together?" he asked, his voice had taken on a hollow tone. "Are they really two different sides of the same emotion?"

Kordelina swallowed hard as she felt his grip stiffen.

"I do not know of what you speak," she replied uncertainly.

He raised one brow, and glared at her as if he resented having to explain himself. "Like this neck," he said, "I want to press my lips to it, savor its texture, its beauty. At the same moment, I could twist it with all of my strength until it snaps."

Kordelina strained to turn her head away. A mist had begun to move through the grove from the shore. It wrapped itself around the oak branches. In an instant of sheer desperation, she feared that it would be the only witness as Aonghus effortlessly devoured her. What foolishness it was to have pushed him this far, for she knew better than anyone the destruction he was capable of when his anger peaked.

Tears showed in his eyes as he pressed his cheek against hers and listened to her breathing. As his skin met hers, she believed he felt more pain than scorn at its touch. Then, without warning, he suddenly loosened his hold, and leaned all of his weight against her, pinning her to the tree. Her heart was racing, and she opened her mouth to scream, but he covered it with his lips. Her cry came out muffled by his tongue, as he stole one last bit of violent affection. Placing his hands to the bend of her knees, he forced her to unlock her legs as he stepped back. Lightheaded, she felt the damp air on her throat.

"Calm yourself," he said. His expression was hard as he looked directly at her. "I could never hurt you. As much as I would like to crush you with my bare hands, I cannot."

Kordelina looked down, her eyes catching sight of his hard desire for her. How much like a prisoner she felt, perpetually trapped between two worlds: the one in which she lived as the outsider who suppressed all her natural instincts; and the one of her own passion, where an eternal burning lived deep in her soul— a burning that said she must be with this man or her life would hold no meaning.

"Why do you suffer me so?" Aonghus asked. "Do you wish to bring us further pain? I have tried to explain to you, even begged you to leave me be, yet you track me as though I were your prey."

Kordelina shook her head, and looked at him boldly. "Our pain is only brought about when we seek happiness away from each other," she answered, her voice quivering. "It brings me no suffering when I am in your arms. When I feel your breath mingling with my own, and our two hearts beat as one, it is not torment. But when you push me away, pretending to love me as your sister—it is then that I am wounded. In my life, I do not desire just any man's pleasure or another woman's beauty. I seek nothing more than to have you as my love and master."

She could see he was grinding his teeth, but his eyes softened as she spoke. Why could he not speak what was on his mind? What could possibly be so terrible that keeping it inside would cause this kind of reaction in him? She took a step closer and he backed away, almost cowering from her.

"How long must I wait for you?" she asked. "Tell me please, Aonghus. You have only to name a time when I can come to you, or I can wait no longer."

His eyes met hers as if it was an exquisite cry for help, then he turned away. "Kordelina, you know the laws," he answered, bending down to pick up his spear.

She sighed heavily. "Yes, but I do not care about them."

Out of the corner of her eye, she saw his weapon slam into the ground between them, and she gasped in surprise. Aonghus stood on the other side of the spear, his face flushed half from desire and half from embarrassment at his rash display of emotion.

"Do you denounce the laws?" he roared, the veins in his forehead swelling. "That is treason! I have sworn, as you have sworn, to die to uphold them. This island exists because of these customs. How can you say they mean nothing?"

Kordelina stared at him incredulously. "You deceive yourself. They are only designed to keep us subservient. You would lay down your life for an edict contrived by another? Perhaps it is comforting to you, to think that your death would have a higher purpose, or make some kind of difference in the eyes of the heavens and the earth, but for me, I do not want to die. I want to live! I want to spend whatever days I have in this world with you. And if that means denial of every law ever created, then so be it. Life means more to me than having a noble burial.

"Aonghus, I believe that when we were created, the gods took one small beam of light and split it in two parts. You were made from one, and I from the other. And even though we take two different forms, we are part of the same ray. That is why I feel what you feel, why we can read each other's minds, and despite all rational inclinations, we cannot help but desire to be together. Our souls have collided and we are one entity. It is not wrong. I am at a loss to understand what is so grave that you feel you must lie about your feelings to conceal it."

Reaching past the unseen barrier he had meant to create, Kordelina touched the side of his face with the back of her hand.

"I love you. If I could I would ask you to be my husband, but I have not the right," she said softly. "Still, I want you to be well again, and I would do anything to help you."

Unable to resist her, he put his hand on hers. "Then I beg of you, stay far from my presence," he replied, then hurriedly mounted his horse.

Dropping her hand to her side, Kordelina's eyes filled with tears. "Then I mean nothing to you?" she asked.

Aonghus looked down at her, expressionless. "No, you mean everything to me," he answered, grinding his heels into Lir's side. The horse reared at the force of it, then bolted away.

Kordelina stared after him. Her vision was so blurred with tears that she could barely make out his shadow as he wove through the trees.

Feeling the cold mist on his sweaty face, Aonghus leaned forward, allowing more slack in the reins so Lir would go faster. He felt like a coward, fleeing from lust. It was pressing on him, crawling up his back, and he could not escape it. He could still feel her body tingling against his, and eyes bulging, he cried out at the sensation. There were no trees in front of him, only her sinewy arms beckoning him, mercilessly, to return to her.

These laws mean nothing, I love you, Kordelina's voice was ringing in his head, and he knew she was purposely invading his thoughts.

Lir was frothing at the bit, and the white, foaming saliva flew back in Aonghus' face. Pushing on the crest of the horse's neck with his fists, he made it run still harder until the pounding of its hooves against the ground made him grunt at the force of their impact.

Sweating and trembling, he let his love boil inside him. He did not know what it was that frightened him so, but he would learn to loathe all that it represented. He would make his heart shrivel in his body until it no longer hungered for her. Only then could he emerge from this carnal wilderness a free man.

I want to go back with you; I want to take you inside of me, her lilting voice echoed loudly through the trees.

Crazed, Aonghus yelled as loudly as he could to drown out her words. Again and again, he howled until there was no air left in his lungs, and then he yelped like an injured pup. Bending forward, he rested his limp torso on Lir's withers, and let loose of the reins. His arms dangled lifelessly on either side of the stallion's shoulders, and his head jerked up and down as the stud slowed to a trot before he finally stopped at a brook. Aonghus felt the horse's neck lower, and with his chest still heaving, heard the slow slurping sound of him drinking water.

"I will sustain myself through this loneliness. I am being tested, and I will prevail," he said aloud.

Without looking up, he slid from the saddle, his knees buckling beneath his weight when his feet touched the ground. He could smell the the wet soil beneath him. Digging his fingers deep into it, he tried to bring himself back to reality. He felt as if he were paralyzed. His entire body was an aching mass, and he toiled with even the simplest of movements.

"What is happening to me?" he wailed, lifting his face to the sky. "Am I dying? I do not want to die!"

He stretched out on his belly, and reached for the water. He cupped his hand, and straining hard to drink, he lapped up each droplet like a thirsty dog. With the other hand, he gripped a stone at the water's edge, and pulled his body closer so that he could bury his face in the liquid. The coldness of it burned his skin.

Splashing his neck and shoulders, he attempted to steady himself enough to get his bearings. He felt like he was clinging to the edge of sanity. Not since he had first been hurt in Wales was he so close to madness.

"Saturnalia, can you hear me?" he called, as if she were somewhere near. "I despise you! I despise you for expecting me to keep this arcane vow! There are no more secrets! I cannot deny my beloved and live half-crazed from loneliness. There is nothing for me to win or lose except for her, and I slowly kill her as I die to my true feelings. If I do not do something, she will truly leave me this time.

"You cannot release me because you say that you cannot make a choice between the laws and your tribe. You claim them to be the same, and because of your exalted place, you cannot afford anyone special treatment, no matter how much you love them. But I will make you choose—make you choose as I have chosen. I will find a way!"

He rested his head on his bicep, and wearily looked at the glassy water flowing before him. "You can hear me, Saturnalia, deceptive vixen that you are," he stopped to take a rasping breath. "I will make a new vow to you, because I will have restitution for this torment. I will make you want to die as I want to die. For if death be the ultimate healer, then together we will be healthy again."

He stared straight ahead as the sweat from his forehead dripped into his stinging eyes. Stretching out his hand, he let the water ripple over his fingertips. In the mist and fading moonlight it appeared as though it were made of tiny wavelets of silver and bronze. He was so lightheaded that he was sure that his mind was abandoning his body, and he could at last see his grim release.

He rolled over on his back, and clutched one knee to his stomach to relieve the cramping inside. As he did this, he heard his horse move a few leery steps away from the bank, and looking up, he found himself staring into the face of a haggard old woman across the stream.

Startled, he sat up and cocked his head back. She was washing clothes in the brook, and seemed oblivious to his presence.

Aonghus studied her lined face; the deep wrinkles, across her forehead and around her mouth appeared dark crevices. She wore a white scarf tied beneath her sagging chin, and a simple blue robe fastened high beneath her breasts. Her neck was withered, and her hands were spotted with age. He looked into the water to see the color of her eyes, but found she had no reflection.

Suddenly, the cresting waves of silver became crimson arches of blood, as to his horror, he saw the clothes she so labored to clean were his own blood-stained garments.

Panic-stricken, he scrambled to his feet. His body numb, he stood, wide-eyed and open-mouthed, staring at the hag. She was as vivid as the first time he had seen her in the Druid sanctuary as a child.

"You are death," he stated, struggling to get the words out. "We are old companions, are we not?"

The crone paid him no heed as she clutched the tunic, and washed it more vigorously.

"Speak to me!" Aonghus demanded in a frenzy. "Have you come for me?"

The old woman looked up passively. Her eyes were opaque yellow with tiny pupils. She offered a benign smile, then turned her attention back to the clothes floating in the gentle red current. Aonghus paled, and backed away from her.

"Not yet," he said, grabbing Lir's mane and vaulting onto the horse's back. "I am not ready yet—and I will not go alone."

chapter four

aturnalia wrapped an unruly lock of Conn's hair around her index finger. She could see his brown eyes sharpen as she moved closer and brushed the side of her face against his cheek. A sense of relief came from him, a softening of his heart as she touched her lips to his ear, then circled it with her tongue.

Conn returned her gesture and took a handful of her red mane. "Hmm," he said in a low, seductive voice. "Have you come to distract me from my duties?"

She pressed her body against his; it warmed him as though it were a hot ember sent to ease the cold. "Absolutely, I have come to tempt you—to steal you away!" she replied, as she stepped back and with arms outstretched, and twirled in a circle.

She wore a robe of red and purple silk held together by a broach fastened at her left hip. As the night breeze enveloped the material, it expanded away from her body, and Conn could see her naked outline beneath it.

"I like that," he said approvingly, as she unclasped the broach and let her garment drop to the ground.

She spun around again and again, laughing as the chill of the night caused her alabaster skin to rise. Her hair flowed in loose strands, falling into her eyes as she ran her fingers down her torso, and seductively stroked the inside of her thigh. Gazing at Conn alluringly, she turned her back to him and bent down just enough to slightly expose the soft pink tissue between her legs.

"You are a wicked woman," he said, approaching her.

She turned her head, and stared at him over her shoulder. "No, I am a woman in love," she replied, and turned so abruptly that she almost slammed into his chest. "I cannot be expected to wait patiently for what I want."

"Oh really," Conn said, amused. "And what do you want, my Sorceress?"

Saturnalia's lips curled into a subdued smile. "My needs are simple," she declared, as she pushed herself into him.

Conn ran his hands down her silky arms. "I find that hard to believe."

Contrary to her mood when he had left her earlier that day, Saturnalia was full of girlish impishness. When she was like this, Conn not only found her impossible to resist, but unpredictable and even reckless in her actions.

"Why?" she asked before he had finished his sentence.

"Because there is nothing simple about you," he answered, wrapping his arms around her. Then he lifted her in the air as he hugged her close.

She threw her head back, laughing as she dangled her feet above the ground. "Yet, the words I speak are not untrue. I do not ask for very much, not riches nor power. At this moment, when the moon burns the slightest hole in the night sky, I gaze upon the object of my simple desire."

"As do I," he replied, kissing her lips before she could say more.

Placing her feet on his so that she would not have to loosen her embrace, Saturnalia awkwardly walked with him over to where his fur was rolled out on the grass. Leaning back, she pulled him down with her as she stretched out.

"What gifts have you for me tonight?" she questioned slyly.

Conn's eyes lit up. "Well, let's see," he reached into his leather pouch, and pulled out a piece of salted pork. "Would you like some meat?"

Saturnalia giggled and shook her head.

"No? Hmm, let me see what else I have here. A piece of bread and cheese would perhaps suffice the lady?"

"That is for peasants," she replied, putting her arms around his neck and kissing him again. "Have you nothing that would interest a Sorceress?"

Conn rolled on top of her. "I have only this handsome face and strong body," he said, with feigned humility. "Perhaps these qualities would be enough to satisfy this Sorceress?"

Saturnalia's eyes deepened with emotion. "Yes, they are enough," she said, touching her finger to his lips. "Conn?"

"Yes?" he responded, kissing the tip of her finger then pressing the inside of her palm to his lips.

"When we are together, I want for nothing. When we are apart, I can think of nothing but your return," she said.

"I know," he answered, moving his mouth to her wrist and nibbling on it affectionately. "That is the way it is supposed to be when two are in love. Such feelings have long afflicted me, Saturnalia."

Placing her hand beneath his chin, she lifted his face, and looked at him. "I do love you," she said softly. "And I would not have you feel that you are unworthy as you told me earlier this day. I have deeply considered what you said, and it is my wish that you should become my husband in the spring."

Conn's eyes shone with joy. "That I should take this Druidess in marriage, would honor me. Saturnalia, you are more precious to me than the treasures of the gods."

Lowering his head, he kissed between her breasts as she lifted her shoulders off the fur to be nearer to him.

"I would have you come yet closer," she whispered, loosening his trousers and pushing them down his hips. She could feel his hardened loins as he pressed against her.

Resting his chin on her breasts, he looked questioningly into her eyes. "Whether it be pleasure or slumber that is the temptation, the punishment to the warrior who would forsake his duty while he watches over his tribe is still death. And even though you are the Druidess who keeps such laws, I still must —"

"Quiet yourself," she interrupted, moving his leather breeches further down his legs with her bare feet. "As you say, I am the keeper of the laws in this tribe. We have failed to live by them thus far. Love cannot be held by arbitrary boundaries at such times as these."

Arching her hips discreetly, she brushed against his sex with her dampness. Conn could sense a forcefulness about her that went beyond beauty alone. She was more than all the declarations of the heavens. She was a power of her own, a chameleon that could adjust to love or hate with incredible ease.

Saturnalia stuck out her luscious rose-colored lips.

"Would you deny me your love?" she questioned.

Conn squinted and bowed his head. His momentary infatuation seemed to fade suddenly. Her words trailed off into a tiny echo, and his mind filled with a throbbing so loud that it finally drowned them out altogether. He felt a sickness rising inside, like some unknown burden was overtaking him.

"It is not what I wish to do," he said, shaking his head. "But I feel that something is very wrong. Not between you and me, rather there is some terrible thing very near to us that wishes us harm."

He put his cheek on her breast, finding security in the gentle thud of her heart and steady breathing. Desire had left him, and he felt utterly fatigued.

"Saturnalia?" he took a deep breath. "What is this illness I feel?"

Stroking his back with her hands, she closed her eyes, and used her power to see into his mind. Flashes of red and yellow outlines vibrated intensely. They came immediately into focus, then faded into murky darkness. She began to feel extremely nauseous, and Conn's body became so heavy against her that she thought she would be crushed by his weight.

The repulsive scent of rotting flesh floated in the air, and her head was pounding as though it were being slammed over and over against the ground. Then the blackness was pierced by an intensely bright light, and she saw the image of Aonghus towering maniacally over them. His bloodshot eyes bulged out of his contorted face, and the contours of his body were rippling like he was looking at her from beneath a pool of water.

"Evil one!" he hissed, raising his spear. "I will kill you for this."

"I dare you to do it," Saturnalia mentally retorted. "You may spear me to my lover for all eternity, but I promise that you will suffer mercilessly in the afterworld for your deeds."

She watched as his eyes turned to black slits, and opening his mouth so widely that she could see the back of his throat, he let loose a blood-curdling scream. Then with both hands clenched around the shaft of his spear, he drove the weapon through Conn's back. Even though she understood that it was only a vision, she watched with horror as her own body jolted when the blade entered her heart, and skewered both her and Conn to the ground.

As if he had seen it too, Conn cried out, jarring Saturnalia from her trance. Taking her by the hand, he abruptly pulled her to her feet. She could see the terror in his eyes as he laced his trousers.

"That thunder—can you hear it?" he questioned, placing his hands over his ears. "It sounds like there are thousands of horses approaching."

"There are not thousands," she answered, hastily putting on her robe, "Only one. Let him come; he will not destroy me."

"No, it is not safe. I will not endanger you," he said, grabbing her by the arm. "I do not know to whom the entities in this grove play host, but I do know that tonight, they move beneath an evil sky. Let me take you home now."

With a single stride forward, he pulled her along with him as he started for the trees.

———

Solomon sat back on the mounds of fur and silk that made Saturnalia's bed. He scanned the room, taking notice of those objects that were familiar to him but was more interested in those things she had acquired since they had been together last.

His gaze rested on the tall oak cabinet opposite the bed. Its doors were open enough for him to see the shelves of bundled herbs and the tiny bottles of scented oil, each having a different purpose in the practice of her craft. The bottom shelf was piled with materials of various weights and hues, and Solomon knew that concealed behind these cloths were three very sacred books of Druidic teachings. They were the only books that he had ever seen besides the ones he vaguely remembered his own mother reading to him as a child. While he could still remember how to read the words the Romans wrote, he had no idea what the symbols meant in these Druidic volumes.

Lazily stretching out his hand, he felt a woolen robe beneath it. Closing his fingers around the garment, he lifted it to his nose and inhaled deeply. It smelled of the familiar jasmine oil that Saturnalia wore. Clutching it to his chest he closed his eyes, and reflected on their visit earlier in the evening.

He could see the urgency in her delicate features as she stared into her courtyard, silently hoping Conn would come to see her before the sun was down. How her eyes had glimmered with love and anticipation as she had tried, without success, to indulge Solomon on what was now a rare visit to her home.

"He is robust and worthy, I should think, of this Druidess' affections," he had finally admitted.

Saturnalia looked back at him, her eyes moist. "We have known each other much too long for me to fool you, Chieftain," she said, kneeling at his feet, and resting her head on his thighs.

Solomon stroked her hair. "I must be honest with you then," he said, softly. "I thought you and I would, somehow, always be together. Perhaps I was naive, but I never considered that you might commit to another."

Sitting back on her heels, she looked lovingly into his eyes. "Nor did I," she replied, her voice rich with compassion. "You were always the only warrior in my heart, Solomon. You gave unwavering devotion to my every whim. How is it that I change now? I cannot tell you. All I know is that, for all of his brashness, I am desperately in love with Conn."

She had tried to be kind to him; Solomon knew that now. It was impossible for her to spare him the pain of his love, caring more for another than she did for him. He felt his blood run cold as he attempted to hide the shock.

"Then you must go to him," Solomon replied, taking a tremulous breath. "True love is not given to everyone, and those few souls, whose silence and solitude have been redeemed by it, are fortunate. For no one knows better than I how true love can slip away, and be corrupted by a wavering heart."

Reaching up, Saturnalia took his weathered face in her hands. Each line reflected such character and struggle. It was so different from Conn's, whose entire countenance declared that one so hardy could never die or grow old.

"Thank you," she whispered, kissing him lightly on the lips.

She stood, and tried to appear unhurried as she walked to the door. As she opened it, she turned only once, and looked at him kindly, then disappeared into the mist, leaving him alone in her cottage.

"Oh, sweet Saturnalia, how I wish I could hate you for this," he said, sadly, "but I cannot."

Now holding the garment like it was an infant, Solomon began to doze, hoping that he would dream of her. Lying quietly in front of the hearth where they used to make love, he hoped he would be comforted by his memories. Then the sound of a horse crashing through the gate startled him. He scarcely had time to stand before the door burst open revealing a muddy, sinister-looking Aonghus.

"Aonghus, you have not been summoned here!" Solomon declared, stepping in front of the younger warrior to block his entry.

"Where is she?" Aonghus snarled. "Do not try to protect that shrew, or I will kill you as well."

Solomon was shocked by his ghastly appearance. Aonghus' skin was so pale it glowed, and his eyes burned for blood.

"You are tormented by your own mind, Aonghus," Solomon tried to reason with him. "You are very sick and you must realize that. I do not know what you have experienced that has brought you to this, but you can blame no one for it, especially Saturnalia."

Aonghus stared at Solomon coldly. His lips were pressed together so tightly that the side of his face twitched each time he blinked his eyes.

"My vision of death was brought on by the conniving wretch who inhabits this house," he bellowed, pushing his way past Solomon and into the room. "If I wish them to end, I must put an end to her!"

"No, you must not. That would be an unforgivable offense," Solomon said. "You have too much to lose to give into such madness. Aonghus, you are going to be a great ruler. Your people need you, and you must not forget that!"

He watched as Aonghus' face darkened with fury. Solomon could see him trembling as he scanned the room for Saturnalia.

"I have seen men like you," Solomon continued. "Madmen, who are desperately seeking salvation from themselves. You think your destiny has been changed by Saturnalia, but you are wrong. You are the master of your fate, and it is by your hand that you have designed your own demise. Aonghus, the sickness that has overtaken you is the filth you harbor in your own heart. Let go of your hate and your deep regret for Kordelina, or it will eat you alive."

Solomon could see that as he spoke, Aonghus' mind drifted. The glow of the embers on his cavernous face made him appear venomous. This was not the young man he had raised from boyhood; this was a troubled being deteriorating before his eyes.

Slowly he reached out to him, hoping that some show of affection would bring him back. Seeing his movement, Aonghus raised his spear and pressed the tip of his weapon into the hollow of Solomon's throat.

"Please, I do not wish to hurt you, but you must not protect her," he warned. "If I am to live, she must die."

"Did you really think you could kill her?" Solomon challenged. "Believe me when I say you cannot. When I was a child living with the Druids, a warrior there had tried to kill a Druidess. He attempted to ambush her in the grove. He charged unsuspectingly, thinking he would spear her while her back was turned, but he failed, and was captured and found guilty by the Order. Do you wish to know what became of that warrior?"

Aonghus shook his head. "Say another word, and I will kill you!"

"I must finish," Solomon replied. "This man was sentenced to a slow and very tortuous death by amputation. His limbs were severed off, one at a time, beginning with his castration. It was a long time before he finally experienced the mercy of death. Do you know why?"

"Silence!" Aonghus yelled. "I do not wish to hear any more. I did not come here to listen to your stories."

Solomon ignored him and went on. "His death was very slow because after every finger, arm, and leg was cut, the fugitive was given enough food and water to heal before another part of his body was severed. He died a horrible, emaciated man. I hope that will not be your fate, as well."

Aonghus considered his words a moment, as if it took great effort for him to understand. Then he lowered his spear, and backed away, almost reverently.

"I do not wish to do any more damage. It is wrong to hurt you and Kordelina when it is Saturnalia's deeds that have brought me to this!" he raved.

Grabbing his head with his hands, he tried to hide the effects of Solomon's warning. "This oath, this loathsome oath is supposed to bring me comfort, but it does not. It is killing me, and it is killing Kordelina, too. Yet, this Druidess who made me promise something for which I despise myself, expects me to be consoled by the knowledge that I have kept my vow to the gods. I am not consoled; I am tormented, and I want to make her suffer for it."

"Never speak such deranged words to me again, Aonghus," Solomon said. "Go far from here tonight, lest you be tempted beyond your own control. Do what you must to get through until sunrise, that by day you may be well again. Many years ago when you were only a child, you saved my life. I promised you then that my loyalty to you would last forever, and it will, but I cannot allow you to do this because you will only injure yourself. I will say nothing of this to anyone, but you must not return until you are free from this malice. Perhaps death will show mercy on this eve, if your spirit is contrite."

Aonghus' eyes flashed back at him for one horrible moment before he grabbed his spear, and turned on his heel. He gave a bitter laugh as he exited the doorway. Solomon realized that his ugliness had only begun to emerge.

CHAPTER FIVE

he earth crumbled slightly beneath their feet as Conn and Saturnalia hurried through the grove. Every few paces Saturnalia would turn to see if the echoing footsteps were really there, or just in her mind. She saw only the shadowy tree trunks behind her and she knew, as Conn knew, that they were separated from their pursuer by only a few brief moments that fate alone had dictated.

Conn moved with reckless speed through the bracken, pausing only long enough to solemnly look at her, beseeching her to keep up with him. Each time he did this, she would sigh and roll her eyes, then continue to humor his chivalry.

She had no fear of this phantom attacker. Why resist him; what purpose was there in blocking the forces of eternity? For in her years, Saturnalia had learned many things, but the most prominent was that destiny cannot be sought out or evaded. Rather, it moves at its own pace, stopping for those who will not stop for it. Either a person struggles to prevail against an unknown force, or works within its boundaries; the results are inevitably the same. And whether she liked it or not, her fate and Aonghus' were intertwined long ago. She had expected to confront him before this, but then she supposed his fury was finally brought to a head with the news of Jara's intentions for Kordelina.

They approached a narrow irrigation ditch with a steady stream of water flowing in it. The banks were overgrown with moss and vines that sprouted tiny purple flowers. Swooping her up in his arms, Conn gallantly leaped across it, and set her down safely on the opposite side.

"I dare not go further, lest I be found in absence of my watch," he said, taking her by the shoulders. "From here, I can see you all the way to your yard. I will wait for you to signal me that all is well within before I leave."

Saturnalia looked around, and realized that she was on the back side of the hill where she lived. She did not understand how he had found this shortcut without her recognizing the way.

"How did we get here so fast?" she asked in a low voice.

"We came the back way," he answered. "You did not notice?"

Saturnalia shook her head. "In all the years I have lived here, I did not know the path between the two points existed, how could you?"

Conn smiled. "It is my duty. A warrior must have more than one way to protect his Druidess. Go now, and I expect to see a lighted candle that shows you are safe."

He bent and kissed her lightly on the lips. "Wait for me, my love. My guard is over at sunrise, then I will return to you."

Turning around, Saturnalia felt him pat her affectionately on her buttocks before she started up the hill. Moving gracefully, she tried not to rustle the shrubbery or crack a single twig beneath her feet. She stared straight ahead, eyes fixed on the tiny cottage atop the knoll, where she sensed that Solomon was still waiting. There was a calm about the grove that happens only after a violent storm has passed. Surely the intruder had already come and gone, leaving only the slightest trace of his once threatening presence.

Halting her pace, she listened for Aonghus, but found that the thundering hoofbeats had ceased. Tilting her face to the sky, she closed her eyes and tried to focus on his whereabouts. His energy was distant now, and not as menacing. Saturnalia was unsure if it was because he was far away or had found a way to ease his fury elsewhere.

She glanced down the hillside at Conn, who watched her expectantly. Then she looked up at her house, and continued to walk toward it.

He has been here already, she thought to herself. What could he have possibly found to soothe him? Surely, Solomon could not have any control over such a demented soul.

She panicked for the first time. Aonghus had more stealth than she had predicted. "Sweet Goddess," she prayed. "You see all. Let Aonghus and I face each other by the time the sun casts its warmth on my house. Let all that is hidden in the darkness come to light with the clear morning glow."

As she approached the gate to her courtyard, she could see where it had been broken from its hinges. The bushes in front of her door were trampled, and the herbs beside it were crushed beneath the imprints of a horse's hoof. Solomon stood in the doorway with a grievous expression.

"He has come and gone, has he not?" she asked with more urgency than she would have preferred.

"If you speak of Aonghus, then yes," Solomon answered.

Saturnalia swallowed her anger. "I would take revenge, but he is not worth it. Either someone else will kill him, or he will kill himself." Pressing her hand to her forehead, she rubbed her temples with her thumb and forefinger.

"I am sorry for this, for he took me by surprise," Solomon said apologetically. "This morning he seemed to be himself again. He was even happy because he was to join his parents for feasting on this eve—but after what I saw in him tonight, I can only pray that the spirits are still in control."

Saturnalia glared at him. For a moment, she resented the way he was always compassionate toward Aonghus' state.

"Yes, Solomon, they are in control. Of that you can rest assured," she responded harshly. "That fool! If he makes it through the night, I will have him on his knees for this. Do not expect me to sympathize with his insanity. I do not care how many wounds to his head he has suffered. He knows exactly what he is doing."

She entered the house and came back out with a lighted candle. Holding it high in the air, she placed her hand in front of the flame, twice blocking its light to tell her lover that she had arrived safely.

———

Lir bounded over the trunk of a fallen oak, frothing at the bit as Aonghus yanked his head to the side to turn him. The stallion huffed and flicked his tail as the warrior cracked him on the hindquarters with his whip.

"Faster, you must go faster!" Aonghus commanded. "I will catch them together, she is surely with Conn. I should have killed him for leaving me to the Romans. Conn, you devious coward, it is over for you now."

Holding the reins in his mouth, Aonghus lifted his arms in the air, and with fists clenched, gave a warrior's battlecry that echoed through the trees.

When it died out, he yelled again. This time with more ferocity as he drew his knife in one hand, and held his spear in the other. The muscles of his biceps rippled, and his long hair flew in the wind.

"I am coming for you, Druidess," he raved through clenched teeth. "I will find you! You have broken the laws of this tribe. You have laid with your warrior while he is on guard, and have failed to uphold the very laws to which you bind me."

He threw his head back, and laughed malevolently. "And when I do get to you, I will have reason to slay you both. No Druid or chieftain will deny that, because I will kill you as I find you, locked in each other's arms."

He quieted himself as he approached the place he knew Conn would be. The adrenalin was rushing through him like he was going into a battle, and he was. It was a battle for his life and his lover's, and he would make Saturnalia disavow the oath that separated him from Kordelina if it took force to do it.

Slowing his horse to a walk, he tied the leather reins around his waist so that he would be able to charge with weapons in both hands.

Cautiously inching the steed forward, he peered through the trees into the clearing. Leaning his weight back, he made his horse stop. Lir seemed to instinctively understand what his master was doing, because he remained perfectly still as the warrior scrutinized the area before him.

Aonghus could see a fur spread out at the meadow's edge, and a leather pouch cast carelessly next to it. It appeared that its contents had been taken out then thrown aside.

Bending over so that his chin was resting on the horse's neck, Aonghus studied the woods as he anticipated some movement. Perhaps they had heard his screams and were waiting to ambush him.

Sitting still for a few moments, he saw no sign of the two. He lighted from his horse and walked deliberately to the center of the clearing. Holding his hands high above his head, he turned in a circle, signaling anyone waiting to attack him, that he was fair game. His gestures went unanswered.

"You have only evaded me for the moment, Saturnalia," he jeered. "There are still many hours of darkness in which I can move unseen, even to you. I will play your little game and win. You will have no choice then but to grant my wishes. You have become complacent all these years, thinking that no one would dare challenge your authority. I can assure you that you are not the first Druidess to be discredited, regardless of your lofty regard of yourself. Deireadh called herself a Druidess as well, and we both know the end that fate dealt her. I have only to make the people see your flaws, and that you have harbored a spy for many months, and called him your lover. And when they have made a spectacle of your guilt, just as they did with my Kordelina, I will be able to tell her the truth, and you will never come between us again."

He went to Conn's fur, and cut off a corner of it with his knife.

"I will make good use of this, my friend," he said, then climbed atop the lathered stallion.

Gathering the reins, he started down the well-trodden path back to the village. Clouds were moving across the sky, defusing the moonlight and covering the stars. Soon it began to sprinkle, and Aonghus enjoyed the water trickling down his chest and arms. He was glad for the rain because he had asked much of Lir, and the chilly droplets cooled the overheated horse.

Nearing the settlement, he noticed most of the huts were dark, and save an occasional stray dog, Aonghus thought he could probably pass through it without being seen. His instincts told him to stay out of sight, so he turned his horse, and remained on the outskirts until he reached his parent's farm.

He kicked his stallion lightly in the flanks, and the horse obediently scaled the low stone wall surrounding the property. Recognizing him instantly, Koven's three hunting dogs surrounded Aonghus as he dismounted. They happily licked his hands, and begged for attention. Petting each one on the head, he waited for them to calm down before leading his horse to the watering trough.

"You are a courageous one," he said, patting Lir's neck. "You serve me well and I am sorry to work you so hard without water. Drink long, I will be back."

With the reins dangling to the ground, Aonghus left the horse and went toward the house. He felt suddenly free of the anger that had burned his insides earlier; perhaps it was the familiarity of his parent's home, because everything around him evoked a feeling of security. Looking about the farm as he walked, he went around the back of the house to Kordelina's window.

Using his knife blade, he jimmied the shutters apart. Opening them only a crack he looked into her chamber to be sure she was there. He could see the outline of her body underneath the mounds of fur. Carefully he stepped inside, closing the window noiselessly behind him.

Kordelina was in a deep slumber, and gazing upon her caused a quiver within him as he knelt at her bedside. The room was warm, and he felt like he had, at last, come home after an exhausting journey. He was suddenly relaxed, even happy at the sight of her sleeping so serenely before him. Laying his cheek against her covering, he closed his stinging eyelids and let his mind drift to pleasant memories.

"Aonghus, look—look at me, I can ride Macha without any hands!"

Suddenly he saw her as a child. It was summer, and the air was muggy from the heat. He had just returned from fighting the Romans, and informed Solomon that he would take her under his charge. Kordelina was atop her horse, arms out-stretched and laughing as she rode toward him and Conn.

"That is wondrous!" Conn exclaimed, pretending to be more impressed with the youngster than he really was. "If your arms are ever cut off in battle you will still be able to ride! What a talented apprentice you have acquired, my friend."

Aonghus laughed heartily as Conn slapped him on the back. "Come, we will all drink to Aonghus' new foster!"

A sentimental tear came to his eyes at the remembrance. "Things seemed easier then," he said softly.

Fingertips suddenly touched the side of his face. "The past always seems easier," Kordelina answered.

Aonghus looked up. "Not always," he replied, his eyes wrinkling with a nos-talgic smile. "How is it that you sleep so peacefully?"

Kordelina lovingly stroked his brow. "Because you labor so."

She closed her heavy lids as she dozed, then opened them again as Aonghus cupped her face in his hand. She touched the mud on his neck, then lifted her fin-gers to her nose, and smelled it to be sure it was not blood.

"Where have you been?" she asked, examining his soiled clothes.

He looked away sheepishly as if he were trying to find the right words.

Kordelina took his hand in hers. "Tell me," she urged, her voice calm.

"To a place where I have never traveled. I have descended to the darkest depths of my being," he answered seriously. "I have troubled the gods, but they are deaf to my cries. I have cursed my dismal state, and have found that I am least contented with that upon which I have built my life. Kordelina, many years have passed in these few hours."

Wrapping her arms around him, she pulled him down on the bed next to her. "You are so weary, rest now."

Aonghus lay his head in the bend of her neck. Her sleep-warmed skin, and the soft elk hides offered such tender refuge. He was sane again, but felt surpris-ingly unrepentant for his fury.

"I was dreaming of you and me; we were together because the gods had been benevolent," she said, as she rhythmically ran her hand over his bicep. "Per-haps I dreamed it because that is what you seek. Mercy for yourself, and not the pain of another."

Aonghus nodded and pulled her closer. Earthly beauty radiated from her and he loved the feel of her against him. Only it was not sexual pleasure that he sought now, it was the feather-soft touch, the understanding spirit of the one he loved. Her peaceful mind, and her heart whose care for him was innocent and unsuspecting of malice.

"How can you know, so well, what I am feeling?" he asked in a whisper.

Kordelina smiled tenderly. "Because I feel every beat of your heart. There is no way you can hold your soul that it will not be touching mine. You could reject me even unto my own death, only to —"

"Surrender to you again," he finished her thought.

"Yes, we both surrender again. For us, there is no other way; by loving each other, we love ourselves. I do not know why we must overcome so much to be together in this life, but surely there must be a reason," she bent her head as she kissed him on the forehead. "There are times when I think it is something far greater than just the love between us. Perhaps it is the love of all things, that by learning not to hurt each other we are really learning not hurt ourselves."

Aonghus looked into her eyes and kissed her gently on the lips. How could he have ever thought he could survive without her?

"I feel as if nothing can touch us here. It is as though you watch over my very mortality. Yet, I know that it is not safe. We will be found if I stay too long," he said.

He closed his eyes and took a deep breath. "Kordelina, there may be no place for us in this tribe. To be together, we may have to forsake all, and begin again. Are you willing to do that?"

"Yes," she answered, running her fingers over his face. She acted as if she had been robbed of her sight as she touched the bridge of his nose, his rugged cheekbones, and his lips before kissing him again. "I have nothing here but Macha. I would go anywhere with you, Aonghus; you know that."

"Even if it is a great distance? Another land perhaps?" he questioned. "We might not have any choice."

She noticed something more austere in this features. "Our souls span across them all. I have no choice but to follow," she said sweetly.

He hugged her tightly. "Then you must help me. Solomon has banished me from his house until I am once again composed. As I am now, I have no control over my emotions, and my vengeance has been great. I would ask you to use the powers Saturnalia has taught you to show me how I may entreat the spirits to gain strength," he said, letting her go as he looked away. "I can tell you no more."

"I will do what you ask," she answered.

"But I must have your word that you will tell no one, not even Saturnalia. It means that perhaps you will have to lie to keep her from knowing, but it is the only way," he said, as he looked at her suspiciously. "Can I trust you?"

"Yes, I give you my word even unto death," she answered, then reached beneath her covers, and brought out a white-leather conjuring pouch.

Aonghus watched curiously as she opened it. She had never before shared its contents with him, and he had always wondered what mysteries it contained. Carefully, she reached inside it, and pulled out a piece of jade.

"This is my most powerful stone; it was given to me by Saturnalia herself. Hold out your hand," she commanded.

Aonghus complied, and she set the smooth green rock in the center of his palm. It felt slippery and cold.

"Listen, carefully," she continued. "You must wrap this in a scrap of cloth, one of great importance to you. Furl the cloth, and hold it tightly between both hands. If it is power that you seek say the words, 'Power is mine, as of this stone. Beware the fire I cast at thee,' then you must say your own name, and no other. If you do not say your name and focus on your own image, then you will enslave the one whose name you speak. You must avoid that above all things because then you have crossed over from light to darkness. Be very careful. After you have spoken this, make your supplication, whether it be for sleep or kindness, or whatever you need. Do you understand?"

Aonghus nodded.

Taking out a knife from beneath her pillow, Kordelina sliced the vein of her left wrist. The blood seeped out, the red stream filling the minute cracks of her ivory skin. Then she took Aonghus' hand that held the stone, and pressed it to her cut.

"Let this be anointed by the sweet river of my body," she said softly.

Her eyes were glassy; Aonghus ached to look into them. He did not want to involve her in this, but he saw no other way to secure their future. He wrapped his fingers tightly around her slender wrist. It was so slight in his hand that he could easily touch all four fingers with his thumb.

Feeling the strength radiating from her, he clasped it tighter. He felt as if he were burning with fever with each tiny beat of her pulse. They were anchored together, and he did not want to release this conduit between them. He wanted to say something, give some further explanation, but he did not speak. He just pulled her to him and kissed her firmly on the mouth.

CHAPTER SIX

he drizzle had stopped by the time Aonghus returned to the grove. The still air was moist, and brisk enough to chill his arms and face. Droplets dotted the leaves of the shrubbery, and the first light of morning made them appear as tiny diamonds dropped from the sky. The ground was soggy, preventing Lir's hooves from making any sound.

He had left Kordelina sleeping as serenely as he had found her, her sliced wrist bound in a shred of the purple sash he wore around his waist. He had not realized how long a time he had spent with her. But it had been one of the most absorbing, tender experiences of his life. With the strength of her loving heart she had listened to him weep and confess his love for her, and his regret at ever hurting her. She had forgiven him, and asked his forgiveness as well, and the two had promised never to let anything come between them again.

Kordelina discovered his secrets, all except the one of her parentage and his recent encounter with Saturnalia in his bedchamber. After listening to his private hungers and transgressions, she had let him sleep like a little boy against her soft breast. He thought it strange how his lust had transformed into a deeper love, simply by entrusting her with his inner truths. No longer did he have the urgency to fulfill forbidden desires, because now, they would have the rest of their lives together. Kordelina seemed to know this as well because she did nothing to initiate lovemaking between them. She merely laid there next to him, stroking his hair and wiping away his tears. What had begun as a tumultuous night metamorphosized into an emotional consummation of their love.

However sympathetic she was to his plight, she was still not capable of fully comprehending the price of the private war he was about to start. He believed it was because she had no real concept of the importance of the laws that provided the foundation of their culture. To her, they were an arbitrary force that influenced others. He realized now that her devotion was not based on philosophical belief, but on unconditional acceptance. As long as those she loved were happy to live by them, so was she. And Aonghus wondered if, perhaps, she was not the most liberated one of them all.

He was near Conn's post, and his instincts told him that this time, the warrior was there alone. Reaching into the pocket of his vest, he removed the shred of Conn's sleeping roll, and commanded Lir to a halt.

As he dismounted, the only sound he made was the small thud as his feet hit the grass beneath him. He took the jade crystal from his saddle pouch, noticing that Kordelina's blood had dried making its deep-green color a muddy brown. Carefully, he wrapped it in the hide, and clenched his fist tightly around it. Then he took the long leather strap tied to his saddle, the one that was normally used to attach the skull of a slain enemy, and put a slip knot in one end. He did not bother to take his spear, these were the only weapons he would need.

Approaching the clearing, he chose his steps deliberately. Closing his eyes for an instant, he took a deep breath and visualized that all of the light surrounding his body was flowing into the pit of his stomach. Like a swirling wind, he gathered this energy within him, and imagined himself to be invisible. He began prowling through the oaks for the best vantage point. He could easily make out Conn sitting lazily against a tree trunk, with one leg bent and his spear resting in his lap. He was preoccupied, and unaware of his surroundings.

Of the two, Conn was the more natural fighter. His skill in battle was effortless, and his charismatic personality made him far more popular among the women of the clan than Aonghus would ever be. It was little wonder that Saturnalia had chosen him as a lover. He had often joked that greatness was likened to a woman; it found him irresistible.

Aonghus was almost at the meadow, when taking another step, a branch cracked beneath his boot. Conn immediately sat up, and Aonghus was forced to drop to the ground where he was.

He saw Conn rise to his feet and walk to the edge of the trees to search the woods just in front of him. Aonghus could see the warrior was fatigued.

Aonghus was on his stomach, perfectly still. If Conn were to find him, he could easily think up an excuse for being there, but it would ruin what might be his only chance to extort Saturnalia. Conn listened a moment longer, then satisfied that it was nothing, returned to where he had been sitting.

Still on his belly, Aonghus crawled closer. The grass was wet with dew, allowing him to slide noiselessly forward. Remaining well hidden behind two boulders, Aonghus stopped a fair distance away from the warrior and peered at him through a space between the rocks.

"This is not personal, my friend. I am only in need of your influence, since you are the treasured amusement of a Druidess," Aonghus said to himself.

Keeping his eyes fixed on Conn, he placed the fur-wrapped stone between his two hands as Kordelina had instructed.

"Power is mine, as of this stone," he whispered. "Beware the fire I cast at thee, Conn. Let you fall into a blinding slumber in my presence."

A few strained moments passed as Aonghus silently watched the yet unaffected warrior. The sun was beginning to rise, the first rays of its light appearing purple and orange among the hovering rain clouds. When the sun could fully be seen over the hill, Conn's duty would be over, and Aonghus began to wonder if this etheric spell was nothing more than another one of the Druids' absurd myths.

The Druids, what a truly strange lot they were, he mused. They claimed that theirs was the craft of the wise. The archaic rituals they handed from one generation to the next were the cherished beliefs of his people. They preached the mystical art that was the merging between self and the life force of all things, built upon love and used for universal good. And none, not even he, dared to question it until now.

Again he held the stone between his hands and repeated the words, "Power is mine as of this stone; beware the fire I cast at thee, Conn. Let you fall into a blinding sleep, now in my presence."

The fiery orange crest of the sun could now be seen pushing its way up from the earth into the sky. All of Aonghus' attention remained focused on his friend, wondering why, by this time, he had not gathered his weapons and prepared to leave. Straining his eyes, he realized that Conn was already asleep. He was so good at cloaking himself, that he had fooled even Aonghus.

Using the cover of the trees, Aonghus made his way to Conn's side. Squatting beside him, he looped one end of the strap through the slip-knot. As he did this, he turned to look at Conn, waiting a moment to be sure he was not feigning his slumber. When he was satisfied that it was not a trick, Aonghus carefully placed the leather lasso around one of Conn's wrists resting limply in his lap. Then, with even greater precision, he took the loose end, placed it around the other wrist, and then through the knot, loosely binding both of them together.

In a moment, Conn's head dropped forward, startling Aonghus. It took all of his control to keep from backing away in surprise even when he realized that the warrior was only going into a deeper sleep.

Trembling, he cautiously rose to his feet and stepped in front of him. He made sure his weight was evenly distributed, positioning himself for a fight. With one hard pull, he yanked on the strap binding Conn's wrists together.

Conn's eyes burst open, and his head jerked up in surprise. Then his startled look faded, and was replaced by sudden amusement as he focused on Aonghus. He flashed a charismatic smile that seemed to say this was another game created for his entertainment.

"Hello, my friend," he greeted him, then laughed. "You have caught me."

Aonghus looked down on him expressionless, and did not reply.

Conn's smile broadened. "Are you in need of a diversion? A release of tension perhaps?" he joked.

Aonghus' eyes narrowed, and he tugged harder on the strap until Conn was clearly in pain.

The cajoling smile left Conn's face. He eyed Aonghus impassively, then abruptly tried to stand. He was halfway to his feet when he felt Aonghus brutally kick him in the abdomen. Trying to clutch his stomach, he lurched forward, gasping for air as he fell to his knees.

Aonghus stood over him and wrapping the tether around one hand, cut the slack between them.

"On your feet," he commanded, his voice a monotone. "I charge you with neglect of your duty. You were sleeping while on watch."

Breathing hard, Conn looked up as he spoke. Aonghus' chest was covered with mud, his eyes were smoldering, and he seemed on the verge of exploding. At times like these, Conn knew all too well that the slightest error could infuriate him. Temperance was a virtue his friend had never possessed.

"Do not take it to heart. It has happened before, and I dare say that it could happen again," he remarked carelessly. "Even the sun sleeps while the moon is awake. Liken me to the sun if it pleases you."

"It does not," Aonghus replied, his mouth hardening as he spoke. "It would please me to have you on your feet, or I will tie you to the back of my stallion, and drag you back to the village."

Conn burst into laughter. "Aonghus, it is me—Conn. I am not your adversary. I do not wish to do battle. You look as though you have had a cursed night, and I do not wish to ruin your morning."

He saw Aonghus' expression shatter, then toughen quickly until it appeared to be carved in stone. An unsettling wickedness lurked about him.

Bowing his head regretfully, Conn pretended to look down at the ground. Then hastily grabbing his bindings with both hands, he used the leather to brace himself as he sprang to his feet. Aonghus stepped away involuntarily, and Conn forced himself forward, trying desperately to get his balance. He saw Aonghus' boots moving at him, and felt the impact of a two-fisted blow on the back of the neck.

Refusing to falter, Conn staggered before settling into a slouching stance. "If you do not restrain yourself, I will have to hurt you," he warned, trying to sound like he was amused at the situation.

Panting furiously, Aonghus seemed to dance in front of him, his eyes glittering like polished gemstones. Jerking on the leather again, he pulled Conn clumsily forward and delivered a sharp kick to his chest. The warrior grunted at the pain, but remained steadfast.

"Why are you doing this? You are my kinsman, not my enemy," he whispered breathlessly.

"You are charged with the crime of slothfulness, and forsaking your duty to your tribe. Do not expect me to grant you pity. That is for Saturnalia to do, not I," Aonghus' face contorted hatefully as he spoke.

Conn threw back his shoulders boldly, both hands still tightly closed around the leather cord separating them.

"I see," he answered, as his voice regained its resonance. "Then it is your jealousy that provokes you."

Aonghus shook his head, causing a strand of his dirty hair to fall into his eyes. "I have no want of your Druidess. She has visited my chamber in the night, and I find her displeasurable," he saw Conn's face redden with jealousy as he spoke. "I only want her to grant me what she grants to you, and it has nothing to do with what is between her thighs."

"What is it then?" Conn demanded. He had begun to move around Aonghus. The two warriors were moving in a circle, stalking each other.

"A release," Aonghus answered.

"From what?" Conn barked back.

He suddenly moved his hands up the line, and pulling Aonghus unwillingly forward, he butted him between the eyes with his forehead.

Stunned, Aonghus backed away, his eyes tearing at the pain. Raking his leg behind Aonghus' knees, Conn knocked his feet out from under him. Aonghus pulled the bound warrior down with him as he fell.

Without wasting a moment, Conn wrapped the line around his attacker's neck like a garrotte and began to strangle him. Aonghus bucked wildly beneath him, trying to free himself. Conn could hear low, gurgling noises as his face went from red to blue.

"We were brothers once, fighting at each other's side. I do not wish to fight against you now," he said, almost sympathetically.

He saw Aonghus' mouth freeze open, and his eyes roll up into his head. The sweat was streaming down Conn's face as he hunched over the suffocating warrior. He knew he was dying, and it sickened him.

"No!" he yelled, saliva dropping out of his mouth and onto Aonghus' face. "You will not provoke me this way!"

He loosened the garrotte and sat back on the ground, trying to catch his breath. The blush returned to Aonghus' cheeks instantly, and he began to take short, labored breaths of air. Then he slowly raised his hand, and unwound the strap from around his neck. The leather had cut into the skin, and blood trickled down the hollow of his throat. He was listless, and moved slowly.

"From what do you wish to be released?" Conn questioned.

Aonghus shook his head. "It is between Saturnalia and me," he said, his voice cracked as he spoke. "Unfortunately for you, you are the bargaining power I need."

Conn eyed him warily as he got to his knees and his chin dropped to his chest. "Let us call a truce as this has gone too far," Conn offered sincerely. "We have kept each other's secrets before. You have said nothing about Blathnaid, and I have never told anyone about the cave. Let it remain so between us now."

Aonghus did not make eye contact as Conn extended his hand.

Savagely locking his fingers around his forearm, Aonghus heaved him forward and punched him in the face, splitting open his lip. Conn barely had time to react when he felt Aonghus' fists pounding into his sides. He was relentless, and Conn groaned piteously with each blow. Still bound and helpless, he slumped back. A loud crack sounded, but he was unsure if it was his ribs or Aonghus' hands as he felt knuckles pummel him again.

———

A muffled voice could be heard in the next room as Koven dressed to begin his work. He had been afforded the comfort of sleeping a while longer since Kordelina had returned, because she rose early to feed the livestock and care for the horses. He had never asked her to do it, and would rather she had offered to help Enda. With three boys at home, and now Kordelina, his wife was beginning to show signs of weariness.

He clenched his fists tightly, then extended his crooked fingers hoping to ease the burning in his joints. With each day that passed, he was able to use his hands less and less. He did not have to be told that this would be his last spring for planting, and his last chance to teach his children what must be done for a healthy crop.

None of his sons had real talent for farming, and even though he did not realize it at the time, Kordelina being stripped of her place in the hierarchy had provided a needed solution. It seemed a bit of a waste to teach her farming though, because more than any man, she was adept with horses and was an impressive huntress. There was little doubt in Koven's mind that it was because she was born of Solomon and not himself. There was, also, some speculation as to how long his daughter would remain with their tribe, considering that Jara would soon take the girl with her to live elsewhere.

Smoothing back his hair, he opened the door and went to see what ambitious visitor had joined them for breakfast.

He was greeted by the sight of Solomon and Diarmudd, who rose from their seats as he entered the room. Solomon offered a pensive smile that told him he had a matter of great importance to discuss. For some time now, the two men had not had the chance to enjoy a simple visit without matters of conflict arising in the conversation—whether it be Aonghus and Kordelina, or the Roman invasion of the surrounding waters. He hoped that it was the latter because last night's dinner had left him more than disappointed with the behavior of his two children.

"Do not rise on my account. Please sit," he said amicably.

Solomon held out his hand, and Koven took it firmly with one hand, and patted him affectionately on the shoulder with the other.

"How are you, old friend?" the Chieftain asked. "Well, I hope."

Koven nodded agreeably. "I am well," he answered, then turned to Diarmudd. "Well, young man, you are looking very fit this day. How is your wife?"

Diarmudd flashed a gallant smile. "She is fine. Our child is due at any time," he said, gushing with pride as he spoke.

"I have hardly left my home these last weeks for fear I will miss the wondrous event. I would not be here if it were not for what Aonghus —" he stopped immediately, embarrassed that he had said more than he should have. Explaining the reason for their visit was the task of the Chieftain.

Koven raised his brows, and looked at Solomon. "What is wrong with Aonghus? Why is he not with you?"

"I was hoping he was here," Solomon answered, taking his seat, trying to appear unworried.

"No, he is not," Koven replied, noticing that Enda had silently entered the room and was standing in the doorway listening. "Why?"

"There was a small dispute last night after he left you. In a rash moment, I asked him not to return to my dwelling until it was settled. I feel now that my judgment was severe. Aonghus is like a son to me," Solomon nervously rubbed his palms together. He was becoming noticeably upset as he spoke. "He has not come back yet, and I am troubled that in his present state he may have left this tribe alone. I have searched his every hiding place, but he is nowhere to be found."

Enda walked over to him, and placed her hand comfortingly on his shoulder. "My son is ill with a great burden that he will not confide to me or his father. Nor has he been truthful about other things. He would have us believe that he is still going to marry Bracorina, yet she tells me that she thinks him taken by spirits. She is afraid to be in his presence."

"I know," Solomon said, resting his hand on hers. "Where is Kordelina? Perhaps she has spoken with him."

"I doubt that," Koven replied. "She can barely stand the sight of him. Last night, he joined us for feasting, and the two hardly looked at each other. There is little love between them now, and it pains me to see it."

Diarmudd shook his head solemnly. "I am sorry to hear that. Even though I have never liked Kordelina, I know that at one time, Aonghus had great hopes for her," he saw Enda's face tighten at his words.

"Just the same," Solomon continued, paying him no heed. "I would like to speak to her if I could."

"Of course, she is probably in the barn," Koven walked to the window. He knew how much Solomon secretly enjoyed a visit with his daughter, and Koven never denied him the opportunity. He lifted his stiff fingers, and clumsily opened the shutters.

"Kordelina," he called. "Come inside."

In an instant, the girl could be seen at the door, her hair tousled, and her cheeks were rosy from the crisp morning air.

"What is it, Father?" she answered, with a smile. The smile was replaced by a sullen expression as she looked at Solomon and Diarmudd.

"Come in, child," Enda coaxed, walking over to her and taking her by the shoulders. "Solomon would like to speak with you."

Kordelina sat down and stared stubbornly at her feet. It was the first time she had seen him since he had found her and Aonghus together. She caught sight of Diarmudd out of the corner of her eye; his expression was filled with contempt.

Solomon reached out and gave her a fatherly pat on her thigh, but she still could not look at him. She feared that he had come to tell her parents about what had happened between her and Aonghus that night.

"Were you with the horses?" he asked, trying to ease the tension.

"Yes," she answered civilly.

"Your face is so red; you must have been working very hard," he continued in a kind voice.

"No, not hard," her words were curt. "What do you want of me?"

Solomon averted his eyes to the fire for a moment, then looked back at her. He was visibly wounded by her impertinence.

"Kordelina! That is no way to speak to this Chieftain; do not be disrespectful!" Enda reproved.

Solomon waved his hand in the air. "No, it is all right. She has much to do, and I am sure I am keeping her from getting it done. Is that not right?"

Kordelina did not answer.

Solomon took his hand from her leg. "I only wish to know if you have seen your brother, Aonghus, since he visited last night."

Referring to Aonghus as her brother sent a chill through Kordelina. Lifting her gaze, she looked Solomon squarely in the eye. She knew that he would know she was lying if she did not.

"No. He feasted with us last night, then left. That is all," she answered, without blinking. "I am not his keeper, nor am I in his charge any longer. Is that not the way you wanted it, Chieftain?"

Solomon glared at her insolence. "That is the way it must be," he responded seriously.

He took a long look at her, waiting for her to look away, but she did not. Instead she boldly met his gaze, and he saw in her young face the reflection of himself, cleverly blended with the image of Deireadh. She could be stoic and strong-willed, yet cloak herself so well that she was the portrait of vulnerability. She was not to be underestimated.

"Then so be it," she replied disdainfully.

Solomon put his hand to his beard and thought a moment. There was something distressing about her sudden aloofness; perhaps it was the bond that exists between a father and his daughter that gave him extra insight at this moment. Yet, he could not pinpoint exactly what it was that caused him to distrust her response.

"I would like to know that I could rely on you as I once did," he said.

Kordelina gave him a half smile. "I would ask the same of you."

She was sly. According to her punishment, she had no voice in this tribe; therefore, consistent to the laws, her word meant nothing. By manipulating the conversation, she would force him to give her his word of confidence while owing him no allegiance whatsoever. If he refused, he would appear an unworthy Chieftain.

"Chieftain? Can I ask the same of you?" she repeated.

"Yes, Kordelina," he answered. "You may count on me as you always have."

Her expression remained unchanged at his words.

For a long uncomfortable moment, the two sat very still. Solomon was waiting for her to slip. Make some nervous gesture, or a suspicious waver of her gaze that would somehow incriminate her. She was sure of it. He was powerful, there was no question of that, but she was more powerful and more resolute than he could ever know.

Solomon touched the tip of his index finger to his lips, and looked back at her intently. "That is all," he said flatly.

Kordelina still refused to blink. "Nothing more? Perhaps I could help you search for him," she offered, feigning sincerity.

Solomon folded his arms across his chest. Having to endure the months of servitude, and forbidden to speak unless spoken to, she had become a master at disguising her feelings. Perhaps she was capable of making others believe she despised Aonghus, but not him. In his mind's eye, he could still picture the two of them in a blissful embrace. Her devotion unabashedly belonged to Aonghus, and no one, not even a chieftain, could penetrate their bond.

"Do not trouble yourself. He will return soon enough," the Chieftain said, his tone suddenly light. "I will not detain you further."

Kordelina stood and slightly bowed her head in acknowledgement. She turned to her father and reassuringly took his hand. "I have taken care of your horses already, Father. Visit as long as you like, there is little left to tend to."

Koven grinned. "You are good to this old man."

"You are not an old man, you are my father," the girl responded genuinely.

Her display of affection struck a tender cord in Solomon. What would she have been like if he had not given her to this farmer and his wife? Would she have cared for him so endearingly? It would all be so simple now if he had raised her as his own. He would not be so alone in his later years having a daughter to care for him. And surely, she and Aonghus would have married, and given him the joy of many grandchildren.

"Mother, you will fetch me when Edainne's time comes?" she asked.

"Of course," Enda answered. "If you are not here, I will send Niall to find you. Go on now and finish your chores."

Solomon's expression softened when he saw her give Enda a kindly glance before exiting.

Koven returned to the place where he had been seated, beckoning his wife to join them. Enda sat down next to her husband.

"The transition has not been easy for her," Koven confided. "She has been very distant and sullen."

"It is true," Enda agreed, her eyes beginning to tear. "She does all that she is asked, and more. Yet, I sometimes feel like she would rather be back as Aonghus' slave, than be here. Then, last night, seeing the way they behaved toward each other, well, it caused my heart to ache."

Solomon looked at the ground. "Much has happened between them. It is little wonder that they even speak at all. Aonghus never wanted her servitude, yet he could not stand to see her burned in the wicker man for her crime. As for Kordelina, she cares more for him than she lets others know."

A tear trickled down Enda's cheek. She hurriedly wiped it away, hoping no one would notice.

"There, there," Koven said, wrapping his arm around her shoulder, and pulling her to him. "It is nothing to fret about. They are young, and the passage of time will cure the ills between them."

Solomon looked up, his eyes filled with compassion. "Your husband is right. Perhaps we worry about them too much. They are old enough to know their own wishes."

He stood and Diarmudd immediately rose to his feet with him. "I must be going now to tend to my duties. The best of mornings to both of you," he said, bending down as he kissed Enda on the cheek.

The older woman reached up to hug him. "Join us tonight. We will feast together for it has been too long," she said, her voice quivering.

"I would like nothing more," he answered, releasing her. "I will be here at dusk." Then he walked to the door with Diarmudd in tow.

"You take special care of that wife of yours, young man," Koven called, as they left.

"I will, sir," Diarmudd replied respectfully.

CHAPTER SEVEN

ill you need my help any further?" Diarmudd asked
Solomon as he mounted his horse.

"No, you have done more than I could expect
considering you are about to be a father at any time. Go
home, I am sure Edainne would want you with her," he
replied, looking about the livestock area for Kordelina.

"What of Aonghus' duties—who will do them in his stead?" Diarmudd
asked. He knew that Aonghus had a lucrative clientele, and if he, indeed, had
abandoned them, Diarmudd wanted to be the first warrior to whom they were
offered. With the beginnings of a family close at hand, it would certainly be
appreciated.

"They are few on this day, I will take care of them," Solomon answered,
then turned to the young man. "Diarmudd?"

"Yes," Diarmudd answered, unable to hide his disappointment.

Solomon scratched his bearded chin. "When we arrived, Macha was in this
front pasture, was she not?"

Diarmudd turned to look at the grass paddock in front of the house.

"Yes, she was. Kordelina probably put her back in the barn," he replied
carelessly. He wanted to get back to the subject of Aonghus' celsine.

Solomon stared at the oversized building for a long moment. "Why would
she do that? After they are fed, they are turned out, not brought back in," he
replied. "No, I think our innocent Kordelina has gone somewhere. She is tricky.
We did not even hear her leave."

Diarmudd gave the Chieftain a guarded look, hoping he would not ask him
to help look for her as well. This was like Kordelina, he thought to himself, always
inconveniencing someone because of her single-mindedness. It mattered little to
Diarmudd that at one time she had greatly helped Edainne. He had never been
able to abide her head-strong ways. He had liked her the most when she was a servant. The only thing that he regretted was that Aonghus gave her freedom before
allowing him to bid for her as chattel. In his opinion, his friend had suffered
greatly as a result of the leniency he had shown to this selfish young girl.

"Perhaps I can help you search for her?" he offered. From his tone, it was
obvious he was offering his help out of obligation.

Solomon climbed into his saddle. "I appreciate your concern, but you
should go to your wife," he responded. "I will find Kordelina myself."

Diarmudd tried to suppress his relief. "Thank you, Chieftain. I am sorry I could not be of more help, but my cares are with my family right now."

"I understand. The next time I see you, I hope you are a father," Solomon said. He looked at him for a brief moment, then turned his horse. "Kordelina is surely with Aonghus, and this is between him and me."

Spurring his animal, the older warrior started down the narrow road toward the center of the village. Diarmudd watched after him a moment, wondering what was so urgent between the Chieftain and Aonghus, and how it involved Kordelina. Things had been conspicuously different these last few days with Aonghus suddenly releasing Kordelina, then becoming ill, and Bracorina's woeful description of his friend had left Diarmudd sure that Aonghus had completely lost his mind. Now he had mysteriously disappeared and Solomon thought he might have left the tribe altogether. Something was definitely amiss, he thought. Then he shrugged his shoulders, and trotted in the opposite direction. It was really none of his affair.

———

Following the fresh hoof tracks, Solomon trotted across the clearing to the east of the settlement. He was heading for the seashore where a tiny stone hut looked out over the strait. It had been used lately to survey the waters for approaching Roman vessels, but Solomon had not bothered to look there for Aonghus because a recent storm had left the dwelling in a state of disrepair. However, the path he was on definitely led to it, and he considered that perhaps Aonghus had spent the night there, and Kordelina was on her way to tell him about Solomon's visit this morning.

Solomon was more convinced than ever that Kordelina definitely knew of Aonghus' condition and whereabouts. There would be no other reason for her covert behavior unless she were protecting him. The Chieftain only hoped that no harm had come to the young man last night, and more importantly, that he had not harmed anyone else in his present state of mind.

The sun was midway in the sky by the time he could see the strait. The moist, salty air blew cold against his face, but neither the breeze nor the sunshine had been able to remove the haze that hung low over the choppy water. At the very edge of the shore, elevated on a jetty, he could see the outline of the dome-shaped building set against the spray of the sloshing waves.

Approaching it, Solomon knew it was empty because the tracks stopped at a freshwater inlet just in front of it. Kordelina had obviously anticipated being followed, and had brought him there as a decoy. By leading him this far out, she could make him think he was on the trail of something while providing herself an easy escape by the stream and keep her tracks covered.

Feeling incredibly foolish, Solomon rolled his eyes and bit the inside of his lip. He was glad Diarmudd was not there to witness his folly. Just because Kordelina had no rank, it did not mean that she had forgotten her training.

"You do me justice, my daughter," he said, secretly pleased by her stealth.

Following the narrow stream back the way he had come, Solomon surveyed the banks looking for any place where she might have crossed up onto dry land. The dirt on either side was so muddy that he was sure he could spot her tracks.

Wading against the swift current, the sound of his horse blended with the water. He felt no urgency about finding either Aonghus or Kordelina because he did not anticipate quarreling with them; he wanted to talk with them. He knew that whatever he had prevented that night when he found them in the barn together had not ended there. What other reason could there be for Aonghus stalking Saturnalia? Only something of incredible passion would have made him lash out like that.

Catching sight of something moving up ahead, he leaned forward to see what it was. He could make out a tan-colored animal just off the banks that was concealed behind dense foliage. He could see it was rather large, and was the same color as Macha. There was no one near it, but that made no difference. Kordelina was smart enough to tie her horse in a conspicuous place to provide her time to reach her destination on foot.

Shifting in the saddle, he started up the muddy bank. The weight of his horse tore the earth beneath him, leaving deep holes in the soil with each step. He took great care to find a path by which he could move around the animal from the back without being heard. If Kordelina was keeping a lookout nearby, he wagered that she would be watching the stream and not the woods.

The Chieftain moved in silence, not even disturbing the dew on the shrubbery around him. When he was only a few paces away, he saw that the animal was not aware of his approach.

Focusing on the tips of its large ears, he continued moving forward, and when he was almost upon it, it reared its head. Large brown eyes flared in fear, and the Chieftain flinched in surprise as with one leap, it was across the brook and was gone. It was not a horse at all. It was a deer.

Solomon sat back in his saddle, feeling very old. This was the work of younger men, he thought to himself as he patted his horse on the neck, and started back to the settlement. It was no use pursuing Kordelina because she did not want to be found. He would have to leave word with Koven that he wished to speak with her.

The path he took home meandered through the grove and up the incline of a hill. The rays of the sun looked like golden pillars dropped from the sky as they stabbed their way through the knotted branches of the oaks. When he reached the hill's crest, he could see a few storm clouds moving in from the north as he looked down on the village. Relaxing his hold on the reins, he descended the gradual incline toward the center of it. Perhaps he would find Aonghus among his tribesmen, and all his worry was for nothing.

He had almost reached flat ground when he saw two men entering the settlement from the opposite end. One of the men was perched atop a huge bay-colored horse. The fatigued animal was bobbing its head as it walked while his rider sat with his shoulders arrogantly thrown back.

The other man was towed by a long rope bound tightly around his wrists, with one end fastened to the back of the rider's saddle. The prisoner's gait was short and uncoordinated. Even at this distance, Solomon could see his ankles were loosely tied as well, causing him to nearly stumble with each step he took. The tribesmen shifted their attention from the bustle of their chores to the approaching men as Solomon urged his horse to a gallop.

When he reached the center yard, he saw Kordelina. She stood in a small passageway between two houses holding Macha, looking expectantly up the road. Solomon stopped alongside her. She looked up acknowledging him, then looked down at her feet shamefully.

Doors opened on all sides as curious onlookers tried to learn what the commotion was about. One by one, they stepped outside, or peered from their windows. There were a few gasps of disbelief from those who recognized the two warriors. Solomon and Kordelina watched with even greater anticipation, each silently hoping that it was not whom they thought it was.

Then they saw Aonghus riding slowly toward them. He sat straight in his saddle, glowering at the small crowd that had gathered. A low muffle of whispers began among the clan as he passed. He looked part demon, with his tangled hair and dirty arms. There was blood dried on the side of his mouth, and save for the blue and green beginnings of a bruise in the center of his forehead, he had no color in his face. He held the reins in one hand, while his other hand rested casually on his thigh.

Naked to the waist, Conn staggered helplessly behind him. Sweat covered his swollen face, and his neck and arms were scraped from where he had obviously fallen in his trek back. As he came closer, it was easy to see that the young warrior could hardly breathe. He wheezed as he laboriously inhaled through his nose, and exhaled from his mouth. One side of his face was horribly swollen, making it appear lopsided. Along his rib cage were swollen pockets of blood that appeared red and purple in the sunlight. There was so many of them that, at first, Kordelina thought he must have been trampled or rolled down an embankment, until she looked at Aonghus' bulging knuckles, and saw that they were raw.

Spotting her, Aonghus stopped. His expression was stern, and looking into his eyes, Kordelina realized a part of him had hardened—not a trace of gentleness in his countenance remained as she forced herself to look away.

Aonghus sat as if he were frozen in time. He waited for her to look back and offer a private verdict for his deed. He had to know if she meant what she had said last night, that she would support him no matter what came about. He could tell by her tense mannerisms how vulnerable she felt. Then she lifted her gaze, and looked at him disapprovingly.

He glared back at her steely-eyed as he reached into his saddle pouch. Taking out her jade stone, he tossed it in the dirt in front of her feet, and continued on his way.

Kordelina dropped to her knees and snatched it up. As she stood, her gaze met Conn's, and the absence of malice in his expression brought tears to her eyes.

Why had Aonghus done this terrible thing, she asked herself. Why had he betrayed his friend?

In the distance, Saturnalia could be seen atop the hill looking down at the entire spectacle. She was a ghostly image, dressed in a pale green frock that flowed in the breeze. Her arms were at her sides, like a celestial pillar draped in the mist.

———

It seemed only an instant had gone by before the two warriors were at her gate. Bracing herself against the oak, Saturnalia turned to face them as they entered. She could feel her stomach quiver and her knees go weak when she looked at them.

Purposely trampling over her garden, Aonghus stopped in the middle of the yard facing her. Her hands were clammy, and she nervously wiped them on the sides of her hips. She hoped there would be a way to deal with him that would somehow ease the circumstances for Conn.

Trying to temper her breathing, she waited a moment for Aonghus to dismount and properly address her, but he did not. Instead, he stayed atop his horse, looking down at her condescendingly.

Summoning her composure, Saturnalia stared back at him. She had never felt such repulsion for anyone in her life. This selfish man was now in possession of the one thing she wanted more desperately than the very air she breathed. Conn was the keeper of her heart, the only man to whom she had ever entirely divulged her soul. To bargain for his life was to bargain for her own because she did not want to live without him.

"Speak to me, warrior," Saturnalia demanded.

Wiping the blood from his mouth with the back of one hand, Aonghus scoffed at her attempt to show superiority.

Saturnalia's composure transformed into contempt, and she could not disguise her hate any longer. Raising both hands in the air like claws, she found herself about to attack him when Conn suddenly dropped to his knees and cried out in pain.

"On your feet," Aonghus commanded, mercilessly pulling on the rope and forcing him to stand.

"What do you want?" Saturnalia questioned, stopping in front of Lir. She still had her fingers outstretched, and was on the verge of angry tears.

Aonghus looked down his nose at her. "You know what I want."

Saturnalia bristled and took a step back. She was being defeated by him, and she had to resist the distress rising inside of her if she was to think clearly.

"State the reason for your visit," she countered firmly.

He looked her up and down, sensing her unwillingness to bargain with him right then. She wanted to see how serious he was about accusing her lover, and he knew that she was too calculating to give anything away.

"Very well," he said. "This warrior was found asleep while on guard."

He reached around and quickly coiled the rope until Conn was beside him. "By forsaking his obligation to protect his tribe, he endangered their welfare. I charge him with slothfulness of his tribal duty," he continued, unfastening the rope from his saddle.

He eyed Saturnalia coolly, and for a brief moment, did nothing. He wanted to prolong her suffering, and make it clear that he would go as far as he had to in order to accomplish his end. He could see her green eyes dart nervously over to Conn before looking back at Aonghus. When he was satisfied that she was completely tormented, he put his foot in the center of Conn's chest and shoved him to the ground in front of her feet.

"Sacrifice him," he snarled, then he broke into triumphant laughter as he exited the gate.

Staring at him in anguish, Saturnalia backed away as Conn held out his hand to her. "Please, help me," he moaned, writhing with pain. "I love you, Saturnalia. I need you to help me."

Looking down at him, she felt as if she were going to explode. The sight of her lover begging for mercy revolted her. Her despair rising, she wanted to kill him right then while she was still in shock. It would be easier than having to wait to kill him with the swift stab of her own dagger at the sacrificial altar.

Rising to his knees, Conn crawled forward and took hold of her gown.

"Please," he whispered pitifully.

Clutching her head, she stumbled backward, ripping away the part of her robe that he was holding. Her vision was starting to dim; this could not be happening, she thought. Aonghus cannot possibly expect me to kill him.

"Help me," Conn pleaded again, tears welling up in his brown eyes.

Her heart was pounding, and she was heaving wretched sighs. The throbbing in her head was so loud it drowned out the sound of his voice. She could see only his mouth moving as he reached out to her. Then she suddenly envisioned herself standing over him at the stone altar. The thought of it was drowning her, and she felt as if she were going to faint. She stumbled again as she turned away from him, and ran to refuge in her cottage.

Leaving Conn on the ground, she fell across her bed and buried her face in the pillows. Then Saturnalia wailed to the gods for redemption.

CHAPTER EIGHT

ou always do everything he asks of you," Solomon admonished in a disappointed tone.

The crowd had already scattered, and the once interested onlookers who had made up its ranks returned to their morning tasks. Their curiosity had been satisfied.

Kordelina stared at the piece of jade in the palm of her hand. She was not sure if she felt betrayed by Aonghus' use of her powers, or if she had in turn betrayed him by not being a better confidante. For whatever reason, he had felt that he could not tell her his plans last night. She wanted to believe it was because he was looking out for her, and did not wish to involve her at all.

"What did he tell you he was going to use it for?" Solomon continued.

Kordelina shook her head. "It was not meant for this. He came to me last night, and said that you had cast him out of your home. He said he needed my help to soothe the ill spirits within him. I offered him this stone, and told him of a spell he could use with it. That is all, Chieftain. That is all!"

The desperate tone in her voice made Solomon realize that she had no idea the sharing of her craft would be used against another.

"Solomon?" her voice was tearful as she spoke. "What is he trying to do—ruin this entire tribe?"

The old warrior took her by the shoulders and shook her to quiet her. He did not want her to say anything incriminating in front of her tribesmen.

"I do not know. As it is now, he is guilty of nothing. Rather, he has charged his kinsman with a crime," he said seriously. "I fear that your brother has found Conn in absence of his watch; nothing else would cause such a struggle between the two. If that be so, he has the right to demand that he be sacrificed or burned, whichever he thinks is deserving of the deed."

"No!" Kordelina protested.

"Quiet child!" Solomon admonished. He could see her fear that she might somehow be responsible for this.

He pulled her closer and looked straight into her eyes. This womanchild suddenly appeared forlorn to him, as her lower lip quivered and she blinked back tears. It was almost as if she would simply fade away into the ethers if he spoke too loudly.

"Listen to me. This is the time you must trust your inner voice above all else. Do not believe what anyone tells you unless you perceive it to be truth. Not

468

me, nor Saturnalia, and hard as it may be, you must separate yourself from Aonghus. View him as an outsider would lest your devotion to him be prostituted," his words were short; his voice hushed. "Cloak your feelings from all others, that is how you will survive this private war."

A vast gloom showed on Kordelina's face as she slightly lowered her head. "I do not understand of what war you speak."

The Chieftain released his grip. She could be so gullible at times, unsuspecting that someone she loved could ever do anything to hurt another.

"What Aonghus has done is to force Saturnalia to choose between her love for Conn and her responsibility to uphold the laws of our people. If she does not sentence him, she will be nothing more than a figurehead for the Druids," he said. He tried to choose his words carefully.

"These are trying times for our people. The threat of Rome is imminent, and if they do make this island a part of their conquest, we will be forced to embrace beliefs that are not ours. They call us heathens and barbarians, Kordelina, and they will stop at nothing less than our total destruction if we do not submit. Perhaps all seems well in our land, but the tides of fortune may soon turn against us. We are clinging to the last vestiges of our civilization by a tiny thread. If Saturnalia casts aside the statutes for her own good, all that our people have fought and died for on the main islands will appear to mean nothing to her. I do not have to explain to you how fickle and unsympathetic the hearts of our kinsmen can be. Will you answer something honestly for me?" he asked.

The girl nodded and nervously bit her bottom lip.

"Do you seek to uphold the laws of this tribe, or to protect your kinsmen?" he asked, slightly raising his voice.

"To protect my kinsmen," she answered without hesitation. "The laws have never helped me, but my kinsmen have."

Solomon sighed heavily. "Do you understand that as a warrior you swore to uphold the laws, even if it was at the expense of your tribe?"

"Yes, but I am no longer a part of your hierarchy," she argued.

"Those are the words of a coward, and quite unbecoming to be spoken by such a one as you," he retorted. "Maybe you are not part of this tribe now, but Aonghus is. He has made a vow to uphold the laws. That means that if he has found Conn in error, it is his duty to ask for sentencing."

"But that will destroy Saturnalia. She is in love with that warrior. To ask her to sentence her own lover, well, not even a sworn enemy would ask such a thing. Surely, Aonghus would not —" Kordelina stopped in midsentence, and looked in alarm at Solomon. "I must speak to him!"

As she turned to leave, Solomon caught her by the arm. "You are too late. If Aonghus did not expect him to be punished, he never would have come this far. He would have settled it elsewhere," he explained. "No, he means to challenge Saturnalia's resolve for reasons of his own."

"Solomon?" Kordelina asked uncertainly.

"Yes."

"Do you think Aonghus has really gone mad?" she asked, looking down at her feet.

He paused a moment. "All I know is that he is on a personal quest, and he will destroy anyone who gets in his way. If he would betray his kinsman of many years as he did with Conn, he would betray you. Watch yourself, child. You care for him far beyond your own good."

Kordelina cheeks flushed as if what he had said had embarrassed her.

"Yes, Chieftain," she replied. "But I must go to Saturnalia; surely Conn will need care. Aonghus will be looking for me on horseback, but I think I would move better on foot."

"I understand," Solomon said, and took the reins from her hand. "I will return Macha to your home."

"Thank you," she answered.

He watched her take only a few steps at her normal pace, then she sprinted away from him.

———

Kordelina hastened up the hillside to Saturnalia's cottage. All she could think of was how Conn had come to her defense when she had failed Aonghus in battle. More than anyone, he had witnessed what a capable assassin she could be. And that night around the bonfire when her tribesmen would have burned her alive, he had demanded she be tried fairly. Kordelina knew then, by the glint in his eyes, that he was fully aware of her and Aonghus' love for each other. He knew that any quarrels between her and her master were only jealous spats, not blatant usurping of his authority, as Diarmudd had interpreted. If it had not been for Conn, Kordelina was sure she would have been executed by now.

She and Conn had never discussed the reasons he had tried to protect her, but she sensed it was because he understood that matters of the heart fell under a different set of rules. How she wished that Aonghus could understand that now.

Stopping by the ditch behind Saturnalia's cottage, Kordelina knelt down and dug her fingers deep into the wet earth. She took a huge handful of mud, rolled it into a ball, then wrapped it carefully into the fold of her sash. She knew she would need it to dress Conn's wounds.

She ran as fast as she could the rest of the way to Saturnalia's, thinking all the while about what she would say to her about this. She wanted to find a way to tell the Druidess that she had not intentionally used her craft against her lover. It would be useless to lie about it anyway because Saturnalia would read her thoughts, and know the truth.

She thought of what Solomon had told her about Rome, and how they viewed her people as savages who needed to be conquered. Kordelina knew that despite their massive infantries, they could not destroy the world of her people; it was too vast. It extended from the very peak of the heavens to the deepest, darkest crevice of the earth. All that was held therein—each flower, animal, and soul—was sacred. This land was precious, and even as the seashore, the lakes, the emerald crests and lush meadows could not be defeated, neither could the spirits that dwelled therein. Whether they were in the form of man or beast, the murmur of the waters, or the heartbeat of the earth, no army could tame an entire universe.

She could understand their desire for their rich farmland, but what need would they have for their sacred groves? They did not follow the Druidic rituals. Rather, they believed in a single man who professed to be the son of a single god. She had heard Solomon explain his teachings to her father; he called them Christians. It was the belief in the doctrine of a man named Jesus Christ, whom Solomon said had been a gentle soul who believed in love and forgiveness. It was not such a strange idea; after all that is what she wanted, to love and to be forgiven. Perhaps it would not be so bad to trust the teachings of this man, she thought, because the laws of her tribe had brought her only sorrow.

She was desperate when she entered the gate and saw Conn lying face down on the grass in front of Saturnalia's door. His hands and arms were covered with fresh dirt, and Kordelina could see the imprints in the soil where he had dragged himself closer to the house. His eyes were so puffy that when he looked at her, only one would open. As Kordelina knelt beside him, she noticed that his expression was vacant with delirium.

"Conn, listen to me," she said. "You must help me turn you over."

The warrior weakly lifted his hand as if trying to push her away.

Gently running her palm over his back, she felt the muscles spasm at her touch. He was a mass of swollen flesh so badly beaten that the sight of the purple and green contusions made her nauseous.

"What happened between you and Aonghus?" she asked, holding back her urge to vomit.

Conn smiled benignly. "He found me sleeping." He tried to laugh at the irony of it, but began to cough instead. It was a low, rasping sound that meant his lungs were heavily congested.

"Stop it," Kordelina scolded. "This is not funny. You are gravely ill, let me tend to you."

"Help me, if you can," he said in a resigned tone, and using what was left of his strength, slowly rolled over on his back.

After examining him briefly, Kordelina could see she was going to need comfrey, black mustard, and dried kelp, all of which the sorceress stocked. She entered the house without knocking, and stopped inside the entryway. She felt as though she were entering a vault of sorrow; the air was heavy with Saturnalia's muffled sobs, the fire was out, and the room was so dim that Kordelina had to wait a moment for her eyes to adjust to it.

"Saturnalia, Conn is in urgent need of your healing!" she said, staring dumbfounded at the sight of the Druidess, who looked so very unlike herself.

Saturnalia's green eyes were masked by dark circles. Squinting, Kordelina could see red lines on her neck where she had scratched her skin with her fingernails. Her face was pale and the set of her mouth was hard; she looked as if she were made of stone.

"That evil one has told me to sacrifice him," she said, her voice rigid with hate. "He found my lover asleep on watch, and he is using it for revenge. Do not ask me to preserve what I will eventually have to destroy. I would rather Conn die now from Aonghus' hand, than later by my own."

Kordelina was openly dismayed at her declaration. "Has everyone lost their minds? You cannot possibly deny Conn your healing. If he dies now, it will not be because of what Aonghus has done. It will be the result of what you have failed to do. Is that what you want?"

"No!" Saturnalia shrieked, picking up an unlit candle and flinging it at Kordelina. "You are too young; you do not understand my burden."

Kordelina stepped sideways, and easily dodged the flying object. "Perhaps I am still young," she argued, "but I know that if you refuse to help save this warrior, you will be more guilty than Aonghus for his passing."

She stormed over to the oak cabinet where the herbs were kept and flung open the doors. She rifled through Saturnalia's things so indiscriminately that she expected the sorceress to try to stop her, but she did not. She sat staring straight ahead, as if in a trance.

Recognizing the black-jeweled bottle of healing oil, Kordelina grabbed it hastily, along with the bags of herbs she needed. Holding them tightly in one hand, she tucked a blanket and a sheet of muslin under her arm, and, grabbing a jug of wine, she went out again.

She found Conn with his brow hidden in his forearm, his lips pursed in pain. Placing her hand behind his neck, Kordelina tilted his head so that he could drink the wine. He swallowed rapidly, then his chin dropped forward and the red liquid gushed out the sides of his mouth. He coughed, then greedily reached out for the jug, and drank more.

The musty aroma of the wine and the putrid smell of his dried blood sickened Kordelina even more. Reaching for the bucket of water on Saturnalia's step and a cloth, she began to gently clean his wounds.

He winced at her touch, but endured the bath, crying out only once in pain. He kept his eyes closed as she removed the cake of mud from her sash, and placed it in the wet cloth. Then she took the comfrey, mustard, and kelp, and mixed it with the mud, dowsing it with just enough water to make it into a poultice.

"This will only hurt for a moment," she reassured him as she rubbed it along his torso.

The warrior's breaths became labored, and a cold sweat broke out on his face. "I thought you said it would only hurt a moment," he offered, trying to make light of his pain.

"I am sorry," Kordelina apologized. "What I am going to do next is worse, I'm afraid. Your ribs must be bound."

Conn opened one eye, and gave her a pleading look. "Can you not just let me lie here awhile? It hurts so."

"The longer you wait, the worse it will hurt," she replied softly.

He let his head fall back against the grass. "I suppose you are right."

Wrapping him in the muslin first, Kordelina then took off her vest, loosening the laces as far as they would go without coming undone. Her wrinkled shirt bunched up around her waist as she lifted Conn's arms above his head, and she saw that even his armpits were bruised.

He moaned as she pulled the vest down over his head and shoulders.

"Lift yourself a little," Kordelina said. When he complied, she swiftly tugged it down over his midriff.

Conn was sweating profusely, and she could see he had tears in the corners of his eyes. "We are almost done," she whispered, wiping his brow with her hand. "This is the worst part so I will do it as fast as I can."

She yanked on the laces, closing the vest as tightly as it would go. She could see the tiny folds in his flesh as the leather pinched it. The warrior lay trembling, his teeth clenched to keep from making any sound.

"You can relax now, I am finished," Kordelina said, covering him with the blanket.

Conn heaved a sigh of relief. "Why are you doing this?" he asked, hoarsely. "Surely you must know that I am now a criminal. Aonghus has rightly charged me, and I have not denied it."

Kordelina picked up the jug, and gave him another long drink. "It does not matter to me since I am still considered a criminal, as well. You helped me once, and I have not forgotten your kindness," she answered.

Picking up the small vial of healing oil, she anointed his forehead with it. "Do you wish me to stay with you until Saturnalia comes out?"

"No, I will care for him now," came Saturnalia's voice.

Kordelina turned and saw the Druidess standing behind her. Her tears were dry and her green eyes burned with determination. She had found her strength and would heal Conn's infirmities in spite of what the future might hold.

CHAPTER NINE

Crouching on a sturdy branch of a leafy oak tree, Aonghus could easily see Saturnalia's cottage. He had watched Kordelina enter the yard after he had left, and he noticed that as she entered the gate, she was looking over her shoulder as though she wanted to be sure she was not being followed. He knew that she must be thinking he had deceived her, and he had, but only because she never would have helped him if he had told her what he had in mind. Now, he would have to find a way to explain it to her, a way that would make her understand that he had only done what was necessary so they could plan a life together.

So much time had passed since her arrival that he was sure she was tending Conn's wounds. Aonghus hated having to hurt him so severely, but he left him no choice. He was too superior a warrior to surrender without a fight. Even bound, he was an awesome battler. Aonghus' bruised body was proof of that.

Looking back on their friendship now, Aonghus had known from the beginning that it would evolve into rivalry. It was even more evident when Conn had become Saturnalia's lover, that their days of trustworthy cavorting were finished. True, each of them had changed, grown up a little too much to find the same enjoyment in carousing and in hunting the way they used to do together. And it was only natural to want to be more settled and committed to a single woman. After all, man was not meant to be alone. The desolation he had felt these last days without Kordelina made that undeniable.

Still, Aonghus could not help but feel saddened, knowing he and his friend would never be close again. It would be impossible to explain to Conn the reasons for his actions, to tell him that he had to accuse him in order to be able to barter with Saturnalia. Even though at one time Aonghus would have killed him for the good of the tribe, that would have been different than ending it like this. There was more nobility in dying a warrior's death than in being executed as a criminal.

In spite of his imperiousness, Aonghus did care for Conn, but he cared more for Kordelina. By doing this, he was putting the Druidess in the same position he was. He did not believe that she would not sacrifice her lover, but she would allow Kordelina to be taken away. It was not because she loved one more and the other less, but because she had absolute control over this tribe while having to be subservient to a Druidess of higher position. Saturnalia could not

474

absolve Kordelina from her destiny, but she could discreetly allow her to get away from this place.

That was all Aonghus wanted now, a life with her and to be free to speak the truth. Kordelina deserved that, and even if it meant playing by the most unethical of rules, he would do it.

Rubbing his tired eyes, he saw she was finally leaving the yard. She walked with her head down, the legs of her trousers stained with grass from where she had been kneeling. Her hair was loose and rebellious, and her tunic was open enough to expose her collarbone. She had her arms folded across her chest, and Aonghus noticed that she was not wearing her vest.

At the sight of this waif, he felt the exhilarating fear and desire which caused him to experience total rapture in her presence—every nerve in his body was rising to the surface of his skin. Gripping the branch in front of him, he waited for this sensation to pass. By her reaction this morning, he knew she must be furious with him. He also knew that equal to her ability to show anger, was her need to forgive, and Aonghus knew that she would forgive him anything.

The nearer she got to him, the more confused she appeared. He felt guilty; she could not know how desperate he was to be free of all of this, the laws, the tribe, and the lie he had to live every moment he looked into her eyes.

He waited until she was almost beneath him, then dropped to the ground in front of her. She jumped back in surprise, sudden fear flashing in her eyes as she gasped out loud.

"Be not afraid, Kordelina, it is only me," he said, trying to calm her.

She turned white and her face hardened. "Go far from me, Aonghus!" she said, backing away from him.

Aonghus smiled gently. "Kordelina, it is all right; you must not be afraid."

She continued moving away from him so hastily that she tripped over a branch, and fell. Aonghus began to laugh at the sight, as still on the ground, she used her hands and feet to scoot further back.

"What is wrong with you?" he laughed. He had never witnessed such a frightened reaction in her.

Her cheeks reddened with humiliation. "You are what is wrong with me," she accused. "You asked me to trust you, then you lied and wounded another. What you did was wrong Aonghus; it was so wrong."

He did not wait for her to say more as he reached out, and grabbed her by the wrists. Pulling her to her feet, he started to run deeper into the woods. He ran and ran, leading her against her will through the trees and over the sloping green hills. He could hear her words of protest, begging him to let her go.

Aonghus knew she feared he was going to harm her, and he could not blame her for it. He had been more than unpredictable and vengeful in his emotions, and she had every right to be confused. But he had hurt her enough already, and he would not hurt her anymore. He would make that perfectly clear; she would never doubt him again.

Splashing through a chilly stream, he continued up the soggy embankment. At this moment, he felt so free, so hopeful for the future once again. He could smell the sea air as they approached the ocean cliffs, and in spite of the way he was beginning to tire, he ran faster. It was as though the sound of the cranes and seagulls, combined with the roaring of the waves, were calling him by name, and he soon found himself on the edge of a cliff with the strait crashing below.

Realizing where they were, Kordelina dropped to her knees, forcing him to let go of her. He turned abruptly and saw that she was sitting back on her heels, her face sweaty and her cheeks red. Her dark hair fell over one eye, and her pink lips opened as she tried to catch her breath.

"Please, do not cast me into the sea," she pleaded. She stared at him uncertainly, waiting to see what he would do next.

Aonghus' face softened. "I did not bring you here to give you over to the ocean gods. I brought you here because I wanted you to look out as far as you could see, and choose any direction in which you wish to sail. Wherever it may be, I will take you there, Kordelina, and we will make it our home."

She looked away, and there was a long, uncomfortable pause. "I cannot go with you now. Not after what you have done to Conn and Saturnalia," she explained in a reproving tone. "I know that it is because of the way I provoked you that this happened, and I feel that I am more guilty for it than you."

Aonghus flushed with anger. "What I have done to them? What she has done to us is the greater transgression!"

"She has done nothing to us," Kordelina argued, glaring back at him. "Truthfully, Aonghus, when has it been acceptable for a brother and sister to be together in the way that we desire? The night Solomon found us together, I was the one who said it did not matter what others thought, and that all that was important was you and me. Now I see that my desire for you has sorely affected everyone."

Aonghus picked up a rock and turning around, cast it into the ocean, then looked back to her.

"What are you thinking of me now?" he questioned, perturbed. "That I am no longer worthy of your devotion?"

She shook her head sorrowfully. "No, it is I that am not worthy. I have pursued you relentlessly, refusing to believe that you did not love me as I loved you. I feel that it is my fault for tempting you so, and making you turn against your kinsmen," she explained, her eyes beginning to shimmer with tears. "This has come about because I have abused my powers for my own selfish ends. Forgive me, Aonghus, but I have made a victim of you, and I am more than sorry for it."

Aonghus got down on his knees in front of her, and she could feel his strength rippling through her as he took her face in his hands. Over and over, he ran his thumbs across her lips, and stroked her cheeks without uttering a word. His affection created such a passionate surge within that she felt like she was fainting and being revived again and again.

"My precious, innocent Kordelina, you cannot begin to know what abuse of power really is. In your chaste soul, you have no concept of the devious ambitions that have vanquished many a man, the insufferable outrage that spurns honor and embraces unworthiness. So sweet is one such as you that you would think the conscience of all men desire truth when they only cower at its heels. For when I look at your beauty, it translates into virtue before my eyes, and I see that I, too, am a breeder of deception. The only way I will escape this disgrace is to make right that which my ignorance has bargained away. What I did this morning was such a deed," he said seriously.

"I did not want to hurt Conn or deceive you, but I had to do so. You see, this poor condition that I am in is only because I thought they had taken you away the night I released you, and I believed that you were gone from me forever. As you are before me now, I know that the gods have shown mercy. They have given me another chance so that I may prevent the dreaded thing from happening at all."

She listened to him with a cynical expression on her face. "Such things as you speak, I have heard for too long a time now," she responded.

"But this is not nonsense, for I know that you are to be taken away from here to another tribe," he replied. "Saturnalia has been made to give you over as the bride for a chieftain. I believe that Jara intends to have you sacrificed because Mother told me that you shall be sanctified at the celebration of Brigantia. I cannot interpret that to mean anything different."

"No," she whispered, as her body stiffened in fear. "Saturnalia would not let them take me."

Aonghus pulled her close. As she pressed against him, he felt the sudden, dizzying thrill of her softness.

"She does not want to," he continued, "but she has no choice. She is bound by the Order to offer a virgin instructed by her when she is asked, and because of your crime, Jara has demanded that it be you."

"But whose bride shall I be?" she asked, starting to tremble. "Aonghus, I do not want to be killed for another when I would willingly die for you."

Aonghus wrapped his arms around her, and held her close. "You shall be my bride; you shall be my bride," he gently reassured her.

"How? Perhaps we can leave this tribe, but if I am under the demand of the Order to wed a chieftain, no tribe will accept us," she argued meekly. "Every Druid in every clan would know of our deeds, and Jara would never allow us to escape. She would rather see us burned than allow us to defy her authority. It would serve no end for us both to die. As it is now, Conn has already suffered for my selfishness, and Saturnalia is afflicted by the thought of having to kill him."

Aonghus' brows came together for only a moment, then his face went blank. "How did you know it is the sentence I demanded?"

"By the way you brought him before her. You did it so that the whole tribe would rebuke him. Saturnalia's spirit is so distraught, I have never seen her in such a state," she answered.

She turned her head to the side, her eyes closed. She did not want to look at him as she tried to push him away. Aonghus grabbed her arms, and shook her once gently.

"But she will not sacrifice him. She loves him greatly, and Saturnalia is much too shrewd to allow something she wants to slip through her fingers," he said, trying to make eye contact with her. "She will find a way to bend the statutes to suit her as she did with you. When she does it with Conn, she will have to make restitution to me because that is the way the laws are constructed. Before you could become my servant, I had to agree that I would rather have your indenturement than see you executed. When I go before her this time, I will only request what I must so that we can be together. It is too complex a circumstance to seek simple solutions, so I promise you that I will only demand what I must for our freedom."

Kordelina looked at him hopefully. "Aonghus, you are risking your entire future for me. Am I really worth that much to you?"

"You are worth more," he answered, his voice trembling with emotion. "I have always dreamed of you and me, but did not want to admit it. I was always at war with my feelings, wanting to care for you less, and caring for my status and Bracorina more, but I could not. The illusion lives not in my heart, rather it poisons my mind. And when I think with my heart and feel with my head, I become crazed. I want to destroy every obstacle that keeps us apart, and that includes Saturnalia, if she so wishes it."

Kordelina placed her finger to his lips to quiet him. "Do not speak such things. She will hear your threats, and will not stand for it."

Aonghus was shaking now, not from fear but from trying to restrain himself. At this moment, he wanted to invade her with his spirit. He felt he had labored through the hellish night, and was finally being born into a world of devout love. He felt strange and excited, and like an infant suckling his mother's milk for the first time, so was he nourished by the very presence of his loved one.

"Let her hear. I do not care anymore. I have no conscience left except when it comes to you," he replied.

It had begun to sprinkle, and droplets of rain trickled down the sides of Kordelina's face. Reaching out, he grabbed a handful of her damp hair and without speaking, stared at her. He saw the pure expression in her eyes, her slightly parted lips, and her long graceful neck that looked out of proportion with her broad shoulders. Her shirt was wet enough to cling to her breasts, and her erect nipples looked like they would pierce straight through the cloth.

She tried to move away from him, but he went with her. He pushed his chest against her bosom until she lay on the ground beneath him, his pelvis resting between her bent legs.

"I will possess you," he whispered, running his hands through her mussed hair. "We will be one; we must be one."

The rain was coming down harder now, and it was so cold that it felt like tiny pebbles hitting his back. He found it insignificant when compared to the intensity of his skin against hers.

"We are one," she said, and began tenderly kissing his face.

She kissed every part of it so delicately that it felt like the tickle of a feather. First his forehead, then nose, both eyelids, the crest of his cheekbones, and then ever so gently, she touched her lips to his. Then she drew away, and gave a little giggle.

Taking her with him as he rolled on his back, Aonghus laughed aloud. He felt so young again, so incredibly alive. Every sensation was magnified; even the contrast of her skin against her raven hair dazzled him.

"I am tired of seeing you in the soiled clothes of a servant," he said. "I want to dress you like a princess."

She looked back at him, her eyes resonant with beauty, and she smiled. He ran the tip of his finger across her teeth, then touched the inside of her bottom lip. He would have taken his virgin right then if he had thought he could conceal the way he felt from the others, but he knew there was no way that, once they had become one, he would ever be able to hide his feelings for her again. He would have to wait and make them believe that everything was back to normal, or he and Kordelina would never stand a chance.

A strand of her hair brushed against his chest as he lifted his mouth to hers, and delicately returned her affection. They both laughed now, rolling across the wet grass, tenderly kissing each other. It was such liberation to be dominated by his instincts once again, the animal lust rising in him becoming hotter and hotter, until his blood blistered in his veins. He realized he was grabbing at her clothes now, but their wetness clung so closely to her body that he was pinching her skin. He was thinking every moment, recording each nuance of their love.

She was cleaving to him, and her reactions were so spontaneous that they were almost clumsy. She had never been touched the way he was touching her. It seemed almost cruel to intrude so blatantly upon her innocence, but she wanted it this way. He wanted it this way.

They kissed each other like it was a secret ritual of ecstasy that had just been revealed to them. She was nibbling on his lips, moaning softly as he opened them wider and wider until they completely encircled hers.

The rain began pouring down on them, soaking their clothes and plastering their hair. He could taste it as drops of water fell from the tip of her nose onto her upper lip. He found his hands were inside of her tunic, gently massaging her firm rib cage, and brushing across her breasts. He wondered how much further he could go before he would be unable to do anything but make love to her. Softly and deliberately he would do it, with no urgency of proving himself, and he would nurture every subtle movement that brought her pleasure.

"Kordelina, is that you?"

Aonghus recognized their younger brother's voice coming from behind them. Kordelina was too consumed with Aonghus to hear it. She pressed herself forward, slightly arching her back as she kissed him harder.

"Aonghus? Kordelina?" came Niall's timid voice again. It had a tone of disbelief coupled with embarrassment as he spoke.

Aonghus stopped kissing her, and glared at him. "What is it, boy?" he growled impatiently.

Niall put his hand over his mouth, and tried to conceal his astonishment at seeing the two of them together.

"Speak up!" Aonghus barked.

Niall flinched at his tone. "It is Edainne. Her child is near. Mother has sent me to fetch Kordelina to help with the birth."

Red-faced, Kordelina nodded. "I will be there," she said in heavy breaths. With sudden obedience, she pushed Aonghus away, and rose to her feet.

She looked compassionately at Niall's boyish face. He had always idolized her, believed that she could do no wrong. How confused he must be now seeing her and Aonghus this way, she thought. He could never understand that to her this was not wrong.

The boy stood frozen, looking at her in mortified silence.

Aonghus stood and walked over to his brother. Taking him by the shoulders, he looked sternly into his eyes. "It shows much cunning that you were able to find us here," he said arrogantly.

"I followed your tracks," Niall replied, intimidated.

Aonghus nodded in approval, and abruptly slapped him hard on both shoulders with his open palms. It was meant to hurt him just enough to show that he was not amused by the intrusion. The younger brother cringed.

"That is good," Aonghus answered with an icy smile. "You would do well to speak nothing of this to any who would ask."

Niall looked down at his feet. "Ask of what, brother?" he replied, looking back up into Aonghus' cold blue eyes. "I only know that I found Kordelina by the strait."

Aonghus chuckled insincerely. "You know much for one so young," he said and released him.

Kordelina stepped nervously between them. "We should hurry," she said, taking Niall by the elbow then turning to Aonghus. "I am sure Diarmudd would like the comfort of an old friend to ease the wait. Perhaps you will join him later."

Aonghus reached out and taking a strand of her wet hair, kissed it. "Perhaps," he answered.

She offered him a tender look and urged her younger brother forward. "Come, Niall; Edainne is waiting."

ChAPTER TEN

ilence. A silence so still it made her shiver. Clutching her hollow stomach, she listened to the desolate sound of complete nothingness. No birds sang, no breeze rustled the leaves on the trees. She felt as though the abyss of the darkness was a reminder of something she desperately needed to forget.

Lifting her head from her tear-dampened pillow, Saturnalia looked out at the cloudless night. Her vision was blurred; the stars did not twinkle, rather they smeared together to look like a mass of lone flames against the transparent sky. She put her head back down.

At that moment, it was hopeless. She would have welcomed death. Only something that final could stop the molten poison inside her from erupting. Why was there an impenetrable bond between pain and pleasure that could not be broken? It was as though they were lethal entities who fed off each other. And she was now the victim of both.

How she wanted to revive the beautiful reassuring illusion of her love for Conn. The smell of him, the taste of him, the rapture when he was inside of her. Had it all been for nothing? She could not believe that, could not believe that their ill-fated love affair was written in the stars.

Staring blankly at the wall, she thought of Aonghus. Had he really outwitted her to such lengths, or had it simply been an accident? Perhaps he did not really know how greatly in love she and Conn were. She shook her head slowly. There are no such things as accidents she told herself. What Aonghus had done was entirely premeditated, and by his actions, she knew his revenge must have been brewing for quite some time. For a moment, she wondered if any sort of retaliation was worth it.

"I will make sure that it is worth it," she said aloud.

She looked over at Conn sleeping beside her, and carefully touched his swollen face. How Aonghus must despise her to do this—but why? She had not bound him to the oath; he had willingly bound himself. Of all the people in the tribe, no one was better acquainted with the laws than he. From a very young age, he understood exactly how important they were, and he had not been misinformed about the gravity of keeping a Druidic promise. These customs were not created to confuse man's destiny, rather to insure it, and no one understood that better than Aonghus. What a fool he was to think he could manipulate her. After all, she did not make the laws, she was only their keeper. She could not change the edicts that had been revered for generations.

However, Saturnalia realized he was much too selfish to accept that. Instead, he wanted to change the customs to suit himself by discrediting her. Yet it involved more than that now; Jara had decided upon Kordelina's terrible fate. The old Druidess had requested she be sanctified at the festival of Brigantia, and Saturnalia did not have to use her intuition to know that the young girl's death was soon to follow. Jara had only given her false reassurances that Kordelina would be given a good home in another tribe because she knew Saturnalia could not live with the thought of surrendering her to such a destiny.

Naturally, Saturnalia had clung to the promises for her own convenience. It was too difficult to live with the knowledge that Kordelina would be killed. There was not a moment, however, that it had not found its way into her thoughts. Each time she looked into the girl's eyes, she made herself look away, hoping that in time, she would come to forget this renegade spirit she so cherished. No longer would she look forward to their afternoon visits, and the changing seasons would eventually diminish the sound of her footsteps coming up the path. And as the festivals came and went, Saturnalia would look for her soul to be born of another. She had even entertained the thought that she would be born to Aonghus and Bracorina, but Saturnalia knew that could never happen. Kordelina was too disgusted by Bracorina, and instead of Aonghus being in love with his sister, he would then be in love with his daughter. Life positions could not alter the course of human emotions. Perhaps Aonghus, in his own savage way, understood that better than she.

That thief! She found the very thought of him repugnant. She was the one who had been used that night in his chamber, not him. He had taken advantage of her, raping her soul and stealing what he found of value. He wanted her secrets. They had been hers to use, and his to use against her. She should have expected such defilement from that one. Now he had successfully turned her own lust against her.

Grabbing fistfuls of her hair in frustration, she began to cry once again.

"Saturnalia, do not cry," the voice was Conn's; he was barely conscious.

"Speak no more to me!" she sobbed, covering her ears. She got out of bed and walked to the window. Opening it, she looked out a moment, then began pounding the sill with her fists.

"I hate this!" she wept. "I hate that I cannot love you without killing you. Aonghus, you wretched fiend, you will die before me, I swear it!"

She picked up her dagger and, in a rage, sliced both wrists. The blood seeped out onto her arms, and dripped from her elbows.

"I will purge this from myself. I will bleed it out, and either I will die or I will become a greater power," she cried out. "Love—the horror of it all! Such cruelty to be toyed with by the gods in such a way! What purpose does this indignity bring you, that we may be constantly reminded of what flawed beings we really are?"

Tears flowed down her face; her seemingly invincible strength completely shattered. What could she do—reason with herself that she was more exalted than the rest of the mortals? It was not true. Her heart was no more seasoned than Kordelina's. She had never been in love like this before, and because of a position she had assumed as a child, she was supposed to be more reverent about her own destiny. Her crying stopped suddenly as she realized that she and Aonghus were not really so different.

"So we are kinsmen, after all, you and I?" she whispered to herself. "We are both victims of our beliefs. Those vows we thought would give us freedom have only paid us with revenge. And here we are, both too vain to give up our truths for the one thing we need the most."

She rose to her knees, and ripped a shred of cloth from the hem of her gown. Using her teeth, she tore it in two pieces and began to bandage her wrists.

"Aonghus, I will not bleed for you, filth that you are," she snarled. "I will make you bleed for me. You are not stronger than me. You may think that for the moment I have lost, but my wrath upon you will be fierce and your anguish will be great."

Cold with anger, she braced herself against the window frame. She was so lightheaded that she had to wait a moment before she could get her balance. Then, as if in a drunken stupor, she staggered to the door and out into the yard. She returned a moment later with a pail of water to bathe Conn.

Taking his face between her hands, she pressed her lips to his swollen mouth, and then drew away to look at him. He stared back, his soft brown eyes so sorrowful that she could not stop her tears.

"You must not cry," he said, as he lifted his hand and ran his thumb along the side of her face.

She wet a cloth and dabbed his face and neck.

"And you must not punish yourself," he went on. "Promise me that you will be strong until the end."

"Be quiet now," she said kindly. Slipping her arms around his body, she cradled him and began to rock gently back and forth.

Conn collapsed against her, his head resting on her chest. Saturnalia was appalled by the indignity of it all, feeling pity for him now instead of respect.

"I will not beg you," he mumbled, placing his hand on her forearm. "I will not beg you to love me until I am taken."

She shook her head, the tears falling onto his face. "You do not have to beg; I will love you willingly while you are here."

He lifted his head and looked wearily into her eyes.

"It is what I want," he said, his voice trembling. "I do not want my sentence to be subdued or bargained for. These laws we live by are for a reason, for the good of everyone, are they not?"

Saturnalia felt a stab of regret at his words. "I am not sure anymore. I think perhaps they are only for the good of a select few. They are for the people who benefit by them. What of you and me, how good can they be if they cause us such suffering? I will not sacrifice you, my love."

Conn gripped her forearm. "It is what I want. I must have an honorable death. I am a warrior and could not stand to live the rest of my life like Kordelina, floundering about to the next person who takes enough pity on me to tolerate my presence. By sparing her life, her honor was destroyed—that is worse than death. The sentence you bestowed upon her is far more cruel than any sacrifice. You should have given her the chance to begin again. Do not make the same mistake with me; let me have the chance to start over even if it means that we will be apart. Let my sacrifice be a sacred thing."

Saturnalia felt a burning in her cheeks, then it faded at his words.

"But I love you," she said in a low voice. "I will not put an end to you."

"No greater love for me could you show than to set my spirit free. Death would be my gift because I will not face this tribe stripped of my dignity," he said as he looked up at her pleadingly. She stared back at him, a glimmer of her red hair visible in the starlight. Even in her remorse, she appeared flawless, but somehow her face was now aged. He knew how guilty she must be feeling.

"Just love me right now," he continued, his voice cracking with emotion. "Love me without the thought of tomorrow, without the notion of good-bye. Let it not be in your eyes or your mannerisms. For while I am with you, let our hearts be full. Love cannot bend to suit destiny. It continues in spite of it. Please, my dear beautiful Saturnalia, let your heart be light because if I were to speak the truth to you, surely you would understand that I have more than brought about my own fate."

Her eyes widened, and surprisingly her tears stopped. She rested her face against his forehead, and tried to speak, but could make no sound.

"I know," Conn said softly, as he laced his fingers in hers. "I feel for you, and I know."

———

"Push, Edainne. Bear down once more, and you can rest awhile," Enda said, pressing firmly on her stomach with the palm of her hand.

The weary young girl cried silently. She was sweating so much that her hair was flat against her head. The perspiration rolled down her forehead onto her cheeks, making it hard to discern the sweat from the tears. She grit her teeth to keep from crying out, as she clutched Kordelina's forearm so tightly her knuckles turned white. She had been travailing for many hours now, and her coverings were stained with blood and soaked with perspiration.

"Come now, child, bear down," Enda encouraged, this time raising her voice. She shoved the moving fetus down further, hoping to help it break free from the womb. "You have to help me; just one more time and you can sleep."

Edainne looked at Kordelina with listless eyes. She was so pale that her brows looked as if they had been painted on.

"I am too tired," she said faintly.

Kordelina took her by both hands. "Once more, I will help you," she said, as she pulled her forward, lifting her shoulders off the bed.

Edainne's face reddened as she strained. She was trembling, and the blood rushing into her cheeks made her look as though she were going to burst if she pushed any harder. Then she screamed so loudly, the entire room echoed with her pain, and her body went limp.

She closed her eyes. "No more," she whimpered. "I can do no more."

Turning her back to them, Enda took a small bronze pot that had been boiling over the fire, and emptied it into a pewter cup. It was obvious that she was trying to mask her worry as she turned back around, and walking over to the bed, she sat beside the laboring young woman.

"Poor child," she said sympathetically, as she placed her hand behind Edainne's neck, and lifted the steaming cup to her lips.

"I do not want it," the girl protested, weakly trying to push it away.

The older woman paid no attention to her. "Drink it," she gently, ordered. "These herbs will ease the birth."

Kordelina looked at her mother in concerned silence. She knew that when a woman had been in labor this long, the chances of both mother and baby surviving were low. The brew that Edainne was drinking was only offered as a last resort. It induced oblivion in case her womb needed to be cut and the fetus removed.

The exhausted girl swallowed it slowly, then turned her head away.

"More," Enda coaxed, forcing the cup to her lips. "You must drink it all. It will help, I promise."

Edainne looked up submissively, and continued drinking.

"That is good. Sleep now," Enda said kindly.

As she turned to face Kordelina, she was gaunt with fatigue. "I need a breath of air," she said, wiping her brow with the back of her hand. "Bathe her, please."

Kordelina went cold; she knew this meant the worst.

"But Mother," she argued, "she is going to be all right, is she not?"

She saw her mother's face tighten. "Just do as I say, child!" she shouted impatiently, then immediately covered her face with her hand.

"I am sorry, Kordelina," she apologized. "Please, just do as I say."

"Yes, Mother," Kordelina answered as the woman left the room.

Taking the pail of hyssop and comfrey water and a cloth, she sat down next to her friend. The salty smell of sweat and bloody discharge filled her nostrils as she pulled back her covering. Poor, beautiful Edainne, she thought sadly as she looked at her swollen body. Enda had said that she was too small to birth such a large child.

Wringing the excess liquid from the cloth, Kordelina began to gently bathe her with the astringent water. The beads of sweat trickled down between her paunchy breasts, and Kordelina could see that the tips of her nipples were lactating. Her distended abdomen was now motionless, the tired infant not even moving when the wet rag passed over it.

"He will be born," Edainne mumbled incoherently.

Kordelina lay the palm of her hand on the round of Edainne's stomach. She pressed it softly and to her relief, she felt the infant push back against her.

"Yes," she smiled. "He still feels strong."

Opening her eyes, Edainne gave a listless smile in response. "I knew the very instant he came into my womb," her smile broadened at the thought of it. "That fullness of another soul growing inside of me. When you feel it, you will know what I mean. It is a warmth that comes from knowing that you and the one you love have called a spirit together."

Kordelina looked away. She felt almost envious of this woman's pain because she wanted so desperately to feel it, the absolute wonder of laboring for the baby that would belong to her and the one she loved.

In the next moment, Edainne flung her arm out, spilling the water, and screeched in agony. Before Kordelina could even stand, the door flew open, and Enda was at the bedside.

"I can see the crown," Enda said. "It is time; help me lift her."

With Kordelina on one side and Enda on the other, they pulled Edainne up to a squatting position. The girl moaned and sobbed at the same time, and it took all of their strength to keep her from falling forward.

"Bear down, it is almost over," Enda shouted. "I can see his face."

Edainne's head was dropped back, with her mouth open to the ceiling as her guttural cries filled the room.

"Kordelina, take her hands," her mother said as she moved behind Edainne, a clean rag in her hand.

Using all her strength, Kordelina urged Edainne forward, forcing her to squat down further as the infant emerged. Taking the babe's tiny shoulders, Enda gently pulled on it until the whole body was visible.

"He is here!" she cried, as Kordelina slowly eased the new mother back down on the bed.

Cradling the newborn in one arm, Enda pried open its rosebud mouth, and cleared the mucous from the throat with her finger. Then, she held it up by the feet, and slapped it firmly on its blood-covered bottom. The infant's face twisted as it opened its mouth and wailed.

"Well, will the heavens be silenced!" Enda laughed. "He is a she!"

Edainne gave a relieved, maternal smile as Enda placed the little girl on her chest. Her eyes glittered as she looked at her, and lifted a tiny little hand to her lips and kissed it.

"My baby," she whispered. "My little baby."

What was left of the mother's fluid had already passed through the umbilical cord, and Kordelina knew it would be her job to sever it. Taking her knife, she went to the fire, and held the blade in the flames until it glowed to be sure both ends of the cord would be cauterized when she cut it.

"I will do that," Enda offered. "You fetch Diarmudd."

Kordelina ran outside. The fresh air felt good against her flushed skin. She had been in that hot, smelly room so long, she felt like a prisoner freed at last.

There was a fire in the stone ring in front of the house, and emptied flasks of ale were scattered on the ground around it. The sound of the crackling flames combined with the rustle of the nearby cattle seemed the song of a bygone reality. It was always like this when a baby was born, Kordelina thought. The sheer miracle of watching a new spirit come into the world made everyday life somehow less impressive.

Stopping a moment, she ran her hand over her breasts as she thought of the way it felt when Aonghus had touched her. It was like being turned inside out with pleasure. Placing both palms on her stomach, she closed her eyes and tried to imagine their child growing inside of her. She felt the familiar mild cramping that said it would be a fortnight until she bled again. It always seemed like a cruel punishment, bleeding because her womb was barren. Pressing on the spot that was painful with her fingertips, she wished as hard as she could that this time, it would not happen. Maybe this time the heavens would answer.

"Please Great Mother," she whispered. "Bring us a child."

She stood still a moment, not knowing what else she could do to want it more. The spirits gave other women children without them even asking, and her request had gone unfulfilled for so long.

Opening her eyes, she saw the group of men at the back of the barn, and started running toward them. They had undoubtedly moved from their place in front of the house when Edainne's cries became too intense. Strange, the way men were about pain. They could inflict it on each other without a second thought, but to listen to the sound of a woman enduring it made them suffer.

Kordelina could make out their shadows ahead of her as she ran. A few of them sat solemnly on the hay bales, and others hunched over like crows on the fence. She hoped that one of them would be Aonghus. She was desperate to see him. This morning seemed to have happened a lifetime ago. They all watched her expectantly as she stopped in front of them, and looking down on the blur of worried faces, she smiled.

"It is a girl," she said proudly.

"And Edainne?" Diarmudd asked cautiously.

"She is fine. Go to her now," Kordelina answered.

He flashed an elated smile, and sprinted to the house. Then all the men began to howl, and slap each other on the back as if they had been the ones who had accomplished something.

Watching them happily, Kordelina felt someone pick her up from behind, and whirl her in the air. Both his arms were wrapped around her as she felt him kiss her cheek.

"Are you still mine?" the voice was hushed, but she recognized Aonghus.

She reached around, and grabbed his face with one hand. Feeling the tears of joy well in her eyes, she nodded without saying a word.

CHAPTER ELEVEN

othing could hide Solomon's frustration as he glared at Aonghus and Kordelina hugging each other. Maybe they could disguise their reason for such an affectionate display to the others, but Solomon knew it was not the birth they were celebrating. He could sense it by the very way they touched, lightly and deliberately, as though it was something they had rehearsed in private. And when they looked into each other's eyes, they were in a world of their own—a place no one else could enter.

Aonghus released her, then put his hands around her waist, and lifting her off the ground, spun her around in a circle. He laughed one of his hearty laughs that came from deep within, the kind that could not conceal the reason for his delight.

Kordelina threw her head back and giggled shyly. It was no use, Solomon thought, what these two had started could not be stopped, regardless of the reasons he had to prevent it. He was not even sure he would stop them if he could; by watching the exchange taking place in front of him, he knew it was better to let fate deal with them. Maybe it would be more generous with this delinquent love than Solomon had thought.

"Have some ale, my friend," Koven said, interrupting his thoughts. "We were going to feast tonight; now we have more than one thing to celebrate."

Solomon turned to look at Koven, as if weighing his words, then looked back at Aonghus and Kordelina.

"They are my children. I will take them any way I can," Koven said, speaking of the two. By this time, Kordelina was hugging Pwyll with one arm while holding onto Aonghus with the other. "I would just like my family back together again, and I do not care how it happens."

Solomon raised his brows and chuckled to himself. "Be careful of that which you ask," he replied, almost amused. "You are a good man, Koven, and the gods may grant it to you."

Taking the cup of ale, Solomon held it high in the air.

"To Edainne's and Diarmudd's child, may the gods bring her much abundance!" he toasted, raising his voice so that it sliced through the stillness of the night.

Shouts of goodwill were heard from everyone, each taking drinks out of the huge stein of corma as it was passed around. When it got to Pwyll, he offered it to Kordelina before drinking from it himself. Blushing, she shook her head in refusal.

"Please, Kordelina, I would share this with you in thanks for helping to bring my first grandchild into the world," he said sincerely.

Her eyes grew large with appreciation, and she blushed even more. "No, I would honor you first," she humbly replied.

"Then honor me by accepting my gratitude," he responded, again offering her the drink. "Come on, girl, it would please me."

Kordelina felt herself smile as she took it from him, and enjoyed a long drink. It was as if she had a place with these people once again. Had she still been in servitude, she would have had to wait until the celebration was over before she could partake of anything.

Handing it back to the elder, she bowed her head in thanks. "Pwyll, I hope your granddaughter will bring you the joy you deserve."

Turning her back before he could reply, she stepped away from him. She did not want him to see the tears of thanks she felt at this moment. Extending her arms out, she began to turn in circles like she was dancing. It felt so good to be accepted by her kinsmen, even if it was only for the moment. She looked up at the stars, and thought of the wonder of it all, the miracle of life and the sweetness of looking into the eyes of the one she loved. Taking a deep breath, she let the smell of the winter night overtake her.

At the sight of her musing, Koven took out his hand flute, and began to play a sparkling tune of celebration. To dance again, how glorious to dance again, Kordelina thought as she happily broke into a jig.

She did not care how foolish she must have looked, dancing alone in the soiled garments of a servant. In her mind, she imagined herself looking the way she did the night of the tribal gathering long ago. It was when Aonghus had given her the brightly-colored outfit with bells sewn to the hem of the skirt. She pretended that the jingle of them filled the night air, and that she could hear the sound of tinkling jewelry as she moved. It was all so wonderful to imagine, and she laughed out loud as she put both hands on her hips, and kicked her feet high in the air.

The others looked on in amusement. Enda had now joined them, the tender nurturing glow having already returned to her pudgy cheeks. Looking over at the group, Kordelina noticed that they all wore paternal expressions of amusement. All of them, except Aonghus—his eyes gleamed as he stared at her, and in a moment he joined in.

Locking his arm through hers, the two danced in a half circle. Stepping apart, they faced each other long enough for Aonghus to dance a solo, and for Kordelina to respond by copying his steady progression of steps. They smiled conspicuously as they took each other by opposite arms, and did it again. This time, Aonghus let Kordelina go first, then he repeated the jig magnificently.

Their eyes remained fixed on each other, as though they were melting together, and this was a private nuptial dance. Aonghus beamed as he stepped back two paces, then with one leap, was alongside her. He faced in one direction, and she in the other, with only their shoulders touching. Then he gave her a look that could not be masked from anyone, a look that seemed to shout to the heavens that he belonged to her, mind, body, and soul.

Kordelina's smile faded as she mirrored his emotions. It was as though the world had stopped and all that remained was their indestructible desire to be one.

"Come on, you two, dance more!" Koven shouted to them cheerfully.

They stood still a moment longer, then Aonghus flashed an impetuous smile. Wrapping one arm around her waist, he picked her up and began dancing for them both.

As he looked into her eyes, he unveiled his mind. No longer caring who saw, Kordelina relaxed against him. This moment and this dance was a primal ritual to seal their love. This was his proposal, his way of making her his bride before the heavens, his sapphire eyes sparkling as he kissed both her cheeks.

I love you, I love you, came his thoughts clearly to her.

Closing her eyes, Kordelina envisioned a sphere of white light where both of their hearts were. The beam was so strong and bright that it formed one continuous ray between them. She could feel Aonghus perceive her vision, and she knew that this telepathic connection would remain between them for all time. From that moment on, no being, human or spirit, would sever their bond.

As they moved closer to each other, the hole began to shrink until it was only a streak of light that finally disappeared when she rested her head on his shoulder. She was so tired that she wanted him to carry her home and tuck her safely into bed. She wished he could lie beside her and warm her while she dreamed of the beautiful things that had escaped her these last months. And when she awakened, he would still be there, waiting to love her again and again until they were both exhausted by their passion.

The music was still playing, and she could hear the sound of his rhythmic breathing in her ear. Then, his body jerked with agitation, and taking her gently by the shoulders, he moved them apart. Opening her eyes, Kordelina felt suddenly conspicuous at their display as she turned to see what had caught his attention.

It was Bracorina. She stood behind Kordelina. Her face was stern, and she was looking straight at Aonghus as though Kordelina did not even exist. For a moment, Kordelina was paralyzed. She felt the panicked urge to offer an explanation, something that would make it seem less than it really was.

Bracorina stood almost panting with rage, her thin lips pursed in a frown, and her dark brown eyes sunk deeply into her brow. She looked so short and plump, and her full breasts appeared much too heavy for one of her height. Her hair was parted on one side, and hung loose and stringy about her shoulders, her chin tucked down enough to conceal what little neck she had.

Everything about her was in contrast to Kordelina. She held the loftiest social status in the tribe, dictating who was held in high esteem by whether or not they were invited to her feasts. Kordelina had never even seen the inside of their extravagant home, since both Bracorina and Diarmudd considered her more lowly than their own servants. Still, Bracorina had everything she could want, and at one time, had possessed what Kordelina cherished the most: Aonghus. But that was no longer so, and at the sight of her plainness, Kordelina felt pretty in spite of her attire.

The music stopped as Aonghus looked back at Bracorina, expressionless. He had no intention of speaking first, and Kordelina knew it. It was very important that there be no evidence of what they had planned, and his dealing with his former fiancee now would likely be scrutinized by everyone. It would take much guile, but she was sure Aonghus had more than was needed.

Bracorina stepped forward, and glared at Kordelina. "Out of my way, slave," she said maliciously. She lifted her hand in the air, and the next moment, Kordelina felt it strike her on the side of the face. "Do not ever think that you are worthy to dance with this warrior. Out of my sight now. Dancing is forbidden to you!"

Kordelina felt stinging embarrassment rise in her, and she wilted as she looked up at Aonghus. She saw his pained look of apology that she must endure this degradation for even a while longer, but he could do nothing. She was still considered unworthy of any rights, even if she was free now.

Covering her face, she began to cry, not at the pain, but at the utter humiliation of being unable to do anything but what she was told. She felt Aonghus take her arm, but she jerked it away and she started running toward the woods.

"Continue playing, Koven," Bracorina said, her words taking on a false charm. "Let us dance to the birth of my brother's child."

Koven gave a sullen but abiding nod, and began to play a much more melancholy tune.

"Perhaps someone should go with her," Solomon said.

"No," Enda replied, looking after her. "She is embarrassed enough. Better to pretend it was not such a crisis. Besides, you know Kordelina. If you went to her now and tried to comfort her, she would probably spit in your face. She deals with these things better if left alone."

Solomon nodded. She was more like him than she knew. Taking another drink, he watched Aonghus and Bracorina dance. It was apparent that Aonghus' efforts were half-hearted. The spontaneity and passion were gone in his eyes. This was his duty.

Solomon could not help but think that if he danced with her this way, he probably made love to her out of duty as well. There was always an indescribable link between the sensuality of dancing and the act of making love.

The Chieftain empathized with Aonghus. What torment to see your object of desire in front of you, yet be dutybound not to take it. It must be easier for Kordelina; she had never been bound by anything. Those she loved were simply those she loved. If she loved Aonghus differently from her other brothers, so be it. Her needs were beautifully uncomplicated.

In a moment, the song had ended and Aonghus returned to his seat in silence. Bracorina followed him, trying to appear at ease where she was unwanted.

Lifting his eyes, Aonghus gave Solomon an empty look, then stared at the ground. What was he trying to say? That he was sorry, or that he did not care? Solomon was unsure, but he wanted things to be good between them again. Aonghus was like his own son, and it pained him that they had not had the chance to settle their differences.

He walked over to stand in front of the young warrior. He looked down at him understandingly, as though Aonghus were the prodigal son unable to find the right words to ask forgiveness.

Aonghus looked up. His gaze was steady and removed until Solomon saw the tears welling in his eyes. He did not blink when one trickled down his face. He sat without speaking, and waited for Solomon to speak first.

His reaction moved Solomon deeply. He knew how much Aonghus loved his daughter; how in his heart, he could not be condemned for it. It was as though he were challenging Solomon to stop their love, because he knew that nothing could keep him from her now.

"What madness we partake of in the night," Solomon said tenderly as he opened his arms to Aonghus.

Rising to his feet, Aonghus embraced him. He did not speak as he tightened his hold for a moment, then released Solomon. Looking at him for only an instant, Aonghus offered an obliging smile and turned away.

"What has happened between you two?" Bracorina asked suspiciously.

Solomon shook his head. "Something from a long time ago," he answered, offering Aonghus his cup.

Aonghus grasped the cup with his still swollen hands, and blinked back his tears. "I am sorry," he said finally. It hurt to say it, pained him to dredge up the futility of all that had taken place. He could not have stopped the fiend that had surfaced the night before, and it was too much a part of him to ask forgiveness for. "I am sorry about everything."

He held the cup limply. It tilted just enough to spill a few drops on the ground, as Solomon waited patiently for him to continue.

"I wish that I could change everything, but it is too late," he mumbled.

"Is it too late?" Solomon asked, folding his arms across his chest.

Aonghus shot him an icy glare; he knew Solomon was referring to Kordelina's virginity.

"We have done nothing. She is still a worthy bride," he answered, trying to disguise how incensed he was at the question.

"I commend your temperance," Solomon replied. "What of Conn?"

Aonghus turned pale, then lifted the cup and gulped down its contents. He wiped the foam from his mouth with his forearm, and sighed heavily.

"It was a vengeful act," he said, noticeably shaken. "I wanted to show Saturnalia that if these laws were arbitrary for Kordelina, then they should be arbitrary for everyone—even Conn."

Solomon shook his head. "She does not make the laws," he argued.

Aonghus looked at the ground. "I know. I will go to her and ask that his sentence be lessened. In return, I will request passage to another island. When Kordelina is gone, well, it will be too difficult to stay. I can no longer make this my home. Too many unfortunate things have come to pass that even a title cannot soothe. I feel I am being beckoned elsewhere."

Solomon was visibly upset by the young man's unexpected declaration. "Do not be so harsh in your judgments. If you truly feel you cannot abide this clan, then I understand. I would only ask you to get a good night's rest and a good meal, as much has happened and your weariness could only be for the moment. Come home, and we will speak of it when the sun is shining," he said, as he wrapped his arms around Aonghus' shoulder in a fatherly way and pulled him close.

Aonghus seemed to melt at his affection. Feeling his remorse, Solomon embraced him with both arms, and held him like a parent easing the brashness of his son's youth.

"It is better that she be taken this way," Aonghus said, referring to Kordelina. "For there is nothing in the land of the living that could keep me from her; she is too precious to me."

"Yes, Aonghus, I truly believe that," he answered faintly, as Enda came and stood protectively over them. Her motherly radiance was comforting.

"It is time we all went home," she said, putting her arms around the two men. "And I will warn you both to act no more as strangers in my house. You understand me?"

"They understand you, Mother," Koven said, taking his wife by the arm. "Let them be. The best of the night to you, Pwyll. Goodnight, Bracorina."

"To you, as well," Pwyll said, taking Bracorina by the hand.

Bracorina nodded her response as she started toward the house at her father's urging. Looking over her shoulder, she watched with a furrowed brow as Aonghus left with his family, still never having said a word to her.

chapter twelve

onn woke to the sight of Saturnalia bent over the fire, stirring a small cast-iron pot of scented herbs. Her dress was pulled tightly around her curves, and he could see the fine muscles in her small shoulders ripple as she stirred.

In a sudden lucid moment, he remembered everything. The awful vision of the attacker, the fight with Aonghus, the humiliation of accusation, and the desperate plea for help as he lay on the chilly ground. What had happened at that moment, when he had fallen before her, had changed him. Now, he was the downcast image of a transgressor whose past conquests had been wiped away forever by slumber.

He recalled her taking him in her arms as he asked to be killed. He had said something about life without honor being meaningless, but what was honor if it meant being without her? For a moment, he wondered if she would really do what he had asked. Of course, she would. She would give him such an elaborate sacrifice that he would be remembered as a divine entity.

After all, what was he to do, live without rank and become a slave whose self-respect was traded like chattel? No, not him. Better to embrace real death, and begin again, for he realized that to die of his flesh was to be born of his spirit. When his body was finished, his consciousness would transcend to a place without blemish.

He had never relished the thought of his death until now. Before this, it had been a foe to be prevailed against, a phantom thief seeking to steal the preciousness of these wonderful lusty days. It no longer signified retreat, but victory. How glorious to be literally consumed by his lover to the point of it overtaking his very existence. He had never envisioned his world to end in such a way, but what better path to the Otherworld than through the bloodstream of his red-haired lover.

Touching his hand to his ribs, he winced at their tenderness. He was completely naked beneath the warm fur coverings, and his once muddy body had been thoroughly cleansed.

He wondered how long he had been sleeping because it seemed that once Saturnalia had taken him in her arms, he had been set adrift in euphoric darkness. There was little doubt in his mind that she had kept him floating with the aid of a nectar now worn off.

Lowering his hands to his thighs, he rubbed them with his open palms until he felt the circulation replace the numbness. Then he brushed across his pubic hair with his hand, and smiled slightly at the tickle of it as he began to fondle himself. He relished the pleasure of the familiar arousal of blood rushing to his limp organ until it was erect. Pressing gently on the protruding veins, he wrapped his fingers around it, and started stroking himself. As he did this, he discreetly watched Saturnalia take a pinch from a bundle of lavender and drop it into the boiling water.

She silently took the steaming pot and strained its contents through a piece of muslin covering a wooden bowl. The bowl had been fashioned from a crude section of the bark of an oak tree. The center of it was carved just deep enough to hold a small portion of liquid.

When she had finished pouring, she gathered the four corners of the muslin, and tied them in a knot. Then she took a small vial of oil, emptied it onto the cloth, and cast it into the fire. As it crackled in the flames, wisps of the sweet lavender and patchouli immediately filled the room.

Conn was entranced by her. His loins were tense with desire, but he did not move because he did not want to break the spell of her vision. He could not take his eyes off her as she moved in front of the open fire, and let her robe drop to the floor. It fell in ripples around her feet, giving the illusion she had risen from a single pool of water in front of him.

He was breathing harder as he gazed upon the gentle contour of her nakedness in the fireglow. She was a silhouette, standing on water with flames blazing behind her. For a moment, he questioned if she was a hallucination, and he was still lying on the cold earth in her courtyard.

Cupping her hands, Saturnalia immersed them in the water, then touched them to her shadowy breasts. She began bathing herself with her palms, and each time she placed them back in the steaming bowl, the chimes of the water echoed through the chamber. Conn was aching for her touch as he pulled back his covering, seductively exposing himself to her.

She made no sound as she sat down with her legs spread, and poured what was left of the steaming water between her thighs. Tilting her head back, she lifted her face to the ceiling, and let out a soft, erotic moan. The pleasure of it was too much for him, and as he stroked himself harder, he was unaware he was spent until he felt his hot fluid on his hand and stomach.

Panting, he closed his eyes, wishing he could have saved himself for her. Then he felt her hair brush over his thighs and her tongue pass over his belly with feather-like movements. Ecstasy overpowered his senses; the softness of her skin and the sweet fragrance of her hair only added to his delight.

"Oh, my dear, beautiful Sorceress," he moaned.

He could taste the salt of himself as she kissed him full on the lips. The excitement of it made him want her again, but he was floating in rapture. Images flickered in his mind—seductive figures of naked women caressing and whispering to him. Yet, he knew that they were not really there; they all existed in this one woman, his lover.

Moving herself beside him, he felt the cold metal of a cup against his lips. "Drink now," she said, in a muted tone.

"No, I only want to lie here, and remember the feel of you," he answered, gently pushing the cup away. "I do not wish this time to slip away."

"I promise I will not drug you, as this time is special to me as well," she reassured him. "This potion is only to ease the discomfort."

She drank it herself, then pressed her lips to his, and let the liquid flow into his open mouth. Surprised, he swallowed the bitter brew. Soon, he would be painlessly floating away from her again, but he did not want it so. He had to tell her something important. Something about Jara, about himself, only his thoughts were too scrambled. He only knew that it involved Rome.

The room began to spin, and his mind emptied itself of fragmented memories. There was the vision of he and Kordelina butchering a camp of Celts that night while on watch. He could see the gleam in her eyes as she drew blood for the first time, and drained the life out of the warrior. He watched it grow as he, too, reveled in the slaughter of these men. One by one, they were dissected, and seeing the precision with which Kordelina did it, brought him such a voyeuristic thrill. How quickly they had moved, soundless through the dark woods like lovers on a clandestine quest.

"Saturnalia," Conn said, out loud. "Do not let Jara have her. She will be a concubine, not a bride."

He felt Saturnalia run her hand across his face, and he suddenly thought of Aonghus, and the carousing they had done in Wales. Conn could see them together again; it was long ago when they had first gone to fight Rome. Banqueting in a Chieftain's house, they had only just arrived on the island.

They were in an elaborate room, beautifully ornamented with tapestries and silken couches. Full of food and drink, Aonghus lay outstretched naked on a mound of animal pelts. Two beautiful golden-haired maidens were on either side of him, kissing his body. He had his hand in the crotch of one while he suckled the breast of the other. Conn could hear him groan softly as he laid his head back and then opened those turbulent blue eyes, and looked at him.

"You make the first choice, my friend," he said, taking each girl by the arm and turning their faces toward him.

The girls giggled as Conn set down his flask of wine, and appraised their enticingly plump young bodies. One had brown eyes and the other green. Fixing his sights on the green-eyed nymph, Conn motioned that she join him. Seeing that he had made his choice, Aonghus released her and drunkenly rolled on top of the other.

The horrid pain of these memories. One by one, they were dislodging themselves from his mind until he lay in utter silence. A beautiful stillness shrouded his thoughts as he curled up in Saturnalia's arms. He wanted to weep out loud, but he was plummeting into a trance. Then he felt her kiss him again, and the urgent need to release his pain dissipated.

"I do not want it to always be like this," he mumbled, almost incoherently. "I will be responsible for my actions."

Saturnalia gathered him close. "Warrior?"

"Yes," he struggled to answer.

"I am your lover and your enemy as well," she whispered.

"No, you are only my lover," he murmured, as he tried to reach out and touch her, but could not.

"Then as your lover," she whispered, even more softly. "Does your heart belong to me?"

"Yes, only to you," he answered, slurring his words.

Saturnalia touched her open hand to his left breast, and she felt the slow throbbing of his heart.

"Ancient belief says the heart is where the consciousness resides. When your life is ended, I would devour it inside me, that I might feel your love through all eternity," her voice was slightly strained as she spoke.

Conn felt the shock of her words, but could not react. He remembered seeing women eat the heart of their loved ones in ancient rituals, but he was uncertain if it was a remembrance from a life past.

Then the reality of it set in. He truly was going to die at her hand, just as the previous sacrifices he had witnessed. There would be music and dancing, then the sheer panic of knowing death was only moments away. And like the others he had seen, he would writhe pathetically as the blood flowed out, and the surrounding mortals would pray to heaven. Yet, he would not be like the others. He would be her lover, and no archaic custom would ever change that.

"Yes, you and I for all eternity," his words trailed off as he lost consciousness.

———

Saturnalia watched the sunlight peer over the horizon and gradually fill the room. She had not slept all night; she was too afraid to waste even a moment with her slumbering lover.

Conn was sleeping peacefully in her arms, and she watched the steady rise and fall of his chest as he took shallow breaths. His face was so placid, so content that he could have already been dead. But he was not. He was still hers, if even for a brief moment more.

As the sun rose, its reflection grew on the wall in front of her until the entire area was bathed in a warmth of golden color. Aonghus would be coming today; she could feel it. She had seen his face in her mind many times this sleepless night. The square jaw, the prominent nose, and the blue eyes that were only part human. At one point, she had dozed off and been awakened by the sound of him weeping, and the vision of him alone in his room. He looked forlorn, as if victimized by his own symbolic demonstration of power.

More than anyone, he understood the consequences of his demands. That is why he was no doubt coming to bid for Conn's life. Surely Aonghus did not really want his death, but he did not want Saturnalia to think he was not serious either.

So, the reason for the elaborate parade through the village, and the audacity in her yard. How impassioned he must be to go to such lengths to get what he wanted. Only a man deeply in love would do such a thing.

What a strange experience love was after all. This emotion that could make a weakling strong, and the sanest man an evil genius. Out of the deepest love, she too, would find the strength to do what she must.

Touching her fingers to his shoulder, she began to gently stroke Conn's skin. How soft it had always been, like the skin of a babe. It had never possessed the leathery texture of so many of the other men. She fancied it to be even softer than her own.

She saw his eyes flutter slightly, as though he were trying to rouse himself. Then he fell into a sounder sleep. He felt so completely a part of her; she felt their bodies fusing together into a single existence. Resting the side of her face against his, she let herself fully relax into him.

"Beloved," she said humbly. "To what ends have we come that I should be here next to you to dream your last dreams? What have I to offer you now, but refuge from the rest of your proud life? To touch your skin while you slumber in the arms of death, and inhale the substance of your soul as you breathe? What glory is there in begging you to stay with me while you beseech me to set you free? Offer me but one more choice, and I will take it, no matter how hard. I would crawl on my hands and knees for a single chance to keep you."

She shifted against him to feel his warmth on her breasts. It cut through the chill of the room like light penetrating darkness. She was not crying now. She could cry no longer. The pain had settled in her veins, its bitterness making her numb and leaving her eyes dry.

"You and I," she whispered, as she delicately stroked his brow. "Across what universe will our spirits soar when we are together again? And how shall I abide this full life without you until that time comes? If my lips were life's elixir, surely I would press them to yours now, and we would both become immortal. Together, in each other's arms, we would fly high above the smallness of this life, and ascend into the heavens, and the gods there would not deny our pleas. No, they would welcome our resolution of this miserable twist in our destinies."

She felt his hand over hers as opening his eyes, he met her gaze. He had heard every word she said.

"One word, sweet lover," he spoke tenderly. "Were I to live without valor, those same gods that would welcome our love, would detest the sight of my cowardice. There is no triumph in living with disgrace, not even your love could ease its sting. Such poor passion it would be for you to let me exist in such a way. My bravery has been great; let it be so remembered. And this love, our love, has been far greater that it should not be buried with me. No, it cannot grow cold in the earth even if shrouded in gold and silver. You, my sweet, only you have the power to fling it like a fiery star streaking across the heavens, and make death proud to take me."

She looked away. She wished she could hold her heart in hand so that he could see the way it shriveled with each word he spoke. Then there would be no need to tell him that she was not as brave as he, nor was she as noble.

"This wound that is my soul shall never heal once my deed is done," she said wearily.

Conn placed his finger under her chin, and forced her to look at him. "What need have we for remorse now?" he questioned, his voice almost playful compared to hers. "We are still together."

Saturnalia nodded, and forced a sad smile as Conn reached up, and took her face in his hands. She closed her eyes at his touch; the warmth of his palms made her skin feel like stone. He lightly kissed her forehead, and lowering his head, buried his face in her breasts.

They reposed in silence, until it was broken by the sound of horses in the yard. Saturnalia could tell by her sudden trepidation that it was Aonghus.

"Who could it be?" Conn asked.

Saturnalia gently moved away from him, and rose from the bed. "It is your accuser," she answered.

Conn's face tightened. It was hard to tell if it was out of anger or embarrassment at having to see him again. "You mean Aonghus?"

"Yes," she answered, putting on her robe.

Conn stared at the ceiling. "I do not wish to see him. I will lie so quietly as to appear to be sleeping."

Saturnalia fluffed her hair, and pinched color into her cheeks. "Yes, I will not let him exchange a word with you," she said, and kissed his cheek.

The knock on the door was almost timid as it echoed through the room.

"I wish to see no one," Saturnalia shouted. "Leave me!"

"Druidess, it is Aonghus. I wish to speak with you about a matter of great importance to us both," came his muffled voice from the other side of the door.

Saturnalia said nothing as she walked into the next room and placed a piece of wood on the now-smoldering embers. She watched as it lit with a tiny flame, then grew into a blaze and engulfed the log completely.

"Druidess," Aonghus called. "I seek an audience with you, please."

Stepping back from the flames, she held her hands out to warm them. Surely the fire would make the glow return to her complexion and she would not seem to be in mourning. If Aonghus had even a hint of how distraught she really was, he would abuse it. He must not think he had anything that she wanted. He had come to her first, and she did not want to lose the advantage.

"We have nothing to talk about, warrior. You have made your accusation, and it has been recognized," she said carelessly. "I will not open my door to you again."

There was a moment of restless silence, and she could practically hear Aonghus' thoughts as he weighed his options. Then the door slowly opened, and he stepped inside and offered her a respectful bow.

"There was a time when you asked me to indulge you a visit when Kordelina had been charged. I did not wish it, yet you asked that I do it in the name of all that was decent. Now I ask the same of you," he said apprehensively.

His handsome face reflected such genuine concern that Saturnalia imagined herself slapping him with all her might. But she stood calmly in front of the fire, and waited for him to continue.

He was dressed in a clean linen shirt with a green and red sash wrapped tightly around his thick waist. His reddish-brown hair was washed, and pushed away from his clean-shaven face. She always found it slightly amusing that for one so virile, he never had a thick enough growth for a proper beard or mustache.

Bracelets adorned both his wrists, with a thicker spiral-shaped one just above his left elbow. Saturnalia recognized it as Kordelina's torque. It had been the one item Saturnalia resented Aonghus having when the girl was sentenced; from that time on, he had never stopped wearing it. Saturnalia had once thought it was his way of flaunting dominance over her, making her look at it each day in humiliation for her deeds. But now, she realized it was a precious part of her that he could not relinquish.

He was well bathed and she could smell his clean skin over the incense of the room. What was it about this man that even in her hate she found so riveting? Perhaps it was that he was always the seductively tormented soul plagued by his own self-doubt.

"Leave me," she said in an even tone, and pointed to the door. "You may not enter my house uninvited."

She saw him open his mouth to speak, but stop when he caught sight of Conn in the other room. He took a step toward him, but Saturnalia immediately blocked his path.

Aonghus' face lost all expression as he stepped around her. Tilting her head slightly, Saturnalia took hold of his bare arm, and dug her nails into his flesh. Aonghus stopped abruptly.

"Do not take another step," she hissed. "You have no cause to speak with him. You have beaten him and accused him, that is enough."

"I wish him no further suffering. That is why I am here," he replied, his eyes downcast.

Saturnalia walked deliberately to the bedroom door and closed it. Then she slowly turned and walked back, her eyes fixed on Aonghus all the while.

"It is too late for that. This warrior wishes his sentence to be as you have stated. He will be sacrificed at Brigantia's festival," she said coolly.

It was as if she had hit Aonghus in the face. The color drained from his skin as he looked back at her, dumbfounded. He tried to protest, but could only utter a few syllables before he swallowed and shook his head. He looked at the closed door as if trying to see through it, then stared at Saturnalia.

"You will not do it," he stated after a moment. "You would have me think that, but he is too dear to you to kill him yourself."

Saturnalia released her hold, and folded her arms across her chest. She was surprised at how unruffled she really was. "That is your error. It is because of my love for him that I will end his life on my altar."

Aonghus suddenly became incensed at her coldheartedness.

"Have you lost your wits? He is a great warrior, and should not be drained of his blood for a petty misunderstanding between us," he argued. "You spared Kordelina, and she had committed the crime of murder as well as cowardice. She is the one who should have been burned, but instead you let her live —"

"You let her live as a lowly slave only to justify yourself!" she interrupted, pointing her finger incriminatingly in his face.

"What?" Aonghus yelled, pushing her hand away. His face reddened, and she saw the veins in his forehead swell. "I made her live as my slave! No, you shrew, you made me live a lie with her my entire life, pretending to be brother and sister to protect your own murderous act! You slaughtered her mother, I saw you do it! Then you made me vow never to tell anyone to whom she was born—when I was too young to know the difference."

Saturnalia threw her head back and laughed. "You knew the difference all along. You could never accept her as your kin. You have always wanted her as your lover," she scoffed. "Of course, you wanted to tell her the truth, wanted to make a fool of her in front of this clan. Do you think for one instant that these people would have let her live if they had known she was born of the Black Druidess? If you do, you are more naive than I thought. I never wanted her parentage known to protect her; that child had a right to happiness outside of her parent's transgressions, only you would not let it be. You discouraged any interests outside of what involved you, even going so far as to train her to be a warrior. How selfish a man you are to have made her so dependent on you! It was cruel to manipulate her heart so that she was never free to give her loyalty to another. You are the murderer, Aonghus, you took her life for your own, and now, you would slay your kinsman as well."

Aonghus turned away from her as though she were physically assaulting him. She could see his arms tense, and the muscles in his back ripple as he hunched over slightly. Then he cocked his head to the side, and turned to look at her, his eyes tapered with hate.

"What do you want me to do?" he asked, his voice had the calculating tone that indicated he was ready for a fight. "Pretend not to care; pretend your words have no effect on me? It is ridiculous to act as if I do not despise all of this. These vicious games of deception we have played far too long, and they will bring only sorrow to everyone if they persist."

"Then stop them," Saturnalia replied flatly. Her intuition told her she had already pushed him too far, but recalling his smugness in her yard the day before, she could not resist venting her anger on him further.

Aonghus stood straight and faced her. He wore the same vulgar countenance he portrayed just before he went into battle. She knew he was not looking at her as just an adversary, but as his prey.

"I cannot stop what I did not start," he said bitterly. "This web of treachery was woven by you, not me. What I did to Conn was the only way I could make you see that I am desperate to end this lie. I would not have him killed, you know that. I have staked my life to save his in battle many times, and he has done the same for me. I wanted you to understand that this time, I would not let these arbitrary customs take that which I cherish."

"But you have accused him, nonetheless," she challenged, raising her voice to fill the chamber. "You took a warrior that has been great in the eyes of the gods, and devoted to his people, and raped him of his dignity. Now you come to me, and tell me it was all wagered against my weakness. Aonghus, I am not weak; I am strong, and I am a Druidess because I am not afraid of the power I possess."

She stepped toward him and he backed away. "What is the matter, great warrior? Are you frightened of me?" she questioned, pretending to be surprised. "What would one so big and strong have to fear from this frail woman?"

Aonghus stopped short, then moved forward, closing the space between them. "Because you are not frail. You are a conniving shrew who makes fools out of all those who honor you," he said.

Saturnalia could smell his breath as he spoke; it had a stale odor of starvation. She had smelled it many times before in dying men. The physical body always found it necessary to purge itself before it relinquished the soul. Aonghus was not well, no matter how he tried to disguise it. Whatever infirmities he had were still with him and growing stronger.

"And you are filth. Remove yourself from my presence," she said disdainfully.

She saw his eyes flare at her words. At first, she thought it was the reflection of the flame in them, then she felt him grab her by the shoulders and shake her hard.

"Not before you give me what I want!" he threatened.

She did not have time to protest before she realized that he had lifted her from the ground, and shoved her against the wall. She gasped at the impact as she slid to the floor.

Aonghus was crouched over her in an instant, and placing his hands beneath her arms, he sat her upright. Grabbing her face roughly, he made her look at him as the ache rose in her head and back.

"I want to take Kordelina away from here," he told her through tight lips. "I want passage to another island where we can be married by the consent of the Order. Without that, we will never be free."

Saturnalia reached out to grab a handful of his hair. Summoning her power, she found him at last vulnerable to her. She was finally able to look into his thoughts, and see what had really happened these last days.

There were images of the fight. Conn's face in a distorted view, pulling the garrotte tight, and Aonghus gasping for air. Then there was Kordelina, trustingly offering him the jade stone, believing that he would do no wrong with it. She saw the two of them opening their hearts to each other as they danced in the open air, bonding themselves together. There was a strong warmth and love between them as he told her with his eyes she was his bride.

All at once, her head stopped throbbing, and she felt a torrent of mental energy. She envisioned his mind to be ripples of shiny water pouring into the space just above her brow. She was the thief now, abducting the power that he had held ransom.

"Do you really think you can hurt me? What will Kordelina think of you then? Not only will you have betrayed her trust by misuse of her magic, but you have the audacity to force yourself on her Sorceress. I know everything that has happened. More than that, I know what a fool you really are."

She felt his body tense at her words, and he scowled back at her until she released her grip.

"You disgust me," she said.

Aonghus squinted as if the firelight caused his eyes to smart. Then he began to shake his head from side to side like he was trying to rouse himself from a nightmare.

"You have really lost your mind, have you not?" she asked bluntly.

He looked up at her, his brow wrinkled and his lips pursed.

"No more than you," he answered, in a rasping voice. "We are both on the edge of destruction."

"Foul warrior that you are," she replied, with a hint of sympathy. "You and fortune will be lovers no more. You will say farewell here for you have sold yourself as a whore to your own greed. In your revenge, you have only cheated yourself; the only triumph you will taste now will be blemished by your deeds."

Staring into his suddenly fearful eyes, she shook her head remorsefully. "Yes, it is true. We both hover on the edge of destruction, but you warrior, will be the one of us who will fall."

She walked to the bedroom door and Aonghus knelt there, looking back at her, stunned.

"I have no shame about what I will do," she said, standing in front of the entry. "Because when the seas rise, they will rise against you. I promise that."

She flattened her body against the wooden door, and looked at him for a moment longer. Then she gracefully turned the handle, and disappeared into the bedroom.

chapter thirteen

or the first time, Aonghus realized what he had taken on. He knelt where Saturnalia had left him, isolated and empty again. He alone had destroyed his world. The things he had once valued slipped through his fingers one by one until there was no way they could be retrieved—all except the most important: Kordelina. She was still his. Even news of this unworthy display would not change that.

Rising slowly, he looked about Saturnalia's room and was at once void of feeling. His hate for her had strangely evaporated with their confrontation. For a moment, he reveled in the thought of what it would have been like to humiliate her altogether. What satisfaction that would have brought, debasing this sorceress.

The thought of Kordelina had prevented it, because there was no way he could have explained it to her how vile he found himself the morning after he and Saturnalia had slept together, when he had dreamed it was her. Despair had made him its prisoner in the days that followed as he tried to convince himself that he could live without her. Now, his insides reeked with guilt over his betrayal of those he loved, but it no longer mattered. He would spend his life with his lover even if it meant defying them all.

If Conn wanted to die righteously, then why deny him that? If Saturnalia found vindication in his elaborate sacrifice, let her have it. All he wanted and all he needed was Kordelina, and when they were away from here for a time, on some faraway island, with children of their own, he would tell her only what she needed to know. He was sure he could live with them until then.

He walked to the door lost in thought, but free of confusion, at last. He could do nothing more, and as he stepped into the morning sun, he realized that in the end, predestination was but a myth. Every man inevitably chose his own fate, and paid the price for it. He could find solace in no other rationalization.

Tying Conn's horse in front of the cottage, he set his weapons and saddle beside it. Even though under the laws, they belonged to Aonghus now, he had no need for them. It would be hard enough to make it across the channel with Macha and Lir, another horse would only slow them down.

He looked at the regal sorrel stallion that had once so befitted his friend. His eyes had the predatory look of an eagle, unintimidated by anything he gazed upon. How like Conn he really was—confident that only the brave should survive. What bitter irony it would be to remember that, and know that he and his horse would lie together buried in the earth, cold and forgotten like all the rest.

"Goodbye, my friend. Perhaps we shall come together again in another life, and I shall have a chance to ask forgiveness for my failures," he said, patting the animal on the neck, then mounting Lir.

He started out the courtyard, but when he reached the gate, he heard the familiar nicker of Conn's horse. Looking to see what it was, Aonghus found Conn standing there, stroking its mane. One arm was wrapped around the animal's neck as he balanced himself precariously against it. He had a blanket thrown over his shoulders, and Aonghus could tell by his paraffin skin that he was still ailing.

Saturnalia stood inside the doorway, her look of concern strikingly different from her icy expression of only moments before. Her green eyes were soft and caring, and she was wringing her hands nervously as she watched Conn's every move. It was easy to see that she did not wish his death any more than Aonghus. What worthy adversaries they were to bluff each other so well.

Conn looked up at him as Aonghus reined his horse, and waited for him to speak. "In truth, brother, what is it that you wanted out of all of this?" he asked, his words slurring together.

Aonghus felt a knot rise in his throat. He and Conn had been friends through many tests of both valor and emotion. Nothing could change that.

"I want, I want—" he choked back his urge to confess everything. It was useless to try to make him understand something that he did not even comprehend himself. "All I want to know is that when I am far away from this place, we will both be at peace."

Conn squinted his eyes as he tried to interpret Aonghus' words. "Saturnalia has told me that you would go before the Order, and relinquish my accountability. Is this the truth?" he asked.

Aonghus rubbed his stinging eyes and nodded. "Your lover's honesty suits you better than my own loyalty. I do not wish you to perish for the work of the fiend dwelling within me. I am a man sickened by his own desire, and I regret my kinsman has suffered my malice. I would plead my own insanity if it would spare your life."

Conn took a labored step forward, almost falling, and Saturnalia came immediately to his aid. Putting his arm around her neck, he leaned against her to steady himself. Aonghus was tortured by the sight of them; they were so deeply devoted to each other.

"What would my life be then? I would slither about in shame until I could find myself an inglorious grave. I am a warrior, and would die a warrior's death. That is my decision," he said, straightening up as much as he could, then bending over at the pain of it.

Aonghus looked up at the sky, and took a quivering breath. How badly he had beaten him, and to what end had it come? No one was the better for it, and he feared now that they would all suffer gravely for his actions.

"Yes, my friend it is your decision. My remorse is that I was a part of it," he replied, looking back at him, then at Saturnalia.

Her gaze wavered slightly when their eyes met, as if to say that she shared his feelings. Then they glassed over, and she was again the hateful woman he so greatly loathed.

"Whether knowingly or unknowingly, we create our own end. I will accept mine," Conn answered between labored breaths. "Beware while you keep watch. That is all I can tell you. Take care to guard and listen."

Aonghus wanted to ask him more, but he could see by the way Conn was swaying that his thoughts were disjointed.

"May the heavens will us comrades again," Conn offered, lifting his hand in friendship.

Aonghus lifted his hand weakly in response. "If they find me worthy."

Turning away, he spurred his horse to an abrupt canter. The pain was too much, and he could not stand to look back at Conn again.

Aonghus galloped Lir to the seashore, his mind unpossessed of all thoughts and motives. The sun's reflection off the water was so bright it made him squint. The waves were transparent blue in its light, with flocks of seagulls gliding like graceful ghosts over their golden crests. An offshore breeze blew coldly against his cheeks as he stopped and gazed into the distance.

He listened to the grating roar of the water flinging itself against the pebbles of the shore again and again. It was a melancholy cadence that sang in sobs and laughter of faraway lands. He was to be liberated from this place soon, and for all the dark farewells, his spirit would be free at last. Privately, he hoped that this change in his life would somehow heal him because his health was steadily deteriorating.

Since he had seen the hag that night, his dreams were filled with horrid visions of a bloody slaughter taking place on this island. So real were they that in his waking hours, he would flash to them, causing him great confusion. Sometimes it not only affected his mental capacity, but his physical strength and coordination. Aonghus feared that after his spells and illness, he could never be cured.

Trotting slowly along the water's edge, he purposely let the breaking waves wash away any evidence of Lir's hoofprints. He headed toward the cove where he and Conn had stowed the crude Roman cavalry transport they had captured a few weeks prior.

When he reached the crag, he dismounted and made it the rest of the way across the slippery rocks on foot. He found that the flat, wooden boat was stored safely where they had left it.

It was only big enough to carry a few men and their horses. He and Conn had hidden it after they had battled with three Roman scouts on a chance encounter one afternoon while hunting. What an awesome display of prowess it had been.

The soldiers had tried to land the vessel in secret, but he and Conn were waiting. He could still see their astonished faces when Conn had nonchalantly stepped out from behind a rock. He wore a friendly smile, like he was welcoming old friends, and looking back on it, Aonghus wondered if that really was the case. Then, without blinking an eye, Conn threw his javelin and killed the commander.

The other two reached for their weapons, but Aonghus closed in from behind, and slit the throat of one, while Conn gutted the other. Except for the gurgling sounds of the dying men, it had all been done in perfect silence.

They sent the three corpses adrift in the strait. Surely the tides would carry them back to their ship with the message that this island was never to be a Roman domain. Both warriors agreed it was better to leave the vessel completely outfitted in the event that they were ever in need of emergency transport. This was just such a time, and Aonghus was thankful for his and Conn's craftiness. What a pity to waste such cunning in its prime. Yet, Aonghus felt some envy—at least Conn knew his end; he was still being tested.

The oars were intact, and except for the saddlebags of grain molding from the dampness, even the leather pouches of supplies were still usable. He was not sure how good a sailor he was. The currents could be tricky, but he was confident that with Kordelina's help, they would make it safely to another land.

He checked the knot once more before he left. He wanted to be sure that if the sea got turbulent, it would not loosen the boat and float away. They would have only one chance to escape, and if something went wrong, Jara would sever both their heads.

———

The week that followed was bustling with preparations for the festival of Brigantia. The women cooked for the banquet and sewed festival garments. The farmers gathered to choose the best goat and fatted calves, and the warriors organized the sacred hunt for the boar. It was a time of togetherness for the tribe, in spite of the fact that their Druidess was conspicuously absent from all gatherings. She would oversee the actual celebration, but Saturnalia had left word with Solomon that she did not want to be bothered, under any circumstances, before then.

Kordelina cherished each passing day of this period, not because of the significance of the ritual, but because of the treasured time she had to spend with Aonghus. During the day, she went about her usual chores waiting with great anticipation for the moon to show its face. It was then that she would leave her shutters open, and he would steal into her chamber.

He would wait until it was very late, when he knew everyone was sleeping, then quietly enter through the window and lie with her in the dark. These visits were adored by them; they would talk to each other in hushed voices, exchanging their innermost secrets and reveries. Strangely, Kordelina felt that she had come to know him better in these few encounters than she had her entire life. The beautiful thoughts he shared with her, and the lovely impressions of what he wanted their life together to be like, caused her to realize what a complicated man he truly was.

More than once, he had confessed his fear about his mental condition, making her promise that she would kill him before he ever went totally insane. At these times, he was so serious it scared her. She did not want to believe that they would ever part. However, she could not help but notice that besides the light-headedness, Aonghus often had difficulty focusing, and his respiration was at times labored.

Still, their time together was like a dream come true for her. How she loved the feel of him lying next to her. The texture of his skin, and the contours of his muscular frame were all so pleasurable. When he would press his bare chest to her naked breasts, Kordelina could barely endure the wait to be completely his. Their foreplay was tender and sensual, and dominated by Aonghus. He would initiate it and decide how far it would go, always stopping just before she begged him to take her. She knew how hard it was for Aonghus to hold back; they had been close to consummation many times.

There were nights when he would say very little, but take great delight in slowly undressing her. How she loved for him to do this. She was hypnotized by the desirous look in his eyes as he took in the sight of her unclothed body.

When she was completely naked, he would caress her, kiss her, taste her, and whisper the gentlest, most passionate phrases in her ear. One night, he lit a candle and closely examined every part of her, nibbling on anything that enticed him. Just by the touch of his hand he gave her such pleasure that at times, Kordelina wanted to cry out with ecstasy. Only she could not, because they were continually aware of their parents' presence in the other room.

Once she begged him to meet her in the woods, but he refused, saying that if they were completely alone, he would abandon all restraint. He explained to her that they had to remain in control of themselves until they had left the island, or surely, someone would find out and inform Jara. He said that if he ever possessed her entirely, he would never be able to stay away.

Kordelina never doubted his honesty, because when she seduced him, his sexuality was thoroughly unbridled. It was sheer bliss to be able to fondle him and inhale his masculine scent while she buried her face between his thighs. When he was spent, they would quietly coo to each other in a lover's tongue until they drifted off to sleep.

Although he was always gone by sunrise, Aonghus never failed to gently rouse her before his departure. He would tell her how much he adored her, and call her his bride, then he would kiss her brow, and leave as quietly as he had arrived.

Everything seemed perfect when he was with her, but with the festival soon to begin, Kordelina was starting to worry. Their plans were ready to be executed, but she feared they might fail. This feeling was compounded by the fact that Aonghus did not come to her the night before, and she could not help but think that he had experienced a sudden change of heart.

"It is a beautiful robe, is it not?" Enda asked Kordelina, holding it up in front of her.

The dress was made of streams of red and purple silk, ornamented with a wide strip of gold embroidery along the hem and atop the shoulder.

Kordelina sat nibbling on her fist and staring off into infinity. One arm was folded across her stomach, and her shoulders were hunched forward. She could not stop thinking about Aonghus, and hoping that leaving with him was not just a dream. She was afraid these furtive encounters were sent from the gods to tease her, and that she would have to live the rest of her days alone with only these few memories of their passion.

Ironically, the one whose interference she most feared was Bracorina. She had power as well as guile, and from the look on her face the night of Edainne's delivery, she was not one to give up when she wanted something. If she had even the slightest idea of what was going on, she would sooner see Aonghus killed than escape to Kordelina's arms.

"I am talking to you, child," Enda said. "Do you not think it is lovely?"

Kordelina distractedly nodded. She watched as Enda picked up a gold coil usually worn in the hair, and held it out to her.

"What about this? You will have to put your hair in braids to wear it. It has been so long since I have seen you done up, I have forgotten how you look," she said, smiling. Then she turned her attention to some gold jewelry she had set out. Many bracelets were arranged on top of a green cloak that completed the outfit.

Kordelina furrowed her brow, and looked questioningly at Koven seated next to her, then back at Enda.

"Braids? Done up? What do you mean?" she asked, perturbed.

Enda looked at her husband uncomfortably, then down at the dress. "Father, tell her," she remarked evasively.

Koven shifted in his seat to face the girl.

"Tell me what?" Kordelina questioned, rising to her feet, and placing both hands on her hips.

"Kordelina, sit down," her father said. His voice had a tone of authority that she had not heard in years.

Arching her brows, Kordelina looked at him impatiently.

"I said sit down," he commanded.

She waited a long moment, then obeyed. The imperious look that had overtaken him faded the instant she acquiesced. Kindly taking one of her hands, he held it with his crooked fingers.

She stared at him in silence, thinking how much Aonghus was like him. He could be petulant and demanding one minute, and gentle the next. None of her other brothers had inherited that temperament. They were far less changeable, and more jovial like their mother.

"This dress is for you to wear to the festival when you dance," he said softly.

"But, Father, I am not going to dance. Only maids ready to be wed dance at the celebration," she answered. "I can never marry; I have no title."

Koven opened his mouth to reply, but his words were arrested as the door opened and Aonghus entered. He was slightly out of breath.

"Aonghus, dear boy," Enda greeted, reaching out to hug him. "We had not expected to see you."

"Does a son need an invitation to visit his mother?" he replied, taking her in his arms and lifting her off the ground.

"Aonghus, please!" she said, smoothing her apron as he set her back down. "You fluster me."

Aonghus chuckled at her shyness, then turned to Koven. "I thought I would find you choosing your best goat for slaughter. The festival is soon," he remarked, extending his hand.

His father offered a half smile as he released Kordelina, and shook his son's hand as best he could. "It is already taken care of," he answered.

Aonghus stole a glance at Kordelina. She noticed he had the mischievous glint in his eye that she so dearly loved. Then he turned his attention to the robe draped across the table in front of him.

"Is this what you are going to wear tonight?" he asked, taking it and holding it up admiringly.

Kordelina nodded. "So I am told."

Aonghus' eyes flashed back at her, and his smile broadened. "What a sight you will be. I might have to be your personal guard against the rest of the dogs in this tribe."

She felt herself blush. Any amount of attention he showed her made her want him madly.

"That will not be necessary," Koven interrupted. "She will be under the protection of the Order. Jara is coming to take her to another tribe."

The smile faded from Aonghus' face so suddenly that for a moment, Kordelina thought there was more to these circumstances than he had counted on. Then she watched him put the robe down carefully, and look directly at her.

"It will be better for you," he said, with feigned sincerity. "As long as you are here, your life will be filled with loneliness. No one in the clan would take you as his wife, and even though you could always have a place working this land, you would be an afterthought when the rest of us had families of our own."

Kordelina's expression went blank. He was so convincing that she wanted to laugh out loud. She could tell by his confident manner, that all was going as he had planned. She only had to do her part to make it believable.

"That is not my desire," she argued, a trace of resentment in her voice. "If I go to another tribe with Jara, it will be as a chieftain's sacrifice. That is all that I am good for now, only I would sooner kill myself than die by her hand."

"You foolish little girl," Enda exhorted, stepping in front of her. "It does not matter how much we love you, you have wronged your tribe. If you die by your own hand, then you will be made to suffer in the afterworld for it. This way, you can give yourself for the good of a chieftain, and your blemished soul will be free to come back and prosper. It is the only way you can atone for your actions. After all, you did come to us on the night of a festival, and that means you were blessed by the gods from the start. I believe this is their way of calling you back to them."

Kordelina's eyes widened. She could not believe that her mother was talking like this.

"If I were still Aonghus' servant would I have to go?" she asked, raising her voice to a fevered pitch.

Aonghus nodded, and looked at the ground. "I am afraid so. I would be paid the sum of six cattle by the chieftain who desires you. Under the laws, I would have no choice but to accept it," he said earnestly.

Kordelina sat back, and folded her arms across her chest. She scowled at all of them a moment, then stood up in disgust and stormed out of the room.

"I think you have all gone mad!" they heard her declare, as she slammed the door behind her.

"Poor girl," Enda said, as she sat down beside Koven. "I do not think she really understands all of this."

Aonghus shook his head. "No, she does not," he agreed. "Perhaps I should go, and try to explain it to her. It is important that she realize that her family has not betrayed her."

Koven looked at him gratefully. "You have always been the only one who can talk any sense to her. Thank you, son, you make me proud."

Aonghus averted his eyes. He did not want to look at his father knowing what shame he would cause him in the end.

"Go on, the festival begins at dusk, and she must be there," Enda said.

Aonghus nodded and walked to the entryway.

"I will do all I can," he replied.

CHAPTER FOURTEEN

onghus kept his grave expression as he went outside to find Kordelina. As a very young child, she never used to run away like this. It was only when her rebelliousness had cost her some fair beatings by Koven and other tribesmen that she started fleeing conflicts. He supposed she behaved in this way not because she was afraid of being hurt, rather, she found the whole situation a waste of time.

Fortunately, Kordelina had vented her frustrations as a hunter, and bestowed her benevolence on animals instead of humans. She was more insidious with a weapon in her hand than most men he knew, and yet, she was entirely empathetic of even the wildest of beasts.

"They are not like us, Aonghus," she would say again and again. "We choose to do battle, but they have no choice."

Heading straight for the barn, Aonghus knew he would predictably find her where he always found her: pouting in Macha's stall.

As he entered the building, he heard the quiet rustle of hay in the loft above. He looked up, but saw nothing as he stepped inside. Stopping in front of the mare's sleeping place, he peeked in cautiously, expecting to see Kordelina, but found no one.

In the next moment, she dropped to the ground next to him. He was so startled that he gasped in surprise, and jumped back clumsily. Kordelina put her fingers to her lips and giggled, then stopped suddenly, not wanting to anger him.

"It is not funny," Aonghus said, instantly regaining his composure. His face hardened as they looked at each other. "What if I had thought you were an attacker, and I had drawn a weapon?"

Kordelina pursed her lips and rolled her eyes. "But you were not expecting an attacker, and you did not have your weapons drawn," she countered. "You are saying that because I tricked you, and you did not like it."

He smiled awkwardly at her subtle rebuke of his vanity, and looked down.

Kordelina liked him like this. He was so pliable and endearing. She thought that once they were together, he would remain this way forever.

"What are you so happy about anyway? Your moments left in this world are too few to rejoice," he said, suddenly serious.

Kordelina dropped her hands stiffly to her sides. The solemn sound in his voice made her nervous.

"I do not understand what you mean," she said hesitantly, as she craned her head forward and tried to meet his eye.

Aonghus continued to look down, not moving a muscle. "It really is for the best," he said.

She placed her hand to her forehead anxiously, then grabbed his arm.

"What are you talking about?" she asked again, raising her voice and shaking him. "Are you telling me that you have changed your mind? I knew this would happen! It is Bracorina; you were with her last night, and she convinced you to stay with her, did she not?"

Releasing her hold, she turned away. Her mind was reeling, and she could feel herself breaking out in a nervous sweat.

"Am I right?" she demanded, whirling around again.

"No," Aonghus mumbled.

"No?" Kordelina repeated after him.

Aonghus looked up at her, and smiled playfully.

"No," he said flatly. He had a prankish look about him that told her instantly that he was repaying her for teasing him.

"Aonghus," she huffed. "Are you joking?"

"Yes," he replied, holding back his laughter.

She breathed a sigh of relief, then was infuriated at his cruelty. Without thinking, she flung herself at him, and began beating on him with her clenched fists. He laughed harder as he effortlessly took both her wrists in his large hands, and flattened her against the wall.

"Calm yourself," he said. "You like to trick others, but you surely do not like it when one is played on you."

Kordelina's face was twisted and red, and she jerked from side to side trying to get loose from him.

"I cannot believe you would jest like that," she said finally, boring through him with a piercing glare. "What is happening is serious. It is my life you are toying with."

Aonghus' laughter ceased. "It is my life as well. Do not forget that. I could not come to you last night because Solomon never went to sleep. He talked to me at great length about matters of little importance. I think he suspects us, so he stayed awake to see if I was going to leave. If I had visited you, there is no doubt in my mind that I would have been followed."

He stared at her a moment longer, unsure if his explanation had sufficed her anger. Then he let her go, and she fell against him and hugged his neck.

"Forgive me," she whispered in his ear. "I was so worried, I thought you had changed your mind."

"Not at all," he replied, holding her closer. Taking a handful of her hair, he lifted it to his nose to breath in its scent. She felt so soft against him, so inviting. "It is all going as I planned."

"And Conn? His life will be spared, will it not?" she asked, with genuine concern as she met his gaze.

Aonghus' expression saddened, and his eyes started to mist. Letting go of her, he walked to the open door. The warm sunlight illuminated his features so that every line and flaw on his handsome face was magnified. An invisible boundary around him told her to keep her distance, and wait for him to speak. Leaning against the doorway, he carefully considered his response.

"I still do not believe she will do it," he murmured.

Kordelina felt panic come over her. Stepping alongside him, she rested her hand on his shoulder and felt his tension rise.

Aonghus looked at her sharply. His blue eyes were slits, and she was not sure if he was squinting from the light or challenging her to rebuke him.

"She will not do it," he stated. "She says she will, if he desires it so. But I cannot believe one as brave as Conn would knowingly walk to his death."

Kordelina stared at him in disbelief. This was not really happening, she thought, as she let her hand drop and backed away from him. Saturnalia could not kill her own lover, such a deed would be like committing suicide.

"Do not look at me that way. I am not a murderer!" Aonghus erupted as he walked toward her, his hand lifted in the air as if he were going to strike her.

She covered the side of her face with one hand, and cowered away from him. "I am sorry. I cannot accept the thought of it," she said timidly.

Aonghus stopped short. What was he doing? He could not hurt her, he thought, as he struggled to subdue his anger. How terrible it would be to feel her soft flesh bruise with his blow after he had so lovingly caressed it. Seeing her react like this distressed him; his spells of violence must have frightened her more than he imagined.

"I tried to reason with Saturnalia, but she laughed in my face. She said that I had made a fool of Conn, and robbed him of his dignity. I even spoke with him before we parted, and he told me that he was willing to receive death at her hand," Aonghus said quickly, his head tilted mournfully to one side. "I am not his murderer, but his fate I cannot prevent."

Kordelina was stunned. How had they ever been born into this arbitrary place where their free will had become their adversary? Turning her back to him, she pressed herself against the inside wall. She was taking short, anxious breaths, and her whole body ached.

Aonghus walked up behind her and wrapped both arms around her waist. Pulling her to him, she felt first his hot breath on the back of her neck, then the wetness of his lips.

"What have we done, my sweet one?" she whispered sadly.

He did not answer as she felt his hand lower to the round of her belly, and begin to gently massage it. Dropping her head back, she closed her eyes at the sensation of his body against hers. They could not help it, and knowing right from wrong did not matter now.

"Take me, I can wait no longer," she said, her voice filled with surrender. "Do not make me go to the festival, and dance for the death of my kinsman."

"I am sorry, but there is no other way. You must partake of the celebration as if it were your last," he said finally.

"No, I will not," she argued. "Not for Conn. The guilt in my heart cannot celebrate his end. However great it is to be received by the gods, I know that it would not be this way for him if he could prevent it."

"Kordelina, listen to me. When we were initiated as young men, I remember what a difficult experience that night in the cave was for Conn," Aonghus said. Taking her by the shoulders, he turned her around to face him. "He wept as he recalled the vision of his parents killed by the Roman soldiers. What pained him the most is that they were stabbed in the back as they fled. He mourned their cowardice more than their memory. I have come to believe that he wants to be bold in his passing, and Saturnalia can insure that for him.

"It is too late for remorse or outrage. The wheels of our future are turning too fast to stop. You must do all that you are asked, and when Jara arrives, you must bow to her, and pretend to willingly accept your place. When I leave to take my watch, you must wait for the right time to follow. It is crucial that you are not seen by anyone. I will meet you at my post, and we will leave straightaway. Kordelina, you must use all your stealth— the price is high for our failure."

Kordelina reached deep into her soul as he spoke, trying to discern if she still had enough courage to go through with it. "Yes, Aonghus, I will do as you say."

He kissed her forehead. "I know you will. I have faith in you, Kordelina."

"Aonghus, does Saturnalia know about us?" she questioned.

"Yes, she always has," he answered, pressing his face against her cheek. "Before your servitude I had requested to take you as my wife. I confessed my feelings for you then, but she would not condone it."

Kordelina gazed at the ground, utterly perplexed. "Then why has she not tried to stop it?"

"Because she loves you greatly," he answered, his voice infinitely strong. "But my love for you is greater."

He pulled her to him and hugged her tightly. "You must go now, and when I hold you again, it will be for ever," he said quietly, as he let her go.

She looked up at him, wounded. "Can I not stay with you to the very last moment? Let us ride to the seashore, and I will return freely at dusk."

Aonghus offered her a warm, apologetic look. For a moment, his expression was exactly the same one she remembered from childhood, and her adoration of him swelled.

"The temptation is too great. I would not let you return, and your absence would be conspicuous. Go now, and adorn yourself for my pleasure. I will be waiting for you," he responded, nuzzling the bend of her neck.

She touched the side of his face with her open palm.

"As you wish," she replied, then walked reluctantly back to the house.

CHAPTER FIFTEEN

here was little left to do except wait for Solomon to come and take her; little left to care for except the matters of her own heart, she thought, as she bathed and prepared to descend the hill into the village. Saturnalia felt a terrible queasiness at the thought of the future, better to drive it from her mind lest she lose her courage altogether.

Soon the sun would be below the horizon and the procession would begin. The preparations and chores were tended to by now, and she had left word with her guards that if Jara were to arrive, she was an intruder, and should be treated as such. At this point, Saturnalia did not care how greatly she offended the Druidess. Perhaps she would have to let Kordelina go, but she would make it clear that it was not with her blessing.

If Kordelina had been more popular in the clan, she would have refused Jara's demands, and challenged the supposed chieftain who wanted her. But since Kordelina's past offenses had not been forgotten, she doubted there would be any real support for it, even if it were an opportunity to do battle and take another chieftain's territory. As for Saturnalia personally, she would have liked the comfort of the young girl's company to ease her loneliness. Life without Conn would be more difficult than she could imagine.

Setting down her cloth, she opened a vial of oil she had made by the full moon especially for this occasion. Inhaling the pleasant aroma of jasmine, patchouli, and sandlewood, she poured it into the center of her palms and rubbed it over her entire body.

The radiating heat of the fire penetrated her pores, giving her an erotic sensation of her own femininity. Her spirit was soon to be away from here, and she felt a sudden urgency to be with her lover as she was for the last time.

Walking into her courtyard, she cut three long strands of ivy from the trunk of the oak and brought them back into her chamber. She carefully wrapped them around an anointed candle, then lit it. Next, she took a small bronze scepter in the shape of a hawk's leg with its talons still attached, and stirred a mortar bowl of ruan set in front of her.

"Red of this blood is as dark as the shadow that makes the ashes of my death. For it is the death of myself," she said. "Death, my seductive ally, what I hold within my womb I shall not fear. So red of my blood transform to my lover's flesh and shadow to ivy leaf, that I may offer him rebirth."

She touched the metal wand to the round of her stomach, and drew one large red circle around her womb. Then in the center, she drew an "X" with a line through the middle, the sign of the grove and eternal life.

She then lifted the three strands of ivy, and began twisting them together as she spoke.

"Bone become my flesh; shadow become this leaf. As death is my love; it bears me life," she continued, tying the ivy rope around her waist.

Naked, she walked to the bedroom where Conn slept. She had given him a dose of nepenthe so that he would sleep through the night. The first eve of the festival was sacred to the tribal women, and it was important that he remain oblivious to what was taking place.

Kneeling beside him, she gently pulled back his covering, and began massaging his body with her oily hands. The bruises were scarcely visible now; her use of poultice and healing oils had worked nicely. She was certain that his ribs were healed enough to afford him a chance to love her once more.

She saw his eyes blink open as she moved her open mouth across the round of his stomach, and she felt his hands in her hair as she began seductively kissing the round of his hips and the insides of his thighs. She heard him sigh as she lightly ran her tongue over his groin. Feeling his flaccid shaft harden against her cheek, she delicately kissed it and he opened his legs wider at the stimulation.

"Lover, I am floating now, away somewhere with you. I am loving you in my dreams, and have little control of this physical world," he said groggily.

"Then, lover, you must let me do it," she responded, as she looked across his stomach into his listless eyes.

Sitting up, she leaned over him on all fours, and brushed her nipples across his chest. She moved back and forth rhythmically, never allowing her gaze to waver from his. In a moment, she lowered her head and kissed him, biting his tongue just hard enough to draw blood. His body tensed, but she began sucking on it until he relaxed.

His blood was on her mouth by the time she drew away. Looking hard into his eyes, she saw the dull shock on his face at the sight of her.

"Give yourself to me," she whispered, placing her hand on the sides of his face and rubbing his temples with her fingertips. "Fill me with your spirit. It is the only way we will survive this."

He gasped at her words. Death was soon to be upon him—it was no longer merely a heroic principle. Reaching out, he ran his hand along the side of her face and over the round of her shoulder.

"Yes," he murmured, taking both her breasts in his hands and firmly squeezing them. "Yes, I want to live again."

Straddling him, she took him inside of her. As she slowly rocked on top of him, she let every sensation of their union scald her insides until she was thoroughly consumed by their heat. Conn appeared spellbound by the image of her graceful movements in the flame's shadow.

Lifting his head off the pillow, he suckled first one breast then the other. He was struggling to prolong it, waiting for that dizzying feeling of her flesh pouncing on him, begging to be relieved.

"Come into me," he heard her say. She seemed to be screaming as he took one of her nipples between his teeth, and pressed a little harder. "Let your soul come into me."

He could feel her throbbing insides as she took his head in her hands, and jerked his face back for her to see him. Sweat was dripping down her brow, and her lips were open enough to let out her pants of desire. Her green eyes were only dim shadows in the firelight.

Conn opened his mouth to cry out, but made only a low grunting noise as his warmth spurted into her. For an instant, he thought he saw etheral images of robed figures surrounding them, then he was spiraling helplessly into a funnel of darkness. Shutting his eyes tightly, he reached out, groping for her as she wrapped her arms around him.

His pleasure had suddenly transformed into a lament. It came out in long mournful cries as she held him closer, trying to soothe him. He sobbed for a few moments more, then dropped into a hypnotic slumber.

"It is well now. You are mine and must live on," she said in a tranquil voice. "I will repay the heavens with a life, but it will not be yours."

Rising from the bed, she went to her cabinet and took out a small dried branch from a hawthorn tree, and three brittle thorns saved from a rose Kordelina had given her months before. She set them down carefully on the floor next to the bedside.

Returning to the cabinet, she reached far back on the top shelf and removed a bronze jar containing the heart of a pheasant she had left seeping in wine since the last full moon. She set it next to the branch and thorns, then lit three beeswax candles, and placed them in a triangle surrounding them.

Acting as if she were in a trance, she went to her conjuring bag and pulled out the tuft of Aonghus' hair she had taken during their struggle. What a fool he was to think that she would let her lover die without trying to destroy him first.

She took a scrap of black cloth and placed it, perfectly smooth, in the middle of the candles. Then she removed the fowl's heart from its holder, and put it in its center. The red wine trickled through her fingers and down her wrist, giving the graven image of blood still flowing from the lifeless organ.

"Aonghus, crude warrior that you are, as this heart is pierced, it shames thy deed. It accuses thy hand, it mars thy heart, and it destroys thyself," she recited in a hushed voice. She repeated the phrase two more times as one by one she took the thorns, and plunged them into the core of the heart.

Then she took Aonghus' hair and wrapped it around the thorned organ as many times as it would go.

"As this heart is pierced, it shames thy deed; it accuses thy hand; it mars thy heart, and it destroys thyself," she said, again raising her voice with each word until she shouted the last syllables so that it echoed through the room.

Holding the charm in her palm, she grabbed Conn's knife from the bedside, and without waking him, pierced the tip of his finger. The blood came out in bright red droplets, and she let them fall onto the thorns. When she was satisfied that enough of his blood had been spent, she gently wrapped his hand in a cloth, and placed it beneath the covers.

Sitting down cross-legged in front of the candles, she stared at the charm like a child holding her most prized possession. Then she carefully covered it with the black cloth, and bound it tightly with a long strand of her own hair. Replacing it in the middle of the candles, she began softly humming and meditating on Aonghus' image.

"As my lover's spirit is kept safe inside of me, so will yours be taken in bondage. Let your breath and life be the mirror of his death. I entreat our ancestral heavens to hear my call," her speech was detached and without feeling. It was happening already—she was leaving this place.

———

Saturnalia awoke to the sight of Solomon kneeling over her. He gently stroked her face to rouse her, then took her hands and helped her to stand.

She staggered at first, then stood in silence as he took her ceremonial robe and draped it over her unclothed body. He moved slowly and deliberately as he fastened the broach atop her left shoulder, then he lightly kissed both her cheeks.

"It is time now," he said paternally.

Saturnalia bent down and picked up the black bundle. Discreetly attaching it to her broach, she looked at Solomon with vacant eyes. Then she walked to Conn's bedside, and delicately kissed his lips. He would remain sequestered in this room until the last moment.

"Let us go then," she replied in a vacuous tone.

Holding hands, Solomon and Saturnalia walked into the courtyard. The fresh night air sobered her as Solomon mounted his well-decorated horse, and pulled her up onto the animal's back. Wrapping her arms tightly around his waist, she nuzzled the back of his neck and lightly kissed his hair.

"Dear Chieftain, do not let anything happen to me," she said meekly.

Solomon turned in his saddle and gave her a puzzled look. "I do not know of what you speak."

She yielded a resigned smile. "Sometimes the gods toy with us, and answer our petitions. As my dearest friend, do not let me falter this time," she answered, her eyes beginning to tear. "It means more than my life alone, it is the life of our people. I feel that what happens at this festival will affect them for generations to come."

He offered her a compassionate look. "If that is so, then this time Sorceress, I know you will not falter," he answered, turning back around and gently spurring his horse to an even trot.

The festival procession was halfway through the settlement when, sitting sidesaddle on the back of Solomon's steed, Saturnalia descended the knoll. The beautifully-dressed women sang joyously as they went from one household to another, collecting the presents meant to pay homage to their goddess, Brigantia. Each girl of marrying age carried a basket filled with fresh herbs and seashells along with the special stones needed for their magical practices on this eve. The already married women, still of childbearing age, carried special cakes baked to the Goddess that were to be eaten by the group before the sun rose the next day.

At the head of the parade, barely recognizable because of her lavish adornments, was Kordelina. Her skin was powdered white, her brows darkened with berry juice, and her cheeks reddened with ruan. Her lips had been outlined to make a smile even when she frowned. The bells on her skirt jingled in unison with the clank of the many bracelets she wore, and as she drew closer, Saturnalia could tell by her suffering expression that she was almost in tears. Still, she held out her basket and bowed as Solomon stopped in the center of the village, and Saturnalia dismounted.

The Druidess held out her arms to welcome the women, and they all bowed in respect.

"Beautiful Brides of the Goddess Brigantia, let us nourish ourselves by celebrating her wonder!" she shouted, lifting her face to the sky.

The women responded by exclaiming the beauty of the bride and twirling around each other in rehearsed steps, all except Kordelina, who remained on her knees in front of her.

"Beautiful child, let us welcome the Goddess who has named you a Chieftain's bride," she said, in a tone of false exhilaration.

Kordelina somberly rose to her feet and Saturnalia stared at her dull eyes. What torture it must be for one so private to be dressed and paraded flagrantly in front of her clan, she thought.

The women all fell into a line behind her, dancing in circles so that the bells on all of their skirts chimed through the air. Their lovely soprano voices rejoiced in song as they proceeded up the hill to Saturnalia's cottage, and once inside, barred the door behind them.

The men of the tribe watched with intrigue as they shared wine and ale among themselves, and prepared the festival pyre that would be lit at dawn.

CHAPTER SIXTEEN

ll of the women crammed themselves into Saturnalia's main chamber. They sat in small circles of three or four on pillows and animal pelts with their herbs and materials combined together in the center. A few had brought drums, harps, or hand flutes and played soft tunes as they were inspired. The others worked in silence, borrowing from one another what they needed to complete their offering. At times, one of the girls would go to another circle and bow politely, wordlessly asking to partake of their supplies, and they were generously shared with a hug and a smile.

Kordelina held the flagon of red wine, and went from one group to another, making sure the communal flasks remained filled to the brim. As the future chosen bride, it was her responsibility to serve the others on this eve out of respect for the Goddess' powers. It was meant to impart humility to her, that she would be a selfless offering for her husband, be he human or spirit. Only when the sun came up would she be free to do as she pleased. It was that promise that made this forced subservience bearable.

Saturnalia was stretched out on an elk hide nearest the fire; she was in a deep hypnotic sleep. What was she seeing in her dreams, Kordelina wondered to herself as she took the ivory pipe full of hemp Edainne offered. Her ears were buzzing with the magnified sounds of the music and the women's shallow breathing. Saturnalia had given her something in a cup, and made her drink it before the ritual began. Whatever the mixture was, it was powerful, and Kordelina was fighting to keep from drifting off completely.

She took a puff of the pipe, then handed it back to Edainne and smiled. Edainne smiled back, then started laughing and hugged Kordelina.

"Thank you for being my friend," she said sweetly.

Kordelina drew away, giggling. She could see where the red makeup had smeared on Edainne's white robe. She tried clumsily to brush it away, but found that she had no feeling in her fingertips.

"It is you whose friendship I value. Even when the others mocked me, you were always kind," she said, looking at her friend sincerely.

Edainne shook her head. "The kindness I showed is little of what you have done for me. I am only worthy to ask that you implore the gods in the happy Otherworld to care for my daughter."

Kordelina nodded. "If I am able," she answered seriously.

"Girl, fetch us more wine," she heard Bracorina's commanding voice from across the room.

Kordelina hardened as she went to the circle where Bracorina sat with her sisters. She could not help but take notice of the material with which Bracorina was working.

Combined neatly in a red, embroidered cloth, were honeysuckle, rue, willow bark, and a slim braid of reddish-brown hair knotted together with a lock of her own. They were set in front of a candle, a vial of wintergreen oil, and a white feather. A strand of black thread encircled the entire area surrounding it.

Kordelina knew immediately that the crude charm she was making was meant to recall the faithless. Bracorina intended to ask the Goddess for Aonghus' return, and the thought of it evoked a sudden feeling of panic.

"Our flask is nearly empty," Bracorina complained.

Kordelina knelt down, and picking it up with trembling hands, filled it to the top. She was so dizzy that she could barely keep her balance as she tried to set it back down, accidently spilling a small amount on Bracorina's candle, extinguishing it.

"Look what you have done!" Bracorina screeched, grabbing her forehead with both hands.

Kordelina crouched low to the ground, appearing contrite. Yet, she was privately relieved that the heavens had interceded, and she believed that this was a good omen.

"Thank you, Goddess," she said under her breath.

"You have purposely ruined my offering," Bracorina accused, lifting one hand in the air to slap her.

Kordelina bowed her head, and waited to be disciplined. She did not care how much it hurt since she knew she had only to endure one more night of this and then she would be free forever.

"Bracorina, it is all right," Edainne said. "You may use my candle."

Kordelina looked up to find that Edainne was holding Bracorina's wrist with one hand, while offering her a burning candle in the other.

Bracorina's eyes softened slightly as she took the candle from her brother's wife.

"She is so careless," she snapped. "It will be a blessing when she is gone."

Kordelina was resolute. "For me as well, Bracorina. For me as well."

She gave Edainne an appreciative nod, then turned away. The smoke and drink were having great effect on her. She looked around the room and reminisced about how often she had sat within its confines feeling safe, and sometimes strangely powerful. At this moment, the walls seemed to be breathing with life, moving steadily back and forth with the pulsating hearts of those within them. Every detail and imperfection of the structure was magnified, as if each one held great significance on this night. Kordelina thought it peculiar that the room seemed to be revolving around her while she was standing perfectly still. Then her attention was drawn to the closed bedroom door, and she found herself standing in front of it.

Glancing at the Saturnalia, she noticed that she lay motionless. Looking back at the closed entryway, she felt a curious desire to trespass into the Druidess' private chamber. Discreetly turning the handle, she slipped inside.

The room was dark, except for three partially melted candles burning near the bed. Standing perfectly still, she waited for her eyes to adjust to the dim light. She could hear low whispers coming from the back of the room, and she strained her vision to see who it was, but saw no one. A faint feminine laughter sounded in her ear, and she turned suddenly, but it was only thin air.

She could see Conn outstretched on the bed with his back to her. Even with the phantom voices now coming from all sides of the room, she could not help but go to him. Kneeling at the bedside, she noticed there was a cat sitting protectively above his head. Kordelina could not help but be intrigued by the preternatural expression of its cool green eyes; they seemed to follow the girl's every movement. Its coat was an odd coloring of orange and gray stripes unlike anything she had ever seen before.

She was distracted by the flickering candlelight as it cast dancing shadows on the walls. It looked like people milling about in all corners of the room as the surrounding voices now mixed with laughter, and grew louder. Soon, it developed into an incessant chant of ancient phrases Kordelina remembered but did not understand, and she saw Conn roll over and look at her. His expression was distant, as though they had never met.

She offered him a drink of wine, and he indulged himself until the liquor ran down his chin and onto the bed. Something unspoken passed between them as he extended his hand. She took it, and he pulled her onto the bed next to him.

No matter how much she wanted to, Kordelina could not stop what was happening. It was as if someone else surfaced from within her. She could not tear herself from his placid eyes as the chanting grew still louder.

She felt an aching arousal as he ran his hand over her breast, then lifted her robe and touched her between the legs. She thought how morbid it was—two damned souls sharing their last pleasures with each other. Was it further mockery that was meant to humiliate them even more in the sunlight?

Her heart rattled against her chest, and her mouth opened wide as he pressed his lips to it. She could not help herself; she wanted to be naked for him, feel him use her, even if it meant he would know her before Aonghus. She tried to picture Aonghus' face, remember his touch, but it was as though he had never existed. Maybe this was the way it was meant to be, she thought, and her plans for freedom were a cruel illusion.

She felt the invisible presence of a throng of souls closing in around them as Conn gently stroked her with his fingers. The tingling filled her body, and she felt carnal and daring, not at all like she had been when she was with Aonghus. Reaching beneath the covers, she ran her hands across his sweaty loins, like a thief steal-ing a moment of forbidden pleasure.

"Who am I?" Conn asked, as he pulled away from her.

Kordelina was shaking as she wrapped her fingers around his hardness. She could not answer.

"Who am I?" he questioned again, raising his voice. His face had a look of frightened urgency, and for a moment, she wished it had been her with whom he had fallen in love, not Saturnalia. Then she would not have committed her crime, and Aonghus would not have accused him. Their lives would have been fruitful and unaffected, and they would have been able to live happily within the tribal laws.

Kordelina closed her eyes and took a tempered breath. She could do nothing but allow the celestial voices to fill her ears with their echoing sighs and mighty prayers. They seemed to be delivering a long sought after peace, as in a sudden thrust of light, she found herself fluttering like a moth through hallowed festivities. She was watching the celebration of witches and crones, all radiant and gorged with pride. They reached their hands out from beneath their shrouds to touch her, and Kordelina saw in their faces the unrevealed beauty of ancient times. Their counte-nances were so resplendent with hope and their hearts so buoyant, that she wanted to fall before them in worship and offer up her youth in homage.

Then, as if they had transformed into a bright body of water, they parted to unveil a woman so divine that Kordelina could barely take in the vision of her. Her expression was open, and her eyes strangely enlarged; she appeared to be pouring forth enormous virtue as well as deep mourning.

As Kordelina looked deeper into them, she perceived moon beams before her. It was as if she were floating on a silken avalanche of stars that beckoned her into a sparkling trance where a young child reigned on a fragrant, sun-filled island that was still Anglesey. He had clouds of dark hair, and great noble eyes which dis-played his self-assurance in a single glance.

Suddenly she saw herself with Aonghus, the two naked together in the oak grove. As they made passionate love, she was taken by how perfectly the curves of their bodies fit together. She watched herself filling up with life as she lovingly sucked the marrow from his bones, and he returned it with tender kisses. He did it as if he were giving himself to her completely, so that their union could bring forth a stronger one than he.

In the next moment, she gazed upon a young, handsome warrior she knew to be her son. He was powerful, yet beautifully compassionate in his every move-ment. Flying like a bird in the breezes above him, she followed him as he walked the clear coastline along the Menai Strait, then into the shelter of the sacred grove where he had been conceived.

Swooping across the settlement, she saw herself seated beside a man with golden hair and tawny skin. His slender hand was resting atop hers as they gazed out on the green wheat fields and the barren stretches of land where the oak trees had once been.

With another breath she was once again looking into Conn's beseeching eyes, as he waited for her to answer him.

"You are Saturnalia's dearest love," she responded breathlessly, as she pushed him away. "The spirits are testing the devotion of our hearts."

Conn looked back at her in confusion, then he began wiping off her makeup with his fingers.

"We are so insignificant—you and I—that they make us their spectacles," he said ruefully.

As he finished his sentence, the cat jumped from the bed and disappeared into the darkness. Relaxing her neck, Kordelina dropped her head back, and let him smear the makeup Enda had so painstakingly applied. It felt like he was stripping off her clothing.

He ran his hand across her forehead and over her cheeks, spreading the red in all directions. Then he suddenly stopped what he was doing, and cocked his head to one side to listen. "Can you hear them?"

"Yes, and we must take heed," she whispered. "We are important, you must believe that. Our gods will not fail us if we honor them."

He did not seem to understand her as he fixed his eyes on her lips. He was not looking at them with lust, but with genuine sensitivity as he kissed her again. Feeling too drained to resist him, she let him move on top of her and she felt the moist tip of his sex against hers. She wanted to scream, but could not find the strength.

She felt hands running through her hair, loosening her braids as he gnawed on her skin with his teeth. He felt so strange to her, so savage, that it was frightening. How she had wanted to save herself for Aonghus. He had tried so hard, given up so much for their love. It was just like the time she had made her first kill. She had shamelessly done it with his best friend. Now, she wanted to prevent herself from giving her chastity to the one whose life her lover had bargained away.

"Goddess help me to be strong," she murmured.

Hearing the chamber door open, she turned her head to find the Druidess was standing in the middle of the three candles. Her hands were held waist high, with her palms open as if welcoming the young girl. Kordelina panicked at first, but Saturnalia's understanding expression calmed her.

"It is time," she said softly. "Come with me now."

The next thing Kordelina knew they were in the main room. She was sitting stiff and upright in front of the fireplace with the women waiting in a line to make their offerings.

One by one, they took their place beside Saturnalia, and made their requests. Kordelina knew that at one time she had known all their names, but in her present state, they were all strangers. The train seemed endless as one after another, they handed Kordelina their offering and whispered their supplication to Saturnalia. At the Druidess' cue, Kordelina would toss their charms into the flames. Then the women would repeat the same phrase in unison.

"Let the bride come in, the Goddess Brigantia is welcome," they would chant and each drink of their wine.

She remembered seeing Edainne's tearful eyes as she made her request, then tightly hugged Kordelina's neck. If it were not for that gesture of affection, she would have remained as indistinguishable as the rest.

When the last request was heard, the cakes were broken, and the women began to eat and drink together. Saturnalia rose from her place, and removed the carved figure from beneath her robe. It depicted a goddess seated on a throne with a baby's head emerging from between her legs. She placed it deliberately on the hearth in front of the fire. The vibrant flames framed the statue as the women broke into step, and sang to the Mother Goddess.

Saturnalia took an uneaten cake and a flask of wine to where she sat down next to Kordelina. The girl watched intently as she took a bite, then offered her the rest.

Kordelina gave a troubled smiled and ate it. Then she picked up the wine and took a drink, before offering it to Saturnalia. The Sorceress' eyes watered as she drank long, and setting it down, took Kordelina's hand in hers.

"The singing and dancing will continue until sunrise, will you wait with me?" she asked kindly.

"Yes," Kordelina answered, sitting back. Closing her eyes, she saw fragments of the same vision: the beautiful women, the child among the stars, then the same loving exchange between her and Aonghus—Kordelina knew instantly that she must not wait until they were gone to lay with him.

The room was stifling hot, and she could feel the sweat from her neck running down between her breasts and onto her stomach. It was so smoky and noisy that she thought she would suffocate, and as she listened to the steady sound of her own heartbeat, she dozed. Holding Saturnalia's hand tightly, the two waited for the dawn.

"The Bride's bed is ready," she heard one woman announce, and rousing herself, she saw the faint morning light filling the room.

"Then let the Bride come," Saturnalia declared, in response.

The Druidess stood slowly, and picking up the statue, smoothed the still smoldering ashes with her hand. She turned abruptly, and looked at Kordelina for a prolonged moment before she faced the congregation of women and held the figure high above her head.

"The Goddess has welcomed and honored us," she stated. "In her charity, Brigantia has chosen a bride to be her ripening vessel."

The women cried out joyously as they exchanged hugs and gifts.

"She has accepted our offerings," one said tearfully.

"And blessed us with prosperity," cried another. "There will be a new king!"

The Druidess waited patiently for them to finish, then set the figure of the goddess in an ornamented cradle made of willow wood.

Kordelina watched the event with cool detachment. These practices seemed fruitless to her now; whether her plans with Aonghus worked out, or if she was to leave with Jara, they were soon to be out of her life completely.

"Kordelina," Saturnalia said wearily. "Remove the last burning ember, and put it in the elk horn. Take care to keep it lit until we reach the grove."

The girl nodded, and took a smoldering coal from the fire and carefully placed it in the hollow of the horn. As she did this, the women gathered their belongings and prepared to make their descent.

With one hand cupped around the smoking end, Kordelina blew lightly on the ember. The wisps of gray smoke looked like curly strands of hair floating in front of her, then disappearing. When she was satisfied that it would not extinguish itself, she took her place behind the Druidess.

Saturnalia turned, and looked at Kordelina only once before opening the door. Her eyes were ablaze, and the rose-color had filled her cheeks once again. She was rejuvenated.

The train of women sang a different song as they crossed the knoll and went deep into the grove. The first light of morning made the mist floating between the trees look like powdered gold. In the distance, the clearing was visible. A huge pyre of wood had been assembled by the men, and the livestock to be slaughtered for feasting were tied in an area tended by Niall.

Warriors encircled the wood, naked from the waist up, their brightly colored cloaks draped behind them. They had spent the night alone painting their bodies with pictures of their anointed animal.

Saturnalia immediately targeted Aonghus. He stood next to Solomon, straight and broadchested, his ceremonial shield resting against one slightly bent knee, with jeweled disks intricately adorning it, reflecting in the light. He had the symbol of a snake writhing across his midriff. Painted in brightly colored blues and greens, it coiled around his waist, and up his torso, with the head in the center of his chest. Its eyes were blazing red, and it was bearing poisonous fangs.

What a taunting sight he was, such a sensuous specimen of what a warrior was supposed to be, Saturnalia thought as she walked straight up to him and stopped. He bowed respectfully, and she could tell by the slight waver of his gaze as he straightened up, that she made him nervous.

Bending down gracefully, she set the cradle at the base of his shield, and removed the bundle from her broach. She stood up slowly, and gave him a sly smile. She took his face in her hands and kissed him hard on the mouth.

She felt him purse his lips and try to pull away, but she prolonged it by running the tip of her tongue along his mouth.

He staggered to one side when she finally released him. Unable to hide his shock, he tipped over his shield so that it lay face down in the dirt. She turned around so quickly that before Kordelina realized what she was doing, Saturnalia had lit the charm with the ember. The bundle burst into flames as she held it high in the air, smiling triumphantly before she tossed it onto the pile of wood.

"Let the festival begin!" she roared with powerful laughter, as she watched the kindling ignite and start the bonfire.

ChAPTER SEVENTEEN

peak not a word," Solomon warned, picking up Aonghus' shield and taking him by the arm.

Hearing his stern tone of voice, Aonghus instinctively resisted the Chieftain's urging. He jerked his head to the side, defensive at first, then seeing that he was not angry, went willingly with him.

Silence settled about the tribe, as they watched their Chieftain escort the young warrior into the grove.

Saturnalia whirled in circles in front of the growing bonfire, oblivious to their exit, and pleased with herself. She hummed softly as she came to a halt, and seeing the wary expressions of her tribesmen, gave them a puzzled look.

"What troubles all of you?" she questioned innocently. "Let the music play, and the animals be prepared for roasting!"

At her command, the women broke from the line to rejoin their families in prearranged places around the oak-hemmed clearing. As they did, tiny murmurings of reaction at the Druidess' display passed among them. Then the music started to play, the lilting notes of harps and flutes rising to the sky as they made their spots comfortable for the day ahead.

Kordelina remained in her original spot, scowling at Saturnalia as she resumed her dance. The more the girl watched, the angrier she became. Waiting for her to stop, Kordelina then went over to her and, without making eye contact, dropped the elk horn at her feet. The ember was still smoldering inside of it as she turned and began to walk away.

"What is this?" Saturnalia demanded, pointing at it. The wisps of smoke were rising around the hem of her gown.

Kordelina disregarded her question, and continued walking. She was headed toward Niall and the livestock, not because she had any real purpose there. Her head was pounding furiously, and she knew she had to put some distance between herself and Saturnalia.

"Kordelina, answer me! What is the purpose of this?" Saturnalia screamed so loudly that her voice cracked, and her soft alabaster skin turned crimson.

The girl stopped, and turning halfway around, just glared at her.

"Answer me!" she roared. She had a desperate look about her, as though she were going to break down completely if she were ignored.

528

Once again the clan grew still and the music stopped. Although there were many stories of Saturnalia's rage, they had never seen her exhibit her wrath publicly.

"You know exactly what it is about," Kordelina answered, flatly as she turned back around, and went over to her younger brother. She sat down facing Saturnalia, and glowered at her.

The tribe remained motionless, eyes fixed on the two women. In all the cycles that the festival had been celebrated, it had never started with such hostility. It was surely a bad omen to display such a lack of respect to the Goddess.

Saturnalia seethed as she stared at Kordelina, who did not seem to blink. Her eyes were barely visible, framed by her dyed brows and the fatigue-darkened circles beneath them. Aonghus had won this part of the battle after all, she thought. He had succeeded in stealing away her loyalty, and although Saturnalia knew she should have expected this, she could not help but be wounded by it.

"Come back, and take this from the soil. It was not meant to be defiled in this way," she admonished, gritting her teeth. "Do not fail to pass on the fire of the Goddess."

Kordelina shook her head. "No, Saturnalia, this silly game you play is over. It is all—" she paused a moment, "over."

Out of the corner of her eye, Kordelina saw Enda coming hurriedly at her. Taking her face roughly in her hands, she looked at her threateningly.

"As the gods have made us, please daughter, do not —" Enda's words were interrupted by Saturnalia.

"Let her finish," she interjected. "Let her tell this tribe why it is over."

"Yes, tell us," Diarmudd said, stepping into the circle beside Saturnalia.

"Of course, slave, let us hear why you disobey the deities!" Turg demanded.

Kordelina felt her stomach knot. These warriors would sooner kill her, than listen to her reasons for disrespect toward their Druidess.

"I think she is afraid," Bracorina taunted, standing alongside her brother. "She is afraid when she should feel privileged to be a sacrifice."

Kordelina looked at them, astounded that they had ever been of any importance to her. Why would she have ever risked her life to save them when they had always despised her? They were worthless to her now, all except Saturnalia. Kordelina felt guilty for hurting her.

"Speak," Diarmudd commanded. "Speak or suffer for your impertinence!"

She saw Niall take his mother's arm and move back, so they would be out of the way if it got violent. There was a feeling of insecurity in his actions, and at that moment, she realized fully that she could count on no one. She had only herself to rely on for survival, and these people she had once desired to please, were ready to eat her alive. It was better to do as they said, and let her freedom be the best revenge.

She looked back at Saturnalia, *I know why you are doing this,* she mentally spoke to her, *and I hate you for it.*

"There was a time when you loved me. I gave you life," she said out loud in response.

"And now you give me death," Kordelina answered caustically, as she stood and imperviously stalked the Sorceress.

She would not let her gaze waver as she approached. Even when Saturnalia's eyes became frigid and glassy, Kordelina gathered all of her spiritual powers and refused to let herself be hypnotized.

I will never share my soul with you again, she was venting her thoughts with each step. *I surround myself in circles of white light, that you may not pass. You are powerless over me.*

Saturnalia's face swelled with rage, her fine, delicate features expanding into one solid mass. For a moment, Kordelina thought she was going to order her death as she filled her lungs, then released it.

Kordelina stopped directly in front of her. She noticed that Saturnalia looked more frail than before, something had changed between them, altering her perception. Without a word, she bent down and picked up the horn from the ground.

The fire was almost out, and she blew on it for a moment until the red-orange ball intensified. Then she bowed, and as she offered it to Saturnalia, she saw her look down as she took it.

"Is this the way you want it?" she asked in a low voice.

"It is the way I want it," Kordelina retorted.

Saturnalia cast her a look of bitter emotion. "I would rather show you charity than abandon your soul."

"Then grant me freedom," Kordelina said under her breath.

Saturnalia softly blew the smoke from the ember into Kordelina's face. "It will be freedom for you alone. I have no love for Aonghus."

Kordelina's body became numb at her words, and not knowing what else to do, she strutted to the opposite end of the clearing. Her moves were smooth; no one knew she was terribly shaken.

Saturnalia looked after her, then went to her honorary place. It was slightly elevated on mounds of hay and animal skins to designate her precedence over the others. A low table to one side was extravagantly arrayed with ornamented flagons of wine, beer, and mead. The center of it was empty, saved for her special portion of roasted meat.

Kneeling down, she placed the horn in the center of the table. Then she took a gourd filled with water, and poured it over her head. She lifted her face upward, and howled wildly as the water flowed down her neck and her breasts. The chill made her hardened nipples visible through her wet gown as she turned to again face her tribe.

"People of my clan, too much time has been spent with petty exchanges," she said, smiling. Her countenance was again radiant, and she appeared to be a different personality. "I hold this child in no offense. The rendering of her soul in the fortunes of eternity is her own. Let us rejoice now, lest the Goddess be offended. The celebration is too long in beginning, and the seas will not rise against us, nor the sky begin to fall."

There was a loud cheer from everyone as Saturnalia sat back, and looked pointedly at the girl.

Kordelina nervously bit the inside of her cheek as she heard the light sound of the music playing again. She was so tense that her knees were knocking together, and she was thankful for the cover of the full robe she wore. She could sense that Saturnalia wanted to tell her more, but she was reluctant to open her thoughts to her, afraid that she might interfere with her and Aonghus' escape. Feeling suddenly anxious, she turned her back to her.

I am sorry, Saturnalia, but my destiny is different than yours.

Yes, I believe that, Saturnalia's thoughts came blaring into Kordelina's mind. *If you want him, take him, and flee if the gods will permit it.*

———

Solomon took a long swig of corma from his drinking bag, and watched Aonghus impatiently shuffle from one foot to the other. His skin looked more pale in the sunlight than he remembered, as his blue eyes focused intensely on the Chieftain.

"What now?" he asked with a bit of pretentiousness.

Solomon could tell by his tone that he was more frustrated than he wanted to let on.

"We wait," he answered, taking another drink and offering it to him.

"For what?" Aonghus asked, shaking his head in refusal and kicking the ground in front of him. "I can do no more to appease her. If I could change the past, I would. I would entreat the gods to give me infancy again, and all that I have done so regretfully, I would recompense. However, I cannot, and I have no more to offer in vindication than what I have already done."

Solomon tied the leather thong around the top of the bag, and set it on the ground next to him. "It is true; Saturnalia will not be pacified now. She is past the point of reason, and that is why we are here," he replied, drawing his knees to his bare chest, and wrapping both his thick arms around them. "It is better that the festival be well underway before we show our faces again. If it will give Saturnalia a chance to forget even the smallest amount of her anger, we will be the better for it."

He could see Aonghus' jaw jut out and his pupils dilate as he spoke.

"What does she want from me; do you even know? What can I do that would cause her to stop this? I do not wish my friend killed, and I have told her as much. She refuses to listen to reason," his voice rose to a hostile pitch.

Solomon stared into the distance; his countenance said it was useless to continue this discussion. "She wants only one simple thing," he said, after a moment. "You have forced her hand against her lover, and she will not rest until the breath is gone from your body."

Aonghus' eyes narrowed, and their once deep color faded. "That is something I will not easily allow."

Solomon stood up and faced him. He took a long look at the young man who had once been his apprentice, and offering a sentimental smile, patted him on the side of the face. "Even though we have not the same blood, you and I have shared much more than many a father and son. I have entrusted you with my life many times, and even the life of my only child, and you have never disappointed me. I only reserve my judgments now because there have been many hard lessons I have had to learn in just this way. I would only tell you that the heavens know our hearts, and recompense us as such. If your heart is pure, then forgive yourself, and let Saturnalia deal with her own decisions. To avoid any further strife between you, keep your distance."

Aonghus listened to the older one attentively. Solomon could tell by the gradual hardening of his features that his words bore deep inside. It was as if with each sentence, the young warrior was increasing his stamina, and regaining control of himself.

"There will be more temptation to confront her than you can even know before this festival is complete," he continued. "But restrain yourself. The more range you can keep between the two of you, the better you will be for it. I would have you take the last watch. It is the most difficult because you will be full of food and drink by then, but you must remain steadfast in your lookout. It will also keep you from having to partake of Conn's ceremony, or Kordelina's departure."

He noticed that Aonghus looked abruptly at the ground as he spoke his last sentence. "You must say your farewell to her because she will be leaving," Solomon said sadly.

"No, she is not," Aonghus murmured, shaking his head. "I cannot let her go, Solomon. Perhaps I should not be telling you this because I have no guarantee that you will not try to prevent it. Yet, as you have spoken, we have shared more than many a father and son, so I do trust you."

He saw a vague look of surprise in the Chieftain's face. "So you are leaving and taking her with you, are you not?" he questioned dryly.

Aonghus nodded. "Yes, I have to," he answered, his eyes silently beseeching Solomon's blessing. "If they were to steal her away from me, what remains of the life within me would wither long before its time. Truly, Chieftain, I have no other choice. I have tried everything I know to make it right for Kordelina and me; it has all resulted in failure. To be together, we must leave this island. I am sorry; for more than anyone else, it is you whom I will gravely miss."

Solomon angrily clenched both fists. "I should have killed her!" he declared, a ghastly hatred coming over him. "I should have destroyed her at birth!"

"If you had ever given yourself a chance to love her, you would not be saying that," Aonghus responded in a placating voice. "And if you had killed her, as you say, you would have denied me the purest love of my entire life. Solomon, listen to me, please. I am not a healthy man, and I would question how many seasons I have left in this world. My mind grows dim too often to ignore, and what I see in the shadows is bleak. I would not be any sort of a leader to you like this. I realize that. Perhaps as your daughter's husband, I could bring her happiness and live long enough to enjoy a portion of my children's lives. That is all I hope for now.

Chieftain, I ask your forgiveness for this because more than anything, I had dreamed of making you proud of me. From the very beginning that is all I desired, to know that you were proud of me."

The Chieftain's mouth went into a frown, and he rubbed his eyes to hide his reaction to Aonghus' confession. "Dear boy," he said emotionally. "Were I ever to have an heir, he would be little of what you have become. As a man and a warrior, you have made me more than proud. As the one who loves you as his son, I could never want anything but happiness for you. If in your heart, you can only find it with Kordelina, then let the heavens bless you both; I too have come to love her these past years. You may trust that I will not betray you for I have not forgotten the vow I made to you long ago when you saved my life. My regret is only that I will lose you, for I do believe, Aonghus, that you would have been the greatest of leaders."

His eyes and nose turned a deep red as he spoke, and tears suddenly streamed down his cheeks.

"It is a sad time we have come to, you and I," he said. Looking fervently into the young man's eyes, he was silent a moment, then kissed the center of his forehead. "Let it be known to the gods who witness this, that you are my anointed King. That wherever you shall be, you will be secure in the fact that your devotion has been worthy of my deepest appreciation and respect."

Before Aonghus could respond, the two men were distracted by the sound of someone approaching. Drawing his knife, Aonghus darted behind a tree, allowing Solomon to greet the stranger. Wiping away his tears, he looked to where the sound was coming from, and could tell by the slow gait that it was Koven. He wore a look of concern which immediately told both men that all was not well.

"Father," Aonghus called, putting his knife back in its sheath. "How goes the celebration?"

Koven paused to collect his thoughts before he answered. "It began with great contention," he replied, shaking his head despairingly. "It is Kordelina again —"

"What happened?" Aonghus said. "They have not taken her yet, have they?"

Koven looked at his son suspiciously. "No, she is still there, but just barely. She got angry about something, and dropped the horn at Saturnalia's feet, and walked away. When Saturnalia beckoned her to return, she blatantly disobeyed, and probably would not have done her duty if she had not been threatened by Diarmudd."

"Is all well now?" Solomon asked, perturbed.

"Yes, but only because Saturnalia is so long suffering with her," he responded. "Even I wanted to see her punished for her arrogance. It is well that Jara will have her."

Solomon laughed aloud. He could not help but be secretly enchanted by her rebelliousness. "That is if Jara is not too old to handle her. I am sure it will only be a matter of time before we hear that Kordelina has commandeered the Druidess' transport," he remarked playfully.

Aonghus put his hand to his forehead, and took an anxious breath.

Kordelina, if you can hear me now, he said in his mind, *subdue yourself; we have only a little further to go.*

In a moment, warmth and security washed over him. He never fully comprehended how this speaking of minds occurred, or even when he was able to do it. Yet, as the sound of the music and revelry drifted louder through the trees, he knew she was telling him that he could still count on her.

———

Across the Menai Strait on the coast of north Wales, the flat-bottomed cavalry transports were being loaded with Roman infantrymen and their horses.

"How long will it take?" Flavius asked Jara as he helped her onto a standard Roman sailing vessel.

Jara looked out at the placid waters. "If the currents are steady," she answered flatly, "your landing should be well concealed by darkness."

Flavius looked at the island in the distance, and crossed his arms arrogantly. "I trust you fully understand all plans, and realize the consequences if you fail me," he said.

"Completely," Jara responded. "And all of my financial arrangements will be kept in capable hands until I rejoin you."

"Of course," he answered, dropping his arms to his sides, and turning away from her.

He walked to the ladder of the boat, and stopped to look at her once more before disembarking.

"These savages really must be contained," he stated. "By destroying the Druids, the rest of these tribes will be too frightened to resist us any longer."

Jara averted her gaze, and looked back at him without turning her head.

"Perhaps," she replied. "Lest the seas rise and the sky begin to fall."

CHAPTER EIGHTEEN

olomon, Aonghus, and Koven did not return to the festival until midday. They had spent the better part of the morning drinking the contents of both Solomon's bags of ale, and two other rather large ones Koven had provided. The trio had swapped stories of past bravery and personal sentimentalities. Taking the few private hours away from the rest of the tribe had allowed them a chance to reacquaint themselves with their special comradery.

It was such a happy, sentimental visit for Aonghus, that being in the company of the two men made him question whether he could ever leave them. He even entertained the thought of staying away for only a short time, and perhaps bringing Kordelina back when their union could be accepted. Of course, he would not be a ruler then, but at least he would be with friends and family.

The sun was straight up in the sky when they staggered into the celebration, arms linked and singing woefully off-key. They gave the bonfire one complete turn before settling down in their allotted place. There was plenty of room to relax in the space Enda had considerately arranged for them. The fur pelts were piled three or four deep in all places, and their table was full of food and drink.

Cunnedag and Erc were seated to one side, their mouths full of food and drink. At the sight of them, Aonghus went over, and clumsily embraced the two. Wrapping one arm around each, he pulled them close, sloshing ale into their laps.

"What has taken hold of you, brother?" Erc asked, half-amused and half-agitated at his older brother's drunken show of emotion.

Aonghus released his hold, and sitting down cross-legged, offered a nostalgic smile. He had never felt close to these two or Niall. Aonghus could not relate to them, and he knew they felt the same way about him.

"Happiness," he laughed, looking for Kordelina, but not finding her. "At long last, I have been infected with true happiness, and she refuses to let me go."

"Here," said Cunnedag, offering Aonghus his stein. "You might as well drink what you did not spill."

The warrior took it, and swallowed it all in one gulp. Then taking a carafe from the table, he lifted it in the air. "To my brothers," he toasted.

As they all drank, Aonghus scanned the tribe for Kordelina. He could not help himself, he had to see her. He wanted to look into her eyes, and know that his hopes and dreams were still alive.

"Aonghus, here," Cunnedag nudged him with the now half-full container.

Taking it in both hands, Aonghus felt the sudden urge to leave his brothers' company. He felt like he was going to miss something if he stayed where he was. Setting down the corma, he rose to a squatting position, and looked at the two men sincerely. Perhaps they would never rise to Chieftain, but they would be decent, caring husbands and fathers. They were obviously not of the warrior spirit, and it comforted Aonghus to know that Koven would have someone to take over his farmland when he had long since gone.

"The two of you," he addressed them, his once slurred speech now clear and well pronounced. "Take care of our mother. Would you do that for me?"

Erc squinted, wary of his brother's request. "Why are you acting like this?" he asked skeptically.

Aonghus shook his head and smiled, trying to hide his rising sentimentality. "No reason," he answered, looking at the ground, then back at them. "Just promise me that no matter what happens, you will take care of our mother."

Cunnedag twisted his face, and looked at Aonghus like he was crazy.

"Of course we will. She is our mother as well, or did you forget that?" he answered sarcastically. "Brother, I love you, but you have always been such a strange one."

Aonghus laughed and patted him on the shoulder before rising. He turned to speak to Enda, but was distracted by the sight of Kordelina approaching.

His stomach tightening, he took an impassioned breath. He was struggling to disguise his enamored reaction, yet he could barely help himself. He felt like the nervous groom gazing upon his wife for the first time. In spite of his efforts, his giddiness must have shown through, because Enda touched him lightly on the elbow to get his attention.

"It has been long a time since she has looked so lovely," she whispered, looking at her daughter.

"Mother, I never remember her looking this lovely," he responded, as he nervously rubbed the back of his neck.

Kordelina was still wearing the same festival dress, but she had washed her face, and had undone her braids so that her unruly hair was loose about her face and shoulders. She was a striking vision of womanliness. With her eyes fixed on her feet, she moved past the place where Saturnalia dozed. She chose her steps with such care that it was as though she were trying to make herself invisible.

"It would make it easier for her if you said your farewells privately. I truly think that you are the only one of us she will miss," Enda remarked, as she released him and clasped her hands in front of her.

"Of course, I will speak with her now," he replied, not looking away.

He watched as she cautiously walked by Bracorina, and as soon as she was out of her way, she quickened her pace, and lifted her eyes. She smiled at him impishly as he held out his arms to her, and she ran to him just like she had when she was a child. Only she was not a child anymore, and hugging her closely, he had the strangest sensation that she would one day carry his children within her. Wrapping her arms tightly around his neck, she let him lift her off the ground. It all felt so right.

He waited until he could feel her warmth, then set her back down. Taking both her hands, he looked soberly into her eyes. He was trying to seem sad, but he knew he was beaming, and the two must have appeared foolish in their half-hearted attempts to hide their infatuation.

"I—I," he stuttered. He felt like laughing.

Glancing at Saturnalia, he saw she was watching them from the corner of her eye. But looking back into Kordelina's glowing countenance, he knew that the Druidess was no longer of any concern.

"What is it, Aonghus? Have you been taken with fever?" Kordelina teased; she could tell he was having a difficult time controlling himself.

He stared at her for a moment, then took her by the wrist and moved only a few paces into the grove. He purposely wanted to remain in view of the rest of the tribe in order to give their farewell credibility.

Kordelina laughed silently. She strained to keep from making noise as the tears of joy welled in her eyes. She did not know why they were so jubilant. Maybe it was the promise of the future.

"Do not cry," Aonghus said, loud enough so everyone could hear him. "I will miss you too, Kordelina."

He turned his back to the clan and walked deeper into the woods. Putting both arms around her shoulders, he pulled her to him. He was glad that no one was able to see the sudden satisfaction on their faces at being alone together. Kordelina's giggling ceased at his touch; she buried her face in the bend of his neck, and breathed in his scent.

"Listen to me carefully," he said in a hushed but serious tone. "I have been given the final watch. That means Jara will be here before we are able to leave. You have to find a way to leave without being noticed."

"I can do that," she reassured him.

Aonghus rested his chin on top of her head, distracted. If something went wrong, this could be the last time he would ever hold her this way.

"Aonghus," she interrupted his thoughts. "I said I can do that."

"Good," he answered, again attentive. "I will take Macha with me when I go for Lir. Look for her tied behind the three boulders near the hawthorne trees. Then meet me at my watch. It will be dark by then, so we must leave immediately."

"I understand," she said, pressing herself closer to him, and rubbing the side of her face against his perspiring skin. "I have left a few things near Macha's saddle. My clothes and boots are there also. Please do not forget to take them."

"I will not forget," he answered. "They will be with her when you arrive. If for some reason we are separated, meet me at the crag near the strait; there is a boat there. Wait for me."

He kissed her lightly on the top of her head. "Kordelina, if we never speak another word to each other after this moment, you must know that since the day

I was born I have been with you with every beat of my heart. I never told you, but when I was ill in Wales and could not even remember my own name, yours was like a prayer to me."

"And yours to me," she answered wistfully.

"Then no matter what happens this day, we must always remember the way it is between us now, so it will always be."

Letting go of her, he reached into his boot, and took out the knife that he had made for her many years before. It was the first weapon she had ever carried. He saw the gleam in her eyes when he handed it to her.

"Use it if you must," was all he said.

Stuffing it in the fold of her robe, they were distracted by the noise of the festivities. The air was thick with the sound of drums and flutes, and around the blazing pyre, warriors were dancing with maidens.

As he came back into the clearing, Aonghus was filled with great pleasure at the sight of the dancers. He laughed out loud as he went over to his mother and put his arm around her. Enda chuckled and patted his hand.

"Go on, dance with them," she coaxed. "You know how much you love it."

Aonghus blushed. He did love it; loved the way the women's hips swayed and their hair, breaking free from braids, flowed loosely down their backs. He loved the scent of the sweaty bodies as they exchanged secret touches and coy smiles. It was all so primitively erotic. Most of all, he loved being the center of attention, flirting with the girls with his suave movements, knowing all the time that they were enjoying the look of his muscles rippling temptingly.

He felt Kordelina's hand in the small of his back pushing him forward. He wanted to spend as much time as possible with her, but for her, dancing was forbidden until the designated time.

"Yes, Aonghus," she said agreeably. "Do not disappoint them."

Her tone was so unaffected that it was hard for him to tell if she really meant it or not. He gave her a questioning look and she returned it with a smile.

"I mean it," she reassured. "Grace this festival; dance for the Goddess."

Mirroring her expression, he stepped forward to join the line of warriors. The outer circle of men took small side steps in one direction while the inner circle of women turned in half circles in the other. The sound of bracelets clanking together, and bells jingling from the bottoms of their dresses acted in percussion with the music. Occasionally, a skirt would lift in the breeze, exposing the naked, tender thighs of a maid. Then the enticing glimpse would be smothered by brightly colored cloth.

Aonghus' hands were on his hips, his face tilted upward. He was captivated by the brilliant blue of the winter sky, and the absolute passion at being alive to appreciate it. Now he completely understood what he had always labored to comprehend: the fullness of life was far better than its duration. This tribe had been good to him, and he had championed its causes many times. Departing was like saying good-bye to a faithful lover he had never planned on leaving but could not help but discard.

As the two promenades crossed, the women took a series of heel-to-toe steps, and encircled the warriors. Aonghus twisted to the side perfectly on cue, and found he was next to Bracorina. His lighthearted countenance faded as he looked into her serious face. The two stared at each other, not missing a step. Then locking arms, they rounded in one direction and two-stepped back to face each other again.

Aonghus saw Bracorina eye Kordelina tediously, as though she had mulled over her every virtue and shortcoming too many times. Then she gave him a petulant look.

"Once she is gone, all will be well with us again," she scolded.

They locked opposite arms, and repeated the jig. Aonghus stared straight ahead, pretending he had not heard her. His eyes had a dreary cast that said this encounter was pointless and predictable. Then he deliberately looked at Kordelina. She was lying on her stomach at the edge of the circle, her chin resting in her hand as she watched him. Their gaze met and his eyes regained their luminous glow.

In the next instant, the music was interrupted by the bantering of a drum. The slow thud came from the tribal drum Saturnalia was playing. It was tilted at an angle to rest on her shoulder, and she held it in place with one hand while she rapped it with the other.

Using only her fingertips to make the pulsating beat, she dashed in and out of the dancers, hair and robe trailing behind her. She was chanting in an ancient language, raising and lowering her intonation as she spoke.

As Saturnalia briefly arrested her steps in front of him, Aonghus could not help but notice that she looked bewitching and gorgeous. She hit the drum hard with her fist, and gave him a malevolent look as he accidently missed a step.

Flustered, Aonghus quickened his moves to the pace as Saturnalia continued weaving among the dancers. Moving to the side in unison with the others, he saw the cluster of white-robed Druids gather close together as the boar was brought in for slaughter and roasting.

Turg and Berrig carried the pole from which it hung with all four legs tied. Its pleas for freedom came out in frantic squeals that rose above the sound of the music. They took the wiggling, rotund animal beneath the sacred oak, and one of the learned men slit the throat of the animal, silencing it instantly.

The sweat was dripping down Aonghus' chest and arms while he watched the crimson life flow out of the beast. Breathless, he wiped his brow with the back of his hand, and looking down, noticed that the streams of perspiration were causing his tattoo to smear. The once bold snake was liquifying; its two venomous fangs were scarlet rivulets fusing together, flowing down his torso.

Turg and Berrig then passed in front of the dancers with the slain beast, and took one turn around the bonfire. The dripping blood made a circle around the blaze before the animal was taken to the end of the clearing, and hung between two Y-shaped copper poles. Kindling and straw were piled beneath it. Saturnalia set down her drum and took the smoldering ceremonial horn from her table. Her robe drooped off one of her slight shoulders as she walked swiftly but carefully to the roasting place, and used it to light the flame.

The tribe cheered and the dancing ceased. The heated men and women hugged and kissed each other before returning to their resting places.

"Chieftain, let us hear a story," called Pwyll to Solomon, who was outstretched on Saturnalia's animal hide. He was playing the amused spectator, enjoying the revelry going on around him.

He sat up to look at his tribe, then rose to his feet good-naturedly and took a seat in the center of the clearing. The clan shuffled to comfortable places around him and became quiet.

"I will speak to you of a time long ago when this tribe was full of lack and discord," he began, his voice deep as thunder. "There was once an island rich with the spirits of the gods. These entities loved the people who worshipped them, and had willingly received their holy offerings of adoration. So endeared were they to their worshippers that they blessed the land with abundant crops and herds of horses that could soar like hill eagles through the sky. It was a sacred place that had become a haven for the refugees of captured tribes, and a sanctuary for brave warriors defeated by Rome."

Despite his drunken state, the Chieftain's words flowed easily and without thought. Crossing his legs, he beckoned someone to give him a drink, and Bracorina willingly complied. She bustled into the clearing and bowed, then gave him a full vessel of unstrained wine before he continued.

"On this island there was a small clan of brave but disheartened Celts. They were ruled by the good King Donnach, who had long since wanted peace to reign among his people. Yet, as good and fair as this King was, he had a son named Laden whose self-serving judgments had brought him much heartache.

"Although Donnach's tribe numbered few, they were a wealthy clan who had successfully protected their vast territory for many generations. For this reason, they had long since been beckoned by Rome to form trade alliances, of which Donnach wanted no part. Although he knew the riches of his tribe would increase, he was a wise man who could see that an alliance with the Imperialists would ultimately bring destruction to his people, and prostitute the abundance that had been showered upon them by the gods."

Pausing to take a drink, Solomon earnestly looked at the attentive faces. He wanted to make it clear that his words were of great value to all of them.

"Still, Laden was an ambitious sort who knew he was soon to assume rule from his aged father. Without the consent of his King or the people, he secretly started to organize trade with the Romans despite Caesar's past history of exploiting the Celtic nations. When this was found out, he explained to Donnach that his Druidess, Deireadh, had entreated the gods about this matter, and they had instructed them to begin acknowledging the Imperialists. It did not take long for a small group of tribesmen to see that Laden's lust for power was undermining the good of the people, and that he had to be stopped before he became King.

"So this small group of warriors, elders, and farmers went to the estranged husband of Laden's Druidess, and implored him to go on a sacred mission to save his clan. Now you must understand that although he was considered the boldest warrior in the tribe, he could never become its King because his mother had been a Roman. Still, he listened to them explain how Laden must not assume power because it would be inviting Rome into their midst. They entrusted him with an offering and a mission to go to the Druid colony on the opposite side of the island, and to bring back to the clan an uncorrupted spiritualist who could redeem their people. After much persuasion, the warrior agreed to take their tokens and riches, and go to the Council of the Druids. There he was to ask them to seek the heavens for another, yet untainted, Druidess to come to their aid."

Solomon stopped again, and glanced over at Aonghus. The handsome warrior sat on a log across from him with one leg bent to the side and the other on the ground. He was twisting a piece of straw between his thumb and forefinger as he looked back at the Chieftain. Then his eyes passed over the rest of the tribe, stopping painfully at Saturnalia, before he looked down at the ground. He seemed somehow embarrassed by the telling of these events.

"The lone warrior and his apprentice left before the sun rose on the very next day. They shared one war-horse and an old gelding between them. Two nights they rode unseen through hostile territories, and their journey was so uneventful, they believed it was the will of the heavens that they reach their destination untested. But on the last day, they stopped to water their horses, and were confronted by three warriors from a warring tribe. Javelins were hurled at the man and the boy, and the two tried to escape, but the warrior was speared in the back, and fell wounded in the stream.

"With only his father's workhorse and his dagger, the young apprentice circled where his wounded master was fighting two enemies. Riding up from behind, he drove his dagger into the base of the skull of one Celt. Jumping to the ground, he took the spear that was lodged in his master's back, and used it to kill the other. Seeing this fierce display from one so young, the last of the group fled in fear.

"The master was astonished at the bravery of his foster, and was convinced, more than ever before, that the gods were watching over them. He thanked the boy, and promised his loyalty for as long as he lived, and the boy wept at the bitter realization that he had ended the life of another.

"When they finally reached the Druid colony, they were filled with despair because they were told that many a Druid had been persecuted with the coming of the Romans, and there were no elders left to assume the responsibility of an entire clan. The warrior entreated the Order, telling them of the attack, and how the gods had watched for them to arrive safely. Surely there was one who was ordained by the heavens to reign in this worthy village. He asked that the Order take the offering in meditation, and certainly one would arrive to answer their prayers.

"When the moon rose one night later, the elder Druid came to the warrior, and said they believed there was one Druidess who would care for his people, but she was of special making. Her existence was brought about by the blending of the earth's clay, the water of the sea, the rays of the sun, and the beauty of the wind. They said she was kind and just, but her spirit was not born of flesh. Rather, it was made of the elements. He could make no promise of her customs, nor could he be held responsible for her actions. Without reservation, the warrior departed the very next day with the beautiful spiritualist and his foster."

Solomon gave a heavy sigh and stretched out. Then propping himself up on one elbow, he noticed the smirk on Aonghus' face at his embellishment, and how he was describing his behavior as more noble than it had been. Afraid he would start to laugh, too, Solomon kept his eyes downcast and continued.

"Even though an inner-tribal war was brewing upon their arrival, the people were thoroughly enamored by this exquisite, young woman with parchment-like skin and shining red hair. Her eyes were the color of the fields after a rain, and her voice was the song of the birds. The people could not tell, at first, if she was strong enough to rule their tribe because her build was slight and her moves quite delicate. Yet, how they adored the sight of her, and believed in the words she spoke.

"From the very beginning, Laden and Deireadh despised her, and the call to do battle came immediately. Deireadh, whom all knew had gone over to the dark side, called upon the black powers to smite the Druidess, and spread rumors of her clandestine meetings with the other women's husbands. Surely they were lies, but as often happens, the conscience of some is not easily pacified, and the tribe was split. More than half the clan went with the warrior who had brought the Druidess. The rest backed Laden, and his hired mercenary army.

"The skirmish between the two sides never came to pass because Laden was betrayed by one of his own men and killed, and the warrior who had completed the sacred mission was declared the tribal leader. He generously pardoned those few who had opposed him because he desperately wanted his people to be united again. The beautiful Druidess, who had stolen the people's hearts, restored peace, and the abundance of the gods to her people with kindness and virtue."

Solomon raised his wine to toast Saturnalia before drinking. She responded with a fatigued smile as she lifted her goblet to him, and the two drank to each other.

"And what became of Deireadh?" Edainne asked.

Setting down the vessel, Solomon sat upright to finish the story.

"Realizing she was defeated, she lived like a beast in the groves. She was seen time and again wearing tattered garments and stealing corn from the fields. They now called her the Black Druidess, and spoke of how she would talk to herself in the voices of others. She had been consumed by the dark spirits she had invoked, and on the night of the festival of Samhain, she was found dead in the grove. The spirits inhabiting her had grown too many for her body to allow, and they had torn open her stomach to escape. It is said that they still hover within the trees hoping that another of evil ways will need them and invite them into their heart."

For a moment, Solomon said nothing more. He sensed the atmosphere was ripe for forgiveness, and hoped it would be Aonghus or Saturnalia who would speak first. After all, they were the only other ones who knew the truth.

Lifting his eyes, he looked at them, then gazed at Kordelina with a long face. He had so hoped that his dream of unity could once again be fulfilled.

A terrible, restless pain began to rise beneath his rib cage. It startled him at first, and he raised his hand up high to ease it. Interpreting it as a cue to worship, the clan rose to their feet around him, and began to sing. The sound of their voices filling the grove made the ache within him unbearable. He got up, and staring at the reminiscent faces, realized that the simple chronicle of their tribe had become a myth, and he was merely a character of its past.

He felt the vibration of the earth beneath him. It was like a rattle coming from its inner core. To his surprise, no one else reacted, and before he could say another word, the boar was set before him, and he found himself slicing it open.

There was an endless line of maidens, their faces shadowed by the setting sun. How quickly the celebrating had slipped by, Solomon thought to himself. They took portions for their families, and returned to their places. He felt as though he were moving through a dream and his world was disappearing before his eyes.

In the next moment, he was again lying beside Saturnalia, and she was feeding him succulent bits of meat. He saw that the sun was even lower in the sky as Kordelina took her place in front of the fire. With her head bowed, she moved brazenly before the flames, swaying her hips to and fro, and sweeping her arms to each side as she turned.

Her movements seemed driven by the pulse of the drums on all sides of the clearing, and still, Solomon was plagued by the throbbing of the earth beneath him. The top of her robe dropped off her shoulder momentarily, exposing her breast. Clutching the cloth with one hand, she turned her back and refastened her broach. The outline of her figure could be seen through the multi-colored cloth, and noticing the curvaceous hips and thighs, Solomon understood why Aonghus could not resist her. As she faced the tribe again, he could not bear to meet her gaze. Instead, he set his head back down and looked at a star spinning above him.

"Oh, great spirits," he lamented. "If only my child could flourish."

He felt the need to look at her once more, and as he sat back up, he saw Aonghus standing next to her.

Taking the spiral bracelet from above his elbow that once was her torque, the warrior placed it on Kordelina's arm. The girl panted as she pretended to pay homage to him, but really bent far enough forward to reveal her cleavage.

Solomon could see Aonghus' shoulders rise as he took a deep breath, and puffing out his cheeks, exhaled as he turned away from her. Catching Solomon's eye as he approached, he gave him an artful look before taking his place next to the other warriors guarding Saturnalia.

ChAPTER NINETEEN

ill you not even rise to greet me?" Jara asked, looking down at Saturnalia with an aloof expression.

Saturnalia was stretched on a mound of fur pelts, her long white legs exposed, and Solomon's red cloak draped carelessly across her shoulders. Her gown was bunched around her hips and its neckline nearly sagged down to her stomach to reveal the shadowy fullness of her breasts. Taking a bite from a tender leg of lamb, she kept her gaze fixed on Kordelina as she danced around the festival pyre.

"Jara," she answered flatly. "You have not been invited to join in this celebration. Since I do not wish you to be here, I will not rise to greet you."

Jara's expression turned contemptuous, and she took a step closer. As she did this, Solomon rose to his feet, and politely offered her his place if she wished. Aonghus, Diarmudd, and Berrig instinctively moved nearer to Saturnalia. They would do anything she commanded, even challenge the authority of the older Druidess.

Seeing their movement, Jara sat down cautiously next to Saturnalia, her eyes scrutinizing the movements of the dancing girl in front of them.

"How did you get this far?" Saturnalia continued. "I left word with my guards that you should be treated as an intruder, and killed if need be."

"They listened to reason, and allowed me to pass. I am still a Druidess of high esteem, and my immunity is guaranteed," she replied. "Saturnalia, why do you not welcome me? To be treated with such animosity pains me, as you are like my own daughter."

Saturnalia glared at her in silence.

Trying to ease the tension, Jara rested her hand on her shoulder. "What troubles you? Confide your feelings to me; perhaps I can be of help."

Looking coldly at Jara's hand, then into her eyes, Saturnalia sat up straight. "You, Jara," she answered, her voice filled with scorn. "It is you that bothers me. This is my clan; you have no authority here."

Pulling her hand away, Jara was speechless for a moment. She knew that Saturnalia would not be pleased with the reasons for her presence, but she had not counted on her being so harsh.

"I have come to you in peace to heal the ills between us," she responded, with feigned sincerity.

Saturnalia threw her head back and gave a bitter laugh.

"You have come with Romans," she countered impatiently. "Do you think me so naive that I would believe you are here because you love me and care for my people? What kind of underling to you perceive me to be? You arrived onshore in a Roman vessel, and were no doubt escorted by Caesar's men. Do they come in peace as well?"

Jara's eyes became icy slits, the wrinkles beneath them contracting suspiciously. "Why are you so distrustful? I have never deceived you before. I came by Roman ship because these are Roman waters. They rule this territory now, or have you been so consumed by your own little empire here that you still do not know that many rich clans have embraced the Imperialist rule?"

Saturnalia shook her head, a few wisps of red hair falling in her eyes. "No Jara. I know only of Caesar's slaughter of our people. This island has offered refuge to many a brave warrior who has lost multitudes in the endless fight against Rome. There is one there," she said, pointing to Turg. "Would you like to hear how they raped his wife and daughters, and cut off their breasts because they refused to speak Caesar's name? They butchered his tribe because they would not lay down their weapons. And even though they had paid the ransom the Imperialists requested, his people were betrayed. Rome wanted to take away the worship of our gods, and leave them dispirited and living like peasants. Yes, Jara, this new ruler you speak of, I am well acquainted with his ways. Many have been lost because of them."

"And you will lose many more," Jara remarked, as she sat back against a log and helped herself to Saturnalia's meat. "You cannot defeat Caesar. His army is too strong. This is the only island left still dominated by Celts, and Rome is determined to take it. If you truly love your people, you will listen to me, and spare their bloody slaughter. I speak to you in all sincerity when I say there is still time to save them if you would but surrender."

Her words incensed Saturnalia; the side of her mouth began to twitch. It was easy to see she was hovering on the bitter edge of reason, and Jara could not help but wonder what had occurred to cause such a change in her.

"Surrender to Caesar!" she blurted out, feeling her head start to throb. "That would be true calamity. We would prostitute our bodies as well as our souls. This band of warriors has outwitted Caesar for years now. He may claim rule over the waters surrounding this island, but he will never set foot on the soil itself. And he surely will never, ever claim the spirit of a true Celt, no matter how great the bloodletting."

Saturnalia could see Jara was unnerved by her heated reaction. She blinked her eyes nervously as each word was spoken, and glanced at the warriors uneasily. Then she dropped her gaze, and scratched the center of one hand with the other.

"Saturnalia," she insisted in a reasonable tone. "What is happening is preordained. If it were not the Romans who brought it about, it would be someone else. Make it easy on yourself. Accept Caesar's rule."

Saturnalia's ears rang with her anger. "You think surrender is the easy way?" she rebutted. "You will find out in your lives to come that in your supposed acceptance of this defiler, you will only perish. We will be the ones who will prevail and continue to fight. Barter away your people, Jara, but I will not partake of such despicable acts."

The older Druidess still would not look at her, and the two women sat without speaking, their eyes fixed on Kordelina twirling in front of them. The young girl's body flowed to the sound of the music as though each step was an epiphany of the gods. She spun in a circle with outstretched arms, making her multicolored robe appear sheer in the firelight. It drooped from one shoulder, exposing most of her pubescent cleavage as she bowed to Jara respectfully.

"Strange how one ugly as a child has grown into such beauty," Jara commented, breaking the silence.

Saturnalia gave no reply. She was preoccupied with Aonghus who had moved conspicuously closer to hear their conversation.

"I will take her at dawn," the older one continued. "It is her time."

The words chilled Saturnalia, who cast her gaze back down at the ground. In spite of Kordelina's vindictiveness that morning, she wanted no harm to come to her. She understood the indescretion of her youth, and was empathetic to the extremes of her passion. Catching sight of the shadow of the young girl's bare feet and legs moving alluringly in the flame's glow, Saturnalia could not help but feel a maternal, forgiving love for her.

"If all the islands are under Caesar's domain, will she be a virgin to a Chieftain, or a Roman concubine?" she asked coldly, looking up at Aonghus as she spoke.

The warrior's compelling blue eyes widened, then he looked away, fighting to disguise his guilt. Oblivious to their exchange, Jara picked up Saturnalia's vessel of wine, and took a long gluttonous drink.

"Are you calling me a liar, Sorceress?" she retorted sharply. She was growing impatient with her lack of respect.

"I am only remarking that virgins bring a high price to the aristocrats in Rome. I have heard many stories of Celtic maids sold into slavery by their elders," she answered slyly. "They are used for amusement, then murdered when they are taken with child and no longer pleasurable to their owners."

"I am not responsible for what happens in Rome," Jara countered.

Saturnalia rolled her eyes, then stared at her disdainfully. "Why do I not believe that? I will fight you to the end of my power on this; Kordelina has been chosen by one more powerful than Caesar or yourself."

Jara could not respond as the drums suddenly broke their tempo and changed to a slow, even beat. It was time to prepare for the offering.

Rising, Saturnalia approached the center clearing. She stood motionless as she gazed out at her tribe. They were a sea of trusting faces looking back at her, and her thoughts were muddled knowing what was soon to take place. There was an instant blinding fear coupled with the urge to retreat, but she calmed herself, and waited for it to pass.

Jara moved behind her, a thin shadow of the one she had created. "I know you are inebriated with their adoration of you, Saturnalia. Still, these simple beings who bow at your feet would not love you so or share in your feast if they knew that by your obstinance, you have guaranteed their deaths."

Saturnalia's gaze remained steadfast. "Do you, Jara, think you would be allowed to breathe yet another breath if they knew you were the one who brought their demise?"

An ominous silence fell about the two women as they let the celebration go on around them. On all sides of the clearing, heads were thrown back in drunken laughter while lovers called out with lusty pleasure. Most of them were only half clothed, and the steam seemed to be rising off their heated bodies in the crisp winter air.

Saturnalia watched somberly as Kordelina continued her steps. A smug look of completeness shone on her face, as if she already knew what it was to be loved as a woman. She was coy, Saturnalia thought, sweating and giggling as she moved, sharing only a few stolen looks of seduction with Aonghus. The only thing that gave her away was the joyful, uncaring manner in which she spun around the clearing. Hers was not the countenance of one defeated; rather, it was the purest reflection of hope and virtue. And Saturnalia's intuition told her that she must protect Kordelina, even if it meant releasing her into Aonghus' care.

Focusing on the very edge of the trees, she saw Aonghus preparing to leave. She was somehow relieved that he would not be present to witness Conn's end. For him to be an observer was a sacrilege, somehow, because in her mind, she held him entirely accountable for what she was about to do.

Taking his shield and spear in hand, he paid his respects to the elders. Then he turned and deliberately glanced at Kordelina for a brief moment. His eyes were so completely consumed with the vision of her that they appeared as luminous jewels. Then he disappeared into the darkness of the oaks.

CHAPTER TWENTY

She had the nagging urge to run after him the way she had done so often as a child. If only it were that simple, Kordelina thought to herself.

The two Druidesses were chilling figures etched in the orange and yellow fireglow. Saturnalia, the ethereal icon of these sacred rituals, and Jara, the parched old hag whose vindictiveness had corroded any natural beauty she had ever possessed.

Kordelina watched indifferently as the rest of the clan clustered around her. They left her no choice but to hover about the outer edges of the trees, keeping her within sight of the two women for only glimpses at a time.

Sauntering to her family's resting place, she put on her green cloak. The chilly night air made her dance-fatigued muscles tighten. Draping it around her shoulders, she caught sight of Jara.

Averting her gaze, she pretended not to notice when Jara beckoned her to stand beside her. Then, out of the corner of her eye, she saw her motion to her two older brothers to bring her forward.

Alarmed, Kordelina turned away from them as they approached. If she had to stand in front of everyone, she would never be able to leave unnoticed, and all of Aonghus' plans would be in vain. She stepped back, attempting to get away from Erc and Cunnedag, but they stood on either side of her, forcing her to stop.

Looking at each of them, and seeing Jara walk toward her, Kordelina simply sat down, and refused to budge. Impatient with her lack of cooperation, Cunnedag grabbed her by the arm, and tried to pull her to her feet, but taking hold of a stein of ale, Kordelina angrily threw it in his face. She would not obey these mindless subordinates, she told herself. She did not care if they were from the same family, they were Jara's servants now and that made them her enemies.

"Kordelina, you have been summoned," Erc commanded. "Take your place."

Cunnedag wiped the liquor from his face and glared at her, but she knew he would not provoke her further. He was far too lazy, and wary of her temper.

"Get away from me!" she snapped, crouching lower. She frantically grabbed hold of the side table still full of food, and was determined to drag it along with her if they made her go.

Erc got down on one knee next to her. "Do not resist what you cannot stop," he reasoned. She could see by the look in his eye that unlike his brother, he would use force if necessary.

"Get away from me, you pig, or I will kill you," she threatened, touching her fingers to the knife hidden in her robe.

Her reaction was openly defiant; he was well within his right to discipline her. Raising his brows, he looked over his shoulder at Jara. She nodded her consent, and in the next moment, he grabbed her roughly by the back of the neck, and pulled her to her feet.

Kordelina kept hold of the table as long as she could, sending the food rolling into the dirt, and spilling the wine and ale. Still, he jerked her up so suddenly that she was eventually forced to release it, and stand against her will. She squirmed, and arched her back painfully as she struggled to get free.

"What is this nonsense?" Saturnalia demanded. "This young one has been sanctified, and should not be manhandled in such a way. Release her!"

Kordelina heard Erc grunt impatiently, then he tightened his hold for an instant, causing her greater pain before he let her go and stepped away.

She stared pleadingly into the Sorceress' eyes. She felt terribly foolish when she saw Saturnalia's forgiving reflection; she needed her now, and this was her way of begging for what she knew she did not deserve. If only she would have confided to her about the vision, then she would understand.

"I would have her with me," Jara argued.

Saturnalia looked at Jara, then cast a tender gaze at Kordelina. "She will be with you soon enough. Let the child watch from afar if she chooses," she replied.

Jara frowned. "Druidess, I said —"

"Let her enjoy the comforts of her family for yet awhile longer," Saturnalia interjected adamantly.

The older woman was silenced by her tone. It was no longer debatable. "Very well," she conceded.

Saturnalia cocked her head, and stared at Kordelina for a heartfelt moment. *Go now, child,* she wordlessly said to her. *I can give you no more chances.*

Tears filling her eyes, Kordelina awkwardly rose to her feet. The attention of the clan was still on her as she nervously wiped her clammy hands on her thighs. Then rubbing her watery eyes with her fists, she tried to collect herself.

After what seemed an eternity, beautiful soprano voices filled the air, and a line of hooded priests locked hands to form a protective, white-robed circle around Saturnalia and Jara. The clan pressed closer, making a human barrier between Kordelina and the Druidesses. It was an eerie, isolated feeling for the young girl to realize that although the space dividing them was little, it was a chasm that could never again be bridged.

When she was sure that she was no longer the object of attention, Kordelina walked cautiously into the denseness of the grove. She was only a few feet out of sight before she started running as fast as her legs would carry her. A subtle wild sensation rose in her as she quickly removed her festival garb.

Recalling the image she had seen of her and Aonghus the night before, she took off her crown and bracelets. Flinging them into the shrubbery on either side, she laughed to herself as she heard them clank against the ground. Then she shook her head and let her hair drop down her back as she unclasped her broach and let her robe slip off, relishing the tantalizing bite of the winter air against her hot skin.

By the time she reached the boulders where Macha was tied, she had the green cloak wrapped around her naked body, and wore only the bracelet Aonghus had given back to her. She gathered the reins, and climbed into the saddle. The touch of the leather between her naked thighs made her feel madly seductive as the hot wanton urges grew stronger.

"We made it, Macha! We really did make it!" she whispered to the mare.

Jabbing her bare heels into the horse's flanks, she broke into a gallop, and started for the place she knew Aonghus was waiting.

Kordelina let the horse leap across the brook, and over the charred trunk of the oak that had been struck by lightning the spring before. She could almost hear the sound of Aonghus' voice saying her name, beckoning her to come to him, at last and forever.

Descending further into the dense cluster of trees, she could finally make out his outline in the distance. By the time she could see the shadow of his face, their thoughts were fused together, and their minds were engaged in the sweet, sensual foreplay they had waited so many years to indulge. As she reined her horse, Aonghus held out his hand to her and told her with one look that at last, at last, she was his alone.

Dismounting, she let her cloak drop to the ground, and stood naked, looking shamelessly back at him. She was so beautiful to him that he felt himself begin to tremble with the overpowering desire to take her for his own.

Kordelina drew closer. He studied her heavy breasts and the lovely dark nipples that were now hard and erect. With his eyes, he followed the line of her broad shoulders down her arms, and found that even their contours were enticing. He undressed without taking his eyes off her. There were no remnants of the child he had once known; to him, she was now solely his virgin.

She moved as though her feet did not touch the ground. Boldly she prowled, a vision of womanliness. In a moment, she was kissing his chest and shoulders, the sensation of her lips against his skin sublime bliss. The scent of her was the sweet perfume of innocence, and as she brushed against his loins, her closeness penetrated his senses and sent him floating, utterly lost in her soft flesh. She wanted freedom, and he would willingly give it to her.

She was so near that he could almost hear the blood rushing through her. Fighting his desire to conquer her completely, he gently kissed first one nipple then the other while he caressed her arms and shoulders with the palms of his calloused hands. Lifting his head, he looked deeply into her eyes, the piercing expression of their passion enslaving him.

They stood facing each other, chests heaving, their eyes transfixed. At that moment, each knew that their destiny stood before them, and no words needed to be spoken.

Kordelina dropped to her knees in front of him, and stretching out her arms, she ran her fingers over his chest, and down his thighs. Her nails scraped against him, yet he could feel no pain, even as the red welts began to rise on his skin. Closing his eyes a moment, he swayed slightly backward when he felt her wet lips slide down his hardened shaft, her soft tongue licking him. He let out a low, seductive moan as she took him into her mouth while she massaged his buttocks.

With the next movement, she pulled him on top of her, inviting him inside of her as if she were begging for salvation. Aonghus could not help but enjoy the complete dominance over such naive beauty.

As he ran his lips down her body, he left round, dewy circles with his mouth. Then he lightly kissed the inside of her thighs while his hand fondled her breasts. Taking her nipples between his fingertips, he squeezed them just hard enough to make them pucker while he outlined the moist opening between her legs with the tip of his tongue.

Moving lower down her inner thighs, Aonghus outstretched her long legs, and kissed the perspiration clinging to the bend of her knees. Then he nibbled on the backs of her calves before suckling the arches of both feet and her toes. Kordelina's excitement was peaked to the point of desperation while Aonghus was drunk with his ability to inflict either pain or pleasure with a single movement.

"Please," she said breathlessly. "Aonghus, I love you. Let me feel you love me."

From the sound of her voice, he knew he should not prolong this seduction, but he could not help himself. He had waited so long to be with her like this that he did not want to rush even the slightest bit of their love.

Urging her on her stomach, he started back up her body by kissing the backs of her legs, the base of her hips, and the shadowy crevice of her buttocks. His own arousal was so intense that he was aching as he seemingly fed on the small of her back, and the tender area between her shoulder blades. Then he took a mouthful of her hair, while he rubbed the hardened part of himself against her.

With her dark tresses still between his teeth, he studied her lovely profile. How he adored the dainty nose, the sultry eyes, and her strong jaw. He touched his fingertips to her mouth, and by the way she began to nurse on them, he knew they could wait no longer. Turning her over to face him, he moved on top of her, crushing her bosom to his chest.

Aonghus forced himself to pause a moment as he gently brushed the hair from her face. As he silently bid farewell to the last of her innocence, he delicately kissed her brow.

Gazing at her, he was thoroughly enamored by the purity of her countenance. It reflected such trust, such love that he knew she would follow him to the far stretches of the universe. What could ever have prevented their love, he asked himself. It seemed such foolishness now to deny this ecstasy. If the bonding of their souls was wrong, then let them perish in each other's arms, for to live without this love from that moment on, was not to live at all.

Closing his eyes, he rested the side of his face against her forehead. The beads of her sweat clung to his skin as he spread her legs with his hips. Holding himself back, he pressed as delicately as he could into her wetness. His lips were quivering as he opened his eyes and focused on her. She stared back vulnerably, her cheeks flushed and her lips barely parted. She offered herself so completely that he wished he could be more gentle than he knew was possible.

Kordelina winced as he penetrated her, pushing deeper as he felt her chaste blood oozing around him, welcoming him. He felt her body tense with sudden pain, instinctively trying to pull away as he pressed harder into the yet untouched flesh. She looked back at him questioningly at first, her eyes watering, then she turned her head away. Sensing her fear, Aonghus did not move for a bit, allowing her time to get used to the feel of him. Bowing his head, he kissed her neck and hair.

"My precious Kordelina," he murmured to her softly, "no one can take you from me now."

At his words, her pelvis tilted upward, and she moved her open mouth to his. Kissing him frantically, she grabbed his buttocks, and urged him further until there was no more of him. Their joining was complete.

Years of passion were suddenly unleashed with each stroke. In his mind's eye, he envisioned the two made of precious gold, and this union a divine sacrament of the gods. He felt as if their bodies melded into one single entity, half-male and half-female, yet forever joined in the realm of true love. The image brought such instinctual animal power that the raw intensity of it drove them together with great force, until their sweaty bodies slapped against each other in utter abandonment.

Gasping for air, Kordelina cried out and dug her nails into his buttocks as the tremors raked her body. Aonghus could feel her turgid flesh drawing upon the currents of his soul, and it was complete exhilaration to give it to her.

Perspiration streaked his face, and Aonghus found himself unable to make a sound. Spellbound, he was suffocating in the pleasure of her as, finally unable to endure it any longer, he arched his hips and let his heat invade her throbbing womb.

So seductive was this rapture that he thought himself insane. She lay beneath him burning with a rare, tender passion that comes only from complete, selfless love. Still one with her, Aonghus bathed in her slippery warmth. Running his palms over the perspiring curves of her body, he began kissing her feverishly as he gently moved inside of her, teasing her. She was divinely hot, and her response was still hungry for him; he knew he had to have her again.

Images of her vanishing, then coming sharply back into view. A whimper slipping from her lips, and her legs clamping desperately around his waist. Like a wild, toxic vine, this sensual euphoria overtook them as he rocked slowly and powerfully, demanding her complete surrender. As he coursed madly over her raw, pulsating insides, there was a sudden hush, and he was suspended in an invigorating stillness. Burying his face in her hair, everything went black. It was at this moment that Aonghus knew his vow was destined to become insignificant.

CHAPTER TWENTY-ONE

heir passion spent, they lay with glistening arms and legs tangled around each other, as though they were still one. Above, the moonlight peered through the knobbed oak branches, and the mistletoe appeared as dark clusters against the night sky.

A calm like Aonghus had never known had come over him, and the fullness of true love covered him as he cradled Kordelina in his arms. She was the answer to the depths of his being, however good or evil they might be. In his heart, he knew he was exalted above all else that existed in her life.

Holding her now, he could feel her warm breath against his skin as she snuggled closer, and tucked her head in the round of his neck. Promises did not matter now. All that was important was this moment, and this love.

"Kordelina?" he whispered.

She did not answer.

He ran his fingers through her hair. Lifting a strand to his lips, he kissed it. "Kordelina, I have something to tell you," his words were thick with uncertainty.

He felt a sudden rush of adrenalin as he thought of telling her the truth. Still, she remained motionless and quiet. There was such insecurity in her silence that he instantly reconsidered what he was about to do.

"Are you sleeping?" he asked, raising his tone from a whisper.

He felt her kiss him softly on the neck. "No," she answered. "But I have something to tell you."

The sound of her voice pierced the surroundings. Reality was far from this place. All that existed was the snugness of the animal fur wrapped around their naked bodies, and the fragrance of her skin.

She looked up at him, her eyes vibrant as she ran her hand across his forehead, brushing the hair from his eyes.

"Aonghus," she said, with a brilliant smile. "Last night when I was in Saturnalia's chamber, I was given a gift of knowledge. It came in a sort of waking dream, almost like a visitation, from a lovely woman who showed me a child. It was a boy who was waiting to be brought into the world. He had wavy hair like mine and eyes a deeper blue than your own, and I loved him instantly. Then I saw us making love right here in the grove, and you were filling me with life."

"Kordelina, the gods will be granted to us," he answered tenderly.

She put his hand on the round of her stomach. "Feel," she told him. "He will be a proud warrior, just like you, Aonghus."

He stared at his hand expressionless, waiting for something to happen. "I do not feel anything," he said uncertainly. "Do you?"

"I am not sure, but Edainne told me you know as soon as the spirit fills your womb," she answered, openly joyful at her discovery. "It is supposed to feel good."

"Well, does it feel good?" he questioned with a smile.

He watched her expectantly as the color blossomed in her cheeks. "It feels good to be with you," she answered sweetly, and nuzzled him.

Aonghus smiled and turned bright red. "It feels good to be with you, Kordelina. If I could only find the words to tell you how precious you are to me."

The playful look faded from his face as he suddenly recalled the night of her birth. Remembering the violence of it, his eyes watered to think that something so awful could transform into something as beautiful as this. He pulled her closer.

"Aonghus, there is something else," she went on. "When I was in servitude, Airann told me the story of a king who used to rule this tribe, called Oisil. He had a very brave son named Roilan, who would have been a great king if he had not been killed by Romans. I think perhaps this warrior inside of me would like to known by that name."

"Then so be it," he said seriously. "We will call him Roilan. You know, children born and conceived on festival nights are begotten of the gods."

Kordelina lifted her head, and looked at him with a perplexed expression. "That is what Mother told me," she said. "I thought it was strange that she would speak to me of such things, and she had the most peculiar look in her eyes when she said it. How would she know to tell me that?"

Sympathy washed across Aonghus' handsome features, and taking her hand in his, he kissed the center of her palm. As he did this, Kordelina cupped the side of his face, and looking into her dazzling eyes, he felt the urge to have her again.

Running his hand down her forearm and over her elbow, he gathered the skin beneath her arm, then fondled her breast. It was so wondrously smooth and alluring that he lost all train of thought as he dropped his head and kissed her neck.

"Aonghus, why would Mother tell me that?" she asked again, as she lifted his chin to meet his eyes. "She could not know it would be important to us."

A warmth rose in him as he looked at her young face. She was so fresh, so naively seductive that he was at once transfused with a burning for her touch.

"Because you are begotten of the gods, Kordelina. You were their gift to me," he murmured, covering her soft, unguarded mouth with his lips.

He sensed that she wanted to say something more to him, but the dizzying intensity he felt would not let him stop kissing her. She grabbed his long hair, then stopped, and taking his face in her hands, lifted his head to get his attention.

Staring back at her, Aonghus had not a thought in his head except to make love to her.

"Do you think so?" she questioned, with a puzzled look.

He did not answer as he bent his head, and ran the tip of his tongue along the part of her lips. He felt her squeeze his face as she tried to stop him, but he kissed her again, wet and full.

"Aonghus, do you really think I was born on a sacred night?" she asked.

He nodded, and lightly kissed her again.

"But how do you know?" she asked, determined. "Maybe they told you that so they would have an excuse to sacrifice me when the time came?"

Aonghus unknowingly smiled at her reasoning, as he let the whirling particles of green and brown in her eyes envelope him until his vision blurred.

"I know it as truth, Kordelina," he replied, thoughtlessly. "I was there."

He saw a flush of anger on her face, and as he felt her body flinch, he realized the gravity of his admission. At that moment, she turned unpliable. What a terrible mistake he had made.

"Why have you never told me this before? I have asked you many times if you knew my parents, and you said you did not. Why did you lie? If only you had told me who they were, we would not have had to keep our love secret," she said angrily. "All this time, I felt I was some kind of vulgar fiend to want you as my lover because everyone insisted we were kin. Why did you let me suffer so?"

She pushed him away, trying to free herself from his embrace. "How can you say you love me, then deceive me again!" she said coldly. "You knew how much my birthright meant to me."

"Wait! Wait!" he said, struggling to hold her. "Listen to me a moment."

Kordelina's face contorted furiously. "No! You are a liar! You toyed with my heart cruelly. I have always loved you, and you have known this all the while. Still, you would not tell me. You would not spare me this misery. What amusement I must have provided for you!" she shrieked. Jerking her head to the side, she bit him hard on the forearm. He could feel her teeth break the skin as she tugged on it hard for a moment, then let go.

"Ah!" he cried, but did not let loose of her. He knew that if she got away from him in this confused state, she would leave him forever. Fearing that she might run before he could explain, he rolled on top of her to keep her still.

Kordelina thrashed violently beneath him. "Leave me alone," she fumed. "You have betrayed me too many times!"

She pushed against him with all her might, but he fought to keep her down. Holding her firmly, he looked into her turbulent eyes. For a moment, he could see her challenging him, and there was no doubt in his mind that if she had a weapon, she would have used it. Then he felt her surrender, and he knew there was no way to spare her anymore.

"I have not betrayed you; please know that. I made a sacred promise to the Druids when you were first born that I would never reveal your parentage. It never would have mattered had it not been for our feelings. I wanted to tell you so many times. I even went to Saturnalia, and asked to be freed of my oath so that I could tell you everything, but she refused me," he entreated, moving his face so close to hers that their lips were almost touching as he spoke.

"No!" Kordelina said sharply. "Saturnalia would not do such a thing. To what good would it bring her to deny my happiness? The only reason I am here with you now, is because she spared me. It is a lie, you want me to hate her because you hate her. Do not do this, Aonghus. I can take no more lies; please do not speak any more lies!"

"I have to do this. If I do not, we will never be free of her," he argued. "What you have been told your entire life has been lies, but the words I speak to you now are truth. In my heart, I cannot withhold this from you any longer. Kordelina, I must be released of my guilt so that I can be your husband."

He watched her expression sadden as she shut her eyes, and bit her bottom lip. "Then who are my parents? Why was I taken from them?" she questioned, her voice heavy with sorrow.

Aonghus did not answer. He feared if he said more, they would both suffer the fury of the heavens.

Kordelina opened her eyes defiantly. "Who?" she screamed, arching her back and pushing her weight against him. "I want to know who they were!"

"Please do not ask that of me. I have already said enough, lest the gods be angered," he replied submissively.

"Were they Romans, is that the mystery? I am really not a Celt at all, am I? And you could not take me as your wife because I was unclean from the beginning. Is that right?" she demanded, again bucking wildly beneath him. Her moves were so abrupt, he almost lost his hold.

"Tell me!" she cried desperately. "Tell me to whom I was born, and then, I will believe what you say. Do not make me beg. Please, Aonghus, do not make me beg!"

Her words bore deeply into his conscience. He so loved her that he could not, and would not, make her grovel for her birthright.

"Solomon," he said, so quickly that it was as if he were afraid that someone else would hear. "You were born of the Chieftain Solomon and Deireadh, the Black Druidess."

Kordelina was speechless, and he could see she was holding back tears. She thought of the story that Solomon had told that earlier night around the fire, about the evil woman who had burst open from the spirits within her, and she was finally able to comprehend why he had chased her into the grove so long ago when Aonghus was being initiated. Surely, he must have loved her mother in spite of her ways because he was contrite when he had spoken Deireadh's name. Then it occured to her how difficult it must have been for Aonghus to keep this a secret for so long. Remembering the sensitive young man who had rescued her years ago when she had run away from her fosterage, and the way he had so patiently taught her to dance in front of the fire and to catch the wild horses, she knew in her heart that his lies were meant to protect her, not to hurt her.

"You must believe me," he implored, his body shaking with repentence. "I am not lying to you this time. Saturnalia wanted it to remain a secret because she believed the clan would kill you if they knew who your mother was."

He watched helplessly as her fury dissolved into anguish, and her body became limp. She was struggling inwardly to make sense of a fallacious lifetime that he was partially responsible for creating. Filled with remorse, he plunged his face into her raven hair and inhaled the smoky odor of the festival pyre mixed with the sweet languor of their past.

"I love you; I never meant to hurt you this way," his voice quivered as he spoke.

Unknowingly, he had released his grip, because in the next moment, she was running her fingertips up and down his back. With one hand, she reached for the fur covering and spread it over him, then held him close.

Aonghus found himself sobbing as he clung to her like a mourner lamenting his own death. She ran her fingers through his hair, then down the side of his face, and lifted his head. Moving her mouth to his, she grimaced at the salty taste of his tears.

"Yes, I know now how much you have always loved me," she whispered, rubbing her face against his to dry his tears. "What a burden you have carried all these years, my dearest love."

They rested in heedful silence, their intimacy blooming despite their unspeakable pain. Kordelina could feel Aonghus' body growing hard and feverish as she pressed herself closer to him. She belonged with this man, and nothing could ever keep them apart again. An immediate contentment came over her as she spread her legs and stared into his urgent blue eyes.

She moaned softly as he again entered her swollen flesh, his rigidness stinging the raw tissue as he moved. She wanted to feel him even deeper inside of her as she imagined the wetness between their thighs to be the cleansing blood brought forth by their passion.

He stroked her gently at first, then with desperate intensity; it was as if her pleasure would atone for his guilt. His hands held her hips down as he thrust. Tears streaked Kordelina's face, and her lips stretched tightly across her mouth as she whimpered with ecstasy.

Aonghus pulled back, almost withdrawing, then pushed hard into her as he completely indulged himself in her being. Drained, he relaxed in her arms, the sound of her soft cries carrying him into a restive sleep.

CHAPTER TWENTY-TWO

e awoke suddenly, his eyes darting from side to side as he tried to get his bearings. His body jerked as he attempted to rouse himself from his slumber, and then for a moment, he felt unable to move. What was it that had broken the spell of his sleep so violently? Panic rose within him, as though something dangerous was near, and he could not help but think he had stirred the ill forces of the deities with his broken oath.

"What is it?" Kordelina asked, in a low but alert tone.

She stretched out her hand, trying to grab his spear, but could not reach it. Such poor planning for a warrior to be without a weapon, she scolded herself.

Aonghus squeezed her shoulder. "We must leave now," he said quietly as he scanned the woods. "The celebration will soon be over."

"What is it?" she asked again.

He pressed his finger to her lips to quiet her. "Get dressed quickly," he answered, pulling back the fur and letting in a rush of cold air.

Hurriedly, Kordelina slipped her fur-lined tunic over her head. She used the green cloak to wipe the dried blood and fluid from the inside of her thighs before pulling on her trousers and boots. A mild but pleasurable soreness radiated from deep within her. Stopping a moment to look for her knife, she found that it was not in her saddle where she had left it.

"Kordelina, the horses!" Aonghus commanded, giving her a sign to move faster as he dressed and gathered the weapons.

"But my knife—I cannot find it," she countered.

Aonghus waved his hand in the air, dismissing what she had said.

"Aonghus, that is the knife you made for me. I will not be able to come back for it after we have left," she reasoned, her brows knitting together.

"Do not worry, Kordelina; I will give you mine. Right now, though, we must move swiftly. There is not much time."

"All right," she said under her breath, and went to the horses.

As she gathered their reins, she noticed the whites of their eyes showed fearfully. Macha took a couple of short steps as if to bolt, then stared at Kordelina impatiently. Lir's nostrils were flared, and his ears pinned straight back. He suddenly pricked up his ears, and looked skittishly into the grove in front of him.

Pawing the ground with his front hoof, he let out a loud squeal of warning. Whatever it was that frightened him, it was just beyond the trees. Kordelina tried to disguise her increasing fear as she turned to Aonghus, and he met her gaze. How she hated the threatened look in his narrow blue eyes. His pupils were pinpoints, and his movements tense as he reached for his spear and shield lying on the ground.

The trees rustled when an owl unexpectedly took flight and spooked the horses as it noiselessly swooped down before them. Both animals tried to dart forward, then abruptly retreated back. Kordelina held their reins tightly and moved with them, not wanting to cause further commotion. Lir fought the bit and tried to rear up, but Kordelina yanked on his reins. He angrily lashed his head in response, and she almost lost her hold.

Aonghus grabbed him before he could bolt, and this time as the stallion reared to get free, he clipped Aonghus on the side of the head with his front hoof. A horrible pain radiated across the warrior's brow, then shot down the back of his neck. His hands temporarily lost all feeling, and with ears ringing, everything became dark for an instant before dimly coming back into view.

Noticing that he could barely grip the reins, Kordelina braced him with one hand until Lir settled down again.

"Can you still ride?" she asked, worried.

He nodded, and all at once, a stillness came over the grove. It was like the chilling desperation of being silently stalked by an invisible but omnipotent predator, and Kordelina prayed that Saturnalia had not sent her guards. Mounting her horse, she motioned for Aonghus to follow, but he handed her Lir's reins instead.

"Hold him. I am going to see what it is," he said, standing alongside her.

An irrational feeling of despair overwhelmed her; she knew their lives depended on his every action.

"No," she contested. "Come with me now. This island does not matter anymore. We are not obligated to defend it. We are free now to live as we wish."

Aonghus ran his hand down the outside of her thigh, and looked up at her compassionately. "I understand how your heart must have hardened. You have learned bitter truths on this night. Still, I should have been watching, not sleeping. My dearest kinsman will die on this eve for just such an error, and it was he who cautioned me to beware in the darkness. What a fool I would be if I ignored his warning, and led us into danger. I cannot risk our welfare, or that of our clan, for many could perish," he reasoned.

Kordelina's expression clouded. "They are no longer my clan; I have no debt to them."

He saw her mouth tighten and her jaw square off, and he felt a deep sadness as he looked at her. Whether by necessity or by her own free will, she had aged many years on this night.

"You are too hasty to denounce those you love," he gently admonished.

Her eyes reflected an inner determination as she looked back at him. "My only concern is for those I love, and that is you and our child," she said sharply.

It was useless to argue with her. It would only waste what little time they had left. Then, as if he were glimpsing a dreaded intruder, he flashed to that night in her room when she had begged him to love her. He could still see her tears and rage as she knelt before him, pleading to share her passion. His mind then wandered to the vision of the gash in his bare chest, and the empty cavern that had once held his heart. Closing his eyes, he shook his aching head to rid himself of it.

Sensing his need, Kordelina stroked his hair, and her affection eased the tension between them. Reaching out, he touched her cheek with his deadened fingertips. He loved her so.

The presence, the icy cold presence—it was there again. A chill ran up his spine as he felt it surrounding them. A hawk cried out from above, and Kordelina firmly grasped his forearm.

"Please, Aonghus, we can get away now. There will not be another chance for us, I know it!" she pleaded. The sense of impending disaster was stifling. "You must listen to me; there was a part of my vision that I did not share with you. It was when I saw myself years from now still living on this island—you were not there with me. I beg you, Aonghus, do not be a fool who walks nobly to his own destruction!"

Her words stung. It was as if they were a confirmation of what he feared the most. The fear that somehow, all of his dreams would remain forever unattainable, and another man would steal the kisses of Kordelina's life. Then he was beset by an indeterminable sound, and a cold sweat broke out over his body. He tried to identify it; he knew this was what Conn had warned him about.

"I must see what it is—wait here," his words were gruff and impatient.

"No, I want to go with you," she insisted. "If we stay together perhaps we will be safe."

Aonghus put his hand over hers and squeezed it, attempting to calm her. It was quivering nervously. "Just let me see if it is clear to cross the meadow," he replied in a more persuasive tone.

Kordelina stared back at him, not wanting to see the hunted expression on his face. As if to reassure her, his features softened, and he looked at her with piercing eyes. In the darkness, they appeared to have an unearthly cast, and she knew he was being called by something she could not prevail against.

"Aonghus, stay with me," she begged. "You alone can make little difference to anyone but me and our baby. We have waited too long, sacrificed too much to be daunted now. You are given a choice, and only by your free will can we survive."

"Kordelina, I am a warrior," he replied firmly. "I have been ordained by the gods to protect their creations, and I do not understand the choice of which you speak. I have a duty, but that does not mean I love you any less. It only means that I should guard you with all my might. So please, wait a brief moment until I am sure it is safe. Do not follow because you could endanger yourself."

Bending his head, he kissed the top of her leg then lifted his face to her. Gazing back at him, Kordelina thought she could never love another as much as she loved him, and she leaned down and pressed her lips to his.

"We will have our life together, I promise you. Just wait for me," he said tenderly and kissed her again. "My precious Kordelina, your name is my prayer."

He walked to the edge of the grove without a sound. His body seemed to have become weightless. Overhead, the hawk screeched again, and circled once before perching on a nearby oak branch. Stopping a moment, Aonghus turned to look at Kordelina. His head moved stiffly until she could see his entire face. His expression was once again gentle, and full of love.

Naked to the waist, his skin appeared slate grey in the moonlight. The shadowy contours of his muscled back rippled evenly with each movement. Kordelina watched with trepidation as the outline of his body merged into the shadows of the trees, and a feeling of desolation came over her. She did not want to consider that he would not return.

———

Aonghus could hear the sound of the river flowing as he stepped into the darkness of the grove and a cold wind swirled around his feet. The rustle of it through the branches was so magnified that, at first, he was unsure if he had completely shaken his slumber.

Rubbing his temples, he felt the earth jolt beneath him, as if the very impact of his foot caused it to move. Then he stopped warily, and attempted to regain his senses. His skin was suddenly sensitive and the cold air was blistering. Something was going wrong, it was as though his mind was caving into itself, and he shook his head from side to side to revive himself.

Slowly, slowly, he walked deeper into the oaks, and he realized they were no longer a sanctuary; they were a maze. His eyes burned as if someone had thrown hot ash into them, and his head was growing heavy. He suddenly felt tormented, like a man whose broken heart was still laboring to beat with life.

His hands started to tingle, and an irrational fear that his body was evaporating caused him to hold them in front of his face. Staring at them, he made a fist and touched it lightly to his lips. His teeth were chattering, and his legs grew weaker with each step.

He sensed the eerie presence coming up behind him as his ringing ears filled with the quiet sobs of a single soul crying out. It sounded as though it were rising from the roots of the oaks, and ascending into the night sky. Turning around, Aonghus desperately wanted to go back to Kordelina, but all the trees looked the same, and he could scarcely retrace his steps.

"This will pass," he reassured himself, as he desperately spread both palms over his chest as though he were trying to prevent his spirit from escaping.

Suddenly he could hear Kordelina's whisper on the breeze, and he knew she was beckoning him to her. Trying to identify the direction from which it came, he caught sight of a strange and beautiful woman with tears in her eyes. She seemed to float on the mist, and his intuition told him to stay away from her, no matter how lovely she appeared. She was a short distance in front of him at first, then directly alongside him. He felt such a pull to her that he was overcome with the need to touch her.

"Goddess," he murmured, and when he reached out his hand, she disappeared instantly.

The sound of a baby's cries came from the very tops of the trees. It was his baby, and the plaints were shrill and tortured. Clamping his hands over his ears, he staggered to the side. He had to return to Kordelina.

The newborn's suffering grew mercilessly louder until it became the wailing sound of the world itself. Aonghus was too distraught; he could not escape the cries. They were coming for him. He now understood fully that his anguished body was soon to be out of its misery.

He was almost convulsing as he watched a stream of sparks flash between the trees. Moving in long, urgent strides, he stared madly down the tree-lined pathways for a way out. He saw a beam of blinding light so vivid that it looked like the rising of the sun. His mind was crumbling, and he could not prevent it.

Feeling as if a multitude of stunned eyes were watching his pitiful display, he stopped abruptly and looked defensively around the vast emptiness of the grove. He could not catch his breath, and droplets of sweat surfaced from his skin like his insides were seeping out of his pores.

Rubbing his eyes with his fists, he was beset with the most horrible of all sounds. It was the grieving of a solitary masculine voice. It was pleading as though each utterance was a single gasp for life. Opening his eyes, he glimpsed the Celt he had killed when he was a child. He was leaning against one of the oaks, grinning back at him with the dagger still lodged in the base of his skull.

Terrified, Aonghus shut his eyes, and when he reopened them, he was greeted by the gruesome sight of the second Celtic warrior he had slain that day with Solomon. He was standing directly in front of him soaked with blood, and his lifeless green eyes had the gravel from the river bottom still in them.

"Kordelina, help me!" he begged, and the warrior immediately vanished. "I cannot find you. Why did I walk away? Oh, my precious love, I want to hear your sweet voice, and feel the beat of your heart. Kordelina!"

His wobbly legs made him teeter in a circle, and the pounding in his head was again filled with infantile cries.

"My baby's crying; save him! Save me, Kordelina; save me, please!" he rambled, putting his face in his hands.

Suddenly it felt like the ground slanted, and the motion forced him forward. Dropping his hands limply to his sides as he moved, his ears echoed with the faint scattering of thousands of pleading voices, and he saw a blurred image of despondent souls.

The wind was like ice now. It spiraled around his legs like a rope as he tried in vain to retrace his steps. His heart raced, and he felt hordes of unseen people rushing at him, pawing at his body as their lamenting transformed into a triumphant call.

Aonghus began running blindly forward. He had to get out of the trees. He could see the meadow in front of him, and as he stopped in its center, he found himself completely surrounded by Roman infantrymen.

As they seized him, he unwillingly reverted to the savage hatred they had evoked in him so many years ago. It seethed in him as he struggled to get free of their hold, but two men held him by his arms, as still another came directly at him. How he loathed their skin against his; it seemed to defile something sacred after lying with Kordelina.

With a desperate surge of strength, he lunged at his attacker. Dragging the two men with him, he butted the oncoming Roman in the stomach with his head. He felt someone wrap their arm around his neck, and the blow of a knee squarely into his kidneys. He was crippled by the pain as he was struck again and again in the same place until he doubled over excruciatingly.

You are going to die, the sound of his subconscious echoed in his head. And in that slice of time between stifling torment and nothingness, he fully comprehended that this was only the beginning of the slaughter. It was useless to believe that his people could always prevail against Caesar. Their fight had been valiant, but these tribes were destined to become like all the others; endlessly persecuted for resisting Imperialist rule. Then he thought of Kordelina and how he must protect her from them.

Taking a powerful breath, he flung his arms wildly to the sides knocking one soldier off balance, and momentarily breaking free. He tried to run, but was kicked again in the small of the back. Lurching forward in agony, he felt as if his spine had been crushed.

"Get on your knees and beg me not to kill you," a voice commanded.

Dazed, Aonghus looked up and found that he was facing a Roman officer in full battle attire. He blinked as he focused in disbelief, and immediately recognized the blunt nose, the pale, malevolent eyes, and the missing front teeth. It was the soldier he had left for dead years before when he had been wounded in Wales.

"On your knees," he demanded, the air whistling through his missing teeth. "I will give you a chance to live, but you must beg for it—you pagan dog."

The sound of the Roman's voice could have been Aonghus' own from long ago, when he had brutally tortured men for the simple thrill of it.

The dull throb moving up his spine, Aonghus began to feel more lightheaded. He tried to touch his feet to the ground, but they were numb. Closing his eyes, he wished he had killed this man when he had the chance. As a sudden stab of pain crucified him, he knew he was bleeding inside. He could not ride like this, and even if he did grovel for his own life, what of Kordelina? Perhaps he would be spared, but she would surely be taken prisoner, and he could not bear to see that happen. Looking up again, he spit in the officer's face. Then he threw his head back, and gave a warrior's battle cry.

The Roman offered a vicious smile as he wiped the saliva from his cheek. "For that, you will die," he said disdainfully.

They pushed down on Aonghus' shoulders, and his knees buckled beneath him. He caught sight of something in the trees. It seemed to calm him before he looked away.

Be still, Kordelina; you cannot help me this time, he soundlessly spoke to her. *I love you, my precious Kordelina. Your name is my prayer.*

Sensing beyond his pain and fear, his mind suddenly pictured her as a young child. She was standing on the cliffs, just the way she had been when he had departed on the ship for Wales. He could see her kiss her fingertips, then hold them up so it would be carried to him on the breeze.

Remembering how much he had wanted to come back to her then made him certain they would find each other again. It did not matter if it was in another life where their names and perhaps the place would be different; the only thing of true importance was that their eternal love for each other would remain as strong and enduring as it had always been. At this thought, he felt her receive him.

Yes, Aonghus, we are as endless as the wind, you and I. As endless as the wind, he heard her sweet, young voice sound in his mind, and then there was the faintest chime of a very tiny heartbeat. He was enveloped with a sense of emanating warmth as euphoria returned, and his muscled shoulders relaxed.

"Do not worry, Celt," the Roman was saying. "I have no use for your head; it means nothing to me. I will not hang it from a post outside my door as a testimony of my manhood. Rather, I would have your heart. Yes, the splendid heart of a simple Celtic dog."

The surrounding men laughed brashly at their superior's comment. One of them came forward and spit on the ailing warrior while still another pulled Aonghus' own knife from his belt and ran it through his bicep. The soldier twisted it deeper before he yanked it out, causing him to yelp at the pain.

Forcing himself to quiet, again Aonghus saw the blade of the commander's sword glimmer in the moonlight. It was useless to resist, he thought. Death eventually came to everyone. He would accept it as a warrior anointed by the gods. Looking up to the sky passively, he let his mind fill with the indescribable mysteries he had shared with his Kordelina.

His death was instantaneous. As the soldier sliced open Aonghus' chest, the draught of blood poured out of him. He made no sound as his head dropped forward and his body went limp. The two men on either side held him up as the officer reached in the gaping wound, and yanked his heart from his body.

Holding it high in the air, the steamy, scarlet liquid flowed down his arm and dripped off his elbow. The rest of the soldiers cheered at the sight of first blood drawn, and Aonghus' lifeless body was cast aside.

Hiding behind an oak, Kordelina would have screamed, but her terror was too great.

chapter twenty-three

he dancing and singing had ended.

The festival clearing had taken on a life of its own as the tribe pushed closer to the ceremonial altar. The myriad of moving figures appeared to wither like flowers against the torchlights, before the bright shades of their garments and the sheen of their supplicated faces blossomed over again. They transformed independently of each other, as if each were singular elements of one multicolored bouquet.

Looking out on the crowd of worshippers, Saturnalia felt she had at last reached her destination. The events since the festival had begun seemed to evaporate, leaving only faint impressions on her memory. Lifting her arms to the sky, she twirled in a circle, while gazing at the immensity of this oak temple. On this, the last night of the sacred festival, she would defy the laws of her own reason, and dedicate her humanness to the gods.

As the people crowded nearer, she felt even more separate, as if frozen by her own power and unearthly connectedness. Mortality was insignificant now, and there was no hint of the earthly being she had once been. Tonight, she was dying to herself as she did every night that she offered a soul to the heavens.

Facing forward, her gaze met Solomon's. Even though Saturnalia knew he did not condone what she was about to do, he was enamored with the sight of her. His scent was thick and musty as if he himself had been changed into a master enraptured by his own power. He was a Christian only by circumstance; in his soul, he was pure Celt.

Beckoning him to touch her, Saturnalia lowered her arms. Solomon's eyes grew large and admiring as he reached out to hold her shoulders with his hands.

"I have lived—I have loved this grove and its people," his words were loud and unanchored to this world. "I am the tribal Chieftain, anointed by the spirit of the hawk. And by his might, I implore the blessing of the Goddess Brigantia. Mother, come into this shrine."

Saturnalia closed her eyes, rocking gently. She was leaving her body, floating above the grove. She saw Solomon reach for a rolled stick of scented herbs and dried mistletoe, and light the end of it with a torch. Forcing herself to spiral down again, she willed herself back into her body as the Chieftain turned to the tribe.

Holding the flaming bundle high in the air, he pointed it first in the direction of north, then south, east, and west. As he did this, he stopped each time to encircle Saturnalia with the pungent smoke, and called upon the keepers of the four elements to bless her.

"I invoke the powers of the heavens to come into this temple!" he declared, his face cast to the sky as he lifted the roll in the air.

"And I cry to the magic of the earth to receive this offering!" he commanded, lowering it to the ground.

When he looked at Saturnalia, she was astonished at how, at this moment, they were completely separate.

"High Priestess," he said, his mouth appearing to move out of time with the sound of his words. "Sanctify us!"

Her body ached with vigilant purpose as he held the smoking herbs out to her. Taking the smoldering stick, she crouched down, and began to encircle herself with it. She started at her feet, and moved over her entire body until her arms were stretched high above her head. When she finished, the Druidess gazed into Solomon's eyes one last time before descending into the inner sanctum of her soul.

The sound of soft hymns sung by the celebrants greeted her. Short beeswax candles were placed in her open palms, and vines of ivy and mistletoe were roped around her. The air began to feel warmer as the songs became chants, and Saturnalia's hips swayed to the percussion of the drums and rattles beating around her.

Lowering her head, she stared into the distant opening of this holy retreat. With a divine rush of strength, she moved in front of the stone slab altar. She could smell the fever of the people pressing closer, and could taste their sweat as she breathed. It would be only a moment before Conn would be present, and for the last time she would allow herself to be infatuated by his broad shoulders and the muscled torso that tapered down to slim hips.

Two white-robed priests came forward and took the candles from Saturnalia's hands. Walking through the crowd, they parted an aisle to the dark threshold of the oaks. The chanting rose to the drumbeat in the background as Saturnalia unsheathed her dagger, then clutched it to her chest. All eyes were fixed on the warrior emerging into the torch glow, waiting to glimpse the one who would honor their Goddess with his life. They raised their hands together as Conn came into view; except where the rest of the tribe saw a virile young man, Saturnalia beheld a completely different sight.

Shimmering before her was a golden image that moved about the trees with otherworldly zeal. Ingeniously shaping itself into glistening ripples of flesh, it came forth like a fantastic, jeweled urn whose designs revealed the curved body of a woman. Her robe was made of honeyed threads and crystals that chimed across its front. As her chest rose and fell, they jingled to make a lilting chorus that sounded like the wind sweeping the ashes from the winter sky.

Her eyes appeared enameled blue-green orbs, with pearls for teardrops that trickled down her porcelain cheeks. Her strangely visible heart emanated sparks with each beat that looked like votives shedding light about the grove. The snowy vapors of her breath were the prayers of her worshippers, and Saturnalia was so taken by her awesomeness that her own eyes gleamed with adoration.

Winter's end will come like blood red ice, the Druidess heard her say without moving her mouth. *And the spring will be black.*

Saturnalia was too stunned to reply as the tribe rustled around her, wondering why she had not yet motioned for Conn to approach the altar.

Soon the shadows of rage will close over us, and the sea will rise with corrupted ships that will maul the kindred and consume their scraps of flesh. This scourge of souls will not mar your beauty though, because I see by the greenish light of your long eyes that you understand. Ring out the call, then say farewell.

"Brigantia!" Saturnalia screamed as the apparition dissipated, then solidified into the figure of Conn. The color drained from her face as she was filled with both fear and infatuation for the Goddess. In the next moment, someone shook her by the shoulders.

"Come, Saturnalia, her will must be completed," Jara's voice sounded from behind her. "Summon the warrior forward."

Still in a trance, Saturnalia did not move. Then she whirled around and pointed the dagger at Jara. "You knew!" she screeched. "They are coming because you brought them here yourself!"

"Saturnalia, what is happening to you?" Jara questioned in a panic. "You must complete the ceremony!"

Climbing atop the altar, Saturalia streaked her dagger across the night sky, and filling her lungs with air, she gave a bloodcurdling howl. The warriors knew instantly it was a call to battle—they broke from the crowd and dashed about to arm themselves with their weapons. Suddenly her ears were filled with the thud of a great many horses approaching, and the immediate shrieking of women in the crowd as a mass of Roman infantrymen invaded the grove.

"No! They are forbidden from this place!" Saturnalia yelled.

Leaping to the ground, she rushed forth to stop them. The clearing became chaos as crying children were scooped up in the arms of their fleeing mothers. Some of the warriors ran headlong into the Roman spears, using their bodies as shields to protect their families.

Saturnalia heard Jara shout for her to stop as the old Druidess grasped her by the arm. She tried to pull herself away, but before she could, she felt the hard, blunt end of something hit her skull, and everything went black.

———

Kordelina waited until the soldiers were out of sight, and staggered to where Aonghus lay. The expression on his face was so peaceful, that were it not for the alabaster shade of his skin and the pale green cast to his lips, he would have appeared to be asleep.

Dropping to her knees beside him, she lightly touched his face with trembling fingertips as if she did not want to wake him. Her eyes stung as she looked at the hideous gash in his chest. Then she gently ran her hand down his shoulder and forearm, and tightly laced her fingers in his.

"Oh, my love," she lamented in tearless sobs as she lifted his hand to her lips, and kissed it tenderly. "Look at what they have done to you."

Leaning forward, she moved on top of him, covering his body with hers. His skin was still warm and she wanted to absorb what was left of it.

Her bosom felt the cavity where his heart had been. With the palm of her hand, she touched it, heaving ragged sighs, but she could not cry. His blood clung to her like a red veil, and whimpering sorrowfully, she caressed him in the darkness.

"Lift me with your spirit away from here, because I am dying now upon your corpse," she sobbed, her eyes finally tearing. She buried her face in the round of his neck, and kissed it again and again. Then she lifted her head and looked at him, as if she were waiting for him to come back to life. She cried silently as she ran her bloody fingertips over his cheekbones, then across his brow and his lips.

"I want your love and kisses to rain on me, not the scarlet of your life," she wept, pressing the side of her face against his. "Oh, Aonghus, my only love, my heart beats loudly, as if beating for you as well. Let me press it closer to you, and warm you with my touch."

She tried to remember the way it had felt to have him sleeping next to her in her chamber these last nights, holding her in a special way so the contours of their bodies fit perfectly together. Closing her eyes, she imagined he was still breathing as she moved his hand to touch her cheek.

Listening to the memories inside her head, she could hear his clear tenor voice as he called her name, and could see his broad smile and his glistening blue eyes. As his blood soaked into her garment, she relived every detail of the nuptial dance they had shared the night Edainne gave birth. It was so real that Kordelina felt herself being sucked into another dimension, where her lover was still alive.

It was not clear how much time had elapsed until his skin turned to cold marble, but whatever essence of his soul it had once held, was now gone. Still Kordelina lay motionless, dozing incoherently with his corpse. She could not bear to leave what was left of him alone in the clearing.

Save your Druidess, a voice said, jarring her from her vigil.

It was so distinct that she thought someone else was there with her. Looking around, she saw only two ravens perched on the tree in front of her. They sat in curious silence, and Kordelina did not know if it was her own blurry eyesight that made them seem unreal. Yet she understood perfectly that these companions of ancient war goddesses were the worst of omens.

Save the Druidess, and you will save yourself, she heard it again; only this time, she could not tell from where it came.

She felt a chill run up her back, and sliding to the ground, she propped herself on one elbow. She wondered if she had strength enough to stand as she picked Aonghus' knife off the ground, and stuffed it into her boot.

"Aonghus, I swear I will be with you again," she said, as she removed the torque from around his neck, and put it on. Sitting back on her heels, she stared at his motionless body, her tears now overflowing.

Wiping them from her cheeks with the back of her hand, she leaned forward, and nuzzling the bend of his neck, inhaled his scent.

"Aonghus, I will wait lifetimes for your love if I must. I vow that we will start over someday," she whispered as she pressed her mouth to his unyielding lips. "And this, I promise you; your death will not go unavenged. Nor will I let the fool Roman who has slain you die without speaking your name in reverence."

She paused, and smoothed his hair lovingly away from his face. Sweating and puffing, she placed his right hand over the wound in his chest, trying to cover it.

"My beloved, can you even know what the love you have shared with me has meant? For deep in my being, I had long desired to know if such truth and beauty could exist in one man, and I found it in you. As I promised, I will wait. I will keep what is in my heart only for your care. For as the darkness still hangs heavy in the sky, I know that when the sun casts its golden rays there will be reason to hope once again," she continued listlessly, as she took a deep, agonizing breath. "I would say farewell, but for us there will never be such a thing. This lifetime is but a moment of forever."

At her first attempt to stand, her knees gave away and she fell into a chilly pool of Aonghus' blood. Frantically rolling away from it, she hit her head against the leg of a horse. Afraid it was a Roman, she drew her knife and jumped to her feet. She was taken aback when she found herself staring into Macha's kind eyes.

Crying out in relief, she hugged the mare's neck and waited for the numbing surge of adrenalin in her limbs to pass. "Dear friend, help me. I must get back to the tribe."

The horse bent her neck, and rubbed against Kordelina's bloody shoulder.

"Lir, where is Lir?" Kordelina asked suddenly. "We must not leave him. We will take him with us; surely, there will be a need for such a good stallion."

With all her energy, she slowly climbed into the saddle. Struggling to maintain her balance, she went back into the grove for the bay stallion. She found him standing dutifully over Aonghus' weapons, looking dangerous and aloof. He watched her keenly as she came alongside him.

"Lir, Aonghus is not coming back," Kordelina said, her lips so dry she could barely get the words out.

Taking his reins in one hand, she tried to pull him forward, but the stallion yanked his head away almost unseating her. A cold sweat broke out on Kordelina's brow as she tugged back on him.

"Please, Lir, Aonghus is dead. I know you understand me, you stubborn horse. He is dead! Do you hear me?" she felt herself suppressing her hysteria. "They killed him!"

Lir's eyes appeared to smolder for a brief moment, then he lowered his head in submission and gave in to her hold.

Kordelina's scrambled sense of direction made it nearly impossible to find the way back to the settlement. Each pathway in the grove seemed to lead her back to the clearing where Aonghus lay. Vainly trying to focus her instincts, she was in constant fear that one of Caesar's men would be waiting behind any one of the massive oaks. Finally, she was so disoriented that she let Macha find the way, trusting that the mare knew the trail back from whence she had come.

chapter twenty-four

A sense of perdition filled her body as she splashed through the stream toward her settlement. Weak and numb, Kordelina galloped up the hill and through the grove until she could hear the sounds of fighting in the distance.

Slowing her pace, she cautiously approached the clearing. Commanding Macha and Lir to a halt, she inched closer until her senses were filled with the nauseating odor of fresh blood. Leaning forward in her saddle, she peered from behind a tree, hoping to catch a glimpse of the clearing, but found herself suddenly confronted with a Roman soldier instead.

He was instantly beside her, trying to yank her off her horse. Spooked, the animals tried to bolt, but the soldier grabbed hold of Kordelina's leg with one hand, and Lir's reins with the other. She drew Aonghus' knife and ran the blade down the Roman's brow, gashing out his eye. Covering his face, the ruddy fluid gushed through his fingers. He tried to cry out at the pain, but the blood flowed into his open mouth, and all that came out was a frantic, gurgling sound.

Kordelina stared at him with a trenchant expression as he staggered back and dropped to his knees. Jumping to the ground, she shoved him the rest of the way down with her foot.

"Roman, do not die yet," she told him, as she pulled his sword from its scabbard. "Not before you understand the wrath of a Celt."

Swinging the weapon, she decapitated him. Then with one swift kick, she sent his head rolling down the incline in front of her. She stood, eyes transfixed on his body as it experienced the throes of death. His legs spasmed, and his torso jolted until a puddle of urine formed beneath him.

She found it strange how Aonghus had suffered none of these morbid convulsions. It was almost as though his spirit had already left his body, and there was no need for this repulsive purging.

Lifting her eyes, she saw a small band of unsaddled horses wildly running at her. She recognized that the grey stallion at the head of the group belonged to Diarmudd. With bulging eyes, and ears pinned back, they were all terror-stricken.

Grabbing both Lir's and Macha's reins tightly, she crouched between the two animals to avoid being trampled. For a brief moment, she thought she would be dragged away by Lir when he tried to join the runaways.

Before the last of the herd was past them, Kordelina was atop Macha, and heading for the festival site. When she reached it, the carnage was so great that Kordelina could not help but look away in disgust. Bodies of men, women, and children were strewn around what had been the center of the celebration. Some of them had been stabbed or hacked to death, while others had been trampled by horses. The charred arms and legs of still others could be seen in the festival pyre.

A handful of armed warriors were still fighting, and she recognized one of them to be Turg. He was staving off a Roman with only his shield and a lighted torch. His sword lay on the ground near his feet, and as he pivoted to pick it up, the Roman speared him in the stomach. Realizing he was about to be killed, Turg hastily sliced his jugular vein before being shoved, half-dead, into the flames of the bonfire.

Frenzied women shrieked as they tried in vain to attack the intruders themselves. Most fell to immediate deaths, and the few brandishing weapons had little expertise at using them. Either they were turned against them, or they lost them and were forced to fight the soldiers with their fists and teeth. They were little more than a nuisance to the powerful Romans, and as often as a woman would assault a soldier, they were effortlessly cast aside or murdered.

Kordelina could see the group of white-robed priests cloistered around the stone altar in prayer. More than one of them had their hands uplifted. With tightly shut eyes, they prayed to the gods in unison. Straining her vision to find Saturnalia, the young girl saw no evidence of either her or Solomon. The stone slab was empty of Conn's sacrifice and she watched as in the next moment a mounted officer rushed forward, and three of the priests flung themselves protectively across it. It was a place of sacred offering, and to be touched by an unholy hand was an abomination.

The Roman's face reddened furiously and he ran his sword across their backs, making a symmetrical red gash. Then he took a torch offered him from a nearby soldier, and lit the wounded men and the altar on fire. Their robes ignited instantly as the white-hot flames climbed up their backs to incinerate their skulls.

Urging the horses on, Kordelina headed in the opposite direction. She could do nothing there but fall to her own death, and she knew she was not meant to die on this day.

Going deep into the woods, she wove through the cover of the trees toward her house. She was hoping that her family was still alive. Her body was stiff with fear, but her rushing adrenalin made her ready to kill anything that moved. She was haunted by the picture of Aonghus' murder, again and again, with his placid blue eyes staring tranquilly up at the moon as he waited to take his last breath. What was he thinking in those last moments that gave him so much peace? Was he content knowing that it was all finally over, and he would labor no more? At this thought, Kordelina felt the tears sting her eyes. Did all of life come down to one final instant of either purpose or futility?

Focusing on the face of the officer who had killed him, she imprinted his every feature and mannerism into her memory. He would die before her; she vowed it. She would hunt him down, look straight into his eyes, and tell him this was to repay the debt of one warrior's life before she slowly killed him.

Nearing her parent's farm, she circled around the back of the barn. She emerged from the corn field, and inside the house, she could see stray soldiers moving about. She could tell by their helmets that they were of low rank, and were probably looking for valuables.

Coming alongside the dwelling, she peered in the window, and found one soldier cavorting grotesquely around the room in her mother's feasting robe. He had it tied around his waist, and was wearing Enda's festival beads. In a moment of panic, Kordelina realized they were the same beads she had worn to the celebration. She must be nearby, she thought, spurring her horse.

She went quickly to the entrance of the house, but she did not find Enda. Rather, to her horror, she found her brother, Cunnedag, lying just outside the doorway. His torso was cut open along the lower abdomen, and a portion of his entrails were uncoiled in the dirt. His mouth and eyes were still open in terror, and one arm reached out to Erc's headless body. Kordelina moaned in anguish, feeling the vomit rising in her throat.

"I do not know who else is left," she heard a voice come from the shadows.

Almost gasping out loud, she swallowed her nausea and gripped her sword. Turning aggressively in the saddle, she grit her teeth as she poised her weapon, and saw Solomon step out into the light. His clothes were dirty and tattered, his face swollen with bruises, and he had bloody gashes down his arms and across his chest. He was badly wounded in one leg.

"Can you still handle a horse?" she asked, offering him Lir's reins.

Solomon looked at Aonghus' horse, stupefied.

"Chieftain, there is little time!" she urged, fearing that the shock of Aonghus' death would overtake him.

"But how could they have killed him?" he questioned, tears falling down his face and trickling onto his mustache. "I thought that surely there was time enough for the two of you to escape."

Kordelina shut her eyes tightly, and bit the inside of both cheeks. At that moment, the unwanted reality of his death hit her like a merciless blow. She would not ever hear Aonghus' voice speak her name in the darkness, or taste his kisses in the rain. They would never again ride horses together, nor would they snuggle in each other's arms beneath a blanket of bright stars.

"We were asleep," she answered finally. "There was no time."

Solomon's crying ceased, and his watery eyes filled with sudden anger. "While you slept, they massacred our people."

Kordelina's face turned red as she looked back at him.

"Yes," she answered sharply. "They murdered Aonghus as well. I am sorry for our tribe, Chieftain, yet my grief is now for my beloved."

Solomon shook his head, then covered his face with his hands. "If we had only had more warning, our losses would not have been so great. How could I have been so foolish as to think the gods would not ask restitution for what I allowed you to do? I knew Aonghus was going to leave with you, and I should have stopped it. If I had only been stronger, he would have kept his guard, and probably still be alive."

Kordelina looked at him ruefully. "You cannot possibly think that we caused all of this. We loved each other. Love does not bring destruction. Perhaps this would have happened anyway, and the gods were merciful to let us share our feelings before we had to part. Aonghus was a brave warrior, brave enough to speak my mother's name for I know my father already."

Solomon was too distressed to find a response.

"Aonghus is dead," she went on, her eyes misting. "And so are the lies we have lived these many years, with all of us pretending to be something we were not. It is such cowardice to continue to fear truth. We are of the same line, you and I. It is well now that we should accept it."

Solomon's gaze turned inward. He felt like he was dying inside, and the pain of it was so great that for a moment, he thought of taking his knife and cutting his own throat to end his misery.

"This tribe would have destroyed you if they had known you were of Deireadh's womb," he explained compassionately. "By the time your feelings for Aonghus were apparent, it was too late. Promises had been made, and vows had to be kept. Yet, you must believe that there is no one I would have rather shared you with than him. I loved him as though he were born of my own flesh."

"I loved him more," she responded, blinking back her tears.

An empathetic cast showed in the eyes of the battle-worn Chieftain, as he realized what strength of character his daughter possessed. He gave her a tender look that said that perhaps, there was still hope for them.

"Kordelina, we must set aside the past for now, and try to save those we can," he said, limping over to the stallion.

Reaching up, he grabbed hold of the horse's mane, and threw himself on top of it. He gave a muted cry of pain, then slouched forward on its withers, waiting for it to subside.

"We must get Saturnalia," he said, carefully sitting upright. He was pale and sweating profusely. "Jara took her when the fighting broke out, and I think she is being held in her cottage. Conn is still alive somewhere, I suppose."

"Yes, we could use his help. Aonghus stored a boat at the strait. It is seaworthy, and can carry a few people safely," Kordelina said. "We will need another horse, and Jara. The Romans will not harm her. She will guarantee safe passage."

Solomon ran his fingers through his sweat-drenched hair, pushing it away from his eyes. Glancing at Kordelina, he saw that her mournful expression now possessed a resolute fury, and he knew she was his closest ally.

"Very well," he responded, spurring Lir to a canter. "Let us find a way to rescue our Druidess."

Still holding her sword, Kordelina gathered her reins and followed him.

CHAPTER TWENTY-FIVE

he Imperialist soldiers were scattered; it was difficult to tell just how many they numbered. Throughout the village were groups of four and five infantrymen moving in a swirl from door-to-door. And more often than not, they were confronted with a frothing Celt who would fight them with whatever weapons he had, even if it was only his fists. No matter how brave the effort, he was inevitably murdered. The only difference was whether he died immediately, or had a chance to do some harm before his death.

Kordelina and Solomon sat on horseback halfway up a hillside. Concealed by a dense cluster of oaks, they watched the men move in well-organized waves.

First there was the fighting advance of the small groups who were followed by the landing parties already at the edge of the village. The mass of soldiers marched together in perfectly disciplined strides, headed by four Centurions on majestic white horses. Behind that, far off in the distance, the cavalry could be seen. They were probably going to secure the village first, then go to the outskirts to find any survivors.

Most of the houses had already been ruined or looted, and even at this distance, Kordelina could hear the violated cries of women still alive inside. A few of the huts were set ablaze, the flaming thatched roofs licking the base of the sky. In the misty early morning air, the strange golden aura of the fire radiated halos around the houses. Dawn would come cold and harsh this day. The same pleasant rays that had warmed yesterday's celebration would now shine on a desperate clan.

"We need another horse," Solomon said, tearing a strip off a linen shirt and wrapping it around his leg.

The ripping sound caused Kordelina to turn, only to find that the shirt he had torn was one of Aonghus' finest.

"Where did you get that?" she asked defensively.

Solomon shot her a questioning look. "It was in the saddle bag," he answered tersely. "I am sorry to ruin it, but my wounds need tending."

Kordelina squinted. "You mean Aonghus had a feasting shirt in there —not traveling clothes? How vain can one man be?" she asked, expecting no response.

The Chieftain twisted the ends of the material together, and knotted them tight. "When he got to wherever it was he was going, he wanted to be sure he made a good first impression, I guess," he said, vaguely amused.

Forgetting herself, Kordelina gave a tiny laugh. "Some things do not change," she replied, staring straight ahead again.

Solomon studied her profile thoughtfully, then reached down the side of the saddle and untied the two leather pouches. "Forgive me," he said, holding them out to her. "Of course, you will want these."

Kordelina shrugged uncomfortably, and he saw her lips start to quiver.

"Here, take them," Solomon urged. "We can give him no burial now. These few things are all that is left of him."

"Not all," Kordelina said emotionally, as she took them and draped them across Macha's withers.

Solomon's eyes softened. He knew she was trying to be brave. How he wished he could take her in his arms, and let her release her sorrow, and he could mourn as well. He had the urge to ask her how Aonghus had died, not for any other reason than to know what had finally snared his courage.

"I know this is not the time for it, but for my own conscience, I wish someday to know what happened to him," Solomon said, grief rising in his tone.

Kordelina tilted her head to the side and painfully shut her eyes. "Someday when there is time to grieve and celebrate again, you shall know, Chieftain," she answered, opening them and looking at him sorrowfully. "But now, now there is little darkness left."

With his eyes downcast, Solomon stared at the back of his horse's head. He could not help but wish that he was the one who had died, not Aonghus. And he knew all the while that it was for the most selfish of reasons because for the first time ever, his soul felt too infirmed to accept the end of one he so greatly loved.

"Yes, we must have another horse for Saturnalia," he stated, his voice again composed. "The infantry is moving from the south, so we would be safest moving east and west, one in either direction. That way if one of us does not make it, hopefully the other will."

"And if the gods are merciful yet," she responded. "I will meet you at the backside of the knoll to Saturnalia's cottage. I will only wait until I see the very first light of day, then I will go on alone. You must do the same."

"Yes," he agreed, nodding his head. "You ride from where the sun rises, and I from where it sets. Go now and fear not."

He reached across and patted the outside of her thigh affectionately, and to his surprise, she rested her slender, trembling hand on his.

"Kordelina, you were never unacceptable to me, you must believe that," he told her sincerely. "So much took place between your mother and me that I could not even begin to justify what happened to you. Yet, there is one thing that you must know. In all of my years, I have never been so possessed by a woman or so affected as I was by Deireadh. She told me many things in the hours that she labored to deliver you. Some of it was not what I wanted to hear, and some was so honest and full of love that I have never heard words like that spoken since. Parts of you remind me of her. You are a lovely child, Kordelina, and I should have done right by you all this time. Forgive me."

He felt her squeeze his hand for only a moment before she let it go.

"I do," she said tenderly. "To what good would it be to hate you; you did what you thought was best at the time."

Then with that same hand, she reached down to pull out the Roman sword. "Wait only until first light," she repeated and turned her horse.

Sitting straight and purposefully in the saddle, she rode unafraid into the woods. The trees in this grove were her friends, her protectors. When she got to the farthest edge of the village, she zig-zagged closer to what she knew was Diarmudd's property. She could only hope that the Romans were looting the houses closer in, and they had not gotten this far. Drawing nearer, she saw no one around the house except for a fully-tacked horse tied outside. She could hear the cries of a baby within, and knew that whether dead or alive, Edainne had to be there as well.

Dismounting, she hid Macha between two large trees, and sprinted to the back of the house. Inching closer to the window, she cautiously peered in. She could see the infant resting safely in its crib. The main chamber was empty, and since the fire was nearly out, it was almost completely dark.

Quickly climbing through the window, she walked with stealth to the bed-chamber. The door was cracked, and she could see Edainne lying on the floor with the bare buttocks of a Roman thrusting between her spread legs. The tears flowed down her cheeks, and her lips were shut tightly in an attempt to suppress her cries.

Wrapping her fingers tightly around the sword, Kordelina pushed open the door and entered the room. Edainne's eyes were glassy, and she did not seem to notice her, but the soldier did. He withdrew hurriedly, and before Kordelina could attack, he picked up his javelin and heaved it. Turning to shield herself, she cringed agonizingly as she felt the burning slice of the blade into her shoulder.

"Kordelina!" Edainne screamed. "Run from here and take my baby!"

Stunned by the pain, Kordelina dropped her sword, and as the soldier groped for another weapon, Edainne scrambled to pick it up. Holding it with all her strength, the young mother lunged at her defiler. She timed it perfectly, and split his skull.

Edainne's eyes fluttered as the red droplets spurt onto her face. Then she covered her face with her hands, and frantically rubbed it.

"Edainne," Kordelina said, dropping to her knees. "We must leave quickly."

Edainne jerked her head up, and grabbed the soldier's knife. "I must get my baby!" she cried, then hurried into the next room.

Kordelina could barely stand the stinging pain radiating down her arm and into her fingertips. She tried to make a fist, but her muscles were frozen.

She broke out in painful tears as she laboriously reached around her back with the opposite arm and yanked the weapon out herself. Gritting her teeth, she growled like an injured animal as her warm blood ran down her waist and onto her hip. Touching her fingertips to the round of her hand, she waited for the feeling to return. Then, bracing herself against the wall, she stood slowly and went to look for her friend. She found Edainne in the next room, sitting back on her heels and rocking her baby daughter.

"I have a child, Kordelina, and I do not care what I have to do to keep her alive." She clutched the infant closer and started crying again. "Tell me what we can do to save ourselves and I will do it."

Kordelina ambled to the door and opened it slightly. The soldier's horse was standing where she had originally seen it. They needed it desperately, yet Kordelina could not leave the young mother and child. The only alternative was to take them with her, and pray that Solomon would have better luck than she.

"Edainne, if you truly do want to live, you must come with me. This settlement is ours no longer."

Edainne furrowed her brow. "Where can we go?" she retorted. "They are all gone. Everyone is dead, Kordelina. Do you hear me; they're dead!"

"Not Saturnalia," she countered firmly. "She is still alive, and will take you to another place where your child may grow up a Celt. There is little time to give you any more assurance than that. I can only tell you that you must have faith that you will carry on, or you will perish like all the rest. And I cannot be more insistent that each moment we spend here is wasted."

She started toward the back window where she had originally entered. "I have Macha outside. Wait until I come to the front of the house, then take the Roman's horse and follow. Solomon is waiting, and Saturnalia is yet to be found. I will only pass by here once before going on, so come quickly," she said in a voice so calm, it belied her.

Edainne nodded, and Kordelina could tell by her abrupt change of expression that she had once again gained control of herself. "I will make it," she responded, as she kissed her baby daughter on the forehead. "I want my baby to live."

Going to the window, Kordelina looked out first to see if it was safe. She could feel her blood trickling down her leg and into her boot, and looking down, she noticed that the leather was soaked. She had better make it all the way on horseback, she thought, climbing outside, because if she was forced to go on foot, she would surely leave a red trail.

With her left arm tucked to her body, she ran across the open livestock area. The startled pigs squealed, and the chickens fluttered out of her path. She could hear the barking of the wolves in the foothills. Daylight would soon be upon them.

———

With Edainne in tow, Kordelina safely reached her meeting place with Solomon. When she got there, she was relieved to see that not only had he gathered a horse for Saturnalia, but he had stolen it from a Roman commander. The beautiful animal stood proudly by Lir, a regal being in his ornamented bronze headset and chestplate. Kordelina could not help but smile at the sight of him. If they did survive this, she was sure the Chieftain would have the most embellished recollection of how he had done it.

He was accompanied by Berrig, who had managed to escape with a chariot and his son, Brendan. Brendan was about the same age as Kordelina, and had a shy, but funny way about him. His fair complexion and clear eyes gave him an innocent, angelic appearance that understated the scrappy temperament he had inherited from his father. He had been anointed the spring before, and had been impressive in his pursuits with the fianna. Now he stood leaning on the hindquarters of one of the horses, appearing more relaxed than the present situation called for.

In the back of the chariot was Diarmudd. He was wrapping a piece of hide around the stub of one hand where his finger had been severed. At the sight of Edainne, he almost burst into tears as he went immediately to her side.

Cupping her face in his one good hand, he looked at her questioningly to see if she was all right. She bowed her head, and he lightly kissed the top of her head, then he kissed his daughter as well.

"Diarmudd," Solomon said quietly. "Take her to the cove along the strait, and wait for us there. There are too many of us now to move swiftly. It will be safer for you both."

Diarmudd waited a moment before responding. He did not want to appear too anxious to leave lest he be thought a coward.

"As you wish, Chieftain," he replied, then hesitantly climbed on the horse behind his wife. "We will be waiting."

"I have told the few tribesman I have seen to meet us there as well. If we do not return by sunrise, you will be in charge of them," Solomon said. "You should set sail immediately, and head to the land west of here, do you understand?"

Diarmudd nodded and started for the seashore with his family. Kordelina watched him ride off, and shook her head. What irony to consider that of all of them, Diarmudd would be the one who would live to tell his one-sided account of these tragic events, she thought to herself.

"Are you sure she is there?" Brendan asked, looking up at Saturnalia's cottage.

Solomon nervously smoothed his mustache with one hand. "No, I am not," he answered. "But my intuition tells me that she knows we are here, and she is waiting for us."

Kordelina closed her eyes and tried to connect with the Druidess, but could not. The girl was unable to discern if the void was due to her own weariness, or Saturnalia's refusal to acknowledge her. However, she was certain of one thing: this plan of escape was definitely her idea. Perhaps it was her voice Kordelina had heard earlier, and she was indeed waiting for them now.

"There are two guards outside the door," Brendan continued. "They should be easy enough to take care of."

"Yes," Berrig interjected, turning to Solomon. "We will drive straight through the front; you come immediately behind us. Do what you need to do, and get on your way. The hill is too steep for us to turn in time to make a second assault."

"I understand," the Chieftain replied, moving alongside Kordelina. He looked at her wounded shoulder, then into her eyes.

"I will leave you with this horse," he said, handing her the reins of the animal. It was so big that Kordelina felt as though she were riding a pony. "Once you get Saturnalia in the saddle, ride on, and do not look back for any reason. Is that clear? I will get Jara myself, even if I have to drag her behind me by the hair."

Kordelina let a nervous laugh escape at the thought of the old shrew swept along by her hair, and Solomon cackling wildly at his deed. Looking down, she met Brendan's gaze for just an instant, then focusing on Aonghus' saddle bags, became serious once again.

"Yes, we will go straight to the crag," she said, taking the equine.

He patted her cheek fondly, and offered her a half smile that told her she must succeed in spite of her infirmities.

"Then let us go," Berrig announced, holding the wide leather chariot straps in his large hands.

Brendan took hold of his shield in one hand, and a javelin in the other. Pausing a moment, he looked Kordelina up and down, and she did not know if it was because of the bloody sight of her, or that he was doubtful of how she would fare.

"Your master was the finest of warriors, do not forget all that he taught you," he told her, then hopped into the back of the cart, and braced himself as his father slapped the horses forward.

———

Inside her house, Saturnalia sat near the window, bathed and clothed. Jara had scented her hair with honeysuckle, not the jasmine oil she usually wore. She had chosen a timid blue frock for her to wear, and failed to tie a sash around her waist for color. Saturnalia had not worn anything so plain since her days of Druidic study.

"Jara, why did you not dress me like a jester for your Romans? After all that is what I am," Saturnalia said, chewing on a fingernail.

Jara turned abruptly from where she stood hunched over the fireplace. She trudged purposefully over to Saturnalia, and with her open palm slapped her across the face.

"Silence, Saturnalia!" she scolded, her face turning a deep red. "You cannot even know how close to death you and I are. That whore of a child has gotten us both into a great deal of trouble."

The side of Saturnalia's face stung, but she refused to touch it, or give any sign whatsoever that Jara had hurt her. After what she had experienced the night before, she was alarmingly numb. She knew the Goddess had appeared to deliver them, and no matter how difficult the circumstances seemed at the present moment, surely some of them would be spared.

"That has always been your trouble, Jara. You rely on the manipulation of others to get what you want, instead of doing the work yourself," she said.

"Silence yourself!" Jara screeched, slapping her hands against her thighs. "Do not cast your judgments on me, not after this calamity. This tribe that you love so much is nothing! And you, my spoiled little Sorceress, will be shown little mercy from Rome either. So if you have any notion of continuing in this world, you had better start to humble yourself now."

Irate, Jara clenched her fists in front of her. "How could I have been so stupid?" she ranted. "You never intended to give her to me at all! It was a clever ploy to exercise your free will. You wanted to make it perfectly clear that you found my demands beneath you when all I was trying to do was to save your life!"

"Do not be ridiculous. You could not save my life and slaughter my people because they are my life. As you wanted to spare me, so do I wish to spare them," Saturnalia replied coolly. "Your precious Rome will be appeased anyway, especially after they see what you have given them on this island."

She pushed the shutters open a crack, and looking outside, caught a brief glimpse of two horsemen waiting just beyond the trees. She saw the horses' forelegs move through the shrubbery, then vanish behind an oak. Surely one of them was Solomon, Saturnalia thought; he had never failed her. She tried to stand so she could look out her front window, but Jara shoved her back down again.

"Sit there," she commanded. "I need some time to think of a way to get us out of this. If I do not have a good explanation by the time Flavius arrives, we will only be more fuel for the bonfire."

Saturnalia heaved a sigh. She had to find some way to get outside. Her head hurt from where she had been knocked unconscious, and Jara's incessant screeching was wearing on her. She thought of Conn and wondered if he had escaped the fighting. If he was meant to die the honorable death he had requested, what better way to do it than by defending his people.

"Forgive me, Druidess," she said, her voice suddenly sweet and yielding. She would pretend to be sympathetic to Jara's needs if that was what it took. "I am not myself; my callousness betrays my true intentions."

Jara stared at her suspiciously.

"Truly," Saturnalia said, extending her hand. "We are of the same body, you and I. All else is of little importance. Come sit beside me, and we will consider this together."

Ignoring her gesture of affection, Jara sat roughly down beside her. Scooting closer, Saturnalia took the old woman's hand.

"I am doing what is best," Jara said plainly. "If you could know the bloodshed I have seen these past months, you would understand why I had to acquiesce to certain things to keep us alive."

The Sorceress nodded empathetically. "Of course, you were of the purest intentions. It is only that —"

Her words were interrupted by the rumbling of an approaching chariot. Without wasting a breath, Saturnalia grasped Jara's little finger, and yanked it back. Bone cracked as Jara's mouth flew open in a silent cry of pain.

"Do not make a sound or I will break the rest," Saturnalia warned.

Pulling Jara to her feet, she kept the older Druidess in front of her as she walked to her door, and opened it. Standing in the entryway, she saw the hurried flash of the chariot, and two well-aimed javelins lodge mortally in the Roman guards. One was struck in the neck, and the other between the eyes as they, almost simultaneously, fell to the ground.

Saturnalia pushed Jara outside. Shoving her to the ground, she kicked dirt in her eyes, momentarily blinding her. The old woman squirmed and spit as she tried to wipe the soil from her face. For an instant, the Sorceress stood looking expectantly around her courtyard, frozen by the sudden thought that perhaps she was too late for her only chance at freedom.

In the next moment, Kordelina came streaking through the gate with a Roman horse, and halted just long enough for Saturnalia to take the reins. The excited animal reared halfway up, then impatiently started trotting as soon as his hooves touched back down. Saturnalia had to run alongside it for a short distance before she was able to climb into the saddle.

Kordelina was in back of her, and she heard the crack of the whip as the girl hit the horse's hindquarters. The animal bucked slightly, then broke into a violent gallop, leaving Kordelina a small distance behind her.

The horse was so tall that Saturnalia had to duck beneath some of the low-hanging oak branches as she rode. She could hear the pounding hooves to the side of her, and glancing over her shoulder, she realized it was Conn. He was riding a Roman horse, and looking very battered.

In what seemed an instant, they were all a safe distance away from her cottage and heading toward the strait. The frenzied beat of her heart filled her head as Saturnalia tried to ease the monstrous equine, but it refused the command and ran still faster. Tugging on the reins, she attempted to stop, but it grabbed the bit so hard that she was almost pulled out of the saddle. Seeing her distress, Conn came alongside her and taking one rein, slowed the horse to a comfortable gait with his own.

Looking back from where they had come, Saturnalia saw Solomon and Kordelina emerge from the grove. Their horses were lathered and puffing, and Kordelina was listing hurtfully to one side. It seemed to take all of her strength to keep pace with Solomon, who had Jara thrown across Lir's withers.

chapter twenty-six

ordelina reached the crag behind the others. She was bleeding so badly that she was forced to stop along the way and bandage herself before going on. When she finally did get there, she found her family and Edainne and Diarmudd.

The rest of the horsemen were just now dismounting, and to the far right of the group, near the boat, Kordelina saw Koven. He sat hunched over, face in his hands, talking to Enda, who was holding Niall close. She could tell he was not aware of what was happening.

"Father," she called to him in a worried voice.

Koven looked up, and smiled naively. His expression had a peculiar vacuous look as he stood to approach the group.

"Good friend," he greeted Solomon, without acknowledging Kordelina. "You made it."

The Chieftain cast him a puzzled glance as he flung Jara down from the saddle like hunted game. The old Druidess hit the ground with a thud. No doubt the arduous ride had weakened her because she sat trying to catch her breath.

"All is well, I hope?" Koven continued, still smiling foolishly.

Solomon slid to the ground, and went to Saturnalia and helped her off her horse. She looked appreciatively back at him and gave him a gentle hug. Then she went to Conn, and putting her arms around his neck, started to cry.

"There now," Conn soothed, holding her near. "You kept my soul safe with you all this time, and we are still together."

Solomon stared at the two lovers a moment, then turned to Koven. "No, Koven, all is not well. Half the clan is dead, and the other half is soon to suffer the same fate. We have to seek refuge elsewhere if we are to survive. I dare say it is not the best of situations, because either we set sail through Imperialist waters in broad daylight, in the hope of escaping, or we wait until dark and pray the Romans do not find us before then."

Koven waved his hand in the air, and gave a polite laugh. "Oh, it will be all right," he said carelessly. "You can stay the night and feast with us. Enda has roast lamb, and surely Aonghus will be here as well."

Kordelina stared at him, expressionless. She knew his condition was a result of what he had seen happen to Cunnedag and Erc. With his two middle sons dead, he needed to believe that his eldest son had prevailed. Looking to Enda, she motioned for her to comfort him. She did not want to tell either of her parents of Aonghus' fate; it would only make things worse.

Pretending to ignore her father's statement, she loosened her horse's cinch, and ran her hand down the mare's front legs checking them for swelling.

"You tell him," Solomon said gruffly. "Aonghus was his first born."

Kordelina ignored his remark as she lifted her horse's hoof, and pryed a rock from it.

"Tell me what, Kordelina?" Koven interjected good-naturedly.

"Nothing, Father," she reassured him; then shot an icy glare at Solomon.

"He has a right to know," the Chieftain persisted.

"Leave him alone," Kordelina snapped. "Let him ease his pain any way he can. I am sure he already knows, and that is why he is like this."

"You are only afraid of the truth," Jara said under her breath, as she sat upright. "Afraid for him to know what a whore his daughter really is."

Kordelina felt her blood boil. Drawing her knife, she went toward the Druidess, who cowered when she saw the weapon. Taking a handful of Jara's hair, Kordelina cut it close to the skull then held it in front of her face.

"Do you see this?" she snarled. "If you do not hold your tongue, I will stuff it down your throat to silence you."

No one moved as Kordelina glared threateningly at Jara a moment longer, then released her and stormed off.

"Enough of these games," Jara stated, as she rose to her feet and brushed the grass from her frock. "Am I to be your prisoner?"

"You are to be our passage," Conn stated matter-of-factly. "You are going to use all your political immunity to get us out of here safely."

"And if I refuse?" she asked imperiously.

"I will kill you, and hang you by the feet from that tree," Solomon responded flatly, as he pointed to a huge oak in the distance. "And I will make certain not to tie down your robe, so that every Roman passing by will point laughingly at your wrinkled ass."

Jara turned red and folded her arms across her chest, careful not to jostle her broken finger. "Do not issue empty threats, Chieftain," she scoffed. "I am no good to you dead. Let us negotiate terms."

Saturnalia stepped in front of Solomon, and glared at her in disbelief. "Terms?" she questioned incredulously. "These people have been massacred, and still you speak of terms. What terms did they get? Certain death from your cowardly Caesar who creeps about in the night defiling the Goddess and her worshippers."

Walking to her, Saturnalia jabbed Jara in the chest with her forefinger. "You knew all along what was going to happen. You let these innocent people celebrate to their own deaths, like pigs going to slaughter. But they were not pigs, nor were they the savages that your Romans would like to think they were. They were living, breathing people that loved this island, and loved me!"

She jabbed her again, and Jara backed away until she found herself flattened against Conn and Berrig, who had moved behind her.

"You will help us," Saturnalia threatened. "Or as the gods have made us, I will take you into the middle of the sea, and cast you out myself."

Jara scowled back at her. "Let us take this up in private," she said. "And I will tell you how your precious warrior, Conn, sold your clan for his own ambitions. He was planning to become Rome's client king to this island."

She saw Saturnalia's eyes blaze as she felt Conn take her by the back of the neck, and squeeze it hard.

"There is no time," he said. "I am with my people now, and you are the traitor."

"And you should have been dead, so silence yourself!" Jara's lips quivered angrily. "Saturnalia, I only ask for a few moments alone with you and the girl. Then we can depart."

"Indulge her if that is the only way we can get on our way," Solomon ordered. "You want to speak with Kordelina, as well?"

Jara nodded, and ducked out from Saturnalia's glare.

"Kordelina," Solomon called. "Come here. The rest of you, wait by the boat."

Jaundiced and weak, Kordelina walked slowly over to them. She had her left arm tucked beneath her breasts, and her clothes were covered with blood, front and back. She took a place on the ground near Saturnalia's feet.

"This is between us, Chieftain," Jara told Solomon.

"As you wish, but remember this is the last privilege you will be granted, so get on with it," he replied sternly.

The old woman turned her attention to Kordelina. "You," she accused, striding over to the young girl. "Do you know how many have died in this blood-bath today? You, who would defy the laws and refuse your duty to a Chieftain. If you had been more yielding, there would have been no need for such a show of force. You are the evil one who would let your people be destroyed!"

The anger crested in Jara's eyes as she bent down and took Kordelina's face in her hands. Full of repulsion, Kordelina's eyes fired back at her, then she felt her body heave. Pushing Jara's hands away, she gasped for air and retched.

"Leave her!" Saturnalia commanded. Going immediately to her side, she gently supported her convulsing shoulders. "She is still only a child."

Jara's eyes widened fiercely. "She was to be a virgin for a Chieftain! Are you saying that she is too young to understand what a privilege that was? How can you pity one who, on a whim, would debauch your entire tribe?"

Saturnalia did not respond. Wiping the perspiration from Kordelina's face, she waited for the girl to stop heaving, then comfortingly took her in her arms. Burying her face in the Sorceress' bosom, Kordelina blindly let her sorrow flow.

"It was not a whim," she wept. "We were in love. I swear we were in love."

Saturnalia looked up at Solomon sadly as she pressed the side of her face against Kordelina's forehead. "I know you were," she said. Opening her heart, Saturnalia felt her unbearable despair. She let its burning enter her veins; the girl's suffering took over her limbs like a demon trying to tear her apart. What horror this child had experienced, she thought, and she was filled with sympathy for her. Closing her eyes, Saturnalia bore the intensity in silence until she felt her relax.

"You have repeatedly challenged my authority, and this time, Saturnalia, you have exhausted my benevolence," Jara ranted, as she paced back and forth in front of them. "I should call up the gods now, and have this child you protect so dearly, annihilated."

Saturnalia looked at her intently. "The only spirits you can entreat are the dark spirits, for shadows cannot dwell in an untainted heart. Your malevolence has no power here."

Jara laughed despicably. "You who profess to have pure light, you are the one who instructed this wretch. You sanctify yourself in lies that make you dabble in the petty destinies of underlings. And you have the audacity to rebuke me!"

"I do not wish to wage my hostilities against yours, for such a battle would only disintegrate what closeness we might still be able to salvage. As it is, anything that remains is being divided at its core with each word we speak," Saturnalia countered. She breathed in deeply, her back straightening, then leaned forward as she exhaled. "I protect this one because as you created me, I am responsible for her having been brought into this world. Kordelina was chosen from the beginning."

Jara stopped, and eyed her dubiously. "Go on," she said with sudden interest. "Perhaps, I will find the words you have to say worthy of my aid. So speak your truths to me, Saturnalia."

Saturnalia sensed that a simple confession on her part might be all Jara would need to spare Kordelina. She could feel herself shiver apprehensively. If she did not chose her words carefully, Jara would refuse to help what was left of her tribe.

"Very well, Jara. I was summoned one night during the celebration of Samhain many years ago by this Chieftain's foster," she began, grimly acknowledging Solomon. "Deireadh, his banished wife, had been travailing for many hours with a child who refused to be born. As Deireadh's strength weakened, she began to call on the dark spirits for her life. Of course, they answered her pleas since she was known as the Black Druidess, and they were well accustomed to her voice. They promised to spare her life, but in recompense, they demanded the baby's soul. When I arrived, I believe the foul woman was trying to enter into her infant's body, and I could not knowingly allow one so evil to be reborn. So, I entreated the heavens for mercy and with all of my power, I screamed the divine prayers, and requested one of pure spirit. As I felt the ethers release its soul, I realized that this child was special. I had visited with her many times in my dreams, and she had spoken in my thoughts long before I had come to this place.

"Realizing she was about to be overtaken, Deireadh began ripping her own flesh with her fingernails, mutilating herself. Fearing that she would harm the infant, I took my dagger, cut open her womb, and removed the babe. The child was so desperate for air that her face was blue, and using my own essence, I breathed life into her body."

She met Solomon's eye as she remembered the somber occasion. He gazed back at her with compassion, finding relief in the truth at last being known.

"With her first gasp of air, I realized she had been waiting for the right time to come into the world because she was destined to serve an important purpose. As I bathed her tiny body, I understood that this little girl had a preordained destiny that I could not hinder. I heard the gods whisper to me the name, Kordelina."

She looked down at the girl listening in silence. What a painful thing it must be for her to hear this. More than anyone, Saturnalia knew how hard she had labored to reduce the mystery of her life, living by trusting in her instincts. Lifting her hand to her brow, Saturnalia felt Kordelina move away from her.

"Kordelina, I did what I believed was right for you then. If anyone had known the circumstances of your birth, I truly believed they would have brought harm to you, and I loved you too much to have that happen. We pay dearly for such powerful emotions," she said contritely.

Putting her face in her hands, Saturnalia took a moment to collect herself. Then she turned to Jara, her face older but decidedly more tenacious than before. "So if you seek vengeance on her, you must seek it on me as well, and we both know that you cannot, and will not, destroy me. You still have political power, and I ask you to use it to preserve what is left of us."

Jara smiled bitterly. "You push me to this? How can you think that my anger could possibly be placated by your woeful tale? Really Saturnalia, how trite a being you have become. All this time you have been nothing but stubborn and unwilling to fulfill anything but your own rebellious vision for your clan, and it has finally amounted to this."

Jara scowled at Kordelina in disgust, believing she was responsible for dividing Saturnalia's loyalty. "You could have had gold and silver at your feet," she said to Kordelina. "But for mortal lust, you have prostituted yourself. I can see it in your face, and I can see the face of the one with whom you laid. It was in your eyes while you danced before him."

Kordelina gave no response as the old Druidess looked at Solomon and Saturnalia, her face brimming with the desire to punish.

"Yes, Saturnalia, I do believe you have seen the error of your ways, and for that, I will cooperate," she said. "I will use my status with Caesar to insure the safety of these refugees—but only on one condition."

"What is that?" Solomon asked defensively.

"This child has made a mockery of me, and has forsaken the laws. I will ensure your passage only if she is left to her own ruin. She shall be an outcast for all eternity, never to be recognized as anything but an abomination by the Celtic people. Perhaps Caesar's army will have some better use for this vermin," she stated.

"No!" Saturnalia argued. "How can you request such a thing after the way even you have betrayed these people? Kordelina has done nothing compared to your deeds."

"Those are my terms," she declared. "You may refuse them if you wish. Still, I would caution you not to risk the lives of the others for your selfishness. For as is plain by this situation, you have done it before, and the ill-fortune it has caused is still with you. Do not make the same mistake twice."

Saturnalia looked at Kordelina helplessly, but to her surprise, she saw no bitterness in the young girl's reflection.

"Saturnalia, it does not matter what Jara says about me," Kordelina told her without resentment. "Because I know that I am in the will of the gods, not her.

The night the festival began, I went into your chamber and was visited there by a dream of the future. It was given to me as a gift from the Goddess, and what I saw made me understand that I do have an important purpose here. As long as I am true to it, no one will bring me harm."

Saturnalia's green eyes fixed on her pensively. "And what was your dream?" she questioned.

Kordelina smiled, and all at once, appeared serene. "I saw my life as it would come to pass, and I realized that through our love, Aonghus and I would bring forth a new ruler who would one day take this island back from Rome. That is why I had to be with Aonghus in the grove; that is where this spirit has dwelt for many years, and it is here on Anglesey that he must be born. I believe that this island has always belonged to him."

Before Saturnalia could reply, Jara came furiously at Kordelina. Kordelina got to her feet immediately, her repose transformed into panic. Her head pounded, and she thought it would surely burst open as Jara stared disdainfully into her eyes. She saw in the hag's dark pupils dim pictures of her slain brothers, and the settlement in flames. The familiar scent of the woods, the sunshine, and fresh grass were replaced by repugnant odors of simmering flesh. Then she sensed the absolute anguish of being filled with the perfume of Aonghus' skin.

Jara was invading her mind; she knew how defenseless Kordelina was at that moment. Everything she loved was being destroyed as punishment. Shadows of naked bodies locked together. At first, they were gentle silhouettes, tenderly making love, then they became heinous visions of demented people tearing each other's flesh from their bodies, and stuffing it gluttonously into their mouths.

Kordelina touched her torso, with the dried blood on her tunic, as if it were a foreign object as she relived the sight of her knife parting the soldier's brow. She was haunted by the butchering of his flawless face, and was consumed by the agony of her kill.

Frozen in Jara's gaze, she felt as if her spirit had disconnected from the surrounding physical world. She was sinking and could not look away. Her mind flashed on Aonghus' decomposing body in the clearing. His fingers were clutching the ground beneath him, and he was writhing in torment as the maggots invaded each orifice of his body.

"There is no deliverance for you," Jara whispered. "This is what your memories have become."

Kordelina wanted to scream, but could not. Holding up her hand as if trying to block the spiritual assault, her thoughts begged silently for mercy.

Realizing what was taking place, Saturnalia came alongside her and wrapped her arm around her shoulder. "What you are seeing is not real," she said in her ear. "Resist her; you were not given the spirit of fear, but of love. Draw on the joy of the life blossoming within you. It is strong."

"Were it not for you, I would crucify this underling. I do not care what she says, she has been given nothing by the Goddess! But for all your insolence, I do still love you, Saturnalia, and will do as you ask, when you ask. I do not respond to orders," Jara taunted.

Saturnalia bit her lip and looked across at Solomon. He stood in anxious silence, incapable of understanding what was taking place.

"Please let her be," she said softly.

"So be it," Jara responded, and turned her back.

Kordelina was on the verge of fainting as Saturnalia embraced her. The sudden weight against her body forced her to step back.

"We cannot help each other any further," she said wiping the perspiration from Kordelina's cheeks. "Our time is near, and this tribe must begin again. I would fight against her, but what power I have left must be used to preserve the others. You have your own power, Kordelina, you must use it now."

"I know," she replied, her throat parched. "It is foolishness to risk the voyage without Jara's help. Truly, Saturnalia, she has issued me no sentence, for I do believe that my lot is to remain here. I know in my heart that the babe must be born to this soil because no matter how many Romans tread on it, it is still sacred to us. And you must understand that despite your wrath toward Aonghus, he gave his life for me, and I cannot bear to see him defiled by Romans. I will put him to rest peacefully, so that when he returns, he can find me again.

"Do not despair for my safety, I have places to hide and I know the skills of a warrior. Perhaps it sounds odd, but I think that this is why the child's spirit finds me worthy, since I can and will protect him with all my might."

The sadness overflowed in Saturnalia as she brushed the hair away from Kordelina's face. As she did this, Kordelina ran her fingertips over Saturnalia's features, watching her green eyes glitter with the awareness of her touch.

"Strange, how we should come to such an end," Kordelina said, her eyes watering. "There were times when I used to think that this world we have shared meant nothing, and at night when we closed our eyes, the beautiful dreams brought by our sleep were the true reality. Yet I do now believe that the heavens allow us to live the secrets of our souls despite what the waking world forbids. And our lives are spent seeking the truths of our dreams. All that I feel inside me now is worth knowing, and I will not repent for my desires."

"Nor should you ever," Saturnalia replied, kissing her cheek. "Be strong, I want you to survive. When you hear my voice, listen closely, it will speak of truths as well. By my very essence, I promise you that."

Kordelina hugged her close. "Speak my name in your new land, and I will forever remember the sound of yours while I am here," she said, releasing her.

She looked at Solomon and forced a melancholy smile as the tears welled in both their eyes. "I know what you are thinking right now, Chieftain," Kordelina told him. "You want to threaten Jara into reconsidering her actions, and that through your physical strength you can force her to take me, but you cannot. By now, these waters are full of Roman ships, and she has the one thing that you need. It is my choice to remain here, not my punishment. And for Aonghus' sake, please know that his loyalty to you and his people remained steadfast. You can be proud of him for the rest of your days in this life. Chieftain, I would have you take Lir, because Aonghus always dreamed of seeing a new land. It would make him happy to know that his horse would carry you across it."

She saw his face take on tremendous despondency as she spoke.

"Kordelina, let me call you Daughter just once. You have my word that I will return for you very soon," he said emotionally. "And in the time we are apart, never forget that like the wind, your soul is without end."

"As is yours, Chieftain," she answered through strained speech. "Let your heart heal itself because the sound of your voice calling me Daughter is enough."

Kordelina turned away from him and went to her family. Kissing Koven and Niall goodbye, she lingered a moment in Enda's arms.

"This is only for a time, Mother. This violence will pass," she said, kissing her.

"Kordelina, if it is your will to stay, please find Aonghus, if you can. Together you will be safe," she said, unaware that her son was dead.

"Yes, Mother, I will," she answered. "You must be on the boat now."

The vessel was launched onto the strait. Everyone turned to look at her, except Koven, who was speaking of a time long ago when he and Aonghus had gone hunting. Weeping, Saturnalia kept her back turned and Conn wrapped his arms around her, pulling her close.

Kordelina saw the boat catch the current. It appeared a tiny but promising image in the morning light, and as she watched the cranes circle above it, she knew that somehow it would arrive safely in another land. Her clan would thrive again, and she had much to do until then, she thought. Hiding her face in Macha's neck, she cried as long as the tears would flow. When she lifted her head again, she found she could no longer see the boat from where she stood.

Forcing herself onto her horse once more, she rode in a daze to the clearing where Aonghus' corpse lay. Dismounting, she neared his body with a kind of blindness, as though it took all of her courage to face him again. The events that had occurred throughout the night had taken place amid such chaos and panic that she could barely grasp them as true. As she struggled to look at her dead lover, she could not fathom that fate had answered their heart's exchange with such an irremediable blow.

She felt the smooth handle of his knife in her belt, and thought that were it not for the child within her, she would have used it on herself to be with him in the Otherworld. Yet she knew, as he had known when he gazed up into the moonlight for the last time, that such potent pleasure as they had known would grow in love and fortify her limbs in the months to come.

Picking up his bronze shield, she extended her fingertips and touched its glass inlays. How handsome he had looked the morning before as he stood beside Solomon and watched her enter the festival. Every step she had taken, from the time she had left Saturnalia's cottage at sunrise, had been to come closer to him.

The magic of his image did not leave her as she took his armor and Macha, and made her way into the shrubbery where they could not be seen. She needed to rest before she could muster enough strength to move Aonghus' body.

Taking the corma from her saddlebag, she drank it slowly, letting it roll down her throat. Closing her eyes for moments between sips, she would peer through the bushes each time she opened them to make certain Aonghus was still there.

"Please do not leave me yet, Aonghus," she murmured. "Watch over me while I rest for awhile."

Setting her sword close by, she slept with Macha standing over her. Kordelina knew if anyone arrived, the mare would awaken her immediately.

Drifting into a dark void of sleep, she was aware of nothing but her hot belly and the power of Aonghus' son. At times, she felt its presence was the only thing that tethered her to the earth, along with the feeling that Aonghus would stay close as long as his seed needed protecting. She had the sense that the two of them had entwined their spirits. Aonghus was the fallen warrior, doomed by destiny, his blades now broken as he passed into death while his son, all youth and bravery, clashed his broad sword together with his father's martyred one in the loud pursuit of life ahead. Then, through the murky desolation of her own fatigue she suddenly heard someone approaching. At first, it was barely detectable. Its vibration gave rise to a panic within her as, gradually, it turned into the obscure pattern of footsteps treading across soft sand. Kordelina felt as if the sound was only audible through the earth, because without her horse ever being aware of it, it grew continually louder in its advance.

In her drowsiness, her eyes felt as if they were sealed shut, and she considered that perhaps she was meant to lie still and let this intruder pass by altogether. Then she felt someone blow lightly on her face to awaken her. It was such a sweet breath that it caused her to reach out to it. When she did, her hand was unmistakably grasped within the strong, warm palm of another, and she instantly recognized the calloused fingers that had, just last night, caressed her naked breasts.

Aonghus, she called to him in her thoughts.

She was entranced by his presence, craving his nepenthe kisses which did not come. Rather, she was lured back by his call to life, the kind of summons that creates desire and jostles the realization of purpose in the outer world. Opening her eyes, she wanted desperately to find him beside her. As the green leaves of the oak trees came sharply into view, she found herself alone gripping the handle of her sword, and she knew she must defend herself once more.

Macha flaunted her full tail as Kordelina raised herself into the saddle and rested low upon her thick mane. She was holding her reins in her left hand despite the throb from her wound; the other, which poised the weapon, felt as strong as if it had absorbed the might of both.

Watching the horse's ears twitch, she stared in the direction they pointed, and her body grew taut and ready for battle. Someone was very near because suddenly, Macha pinned her ears and her flesh started to quiver. Trained as a war-horse, the mare remained absolutely motionless as a Roman commander entered the clearing.

Although it was black with smoke, Kordelina instantly recognized the hateful lines of his face and the ugly mouth that grimaced to reveal his missing front teeth. She assumed he had returned to look for armor since he no longer wore a chest plate, nor carried a weapon. Searching the area around the inert warrior, he stopped with his back to her and gave a cold-blooded snicker.

"You Celts die so easily," he remarked, and kicked Aonghus in the ribs. "It's like slaughtering sheep."

At that moment it was as if an abhorrent spell had been cast over Kordelina. The hatred she had for this man was so fierce, that unable to utter a single sound, she boldly charged out of the bushes to attack. She moved with such speed that he did not have time to defend himself before she swooped down on him, and ran her sword across the back of his knees, slashing his tendons. Crippled instantly, he dropped forward, his eyes wide with the light of helpless surprise as Kordelina turned her horse, and came at him again, this time inflicting a deep gash above his elbow.

The commander grunted, and reached around with one arm before crying out at the realization that she had maimed the other.

Kordelina rode around him in dizzying circles as his single, useful arm flailed about trying to protect himself from her mock assaults. She pretended to go for his head first, then she charged back at him with the tip of her sword pointed directly at his groin. It created a surge of dominance in her to see such a huge bulk of a man cower to her punishment. Masterfully prolonging it, she did not stop until the blood from his legs formed circles in the grass around his knees and the scarlet streaked his torso. Only then did she stop her horse opposite him, and savor his disabled gasp as his eyes met hers.

She was a chilling sight to behold with her blanched face shadowed by smudges of dried blood that ceased at the collar of her red-stained jerkin. The dark borders of her eyes intensified their ghostly green cast, and the fact that she had not vocalized a single sound during her assault gripped the soldier with unbounded terror.

Lowering her gaze to the dead Celt stretched out like an altar in front of the injured Roman, she raised her eyes and her weapon simultaneously, and stared at him with calloused resolve.

"Aonghus was a great warrior. He would have been King," she said. "Speak this truth and I promise to kill you swiftly."

The man responded with a vacant look, as though it took a moment for him to understand what she meant. Then his ugly mouth curled into an invidious snarl. "You are only a child—you could never kill me!"

At that, Kordelina dug her heels into Macha's sides, spurring the horse forward so that it leaped over Aonghus and touched down dangerously close to the Roman. Thinking he was going to be trampled, he cried out and she answered him with a clean slice across his shoulder blades.

The red oozed down his back as she circled, waving her sword close to his head to unnerve him. She was silent, save the swish of the bronze blade and the thud of horse hooves as she came at him again, clipping off his ear lobe. The warm fluid drained down his neck, as she charged one last time using her weapon to rip open the flesh of his good arm. Then she stopped in the same place as before.

"Aonghus was a great warrior. He would have been King," she repeated over the grinding of Macha's teeth on the metal bit. "Speak this truth and I promise to kill you swiftly."

The Roman's face twisted with pain, and for a moment she thought she detected a hint of sadness in his pale eyes as she slid out of the saddle, and slowly walked toward him. He offered one feeble attempt to ward her off, but he was pitifully defenseless. And for him to realize that it was a young woman standing over him, strong and galling, was more intolerable than any of his seeping wounds.

Kordelina's appearance intensified as she looked down on her mangled victim. She would fulfill her promise to Aonghus now, she thought, as she yanked the knife from her belt and roughly drove it into the Roman's bicep.

"I have no use for your head because you have destroyed my village, and I no longer have a doorway to hang it from," she told him, twisting it deeper into his muscle as he yelped with pain. "Instead, I would have your heart to take back the power that you stole from Aonghus and to bring strength to his unborn heir within me."

The soldier's chin dropped to his chest causing the cut on his back to pull apart and bleed even more. It soaked into the material of his shirt as he stared at the hideous opening in Aonghus' chest, then shook his head in refusal.

Roughly seizing the back of his hair, Kordelina jerked his face up and made him look at her. "Have mercy on yourself; since I have none for you, your death will be a slow, torturous one."

The Roman's eyes grew dim and as he slouched forward, Kordelina took on a more rigid form.

"You were there," he mumbled, his body trembling for the first time. "Why did I not kill you as well?"

"Because my will is stronger than yours," she answered.

"So it is," he admitted, then paused as if contemplating his own defeat. "Aonghus was a great warrior. He would have been King."

Stepping in front of him, Kordelina raised her sword with both hands, and let out a lamentable howl that sounded like a devoted hound mourning the loss of its master.

———

"They will be burning the oak groves soon," Saturnalia murmured as she stared at the blanket of fumes rising from the burning villages. "Caesar will humiliate us for believing in our gods."

The eastern sun perforated the smoke to cast a heavenly light on the all but tranquil currents of the Menai Strait. The water was choppy with the gloomy presence of Roman vessels ahead, and the one lone transport of refugees seemed a strange spectacle among them.

Koven, Conn, Brendan, and Berrig manned the oars, the straining sound of the wooden sculls barely endurable as they anxiously approached the mouth of the channel. Solomon was at the stern, guiding the rudder through the treacherous tides. Were it not for the Imperialist ship blocking their path, they would be out on the open sea soon enough. But as the Chieftain turned to speak a word of comfort to Saturnalia, the heavy ocean breeze blew the hair away from his eyes, and he caught sight of the soldiers on deck arming themselves with bows and arrows. Forgetting what he was about to say, he hurriedly offered the helm to Conn and approached Jara instead.

"What are you planning to do about this?" he barked, as he shoved the old Druidess to the front of the craft and pointed. "You better give them your best smile because they do not seem to recognize your face."

Jara turned to him contemptuously. "Do not handle me like that again," she reprimanded.

"That's only the beginning," Solomon huffed. "Tell them that you are Rome's whore so that they will let us pass."

Jara raised a hand to slap him, but Solomon caught her by the wrist. He could feel her trembling and he knew that it was not because she was afraid of him, but of the Romans.

"You have no influence at all, do you?" he challenged, shaking her by one arm. "Your centurion had no intention of saving you. It was all a farce to get you off Anglesey before they killed you, too."

Saturnalia faced her elder with a look of bewilderment. "Is that true? Was Flavius going to kill you as well, and you only lied your way onto this boat to save yourself? That is why you were so determined to leave Kordelina behind; if she had come there would not have been a place for you."

The old woman looked frantic as a crash of water unexpectedly spilled over the bow and drenched her robe. Startled, she fell forward and found herself clinging to Solomon for protection.

"Get away!" he growled, and yanked his arm from her grasp. "You would sacrifice anything or anyone to save yourself. Are you planning to turn us over as prisoners? I am sure Flavius would find that endearing!"

Jara's eyes showed sudden fright as she let out a laugh that was almost a sob. "No, that is not it! I am under the protection of Rome. My well-being is guaranteed as is the well-being of anyone whom I deem worthy."

Solomon felt a madness swelling in him at the very sight of her. He shoved her away from him with such force that only the wooden railing prevented her from falling overboard.

"You are an imposter!" he bellowed. "You are responsible for the death of my people. You took my daughter from me, and because of you, Aonghus is gone as well! Offer me no further reasons why I should respect your influence with

Rome, Jara. You are lower than the most vile beast. If we survive this, I swear by the gods that I'm going to sell you to the first merchant I find. And if he will not buy you from me, I will offer him my sword to take you."

Jara's expression remained unchanged as the enemy vessel came closer. Aware that its imposing figure now dominated the wavering wrinkles of the strait, the tribe clustered together for safety. Crouching low, they held the warrior's shields over their heads to protect themselves.

Lir began to nervously paw the bottom of the transport with his front hoof as it bowed and plunged through the turbulent water. They could hear commands shouted out above them, then the first arrow hit the deck like a flash of lightning, and Conn rushed in front of Saturnalia with his shield.

"Get low and stay behind me," he told her, as he knelt and angled it to deflect the sudden onslaught of arrows.

Jara lay flat on her belly and tried to crawl behind Lir for cover, but Solomon caught her by the ankle and dragged her to the bow. Grabbing her by the collar, he forced her to stand while the soldiers reloaded.

"Tell them that Flavius has permitted our passage!" he shouted, removing his dagger from its sheath. "Because if you really are of no use to us, I think this boat would travel much faster with a little less weight."

"How dare you threaten me," she countered, her eyes angrily glinting back at him. He had pushed her too far. She had not come to this point in her life to lose her power to an impudent chieftain, after having dealt with the eminent forces of Rome. And she knew that if she did not master this situation and assert her position, she would not stand a chance once they reached land. Her instincts became suddenly calm, and she offered a mockish grin to hide the fury that she felt. "Being so troublesome will come at great expense to you, Chieftain."

"I am waiting, Druidess," Solomon dared, loathing the twinkling of malice that now showed in her cunning gaze. "We are running out of time."

He got down on one knee, holding his shield in front of him, and Jara stood still with indignation.

"When you see just how much authority I have with your conquerers, on your knees is where you will stay," she declared, choking back rage.

The old Druidess advanced to the front of the boat in a lordly fashion, and waving both arms in the air, demanded that the attack be stopped.

"We are under the protection of the Imperialist rule!" she yelled, authoritatively. "This is a Roman vessel of the centurion, Flavius. Hail Caesar!"

The soldiers had already released their bows, and one of the bolts lodged in her arm, causing her to cry out.

"I am a Druidess under the protection of the centurion, Flavius. I aided in this invasion. Hail, Caesar!" she screeched. Then, she was silent and Solomon felt her body sag against his shield. One limp arm hooked itself over the top of his armor, and he saw her fingers spasm, then immediately relax.

Certain that there would be another siege of arrows, the Chieftain held his breath and waited for the deadly whine of their shafts to penetrate the salty air, but it did not come. All he heard was Lir snort as he tried to break his shank. A single dart, wrapped in cloth, landed beside him.

"We did not see your emblem at a distance," a voice called from the ship. "Use this next time to show your allegiance."

Solomon looked up and saw the boat's commander. He stared at him suspiciously as Saturnalia unraveled the fabric and held out the Roman flag.

"Hail, Caesar!" the commander bellowed.

"Hail, Caesar!" the voices of his men echoed, as the transport passed.

Still bearing the weight of Jara's body upon his armor, Solomon lowered it to find that an arrow had pierced her heart. Saturnalia rushed to her side and attempted to revive her, but it was useless. Jara was dead.

"Caesar's emblem is burnt into the wood," Conn said, looking over the bow. "We never needed to bring Jara with us at all."

Saturnalia removed the arrow and held her close. "Perhaps we did. Perhaps Jara needed this chance to make restitution for her deeds. Too much power can corrupt anyone. She was not always evil, and I will mourn the Druidess she used to be."

Absorbed in Jara's lifeless face, Saturnalia started to pray in the ancient tongue known only to the druids. With tears rolling down her creamy cheeks, she drew holy symbols across the dead woman's forehead with her thumb, then lifted her body in her arms. Resisting any help from either Conn or Solomon, she dropped the corpse overboard into the strait.

A mass of bubbles erupted around the body as it plunged below the surface. Twisting the end of his mustache between his fingers, Solomon stared at it a moment, then turned questioningly to Saturnalia.

"It is an offering to the Goddess," she said softly, then made her way to the stern and sat alone in prayer.

———

As Jara's body was left bobbing face down in the rough waters of the strait, Kordelina ate the last piece of the Roman's heart. She had cut it in half, consuming one part to nourish her unborn child while saving the other for Aonghus' body. She knew that if she replaced his heart with the heart of his enemy, when he returned to the world his power would not be diminished.

With Macha's aid, she moved his body into the bushes where it would be concealed until nightfall. And taking a long swig of corma to wash down the salty taste of Roman blood, she tied her drinking bag closed then picked up the piece of the heart that remained. Gently placing it in the empty cavity of her lover's chest, she held her hand over it for a long time, and envisioned that her body gave it heat. Neither the living nor the dead could claim him now, for he belonged only to her.

"We share the same heart, you and I," she told him, tears filling her eyes. "It will beat as one in our child."

Covering him with the animal fur that had warmed them while they made love in the darkness, she lay down beside him. The sun was as bright on this morning as it had been the morning before when the festival had just begun. In a single night, life had changed. Now the earth would feel different beneath her feet when she walked through the fields of wheat and heather, and as long as the Romans remained, the fragrance of the spring flowers in bloom would not seem as sweet. No longer would the azure sky hover above an unspoiled tribe who quarreled among themselves about personal valors, then fell humbly before their gods. Nor would the hunted boar be slain to honor the first full moon following Brigantia's celebration. Soon, Caesar's people would conduct their own rituals and harvest the autumn fields. And the festivals of Beltaine and Samhain would be perceived as nothing more than the fervent display of heathens who did not know how to act more noble.

The consecrated oak groves that had played host to deities and dreams for generations would cease to be the hallowed cathedrals of passionate Celts who honored the elements and rejoiced at the season's change. And for a time, the darkening rain clouds and thunderbolts would come down on a fetid landscape with troubled hearts.

How could one night change so much, she wondered, looking at Aonghus and smoothing her hand across his face. Even in death she could not help but love the look of him, as she leaned over and kissed his lips. She thought of how, in spite of his slaughter, he still possessed an impenetrable dignity she would always worship.

Feeling exhaustion start to overtake her, Kordelina knew she must remain still and wait for nightfall so that she could return to her hiding place until she was healed and could prepare for their child. A mild ocean breeze brushed over her, and she imagined it blowing through each pore of her skin, cleansing and fortifying her for the uncertain days ahead. Looking up, she saw two hawks circling above her. Their lovely tricolored wings were spread against the gray-blue sky, and knowing these birds of prey mated for life, Kordelina was filled with a euphoric sense of peace. In their souls, she and Aonghus would be united forever.

The sound of distant hoofbeats headed away from her toward the strait, and gently placing her head on Aonghus' shoulder, she closed her eyes and imagined them to be the gentle beating of his heart.

Glossary

Beltaine: A feast at the beginning of May, honoring the Celtic sun god and healer, Belenos. It signified the arrival of summer and the time when the cattle left their winter shelter for open pastures. The celebration included a fertility ritual, a sacrifice, and the lighting of huge bonfires between which the cattle were herded in order to rid them of any evil spirits that might have come into their midst during the dark winter months.

Boudicca: Icenian Queen of East Anglia, who was so outraged by the Roman injustices to her people that she commanded a bloody uprising against them in A.D. 61.

Brigantes: Celtic tribe whose patron goddess was Brigantia. Under the rule of Queen Cartimandua, they primarily inhabited northern England, with the exception of a tribe on Anglesey who named the Afron Braint (River Brigantia) in her honor, for nourishing their livestock and farmland with her waters.

Brigantia: The sacred mother-goddess of fertility and patronness of childbirth. It is said that she was born at sunrise in a dwelling that burned with blazes that reached to the heavens, and her breath gave life to the dead. In her multiple form she signifies the virgin bride, matron, and old hag.

celsine: The clients of a warrior who placed themselves under his protection rendering payment for armed guard. The prestige and wealth of a warrior was gauged by how many celes (clients) he watched over.

client kingdoms: Celtic settlements whose leaders maintained tribal rule while becoming politically associated with Rome.

corma: A thick wheaten ale sweetened with honey that was a common drink of the Celts.

cowbane: An extremely poisonous herb also referred to as water hemlock. It was once used to treat various brain disorders causing side effects of abdominal cramps, dilated pupils, delirium, and convulsions.

Druids: A powerful religious order whose role was that of diplomats, astrologers, teachers, and healers. They interceded with the gods on behalf of the Celtic people, as well as overseeing sacred ceremonies. Although it was not unusual for a king to have a personal druid to attend him, most members of the order spent their time traveling between tribes, administering civil rights and worship.

Festival of Brigantia: The sacred Fire Festival of the mother-goddess in early February. Also called Imbolc (derived from the word "oimelc," meaning sheep's milk), it proclaims the coming of spring and the appearance of newborn lambs with a fertility ritual to the virgin bride and childbirth.

fianna: Groups of young warriors who, after their initiation into warriorhood, left tribal areas for a designated period of time to hunt and fight. It was designed to give them military training by making warfare into a sport, while affording the opportunity to gain distinction through individual combat.

fidcheall: A wooden board game designed with sockets and movable pegs.

fibulae: Small broaches attached by a chain to close V-necked tunics.

fosterage: A Celtic practice of bringing up and educating a child by others. The foster was taught a skill as well as formed close bonds with another family that would be beneficial later in life. Beginning in early childhood, the foster did not return to his own household until puberty.

Hyssop: A flowering plant that was used as an astringent and to treat gripping pains in the stomach and bowels.

jerkin: A sleeveless leather waistcoat.

Macha: Pagan reference to the horse goddess also known as Epona, or the Welsh, Rhiannon. An important deity who protected the horses in battle and was associated with the aspects of fertility.

Otherworld: A world beneath the earth's surface that was accessible through lakes and caves, making them sacred places for offerings. The journey to the Otherworld was not considered an ending, but a beginning. It was believed to be a land of innocence and pleasure.

reincarnation: The Celts upheld the religious belief that the soul never died, rather, it proceeded into another body for rebirth. It was preferable to have a short, but courageous, life rather than one that was long and without valor.

Samhain: The Celtic celebration of the Dead, observing the end of summer. It was customary to gather a large bulk of wood and dress it in the clothes of those who had passed to the Otherworld on the last night of the year, then light it on fire. The period from the end of one Celtic year, October 31, to the start of a new one, November 1, was a time when the barriers between mortals and the supernatural world did not exist. It also related to the rite of sacred kingship.

sacrifice: Oblations made in specific holy places or divine ceremonies which were meant to procure the favor of the gods on behalf of the people. They ordinarily came in the form of silver ornaments, jewelry, weapons, and votive offerings. Although human and animal sacrifice was associated with the Druids, it was not a common ritual. Rather it was a special occurrence in which divine rites, were administered so that the individual was extremely honored to be chosen to act as a messenger to the gods.

torque: A collar made of precious metal that had great social and religious significance. It was an indication of status, rank, and power, and was usually adorned with specific dieties to protect and empower the wearer.

woad: An herb used to make a blue dye which the Celtic warrriors applied to their shaven bodies before going into battle.

women in Celtic society: The position of women was held in high regard. They were entitled to be landowners, enter the political arena, choose their own husbands, divorce at will, fight in battles, and take advantage of every social opportunity afforded to men.

wormwood: A bitter herb used as a medicinal tonic to treat a variety of health disorders, and as a compress for bruises.

PRοnuncιλτιοn Guide

Consonants:
b d h l m n p t are pronounced the same as in English
c is hard as in the letter "k"
ch is like the Scottish word "loch"
dd very much like a soft "th" in English
f is like the letter "v" in English
ff is the English "f"
g is hard as in the word "go"
i sounds like "ea" in the word "eat"
ll is pronounced by putting the tip of the tongue behind the teeth and speaking
      the letter "l" while raising the tongue and expelling air
ph is spoken as a phonetic "f" as in photograph
r is the rolled "r" with an aspirate
s is hard as in "sell"

Vowels:
The emphasis of the words is normally on the last syllable, which would determine whether the vowel is long or short. Although there are variants, the first
syllable is ordinarily long, and the last syllable is usually short.

a short is as in the word "cat"
   long is as in the word "part"
e short is as in the word "pet"
   long is as in the word "sane"
i short is as in the word "ring"
   long is as in the word "sea"
o short is as in the word "pot"
   long is a guttural sound similar to the word "dawn"
u has only one sound that is similar to the "y" in the word, "mystery," but with
      more emphasis
w short is as in the word "book"
    long is as in the word "moon"
y represents many diverse sounds that change in certain situations, including:
      "u" as in the word "hungry"; "i" as in the word "spin"; or "e" as in the
      word "tea"

STAY IN TOUCH

On the following pages you will find listed, with their current prices, some of the books now available on related subjects. Your book dealer stocks most of these and will stock new titles in the Llewellyn series as they become available. We urge your patronage.

To obtain our full catalog, to keep informed about new titles as they are released and to benefit from informative articles and helpful news, you are invited to write for our bi-monthly news magazine/catalog, *Llewellyn's New Worlds of Mind and Spirit*. A sample copy is free, and it will continue coming to you at no cost as long as you are an active mail customer. Or you may subscribe for just $10.00 in U.S.A. and Canada ($20.00 overseas, first class mail). Many bookstores also have *New Worlds* available to their customers. Ask for it.

Stay in touch! In *New Worlds'* pages you will find news and features about new books, tapes and services, announcements of meetings and seminars, articles helpful to our readers, news of authors, products and services, special money-making opportunities, and much more.

Llewellyn's New Worlds of Mind and Spirit
P.O. Box 64383-156, St. Paul, MN 55164-0383, U.S.A.
* * *

TO ORDER BOOKS AND TAPES

If your book dealer does not have the books described on the following pages readily available, you may order them direct from the publisher by sending full price in U.S. funds, plus $3.00 for postage and handling for orders *under* $10.00; $4.00 for orders *over* $10.00. There are no postage and handling charges for orders over $50.00. Postage and handling rates are subject to change. UPS Delivery: We ship UPS whenever possible. Delivery guaranteed. Provide your street address as UPS does not deliver to P.O. Boxes. UPS to Canada requires a $50.00 minimum order. Allow 4-6 weeks for delivery. Orders outside the U.S.A. and Canada: Air-mail—add retail price of book; add $5.00 for each non-book item (tapes, etc.); add $1.00 per item for surface mail.

FOR GROUP STUDY AND PURCHASE

Because there is a great deal of interest in group discussion and study of the subject matter of this book, we feel that we should encourage the adoption and use of this particular book by such groups by offering a special quantity price to group leaders or agents.

Our Special Quantity Price for a minimum order of five copies of *The Celtic Heart* is $44.85 cash-with-order. This price includes postage and handling within the United States. Minnesota residents must add 6.5% sales tax. For additional quantities, please order in multiples of five. For Canadian and foreign orders, add postage and handling charges as above. Credit card (VISA, MasterCard, American Express) orders are accepted. Charge card orders only may be phoned in free within the U.S.A. or Canada by dialing 1-800-THE-MOON. For customer service, call 1-612-291-1970. Mail orders to:

LLEWELLYN PUBLICATIONS
P.O. Box 64383-156, St. Paul, MN 55164-0383, U.S.A.

THE 21 LESSONS OF MERLYN
A Study in Druid Magic & Lore
by Douglas Monroe

For those with an inner drive to touch genuine Druidism—or who feel that the lore of King Arthur touches them personally—*The 21 Lessons of Merlyn* will come as an engrossing adventure and psychological journey into history and magic. This is a complete introductory course in Celtic Druidism, packaged within the framework of 21 authentic and expanded folk story/ lessons that read like a novel. These lessons, set in late Celtic Britain ca A.D. 500, depict the training and initiation of the real King Arthur at the hands of the real Merlyn-the-Druid: one of the last great champions of Paganism within the dawning age of Christianity. As you follow the boy Arthur's apprenticeship from his first encounter with Merlyn in the woods, you can study your own program of Druid apprentiship with the detailed practical ritual applications that follow each story. The 21 folk tales were collected by the author in Britain and Wales during a ten-year period; the Druidic teachings are based on the actual, never-before-published 16th-century manuscript entitled *The Book of Pheryllt*.

0-87542-496-1, 420 pgs., 6 x 9, illus., photos, softcover $12.95

YEAR OF MOONS, SEASON OF TREES
Mysteries and Rites of Celtic Tree Magick
by Pattalee Glass-Koentop

Many of you are drawn to Wicca, or the Craft, but do not have teachers or like-minded people around to show you how the religion is practiced. *Year of Moons, Season of Trees* serves as that teacher and as a sourcebook. Most of Witchcraft in America comes from or has been influenced by that of the British Isles. The Druidic sacred trees native to that culture are the focus of this book. The essence, imagery and mythology behind the trees and seasons is vividly portrayed. The author provides the how-to for rituals celebrating Nature through its Moons, its Seasons and Months of Trees. Here is the history, the lore of each tree, the rituals of Temple Workings, songs and chants, even recipes for foods that complete these celebrations. Also included are Ogham correspondence charts, and descriptive lists of solar and lunar trees. This is a valuable sourcebook of material and inspiration.

0-87542-269-1, 264 pgs., 7 x 10, illus., softcover $14.95

CELTIC MAGIC
by D. J. Conway

Many people, not all of Irish descent, have a great interest in the ancient Celts and the Celtic pantheon, and *Celtic Magic* is the map they need for exploring this ancient and fascinating magical culture.

Celtic Magic is for the reader who is either a beginner or intermediate in the field of magic. It provides an extensive "how-to" of practical spell-working. There are many books on the market dealing with the Celts and their beliefs, but none guide the reader to a practical application of magical knowledge for use in everyday life. There is also an in-depth discussion of Celtic deities and the Celtic way of life and worship, so that an intermediate practitioner can expand upon the spellwork to build a series of magical rituals. Presented in an easy-to-understand format, *Celtic Magic* is for anyone searching for new spells that can be worked immediately, without elaborate or rare materials, and with minimal time and preparation.

0-87542-136-9, 240 pgs., mass market, illus.   **$3.95**

THE SACRED CAULDRON
Secrets of the Druids
by Tadhg MacCrossan

Here is a comprehensive course in the history and development of Celtic religious lore, the secrets taught by the Druids, and a guide to the modern performance of the rites and ceremonies as practiced by members of the "Druidactos," a spiritual organization devoted to the revival of this ancient way of life.

The Sacred Cauldron evolved out of MacCrossan's extensive research in comparative mythology and Indo-European linguistics, etymology and archaeology. He has gone beyond the stereotypical image of standing stones and white-robed priests to piece together the truth about Druidism.The reader will find detailed interpretations of the words, phrases and titles that are indigenous to this ancient religion. Here also are step-by-step instructions for ceremonial rites for modern-day practice.

0-87542-103-2, 302 pgs., 5.25 x 8, illus., softcover   **$10.95**

THE HANDBOOK OF CELTIC ASTROLOGY
The 13-Sign Lunar Zodiac of the Ancient Druids
Helena Paterson

Discover your lunar self with *The Handbook of Celtic Astrology!* Solar-oriented astrology has dominated Western astrological thought for centuries, but lunar-based Celtic astrology provides the "Yin" principle that has been neglected in the West—and author Helena Paterson presents new concepts based on ancient Druidic observations, lore and traditions that will redefine Western astrology.

This reference work will take you through the Celtic lunar zodiac, where each lunar month is associated with one of the 13 trees sacred to the Druids: birch, rowan, ash, alder, willow, hawthorn, oak, holly, hazel, vine, ivy, reed and elder. Chapters on each "tree sign" provide comprehensive text on Celtic mythology and gods/desses associated with the sign's ruling tree and planet; general characteristics of natives of the sign; and interpretive notes on the locations of the planets, the Moon, the ascendant and Midheaven as they are placed in any of the three decans of each tree sign. A thorough introduction on chart construction, sign division and the importance of solstices, equinoxes, eclipses and aspects to the Moon guarantees this book will become *the* definitive work on Celtic astrology.

ISBN: 1-56718-509-6, 7 x 10, est. 256 pp., illus.   **$15.00**

WITTA
An Irish Pagan Tradition
by Edain McCoy

The beauty and simplicity which is paganism may never be more evident than in Witta. The Old Religion of Ireland was born of simplicity, of a people who loved their rugged, green Earth Mother and sought to worship her through the resources she provided. Witta prescribes no elaborate tools, ritual dress or rigid and intimidating initiation rites. The magick and the ritual words come, as they did thousands of years ago, from within the heart of the practitioner.

Until now, no practical guide has presented Irish paganism as a religious system within the framework of its history. In *Witta*, you will learn who and what influenced the Wittan religion as we know it today. You will discover the mythology that shaped their deities and learn about the Sabbats which honor them. See how the Druids bridged the gap between the old ways and the new, and understand the inherent power of homespun spellcrafting. Learn about the Celtic Tree system and how the trees relate to magickal practice. Plus, learn how to construct your own rituals in accordance with Wittan tradition.

0-87542-732-4, 288 pgs., 6 x 9, illus., softcover $12.95

MODERN MAGICK
Eleven Lessons in the High Magickal Arts
by Donald Michael Kraig

Modern Magick is the most comprehensive step-by-step introduction to the art of ceremonial magic ever offered. The eleven lessons in this book will guide you from the easiest of rituals and the construction of your magickal tools through the highest forms of magick: designing your own rituals and doing pathworking. Along the way you will learn the secrets of the Kabbalah in a clear and easy-to-understand manner. You will discover the true secrets of invocation (channeling) and evocation, and the missing information that will finally make the ancient grimoires, such as the "Keys of Solomon," not only comprehensible, but usable. This book also contains one of the most in-depth chapters on sex magick ever written. *Modern Magick* is designed so anyone can use it, and it is the perfect guidebook for students and classes. It will also help to round out the knowledge of long-time practitioners of the magickal arts.

0-87542-324-8, 592 pgs., 6 x 9, illus., index, softcover $14.95

THE BOOK OF OGHAM
The Celtic Tree Oracle
by Edred Thorsson

Drink deeply from the very source of the Druids' traditional lore. The oghamic Celtic tradition represents an important breakthrough in the practical study of Celtic religion and magick. Within the pages of *The Book of Ogham* you will find the *complete and authentic* system of divination based on the letters of the Celtic ogham alphabet (commonly designated by tree names), and a whole world of experiential Celtic spirituality.

Come to understand the Celtic Way to new depths, discover methodological secrets shared by the Druids and Drightens of old, receive complete instructions for the practice of ogham divination, and find objective inner truths concealed deep within yourself.

The true and inner learning of oghams is a pathway to awakening the deeply rooted structural patterns of the Celtic psyche or soul. Read, study and work with the ogham oracle. . . open up the mysterious and hidden world within . . . and become part of the eternal stream of tradition that transcends the individual self. Come, and drink directly from the true cauldron of inspiration: the secret lore and practices of the ancient Celtic Druids.

0-87542-783-9, 224 pgs., 6 x 9, illus., glossary, softcover $12.95

ROBIN WOOD TAROT DECK
created and illustrated by Robin Wood
Instructions by Robin Wood and Michael Short

Tap into the wisdom of your subconscious with one of the most beautiful Tarot decks on the market today! Reminiscent of the Rider-Waite deck, the Robin Wood Tarot is flavored with nature imagery and luminous energies that will enchant you and the querant. Even the novice reader will find these cards easy and enjoyable to interpret.

Radiant and rich, these cards were illustrated with a unique technique that brings out the resplendent color of the prismacolor pencils. The shining strength of this Tarot deck lies in its depiction of the Minor Arcana. Unlike other Minor Arcana decks, this one springs to pulsating life. The cards are printed in quality card stock and boxed complete with instruction booklet, which provides the upright and reversed meanings of each card, as well as three basic card layouts. Beautiful and brilliant, the Robin Wood Tarot is a must-have deck!

0-87542-894-0, boxed set: 78-cards with booklet $19.95

THE CRAFTED CUP
Ritual Mysteries of the Goddess and the Grail
by Shadwynn

The Holy Grail—fabled depository of wonder, enchantment and ultimate spiritual fulfillment—is the key by which the wellsprings of a Deeper Life can be tapped for the enhancement of our inner growth. *The Crafted Cup* is a compendium of the teachings and rituals of a distinctly Pagan religious Order—the *Ordo Arcanorum Gradalis*—which incorporates into its spiritual way of worship ritual imagery based upon the Arthurian Grail legends, a reverence towards the mythic Christ, and an appreciation of the core truths and techniques found scattered throughout the New Age movement.

The Crafted Cup is divided into two parts. The first deals specifically with the teachings and general concepts which hold a central place within the philosophy of the *Ordo Arcanorum Gradalis*. The second and larger of the two parts is a complete compilation of the sacramental rites and seasonal rituals which make up the liturgical calendar of the Order. It contains one of the largest collections of Pagan, Grail-oriented rituals yet published.

0-87542-739-1, 420 pgs., 7 X 10, illus., softcover $18.00

THE COMMITTEE
by Raymond Buckland

"Duncan's eyes were glued to the destruct button. He saw that the colonel's hand never did get to it. Yet, even as he watched, he saw the red button move downwards, apparently of its own volition. The rocket blew into a million pieces, and the button came back up. No one, Duncan would swear, had physically touched the button, yet it had been depressed."

The Cold War is back in this psi-techno suspense thriller where international aggressors use psychokinesis, astral projection and other psychic means to circumvent the U.S. intelligence network. When two routine communications satellite launches are inexplicably aborted at Vandenberg Air Force Base in California, one senator suspects paranormal influences. He calls in a writer, two parapsychologists and a psychic housewife—and The Committee is formed. Together, they piece together a sinister occult plot against the United States. The Committee then embarks on a supernatural adventure of a lifetime as they attempt to beat the enemy at its own game.

Llewellyn Psi-Fi Fiction Series
1-56718-100-7, 240 pgs., mass market $4.99

THE MESSENGER
by Donald Tyson

"She went to the doorway and took Eliza by her shoulders. 'But you mind what I tell you. Something in this house is watching us, and its thoughts are not kindly. It's all twisted up and bitter inside. It means to make us suffer. Then it means to kill us, one by one.'"

Sealed inside a secret room of an old mansion in Nova Scotia is a cruel and uncontrollable entity, created years earlier by an evil magician. When the new owner of the mansion unknowingly releases the entity, it renews its malicious and murderous rampage. Called on to investigate the strange phenomena are three women and four men—each with their own occult talents. As their investigation proceeds, the group members enter into a world of mystery and horror as they encounter astral battles, spirit possession—even death. In their efforts to battle the evil spirit, they use seance, hypnotic trance and magical rituals, the details of which are presented in fascinating and accurate detail.

Llewellyn Psi-Fi Fiction Series
0-87542-836-3, 240 pgs., mass market   **$4.99**

THE FAMILY WICCA BOOK
The Craft for Parents & Children
by Ashleen O'Gaea

Enjoy the first book written for Pagan parents! The number of Witches raising children to the Craft is growing. The need for mutual support is rising—yet until now, there have been no books that speak to a Wiccan family's needs and experience. Finally, here is *The Family Wicca Book*, full to the brim with rituals, projects, encouragement and practical discussion of real-life challenges. You'll find lots of ideas to use right away.

Is magic safe for children? Why do some people think Wiccans are Satanists? How do you make friends with spirits and little people in the local woods? Find out how one Wiccan family gives clear and honest answers to questions that intrigue pagans all over the world.

When you want to ground your family in Wicca without ugly "bashing;" explain life, sex, and death without embarrassment; and add to your Sabbats without much trouble or expense, *The Family Wicca Book* is required reading. You'll refer to it again and again as your traditions grow with your family.

0-87542-591-7, 240 pgs., 5 1/4 x 8, illus., softcover   **$9.95**

MODERN MAGICK
Eleven Lessons in the High Magickal Arts
by Donald Michael Kraig

Modern Magick is the most comprehensive step-by-step introduction to the art of ceremonial magic ever offered. The eleven lessons in this book will guide you from the easiest of rituals and the construction of your magickal tools through the highest forms of magick: designing your own rituals and doing pathworking. Along the way you will learn the secrets of the Kabbalah in a clear and easy-to-understand manner. You will discover the true secrets of invocation (channeling) and evocation, and the missing information that will finally make the ancient grimoires, such as the "Keys of Solomon," not only comprehensible, but usable. This book also contains one of the most in-depth chapters on sex magick ever written. *Modern Magick* is designed so anyone can use it, and it is the perfect guidebook for students and classes. It will also help to round out the knowledge of long-time practitioners of the magickal arts.

0-87542-324-8, 592 pgs., 6 x 9, illus., index, softcover   **$14.95**

THE RAG BONE MAN
A Chilling Mystery of Self-Discovery
Charlotte Lawrence

This occult fiction, mystery and fantasy is a tale of the subtle ways psychic phenomena can intrude into anyone's life—and influence the even the most rational of people!

The Rag Bone Man mixes together a melange of magickal ingredients—from amulets, crystals, the tarot, past lives and elemental beings to near death experiences, shapeshifting and modern magickal ritual—to create a simmering blend of occult mystery and suspense.

Rian McGuire is a seemingly ordinary young woman who owns a New Age book and herb shop in a small Maryland town. When a disturbing man leaves a mysterious old book in Rian's shop and begins to invade her dreams, she is launched into a bizarre, often terrifying journey into the arcane. Why is this book worth committing murder to recover? As Rian's family and friends gather psychic forces to penetrate the mysteries that surround her, Rian finally learns the Rag Bone Man's true identity—but will she be able to harness the undreamt-of power of her own magickal birthright before the final terrifying confrontation?

ISBN: 1-56718-412-X, mass market, 336 pp.   **$4.99**

RITUAL MAGIC
What It Is & How To Do It
by Donald Tyson

For thousands of years men and women have practiced it despite the severe repression of sovereigns and priests. Now, *Ritual Magic* takes you into the heart of that entrancing, astonishing and at times mystifying secret garden of *magic*.

What is this ancient power? Where does it come from? How does it work? Is it mere myth and delusion, or can it truly move mountains and make the dead speak. . . bring rains from a clear sky and calm the seas. . . turn the outcome of great battles and call down the Moon from Heaven? Which part of the claims made for magic are true in the most literal sense, and which are poetic exaggerations that must be interpreted symbolically? How can magic be used to improve *your* life?

This book answers these and many other questions in a clear and direct manner. Its purpose is to separate the wheat from the chaff and make sense of the non-sense. It explains what the occult revival is all about, reveals the foundations of practical ritual magic, showing how modern occultism grew from a single root into a number of clearly defined esoteric schools and pagan sects.

0-87542-835-5, 288 pgs., 6 x 9, illus., index, softcover **$12.95**

FAERY WICCA
BOOK ONE
Theory & Magick • *A Book of Shadows & Lights*
Kisma K. Stepanich

Many books have been written on Wicca, but never until now has there been a book on the tradition of Irish Faery Wicca. If you have been drawn to the kingdom of Faery and want to gain a comprehensive understanding of this old folk faith, *Faery Wicca* offers you a thorough apprenticeship in the beliefs, history and practice of this rich and fulfilling tradition.

First, you'll explore the Irish history of Faery Wicca, its esoteric beliefs and its survival and evolution into its modern form; the Celtic pantheon; the Celtic division of the year; and the fairies of the Tuatha De Danann and their descendants. Each enlightening and informative lesson ends with a journal exercise and list of suggested readings.

The second part of *Faery Wicca* describes in detail magickal applications of the basic material presented in the first half: Faery Wicca ceremonies and rituals; utilizing magickal Faery tools, symbols and alphabets; creating sacred space; contacting and working with Faery allies; and guided visualizations and exercises suitable for beginners.

This fascinating guide will give you a firm foundation in the Faery Wicca tradition, which the upcoming *Faery Wicca, Book Two: The Shamanic Practices of Herbcraft, Spellcraft and Divination* will build upon.

ISBN: 1-56718-694-7, 7 x 10, 320 pp., illus., softbound $17.50

THE LLEWELLYN PRACTICAL GUIDE TO THE DEVELOPMENT OF PSYCHIC POWERS
by Denning & Phillips

You may not realize it, but you already have the ability to use ESP, Astral Vision and Clairvoyance, Divination, Dowsing, Prophecy, and Communication with Spirits.

Written by two of the most knowledgeable experts in the world of psychic development, this book is a complete course—teaching you, step-by-step, how to develop these powers that actually have been yours since birth. Using the techniques, you will soon be able to move objects at a distance, see into the future, know the thoughts and feelings of another person, find lost objects and locate water using your no-longer latent talents.

Psychic powers are as much a natural ability as any other talent. You'll learn to play with these new skills, working with groups of friends to accomplish things you never would have believed possible before reading this book. The text shows you how to make the equipment you can use, the exercises you can do—many of them at any time, anywhere—and how to use your abilities to change your life and the lives of those close to you. Many of the exercises are presented in forms that can be adapted as games for pleasure and fun, as well as development.

0-87542-191-1, 272 pgs., 5 1/4 x 8, illus., softcover   **$8.95**